Faithfully yours
Wilkie Collins

# MAN AND WIFE

By WILKIE COLLINS

DOVER PUBLICATIONS, INC.
NEW YORK

"May I not write in such a style as this?
In such a method too, and yet not miss
My end, thy good? Why may it not be done?
Dark clouds bring waters, when the bright bring none."
                    JOHN BUNYAN'S *Apology for his Book*.

Published in Canada by General Publishing Company, Ltd., 30 Lesmill Road, Don Mills, Toronto, Ontario.

Published in the United Kingdom by Constable and Company, Ltd., 10 Orange Street, London WC2H 7EG.

This Dover edition, first published in 1983, is an unabridged republication of the work as published by Harper & Brothers, New York, 1870, with the addition of the Preface, the epigraph, the dedication, and Appendix "Note A" from the English edition published in three volumes by F. S. Ellis, London, 1870, and a new table of contents written for the present edition (with the title of Chapter LIII taken from the English edition). *Man and Wife* was originally published serially in *Harper's Weekly*, New York, 1869–70.

Manufactured in the United States of America
Dover Publications, Inc., 180 Varick Street, New York, N.Y. 10014

**Library of Congress Cataloging in Publication Data**

Collins, Wilkie, 1824–1889.
  Man and wife.

  I. Title.
PR4494.M3   1983      823'.8                      82-17809
ISBN 0-486-24451-2

AFFECTIONATELY  DEDICATED

TO

# MR. AND MRS. FREDERICK LEHMANN.

# PREFACE.

The Story here offered to the reader differs in one respect from the stories which have preceded it by the same hand. This time the fiction is founded on facts, and aspires to afford what help it may towards hastening the reform of certain abuses which have been too long suffered to exist among us unchecked.

As to the present scandalous condition of the Marriage Laws of the United Kingdom, there can be no dispute. The Report of the Royal Commission appointed to examine the working of those laws, has supplied the solid foundation on which I have built my book. Such references to this high authority as may be necessary to convince the reader that I am not leading him astray, will be found collected in the [note on page 91]. I have only to add that, while I write these lines, Parliament is bestirring itself to remedy the cruel abuses which are here exposed in the story of "Hester Dethridge." There is a prospect, at last, of lawfully establishing the right of a married woman, in England, to possess her own property, and to keep her own earnings. Beyond this, no attempt has been made by the Legislature, that I know of, to purify the corruptions which exist in the Marriage Laws of Great Britain and Ireland. The Royal Commissioners have called for State interference, in no uncertain voice — thus far, without prevailing on Parliament to make any reply.

As to the other social question which has found its way into these pages—the question of the influence of the present rage for muscular exercises on the health and morals of the rising generation of Englishmen—I do not disguise from myself that I am treading on delicate ground, and that certain persons will strongly resent what I have written on this head.

Although I have, here, no Royal Commission to appeal to, I submit, nevertheless, that I am still dealing with plain and producible facts. As to the physical results of the mania for muscular cultivation which has seized on us of late years, it is a fact that the opinions expressed in this book are the opinions of the medical profession in general—with the high authority of Mr. Skey at their head. And (if the medical evidence is to be disputed as evidence based on theory only) it is also a fact that the view taken by the doctors is a view which the experience of fathers in all parts of England can practically confirm by reference to the cases of their sons. This last new form of our "national eccentricity" has its victims to answer for—victims who are broken for life.

As to the moral results, I may be right or I may be wrong, in seeing as I do a connection between the recent unbridled developement of physical cultivation in England, and the recent spread of grossness and brutality among certain classes of the English population. But, is it to be denied that the grossness and the brutality exist? and, more, that they have assumed formidable proportions among us of late years? We have become so shamelessly familiar with violence and outrage, that we recognise them as a necessary ingredient in our social system, and class our savages as a representative part of our population, under the newly invented name of "Roughs." Public attention has been directed by hundreds of other writers to the dirty Rough in fustian. If the present writer had confined himself within those limits, he would have carried all his readers with him. But he is bold enough to direct attention to the washed Rough in broadcloth—and he must stand on his defence with readers who have not noticed this variety, or who, having noticed, prefer to ignore it.

The Rough with the clean skin and the good coat on his back, is easily traced through the various grades of English society, in the middle and the upper classes. To quote a few instances only. The medical division not long since diverted itself, on its return from a public amusement, by destroying house-property, extinguishing street lights, and terrifying the decent inhabitants of a London suburb. The military division—also, not long since—committed atrocities (in certain regiments) which forced the authorities at the Horse Guards to interfere. The mercantile division, only the other day, mobbed, hustled and violently ejected from the Stock Exchange an eminent foreign banker, who had been taken to see the place by one of its oldest and most respectable members. The University Division (at Oxford) hooted the Vice-Chancellor, the heads of colleges, and the visitors, out of doors, at the Commemoration of 1869—and have since broken into the Christchurch Library, and burnt the busts and works of sculpture which it contained. It is a fact that these outrages have been committed. It is a fact that the persons concerned in them are largely represented among the patrons, and sometimes among the heroes, of Athletic Sports. Is there no material here for the making of such a character as "Geoffrey Delamayn?" Have I drawn entirely on my imagination for the scene which takes place in the athletic house of assembly at the "Cock and Bottle," Putney? Is no protest needed, in the interests of civilization, against a revival of barbarism among us, which asserts itself to be a revival of manly virtue, and finds human stupidity actually dense enough to admit the claim?

Reverting, for one moment, before I close these prefatory words, to the question of Art, I hope the reader of these pages will find that the purpose of the story is always an integral part of the story itself. The foremost condition of success, in a work of this sort, is that the fact and the fiction shall never be separable one from the other. I have wrought hard to reach this end; and I trust I have not wrought in vain.

W. C.

*June,* 1870.

# CONTENTS

## PROLOGUE

### THE IRISH MARRIAGE

## THE STORY

### FIRST SCENE—THE SUMMER-HOUSE

### SECOND SCENE—THE INN

### THIRD SCENE—LONDON

### FOURTH SCENE—WINDYGATES

### FIFTH SCENE—GLASGOW

# MAN AND WIFE.

PROLOGUE.—The Irish Marriage.

## Part the First.

### THE VILLA AT HAMPSTEAD.

#### I.

On a summer's morning, between thirty and forty years ago, two girls were crying bitterly in the cabin of an East Indian passenger ship, bound outward, from Gravesend to Bombay.

They were both of the same age—eighteen. They had both, from childhood upward, been close and dear friends at the same school. They were now parting for the first time—and parting, it might be, for life.

The name of one was Blanche. The name of the other was Anne.

Both were the children of poor parents; both had been pupil-teachers at the school; and both were destined to earn their own bread. Personally speaking, and socially speaking, these were the only points of resemblance between them.

Blanche was passably attractive and passably intelligent, and no more. Anne was rarely beautiful and rarely endowed. Blanche's parents were worthy people, whose first consideration was to secure, at any sacrifice, the future well-being of their child. Anne's parents were heartless and depraved. Their one idea, in connection with their daughter, was to speculate on her beauty, and to turn her abilities to profitable account.

The girls were starting in life under widely different conditions. Blanche was going to India, to be governess in the household of a Judge, under care of the Judge's wife. Anne was to wait at home until the first opportunity offered of sending her cheaply to Milan. There, among strangers, she was to be perfected in the actress's and the singer's art; then to return to England, and make the fortune of her family on the lyric stage.

Such were the prospects of the two as they sat together in the cabin of the Indiaman locked fast in each other's arms, and crying bitterly. The whispered farewell talk exchanged between them—exaggerated and impulsive as girls' talk is apt to be—came honestly, in each case, straight from the heart.

"Blanche! you may be married in India. Make your husband bring you back to England."

"Anne! you may take a dislike to the stage. Come out to India if you do."

"In England or out of England, married or not married, we will meet, darling—if it's years hence—with all the old love between us; friends who help each other, sisters who trust each other, for life! Vow it, Blanche!"

"I vow it, Anne!"

"With all your heart and soul?"

"With all my heart and soul!"

The sails were spread to the wind, and the ship began to move in the water. It was necessary to appeal to the captain's authority before the girls could be parted. The captain interfered gently and firmly. "Come, my dear," he said, putting his arm round Anne; "you won't mind *me!* I have got a daughter of my own." Anne's head fell on the sailor's shoulder. He put her, with his own hands, into the shore-boat alongside. In five minutes more the ship had gathered way; the boat was at the landing-stage—and the girls had seen the last of each other for many a long year to come.

This was in the summer of eighteen hundred and thirty-one.

#### II.

Twenty-four years later—in the summer of eighteen hundred and fifty-five—there was a villa at Hampstead to be let, furnished.

The house was still occupied by the persons who desired to let it. On the evening on which this scene opens a lady and two gentlemen were seated at the dinner-table. The lady had reached the mature age of forty-two. She was still a rarely beautiful woman. Her husband, some years younger than herself, faced her at the table, sitting silent and constrained, and never, even by accident, looking at his wife. The third person was a guest. The husband's name was Vanborough. The guest's name was Kendrew.

It was the end of the dinner. The fruit and the wine were on the table. Mr. Vanborough pushed the bottles in silence to Mr. Kendrew. The lady of the house looked round at the servant who was waiting, and said, "Tell the children to come in."

The door opened, and a girl twelve years old entered, leading by the hand a younger girl of five. They were both prettily dressed in white, with sashes of the same shade of light blue. But there was no family resemblance between them. The elder girl was frail and delicate, with a pale, sensitive face. The younger was light and florid, with round red cheeks and bright, saucy eyes— a charming little picture of happiness and health.

Mr. Kendrew looked inquiringly at the younger of the two girls.

"Here is a young lady," he said, "who is a total stranger to me."

"If you had not been a total stranger yourself for a whole year past," answered Mrs. Vanborough, "you would never have made that confession. This is little Blanche—the only child of the dearest friend I have. When Blanche's mother and I last saw each other we were two poor school-girls beginning the world. My friend went to India, and married there late in life. You may have heard of her husband—the famous Indian officer, Sir Thomas Lundie? Yes: 'the rich Sir Thomas,' as you call him. Lady Lundie is now on her way back to England, for the first time since she left it—I am afraid to say how many years since. I expected her yesterday; I expect her to-day—she may come at any moment. We exchanged promises to meet, in the ship that took her to India—'vows' we called them in the dear old times. Imagine how changed we shall find each other when we *do* meet again at last!"

"In the mean time," said Mr. Kendrew, "your friend appears to have sent you her little daughter to represent her? It's a long journey for so young a traveler."

"A journey ordered by the doctors in India a year since," rejoined Mrs. Vanborough. "They said Blanche's health required English air. Sir Thomas was ill at the time, and his wife couldn't leave him. She had to send the child to England, and who should she send her to but me? Look at her now, and say if the English air hasn't agreed with her! We two mothers, Mr. Kendrew, seem literally to live again in our children. I have an only child. My friend has an only child. My daughter is little Anne—as *I* was. My friend's daughter is little Blanche—as *she* was. And, to crown it all, those two girls have taken the same fancy to each other which *we* took to each other in the by-gone days at school. One has often heard of hereditary hatred. Is there such a thing as hereditary love as well?"

Before the guest could answer, his attention was claimed by the master of the house.

"Kendrew," said Mr. Vanborough, "when you have had enough of domestic sentiment, suppose you take a glass of wine?"

The words were spoken with undisguised contempt of tone and manner. Mrs. Vanborough's color rose. She waited, and controlled the momentary irritation. When she spoke to her husband it was evidently with a wish to soothe and conciliate him.

"I am afraid, my dear, you are not well this evening?"

"I shall be better when those children have done clattering with their knives and forks."

The girls were peeling fruit. The younger one went on. The elder stopped, and looked at her mother. Mrs. Vanborough beckoned to Blanche to come to her, and pointed toward the French window opening to the floor.

"Would you like to eat your fruit in the garden, Blanche?"

"Yes," said Blanche, "if Anne will go with me."

Anne rose at once, and the two girls went away together into the garden, hand in hand. On their departure Mr. Kendrew wisely started a new subject. He referred to the letting of the house.

"The loss of the garden will be a sad loss to those two young ladies," he said. "It really seems to be a pity that you should be giving up this pretty place."

"Leaving the house is not the worst of the sacrifice," answered Mrs. Vanborough. "If John finds Hampstead too far for him from London, of course we must move. The only hardship that I complain of is the hardship of having the house to let."

Mr. Vanborough looked across the table, as ungraciously as possible, at his wife.

"What have *you* to do with it?" he asked.

Mrs. Vanborough tried to clear the conjugal horizon by a smile.

"My dear John," she said, gently, "you forget that, while you are at business, I am here all day. I can't help seeing the people who come to look at the house. Such people!" she continued, turning to Mr. Kendrew. "They distrust every thing, from the scraper at the door to the chimneys on the roof. They force their way in at all hours. They ask all sorts of impudent questions—and they show you plainly that they don't mean to believe your answers, before you have time to make them. Some wretch of a woman says, 'Do you think the drains are right?'—and sniffs suspiciously, before I can say Yes. Some brute of a man asks, 'Are you quite sure this house is solidly built, ma'am?'—and jumps on the floor at the full stretch of his legs, without waiting for me to reply. Nobody believes in our gravel soil and our south aspect. Nobody wants any of our improvements. The moment they hear of John's Artesian well, they look as if they never drank water. And, if they happen to pass my poultry-yard, they instantly lose all appreciation of the merits of a fresh egg!"

Mr. Kendrew laughed. "I have been through it all in my time," he said. "The people who want to take a house are the born enemies of the people who want to let a house. Odd—isn't it, Vanborough?"

Mr. Vanborough's sullen humor resisted his friend as obstinately as it had resisted his wife.

"I dare say," he answered. "I wasn't listening."

This time the tone was almost brutal. Mrs. Vanborough looked at her husband with unconcealed surprise and distress.

"John!" she said. "What *can* be the matter with you? Are you in pain?"

"A man may be anxious and worried, I suppose, without being actually in pain."

"I am sorry to hear you are worried. Is it business?"

"Yes—business."

"Consult Mr. Kendrew."

"I am waiting to consult him."

Mrs. Vanborough rose immediately. "Ring, dear," she said, "when you want coffee." As she passed her husband she stopped and laid her hand tenderly on his forehead. "I wish I could smooth out that frown!" she whispered. Mr. Vanborough impatiently shook his head. Mrs. Vanborough sighed as she turned to the door. Her husband called to her before she could leave the room.

"Mind we are not interrupted!"

"I will do my best, John." She looked at Mr. Kendrew, holding the door open for her; and resumed, with an effort, her former lightness of tone. "But don't forget our 'born enemies!' Somebody may come, even at this hour of the evening, who wants to see the house."

The two gentlemen were left alone over their wine. There was a strong personal contrast between them. Mr. Vanborough was tall and dark —a dashing, handsome man; with an energy in his face which all the world saw; with an inbred falseness under it which only a special observer could detect. Mr. Kendrew was short and light —slow and awkward in manner, except when something happened to rouse him. Looking in *his* face, the world saw an ugly and undemonstrative little man. The special observer, penetrating under the surface, found a fine nature beneath, resting on a steady foundation of honor and truth.

Mr. Vanborough opened the conversation.

"If you ever marry," he said, "don't be such a fool, Kendrew, as I have been. Don't take a wife from the stage."

"If I could get such a wife as yours," replied the other, "I would take her from the stage to-morrow. A beautiful woman, a clever woman, a woman of unblemished character, and a woman who truly loves you. Man alive! what do you want more?"

"I want a great deal more. I want a woman highly connected and highly bred—a woman who can receive the best society in England, and open her husband's way to a position in the world."

"A position in the world!" cried Mr. Kendrew. "Here is a man whose father has left him half a million of money—with the one condition annexed to it of taking his father's place at the head of one of the greatest mercantile houses in England. And he talks about a position, as if he was a junior clerk in his own office! What on earth does your ambition see, beyond what your ambition has already got?"

Mr. Vanborough finished his glass of wine, and looked his friend steadily in the face.

"My ambition," he said, "sees a Parliamentary career, with a Peerage at the end of it—and with no obstacle in the way but my estimable wife."

Mr. Kendrew lifted his hand warningly. "Don't talk in that way," he said. "If you're joking—it's a joke I don't see. If you're in earnest—you force a suspicion on me which I would rather not feel. Let us change the subject."

"No! Let us have it out at once. What do you suspect?"

"I suspect you are getting tired of your wife."

"She is forty-two, and I am thirty-five; and I have been married to her for thirteen years. You know all that—and you only *suspect* I am tired of her. Bless your innocence! Have you any thing more to say?"

"If you force me to it, I take the freedom of an old friend, and I say you are not treating her fairly. It's nearly two years since you broke up your establishment abroad, and came to England on your father's death. With the exception of myself, and one or two other friends of former days, you have presented your wife to nobody. Your new position has smoothed the way for you into the best society. You never take your wife with you. You go out as if you were a single man. I have reason to know that you are actually believed to be a single man, among these new acquaintances of yours, in more than one quarter. Forgive me for speaking my mind bluntly—I say what I think. It's unworthy of you to keep your wife buried here, as if you were ashamed of her."

"I *am* ashamed of her."

"Vanborough!"

"Wait a little! you are not to have it all your own way, my good fellow. What are the facts? Thirteen years ago I fell in love with a handsome public singer, and married her. My father was angry with me; and I had to go and live with her abroad. It didn't matter, abroad. My father forgave me on his death-bed, and I had to bring her home again. It does matter, at home. I find myself, with a great career opening before me, tied to a woman whose relations are (as you well know) the lowest of the low. A woman without the slightest distinction of manner, or the slightest aspiration beyond her nursery and her kitchen, her piano and her books. Is *that* a wife who can help me to make my place in society?—who can smooth my way, through social obstacles and political obstacles, to the House of Lords? By Jupiter! if ever there was a woman to be 'buried' (as you call it), that woman is my wife. And, what's more, if you want the truth, it's because I *can't* bury her here that I'm going to leave this house. She has got a cursed knack of making acquaintances wherever she goes. She'll have a circle of friends about her if I leave her in this neighborhood much longer. Friends who remember her as the famous opera-singer. Friends who will see her swindling scoundrel of a father (when my back is turned) coming drunk to the door to borrow money of her! I tell you, my marriage has wrecked my prospects. It's no use talking to me of my wife's virtues. She is a millstone round my neck, with all her virtues. If I had not been a born idiot I should have waited, and married a woman who would have been of some use to me; a woman with high connections—"

Mr. Kendrew touched his host's arm, and suddenly interrupted him.

"To come to the point," he said—"a woman like Lady Jane Parnell."

Mr. Vanborough started. His eyes fell, for the first time, before the eyes of his friend.

"What do you know about Lady Jane?" he asked.

"Nothing. I don't move in Lady Jane's world—but I do go sometimes to the opera. I saw you with her last night in her box; and I heard what was said in the stalls near me. You were openly spoken of as the favored man who was singled out from the rest by Lady Jane. Imagine what would happen if your wife heard that! You are wrong, Vanborough—you are in every way wrong. You alarm, you distress, you disappoint me. I never sought this explanation —but now it has come, I won't shrink from it. Reconsider your conduct; reconsider what you have said to me—or you count me no longer among your friends. No! I want no further talk about it now. We are both getting hot— we may end in saying what had better have been left unsaid. Once more, let us change the subject. You wrote me word that you wanted me here to-day, because you needed my advice on a matter of some importance. What is it?"

Silence followed that question. Mr. Vanborough's face betrayed signs of embarrassment. He poured himself out another glass of wine, and drank it at a draught before he replied.

"It's not so easy to tell you what I want,"

he said, "after the tone you have taken with me about my wife."

Mr. Kendrew looked surprised.

"Is Mrs. Vanborough concerned in the matter?" he asked.

"Yes."

"Does she know about it?"

"No."

"Have you kept the thing a secret out of regard for *her*?"

"Yes."

"Have I any right to advise on it?"

"You have the right of an old friend."

"Then, why not tell me frankly what it is?"

There was another moment of embarrassment on Mr. Vanborough's part.

"It will come better," he answered, "from a third person, whom I expect here every minute. He is in possession of all the facts—and he is better able to state them than I am."

"Who is the person?"

"My friend, Delamayn."

"Your lawyer?"

"Yes—the junior partner in the firm of Delamayn, Hawke, and Delamayn. Do you know him?"

"I am acquainted with him. His wife's family were friends of mine before he married. I don't like him."

"You're rather hard to please to-day! Delamayn is a rising man, if ever there was one yet. A man with a career before him, and with courage enough to pursue it. He is going to leave the Firm, and try his luck at the Bar. Every body says he will do great things. What's your objection to him?"

"I have no objection whatever. We meet with people occasionally whom we dislike without knowing why. Without knowing why, I dislike Mr. Delamayn."

"Whatever you do, you must put up with him this evening. He will be here directly."

He was there at that moment. The servant opened the door, and announced—"Mr. Delamayn."

### III.

Externally speaking, the rising solicitor, who was going to try his luck at the Bar, looked like a man who was going to succeed. His hard, hairless face, his watchful gray eyes, his thin, resolute lips, said plainly, in so many words, "I mean to get on in the world; and, if you are in my way, I mean to get on at your expense." Mr. Delamayn was habitually polite to every body—but he had never been known to say one unnecessary word to his dearest friend. A man of rare ability; a man of unblemished honor (as the code of the world goes); but not a man to be taken familiarly by the hand. You would never have borrowed money of him—but you would have trusted him with untold gold. Involved in private and personal troubles, you would have hesitated at asking him to help you. Involved in public and producible troubles, you would have said, Here is my man. Sure to push his way—nobody could look at him and doubt it—sure to push his way.

"Kendrew is an old friend of mine," said Mr. Vanborough, addressing himself to the lawyer. "Whatever you have to say to *me* you may say before *him*. Will you have some wine?"

"No—thank you."

"Have you brought any news?"

"Yes."

"Have you got the written opinions of the two barristers?"

"No."

"Why not?"

"Because nothing of the sort is necessary. If the facts of the case are correctly stated there is not the slightest doubt about the law."

With that reply Mr. Delamayn took a written paper from his pocket, and spread it out on the table before him.

"What is that?" asked Mr. Vanborough.

"The case relating to your marriage."

Mr. Kendrew started, and showed the first tokens of interest in the proceedings which had escaped him yet. Mr. Delamayn looked at him for a moment, and went on.

"The case," he resumed, "as originally stated by you, and taken down in writing by our head-clerk."

Mr. Vanborough's temper began to show itself again.

"What have we got to do with that now?" he asked. "You have made your inquiries to prove the correctness of my statement—haven't you?"

"Yes."

"And you have found out that I am right?"

"I have found out that you are right—if the case is right. I wish to be sure that no mistake has occurred between you and the clerk. This is a very important matter. I am going to take the responsibility of giving an opinion which may be followed by serious consequences; and I mean to assure myself that the opinion is given on a sound basis, first. I have some questions to ask you. Don't be impatient, if you please. They won't take long."

He referred to the manuscript, and put the first question.

"You were married at Inchmallock, in Ireland, Mr. Vanborough, thirteen years since?"

"Yes."

"Your wife—then Miss Anne Silvester—was a Roman Catholic?"

"Yes."

"Her father and mother were Roman Catholics?"

"They were."

"*Your* father and mother were Protestants? and *you* were baptized and brought up in the Church of England?"

"All right!"

"Miss Anne Silvester felt, and expressed, a strong repugnance to marrying you, because you and she belonged to different religious communities?"

"She did."

"You got over her objection by consenting to become a Roman Catholic, like herself?"

"It was the shortest way with her—and it didn't matter to *me*."

"You were formally received into the Roman Catholic Church?"

"I went through the whole ceremony."

"Abroad or at home?"

"Abroad."

"How long was it before the date of your marriage?"

"Six weeks before I was married."

Referring perpetually to the paper in his hand,

Mr. Delamayn was especially careful in comparing that last answer with the answer given to the head-clerk.

"Quite right," he said, and went on with his questions.

"The priest who married you was one Ambrose Redman—a young man recently appointed to his clerical duties?"

"Yes."

"Did he ask if you were both Roman Catholics?"

"Yes."

"Did he ask any thing more?"

"No."

"Are you sure he never inquired whether you had both been Catholics *for more than one year before you came to him to be married?*"

"I am certain of it."

"He must have forgotten that part of his duty—or, being only a beginner, he may well have been ignorant of it altogether. Did neither you nor the lady think of informing him on the point?"

"Neither I nor the lady knew there was any necessity for informing him."

Mr. Delamayn folded up the manuscript, and put it back in his pocket.

"Right," he said, "in every particular."

Mr. Vanborough's swarthy complexion slowly turned pale. He cast one furtive glance at Mr. Kendrew, and turned away again.

"Well," he said to the lawyer, "now for your opinion! What is the law?"

"The law," answered Mr. Delamayn, "is beyond all doubt or dispute. Your marriage with Miss Anne Silvester is no marriage at all."

Mr. Kendrew started to his feet.

"What do you mean?" he asked, sternly.

The rising solicitor lifted his eyebrows in polite surprise. If Mr. Kendrew wanted information, why should Mr. Kendrew ask for it in that way? "Do you wish me to go into the law of the case?" he inquired.

"I do."

Mr. Delamayn stated the law, as that law still stands—to the disgrace of the English Legislature and the English Nation.

"By the Irish Statute of George the Second," he said, "every marriage celebrated by a Popish priest between two Protestants, or between a Papist and any person who has been a Protestant within twelve months before the marriage, is declared null and void. And by two other Acts of the same reign such a celebration of marriage is made a felony on the part of the priest. The clergy in Ireland of other religious denominations have been relieved from this law. But it still remains in force so far as the Roman Catholic priesthood is concerned."

"Is such a state of things possible in the age we live in!" exclaimed Mr. Kendrew.

Mr. Delamayn smiled. He had outgrown the customary illusions as to the age we live in.

"There are other instances in which the Irish marriage-law presents some curious anomalies of its own," he went on. "It is felony, as I have just told you, for a Roman Catholic priest to celebrate a marriage which may be lawfully celebrated by a parochial clergyman, a Presbyterian minister, and a Non-conformist minister. It is also felony (by another law) on the part of a parochial clergyman to celebrate a marriage that may be lawfully celebrated by a Roman Catholic priest. And it is again felony (by yet another law) for a Presbyterian minister and a Non-conformist minister to celebrate a marriage which may be lawfully celebrated by a clergyman of the Established Church. An odd state of things. Foreigners might possibly think it a scandalous state of things. In this country we don't appear to mind it. Returning to the present case, the results stand thus: Mr. Vanborough is a single man; Mrs. Vanborough is a single woman; their child is illegitimate, and the priest, Ambrose Redman, is liable to be tried, and punished, as a felon, for marrying them."

"An infamous law!" said Mr. Kendrew.

"It *is* the law," returned Mr. Delamayn, as a sufficient answer to him.

Thus far not a word had escaped the master of the house. He sat with his lips fast closed and his eyes riveted on the table, thinking.

Mr. Kendrew turned to him, and broke the silence.

"Am I to understand," he asked, "that the advice you wanted from me related to *this?*"

"Yes."

"You mean to tell me that, foreseeing the present interview and the result to which it might lead, you felt any doubt as to the course you were bound to take? Am I really to understand that you hesitate to set this dreadful mistake right, and to make the woman who is your wife in the sight of Heaven your wife in the sight of the law?"

"If you choose to put it in that light," said Mr. Vanborough; "if you won't consider—"

"I want a plain answer to my question—'yes,' or no.'"

"Let me speak, will you! A man has a right to explain himself, I suppose?"

Mr. Kendrew stopped him by a gesture of disgust.

"I won't trouble you to explain yourself," he said. "I prefer to leave the house. You have given me a lesson, Sir, which I shall not forget. I find that one man may have known another from the days when they were both boys, and may have seen nothing but the false surface of him in all that time. I am ashamed of having ever been your friend. You are a stranger to me from this moment."

With those words he left the room.

"That is a curiously hot-headed man," remarked Mr. Delamayn. "If you will allow me, I think I'll change my mind. I'll have a glass of wine."

Mr. Vanborough rose to his feet without replying, and took a turn in the room impatiently. Scoundrel as he was—in intention, if not yet in act—the loss of the oldest friend he had in the world staggered him for the moment.

"This is an awkward business, Delamayn," he said. "What would you advise me to do?"

Mr. Delamayn shook his head, and sipped his claret.

"I decline to advise you," he answered. "I take no responsibility, beyond the responsibility of stating the law as it stands, in your case."

Mr. Vanborough sat down again at the table, to consider the alternative of asserting or not asserting his freedom from the marriage tie. He had not had much time thus far for turning the matter over in his mind. But for his residence on the Continent the question of the flaw in his marriage might no doubt have been raised long since. As things were, the question had only taken its rise in a chance conversation with Mr. Delamayn in the summer of that year.

For some minutes the lawyer sat silent, sipping his wine, and the husband sat silent, thinking his own thoughts. The first change that came over the scene was produced by the appearance of a servant in the dining-room.

Mr. Vanborough looked up at the man with a sudden outbreak of anger.

"What do you want here?"

The man was a well-bred English servant. In other words, a human machine, doing its duty impenetrably when it was once wound up. He had his words to speak, and he spoke them.

"There is a lady at the door, Sir, who wishes to see the house."

"The house is not to be seen at this time of the evening."

The machine had a message to deliver, and delivered it.

"The lady desired me to present her apologies, Sir. I was to tell you she was much pressed for time. This was the last house on the house agent's list, and her coachman is stupid about finding his way in strange places."

"Hold your tongue, and tell the lady to go to the devil!"

Mr. Delamayn interfered—partly in the interests of his client, partly in the interests of propriety.

"You attach some importance, I think, to letting this house as soon as possible?" he said.

"Of course I do!"

"Is it wise—on account of a momentary annoyance—to lose an opportunity of laying your hand on a tenant?"

"Wise or not, it's an infernal nuisance to be disturbed by a stranger."

"Just as you please. I don't wish to interfere. I only wish to say—in case you are thinking of my convenience as your guest—that it will be no nuisance to me."

The servant impenetrably waited. Mr. Vanborough impatiently gave way.

"Very well. Let her in. Mind, if she comes here, she's only to look into the room, and go out again. If she wants to ask questions, she must go to the agent."

Mr. Delamayn interfered once more, in the interests, this time, of the lady of the house.

"Might it not be desirable," he suggested, "to consult Mrs. Vanborough before you quite decide?"

"Where's your mistress?"

"In the garden, or the paddock, Sir—I am not sure which."

"We can't send all over the grounds in search of her. Tell the house-maid, and show the lady in."

The servant withdrew. Mr. Delamayn helped himself to a second glass of wine.

"Excellent claret," he said. "Do you get it direct from Bordeaux?"

There was no answer. Mr. Vanborough had returned to the contemplation of the alternative between freeing himself or not freeing himself from the marriage tie. One of his elbows was on the table; he bit fiercely at his finger-nails. He muttered between his teeth, "What am I to do?"

A sound of rustling silk made itself gently audible in the passage outside. The door opened, and the lady who had come to see the house appeared in the dining-room.

## IV.

She was tall and elegant; beautifully dressed, in the happiest combination of simplicity and splendor. A light summer veil hung over her face. She lifted it, and made her apologies for disturbing the gentlemen over their wine, with the unaffected ease and grace of a highly-bred woman.

"Pray accept my excuses for this intrusion. I am ashamed to disturb you. One look at the room will be quite enough."

Thus far she had addressed Mr. Delamayn, who happened to be nearest to her. Looking round the room her eye fell on Mr. Vanborough. She started, with a loud exclamation of astonishment. "*You!*" she said. "Good Heavens! who would have thought of meeting *you* here?"

Mr. Vanborough, on his side, stood petrified.

"Lady Jane!" he exclaimed. "Is it possible?"

He barely looked at her while she spoke. His eyes wandered guiltily toward the window which led into the garden. The situation was a terrible one—equally terrible if his wife discovered Lady Jane, or if Lady Jane discovered his wife. For the moment nobody was visible on the lawn. There was time, if the chance only offered—there was time for him to get the visitor out of the house. The visitor, innocent of all knowledge of the truth, gayly offered him her hand.

"I believe in mesmerism for the first time," she said. "This is an instance of magnetic sympathy, Mr. Vanborough. An invalid friend of mine wants a furnished house at Hampstead. I undertake to find one for her, and the day *I* select to make the discovery is the day *you* select for dining with a friend. A last house at Hampstead is left on my list—and in that house I meet you. Astonishing!" She turned to Mr. Delamayn. "I presume I am addressing the owner of the house?" Before a word could be said by either of the gentlemen she noticed the garden. "What pretty grounds! Do I see a lady in the garden? I hope I have not driven her away." She looked round, and appealed to Mr. Vanborough. "Your friend's wife?" she asked, and, on this occasion, waited for a reply.

In Mr. Vanborough's situation what reply was possible?

Mrs. Vanborough was not only visible—but audible—in the garden; giving her orders to one of the out-of-door servants with the tone and manner which proclaimed the mistress of the house. Suppose he said, "She is *not* my friend's wife?" Female curiosity would inevitably put the next question, "Who is she?" Suppose he invented an explanation? The explanation would take time, and time would give his wife an opportunity of discovering Lady Jane. Seeing all these considerations in one breathless moment, Mr. Vanborough took the shortest and the boldest way out of the difficulty. He answered silently by an affirmative inclination of the head, which dextrously turned Mrs. Vanborough into Mrs. Delamayn, without allowing Mr. Delamayn the opportunity of hearing it.

But the lawyer's eye was habitually watchful, and the lawyer saw him.

Mastering in a moment his first natural astonishment at the liberty taken with him, Mr. Delamayn drew the inevitable conclusion that there was something wrong, and that there was an attempt (not to be permitted for a moment) to mix him up in it. He advanced, resolute to contradict his client, to his client's own face.

The voluble Lady Jane interrupted him before he could open his lips.

"Might I ask one question? Is the aspect south? Of course it is! I ought to see by the sun that the aspect is south. These and the other two are, I suppose, the only rooms on the ground-floor? And is it quiet? Of course it's quiet! A charming house. Far more likely to suit my friend than any I have seen yet. Will you give me the refusal of it till to-morrow?" There she stopped for breath, and gave Mr. Delamayn his first opportunity of speaking to her.

"I beg your ladyship's pardon," he began. "I really can't—"

Mr. Vanborough—passing close behind him, and whispering as he passed—stopped the lawyer before he could say a word more.

"For God's sake, don't contradict me! My wife is coming this way!"

At the same moment (still supposing that Mr. Delamayn was the master of the house) Lady Jane returned to the charge.

"You appear to feel some hesitation," she said. "Do you want a reference?" She smiled satirically, and summoned her friend to her aid. "Mr. Vanborough!"

Mr. Vanborough, stealing step by step nearer to the window—intent, come what might of it, on keeping his wife out of the room—neither heeded nor heard her. Lady Jane followed him, and tapped him briskly on the shoulder with her parasol.

At that moment Mrs. Vanborough appeared on the garden side of the window.

"Am I in the way?" she asked, addressing her husband, after one steady look at Lady Jane. "This lady appears to be an old friend of yours." There was a tone of sarcasm in that allusion to the parasol, which might develop into a tone of jealousy at a moment's notice.

Lady Jane was not in the least disconcerted. She had her double privilege of familiarity with the men whom she liked—her privilege as a woman of high rank, and her privilege as a young widow. She bowed to Mrs. Vanborough, with all the highly-finished politeness of the order to which she belonged.

"The lady of the house, I presume?" she said, with a gracious smile.

Mrs. Vanborough returned the bow coldly—entered the room first—and then answered, "Yes."

Lady Jane turned to Mr. Vanborough.

"Present me!" she said, submitting resignedly to the formalities of the middle classes.

Mr. Vanborough obeyed, without looking at his wife, and without mentioning his wife's name.

"Lady Jane Parnell," he said, passing over the introduction as rapidly as possible. "Let me see you to your carriage," he added, offering his arm. "I will take care that you have the refusal of the house. You may trust it all to me."

No! Lady Jane was accustomed to leave a favorable impression behind her wherever she went. It was a habit with her to be charming (in widely different ways) to both sexes. The social experience of the upper classes is, in England, an experience of universal welcome. Lady Jane declined to leave until she had thawed the icy reception of the lady of the house.

"I must repeat my apologies," she said to Mrs. Vanborough, "for coming at this inconvenient time. My intrusion appears to have sadly disturbed the two gentlemen. Mr. Vanborough looks as if he wished me a hundred miles away. And as for your husband—" She stopped and glanced toward Mr. Delamayn. "Pardon me for speaking in that familiar way. I have not the pleasure of knowing your husband's name."

In speechless amazement Mrs. Vanborough's eyes followed the direction of Lady Jane's eyes—and rested on the lawyer, personally a total stranger to her.

Mr. Delamayn, resolutely waiting his opportunity to speak, seized it once more—and held it this time.

"I beg your pardon," he said. "There is some misapprehension here, for which I am in no way responsible. I am *not* that lady's husband."

It was Lady Jane's turn to be astonished. She looked at the lawyer. Useless! Mr. Delamayn had set himself right—Mr. Delamayn declined to interfere further. He silently took a chair at the other end of the room. Lady Jane addressed Mr. Vanborough.

"Whatever the mistake may be," she said, "you are responsible for it. You certainly told me this lady was your friend's wife."

"What!!!" cried Mrs. Vanborough—loudly, sternly, incredulously.

The inbred pride of the great lady began to appear behind the thin outer veil of politeness that covered it.

"I will speak louder if you wish it," she said. "Mr. Vanborough told me you were that gentleman's wife."

Mr. Vanborough whispered fiercely to his wife through his clenched teeth.

"The whole thing is a mistake. Go into the garden again!"

Mrs. Vanborough's indignation was suspended for the moment in dread, as she saw the passion and the terror struggling in her husband's face.

"How you look at me!" she said. "How you speak to me!"

He only repeated, "Go into the garden!"

Lady Jane began to perceive, what the lawyer had discovered some minutes previously—that there was something wrong in the villa at Hampstead. The lady of the house was a lady in an anomalous position of some kind. And as the house, to all appearance, belonged to Mr. Vanborough's friend, Mr. Vanborough's friend must (in spite of his recent disclaimer) be in some way responsible for it. Arriving, naturally enough, at this erroneous conclusion, Lady Jane's eyes rested for an instant on Mrs. Vanborough with a finely contemptuous expression of inquiry which would have roused the spirit of the tamest woman in existence. The implied insult stung the wife's sensitive nature to the quick. She turned once more to her husband—this time without flinching.

"Who is that woman?" she asked.

Lady Jane was equal to the emergency. The manner in which she wrapped herself up in her own virtue, without the slightest pretension on the one hand, and without the slightest compromise on the other, was a sight to see.

"Mr. Vanborough," she said, "you offered to take me to my carriage just now. I begin to understand that I had better have accepted the offer at once. Give me your arm."

"Stop!" said Mrs. Vanborough, "your ladyship's looks are looks of contempt; your ladyship's words can bear but one interpretation. I am innocently involved in some vile deception which I don't understand. But this I do know —I won't submit to be insulted in my own house. After what you have just said I forbid my husband to give you his arm."

Her husband!

Lady Jane looked at Mr. Vanborough—at Mr. Vanborough, whom she loved; whom she had honestly believed to be a single man; whom she had suspected, up to that moment, of nothing worse than of trying to screen the frailties of his friend. She dropped her highly-bred tone; she lost her highly-bred manners. The sense of her injury (if this was true), the pang of her jealousy (if that woman *was* his wife), stripped the human nature in her bare of all disguises, raised the angry color in her cheeks, and struck the angry fire out of her eyes.

"If you can tell the truth, Sir," she said, haughtily, "be so good as to tell it now. Have you been falsely presenting yourself to the world —falsely presenting yourself to *me*—in the character and with the aspirations of a single man? Is that lady your wife?"

"Do you hear her? do you see her?" cried Mrs. Vanborough, appealing to her husband, in her turn. She suddenly drew back from him, shuddering from head to foot. "He hesitates!" she said to herself, faintly. "Good God! he hesitates!"

Lady Jane sternly repeated her question.

"Is that lady your wife?"

He roused his scoundrel-courage, and said the fatal word:

"No!"

Mrs. Vanborough staggered back. She caught at the white curtains of the window to save herself from falling, and tore them. She looked at her husband, with the torn curtain clenched fast in her hand. She asked herself, "Am I mad? or is he?"

Lady Jane drew a deep breath of relief. He was not married! He was only a profligate single man. A profligate single man is shocking—but reclaimable. It is possible to blame him severely, and to insist on his reformation in the most uncompromising terms. It is also possible to forgive him, and marry him. Lady Jane took the necessary position under the circumstances with perfect tact. She inflicted reproof in the present without excluding hope in the future.

"I have made a very painful discovery," she said, gravely, to Mr. Vanborough. "It rests with *you* to persuade me to forget it! Good-evening!"

She accompanied the last words by a farewell look which aroused Mrs. Vanborough to frenzy. She sprang forward and prevented Lady Jane from leaving the room.

"No!" she said. "You don't go yet!"

Mr. Vanborough came forward to interfere.

His wife eyed him with a terrible look, and turned from him with a terrible contempt. "That man has lied!" she said. "In justice to myself, I insist on proving it!" She struck a bell on a table near her. The servant came in. "Fetch my writing-desk out of the next room." She waited—with her back turned on her husband, with her eyes fixed on Lady Jane. Defenseless and alone she stood on the wreck of her married life, superior to the husband's treachery, the lawyer's indifference, and her rival's contempt. At that dreadful moment her beauty shone out again with a gleam of its old glory. The grand woman, who in the old stage days had held thousands breathless over the mimic woes of the scene, stood there grander than ever, in her own woe, and held the three people who looked at her breathless till she spoke again.

The servant came in with the desk. She took out a paper and handed it to Lady Jane.

"I was a singer on the stage," she said, "when I was a single woman. The slander to which such women are exposed doubted my marriage. I provided myself with the paper in your hand. It speaks for itself. Even the highest society, madam, respects *that!*"

Lady Jane examined the paper. It was a marriage-certificate. She turned deadly pale, and beckoned to Mr. Vanborough. "Are you deceiving me?" she asked.

Mr. Vanborough looked back into the far corner of the room, in which the lawyer sat, impenetrably waiting for events. "Oblige me by coming here for a moment," he said.

Mr. Delamayn rose and complied with the request. Mr. Vanborough addressed himself to Lady Jane.

"I beg to refer you to my man of business. *He* is not interested in deceiving you."

"Am I required simply to speak to the fact?" asked Mr. Delamayn. "I decline to do more."

"You are not wanted to do more."

Listening intently to that interchange of question and answer, Mrs. Vanborough advanced a step in silence. The high courage that had sustained her against outrage which had openly declared itself shrank under the sense of something coming which she had not foreseen. A nameless dread throbbed at her heart and crept among the roots of her hair.

Lady Jane handed the certificate to the lawyer.

"In two words, Sir," she said, impatiently, "what is this?"

"In two words, madam," answered Mr. Delamayn; "waste paper."

"He is *not* married?"

"He is *not* married."

After a moment's hesitation Lady Jane looked round at Mrs. Vanborough, standing silent at her side—looked, and started back in terror. "Take me away!" she cried, shrinking from the ghastly face that confronted her with the fixed stare of agony in the great, glittering eyes. "Take me away! That woman will murder me!"

Mr. Vanborough gave her his arm and led her to the door. There was dead silence in the room as he did it. Step by step the wife's eyes followed them with the same dreadful stare, till the door closed and shut them out. The lawyer, left alone with the disowned and deserted woman, put the useless certificate silently on the table. She looked from him to the paper, and dropped,

"IS THAT LADY YOUR WIFE?"

without a cry to warn him, without an effort to save herself, senseless at his feet.

He lifted her from the floor and placed her on the sofa, and waited to see if Mr. Vanborough would come back. Looking at the beautiful face —still beautiful, even in the swoon—he owned it was hard on her. Yes! in his own impenetrable way, the rising lawyer owned it was hard on her.

But the law justified it. There was no doubt in this case. The law justified it.

The trampling of horses and the grating of wheels sounded outside. Lady Jane's carriage was driving away. Would the husband come back? (See what a thing habit is! Even Mr. Delamayn still mechanically thought of him as the husband—in the face of the law! in the face of the facts!)

No. The minutes passed. And no sign of the husband coming back.

It was not wise to make a scandal in the house. It was not desirable (on his own sole responsibility) to let the servants see what had happened. Still, there she lay senseless. The cool evening air came in through the open window and lifted the light ribbons in her lace cap, lifted the little lock of hair that had broken loose and drooped over her neck. Still, there she lay—the wife who had loved him, the mother of his child—there she lay.

He stretched out his hand to ring the bell and summon help.

At the same moment the quiet of the summer evening was once more disturbed. He held his hand suspended over the bell. The noise outside came nearer. It was again the trampling of horses and the grating of wheels. Advancing—rapidly advancing—stopping at the house.

Was Lady Jane coming back?

Was the husband coming back?

There was a loud ring at the bell—a quick opening of the house-door—a rustling of a woman's dress in the passage. The door of the room opened, and the woman appeared—alone. Not Lady Jane. A stranger—older, years older, than Lady Jane. A plain woman, perhaps, at other times. A woman almost beautiful, now, with the eager happiness that beamed in her face.

She saw the figure on the sofa. She ran to it with a cry—a cry of recognition and a cry of terror in one. She dropped on her knees—and laid that helpless head on her bosom, and kissed, with a sister's kisses, that cold, white cheek.

"Oh, my darling!" she said. "Is it thus we meet again?"

Yes! After all the years that had passed since the parting in the cabin of the ship, it was thus the two school-friends met again.

---

## Part the Second.

### THE MARCH OF TIME.

#### V.

ADVANCING from time past to time present, the Prologue leaves the date last attained (the summer of eighteen hundred and fifty-five), and travels on through an interval of twelve years—tells who lived, who died, who prospered, and who failed among the persons concerned in the tragedy at the Hampstead villa—and, this done, leaves the reader at the opening of THE STORY, in the spring of eighteen hundred and sixty-eight.

The record begins with a marriage—the marriage of Mr. Vanborough and Lady Jane Parnell.

In three months from the memorable day when his solicitor had informed him that he was a free man, Mr. Vanborough possessed the wife he desired, to grace the head of his table and to push his fortunes in the world—the Legislature of Great Britain being the humble servant of his treachery, and the respectable accomplice of his crime.

He entered Parliament. He gave (thanks to his wife) six of the grandest dinners, and two of the most crowded balls of the season. He made a successful first speech in the House of Commons. He endowed a church in a poor neighborhood. He wrote an article which attracted attention in a quarterly review. He discovered, denounced, and remedied a crying abuse in the administration of a public charity. He received (thanks once more to his wife) a member of the Royal family among the visitors at his country house in the autumn recess. These were his triumphs, and this his rate of progress on the way to the peerage, during the first year of his life as the husband of Lady Jane.

There was but one more favor that Fortune could confer on her spoiled child—and Fortune bestowed it. There was a spot on Mr. Vanborough's past life as long as the woman lived whom he had disowned and deserted. At the end of the first year Death took her—and the spot was rubbed out.

She had met the merciless injury inflicted on her with a rare patience, with an admirable courage. It is due to Mr. Vanborough to admit that he broke her heart, with the strictest attention to propriety. He offered (through his lawyer) a handsome provision for her and for her child. It was rejected, without an instant's hesitation. She repudiated his money—she repudiated his name. By the name which she had borne in her maiden days—the name which she had made illustrious in her Art—the mother and daughter were known to all who cared to inquire after them when they had sunk in the world.

There was no false pride in the resolute attitude which she thus assumed after her husband had forsaken her. Mrs. Silvester (as she was now called) gratefully accepted for herself, and for Miss Silvester, the assistance of the dear old friend who had found her again in her affliction, and who remained faithful to her to the end. They lived with Lady Lundie until the mother was strong enough to carry out the plan of life which she had arranged for the future, and to earn her bread as a teacher of singing. To all appearance she rallied, and became herself again, in a few months' time. She was making her way; she was winning sympathy, confidence, and respect every where—when she sank suddenly at the opening of her new life. Nobody could account for it. The doctors themselves were divided in opinion. Scientifically speaking, there was no reason why she should die. It was a mere figure of speech—in no degree satisfactory to any reasonable mind—to say, as Lady Lundie said, that she had got her death-blow on the day when her husband deserted her. The one thing certain was the fact—account for it as you might. In spite of science (which meant little), in spite of her own courage (which meant much), the woman dropped at her post and died.

In the latter part of her illness her mind gave way. The friend of her old school-days, sitting at the bedside, heard her talking as if she thought herself back again in the cabin of the ship. The poor soul found the tone, almost the look, that had been lost for so many years—the tone of the past time when the two girls had gone their dif-

"WILL SHE END LIKE ME?"

ferent ways in the world. She said, "we will meet, darling, with all the old love between us," just as she had said almost a lifetime since. Before the end her mind rallied. She surprised the doctor and the nurse by begging them gently to leave the room. When they had gone she looked at Lady Lundie, and woke, as it seemed, to consciousness from a dream.

"Blanche," she said, "you will take care of my child?"

"She shall be *my* child, Anne, when you are gone."

The dying woman paused, and thought for a little. A sudden trembling seized her.

"Keep it a secret!" she said. "I am afraid for my child."

"Afraid? After what I have promised you?"

She solemnly repeated the words, "I am afraid for my child."

"Why?"

"My Anne is my second self—isn't she?"

"Yes."

"She is as fond of your child as I was of you?"

"Yes."

"She is not called by her father's name—she is called by mine. She is Anne Silvester as I was. Blanche! *Will she end like Me?*"

The question was put with the laboring breath, with the heavy accents which tell that death is near. It chilled the living woman who heard it to the marrow of her bones.

"Don't think that!" she cried, horror-struck. "For God's sake, don't think that!"

The wildness began to appear again in Anne Silvester's eyes. She made feebly - impatient signs with her hands. Lady Lundie bent over her, and heard her whisper, "Lift me up."

She lay in her friend's arms; she looked up in her friend's face; she went back wildly to her fear for her child.

"Don't bring her up like Me! She must be a governess—she must get her bread. Don't let her act! don't let her sing! don't let her go on the stage!" She stopped—her voice suddenly recovered its sweetness of tone—she smiled faintly—she said the old girlish words once more, in the old girlish way, "Vow it, Blanche!" Lady Lundie kissed her, and answered, as she had answered when they parted in the ship, "I vow it, Anne!"

The head sank, never to be lifted more. The last look of life flickered in the filmy eyes and went out. For a moment afterward her lips moved. Lady Lundie put her ear close to them, and heard the dreadful question reiterated, in the same dreadful words: "She is Anne Silvester—as I was. *Will she end like Me?*"

## VI.

Five years passed—and the lives of the three men who had sat at the dinner-table in the Hampstead villa began, in their altered aspects, to reveal the progress of time and change.

Mr. Kendrew; Mr. Delamayn; Mr. Vanborough. Let the order in which they are here named be the order in which their lives are reviewed, as seen once more after a lapse of five years.

How the husband's friend marked his sense of the husband's treachery has been told already. How he felt the death of the deserted wife is still left to tell. Report, which sees the inmost hearts of men, and delights in turning them outward to the public view, had always declared that Mr. Kendrew's life had its secret, and that the secret was a hopeless passion for the beautiful woman who had married his friend. Not a hint ever dropped to any living soul, not a word ever spoken to the woman herself, could be produced in proof of the assertion while the woman lived. When she died Report started up again more confidently than ever, and appealed to the man's own conduct as proof against the man himself.

He attended the funeral—though he was no relation. He took a few blades of grass from the turf with which they covered her grave—when he thought that nobody was looking at him. He disappeared from his club. He traveled. He came back. He admitted that he was weary of England. He applied for, and obtained, an appointment in one of the colonies. To what conclusion did all this point? Was it not plain that his usual course of life had lost its attraction for him, when the object of his infatuation had ceased to exist? It might have been so—guesses less likely have been made at the truth, and have hit the mark. It is, at any rate, certain that he left England, never to return again. Another man lost, Report said. Add to that, a man in ten thousand—and, for once, Report might claim to be right.

Mr. Delamayn comes next.

The rising solicitor was struck off the roll, at his own request—and entered himself as a student at one of the Inns of Court. For three years nothing was known of him but that he was reading hard and keeping his terms. He was called to the Bar. His late partners in the firm knew they could trust him, and put business into his hands. In two years he made himself a position in Court. At the end of the two years he made himself a position *out* of Court. He appeared as "Junior" in "a famous case," in which the honor of a great family, and the title to a great estate were concerned. His "Senior" fell ill on the eve of the trial. He conducted the case for the defendant and won it. The defendant said, "What can I do for you?" Mr. Delamayn answered, "Put me into Parliament." Being a landed gentleman, the defendant had only to issue the necessary orders—and behold, Mr. Delamayn was in Parliament!

In the House of Commons the new member and Mr. Vanborough met again.

They sat on the same bench, and sided with the same party. Mr. Delamayn noticed that Mr. Vanborough was looking old and worn and gray. He put a few questions to a well-informed person. The well-informed person shook his head. Mr. Vanborough was rich; Mr. Vanborough was well-connected (through his wife); Mr. Vanborough was a sound man in every sense of the word; *but*—nobody liked him. He had done very well the first year, and there it had ended. He was undeniably clever, but he produced a disagreeable impression in the House. He gave splendid entertainments, but he wasn't popular in society. His party respected him, but when they had any thing to give they passed him over. He had a temper of his own, if the truth must be told; and with nothing against him—on the contrary, with every thing in his favor—he didn't make friends. A soured man. At home and abroad, a soured man.

## VII.

Five years more passed, dating from the day when the deserted wife was laid in her grave. It was now the year eighteen hundred and sixty-six.

On a certain day in that year two special items of news appeared in the papers—the news of an elevation to the peerage, and the news of a suicide.

Getting on well at the Bar, Mr. Delamayn got on better still in Parliament. He became one of the prominent men in the House. Spoke clearly, sensibly, and modestly, and was never too long. Held the House, where men of higher abilities "bored" it. The chiefs of his party said openly, "We must do something for Delamayn." The opportunity offered, and the chiefs kept their word. Their Solicitor-General was advanced a step, and they put Delamayn in his place. There was an outcry on the part of the older members of the Bar. The Ministry answered, "We want a man who is listened to in the House, and we have got him." The papers supported the new nomination. A great debate came off, and the new Solicitor-General justified the Ministry and the papers. His enemies said, derisively, "He will be Lord Chancellor in a year or two!" His friends made genial jokes in his domestic circle, which pointed to the same conclusion. They warned his two sons, Julius and Geoffrey (then at college), to be careful what acquaintances they made, as they might find themselves the sons of a lord at a moment's notice. It really began to look like something of the sort. Always rising, Mr. Delamayn rose next to be Attorney-General. About the same time—so true it is that "nothing succeeds like success"—a childless relative died and left him a fortune. In the summer of 'sixty-six a Chief Judgeship fell vacant. The Ministry had made a previous appointment which had been universally unpopular. They saw their way to supplying the place of their Attorney-General, and they offered the judicial appointment to Mr. Delamayn. He preferred remaining in the House of Commons, and refused to accept it. The Ministry declined to take No for an answer. They whispered confidentially, "Will you take it with a peerage?" Mr. Delamayn consulted his wife, and took it with a peerage. The London *Gazette* announced him to the world as Baron Holchester of Holchester. And the friends of the family rubbed their hands and said, "What did we tell you? Here are our two young friends, Julius and Geoffrey, the sons of a lord!"

And where was Mr. Vanborough all this time? Exactly where we left him five years since.

He was as rich, or richer, than ever. He was as well-connected as ever. He was as ambitious as ever. But there it ended. He stood still in the House; he stood still in society; nobody liked him; he made no friends. It was all the old story over again, with this difference, that the soured man was sourer; the gray head, grayer; and the irritable temper more unendurable than ever. His wife had her rooms in the house and he had his, and the confidential servants took care that they never met on the stairs. They had no children. They only saw each other at their grand dinners and balls. People ate at their table, and danced on their floor, and compared notes afterward, and said how dull it was. Step by step the man who had once been Mr. Vanborough's lawyer rose, till the peerage received him, and he could rise no longer; while Mr. Vanborough, on the lower round of the ladder, looked up, and noted it, with no more chance (rich as he was and well-connected as he was) of climbing to the House of Lords than your chance or mine.

The man's career was ended; and on the day when the nomination of the new peer was announced, the man ended with it.

He laid the newspaper aside without making any remark, and went out. His carriage set

"THEY BROKE OPEN THE DOOR, AND SAW HIM LYING ON THE SOFA."

him down, where the green fields still remain, on the northwest of London, near the foot-path which leads to Hampstead. He walked alone to the villa where he had once lived with the woman whom he had so cruelly wronged. New houses had risen round it, part of the old garden had been sold and built on. After a moment's hesitation he went to the gate and rang the bell. He gave the servant his card. The servant's master knew the name as the name of a man of great wealth, and of a Member of Parliament. He asked politely to what fortunate circumstance he owed the honor of that visit. Mr. Vanborough answered, briefly and simply, "I once lived here; I have associations with the place with which it is not necessary for me to trouble you. Will you excuse what must seem to you a very strange request? I should like to see the dining-room again, if there is no objection, and if I am disturbing nobody."

The "strange requests" of rich men are of the nature of "privileged communications," for this excellent reason, that they are sure not to be requests for money. Mr. Vanborough was shown into the dining-room. The master of the house, secretly wondering, watched him.

He walked straight to a certain spot on the carpet, not far from the window that led into the garden, and nearly opposite the door. On that spot he stood silently, with his head on his breast —thinking. Was it *there* he had seen her for the last time, on the day when he left the room forever? Yes; it was there. After a minute or so he roused himself, but in a dreamy, absent manner. He said it was a pretty place, and expressed his thanks, and looked back before the door closed, and then went his way again. His carriage picked him up where it had set him down. He drove to the residence of the new Lord Holchester, and left a card for him. Then he went home. Arrived at his house, his secretary reminded him that he had an appointment in ten minutes' time. He thanked the secretary in the same dreamy, absent manner in which he had thanked the owner of the villa, and went into his dressing-room. The person with whom he had made the appointment came, and the secretary sent the valet up stairs to knock at the door. There was no answer. On trying the lock it proved to be turned inside. They broke open the door, and saw him lying on the sofa. They went close to look—and found him dead by his own hand.

## VIII.

Drawing fast to its close, the Prologue reverts to the two girls—and tells, in a few words, how the years passed with Anne and Blanche.

Lady Lundie more than redeemed the solemn pledge that she had given to her friend. Preserved from every temptation which might lure her into a longing to follow her mother's career; trained for a teacher's life, with all the arts and all the advantages that money could procure, Anne's first and only essays as a governess were made, under Lady Lundie's own roof, on Lady Lundie's own child. The difference in the ages of the girls—seven years—the love between them, which seemed, as time went on, to grow with their growth, favored the trial of the experiment. In the double relation of teacher and friend to little Blanche, the girl-

hood of Anne Silvester the younger passed safely, happily, uneventfully, in the modest sanctuary of home. Who could imagine a contrast more complete than the contrast between her early life and her mother's? Who could see any thing but a death-bed delusion in the terrible question which had tortured the mother's last moments: "Will she end like Me?"

But two events of importance occurred in the quiet family circle during the lapse of years which is now under review. In eighteen hundred and fifty-eight the household was enlivened by the arrival of Sir Thomas Lundie. In eighteen hundred and sixty-five the household was broken up by the return of Sir Thomas to India, accompanied by his wife.

Lady Lundie's health had been failing for some time previously. The medical men, consulted on the case, agreed that a sea-voyage was the one change needful to restore their patient's wasted strength—exactly at the time, as it happened, when Sir Thomas was due again in India. For his wife's sake, he agreed to defer his return, by taking the sea-voyage with her. The one difficulty to get over was the difficulty of leaving Blanche and Anne behind in England.

Appealed to on this point, the doctors had declared that at Blanche's critical time of life they could not sanction her going to India with her mother. At the same time, near and dear relatives came forward, who were ready and anxious to give Blanche and her governess a home—Sir Thomas, on his side, engaging to bring his wife back in a year and a half, or, at most, in two years' time. Assailed in all directions, Lady Lundie's natural unwillingness to leave the girls was overruled. She consented to the parting— with a mind secretly depressed, and secretly doubtful of the future.

At the last moment she drew Anne Silvester on one side, out of hearing of the rest. Anne was then a young woman of twenty-two, and Blanche a girl of fifteen.

"My dear," she said, simply, "I must tell *you* what I can not tell Sir Thomas, and what I am afraid to tell Blanche. I am going away, with a mind that misgives me. I am persuaded I shall not live to return to England; and, when I am dead, I believe my husband will marry again. Years ago your mother was uneasy, on her death-bed, about *your* future. I am uneasy, now, about Blanche's future. I promised my dear dead friend that you should be like my own child to me—and it quieted her mind. Quiet *my* mind, Anne, before I go. Whatever happens in years to come—promise me to be always, what you are now, a sister to Blanche."

She held out her hand for the last time. With a full heart Anne Silvester kissed it, and gave the promise.

## IX.

In two months from that time one of the forebodings which had weighed on Lady Lundie's mind was fulfilled. She died on the voyage, and was buried at sea.

In a year more the second misgiving was confirmed. Sir Thomas Lundie married again. He brought his second wife to England toward the close of eighteen hundred and sixty-six.

Time, in the new household, promised to pass as quietly as in the old. Sir Thomas remembered and respected the trust which his first wife had placed in Anne. The second Lady Lundie, wisely guiding her conduct in this matter by the conduct of her husband, left things as she found them in the new house. At the opening of eighteen hundred and sixty-seven the relations between Anne and Blanche were relations of sisterly sympathy and sisterly love. The prospect in the future was as fair as a prospect could be.

At this date, of the persons concerned in the tragedy of twelve years since at the Hampstead villa, three were dead; and one was self-exiled in a foreign land. There now remained living Anne and Blanche, who had been children at the time; and the rising solicitor who had discovered the flaw in the Irish marriage—once Mr. Delamayn: now Lord Holchester.

---

# The Story.

## FIRST SCENE.—THE SUMMER-HOUSE.

## CHAPTER THE FIRST.

### THE OWLS.

In the spring of the year eighteen hundred and sixty-eight there lived, in a certain county of North Britain, two venerable White Owls.

The Owls inhabited a decayed and deserted summer-house. The summer-house stood in grounds attached to a country seat in Perthshire, known by the name of Windygates.

The situation of Windygates had been skillfully chosen in that part of the county where the fertile lowlands first begin to merge into the mountain region beyond. The mansion-house was intelligently laid out, and luxuriously furnished. The stables offered a model for ventilation and space; and the gardens and grounds were fit for a prince.

Possessed of these advantages, at starting, Windygates, nevertheless, went the road to ruin in due course of time. The curse of litigation fell on house and lands. For more than ten years an interminable lawsuit coiled itself closer and closer round the place, sequestering it from human habitation, and even from human approach. The mansion was closed. The garden became a wilderness of weeds. The summer-house was choked up by creeping plants; and the appearance of the creepers was followed by the appearance of the birds of night.

For years the Owls lived undisturbed on the property which they had acquired by the oldest of all existing rights—the right of taking. Throughout the day they sat peaceful and solemn, with closed eyes, in the cool darkness shed round them by the ivy. With the twilight they roused themselves softly to the business of life. In sage and silent companionship of two, they went flying, noiseless, along the quiet lanes in search of a meal. At one time they would beat a field like a setter dog, and drop down in an instant on a mouse unaware of them. At another time—moving spectral over the black surface of the water—they would try the lake for a change, and catch a perch as they had caught the mouse. Their catholic digestions were equally tolerant of a rat or an insect. And there were moments, proud moments, in their lives, when they were clever enough to snatch a small bird at roost off his perch. On those occasions the sense of superiority which the large bird feels every where over the small, warmed their cool blood, and set them screeching cheerfully in the stillness of the night.

So, for years, the Owls slept their happy sleep by day, and found their comfortable meal when darkness fell. They had come, with the creepers, into possession of the summer-house. Consequently, the creepers were a part of the constitution of the summer-house. And consequently the Owls were the guardians of the Constitution. There are some human owls who reason as they did, and who are, in this respect—as also in respect of snatching smaller birds off their roosts —wonderfully like them.

The constitution of the summer-house had lasted until the spring of the year eighteen hundred and sixty-eight, when the unhallowed footsteps of innovation passed that way; and the venerable privileges of the Owls were assailed, for the first time, from the world outside.

Two featherless beings appeared, uninvited, at the door of the summer-house, surveyed the constitutional creepers, and said, "These must come down"—looked around at the horrid light of noonday, and said, "That must come in"— went away, thereupon, and were heard, in the distance, agreeing together, "To-morrow it shall be done."

And the Owls said, "Have we honored the summer-house by occupying it all these years— and is the horrid light of noonday to be let in on us at last? My lords and gentlemen, the Constitution is destroyed!"

They passed a resolution to that effect, as is the manner of their kind. And then they shut their eyes again, and felt that they had done their duty.

The same night, on their way to the fields, they observed with dismay a light in one of the windows of the house. What did the light mean?

It meant, in the first place, that the lawsuit was over at last. It meant, in the second place, that the owner of Windygates, wanting money, had decided on letting the property. It meant, in the third place, that the property had found a tenant, and was to be renovated immediately out of doors and in. The Owls shrieked as they flapped along the lanes in the darkness. And that night they struck at a mouse—and missed him.

The next morning, the Owls—fast asleep in charge of the Constitution—were roused by voices of featherless beings all round them. They opened their eyes, under protest, and saw instruments of destruction attacking the creepers. Now in one direction, and now in another, those instruments let in on the summer-house the horrid light of day. But the Owls were equal to the occasion. They ruffled their feathers, and cried, "No surrender!" The featherless beings plied their work cheerfully, and answered, "Reform!" The creepers were torn down this way and that. The horrid daylight poured in brighter and brighter. The Owls had barely time to pass a new resolution, namely, "That we do stand by the Constitution," when a ray of the outer sunlight flashed into their eyes, and sent them flying headlong to the nearest shade. There they sat winking, while the summer-house was cleared of the rank growth that had choked it up, while the rotten wood-work was renewed, while all the murky place was purified with air and light. And when the world saw it, and said, "Now we shall do!" the Owls shut their eyes in pious remembrance of the darkness, and answered, " My lords and gentlemen, the Constitution is destroyed!"

---

## CHAPTER THE SECOND.

### THE GUESTS.

WHO was responsible for the reform of the summer-house?

The new tenant at Windygates was responsible.

And who was the new tenant?

Come, and see.

In the spring of eighteen hundred and sixty-eight the summer-house had been the dismal dwelling-place of a pair of owls. In the autumn of the same year the summer-house was the lively gathering-place of a crowd of ladies and gentlemen, assembled at a lawn party—the guests of the tenant who had taken Windygates.

The scene—at the opening of the party—was as pleasant to look at as light and beauty and movement could make it.

Inside the summer-house the butterfly-brightness of the women in their summer dresses shone radiant out of the gloom shed round it by the dreary modern clothing of the men. Outside the summer-house, seen through three arched openings, the cool green prospect of a lawn led away, in the distance, to flower-beds and shrubberies, and, farther still, disclosed, through a break in the trees, a grand stone house which closed the view, with a fountain in front of it playing in the sun.

They were half of them laughing, they were all of them talking—the comfortable hum of the voices was at its loudest; the cheery pealing of the laughter was soaring to its highest notes—when one dominant voice, rising clear and shrill above all the rest, called imperatively for silence. The moment after, a young lady stepped into the vacant space in front of the summer-house, and surveyed the throng of guests as a general in command surveys a regiment under review.

She was young, she was pretty, she was plump, she was fair. She was not the least embarrassed by her prominent position. She was dressed in the height of the fashion. A hat, like a cheese-plate, was tilted over her forehead. A balloon of light brown hair soared, fully inflated, from the crown of her head. A cataract of beads poured over her bosom. A pair of cock-chafers in enamel (frightfully like the living originals) hung at her ears. Her scanty skirts shone splendid with the blue of heaven. Her ankles twinkled in striped stockings. Her shoes were of the sort called "Watteau." And her heels were of the height at which men shudder, and ask themselves (in contemplating an otherwise lovable woman), "Can this charming person straighten her knees?"

The young lady thus presenting herself to the general view was Miss Blanche Lundie—once the little rosy Blanche whom the Prologue has introduced to the reader. Age, at the present time, eighteen. Position, excellent. Money, certain. Temper, quick. Disposition, variable.

In a word, a child of the modern time—with the merits of the age we live in, and the failings of the age we live in—and a substance of sincerity and truth and feeling underlying it all.

"Now then, good people," cried Miss Blanche, "silence, if you please! We are going to choose sides at croquet. Business, business, business!"

Upon this, a second lady among the company assumed a position of prominence, and answered the young person who had just spoken with a look of mild reproof, and in a tone of benevolent protest.

The second lady was tall, and solid, and five-and-thirty. She presented to the general observation a cruel aquiline nose, an obstinate straight chin, magnificent dark hair and eyes, a serene splendor of fawn-colored apparel, and a lazy grace of movement which was attractive at first sight, but inexpressibly monotonous and wearisome on a longer acquaintance. This was Lady Lundie the Second, now the widow (after four months only of married life) of Sir Thomas Lundie, deceased. In other words, the step-mother of Blanche, and the enviable person who had taken the house and lands of Windygates.

"My dear," said Lady Lundie, "words have their meanings—even on a young lady's lips. Do you call Croquet, ' business?'"

"You don't call it pleasure, surely?" said a gravely ironical voice in the back-ground of the summer-house.

The ranks of the visitors parted before the last speaker, and disclosed to view, in the midst of that modern assembly, a gentleman of the by-gone time.

The manner of this gentleman was distinguished by a pliant grace and courtesy unknown to the present generation. The attire of this gentleman was composed of a many-folded white cravat, a close-buttoned blue dress-coat, and nankeen trowsers with gaiters to match, ridiculous to the present generation. The talk of this gentleman ran in an easy flow—revealing an independent habit of mind, and exhibiting a carefully-polished capacity for satirical retort—dreaded and disliked by the present generation. Personally, he was little and wiry and slim—with a bright white head, and sparkling black eyes, and a wry twist of humor curling sharply at the corners of his lips. At his lower extremities, he exhibited the deformity which is popularly known as "a club-foot." But he carried his lameness, as he carried his years, gayly. He was socially celebrated for his ivory cane, with a snuff-box artfully let into the knob at the top—and he was socially dreaded for a hatred of modern institutions, which expressed itself in season and out of season, and which always showed the same fatal knack of hitting smartly on the weakest place. Such was Sir Patrick Lundie; brother of the late baronet, Sir Thomas; and inheritor, at Sir Thomas's death, of the title and estates.

Miss Blanche—taking no notice of her step-mother's reproof, or of her uncle's commentary on it—pointed to a table on which croquet mallets and balls were laid ready, and recalled the attention of the company to the matter in hand.

"I head one side, ladies and gentlemen," she resumed. "And Lady Lundie heads the other. We choose our players turn and turn about. Mamma has the advantage of me in years. So mamma chooses first."

With a look at her step-daughter—which, being interpreted, meant, "I would send you back to the nursery, miss, if I could !"—Lady Lundie turned, and ran her eye over her guests. She had evidently made up her mind, beforehand, what player to pick out first.

"I choose Miss Silvester," she said—with a special emphasis laid on the name.

At that there was another parting among the crowd. To us (who know her), it was Anne who now appeared. Strangers, who saw her for the first time, saw a lady in the prime of her life —a lady plainly dressed in unornamented white —who advanced slowly, and confronted the mistress of the house.

A certain proportion—and not a small one— of the men at the lawn-party had been brought there by friends who were privileged to introduce them. The moment she appeared every one of those men suddenly became interested in the lady who had been chosen first.

"That's a very charming woman," whispered one of the strangers at the house to one of the friends of the house. "Who is she ?"

The friend whispered back :

"Miss Lundie's governess—that's all."

The moment during which the question was put and answered was also the moment which brought Lady Lundie and Miss Silvester face to face, in the presence of the company.

The stranger at the house looked at the two women, and whispered again.

"Something wrong between the lady and the governess," he said.

The friend looked also, and answered, in one emphatic word :

"Evidently !"

There are certain women whose influence over men is an unfathomable mystery to observers of their own sex. The governess was one of those women. She had inherited the charm, but not the beauty, of her unhappy mother. Judge her by the standard set up in the illustrated gift-books and the print-shop windows— and the sentence must have inevitably followed. "She has not a single good feature in her face." There was nothing individually remarkable about Miss Silvester, seen in a state of repose. She was of the average height. She was as well made as most women. In hair and complexion, she was neither light nor dark, but provokingly neutral, just between the two. Worse even than this, there were positive defects in her face, which it was impossible to deny. A nervous contraction at one corner of her mouth drew up the lips out of the symmetrically right line, when they moved. A nervous uncertainty in the eye on the same side narrowly escaped presenting the deformity of a "cast." And yet, with these indisputable drawbacks, here was one of those women — the formidable few — who have the hearts of men and the peace of families at their mercy. She moved—and there was some subtle charm, Sir, in the movement, that made you look back, and suspend your conversation with your friend, and watch her silently while she walked. She sat by you and talked to you—and behold, a sensitive something passed into that little twist at the corner of the mouth, and into that nervous uncertainty in the soft gray eye, which turned defect into beauty —which enchained your senses —which made your nerves thrill if she touched you by accident, and set your heart beating if you looked at the same book with her, and felt her breath on your face. All this, let it be well understood, only happened if you were a man. If you saw her with the eyes of a woman, the results were of quite another kind. In that case, you merely turned to your nearest female friend, and said, with unaffected pity for the other sex, "What can the men see in her !"

The eyes of the lady of the house and the eyes of the governess met, with marked distrust on either side. Few people could have failed to see, what the stranger and the friend had noticed alike — that there was something smouldering under the surface here. Miss Silvester spoke first.

"Thank you, Lady Lundie," she said. "I would rather not play."

Lady Lundie assumed an extreme surprise which passed the limits of good-breeding.

"Oh, indeed ?" she rejoined, sharply. "Considering that we are all here for the purpose of playing, that seems rather remarkable. Is any thing wrong, Miss Silvester ?"

A flush appeared on the delicate paleness of Miss Silvester's face. But she did her duty as a woman and a governess. She submitted, and so preserved appearances, for that time.

"Nothing is the matter," she answered. "I am not very well this morning. But I will play if you wish it."

"I do wish it," answered Lady Lundie.

Miss Silvester turned aside toward one of the entrances into the summer-house. She waited for events, looking out over the lawn, with a visible inner disturbance, marked over the bosom by the rise and fall of her white dress.

It was Blanche's turn to select the next player.

In some preliminary uncertainty as to her choice, she looked about among the guests, and caught the eye of a gentleman in the front ranks. He stood side by side with Sir Patrick—a striking representative of the school that is among us—as Sir Patrick was a striking representative of the school that has passed away.

The modern gentleman was young and florid, tall and strong. The parting of his curly Saxon locks began in the centre of his forehead, traveled over the top of his head, and ended, rigidly-central, at the ruddy nape of his neck. His features were as perfectly regular and as perfectly unintelligent as human features can be. His expression preserved an immovable composure wonderful to behold. The muscles of his brawny arms showed through the sleeves of his light summer coat. He was deep in the chest, thin in the flanks, firm on the legs—in two words, a magnificent human animal, wrought up to the highest pitch of physical development, from head to foot. This was Mr. Geoffrey Delamayn—commonly called "the honorable ;" and meriting that distinction in more ways than one. He was honorable, in the first place, as being the son (second son) of that once-rising solicitor, who was now Lord Holchester. He was honorable, in the second place, as having won the highest popular distinction which the educational system of modern England can bestow—he had pulled the stroke-oar in a University boat-race. Add to this, that nobody had ever seen him read any thing but a newspaper, and that nobody had ever known him to be backward in settling a bet—and the picture of this distinguished young Englishman will be, for the present, complete.

Blanche's eye naturally rested on him. Blanche's voice naturally picked him out as the first player on her side.

"I choose Mr. Delamayn," she said.

As the name passed her lips the flush on Miss Silvester's face died away, and a deadly paleness took its place. She made a movement to leave the summer-house—checked herself abruptly—and laid one hand on the back of a rustic seat at her side. A gentleman behind her, looking at the hand, saw it clench itself so suddenly and so fiercely that the glove on it split. The gentleman made a mental memorandum, and registered Miss Silvester in his private books as "the devil's own temper."

Meanwhile Mr. Delamayn, by a strange coincidence, took exactly the same course which Miss Silvester had taken before him. He, too, attempted to withdraw from the coming game.

"Thanks very much," he said. "Could you additionally honor me by choosing somebody else? It's not in my line."

Fifty years ago such an answer as this, addressed to a lady, would have been considered inexcusably impertinent. The social code of the present time hailed it as something frankly amusing. The company laughed. Blanche lost her temper.

"Can't we interest you in any thing but severe muscular exertion, Mr. Delamayn?" she asked, sharply. "Must you always be pulling in a boat-race, or flying over a high jump? If you had a mind, you would want to relax it. You have got muscles instead. Why not relax *them?*"

The shafts of Miss Lundie's bitter wit glided off Mr. Geoffrey Delamayn like water off a duck's back.

"Just as you please," he said, with stolid good-humor. "Don't be offended. I came here with ladies—and they wouldn't let me smoke. I miss my smoke. I thought I'd slip away a bit and have it. All right! I'll play."

"Oh! smoke by all means!" retorted Blanche. "I shall choose somebody else. I won't have you!"

The honorable young gentleman looked unaffectedly relieved. The petulant young lady turned her back on him, and surveyed the guests at the other extremity of the summer-house.

"Who shall I choose?" she said to herself.

A dark young man—with a face burned gipsy-brown by the sun; with something in his look and manner suggestive of a roving life, and perhaps of a familiar acquaintance with the sea—advanced shyly, and said, in a whisper:

"Choose me!"

Blanche's face broke prettily into a charming smile. Judging from appearances, the dark young man had a place in her estimation peculiarly his own.

"You!" she said, coquettishly. "You are going to leave us in an hour's time!"

He ventured a step nearer. "I am coming back," he pleaded, "the day after to-morrow."

"You play very badly!"

"I might improve—if you would teach me."

"Might you? Then I *will* teach you!" She turned, bright and rosy, to her step-mother. "I choose Mr. Arnold Brinkworth," she said.

Here, again, there appeared to be something in a name unknown to celebrity, which nevertheless produced its effect—not, this time, on Miss Silvester, but on Sir Patrick. He looked at Mr. Brinkworth with a sudden interest and curiosity. If the lady of the house had not claimed his attention at the moment he would evidently have spoken to the dark young man.

But it was Lady Lundie's turn to choose a second player on her side. Her brother-in-law was a person of some importance; and she had her own motives for ingratiating herself with the head of the family. She surprised the whole company by choosing Sir Patrick.

"Mamma!" cried Blanche. "What can you be thinking of? Sir Patrick won't play. Croquet wasn't discovered in his time."

Sir Patrick never allowed "his time" to be made the subject of disparaging remarks by the younger generation without paying the younger generation back in its own coin.

"In *my* time, my dear," he said to his niece, "people were expected to bring some agreeable quality with them to social meetings of this sort. In *your* time you have dispensed with all that. Here," remarked the old gentleman, taking up a croquet mallet from the table near him, "is one of the qualifications for success in modern society. And here," he added, taking up a ball, "is another. Very good. Live and learn. I'll play! I'll play!"

Lady Lundie (born impervious to all sense of irony) smiled graciously. "I knew Sir Patrick would play," she said, "to please *me.*"

Sir Patrick bowed with satirical politeness.

"Lady Lundie," he answered, "you read me like a book." To the astonishment of all persons present under forty he emphasized those words by laying his hand on his heart, and quoting poetry. "I may say with Dryden," added the gallant old gentleman:

"'Old as I am, for ladies' love unfit,
The power of beauty I remember yet.'"

Lady Lundie looked unaffectedly shocked. Mr. Delamayn went a step farther. He interfered on the spot—with the air of a man who feels himself imperatively called upon to perform a public duty.

"Dryden never said that," he remarked, "I'll answer for it."

Sir Patrick wheeled round with the help of his ivory cane, and looked Mr. Delamayn hard in the face.

"Do you know Dryden, Sir, better than I do?" he asked.

The Honorable Geoffrey answered, modestly, "I should say I did. I have rowed three races with him, and we trained together."

Sir Patrick looked round him with a sour smile of triumph.

"Then let me tell you, Sir," he said, "that you trained with a man who died nearly two hundred years ago."

Mr. Delamayn appealed, in genuine bewilderment, to the company generally:

"What does this old gentleman mean?" he asked. "I am speaking of Tom Dryden, of Corpus. Every body in the University knows *him.*"

"I am speaking," echoed Sir Patrick, "of

John Dryden the Poet. Apparently, every body in the University does *not* know *him!*"

Mr. Delamayn answered, with a cordial earnestness very pleasant to see:

"Give you my word of honor, I never heard of him before in my life! Don't be angry, Sir. *I'm* not offended with *you*." He smiled, and took out his brier-wood pipe. "Got a light?" he asked, in the friendliest possible manner.

Sir Patrick answered, with a total absence of cordiality:

"I don't smoke, Sir."

Mr. Delamayn looked at him, without taking the slightest offense:

"You don't smoke!" he repeated. "I wonder how you get through your spare time?"

Sir Patrick closed the conversation:

"Sir," he said, with a low bow, "you *may* wonder."

While this little skirmish was proceeding Lady Lundie and her step-daughter had organized the game; and the company, players and spectators, were beginning to move toward the lawn. Sir Patrick stopped his niece on her way out, with the dark young man in close attendance on her.

"Leave Mr. Brinkworth with me," he said. "I want to speak to him."

Blanche issued her orders immediately. Mr. Brinkworth was sentenced to stay with Sir Patrick until she wanted him for the game. Mr. Brinkworth wondered, and obeyed.

During the exercise of this act of authority a circumstance occurred at the other end of the summer-house. Taking advantage of the confusion caused by the general movement to the lawn, Miss Silvester suddenly placed herself close to Mr. Delamayn.

"In ten minutes," she whispered, "the summer-house will be empty. Meet me here."

The Honorable Geoffrey started, and looked furtively at the visitors about him.

"Do you think it's safe?" he whispered back.

The governess's sensitive lips trembled, with fear or with anger, it was hard to say which.

"I insist on it!" she answered, and left him.

Mr. Delamayn knitted his handsome eyebrows as he looked after her, and then left the summer-house in his turn. The rose-garden at the back of the building was solitary for the moment. He took out his pipe and hid himself among the roses. The smoke came from his mouth in hot and hasty puffs. He was usually the gentlest of masters—to his pipe. When he hurried that confidential servant, it was a sure sign of disturbance in the inner man.

---

## CHAPTER THE THIRD.

### THE DISCOVERIES.

BUT two persons were now left in the summer-house—Arnold Brinkworth and Sir Patrick Lundie.

"Mr. Brinkworth," said the old gentleman, "I have had no opportunity of speaking to you before this; and (as I hear that you are to leave us to-day) I may find no opportunity at a later time. I want to introduce myself. Your father was one of my dearest friends—let me make a friend of your father's son."

He held out his hand, and mentioned his name.

Arnold recognized it directly. "Oh, Sir Patrick!" he said, warmly, "if my poor father had only taken your advice—"

"He would have thought twice before he gambled away his fortune on the turf; and he might have been alive here among us, instead of dying an exile in a foreign land," said Sir Patrick, finishing the sentence which the other had begun. "No more of that! Let's talk of something else. Lady Lundie wrote to me about you the other day. She told me your aunt was dead, and had left you heir to her property in Scotland. Is that true?—It is?—I congratulate you with all my heart. Why are you visiting here, instead of looking after your house and lands? Oh! it's only three-and-twenty miles from this; and you're going to look after it to-day, by the next train? Quite right. And—what? what?—coming back again the day after to-morrow? Why should you come back? Some special attraction here, I suppose? I hope it's the right sort of attraction. You're very young—you're exposed to all sorts of temptations. Have you got a solid foundation of good sense at the bottom of you? It is not inherited from your poor father, if you have. You must have been a mere boy when he ruined his children's prospects. How have you lived from that time to this? What were you doing when your aunt's will made an idle man of you for life?"

The question was a searching one. Arnold answered it, without the slightest hesitation; speaking with an unaffected modesty and simplicity which at once won Sir Patrick's heart.

"I was a boy at Eton, Sir," he said, "when my father's losses ruined him. I had to leave school, and get my own living; and I have got it, in a roughish way, from that time to this. In plain English, I have followed the sea—in the merchant-service."

"In plainer English still, you met adversity like a brave lad, and you have fairly earned the good luck that has fallen to you," rejoined Sir Patrick. "Give me your hand—I have taken a liking to you. You're not like the other young fellows of the present time. I shall call you 'Arnold.' You mus'n't return the compliment, and call me 'Patrick,' mind—I'm too old to be treated in that way. Well, and how do you get on here? What sort of a woman is my sister-in-law? and what sort of a house is this?"

Arnold burst out laughing.

"Those are extraordinary questions for you to put to me," he said. "You talk, Sir, as if you were a stranger here!"

Sir Patrick touched a spring in the knob of his ivory cane. A little gold lid flew up, and disclosed the snuff-box hidden inside. He took a pinch, and chuckled satirically over some passing thought, which he did not think it necessary to communicate to his young friend.

"I talk as if I was a stranger here, do I?" he resumed. "That's exactly what I am. Lady Lundie and I correspond on excellent terms; but we run in different grooves, and we see each other as seldom as possible. My story," continued the pleasant old man, with a charming frankness which leveled all differences of age and rank between Arnold and himself, "is not entirely unlike yours; though I *am* old enough to be your grandfather. I was getting my living, in *my* way (as a crusty old Scotch lawyer), when my brother married again. His death, without leaving a son by either of his wives, gave *me* a lift in the world, like you. Here I am (to my own sincere regret) the present baronet. Yes, to my sincere regret! All sorts of responsibilities which I never bargained for are thrust on my shoulders. I am the head of the family; I am my niece's guardian; I am compelled to appear at this lawn-party—and (between ourselves) I am as completely out of my element as a man can be. Not a single familiar face meets *me* among all these fine people. Do *you* know anybody here?"

"I have one friend at Windygates," said Arnold. "He came here this morning, like you. Geoffrey Delamayn."

As he made the reply, Miss Silvester appeared at the entrance to the summer-house. A shadow of annoyance passed over her face when she saw that the place was occupied. She vanished, unnoticed, and glided back to the game.

Sir Patrick looked at the son of his old friend, with every appearance of being disappointed in the young man for the first time.

"Your choice of a friend rather surprises me," he said.

Arnold artlessly accepted the words as an appeal to him for information.

"I beg your pardon, Sir—there's nothing surprising in it," he returned. "We were school-fellows at Eton, in the old times. And I have met Geoffrey since, when he was yachting, and when I was with my ship. Geoffrey saved my life, Sir Patrick," he added, his voice rising, and his eyes brightening with honest admiration of his friend. "But for him, I should have been drowned in a boat-accident. Isn't *that* a good reason for his being a friend of mine?"

"It depends entirely on the value you set on your life," said Sir Patrick.

"The value I set on my life?" repeated Arnold. "I set a high value on it, of course!"

"In that case, Mr. Delamayn has laid you under an obligation."

"Which I can never repay!"

"Which you will repay one of these days, with interest—if I know any thing of human nature," answered Sir Patrick.

He said the words with the emphasis of strong conviction. They were barely spoken when Mr. Delamayn appeared (exactly as Miss Silvester had appeared) at the entrance to the summer-house. He, too, vanished, unnoticed—like Miss Silvester again. But there the parallel stopped. The Honorable Geoffrey's expression, on discovering the place to be occupied, was, unmistakably, an expression of relief.

Arnold drew the right inference, this time, from Sir Patrick's language and Sir Patrick's tones. He eagerly took up the defense of his friend.

"You said that rather bitterly, Sir," he remarked. "What has Geoffrey done to offend you?"

"He presumes to exist—that's what he has done," retorted Sir Patrick. "Don't stare! I am speaking generally. Your friend is the model young Briton of the present time. I don't like the model young Briton. I don't see the sense of crowing over him as a superb national production, because he is big and strong, and drinks beer with impunity, and takes a cold shower-bath all the year round. There is far too much glorification in England, just now, of the mere physical qualities which an Englishman shares with the savage and the brute. And the ill results are beginning to show themselves already! We are readier than we ever were to practice all that is rough in our national customs, and to excuse all that is violent and brutish in our national acts. Read the popular books—attend the popular amusements; and you will find at the bottom of them all a lessening regard for the gentler graces of civilized life, and a growing admiration for the virtues of the aboriginal Britons!"

Arnold listened in blank amazement. He had been the innocent means of relieving Sir Patrick's mind of an accumulation of social protest, unprovided with an issue for some time past. "How hot you are over it, Sir!" he exclaimed, in irrepressible astonishment.

Sir Patrick instantly recovered himself. The genuine wonder expressed in the young man's face was irresistible.

"Almost as hot," he said, "as if I was cheering at a boat-race, or wrangling over a betting-book—eh? Ah, we were so easily heated when I was a young man! Let's change the subject. I know nothing to the prejudice of your friend, Mr. Delamayn. It's the cant of the day," cried Sir Patrick, relapsing again, "to take these physically-wholesome men for granted as being morally-wholesome men into the bargain. Time will show whether the cant of the day is right. —So you are actually coming back to Lady Lundie's after a mere flying visit to your own property? I repeat, that is a most extraordinary proceeding on the part of a landed gentleman like you. What's the attraction here—eh?"

Before Arnold could reply Blanche called to him from the lawn. His color rose, and he turned eagerly to go out. Sir Patrick nodded his head with the air of a man who had been answered to his own entire satisfaction. "Oh!" he said, "*that's* the attraction, is it?"

Arnold's life at sea had left him singularly ignorant of the ways of the world on shore. Instead of taking the joke, he looked confused. A deeper tinge of color reddened his dark cheeks. "I didn't say so," he answered, a little irritably.

Sir Patrick lifted two of his white, wrinkled old fingers, and good-humoredly patted the young sailor on the cheek.

"Yes you did," he said. "In red letters."

The little gold lid in the knob of the ivory cane flew up, and the old gentleman rewarded himself for that neat retort with a pinch of snuff. At the same moment Blanche made her appearance on the scene.

"Mr. Brinkworth," she said, "I shall want you directly. Uncle, it's your turn to play."

"Bless my soul!" cried Sir Patrick, "I forgot the game." He looked about him, and saw his mallet and ball left waiting on the table. "Where are the modern substitutes for conversation? Oh, here they are!" He bowled the ball out before him on to the lawn, and tucked the mallet, as if it was an umbrella, under his arm. "Who was the first mistaken person," he said to himself, as he briskly hobbled out, "who discovered that human life was a serious thing? Here am I, with one foot in the grave; and the most serious question before me at the present moment is, Shall I get through the Hoops?"

Arnold and Blanche were left together.

Among the personal privileges which Nature has accorded to women, there are surely none more enviable than their privilege of always looking their best when they look at the man they love. When Blanche's eyes turned on Arnold, after her uncle had gone out, not even the hideous fashionable disfigurements of the inflated "chignon" and the tilted hat that could destroy the triple charm of youth, beauty, and tenderness beaming in her face. Arnold looked at her—and remembered, as he had never remembered yet, that he was going by the next train, and that he was leaving her in the society of more than one admiring man of his own age. The experience of a whole fortnight passed under the same roof with her had proved Blanche to be the most charming girl in existence. It was possible that she might not be mortally offended with him if he told her so. He determined that he *would* tell her so at that auspicious moment.

But who shall presume to measure the abyss that lies between the Intention and the Execution? Arnold's resolution to speak was as firmly settled as a resolution could be. And what came of it? Alas for human infirmity! Nothing came of it but silence.

"You don't look quite at your ease, Mr. Brinkworth," said Blanche. "What has Sir Patrick been saying to you? My uncle sharpens his wit on every body. He has been sharpening it on *you?*"

Arnold began to see his way. At an immeasurable distance—but still he saw it.

"Sir Patrick is a terrible old man," he answered. "Just before you came in he discovered one of my secrets by only looking in my face." He paused, rallied his courage, pushed on at all hazards, and came headlong to the point. "I wonder," he asked, bluntly, "whether you take after your uncle?"

Blanche instantly understood him. With time at her disposal, she would have taken him lightly in hand, and led him, by fine gradations, to the object in view. But in two minutes or less it would be Arnold's turn to play. "He is going to make me an offer," thought Blanche; "and he has about a minute to do it in. He *shall* do it!"

"What!" she exclaimed, "do you think the gift of discovery runs in the family?"

Arnold made a plunge.

"I wish it did!" he said.

Blanche looked the picture of astonishment.

"Why?" she asked.

"If you could see in my face what Sir Patrick saw—"

He had only to finish the sentence, and the thing was done. But the tender passion perversely delights in raising obstacles to itself. A sudden timidity seized on Arnold exactly at the wrong moment. He stopped short, in the most awkward manner possible.

Blanche heard from the lawn the blow of the mallet on the ball, and the laughter of the company at some blunder of Sir Patrick's. The precious seconds were slipping away. She could have boxed Arnold on both ears for being so unreasonably afraid of her.

"Well," she said, impatiently, "if I did look in your face, what should I see?"

Arnold made another plunge. He answered:

"You would see that I want a little encouragement."

"From *me?*"

"Yes—if you please."

Blanche looked back over her shoulder. The summer-house stood on an eminence, approached by steps. The players on the lawn beneath were audible, but not visible. Any one of them might appear, unexpectedly, at a moment's notice. Blanche listened. There was no sound of approaching footsteps—there was a general hush, and then another bang of the mallet on the ball, and then a clapping of hands. Sir Patrick was a privileged person. He had been allowed, in all probability, to try again; and he was succeeding at the second effort. This implied a reprieve of some seconds. Blanche looked back again at Arnold.

"Consider yourself encouraged," she whispered; and instantly added, with the ineradicable female instinct of self-defense, "within limits!"

Arnold made a last plunge—straight to the bottom, this time.

"Consider yourself loved," he burst out, "without any limits at all."

It was all over—the words were spoken—he had got her by the hand. Again the perversity of the tender passion showed itself more strongly than ever. The confession which Blanche had been longing to hear, had barely escaped her lover's lips before Blanche protested against it! She struggled to release her hand. She formally appealed to Arnold to let her go.

Arnold only held her the tighter.

"Do try to like me a little!" he pleaded. "I am so fond of *you!*"

Who was to resist such wooing as this?—when you were privately fond of him yourself, remember! and when you were certain to be interrupted in another moment! Blanche left off struggling, and looked up at her young sailor with a smile.

"Did you learn this method of making love in the merchant-service?" she inquired, saucily.

Arnold persisted in contemplating his prospects from the serious point of view.

"I'll go back to the merchant-service," he said, "if I have made you angry with me."

Blanche administered another dose of encouragement.

"Anger, Mr. Brinkworth, is one of the bad passions," she answered, demurely. "A young lady who has been properly brought up has no bad passions."

There was a sudden cry from the players on the lawn—a cry for "Mr. Brinkworth." Blanche tried to push him out. Arnold was immovable.

"Say something to encourage me before I go," he pleaded. "One word will do. Say, Yes."

Blanche shook her head. Now she had got him, the temptation to tease him was irresistible.

"Quite impossible!" she rejoined. "If you want any more encouragement, you must speak to my uncle."

"I'll speak to him," returned Arnold, "before I leave the house."

There was another cry for "Mr. Brinkworth." Blanche made another effort to push him out.

"Go!" she said. "And mind you get through the hoop!"

"ARNOLD CAUGHT HER ROUND THE WAIST AND KISSED HER."

She had both hands on his shoulders—her face was close to his—she was simply irresistible. Arnold caught her round the waist and kissed her. Needless to tell him to get through the hoop. He had surely got through it already! Blanche was speechless. Arnold's last effort in the art of courtship had taken away her breath. Before she could recover herself a sound of approaching footsteps became plainly audible. Arnold gave her a last squeeze, and ran out.

She sank on the nearest chair, and closed her eyes in a flutter of delicious confusion.

The footsteps ascending to the summer-house came nearer. Blanche opened her eyes, and saw Anne Silvester, standing alone, looking at her. She sprang to her feet, and threw her arms impulsively round Anne's neck.

"You don't know what has happened," she whispered. "Wish me joy, darling. He has said the words. He is mine for life!"

All the sisterly love and sisterly confidence of many years was expressed in that embrace, and in the tone in which the words were spoken. The hearts of the mothers, in the past time, could hardly have been closer to each other—as it seemed—than the hearts of the daughters were now. And yet, if Blanche had looked up in Anne's face at that moment, she must have seen that Anne's mind was far away from her little love-story.

"You know who it is?" she went on, after waiting for a reply.

"Mr. Brinkworth?"

"Of course! Who else should it be?"

"And you are really happy, my love?"

"Happy?" repeated Blanche. "Mind! this is strictly between ourselves. I am ready to jump out of my skin for joy. I love him! I love him! I love him!" she cried, with a childish pleasure in repeating the words. They were echoed by a heavy sigh. Blanche instantly looked up into Anne's face. "What's the matter?" she asked, with a sudden change of voice and manner.

"Nothing."

Blanche's observation saw too plainly to be blinded in that way.

"There *is* something the matter," she said. "Is it money?" she added, after a moment's consideration. "Bills to pay? I have got plenty of money, Anne. I'll lend you what you like."

"No, no, my dear!"

Blanche drew back, a little hurt. Anne was keeping her at a distance for the first time in Blanche's experience of her.

"I tell you all my secrets," she said. "Why are *you* keeping a secret from *me*? Do you know that you have been looking anxious and out of spirits for some time past? Perhaps you don't like Mr. Brinkworth? No? you *do* like him? Is it my marrying, then? I believe it is! You fancy we shall be parted, you goose? As if I could do without you! Of course, when I am married to Arnold, you will come and live with us. That's quite understood between us—isn't it?"

Anne drew herself suddenly, almost roughly, away from Blanche, and pointed out to the steps.

"There is somebody coming," she said. "Look!"

The person coming was Arnold. It was Blanche's turn to play, and he had volunteered to fetch her.

Blanche's attention—easily enough distracted on other occasions—remained steadily fixed on Anne.

"You are not yourself," she said, "and I must know the reason of it. I will wait till to-night; and then you will tell me, when you come into my room. Don't look like that! You *shall* tell me. And there's a kiss for you in the mean time!"

She joined Arnold, and recovered her gayety the moment she looked at him.

"Well? Have you got through the hoops?"

"Never mind the hoops. I have broken the ice with Sir Patrick."

"What! before all the company!"

"Of course not! I have made an appointment to speak to him here."

They went laughing down the steps, and joined the game.

Left alone, Anne Silvester walked slowly to the inner and darker part of the summer-house. A glass, in a carved wooden frame, was fixed against one of the side walls. She stopped and looked into it—looked, shuddering, at the reflection of herself.

"Is the time coming," she said, "when even Blanche will see what I am in my face?"

She turned aside from the glass. With a sudden cry of despair she flung up her arms and laid them heavily against the wall, and rested her head on them with her back to the light. At the same moment a man's figure appeared—standing dark in the flood of sunshine at the entrance to the summer-house. The man was Geoffrey Delamayn.

---

## CHAPTER THE FOURTH.

### THE TWO.

HE advanced a few steps, and stopped. Absorbed in herself, Anne failed to hear him. She never moved.

"I have come, as you made a point of it," he said, sullenly. "But, mind you, it isn't safe."

At the sound of his voice, Anne turned toward him. A change of expression appeared in her face, as she slowly advanced from the back of the summer-house, which revealed a likeness to her mother, not perceivable at other times. As the mother had looked, in by-gone days, at the man who had disowned her, so the daughter looked at Geoffrey Delamayn—with the same terrible composure, and the same terrible contempt.

"Well?" he asked. "What have you got to say to me?"

"Mr. Delamayn," she answered, "you are one of the fortunate people of this world. You are a nobleman's son. You are a handsome man. You are popular at your college. You are free of the best houses in England. Are you something besides all this? Are you a coward and a scoundrel as well?"

He started—opened his lips to speak—checked himself—and made an uneasy attempt to laugh it off. "Come!" he said, "keep your temper."

The suppressed passion in her began to force its way to the surface.

"'Keep my temper?'" she repeated. "Do *you* of all men expect me to control myself? What a memory yours must be! Have you forgotten the time when I was fool enough to think you were fond of me? and mad enough to believe you could keep a promise?"

He persisted in trying to laugh it off. "Mad is a strongish word to use, Miss Silvester!"

"Mad is the right word! I look back at my own infatuation—and I can't account for it; I can't understand myself. What was there in *you*," she asked, with an outbreak of contemptuous surprise, "to attract such a woman as I am?"

His inexhaustible good-nature was proof even against this. He put his hands in his pockets, and said, "I'm sure I don't know."

She turned away from him. The frank brutality of the answer had not offended her. It forced her, cruelly forced her, to remember that she had nobody but herself to blame for the position in which she stood at that moment. She was unwilling to let him see how the remembrance hurt her—that was all. A sad, sad story; but it must be told. In her mother's time, she had been the sweetest, the most lovable of children. In later days, under the care of her mother's friend, her girlhood had passed so harmlessly and so happily—it seemed as if the sleeping passions might sleep forever! She had lived on to the prime of her womanhood—and then, when the treasure of her life was at its richest, in one fatal moment she had flung it away on the man in whose presence she now stood.

Was she without excuse? No: not utterly without excuse.

She had seen him under other aspects than the aspect which he presented now. She had seen him, the hero of the river-race, the first and foremost man in a trial of strength and skill which had roused the enthusiasm of all England. She had seen him, the central object of the interest of a nation; the idol of the popular worship and the popular applause. *His* were the arms whose muscle was celebrated in the newspapers. *He* was first among the heroes hailed by ten thousand roaring throats as the pride and flower of England. A woman, in an atmosphere of red-hot enthusiasm, witnesses the apotheosis of Physical Strength. Is it reasonable—is it just—to expect her to ask herself, in cold blood, What (morally and intellectually) is all this worth?—and that, when the man who is the object of the apotheosis, notices her, is presented to her, finds her to his taste, and singles her out from the rest? No. While humanity is humanity, the woman is not utterly without excuse.

Has she escaped, without suffering for it?

Look at her as she stands there, tortured by the knowledge of her own secret—the hideous secret which she is hiding from the innocent girl, whom she loves with a sister's love. Look at her, bowed down under a humiliation which is unutterable in words. She has seen him below the surface—now, when it is too late. She rates him at his true value—now, when her reputation is at his mercy. Ask her the question: What was there to love in a man who can speak

"THE MAN WAS GEOFFREY DELAMAYN."

to you as that man has spoken, who can treat you as that man is treating you now? you so clever, so cultivated, so refined—what, in Heaven's name, could *you* see in him? Ask her that, and she will have no answer to give. She will not even remind you that he was once your model of manly beauty, too—that you waved your handkerchief till you could wave it no longer, when he took his seat, with the others, in the boat—that your heart was like to jump out of your bosom, on that later occasion when he leaped the last hurdle at the foot-race, and won it by a head.

In the bitterness of her remorse, she will not even seek for *that* excuse for herself. Is there no atoning suffering to be seen here? Do your sympathies shrink from such a character as this? Follow her, good friends of virtue, on the pilgrimage that leads, by steep and thorny ways, to the purer atmosphere and the nobler life. Your fellow-creature, who has sinned and has repented—you have the authority of the Divine Teacher for it—is your fellow-creature, purified and ennobled. A joy among the angels of heaven—oh, my brothers and sisters of the earth, have I not laid my hand on a fit companion for You?

There was a moment of silence in the summer-house. The cheerful tumult of the lawn-party was pleasantly audible from the distance. Outside, the hum of voices, the laughter of girls, the thump of the croquet-mallet against the ball. Inside, nothing but a woman forcing back the bitter tears of sorrow and shame—and a man who was tired of her.

She roused herself. She was her mother's daughter; and she had a spark of her mother's spirit. Her life depended on the issue of that interview. It was useless—without father or brother to take her part—to lose the last chance of appealing to him. She dashed away the tears—time enough to cry, is time easily found in a woman's existence—she dashed away the tears, and spoke to him again, more gently than she had spoken yet.

"You have been three weeks, Geoffrey, at your brother Julius's place, not ten miles from here; and you have never once ridden over to see me. You would not have come to-day, if I had not written to you to insist on it. Is that the treatment I have deserved?"

She paused. There was no answer.

"Do you hear me?" she asked, advancing, and speaking in louder tones.

He was still silent. It was not in human endurance to bear his contempt. The warning of a coming outbreak began to show itself in her face. He met it, beforehand, with an impenetrable front. Feeling nervous about the interview, while he was waiting in the rose-garden—now that he stood committed to it, he was in full possession of himself. He was composed enough to remember that he had not put his pipe in its case—composed enough to set that little matter right before other matters went any farther. He took the case out of one pocket, and the pipe out of another.

"Go on," he said, quietly. "I hear you."

She struck the pipe out of his hand at a blow. If she had had the strength she would have struck him down with it on the floor of the summer-house.

"How dare you use me in this way?" she burst out, vehemently. "Your conduct is infamous. Defend it if you can!"

He made no attempt to defend it. He looked, with an expression of genuine anxiety, at the fallen pipe. It was beautifully colored—it had cost him ten shillings. "I'll pick up my pipe first," he said. His face brightened pleasantly—he looked handsomer than ever—as he examined the precious object, and put it back in the case. "All right," he said to himself. "She hasn't broken it." His attitude, as he looked at her again, was the perfection of easy grace—the grace that attends on cultivated strength in a state of repose. "I put it to your own common-sense," he said, in the most reasonable manner, "what's the good of bullying me? You don't want them to hear you, out on the lawn there—do you? You women are all alike. There's no beating a little prudence into your heads, try how one may."

There he waited, expecting her to speak. She waited, on her side, and forced him to go on.

"Look here," he said, "there's no need to quarrel, you know. I don't want to break my promise; but what can I do? I'm not the eldest son. I'm dependent on my father for every farthing I have; and I'm on bad terms with him already. Can't you see it yourself? You're a lady, and all that, I know. But you're only a governess. It's your interest as well as mine to wait till my father has provided for me. Here it is in a nut-shell: if I marry you now, I'm a ruined man."

The answer came, this time.

"You villain! if you *don't* marry me, I am a ruined woman!"

"What do you mean?"

"You know what I mean. Don't look at me in that way."

"How do you expect me to look at a woman who calls me a villain to my face?"

She suddenly changed her tone. The savage element in humanity—let the modern optimists who doubt its existence look at any uncultivated man (no matter how muscular), woman (no matter how beautiful), or child (no matter how young)—began to show itself furtively in his eyes, to utter itself furtively in his voice. Was he to blame for the manner in which he looked at her and spoke to her? Not he! What had there been in the training of *his* life (at school or at college) to soften and subdue the savage element in him? About as much as there had been in the training of his ancestors (without the school or the college) five hundred years since.

It was plain that one of them must give way. The woman had the most at stake—and the woman set the example of submission.

"Don't be hard on me," she pleaded. "I don't mean to be hard on *you*. My temper gets the better of me. You know my temper. I am sorry I forgot myself. Geoffrey, my whole future is in your hands. Will you do me justice?"

She came nearer, and laid her hand persuasively on his arm.

"Haven't you a word to say to me? No answer? Not even a look?" She waited a moment more. A marked change came over her. She turned slowly to leave the summer-house. "I am sorry to have troubled you, Mr. Delamayn. I won't detain you any longer."

He looked at her. There was a tone in her voice that he had never heard before. There was a light in her eyes that he had never seen in them before. Suddenly and fiercely he reached out his hand, and stopped her.

"Where are you going?" he asked.

She answered, looking him straight in the face, "Where many a miserable woman has gone before me. Out of the world."

He drew her nearer to him, and eyed her closely. Even *his* intelligence discovered that he had brought her to bay, and that she really meant it!

"Do you mean you will destroy yourself?" he said.

"Yes. I mean I will destroy myself."

He dropped her arm. "By Jupiter, she *does* mean it!"

With that conviction in him, he pushed one of the chairs in the summer-house to her with his foot, and signed to her to take it. "Sit down!" he said, roughly. She had frightened him—and fear comes seldom to men of his type. They feel it, when it does come, with an angry distrust; they grow loud and brutal, in instinctive protest against it. "Sit down!" he repeated. She obeyed him. "Haven't you got a word to say to me?" he asked, with an oath. No! there she sat, immovable, reckless how it ended—as only women can be, when women's minds are made up. He took a turn in the summer-house and came back, and struck his hand angrily on the rail of her chair. "What do you want?"

"You know what I want."

He took another turn. There was nothing for it but to give way on his side, or run the risk of something happening which might cause an awkward scandal, and come to his father's ears. "Look here, Anne," he began, abruptly. "I have got something to propose."

She looked up at him.

"What do you say to a private marriage?"

Without asking a single question, without making objections, she answered him, speaking as bluntly as he had spoken himself:

"I consent to a private marriage."

He began to temporize directly.

"I own I don't see how it's to be managed—"

She stopped him there.

"I do!"

"What!" he cried out, suspiciously. "You have thought of it yourself, have you?"

"Yes."

"And planned for it?"

"And planned for it!"

"Why didn't you tell me so before?"

She answered haughtily; insisting on the respect which is due to women—the respect which was doubly due from *him*, in her position.

"Because *you* owed it to *me*, Sir, to speak first."

"Very well. I've spoken first. Will you wait a little?"

"Not a day!"

The tone was positive. There was no mistaking it. Her mind was made up.

"Where's the hurry?"

"Have you eyes?" she asked, vehemently. "Have you ears? Do you see how Lady Lundie looks at me? Do you hear how Lady Lundie speaks to me? I am suspected by that woman. My shameful dismissal from this house may be a question of a few hours." Her head sunk on her bosom; she wrung her clasped hands as they rested on her lap. "And, oh, Blanche!" she moaned to herself, the tears gathering again, and falling, this time, unchecked. "Blanche, who looks up to me! Blanche, who loves me! Blanche, who told me, in this very place, that I was to live with her when she was married!" She started up from the chair; the tears dried suddenly; the hard despair settled again, wan

and white, on her face. "Let me go! What is death, compared to such a life as is waiting for *me?*" She looked him over, in one disdainful glance from head to foot; her voice rose to its loudest and firmest tones. "Why, even *you* would have the courage to die if you were in my place!"

Geoffrey glanced round toward the lawn.

"Hush!" he said. "They will hear you!"

"Let them hear me! When *I* am past hearing *them*, what does it matter?"

He put her back by main force on the chair. In another moment they must have heard her, through all the noise and laughter of the game.

"Say what you want," he resumed, "and I'll do it. Only be reasonable. I can't marry you to-day."

"You can!"

"What nonsense you talk! The house and grounds are swarming with company. It can't be!"

"It can! I have been thinking about it ever since we came to this house. I have got something to propose to you. Will you hear it, or not?"

"Speak lower!"

"Will you hear it, or not?"

"There's somebody coming!"

"Will you hear it, or not?"

"The devil take your obstinacy! Yes!"

The answer had been wrung from him. Still, it was the answer she wanted—it opened the door to hope. The instant he had consented to hear her her mind awakened to the serious necessity of averting discovery by any third person who might stray idly into the summer-house. She held up her hand for silence, and listened to what was going forward on the lawn.

The dull thump of the croquet-mallet against the ball was no longer to be heard. The game had stopped.

In a moment more she heard her own name called. An interval of another instant passed, and a familiar voice said, "I know where she is. I'll fetch her."

She turned to Geoffrey, and pointed to the back of the summer-house.

"It's my turn to play," she said. "And Blanche is coming here to look for me. Wait there, and I'll stop her on the steps."

She went out at once. It was a critical moment. Discovery, which meant moral-ruin to the woman, meant money-ruin to the man. Geoffrey had not exaggerated his position with his father. Lord Holchester had twice paid his debts, and had declined to see him since. One more outrage on his father's rigid sense of propriety, and he would be left out of the will as well as kept out of the house. He looked for a means of retreat, in case there was no escaping unperceived by the front entrance. A door—intended for the use of servants, when picnics and gipsy tea-parties were given in the summer-house—had been made in the back wall. It opened outward, and it was locked. With his strength it was easy to remove that obstacle. He put his shoulder to the door. At the moment when he burst it open he felt a hand on his arm. Anne was behind him, alone.

"You may want it before long," she said, observing the open door, without expressing any surprise. "You don't want it now. Another person will play for me—I have told Blanche I am not well. Sit down. I have secured a respite of five minutes, and I must make the most of it. In that time, or less, Lady Lundie's suspicions will bring her here—to see how I am. For the present, shut the door."

She seated herself, and pointed to a second chair. He took it—with his eye on the closed door.

"Come to the point!" he said, impatiently. "What is it?"

"You can marry me privately to-day," she answered. "Listen—and I will tell you how!"

---

## CHAPTER THE FIFTH.

### THE PLAN.

SHE took his hand, and began with all the art of persuasion that she possessed.

"One question, Geoffrey, before I say what I want to say. Lady Lundie has invited you to stay at Windygates. Do you accept her invitation? or do you go back to your brother's in the evening?"

"I can't go back in the evening—they've put a visitor into my room. I'm obliged to stay here. My brother has done it on purpose. Julius helps me when I'm hard up—and bullies me afterward. He has sent me here, on duty for the family. Somebody must be civil to Lady Lundie—and I'm the sacrifice."

She took him up at his last word. "Don't make the sacrifice," she said. "Apologize to Lady Lundie, and say you are obliged to go back."

"Why?"

"Because we must both leave this place to-day."

There was a double objection to that. If he left Lady Lundie's, he would fail to establish a future pecuniary claim on his brother's indulgence. And if he left with Anne, the eyes of the world would see them, and the whispers of the world might come to his father's ears.

"If we go away together," he said, "good-by to my prospects, and yours too."

"I don't mean that we shall leave together," she explained. "We will leave separately—and I will go first."

"There will be a hue and cry after you, when you are missed."

"There will be a dance when the croquet is over. I don't dance—and I shall not be missed. There will be time, and opportunity, to get to my own room. I shall leave a letter there for Lady Lundie, and a letter"—her voice trembled for a moment—"and a letter for Blanche. Don't interrupt me! I have thought of this, as I have thought of every thing else. The confession I shall make will be the truth in a few hours, if it's not the truth now. My letters will say I am privately married, and called away unexpectedly to join my husband. There will be a scandal in the house, I know. But there will be no excuse for sending after me, when I am under my husband's protection. So far as you are personally concerned there are no discoveries to fear—and nothing which it is not perfectly safe and perfectly easy to do. Wait here an hour after I have gone to save appearances; and then follow me."

"Follow you?" interposed Geoffrey. "Where?"

She drew her chair nearer to him, and whispered the next words in her ear.

"To a lonely little mountain inn—four miles from this."

"An inn!"

"Why not?"

"An inn is a public place."

A movement of natural impatience escaped her—but she controlled herself, and went on as quietly as before:

"The place I mean is the loneliest place in the neighborhood. You have no prying eyes to dread there. I have picked it out expressly for that reason. It's away from the railway; it's away from the high-road: it's kept by a decent, respectable Scotchwoman—"

"Decent, respectable Scotchwomen who keep inns," interposed Geoffrey, "don't cotton to young ladies who are traveling alone. The landlady won't receive you."

It was a well-aimed objection—but it missed the mark. A woman bent on her marriage is a woman who can meet the objections of the whole world, single-handed, and refute them all.

"I have provided for every thing," she said; "and I have provided for that. I shall tell the landlady I am on my wedding-trip. I shall say my husband is sight-seeing, on foot, among the mountains in the neighborhood—"

"She is sure to believe that!" said Geoffrey.

"She is sure to disbelieve it, if you like. Let her! You have only to appear, and to ask for your wife—and there is my story proved to be true! She may be the most suspicious woman living, as long as I am alone with her. The moment you join me, you set her suspicions at rest. Leave me to do my part. My part is the hard one. Will you do yours?"

It was impossible to say No: she had fairly cut the ground from under his feet. He shifted his ground. Any thing rather than say Yes!

"I suppose you know how we are to be married?" he asked. "All I can say is—I don't."

"You do!" she retorted. "You know that we are in Scotland. You know that there are neither forms, ceremonies, nor delays in marriage, here. The plan I have proposed to you secures my being received at the inn, and makes it easy and natural for you to join me there afterward. The rest is in our own hands. A man and a woman who wish to be married (in Scotland) have only to secure the necessary witnesses and the thing is done. If the landlady chooses to resent the deception practiced on her, after that, the landlady may do as she pleases. We shall have gained our object in spite of her—and, what is more, we shall have gained it without risk to you."

"Don't lay it all on my shoulders," Geoffrey rejoined. "You women go headlong at every thing. Say we are married. We must separate afterward—or how are we to keep it a secret?"

"Certainly. You will go back, of course, to your brother's house, as if nothing had happened."

"And what is to become of you?"

"I shall go to London."

"What are you to do in London?"

"Haven't I already told you that I have thought of every thing? When I get to London I shall apply to some of my mother's old friends

—friends of hers in the time when she was a musician. Every body tells me I have a voice—if I had only cultivated it. I *will* cultivate it! I can live, and live respectably, as a concert singer. I have saved money enough to support me, while I am learning—and my mother's friends will help me, for her sake."

So, in the new life that she was marking out, was she now unconsciously reflecting in herself the life of her mother before her. Here was the mother's career as a public singer, chosen (in spite of all efforts to prevent it) by the child! Here (though with other motives, and under other circumstances) was the mother's irregular marriage in Ireland, on the point of being followed by the daughter's irregular marriage in Scotland! And here, stranger still, was the man who was answerable for it—the son of the man who had found the flaw in the Irish marriage, and had shown the way by which her mother was thrown on the world! "My Anne is my second self. She is not called by her father's name; she is called by mine. She is Anne Silvester as I was. Will she end like Me?"—The answer to those words—the last words that had trembled on the dying mother's lips—was coming fast. Through the chances and changes of many years, the future was pressing near—and Anne Silvester stood on the brink of it.

"Well?" she resumed. "Are you at the end of your objections? Can you give me a plain answer at last?"

No! He had another objection ready as the words passed her lips.

"Suppose the witnesses at the inn happen to know me?" he said. "Suppose it comes to my father's ears in that way?"

"Suppose you drive me to my death?" she retorted, starting to her feet. "Your father shall know the truth, in that case—I swear it!"

He rose, on his side, and drew back from her. She followed him up. There was a clapping of hands, at the same moment, on the lawn. Somebody had evidently made a brilliant stroke which promised to decide the game. There was no security now that Blanche might not return again. There was every prospect, the game being over, that Lady Lundie would be free. Anne brought the interview to its crisis, without wasting a moment more.

"Mr. Geoffrey Delamayn," she said. "You have bargained for a private marriage, and I have consented. Are you, or are you not, ready to marry me on your own terms?"

"Give me a minute to think!"

"Not an instant. Once for all, is it Yes, or No?"

He couldn't say "Yes," even then. But he said what was equivalent to it. He asked, savagely, "Where is the inn?"

She put her arm in his, and whispered, rapidly,

"Pass the road on the right that leads to the railway. Follow the path over the moor, and the sheep-track up the hill. The first house you come to after that is the inn. You understand!"

He nodded his head, with a sullen frown, and took his pipe out of his pocket again.

"Let it alone this time," he said, meeting her eye. "My mind's upset. When a man's mind's upset, a man must smoke. What's the name of the place?"

"Craig Fernie."

"Who am I to ask for at the door?"

"For your wife."

"Suppose they want you to give your name when you get there?"

"If I must give a name, I shall call myself Mrs., instead of Miss, Silvester. But I shall do my best to avoid giving any name. And you will do your best to avoid making a mistake, by only asking for me as your wife. Is there any thing else you want to know?"

"Yes."

"Be quick about it! What is it?"

"How am I to know you have got away from here?"

"If you don't hear from me in half an hour from the time when I have left you, you may be sure I have got away. Hush!"

Two voices, in conversation, were audible at the bottom of the steps—Lady Lundie's voice and Sir Patrick's. Anne pointed to the door in the back wall of the summer-house. She had just pulled it to again, after Geoffrey had passed through it, when Lady Lundie and Sir Patrick appeared at the top of the steps.

---

## CHAPTER THE SIXTH.

### THE SUITOR.

LADY LUNDIE pointed significantly to the door, and addressed herself to Sir Patrick's private ear.

"Observe!" she said. "Miss Silvester has just got rid of somebody."

Sir Patrick deliberately looked in the wrong direction, and (in the politest possible manner) observed—nothing.

Lady Lundie advanced into the summer-house. Suspicious hatred of the governess was written legibly in every line of her face. Suspicious distrust of the governess's illness spoke plainly in every tone of her voice.

"May I inquire, Miss Silvester, if your sufferings are relieved?"

"I am no better, Lady Lundie."

"I beg your pardon?"

"I said I was no better."

"You appear to be able to stand up. When *I* am ill, I am not so fortunate. I am obliged to lie down."

"I will follow your example, Lady Lundie. If you will be so good as to excuse me, I will leave you, and lie down in my own room."

She could say no more. The interview with Geoffrey had worn her out; there was no spirit left in her to resist the petty malice of the woman, after bearing, as she had borne it, the brutish indifference of the man. In another moment the hysterical suffering which she was keeping down would have forced its way outward in tears. Without waiting to know whether she was excused or not, without stopping to hear a word more, she left the summer-house.

Lady Lundie's magnificent black eyes opened to their utmost width, and blazed with their most dazzling brightness. She appealed to Sir Patrick, poised easily on his ivory cane, and looking out at the lawn-party, the picture of venerable innocence.

"After what I have already told you, Sir Patrick, of Miss Silvester's conduct, may I ask whether you consider *that* proceeding at all extraordinary?"

The old gentleman touched the spring in the knob of his cane, and answered, in the courtly manner of the old school:

"I consider no proceeding extraordinary, Lady Lundie, which emanates from your enchanting sex."

He bowed, and took his pinch. With a little jaunty flourish of the hand, he dusted the stray grains of snuff off his finger and thumb, and looked back again at the lawn-party, and became more absorbed in the diversions of his young friends than ever.

Lady Lundie stood her ground, plainly determined to force a serious expression of opinion from her brother-in-law. Before she could speak again, Arnold and Blanche appeared together at the bottom of the steps. "And when does the dancing begin?" inquired Sir Patrick, advancing to meet them, and looking as if he felt the deepest interest in a speedy settlement of the question.

"The very thing I was going to ask mamma," returned Blanche. "Is she in there with Anne? Is Anne better?"

Lady Lundie forthwith appeared, and took the answer to that inquiry on herself.

"Miss Silvester has retired to her room. Miss Silvester persists in being ill. Have you noticed, Sir Patrick, that these half-bred sort of people are almost invariably rude when they are ill?"

Blanche's bright face flushed up. "If you think Anne a half-bred person, Lady Lundie, you stand alone in your opinion. My uncle doesn't agree with you, I'm sure."

Sir Patrick's interest in the first quadrille became almost painful to see. "*Do* tell me, my dear, when *is* the dancing going to begin?"

"The sooner the better," interposed Lady Lundie; "before Blanche picks another quarrel with me on the subject of Miss Silvester."

Blanche looked at her uncle. "Begin! begin! Don't lose time!" cried the ardent Sir Patrick, pointing toward the house with his cane. "Certainly, uncle! Any thing that *you* wish!" With that parting shot at her step-mother, Blanche withdrew. Arnold, who had thus far waited in silence at the foot of the steps, looked appealingly at Sir Patrick. The train which was to take him to his newly inherited property would start in less than an hour; and he had not presented himself to Blanche's guardian in the character of Blanche's suitor yet! Sir Patrick's indifference to all domestic claims on him—claims of persons who loved, and claims of persons who hated, it didn't matter which—remained perfectly unassailable. There he stood, poised on his cane, humming an old Scotch air. And there was Lady Lundie, resolute not to leave him till he had seen the governess with *her* eyes and judged the governess with *her* mind. She returned to the charge—in spite of Sir Patrick, humming at the top of the steps, and of Arnold, waiting at the bottom. (Her enemies said, "No wonder poor Sir Thomas died in a few months after his marriage!" And, oh dear me, our enemies *are* sometimes right!)

"I must once more remind you, Sir Patrick, that I have serious reason to doubt whether Miss Silvester is a fit companion for Blanche. My governess has something on her mind. She has

fits of crying in private. She is up and walking about her room when she ought to be asleep. She posts her own letters—*and*, she has lately been excessively insolent to Me. There is something wrong. I must take some steps in the matter—and it is only proper that I should do so with your sanction, as head of the family."

"Consider me as abdicating my position, Lady Lundie, in your favor."

"Sir Patrick, I beg you to observe that I am speaking seriously, and that I expect a serious reply."

"My good lady, ask me for any thing else and it is at your service. I have not made 'a serious reply' since I gave up practice at the Scottish Bar. At my age," added Sir Patrick, cunningly drifting into generalities, "nothing is serious—except Indigestion. I say, with the philosopher, 'Life is a comedy to those who think, and a tragedy to those who feel.'" He took his sister-in-law's hand, and kissed it. "Dear Lady Lundie, why feel?"

Lady Lundie, who had never "felt" in her life, appeared perversely determined to feel, on this occasion. She was offended—and she showed it plainly.

"When you are next called on, Sir Patrick, to judge of Miss Silvester's conduct," she said, "unless I am entirely mistaken, you will find yourself *compelled* to consider it as something beyond a joke." With those words, she walked out of the summer-house—and so forwarded Arnold's interests by leaving Blanche's guardian alone at last.

It was an excellent opportunity. The guests were safe in the house—there was no interruption to be feared. Arnold showed himself. Sir Patrick (perfectly undisturbed by Lady Lundie's parting speech) sat down in the summer-house, without noticing his young friend, and asked himself a question founded on profound observation of the female sex. "Were there ever two women yet with a quarrel between them," thought the old gentleman, "who didn't want to drag a man into it? Let them drag *me* in, if they can!"

Arnold advanced a step, and modestly announced himself. "I hope I am not in the way, Sir Patrick?"

"In the way? of course not! Bless my soul, how serious the boy looks! Are *you* going to appeal to me as the head of the family next?"

It was exactly what Arnold was about to do. But it was plain that if he admitted it just then Sir Patrick (for some unintelligible reason) would decline to listen to him. He answered cautiously, "I asked leave to consult you in private, Sir; and you kindly said you would give me the opportunity before I left Windygates?"

"Ay! ay! to be sure. I remember. We were both engaged in the serious business of croquet at the time—and it was doubtful which of us did that business most clumsily. Well, here is the opportunity; and here am I, with all my worldly experience, at your service. I have only one caution to give you. Don't appeal to me as 'the head of the family.' My resignation is in Lady Lundie's hands."

He was, as usual, half in jest, half in earnest. The wry twist of humor showed itself at the corners of his lips. Arnold was at a loss how to approach Sir Patrick on the subject of his niece without reminding him of his domestic responsibilities on the one hand, and without setting himself up as a target for the shafts of Sir Patrick's wit on the other. In this difficulty, he committed a mistake at the outset. He hesitated.

"Don't hurry yourself," said Sir Patrick. "Collect your ideas. I can wait! I can wait!"

Arnold collected his ideas—and committed a second mistake. He determined on feeling his way cautiously at first. Under the circumstances (and with such a man as he had now to deal with), it was perhaps the rashest resolution at which he could possibly have arrived—it was the mouse attempting to outmanœuvre the cat.

"You have been very kind, Sir, in offering me the benefit of your experience," he began. "I want a word of advice."

"Suppose you take it sitting?" suggested Sir Patrick. "Get a chair." His sharp eyes followed Arnold with an expression of malicious enjoyment. "Wants my advice?" he thought. "The young humbug wants nothing of the sort —he wants my niece."

Arnold sat down under Sir Patrick's eye, with a well-founded suspicion that he was destined to suffer, before he got up again, under Sir Patrick's tongue.

"I am only a young man," he went on, moving uneasily in his chair; "and I am beginning a new life—"

"Any thing wrong with the chair?" asked Sir Patrick. "Begin your new life comfortably, and get another."

"There's nothing wrong with the chair, Sir. Would you—"

"Would I keep the chair, in that case? Certainly."

"I mean, would you advise me—"

"My good fellow, I'm waiting to advise you. (I'm sure there's something wrong with that chair. Why be obstinate about it? Why not get another?)"

"Please don't notice the chair, Sir Patrick— you put me out. I want—in short—perhaps it's a curious question—"

"I can't say till I have heard it," remarked Sir Patrick. "However, we will admit it, for form's sake, if you like. Say it's a curious question. Or let us express it more strongly, if that will help you. Say it's the most extraordinary question that ever was put, since the beginning of the world, from one human being to another."

"It's this!" Arnold burst out, desperately. "I want to be married!"

"That isn't a question," objected Sir Patrick. "It's an assertion. You say, I want to be married. And I say, Just so! And there's an end of it."

Arnold's head began to whirl. "Would you advise me to get married, Sir?" he said, piteously.

"That's what I meant."

"Oh! That's the object of the present interview, is it? Would I advise you to marry, eh?"

(Having caught the mouse by this time, the cat lifted his paw and let the luckless little creature breathe again. Sir Patrick's manner suddenly freed itself from any slight signs of impatience which it might have hitherto shown, and became as pleasantly easy and confidential as a manner could be. He touched the knob of his cane, and helped himself, with infinite zest and enjoyment, to a pinch of snuff.)

"Would I advise you to marry?" repeated Sir Patrick. "Two courses are open to us, Mr. Arnold, in treating that question. We may put it briefly, or we may put it at great length. I am for putting it briefly. What do you say?"

"What *you* say, Sir Patrick."

"Very good. May I begin by making an inquiry relating to your past life?"

"Certainly!"

"Very good again. When you were in the merchant service, did you ever have any experience in buying provisions ashore?"

Arnold stared. If any relation existed between that question and the subject in hand it was an impenetrable relation to *him*. He answered, in unconcealed bewilderment,

"Plenty of experience, Sir."

"I'm coming to the point," pursued Sir Patrick. "Don't be astonished. I'm coming to the point. What did you think of your moist sugar when you bought it at the grocer's?"

"Think?" repeated Arnold. "Why, I thought it was moist sugar, to be sure!"

"Marry, by all means!" cried Sir Patrick. "You are one of the few men who can try that experiment with a fair chance of success."

The suddenness of the answer fairly took away Arnold's breath. There was something perfectly electric in the brevity of his venerable friend. He stared harder than ever.

"Don't you understand me?" asked Sir Patrick.

"I don't understand what the moist sugar has got to do with it, Sir."

"You don't see that?"

"Not a bit!"

"Then I'll show you," said Sir Patrick, crossing his legs, and setting in comfortably for a good talk. "You go to the tea-shop, and get your moist sugar. You take it on the understanding that it *is* moist sugar. But it isn't any thing of the sort. It's a compound of adulterations made up to look like sugar. You shut your eyes to that awkward fact, and swallow your adulterated mess in various articles of food; and you and your sugar get on together in that way as well as you can. Do you follow me, so far?"

Yes. Arnold (quite in the dark) followed, so far.

"Very good," pursued Sir Patrick. "You go to the marriage-shop, and get a wife. You take her on the understanding—let us say—that she has lovely yellow hair, that she has an exquisite complexion, that her figure is the perfection of plumpness, and that she is just tall enough to carry the plumpness off. You bring her home, and you discover that it's the old story of the sugar over again. Your wife is an adulterated article. Her lovely yellow hair is—dye. Her exquisite skin is — pearl powder. Her plumpness is—padding. And three inches of her height are—in the boot-maker's heels. Shut your eyes, and swallow your adulterated wife as you swallow your adulterated sugar—and, I tell you again, you are one of the few men who can try the marriage experiment with a fair chance of success."

With that he uncrossed his legs again, and looked hard at Arnold. Arnold read the lesson, at last, in the right way. He gave up the hopeless attempt to circumvent Sir Patrick, and—come what might of it—dashed at a direct allusion to Sir Patrick's niece.

"HE TOUCHED THE KNOB OF HIS CANE, AND HELPED HIMSELF, WITH INFINITE ZEST AND ENJOYMENT, TO A PINCH OF SNUFF."

"That may be all very true, Sir, of some young ladies," he said. "There is one I know of, who is nearly related to you, and who doesn't deserve what you have said of the rest of them."

This was coming to the point. Sir Patrick showed his approval of Arnold's frankness by coming to the point himself, as readily as his own whimsical humor would let him.

"Is this female phenomenon my niece?" he inquired.

"Yes, Sir Patrick."

"May I ask how you know that my niece is not an adulterated article, like the rest of them?"

Arnold's indignation loosened the last restraints that tied Arnold's tongue. He exploded in the three words which mean three volumes in every circulating library in the kingdom.

"I love her."

Sir Patrick sat back in his chair, and stretched out his legs luxuriously.

"That's the most convincing answer I ever heard in my life," he said.

"I'm in earnest!" cried Arnold, reckless by this time of every consideration but one. "Put me to the test, Sir! put me to the test!"

"Oh, very well. The test is easily put." He looked at Arnold, with the irrepressible humor twinkling merrily in his eyes, and twitching sharply at the corners of his lips. "My niece has a beautiful complexion. Do you believe in her complexion?"

"There's a beautiful sky above our heads," returned Arnold. "I believe in the sky."

"Do you?" retorted Sir Patrick. "You were evidently never caught in a shower. My niece has an immense quantity of hair. Are you convinced that it all grows on her head?"

"I defy any other woman's head to produce the like of it!"

"My dear Arnold, you greatly underrate the existing resources of the trade in hair! Look into the shop-windows. When you next go to London pray look into the shop-windows. In the mean time, what do you think of my niece's figure?"

"Oh, come! there can't be any doubt about *that!* Any man, with eyes in his head, can see it's the loveliest figure in the world."

Sir Patrick laughed softly, and crossed his legs again.

"My good fellow, of course it is! The loveliest figure in the world is the commonest thing in the world. At a rough guess, there are forty ladies at this lawn-party. Every one of them possesses a beautiful figure. It varies in price; and when it's particularly seductive, you may swear it comes from Paris. Why, how you stare! When I asked you what you thought of my niece's figure, I meant—how much of it comes from Nature, and how much of it comes from the Shop? I don't know, mind! Do you?"

"I'll take my oath to every inch of it!"

"Shop?"

"Nature!"

Sir Patrick rose to his feet; his satirical humor was silenced at last.

"If ever I have a son," he thought to himself, "that son shall go to sea!" He took Arnold's arm, as a preliminary to putting an end to Arnold's suspense. "If I *can* be serious about any thing," he resumed, "it's time to be serious with you. I am convinced of the sincerity of your attachment. All I know of you is in your favor, and your birth and position are beyond dispute. If you have Blanche's consent, you have mine." Arnold attempted to express his gratitude. Sir Patrick, declining to hear him, went on. "And remember this, in the future. When you next want any thing that I can give you, ask for it plainly. Don't attempt to mystify *me* on the next occasion, and I will promise, on my side, not to mystify *you*. There, that's understood. Now about this journey of yours to see your estate. Property has its duties, Master Arnold, as well as its rights. The time is fast coming when its rights will be disputed, if its duties are not performed. I have got a new interest in you, and I mean to see that you do your duty. It's settled you are to leave Windygates to-day. Is it arranged how you are to go?"

"Yes, Sir Patrick. Lady Lundie has kindly ordered the gig to take me to the station, in time for the next train."

"When are you to be ready?"

Arnold looked at his watch. "In a quarter of an hour."

"Very good. Mind you *are* ready. Stop a minute! you will have plenty of time to speak to Blanche when I have done with you. You don't appear to me to be sufficiently anxious about seeing your own property."

"I am not very anxious to leave Blanche, Sir —that's the truth of it."

"Never mind Blanche. Blanche is not business. They both begin with a B—and that's the only connection between them. I hear you have got one of the finest houses in this part of Scotland. How long are you going to stay in it?"

"I have arranged (as I have already told you, Sir) to return to Windygates the day after to-morrow."

"What! Here is a man with a palace waiting to receive him—and he is only going to stop one clear day in it!"

"I am not going to stop in it at all, Sir Patrick—I am going to stay with the steward. I'm only wanted to be present to-morrow at a dinner to my tenants—and, when that's over, there's nothing in the world to prevent my coming back here. The steward himself told me so in his last letter."

"Oh, if the steward told you so, of course there is nothing more to be said!"

"Don't object to my coming back! pray don't, Sir Patrick! I'll promise to live in my new house, when I have got Blanche to live in it with me. If you won't mind, I'll go and tell her at once that it all belongs to her as well as to me."

"Gently! gently! you talk as if you were married to her already!"

"It's as good as done, Sir! Where's the difficulty in the way now?"

As he asked the question the shadow of some third person, advancing from the side of the summer-house, was thrown forward on the open sunlit space at the top of the steps. In a moment more the shadow was followed by the substance—in the shape of a groom in his riding livery. The man was plainly a stranger to the place. He started, and touched his hat, when he saw the two gentlemen in the summer-house.

"What do you want?" asked Sir Patrick.

"I beg your pardon, Sir; I was sent by my master—"

"Who is your master?"

"The Honorable Mr. Delamayn, Sir."

"Do you mean Mr. Geoffrey Delamayn?" asked Arnold.

"No, Sir. Mr. Geoffrey's brother—Mr. Julius. I have ridden over from the house, Sir, with a message from my master to Mr. Geoffrey."

"Can't you find him?"

"They told me I should find him hereabouts, Sir. But I'm a stranger, and don't rightly know where to look." He stopped, and took a card out of his pocket. "My master said it was very important I should deliver this immediately. Would you be pleased to tell me, gentlemen, if you happen to know where Mr. Geoffrey is?"

Arnold turned to Sir Patrick. "I haven't seen him. Have you?"

"I have smelt him," answered Sir Patrick, "ever since I have been in the summer-house. There is a detestable taint of tobacco in the air— suggestive (disagreeably suggestive to *my* mind) of your friend, Mr. Delamayn."

Arnold laughed, and stepped outside the summer-house.

"If you are right, Sir Patrick, we will find him at once." He looked around, and shouted, "Geoffrey!"

A voice from the rose-garden shouted back, "Hullo!"

"You're wanted. Come here!"

Geoffrey appeared, sauntering doggedly, with his pipe in his mouth, and his hands in his pockets.

"Who wants me?"

"A groom—from your brother."

That answer appeared to electrify the lounging and lazy athlete. Geoffrey hurried, with eager steps, to the summer-house. He addressed the groom before the man had time to speak. With horror and dismay in his face, he exclaimed:

"By Jupiter! Ratcatcher has relapsed!"

Sir Patrick and Arnold looked at each other in blank amazement.

"The best horse in my brother's stables!" cried Geoffrey, explaining, and appealing to them, in a breath. "I left written directions with the coachman; I measured out his physic for three days; I bled him," said Geoffrey, in a voice broken by emotion—"I bled him myself, last night."

"I beg your pardon, Sir—" began the groom.

"What's the use of begging my pardon? You're a pack of infernal fools! Where's your horse? I'll ride back, and break every bone in the coachman's skin! Where's your horse?"

"If you please, Sir, it isn't Ratcatcher. Ratcatcher's all right."

"Ratcatcher's all right? Then what the devil is it?"

"It's a message, Sir."

"About what?"

"About my lord."

"Oh! About my father?" He took out his handkerchief, and passed it over his forehead, with a deep gasp of relief. "I thought it was Ratcatcher," he said, looking at Arnold, with a smile. He put his pipe into his mouth, and re-kindled the dying ashes of the tobacco. "Well?" he went on, when the pipe was in working order, and his voice was composed again: "What's up with my father?"

"A telegram from London, Sir. Bad news of my lord."

The man produced his master's card.

Geoffrey read on it (written in his brother's handwriting) these words:

"I have only a moment to scribble a line on my card. Our father is dangerously ill—his lawyer has been sent for. Come with me to London by the first train. Meet at the junction."

Without a word to any one of the three persons present, all silently looking at him, Geoffrey consulted his watch. Anne had told him to wait half an hour, and to assume that she had gone if he failed to hear from her in that time. The interval had passed—and no communication of any sort had reached him. The flight from the house had been safely accomplished. Anne Silvester was, at that moment, on her way to the mountain inn.

---

## CHAPTER THE SEVENTH.

### THE DEBT.

ARNOLD was the first who broke the silence. "Is your father seriously ill?" he asked.

Geoffrey answered by handing him the card.

Sir Patrick, who had stood apart (while the question of Ratcatcher's relapse was under discussion) sardonically studying the manners and customs of modern English youth, now came forward, and took his part in the proceedings. Lady Lundie herself must have acknowledged that he spoke and acted as became the head of the family, on this occasion.

"Am I right in supposing that Mr. Delamayn's father is dangerously ill?" he asked, addressing himself to Arnold.

"Dangerously ill, in London," Arnold answered. "Geoffrey must leave Windygates with me. The train I am traveling by meets the train his brother is traveling by, at the junction. I shall leave him at the second station from here."

"Didn't you tell me that Lady Lundie was going to send you to the railway in a gig?"

"Yes."

"If the servant drives, there will be three of you—and there will be no room."

"We had better ask for some other vehicle," suggested Arnold.

Sir Patrick looked at his watch. There was no time to change the carriage. He turned to Geoffrey. "Can you drive, Mr. Delamayn?"

Still impenetrably silent, Geoffrey replied by a nod of the head.

Without noticing the unceremonious manner in which he had been answered, Sir Patrick went on:

"In that case, you can leave the gig in charge of the station-master. I'll tell the servant that he will not be wanted to drive."

"Let me save you the trouble, Sir Patrick," said Arnold.

Sir Patrick declined, by a gesture. He turned again, with undiminished courtesy, to Geoffrey. "It is one of the duties of hospitality, Mr. Delamayn, to hasten your departure, under these sad circumstances. Lady Lundie is engaged with her guests. I will see myself that there is no unnecessary delay in sending you to the station." He bowed—and left the summer house.

Arnold said a word of sympathy to his friend, when they were alone.

"I am sorry for this, Geoffrey. I hope and trust you will get to London in time."

He stopped. There was something in Geoffrey's face—a strange mixture of doubt and bewilderment, of annoyance and hesitation—which was not to be accounted for as the natural result of the news that he had received. His color shifted and changed; he picked fretfully at his finger-nails; he looked at Arnold as if he was going to speak—and then looked away again, in silence.

"Is there something amiss, Geoffrey, besides this bad news about your father?" asked Arnold.

"I'm in the devil's own mess," was the answer.

"Can I do any thing to help you?"

Instead of making a direct reply, Geoffrey lifted his mighty hand, and gave Arnold a friendly slap on the shoulder which shook him from head to foot. Arnold steadied himself, and waited—wondering what was coming next.

"I say, old fellow!" said Geoffrey.

"Yes."

"Do you remember when the boat turned keel upward in Lisbon Harbor?"

Arnold started. If he could have called to mind his first interview in the summer-house with his father's old friend, he might have remembered Sir Patrick's prediction that he would sooner or later pay, with interest, the debt he owed to the man who had saved his life. As it was, his memory reverted at a bound to the time of the boat-accident. In the ardor of his gratitude and the innocence of his heart, he almost resented his friend's question as a reproach which he had not deserved.

"Do you think I can ever forget," he cried, warmly, "that you swam ashore with me and saved my life?"

Geoffrey ventured a step nearer to the object that he had in view.

"One good turn deserves another," he said, "don't it?"

Arnold took his hand. "Only tell me!" he eagerly rejoined—"only tell me what I can do!"

"You are going to-day to see your new place, ain't you?"

"Yes."

"Can you put off going till to-morrow?"

"If it's any thing serious—of course I can!"

Geoffrey looked round at the entrance to the summer-house, to make sure that they were alone.

"You know the governess here, don't you?" he said, in a whisper.

"Miss Silvester?"

"Yes. I've got into a little difficulty with Miss Silvester. And there isn't a living soul I can ask to help me but *you*."

"You know I will help you. What is it?"

"It isn't so easy to say. Never mind—you're no saint either, are you? You'll keep it a secret, of course? Look here! I've acted like an infernal fool. I've gone and got the girl into a scrape—"

Arnold drew back, suddenly understanding him.

"Good heavens, Geoffrey! You don't mean—"

"I do! Wait a bit—that's not the worst of it. She has left the house."

"Left the house?"

"Left, for good and all. She can't come back again."

"Why not?"

"Because she's written to her missus. Women (hang 'em!) never do these things by halves. She's left a letter to say she's privately married, and gone off to her husband. Her husband is—Me. Not that I'm married to her yet, you understand. I have only promised to marry her. She has gone on first (on the sly) to a place four miles from this. And we settled I was to follow, and marry her privately this afternoon. That's out of the question now. While she's expecting me at the inn I shall be bowling along to London. Somebody must tell her what has happened—or she'll play the devil, and the whole business will burst up. I can't trust any of the people here. I'm done for, old chap, unless you help me."

Arnold lifted his hands in dismay. "It's the most dreadful situation, Geoffrey, I ever heard of in my life!"

Geoffrey thoroughly agreed with him. "Enough to knock a man over," he said, "isn't it? I'd give something for a drink of beer." He produced his everlasting pipe, from sheer force of habit. "Got a match?" he asked.

Arnold's mind was too preoccupied to notice the question.

"I hope you won't think I'm making light of your father's illness," he said, earnestly. "But it seems to me—i must say it—it seems to me that the poor girl has the first claim on you."

Geoffrey looked at him in surly amazement.

"The first claim on me? Do you think I'm going to risk being cut out of my father's will? Not for the best woman that ever put on a petticoat!"

Arnold's admiration of his friend was the solidly-founded admiration of many years; admiration for a man who could row, box, wrestle, jump—above all, who could swim—as few other men could perform those exercises in contemporary England. But that answer shook his faith. Only for the moment—unhappily for Arnold, only for the moment.

"You know best," he returned, a little coldly. "What can I do?"

Geoffrey took his arm—roughly, as he took every thing; but in a companionable and confidential way.

"Go, like a good fellow, and tell her what has happened. We'll start from here as if we were both going to the railway; and I'll drop you at the foot-path, in the gig. You can get on to your own place afterward by the evening train. It puts you to no inconvenience; and it's doing the kind thing by an old friend. There's no risk of being found out. I'm to drive, remember! There's no servant with us, old boy, to notice, and tell tales."

Even Arnold began to see dimly by this time that he was likely to pay his debt of obligation with interest—as Sir Patrick had foretold.

"What am I to say to her?" he asked. "I'm bound to do all I can do to help you, and I will. But what am I to say?"

It was a natural question to put. It was not an easy question to answer. What a man, under given muscular circumstances, could do, no person living knew better than Geoffrey Delamayn. Of what a man, under given social circumstances, could say, no person living knew less.

"Say?" he repeated. "Look here! say I'm half distracted, and all that. And—wait a bit—tell her to stop where she is till I write to her."

Arnold hesitated. Absolutely ignorant of that low and limited form of knowledge which is called "knowledge of the world," his inbred delicacy of mind revealed to him the serious difficulty of the position which his friend was asking him to occupy as plainly as if he was looking at it through the warily-gathered experience of society of a man of twice his age.

"Can't you write to her now, Geoffrey?" he asked.

"What's the good of that?"

"Consider for a minute, and you will see. You have trusted me with a very awkward secret. I may be wrong—I never was mixed up in such a matter before—but to present myself to this lady as your messenger seems exposing her to a dreadful humiliation. Am I to go and tell her to her face: 'I know what you are hiding from the knowledge of all the world;' and is she to be expected to endure it?"

"Bosh!" said Geoffrey. "They can endure a deal more than you think for. I wish you had heard how she bullied me, in this very place. My good fellow, you don't understand women. The grand secret, in dealing with a woman, is to take her as you take a cat, by the scruff of the neck—"

"I can't face her—unless you will help me by breaking the thing to her first. I'll stick at no sacrifice to serve you; but—hang it!—make allowances, Geoffrey, for the difficulty you are putting me in. I am almost a stranger; I don't know how Miss Silvester may receive me, before I can open my lips."

Those last words touched the question on its practical side. The matter-of-fact view of the difficulty was a view which Geoffrey instantly recognized and understood.

"She has the devil's own temper," he said. "There's no denying that. Perhaps I'd better write. Have we time to go into the house?"

"No. The house is full of people, and we haven't a minute to spare. Write at once, and write here. I have got a pencil."

"What am I to write on?"

"Any thing—your brother's card."

Geoffrey took the pencil which Arnold offered to him, and looked at the card. The lines his brother had written covered it. There was no room left. He felt in his pocket, and produced a letter—the letter which Anne had referred to at the interview between them; the letter which she had written to insist on his attending the lawn-party at Windygates.

"This will do," he said. "It's one of Anne's own letters to me. There's room on the fourth page. If I write," he added, turning suddenly on Arnold, "you promise to take it to her? Your hand on the bargain!"

"THAT WILL DO THE BUSINESS! READ IT YOURSELF, ARNOLD—IT'S NOT SO
BADLY WRITTEN."

He held out the hand which had saved Arnold's life in Lisbon Harbor, and received Arnold's promise, in remembrance of that time.

"All right, old fellow. I can tell you how to find the place as we go along in the gig. By-the-by, there's one thing that's rather important. I'd better mention it while I think of it."

"What is that?"

"You mustn't present yourself at the inn in your own name; and you mustn't ask for her by *her* name."

"Who am I to ask for?"

"It's a little awkward. She has gone there as a married woman, in case they're particular about taking her in—"

"I understand. Go on."

"And she has planned to tell them (by way of making it all right and straight for both of us, you know) that she expects her husband to join her. If I had been able to go I should have asked at the door for 'my wife.' You are going in my place—"

"And I must ask at the door for 'my wife,' or I shall expose Miss Silvester to unpleasant consequences?"

"You don't object?"

"Not I! I don't care what I say to the people of the inn. It's the meeting with Miss Silvester that I'm afraid of."

"I'll put that right for you—never fear!"

He went at once to the table and rapidly scribbled a few lines—then stopped and considered. "Will that do?" he asked himself. "No; I'd better say something spooney to quiet her." He considered again, added a line, and brought his hand down on the table with a cheery smack. "That will do the business! Read it yourself, Arnold—it's not so badly written."

Arnold read the note without appearing to share his friend's favorable opinion of it.

"This is rather short," he said.

"Have I time to make it longer?"

"Perhaps not. But let Miss Silvester see for herself that you have no time to make it longer. The train starts in less than half an hour. Put the time."

"Oh, all right! and the date too, if you like."

He had just added the desired words and figures, and had given the revised letter to Arnold, when Sir Patrick returned to announce that the gig was waiting.

"Come!" he said. "You haven't a moment to lose!"

Geoffrey started to his feet. Arnold hesitated.

"I must see Blanche!" he pleaded. "I can't leave Blanche without saying good-by. Where is she?"

Sir Patrick pointed to the steps, with a smile. Blanche had followed him from the house. Arnold ran out to her instantly.

"Going?" she said, a little sadly.

"I shall be back in two days," Arnold whispered. "It's all right! Sir Patrick consents."

She held him fast by the arm. The hurried parting before other people seemed to be not a parting to Blanche's taste.

"You will lose the train!" cried Sir Patrick.

Geoffrey seized Arnold by the arm which Blanche was holding, and tore him—literally tore him—away. The two were out of sight, in the shrubbery, before Blanche's indignation found words, and addressed itself to her uncle.

"Why is that brute going away with Mr. Brinkworth?" she asked.

"Mr. Delamayn is called to London by his father's illness," replied Sir Patrick. "You don't like him?"

"I hate him!"

Sir Patrick reflected a little.

"She is a young girl of eighteen," he thought to himself. "And I am an old man of seventy. Curious, that we should agree about any thing. More than curious that we should agree in disliking Mr. Delamayn."

He roused himself, and looked again at Blanche. She was seated at the table, with her head on her hand; absent, and out of spirits—thinking of Arnold, and yet, with the future all smooth before her, not thinking happily.

"Why, Blanche! Blanche!" cried Sir Patrick, "one would think he had gone for a voyage round the world. You silly child! he will be back again the day after to-morrow."

"I wish he hadn't gone with that man!" said Blanche. "I wish he hadn't got that man for a friend!"

"There! there! the man was rude enough, I own. Never mind! he will leave the man at the second station. Come back to the ball-room with me. Dance it off, my dear—dance it off!"

"No," returned Blanche. "I'm in no humor for dancing. I shall go up stairs, and talk about it to Anne."

"You will do nothing of the sort!" said a third voice, suddenly joining in the conversation.

Both uncle and niece looked up, and found Lady Lundie at the top of the summer-house steps.

"I forbid you to mention that woman's name again in my hearing," pursued her ladyship. "Sir Patrick! I warned you (if you remember?) that the matter of the governess was not a matter to be trifled with. My worst anticipations are realized. Miss Silvester has left the house!"

## CHAPTER THE EIGHTH.

### THE SCANDAL.

It was still early in the afternoon when the guests at Lady Lundie's lawn-party began to compare notes together in corners, and to agree in arriving at a general conviction that "something was wrong."

Blanche had mysteriously disappeared from her partners in the dance. Lady Lundie had mysteriously abandoned her guests. Blanche had not come back. Lady Lundie had returned with an artificial smile, and a preoccupied manner. She acknowledged that she was "not very well." The same excuse had been given to account for Blanche's absence—and, again (some time previously), to explain Miss Silvester's withdrawal from the croquet! A wit among the gentlemen declared it reminded him of declining a verb. "I am not very well; thou art not very well; she is not very well"—and so on. Sir Patrick too! Only think of the sociable Sir Patrick being in a state of seclusion—pacing up and down by himself in the loneliest part of the garden. And the servants again! it had even spread to the servants! *They* were presuming to whisper in corners, like their betters. The house-maids appeared, spasmodically, where house-maids had no business to be. Doors banged and petticoats whisked in the upper regions. Something going wrong—depend upon it, something wrong! "We had much better go away. My dear, order the carriage."—"Louisa, love, no more dancing; your papa is going."—"*Good*-afternoon, Lady Lundie!"—"Haw! thanks very much!"—"*So* sorry for dear Blanche!"—"Oh, it's been *too* charming!" So Society jabbered its poor, nonsensical little jargon, and got itself politely out of the way before the storm came.

This was exactly the consummation of events for which Sir Patrick had been waiting in the seclusion of the garden.

There was no evading the responsibility which was now thrust upon him. Lady Lundie had announced it as a settled resolution, on her part, to trace Anne to the place in which she had taken refuge, and discover (purely in the interests of virtue) whether she actually was married or not. Blanche (already overwrought by the excitement of the day) had broken into an hysterical passion of tears on hearing the news, and had then, on recovering, taken a view of her own of Anne's flight from the house. Anne would never have kept her marriage a secret from Blanche; Anne would never have written such a formal farewell letter as she had written to Blanche—if things were going as smoothly with her as she was trying to make them believe at Windygates. Some dreadful trouble had fallen on Anne—and Blanche was determined (as Lady Lundie was determined) to find out where she had gone, and to follow, and help her.

It was plain to Sir Patrick (to whom both ladies had opened their hearts, at separate interviews) that his sister-in-law, in one way, and his niece in another, were equally likely—if not duly restrained—to plunge headlong into acts of indiscretion which might lead to very undesirable results. A man in authority was sorely needed at Windygates that afternoon—and Sir Patrick was fain to acknowledge that he was the man.

"Much is to be said for, and much is to be said against, a single life," thought the old gentleman, walking up and down the sequestered garden-path to which he had retired, and applying himself at shorter intervals than usual to the knob of his ivory cane. "This, however, is, I take it, certain. A man's married friends can't prevent him from leading the life of a bachelor, if he pleases. But they can, and do, take devilish good care that he sha'n't enjoy it!"

Sir Patrick's meditations were interrupted by the appearance of a servant, previously instructed to keep him informed of the progress of events at the house.

"They're all gone, Sir Patrick," said the man.

"That's a comfort, Simpson. We have no visitors to deal with now, except the visitors who are staying in the house?"

"None, Sir Patrick."

"They're all gentlemen, are they not?"

"Yes, Sir Patrick."

"That's another comfort, Simpson. Very good. I'll see Lady Lundie first."

Does any other form of human resolution approach the firmness of a woman who is bent on discovering the frailties of another woman whom she hates? You may move rocks, under a given set of circumstances. But here is a delicate being in petticoats, who shrieks if a spider drops on her neck, and shudders if you approach her after having eaten an onion. Can you move *her*, under a given set of circumstances, as set forth above? Not you!

Sir Patrick found her ladyship instituting her inquiries on the same admirably exhaustive system which is pursued, in cases of disappearance, by the police. Who was the last witness who had seen the missing person? Who was the last servant who had seen Anne Silvester? Begin with the men-servants, from the butler at the top to the stable-boy at the bottom. Go on with the women-servants, from the cook in all her glory to the small female child who weeds the garden. Lady Lundie had cross-examined her way downward as far as the page, when Sir Patrick joined her.

"My dear lady! pardon me for reminding you again, that this is a free country, and that you have no claim whatever to investigate Miss Silvester's proceedings after she has left your house."

Lady Lundie raised her eyes, devotionally, to the ceiling. She looked like a martyr to duty. If you had seen her ladyship at that moment, you would have said yourself, "A martyr to duty."

"No, Sir Patrick! As a Christian woman, that is not *my* way of looking at it. This unhappy person has lived under my roof. This unhappy person has been the companion of Blanche. I am responsible—I am, in a manner, morally responsible. I would give the world to be able to dismiss it as you do. But no! I must be satisfied that she *is* married. In the interests of propriety. For the quieting of my own conscience. Before I lay my head on my pillow to-night, Sir Patrick—before I lay my head on my pillow to-night!"

"One word, Lady Lundie—"

"No!" repeated her ladyship, with the most pathetic gentleness. "You are right, I dare say, from the worldly point of view. I can't take the worldly point of view. The worldly point of view hurts me." She turned, with impressive gravity, to the page. "You know where you will go, Jonathan, if you tell lies!"

Jonathan was lazy, Jonathan was pimply, Jonathan was fat—*but* Jonathan was orthodox.

He answered that he did know; and, what is more, he mentioned the place.

Sir Patrick saw that further opposition on his part, at that moment, would be worse than useless. He wisely determined to wait, before he interfered again, until Lady Lundie had thoroughly exhausted herself and her inquiries. At the same time—as it was impossible, in the present state of her ladyship's temper, to provide against what might happen if the inquiries after Anne unluckily proved successful — he decided on taking measures to clear the house of the guests (in the interests of all parties) for the next four-and-twenty hours.

"I only want to ask you a question, Lady Lundie," he resumed. "The position of the gentlemen who are staying here is not a very pleasant one while all this is going on. If you had been content to let the matter pass without notice, we should have done very well. As things are, don't you think it will be more convenient to every body if I relieve you of the responsibility of entertaining your guests?"

"As head of the family?" stipulated Lady Lundie.

"As head of the family!" answered Sir Patrick.

"I gratefully accept the proposal," said Lady Lundie.

"I beg you won't mention it," rejoined Sir Patrick.

He quitted the room, leaving Jonathan under examination. He and his brother (the late Sir Thomas) had chosen widely different paths in life, and had seen but little of each other since the time when they had been boys. Sir Patrick's recollections (on leaving Lady Lundie) appeared to have taken him back to that time, and to have inspired him with a certain tenderness for his brother's memory. He shook his head, and sighed a sad little sigh. "Poor Tom!" he said to himself, softly, after he had shut the door on his brother's widow. "Poor Tom!"

On crossing the hall, he stopped the first servant he met, to inquire after Blanche. Miss Blanche was quiet, up stairs, closeted with her maid in her own room. "Quiet?" thought Sir Patrick. "That's a bad sign. I shall hear more of my niece."

Pending that event, the next thing to do was to find the guests. Unerring instinct led Sir Patrick to the billiard-room. There he found them, in solemn conclave assembled, wondering what they had better do. Sir Patrick put them all at their ease in two minutes.

"What do you say to a day's shooting to-morrow?" he asked.

Every man present—sportsman or not—said yes.

"You can start from this house," pursued Sir Patrick; "or you can start from a shooting-cottage which is on the Windygates property—among the woods, on the other side of the moor. The weather looks pretty well settled (for Scotland), and there are plenty of horses in the stables. It is useless to conceal from you, gentlemen, that events have taken a certain unexpected turn in my sister-in-law's family circle. You will be equally Lady Lundie's guests, whether you choose the cottage or the house. For the next twenty-four hours (let us say)—which shall it be?"

Every body—with or without rheumatism—answered "the cottage!"

"Very good," pursued Sir Patrick. "It is arranged to ride over to the shooting-cottage this evening, and to try the moor, on that side, the first thing in the morning. If events here will allow me, I shall be delighted to accompany you, and do the honors as well as I can. If not, I am sure you will accept my apologies for to-night, and permit Lady Lundie's steward to see to your comfort in my place."

Adopted unanimously. Sir Patrick left the guests to their billiards, and went out to give the necessary orders at the stables.

In the mean time Blanche remained portentously quiet in the upper regions of the house; while Lady Lundie steadily pursued her inquiries down stairs. She got on from Jonathan (last of the males, indoors) to the coachman (first of the males, out-of-doors), and dug down, man by man, through that new stratum, until she struck the stable-boy at the bottom. Not an atom of information having been extracted, in the house or out of the house, from man or boy, her ladyship fell back on the women next. She pulled the bell, and summoned the cook—Hester Dethridge.

A very remarkable-looking person entered the room.

Elderly and quiet; scrupulously clean; eminently respectable; her gray hair neat and smooth under her modest white cap; her eyes, set deep in their orbits, looking straight at any person who spoke to her—here, at a first view, was a steady, trust-worthy woman. Here also, on closer inspection, was a woman with the seal of some terrible past suffering set on her for the rest of her life. You felt it, rather than saw it, in the look of immovable endurance which underlaid her expression—in the deathlike tranquillity which never disappeared from her manner. Her story was a sad one—so far as it was known. She had entered Lady Lundie's service at the period of Lady Lundie's marriage to Sir Thomas. Her character (given by the clergyman of her parish) described her as having been married to an inveterate drunkard, and as having suffered unutterably during her husband's lifetime. There were drawbacks to engaging her, now that she was a widow. On one of the many occasions on which her husband had personally ill-treated her, he had struck her a blow which had produced very remarkable nervous results. She had lain insensible many days together, and had recovered with the total loss of her speech. In addition to this objection, she was odd, at times, in her manner; and she made it a condition of accepting any situation, that she should be privileged to sleep in a room by herself. As a set-off against all this, it was to be said, on the other side of the question, that she was sober; rigidly honest in all her dealings; and one of the best cooks in England. In consideration of this last merit, the late Sir Thomas had decided on giving her a trial, and had discovered that he had never dined in his life as he dined when Hester Dethridge was at the head of his kitchen. She remained, after his death, in his widow's service. Lady Lundie was far from liking her. An unpleasant suspicion attached to the cook, which Sir Thomas had overlooked, but which persons less sensible of the immense importance of dining well could not fail to regard as a serious objection to her. Medical men, consulted about her case, discovered certain physiological anomalies in it which led them to suspect the woman of feigning dumbness, for some reason best known to herself. She obstinately declined to learn the deaf and dumb alphabet—on the ground that dumbness was not associated with deafness in her case. Stratagems were invented (seeing that she really did possess the use of her ears) to entrap her into also using her speech, and failed. Efforts were made to induce her to answer questions relating to her past life in her husband's time. She flatly declined to reply to them, one and all. At certain intervals, strange impulses to get a holiday away from the house appeared to seize her. If she was resisted, she passively declined to do her work. If she was threatened with dismissal, she impenetrably bowed her head, as much as to say, "Give me the word, and I go." Over and over again, Lady Lundie had decided, naturally enough, on no longer keeping such a servant as this; but she had never yet carried the decision to execution. A cook who is a perfect mistress of her art, who asks for no perquisites, who allows no waste, who never quarrels with the other servants, who drinks nothing stronger than tea, who is to be trusted with untold gold—is not a cook easily replaced. In this mortal life we put up with many persons and things, as Lady Lundie put up with her cook. The woman lived, as it were, on the brink of dismissal; but thus far the woman kept her place—getting her holidays when she asked for them (which, to do her justice, was not often), and sleeping always (go where she might with the family) with a locked door, in a room by herself.

Hester Dethridge advanced slowly to the table at which Lady Lundie was sitting. A slate and pencil hung at her side, which she used for making such replies as were not to be expressed by a gesture or by a motion of the head. She took up the slate and pencil, and waited with stony submission for her mistress to begin.

Lady Lundie opened the proceedings with the regular formula of inquiry which she had used with all the other servants.

"Do you know that Miss Silvester has left the house?"

The cook nodded her head affirmatively.

"Do you know at what time she left it?"

Another affirmative reply. The first which Lady Lundie had received to that question yet. She eagerly went on to the next inquiry.

"Have you seen her since she left the house?"

A third affirmative reply.

"Where?"

Hester Dethridge wrote slowly on the slate, in singularly firm upright characters for a woman in her position of life, these words:

"On the road that leads to the railway. Nigh to Mistress Chew's Farm."

"What did you want at Chew's Farm?"

Hester Dethridge wrote: "I wanted eggs for the kitchen, and a breath of fresh air for myself."

"Did Miss Silvester see you?"

A negative shake of the head.

"Did she take the turning that leads to the railway?"

Another negative shake of the head.

"SHE TOOK UP THE SLATE AND PENCIL, AND WAITED WITH STONY SUBMISSION FOR HER MISTRESS TO BEGIN."

"She went on, toward the moor?"

An affirmative reply.

"What did she do when she got to the moor?"

Hester Dethridge wrote: "She took the foot-path which leads to Craig Fernie."

Lady Lundie rose excitedly to her feet. There was but one place that a stranger could go to at Craig Fernie. "The inn!" exclaimed her ladyship. "She has gone to the inn!"

Hester Dethridge waited immovably. Lady Lundie put a last precautionary question, in these words:

"Have you reported what you have seen to any body else?"

An affirmative reply. Lady Lundie had not bargained for that. Hester Dethridge (she thought) must surely have misunderstood her.

"Do you mean that you have told somebody else what you have just told me?"

Another affirmative reply.

"A person who questioned you, as I have done?"

A third affirmative reply.

"Who was it?"

Hester Dethridge wrote on her slate: "Miss Blanche."

Lady Lundie stepped back, staggered by the discovery that Blanche's resolution to trace Anne Silvester was, to all appearance, as firmly settled as her own. Her step-daughter was keeping her own counsel, and acting on her own responsibility—her step-daughter might be an awkward obstacle in the way. The manner in which Anne had left the house had mortally offended Lady Lundie. An inveterately vindictive woman, she had resolved to discover whatever compromising elements might exist in the governess's secret, and to make them public property (from a paramount sense of duty, of course) among her own circle of friends. But to do this—with Blanche acting (as might certainly be anticipated) in direct opposition to her, and openly espousing Miss Silvester's interests—was manifestly impossible.

The first thing to be done—and that instantly—was to inform Blanche that she was discovered, and to forbid her to stir in the matter.

Lady Lundie rang the bell twice—thus intimating, according to the laws of the household, that she required the attendance of her own maid. She then turned to the cook—still waiting her pleasure, with stony composure, slate in hand.

"You have done wrong," said her ladyship, severely. "I am your mistress. You are bound to answer your mistress—"

Hester Dethridge bowed her head, in icy acknowledgment of the principle laid down—so far.

The bow was an interruption. Lady Lundie resented it.

"But Miss Blanche is not your mistress," she went on, sternly. "You are very much to blame for answering Miss Blanche's inquiries about Miss Silvester."

Hester Dethridge, perfectly unmoved, wrote her justification on her slate, in two stiff sentences: "I had no orders not to answer. I keep nobody's secrets but my own."

That reply settled the question of the cook's dismissal—the question which had been pending for months past.

"You are an insolent woman! I have borne with you long enough—I will bear with you no longer. When your month is up, you go!"

In those words Lady Lundie dismissed Hester Dethridge from her service.

Not the slightest change passed over the sinister tranquillity of the cook. She bowed her head again, in acknowledgment of the sentence pronounced on her—dropped her slate at her side—turned about—and left the room. The woman was alive in the world, and working in the world; and yet (so far as all human interests were concerned) she was as completely out of the world as if she had been screwed down in her coffin, and laid in her grave.

Lady Lundie's maid came into the room as Hester left it.

"Go up stairs to Miss Blanche," said her mistress, "and say I want her here. Wait a minute!" She paused, and considered. Blanche might decline to submit to her step-mother's interference with her. It might be necessary to appeal to the higher authority of her guardian. "Do you know where Sir Patrick is?" asked Lady Lundie.

"I heard Simpson say, my lady, that Sir Patrick was at the stables."

"Send Simpson with a message. My compliments to Sir Patrick—and I wish to see him immediately."

\*     \*     \*     \*     \*     \*

The preparations for the departure to the shooting-cottage were just completed; and the one question that remained to be settled was, whether Sir Patrick could accompany the party—when the man-servant appeared with the message from his mistress.

"Will you give me a quarter of an hour, gentlemen?" asked Sir Patrick. "In that time I shall know for certain whether I can go with you or not."

As a matter of course, the guests decided to wait. The younger men among them (being Englishmen) naturally occupied their leisure time in betting. Would Sir Patrick get the better of the domestic crisis? or would the domestic crisis get the better of Sir Patrick? The domestic crisis was backed, at two to one, to win.

Punctually at the expiration of the quarter of an hour, Sir Patrick reappeared. The domestic crisis had betrayed the blind confidence which youth and inexperience had placed in it. Sir Patrick had won the day.

"Things are settled and quiet, gentlemen; and I am able to accompany you," he said. "There are two ways to the shooting-cottage. One—the longest—passes by the inn at Craig Fernie. I am compelled to ask you to go with me by that way. While you push on to the cottage, I must drop behind, and say a word to a person who is staying at the inn."

He had quieted Lady Lundie—he had even quieted Blanche. But it was evidently on the condition that he was to go to Craig Fernie in their places, and to see Anne Silvester himself. Without a word more of explanation he mounted his horse, and led the way out. The shooting-party left Windygates.

## SECOND SCENE.—THE INN.

## CHAPTER THE NINTH.

### ANNE.

"YE'LL just permit me to remind ye again, young leddy, that the hottle's full—exceptin' only this settin'-room, and the bedchamber yonder belonging to it."

So spoke "Mistress Inchbare," landlady of the Craig Fernie Inn, to Anne Silvester, standing in the parlor, purse in hand, and offering the price of the two rooms before she claimed permission to occupy them.

The time of the afternoon was about the time when Geoffrey Delamayn had started in the train, on his journey to London. About the time also, when Arnold Brinkworth had crossed the moor, and was mounting the first rising ground which led to the inn.

Mistress Inchbare was tall and thin, and decent and dry. Mistress Inchbare's unlovable hair clung fast round her head in wiry little yellow curls. Mistress Inchbare's hard bones showed themselves, like Mistress Inchbare's hard Presbyterianism, without any concealment or compromise. In short, a savagely-respectable woman, who plumed herself on presiding over a savagely-respectable inn.

There was no competition to interfere with Mistress Inchbare. She regulated her own prices, and made her own rules. If you objected to her prices, and revolted from her rules, you were free to go. In other words, you were free to cast yourself, in the capacity of houseless wanderer, on the scanty mercy of a Scotch wilderness. The village of Craig Fernie was a collection of hovels. The country about Craig Fernie, mountain on one side and moor on the other, held no second house of public entertainment, for miles and miles round, at any point of the compass. No rambling individual but the helpless British Tourist wanted food and shelter from strangers, in that part of Scotland; and nobody but Mistress Inchbare had food and shelter to sell. A more thoroughly independent person than this was not to be found on the face of the hotel-keeping earth. The most universal of all civilized terrors—the terror of appearing unfavorably in the newspapers—was a sensation absolutely unknown to the Empress of the Inn. You lost your temper, and threatened to send her bill for exhibition in the public journals. Mistress Inchbare raised no objection to your taking any course you pleased with it. "Eh, man! send the bill whar' ye like, as long as ye pay it first. There's nae such thing as a newspaper ever darkens my doors. Ye've got the Auld and New Testaments in your bedchambers, and the natural history o' Pairthshire on the coffee-room table—and if that's no' reading eneugh for ye, ye may een gae back South again, and get the rest of it there."

This was the inn at which Anne Silvester had appeared alone, with nothing but a little bag in her hand. This was the woman whose reluctance to receive her she innocently expected to overcome by showing her purse.

"Mention your charge for the rooms," she said. "I am willing to pay for them beforehand."

Her majesty, Mrs. Inchbare, never even looked at her subject's poor little purse.

"It just comes to this, mistress," she answered. "I'm no' free to tak' your money, if I'm no' free to let ye the last rooms left in the hoose. The Craig Fernie hottle is a faimily hottle—and has its ain gude name to keep up. Ye're ower-well-looking, my young leddy, to be traveling alone."

The time had been when Anne would have answered sharply enough. The hard necessities of her position made her patient now.

"I have already told you," she said, "my husband is coming here to join me." She sighed wearily as she repeated her ready-made story—and dropped into the nearest chair, from sheer inability to stand any longer.

Mistress Inchbare looked at her, with the exact measure of compassionate interest which she might have shown if she had been looking at a stray dog who had fallen footsore at the door of the inn.

"Weel! weel! sae let it be. Bide awhile, and rest ye. We'll no' chairge ye for that—and we'll see if your husband comes. I'll just let the rooms, mistress, to *him*, instead o' lettin' them to *you*. And, sae, good-morrow t' ye." With that final announcement of her royal will and pleasure, the Empress of the Inn withdrew.

Anne made no reply. She watched the landlady out of the room—and then struggled to control herself no longer. In her position, suspicion was doubly insult. The hot tears of shame gathered in her eyes; and the heartache wrung her, poor soul—wrung her without mercy.

A trifling noise in the room startled her. She looked up, and detected a man in a corner, dusting the furniture, and apparently acting in the capacity of attendant at the inn. He had shown her into the parlor on her arrival; but he had remained so quietly in the room that she had never noticed him since, until that moment.

He was an ancient man—with one eye filmy and blind, and one eye moist and merry. His head was bald; his feet were gouty; his nose was justly celebrated as the largest nose and the reddest nose in that part of Scotland. The mild wisdom of years was expressed mysteriously in his mellow smile. In contact with this wicked world, his manner revealed that happy mixture of two extremes—the servility which just touches independence, and the independence which just touches servility—attained by no men in existence but Scotchmen. Enormous native impudence, which amused but never offended; immeasurable cunning, masquerading habitually under the double disguise of quaint prejudice and dry humor, were the solid moral foundations on which the character of this elderly person was built. No amount of whisky ever made him drunk; and no violence of bell-ringing ever hurried his movements. Such was the head-waiter at the Craig Fernie Inn; known, far and wide, to local fame, as "Maister Bishopriggs, Mistress Inchbare's right-hand man."

"What are you doing there?" Anne asked, sharply.

Mr. Bishopriggs turned himself about on his gouty feet; waved his duster gently in the air; and looked at Anne, with a mild, paternal smile.

"Eh! Am just doostin' the things; and settin' the room in decent order for ye."

"For *me?* Did you hear what the landlady said?"

Mr. Bishopriggs advanced confidentially, and pointed with a very unsteady forefinger to the purse which Anne still held in her hand.

"Never fash yoursel' aboot the landleddy!" said the sage chief of the Craig Fernie waiters. "Your purse speaks for you, my lassie. Pet it up!" cried Mr. Bishopriggs, waving temptation away from him with the duster. "In wi' it into yer pocket! Sae long as the warld's the warld, I'll uphaud it any where—while there's siller in the purse, there's gude in the woman!"

Anne's patience, which had resisted harder trials, gave way at this.

"What do you mean by speaking to me in that familiar manner?" she asked, rising angrily to her feet again.

Mr. Bishopriggs tucked his duster under his arm, and proceeded to satisfy Anne that he shared the landlady's view of her position, without sharing the severity of the landlady's principles. "There's nae man livin'," said Mr. Bishopriggs, "looks with mair indulgence at human frailty than my ain sel'. Am I no' to be familiar wi' ye—when I'm auld eneugh to be a fether to ye, and ready to be a fether to ye till further notice? Hech! hech! Order your bit dinner, lassie. Husband or no husband, ye've got a stomach, and ye must een eat. There's fesh and there's fowl—or, maybe, ye'll be for the sheep's head singit, when they've done with it at the tabble dot?"

There was but one way of getting rid of him: "Order what you like," Anne said, "and leave the room." Mr. Bishopriggs highly approved of the first half of the sentence, and totally overlooked the second.

"Ay, ay—just pet a' yer little interests in my hands; it's the wisest thing ye can do. Ask for Maister Bishopriggs (that's me) when ye want a decent 'sponsible man to gi' ye a word of advice. Set ye doon again—set ye doon. And don't tak' the arm-chair. Hech! hech! yer husband will be coming, ye know, and he's sure to want it!" With that seasonable pleasantry the venerable Bishopriggs winked, and went out.

Anne looked at her watch. By her calculation it was not far from the hour when Geoffrey might be expected to arrive at the inn, assuming Geoffrey to have left Windygates at the time agreed on. A little more patience, and the landlady's scruples would be satisfied, and the ordeal would be at an end.

Could she have met him nowhere else than at this barbarous house, and among these barbarous people?

No. Outside the doors of Windygates she had not a friend to help her in all Scotland. There was no place at her disposal but the inn; and she had only to be thankful that it occupied a sequestered situation, and was not likely to be visited by any of Lady Lundie's friends. Whatever the risk might be, the end in view justified her in confronting it. Her whole future depended on Geoffrey's making an honest woman of her. Not her future with *him*—that way there was no hope; that way her life was wasted. Her future with Blanche—she looked forward to nothing now but her future with Blanche.

Her spirits sank lower and lower. The tears rose again. It would only irritate him if he came and found her crying. She tried to divert her mind by looking about the room.

There was very little to see.  Except that it was solidly built of good sound stone, the Craig Fernie hotel differed in no other important respect from the average of second-rate English inns.  There was the usual slippery black sofa—constructed to let you slide when you wanted to rest.  There was the usual highly-varnished arm-chair, expressly manufactured to test the endurance of the human spine.  There was the usual paper on the walls, of the pattern designed to make your eyes ache and your head giddy.  There were the usual engravings, which humanity never tires of contemplating.  The Royal Portrait, in the first place of honor.  The next greatest of all human beings—the Duke of Wellington—in the second place of honor.  The third greatest of all human beings—the local member of parliament—in the third place of honor; and, a hunting scene, in the dark.  A door opposite the door of admission from the passage opened into the bedroom; and a window at the side looked out on the open space in front of the hotel, and commanded a view of the vast expanse of the Craig Fernie moor, stretching away below the rising ground on which the house was built.

Anne turned in despair from the view in the room to the view from the window.  Within the last half hour it had changed for the worse.  The clouds had gathered; the sun was hidden; the light on the landscape was gray and dull.  Anne turned from the window, as she had turned from the room.  She was just making the hopeless attempt to rest her weary limbs on the sofa, when the sound of voices and footsteps in the passage caught her ear.

Was Geoffrey's voice among them?  No.

Were the strangers coming in?

The landlady had declined to let her have the rooms: it was quite possible that the strangers might be coming to look at them.  There was no knowing who they might be.  In the impulse of the moment she flew to the bedchamber and locked herself in.

The door from the passage opened, and Arnold Brinkworth—shown in by Mr. Bishopriggs—entered the sitting-room.

"Nobody here!" exclaimed Arnold, looking round.  "Where is she?"

Mr. Bishopriggs pointed to the bedroom door.  "Eh!  yer good leddy's joost in the bedchamber, nae doot!"

Arnold started.  He had felt no difficulty (when he and Geoffrey had discussed the question at Windygates) about presenting himself at the inn in the assumed character of Anne's husband.  But the result of putting the deception in practice was, to say the least of it, a little embarrassing at first.  Here was the waiter describing Miss Silvester as his "good lady;" and leaving it (most naturally and properly) to the "good lady's" husband to knock at her bedroom door, and tell her that he was there.  In despair of knowing what else to do at the moment, Arnold asked for the landlady, whom he had not seen on arriving at the inn.

"The landleddy's just tottin' up the ledgers o' the hottle in her ain room," answered Mr. Bishopriggs.  "She'll be here anon—the wearyful woman!—speerin' who ye are and what ye are, and takin' a' the business o' the hoose on her ain pair o' shouthers."  He dropped the subject of the landlady, and put in a plea for himself.  "I

ha' lookit after a' the leddy's little comforts, Sir," he whispered.  "Trust in me! trust in me!"

Arnold's attention was absorbed in the very serious difficulty of announcing his arrival to Anne.  "How am I to get her out?" he said to himself, with a look of perplexity directed at the bedroom door.

He had spoken loud enough for the waiter to hear him.  Arnold's look of perplexity was instantly reflected on the face of Mr. Bishopriggs.  The head-waiter at Craig Fernie possessed an immense experience of the manners and customs of newly-married people on their honey-moon trip.  He had been a second father (with excellent pecuniary results) to innumerable brides and bridegrooms.  He knew young married couples in all their varieties:—The couples who try to behave as if they had been married for many years; the couples who attempt no concealment, and take advice from competent authorities about them.  The couples who are bashfully talkative before third persons; the couples who are bashfully silent under similar circumstances.  The couples who don't know what to do; the couples who wish it was over; the couples who must never be intruded upon without careful preliminary knocking at the door; the couples who *can* eat and drink in the intervals of "bliss," and the other couples who *can't*.  But the bridegroom who stood helpless on one side of the door, and the bride who remained locked in on the other, were new varieties of the nuptial species, even in the vast experience of Mr. Bishopriggs himself.

"Hoo are ye to get her oot?" he repeated.  "I'll show ye hoo!"  He advanced as rapidly as his gouty feet would let him, and knocked at the bedroom door.  "Eh, my leddy! here he is in flesh and bluid.  Mercy preserve us! do ye lock the door of the nuptial chamber in your husband's face?"

At that unanswerable appeal the lock was heard turning in the door.  Mr. Bishopriggs winked at Arnold with his one available eye, and laid his forefinger knowingly along his enormous nose.  "I'm away before she falls into your arms!  Rely on it I'll no come in again without knocking first!"

He left Arnold alone in the room.  The bedroom door opened slowly by a few inches at a time.  Anne's voice was just audible, speaking cautiously behind it.

"Is that you, Geoffrey?"

Arnold's heart began to beat fast, in anticipation of the disclosure which was now close at hand.  He knew neither what to say or do—he remained silent.

Anne repeated the question in louder tones:  "Is that you?"

There was the certain prospect of alarming her, if some reply was not given.  There was no help for it.  Come what come might, Arnold answered, in a whisper:  "Yes."

The door was flung wide open.  Anne Silvester appeared on the threshold, confronting him.

"Mr. Brinkworth!!!" she exclaimed, standing petrified with astonishment.

For a moment more neither of them spoke.  Anne advanced one step into the sitting-room, and put the next inevitable question, with an instantaneous change from surprise to suspicion.

"EH, MY LEDDY! HERE HE IS IN FLESH AND BLUID."

"What do you want here?"

Geoffrey's letter represented the only possible excuse for Arnold's appearance in that place, and at that time.

"I have got a letter for you," he said—and offered it to her.

She was instantly on her guard. They were little better than strangers to each other, as Arnold had said. A sickening presentiment of some treachery on Geoffrey's part struck cold to her heart. She refused to take the letter.

"I expect no letter," she said. "Who told you I was here?" She put the question, not only with a tone of suspicion, but with a look of contempt. The look was not an easy one for a man to bear. It required a momentary exertion of self-control on Arnold's part, before he could trust himself to answer with due consideration for her. "Is there a watch set on my actions?" she went on, with rising anger. "And are *you* the spy?"

"You haven't known me very long, Miss Silvester," Arnold answered, quietly. "But you ought to know me better than to say that. I am the bearer of a letter from Geoffrey."

She was on the point of following his example, and of speaking of Geoffrey by his Christian name, on her side. But she checked herself, before the word had passed her lips.

"Do you mean Mr. Delamayn?" she asked, coldly.

"Yes."

"What occasion have *I* for a letter from Mr. Delamayn?"

She was determined to acknowledge nothing— she kept him obstinately at arm's-length. Ar-

nold did, as a matter of instinct, what a man of larger experience would have done, as a matter of calculation—he closed with her boldly, then and there.

"Miss Silvester! it's no use beating about the bush. If you won't take the letter, you force me to speak out. I am here on a very unpleasant errand. I begin to wish, from the bottom of my heart, I had never undertaken it."

A quick spasm of pain passed across her face. She was beginning, dimly beginning, to understand him. He hesitated. His generous nature shrank from hurting her.

"Go on," she said, with an effort.

"Try not to be angry with me, Miss Silvester. Geoffrey and I are old friends. Geoffrey knows he can trust me—"

"Trust you?" she interposed. "Stop!"

Arnold waited. She went on, speaking to herself, not to him.

"When I was in the other room I asked if Geoffrey was there. And this man answered for him." She sprang forward with a cry of horror.

"Has he told you—"

"For God's sake, read his letter!"

She violently pushed back the hand with which Arnold once more offered the letter. "You don't look at me! He *has* told you!"

"Read his letter," persisted Arnold. "In justice to him, if you won't in justice to me."

The situation was too painful to be endured. Arnold looked at her, this time, with a man's resolution in his eyes—spoke to her, this time, with a man's resolution in his voice. She took the letter.

"I beg your pardon, Sir," she said, with a sudden humiliation of tone and manner, inexpressibly shocking, inexpressibly pitiable to see. "I understand my position at last. I am a woman doubly betrayed. Please to excuse what I said to you just now, when I supposed myself to have some claim on your respect. Perhaps you will grant me your pity? I can ask for nothing more."

Arnold was silent. Words were useless in the face of such utter self-abandonment as this. Any man living—even Geoffrey himself—must have felt for her at that moment.

She looked for the first time at the letter. She opened it on the wrong side. "My own letter!" she said to herself. "In the hands of another man!"

"Look at the last page," said Arnold.

She turned to the last page, and read the hurried penciled lines. "Villain! villain! villain!" At the third repetition of the word, she crushed the letter in the palm of her hand, and flung it from her to the other end of the room. The instant after, the fire that had flamed up in her died out. Feebly and slowly she reached out her hand to the nearest chair, and sat down in it with her back to Arnold. "He has deserted me!" was all she said. The words fell low and quiet on the silence: they were the utterance of an immeasurable despair.

"You are wrong!" exclaimed Arnold. "Indeed, indeed you are wrong! It's no excuse—it's the truth. I was present when the message came about his father."

She never heeded him, and never moved. She only repeated the words:

"He has deserted me!"

"Don't take it in that way!" pleaded Arnold—"pray don't! It's dreadful to hear you; it is indeed. I am sure he has *not* deserted you." There was no answer; no sign that she heard him; she sat there, struck to stone. It was impossible to call the landlady in at such a moment as this. In despair of knowing how else to rouse her, Arnold drew a chair to her side, and patted her timidly on the shoulder. "Come!" he said, in his single-hearted, boyish way. "Cheer up a little!"

She slowly turned her head, and looked at him with a dull surprise.

"Didn't you say he had told you every thing?" she asked.

"Yes."

"Don't you despise a woman like me?"

Arnold's heart went back, at that dreadful question, to the one woman who was eternally sacred to him—to the woman from whose bosom he had drawn the breath of life.

"Does the man live," he said, "who can think of his mother—and despise women?"

That answer set the prisoned misery in her free. She gave him her hand — she faintly thanked him. The merciful tears came to her at last.

Arnold rose, and turned away to the window in despair. "I mean well," he said. "And yet I only distress her!"

She heard him, and struggled to compose herself. "No," she answered, "you comfort me. Don't mind my crying—I'm the better for it." She looked round at him gratefully. "I won't distress you, Mr. Brinkworth. I ought to thank you—and I do. Come back, or I shall think you are angry with me." Arnold went back to her. She gave him her hand once more. "One doesn't understand people all at once," she said, simply. "I thought you were like other men—I didn't know till to-day how kind you could be. Did you walk here?" she added, suddenly, with an effort to change the subject. "Are you tired? I have not been kindly received at this place—but I'm sure I may offer you whatever the inn affords."

It was impossible not to feel for her—it was impossible not to be interested in her. Arnold's honest longing to help her expressed itself a little too openly when he spoke next. "All I want, Miss Silvester, is to be of some service to you, if I can," he said. "Is there any thing I can do to make your position here more comfortable? You will stay at this place, won't you? Geoffrey wishes it."

She shuddered, and looked away. "Yes! yes!" she answered, hurriedly.

"You will hear from Geoffrey," Arnold went on, "to-morrow or next day. I know he means to write."

"For Heaven's sake, don't speak of him any more!" she cried out. "How do you think I can look you in the face—" Her cheeks flushed deep, and her eyes rested on him with a momentary firmness. "Mind this! I am his wife, if promises can make me his wife! He has pledged his word to me by all that is sacred!" She checked herself impatiently. "What am I saying? What interest can *you* have in this miserable state of things? Don't let us talk of it! I have something else to say to you. Let us go back to my troubles here. Did you see the landlady when you came in?"

"No. I only saw the waiter."

"The landlady has made some absurd difficulty about letting me have these rooms because I came here alone."

"She won't make any difficulty now," said Arnold. "I have settled that."

"*You!*"

Arnold smiled. After what had passed, it was an indescribable relief to him to see the humorous side of his own position at the inn.

"Certainly," he answered. "When I asked for the lady who had arrived here alone this afternoon—"

"Yes."

"I was told, in your interests, to ask for her as my wife."

Anne looked at him—in alarm as well as in surprise.

"You asked for me as your wife?" she repeated.

"Yes. I haven't done wrong—have I? As I understood it, there was no alternative. Geoffrey told me you had settled with him to present yourself here as a married lady, whose husband was coming to join her."

"I thought of *him* when I said that. I never thought of *you*."

"Natural enough. Still, it comes to the same thing (doesn't it?) with the people of this house."

"I don't understand you."

"I will try and explain myself a little better. Geoffrey said your position here depended on my asking for you at the door (as *he* would have asked for you if he had come) in the character of your husband."

"He had no right to say that."

"No right? After what you have told me of the landlady, just think what might have happened if he had *not* said it! I haven't had much experience myself of these things. But—allow me to ask—wouldn't it have been a little awkward (at my age) if I had come here and inquired for you as a friend? Don't you think, in that case, the landlady might have made some additional difficulty about letting you have the rooms?"

It was beyond dispute that the landlady would have refused to let the rooms at all. It was equally plain that the deception which Arnold had practiced on the people of the inn was a deception which Anne had herself rendered necessary, in her own interests. She was not to blame; it was clearly impossible for her to have foreseen such an event as Geoffrey's departure for London. Still, she felt an uneasy sense of responsibility—a vague dread of what might happen next. She sat nervously twisting her handkerchief in her lap, and made no answer.

"Don't suppose I object to this little stratagem," Arnold went on. "I am serving my old friend, and I am helping the lady who is soon to be his wife."

Anne rose abruptly to her feet, and amazed him by a very unexpected question.

"Mr. Brinkworth," she said, "forgive me the rudeness of something I am about to say to you. When are you going away?"

Arnold burst out laughing.

"When I am quite sure I can do nothing more to assist you," he answered.

"Pray don't think of *me* any longer."

"In your situation! who else am I to think of?"

Anne laid her hand earnestly on his arm, and answered:

"Blanche!"

"Blanche?" repeated Arnold, utterly at a loss to understand her.

"Yes—Blanche. She found time to tell me what had passed between you this morning before I left Windygates. I know you have made her an offer. I know you are engaged to be married to her."

Arnold was delighted to hear it. He had been merely unwilling to leave her thus far. He was absolutely determined to stay with her now.

"Don't expect me to go after that!" he said. "Come and sit down again, and let's talk about Blanche."

Anne declined impatiently, by a gesture. Arnold was too deeply interested in the new topic to take any notice of it.

"You know all about her habits and her tastes," he went on, "and what she likes, and what she dislikes. It's most important that I should talk to you about her. When we are husband and wife, Blanche is to have all her own way in every thing. That's my idea of the Whole Duty of Man—when Man is married. You are still standing? Let me give you a chair."

It was cruel—under other circumstances it would have been impossible—to disappoint him. But the vague fear of consequences which had taken possession of Anne was not to be trifled with. She had no clear conception of the risk (and it is to be added, in justice to Geoffrey, that *he* had no clear conception of the risk) on which Arnold

had unconsciously ventured, in undertaking his errand to the inn. Neither of them had any adequate idea (few people have) of the infamous absence of all needful warning, of all decent precaution and restraint, which makes the marriage law of Scotland a trap to catch unmarried men and women, to this day. But, while Geoffrey's mind was incapable of looking beyond the present emergency, Anne's finer intelligence told her that a country which offered such facilities for private marriage as the facilities of which she had proposed to take advantage in her own case, was not a country in which a man could act as Arnold had acted, without danger of some serious embarrassment following as the possible result. With this motive to animate her, she resolutely declined to take the offered chair, or to enter into the proposed conversation.

"Whatever we have to say about Blanche, Mr. Brinkworth, must be said at some fitter time. I beg you will leave me."

"Leave you!"

"Yes. Leave me to the solitude that is best for me, and to the sorrow that I have deserved. Thank you—and good-by."

Arnold made no attempt to disguise his disappointment and surprise.

"If I must go, I must," he said. "But why are you in such a hurry?"

"I don't want you to call me your wife again before the people of this inn."

"Is *that* all? What on earth are you afraid of?"

She was unable fully to realize her own apprehensions. She was doubly unable to express them in words. In her anxiety to produce some reason which might prevail on him to go, she drifted back into that very conversation about Blanche into which she had declined to enter but the moment before.

"I have reasons for being afraid," she said. "One that I can't give; and one that I can. Suppose Blanche heard of what you have done? The longer you stay here—the more people you see—the more chance there is that she *might* hear of it."

"And what if she did?" asked Arnold, in his own straightforward way. "Do you think she would be angry with me for making myself useful to *you?*"

"Yes," rejoined Anne, sharply, "if she was jealous of me."

Arnold's unlimited belief in Blanche expressed itself, without the slightest compromise, in two words:

"That's impossible!"

Anxious as she was, miserable as she was, a faint smile flitted over Anne's face.

"Sir Patrick would tell you, Mr. Brinkworth, that nothing is impossible where women are concerned." She dropped her momentary lightness of tone, and went on as earnestly as ever. "You can't put yourself in Blanche's place—I can. Once more, I beg you to go. I don't like your coming here, in this way! I don't like it at all!"

She held out her hand to take leave. At the same moment there was a loud knock at the door of the room.

Anne sank into the chair at her side, and uttered a faint cry of alarm. Arnold, perfectly impenetrable to all sense of his position, asked what there was to frighten her—and answered the knock in the two customary words:

"Come in!"

---

## CHAPTER THE TENTH.

### MR. BISHOPRIGGS.

THE knock at the door was repeated—a louder knock than before.

"Are you deaf?" shouted Arnold.

The door opened, little by little, an inch at a time. Mr. Bishopriggs appeared mysteriously, with the cloth for dinner over his arm, and with his second in command behind him, bearing "the furnishing of the table" (as it was called at Craig Fernie) on a tray.

"What the deuce were you waiting for?" asked Arnold. "I told you to come in."

"And *I* tauld *you*," answered Mr. Bishopriggs, "that I wadna come in without knocking first. Eh, man!" he went on, dismissing his second in command, and laying the cloth with his own venerable hands, "d'ye think I've lived in this hottle in blinded eegnorance of hoo young married couples pass the time when they're left to themselves? Twa knocks at the door—and an unco trouble in opening it, after that—is joost the least ye can do for them! Whar' do ye think, noo, I'll set the places for you and your leddy there?"

Anne walked away to the window, in undisguised disgust. Arnold found Mr. Bishopriggs to be quite irresistible. He answered, humoring the joke,

"One at the top and one at the bottom of the table, I suppose?"

"One at tap and one at bottom?" repeated Mr. Bishopriggs, in high disdain. "De'il a bit of it! Baith yer chairs as close together as chairs can be. Hech! hech!—haven't I caught 'em, after goodness knows hoo many preleeminary knocks at the door, dining on their husbands' knees, and steemulating a man's appetite by feeding him at the fork's end like a child? Eh!" sighed the sage of Craig Fernie, "it's a short life wi' that nuptial business, and a merry one! A month for yer billin' and cooin'; and a' the rest o' yer days for wondering ye were ever such a fule, and wishing it was a' to be done ower again.—Ye'll be for a bottle o' sherry wine, nae doot? and a drap toddy afterwards, to do yer digestin' on?"

Arnold nodded—and then, in obedience to a signal from Anne, joined her at the window. Mr. Bishopriggs looked after them attentively—observed that they were talking in whispers—and approved of that proceeding, as representing another of the established customs of young married couples at inns, in the presence of third persons appointed to wait on them.

"Ay! ay!" he said, looking over his shoulder at Arnold, "gae to your deerie! gae to your deerie! and leave a' the solid business o' life to Me. Ye've Screepture warrant for it. A man maun leave fether and mother (I'm yer fether), and cleave to his wife. My certie! 'cleave' is a strong word—there's nae sort o' doot aboot it, when it comes to 'cleaving!'" He wagged his head thoughtfully, and walked to the side-table in a corner, to cut the bread.

As he took up the knife, his one wary eye detected a morsel of crumpled paper, lying lost between the table and the wall. It was the letter from Geoffrey, which Anne had flung from her, in the first indignation of reading it—and which neither she nor Arnold had thought of since.

"What's that I see yonder?" muttered Mr. Bishopriggs, under his breath. "Mair litter in the room, after I've doosted and tidied it wi' my ain hands!"

He picked up the crumpled paper, and partly opened it. "Eh! what's here? Writing on it in ink? and writing on it in pencil? Who may this belong to?" He looked round cautiously toward Arnold and Anne. They were both still talking in whispers, and both standing with their backs to him, looking out of the window. "Here it is, clean forgotten and dune with!" thought Mr. Bishopriggs. "Noo what would a fule do, if he fund this? A fule wad light his pipe wi' it, and then wonder whether he wadna ha' dune better to read it first. And what wad a wise man do, in a seemilar position?" He practically answered that question by putting the letter into his pocket. It might be worth keeping, or it might not; five minutes' private examination of it would decide the alternative, at the first convenient opportunity. "Am gaun' to breeng the dinner in!" he called out to Arnold. "And, mind ye, there's nae knocking at the door possible, when I've got the tray in baith my hands, and, mairs the pity, the gout in baith my feet." With that friendly warning, Mr. Bishopriggs went his way to the regions of the kitchen.

Arnold continued his conversation with Anne, in terms which showed that the question of his leaving the inn had been the question once more discussed between them while they were standing at the window.

"You see we can't help it," he said. "The waiter has gone to bring the dinner in. What will they think in the house, if I go away already, and leave 'my wife' to dine alone?"

It was so plainly necessary to keep up appearances for the present, that there was nothing more to be said. Arnold was committing a serious imprudence—and yet, on this occasion, Arnold was right. Anne's annoyance at feeling that conclusion forced on her produced the first betrayal of impatience which she had shown yet. She left Arnold at the window, and flung herself on the sofa. "A curse seems to follow me!" she thought, bitterly. "This will end ill—and I shall be answerable for it!"

In the mean time Mr. Bishopriggs had found the dinner in the kitchen, ready, and waiting for him. Instead of at once taking the tray on which it was placed into the sitting-room, he conveyed it privately into his own pantry, and shut the door.

"Lie ye there, my freend, till the spare moment comes—and I'll look at ye again," he said, putting the letter away carefully in the dresser-drawer. "Noo aboot the dinner o' they twa turtle-doves in the parlor?" he continued, directing his attention to the dinner-tray. "I maun joost see that the cook's dune her duty—the creatures are no' capable o' decidin' that knotty point for their ain selves." He took off one of the covers, and picked bits, here and there, out of the dish with the fork. "Eh! eh! the collops are no' that bad!" He took off another cover, and shook his head in solemn doubt.

"Here's the green meat. I doot green meat's windy diet for a man at my time o' life!" He put the cover on again, and tried the next dish. "The fesh? What the de'il does the woman fry the trout for? Boil it next time, ye betch, wi' a pinch o' saut and a spunefu' o' vinegar." He drew the cork from a bottle of sherry, and decanted the wine. "The sherry wine?" he said, in tones of deep feeling, holding the decanter up to the light. "Hoo do I know but what it may be corkit? I maun taste and try. It's on my conscience, as an honest man, to taste and try." He forthwith relieved his conscience—copiously. There was a vacant space, of no inconsiderable dimensions, left in the decanter. Mr. Bishopriggs gravely filled it up from the water-bottle. "Eh! it's joost addin' ten years to the age o' the wine. The turtle-doves will be nane the waur—and I mysel' am a glass o' sherry the better. Praise Providence for a' its maircies!" Having relieved himself of that devout aspiration, he took up the tray again, and decided on letting the turtle-doves have their dinner.

The conversation in the parlor (dropped for the moment) had been renewed, in the absence of Mr. Bishopriggs. Too restless to remain long in one place, Anne had risen again from the sofa, and had rejoined Arnold at the window.

"Where do your friends at Lady Lundie's believe you to be now?" she asked, abruptly.

"I am believed," replied Arnold, "to be meeting my tenants, and taking possession of my estate."

"How are you to get to your estate to-night?"

"By railway, I suppose. By-the-by, what excuse am I to make for going away after dinner? We are sure to have the landlady in here before long. What will she say to my going off by myself to the train, and leaving 'my wife' behind me?"

"Mr. Brinkworth! that joke—if it is a joke—is worn out!"

"I beg your pardon," said Arnold.

"You may leave your excuse to me," pursued Anne. "Do you go by the up train, or the down?"

"By the up train."

The door opened suddenly; and Mr. Bishopriggs appeared with the dinner. Anne nervously separated herself from Arnold. The one available eye of Mr. Bishopriggs followed her reproachfully, as he put the dishes on the table.

"I warned ye baith, it was a clean impossibility to knock at the door this time. Don't blame me, young madam—don't blame me!"

"Where will you sit?" asked Arnold, by way of diverting Anne's attention from the familiarities of Father Bishopriggs.

"Any where!" she answered, impatiently; snatching up a chair, and placing it at the bottom of the table.

Mr. Bishopriggs politely, but firmly, put the chair back again in its place.

"Lord's sake! what are ye doin'? It's clean contrary to a' the laws and customs o' the honey-mune, to sit as far away from your husband as that!"

He waved his persuasive napkin to one of the two chairs placed close together at the table. Arnold interfered once more, and prevented another outbreak of impatience from Anne.

"What does it matter?" he said. "Let the man have his way."

"Get it over as soon as you can," she returned. "I can't, and won't, bear it much longer."

They took their places at the table, with Father Bishopriggs behind them, in the mixed character of major domo and guardian angel.

"Here's the trout!" he cried, taking the cover off with a flourish. "Half an hour since, he was loupin' in the water. There he lies noo, fried in the dish. An emblem o' human life for ye! When ye can spare any leisure time from yer twa selves, meditate on that."

Arnold took up the spoon, to give Anne one of the trout. Mr. Bishopriggs clapped the cover on the dish again, with a countenance expressive of devout horror.

"Is there naebody gaun' to say grace?" he asked.

"Come! come!" said Arnold. "The fish is getting cold."

Mr. Bishopriggs piously closed his available eye, and held the cover firmly on the dish. "For what ye're gaun' to receive, may ye baith be truly thankful!" He opened his available eye, and whipped the cover off again. "My conscience is easy noo. Fall to! Fall to!"

"Send him away!" said Anne. "His familiarity is beyond all endurance."

"You needn't wait," said Arnold.

"Eh! but I'm here to wait," objected Mr. Bishopriggs. "What's the use o' my gaun' away, when ye'll want me anon to change the plates for ye?" He considered for a moment (privately consulting his experience); and arrived at a satisfactory conclusion as to Arnold's motive for wanting to get rid of him. "Tak' her on yer knee," he whispered in Arnold's ear, "as soon as ye like! Feed him at the fork's end," he added to Anne, "whenever ye please! I'll think of something else, and look out at the proaspect." He winked—and went to the window.

"Come! come!" said Arnold to Anne. "There's a comic side to all this. Try and see it as I do."

Mr. Bishopriggs returned from the window, and announced the appearance of a new element of embarrassment in the situation at the inn.

"My certie!" he said, "it's weel ye cam' when ye did. It's ill getting to this hottle in a storm."

Anne started, and looked round at him. "A storm coming!" she exclaimed.

"Eh! ye're well hoosed here—ye needn't mind it. There's the cloud down the valley," he added, pointing out of the window, "coming up one way, when the wind's blawing the other. The storm's brewing, my leddy, when ye see that!"

There was another knock at the door. As Arnold had predicted, the landlady made her appearance on the scene.

"I ha' just lookit in, Sir," said Mrs. Inchbare, addressing herself exclusively to Arnold, "to see ye've got what ye want."

"Oh! you are the landlady? Very nice, ma'am—very nice."

Mistress Inchbare had her own private motive for entering the room, and came to it without further preface.

"Ye'll excuse me, Sir," she proceeded. "I wasna in the way when ye cam' here, or I suld

"FOR WHAT YE'RE GAUN' TO RECEIVE, MAY YE BAITH BE TRULY THANKFUL!"

ha' made bauld to ask ye the question which I maun e'en ask noo. Am I to understand that ye hire these rooms for yersel', and this leddy here—yer wife?"

Anne raised her head to speak. Arnold pressed her hand warningly, under the table, and silenced her.

"Certainly," he said. "I take the rooms for myself, and this lady here—my wife!"

Anne made a second attempt to speak.

"This gentleman—" she began.

Arnold stopped her for the second time.

"This gentleman?" repeated Mrs. Inchbare, with a broad stare of surprise. "I'm only a puir woman, my leddy—d'ye mean yer husband here?"

Arnold's warning hand touched Anne's, for the third time. Mistress Inchbare's eyes remained fixed on her in merciless inquiry. To have given utterance to the contradiction which trembled on her lips would have been to involve Arnold (after all that he had sacrificed for her) in the scandal which would inevitably follow—a scandal which would be talked of in the neighborhood, and which might find its way to Blanche's ears. White and cold, her eyes never moving from the table, she accepted the landlady's implied correction, and faintly repeated the words: "My husband."

Mistress Inchbare drew a breath of virtuous relief, and waited for what Anne had to say next. Arnold came considerately to the rescue, and got her out of the room.

"Never mind," he said to Anne; "I know what it is, and I'll see about it. She's always like this, ma'am, when a storm's coming," he went on, turning to the landlady. "No, thank

you—I know how to manage her. We'll send to you, if we want your assistance."

"At yer ain pleasure, Sir," answered Mistress Inchbare. She turned, and apologized to Anne (under protest), with a stiff courtesy. "No offense, my leddy! Ye'll remember that ye cam' here alane, and that the hottle has its ain gude name to keep up." Having once more vindicated "the hottle," she made the long-desired move to the door, and left the room.

"I'm faint!" Anne whispered. "Give me some water."

There was no water on the table. Arnold ordered it of Mr. Bishopriggs—who had remained passive in the back-ground (a model of discreet attention) as long as the mistress was in the room.

"Mr. Brinkworth!" said Anne, when they were alone, "you are acting with inexcusable rashness. That woman's question was an impertinence. Why did you answer it? Why did you force me—?"

She stopped, unable to finish the sentence. Arnold insisted on her drinking a glass of wine—and then defended himself with the patient consideration for her which he had shown from the first.

"Why didn't I have the inn door shut in your face"—he asked, good-humoredly—"with a storm coming on, and without a place in which you can take refuge? No, no, Miss Silvester! I don't presume to blame you for any scruples you may feel—but scruples are sadly out of place with such a woman as that landlady. I am responsible for your safety to Geoffrey; and Geoffrey expects to find you here. Let's change the subject. The water is a long time coming. Try another glass of wine. No? Well—here is Blanche's health" (he took some of the wine himself), "in the weakest sherry I ever drank in my life." As he set down his glass, Mr. Bishopriggs came in with the water. Arnold hailed him satirically. "Well? have you got the water? or have you used it all for the sherry?"

Mr. Bishopriggs stopped in the middle of the room, thunder-struck at the aspersion cast on the wine.

"Is that the way ye talk of the auldest bottle o' sherry wine in Scotland?" he asked, gravely. "What's the warld coming to? The new generation's a foot beyond my fathoming. The maircies o' Providence, as shown to man in the choicest veentages o' Spain, are clean thrown away on 'em."

"Have you brought the water?"

"I ha' brought the water—and mair than the water. I ha' brought ye news from ootside. There's a company o' gentlemen on horseback, joost cantering by to what they ca' the shootin' cottage, a mile from this."

"Well—and what have we got to do with it?"

"Bide a wee! There's ane o' them has drawn bridle at the hottle, and he's speerin' after the leddy that cam' here alane. The leddy's your leddy, as sure as saxpence. I doot," said Mr. Bishopriggs, walking away to the window, "*that's* what ye've got to do with it."

Arnold looked at Anne.

"Do you expect any body?"

"Is it Geoffrey?"

"Impossible. Geoffrey is on his way to London."

"There he is, any way," resumed Mr. Bishopriggs, at the window. "He's loupin' down from his horse. He's turning this way. Lord save us!" he exclaimed, with a start of consternation, "what do I see? That incarnate deevil, Sir Paitrick himself!"

Arnold sprang to his feet.

"Do you mean Sir Patrick Lundie?"

Anne ran to the window.

"It *is* Sir Patrick!" she said. "Hide yourself before he comes in!"

"Hide myself?"

"What will he think if he sees you with *me?*"

He was Blanche's guardian, and he believed Arnold to be at that moment visiting his new property. What he would think was not difficult to foresee. Arnold turned for help to Mr. Bishopriggs.

"Where can I go?"

Mr. Bishopriggs pointed to the bedroom door.

"Whar' can ye go? There's the nuptial chamber!"

"Impossible!"

Mr. Bishopriggs expressed the utmost extremity of human amazement by a long whistle, on one note.

"Whew! Is that the way ye talk o' the nuptial chamber already?"

"Find me some other place—I'll make it worth your while."

"Eh! there's my paintry! I trow that's some other place; and the door's at the end o' the passage."

Arnold hurried out. Mr. Bishopriggs—evidently under the impression that the case before him was a case of elopement, with Sir Patrick mixed up in it in the capacity of guardian—addressed himself, in friendly confidence, to Anne.

"My certie, mistress! it's ill wark deceivin' Sir Paitrick, if that's what ye've dune. Ye must know, I was ance a bit clerk body in his chambers at Embro—"

The voice of Mistress Inchbare, calling for the head-waiter, rose shrill and imperative from the regions of the bar. Mr. Bishopriggs disappeared. Anne remained, standing helpless by the window. It was plain by this time that the place of her retreat had been discovered at Windygates. The one doubt to decide, now, was whether it would be wise or not to receive Sir Patrick, for the purpose of discovering whether he came as friend or enemy to the inn.

---

## CHAPTER THE ELEVENTH.

### SIR PATRICK.

THE doubt was practically decided before Anne had determined what to do. She was still at the window when the sitting-room door was thrown open, and Sir Patrick appeared, obsequiously shown in by Mr. Bishopriggs.

"Ye're kindly welcome, Sir Paitrick. Hech, Sirs! the sight of you is gude for sair eyne."

Sir Patrick turned and looked at Mr. Bishopriggs—as he might have looked at some troublesome insect which he had driven out of the window, and which had returned on him again.

"What, you scoundrel! have you drifted into an honest employment at last?"

Mr. Bishopriggs rubbed his hands cheerfully, and took his tone from his superior, with supple readiness.

"Ye're always in the right of it, Sir Paitrick! Wut, raal wut in that aboot the honest employment, and me drifting into it. Lord's sake, Sir, hoo well ye wear!"

Dismissing Mr. Bishopriggs by a sign, Sir Patrick advanced to Anne.

"I am committing an intrusion, madam, which must, I am afraid, appear unpardonable in your eyes," he said. "May I hope you will excuse me when I have made you acquainted with my motive?"

He spoke with scrupulous politeness. His knowledge of Anne was of the slightest possible kind. Like other men, he had felt the attraction of her unaffected grace and gentleness on the few occasions when he had been in her company—and that was all. If he had belonged to the present generation he would, under the circumstances, have fallen into one of the besetting sins of England in these days—the tendency (to borrow an illustration from the stage) to "strike an attitude" in the presence of a social emergency. A man of the present period, in Sir Patrick's position, would have struck an attitude of (what is called) chivalrous respect; and would have addressed Anne in a tone of ready-made sympathy, which it was simply impossible for a stranger really to feel. Sir Patrick affected nothing of the sort. One of the besetting sins of *his* time was the habitual concealment of our better selves —upon the whole, a far less dangerous national error than the habitual advertisement of our better selves, which has become the practice, publicly and privately, of society in this age. Sir

Patrick assumed, if any thing, less sympathy on this occasion than he really felt. Courteous to all women, he was as courteous as usual to Anne —and no more.

"I am quite at a loss, Sir, to know what brings you to this place. The servant here informs me that you are one of a party of gentlemen who have just passed by the inn, and who have all gone on except yourself." In those guarded terms Anne opened the interview with the unwelcome visitor, on her side.

Sir Patrick admitted the fact, without betraying the slightest embarrassment.

"The servant is quite right," he said. "I am one of the party. And I have purposely allowed them to go on to the keeper's cottage without me. Having admitted this, may I count on receiving your permission to explain the motive of my visit?"

Necessarily suspicious of him, as coming from Windygates, Anne answered in few and formal words, as coldly as before.

"Explain it, Sir Patrick, if you please, as briefly as possible."

Sir Patrick bowed. He was not in the least offended; he was even (if the confession may be made without degrading him in the public estimation) privately amused. Conscious of having honestly presented himself at the inn in Anne's interests, as well as in the interests of the ladies at Windygates, it appealed to his sense of humor to find himself kept at arm's-length by the very woman whom he had come to benefit. The temptation was strong on him to treat his errand from his own whimsical point of view. He gravely took out his watch, and noted the time to a second, before he spoke again.

"I have an event to relate in which you are interested," he said. "And I have two messages to deliver, which I hope you will not object to receive. The event I undertake to describe in one minute. The messages I promise to dispose of in two minutes more. Total duration of this intrusion on your time—three minutes."

He placed a chair for Anne, and waited until she had permitted him, by a sign, to take a second chair for himself.

"We will begin with the event," he resumed. "Your arrival at this place is no secret at Windygates. You were seen on the foot-road to Craig Fernie by one of the female servants. And the inference naturally drawn is, that you were on your way to the inn. It may be important for you to know this; and I have taken the liberty of mentioning it accordingly." He consulted his watch. "Event related. Time, one minute."

He had excited her curiosity, to begin with. "Which of the women saw me?" she asked, impulsively.

Sir Patrick (watch in hand) declined to prolong the interview by answering any incidental inquiries which might arise in the course of it.

"Pardon me," he rejoined; "I am pledged to occupy three minutes only. I have no room for the woman. With your kind permission, I will get on to the messages next."

Anne remained silent. Sir Patrick went on.

"First message: 'Lady Lundie's compliments to her step-daughter's late governess—with whose married name she is not acquainted. Lady Lundie regrets to say that Sir Patrick, as head of the family, has threatened to return to Edinburgh unless she consents to be guided by his advice in the course she pursues with the late governess. Lady Lundie, accordingly, foregoes her intention of calling at the Craig Fernie inn, to express her sentiments and make her inquiries in person, and commits to Sir Patrick the duty of expressing her sentiments; reserving to herself the right of making her inquiries at the next convenient opportunity. Through the medium of her brother-in-law, she begs to inform the late governess that all intercourse is at an end between them, and that she declines to act as reference in case of future emergency.'—Message textually correct. Expressive of Lady Lundie's view of your sudden departure from the house. Time, two minutes."

Anne's color rose. Anne's pride was up in arms on the spot.

"The impertinence of Lady Lundie's message is no more than I should have expected from her," she said. "I am only surprised at Sir Patrick's delivering it."

"Sir Patrick's motives will appear presently," rejoined the incorrigible old gentleman. "Second message: 'Blanche's fondest love. Is dying to be acquainted with Anne's husband, and to be informed of Anne's married name. Feels indescribable anxiety and apprehension on Anne's account. Insists on hearing from Anne immediately. Longs, as she never longed for any thing yet, to order her pony-chaise and drive full gallop to the inn. Yields, under irresistible pressure, to the exertion of her guardian's authority, and commits the expression of her feelings to Sir Patrick, who is a born tyrant, and doesn't in the least mind breaking other people's hearts.' Sir Patrick (speaking for himself) places his sister-in-law's view and his niece's view, side by side, before the lady whom he has now the honor of addressing, and on whose confidence he is especially careful not to intrude. Reminds the lady that his influence at Windygates, however strenuously he may exert it, is not likely to last forever. Requests her to consider whether his sister-in-law's view and his niece's view, in collision, may not lead to very undesirable domestic results; and leaves her to take the course which seems best to herself under those circumstances. —Second message delivered textually. Time, three minutes. A storm coming on. A quarter of an hour's ride from here to the shooting-cottage. Madam, I wish you good-evening."

He bowed lower than ever—and, without a word more, quietly left the room.

Anne's first impulse was (excusably enough, poor soul) an impulse of resentment.

"Thank you, Sir Patrick!" she said, with a bitter look at the closing door. "The sympathy of society with a friendless woman could hardly have been expressed in a more amusing way!"

The little irritation of the moment passed off with the moment. Anne's own intelligence and good sense showed her the position in its truer light.

She recognized in Sir Patrick's abrupt departure Sir Patrick's considerate resolution to spare her from entering into any details on the subject of her position at the inn. He had given her a friendly warning; and he had delicately left her to decide for herself as to the assistance which she might render him in maintaining tranquillity at Windygates. She went at once to a side-table in the room, on which writing materials were placed, and sat down to write to Blanche.

"I can do nothing with Lady Lundie," she thought. "But I have more influence than any body else over Blanche; and I can prevent the collision between them which Sir Patrick dreads."

She began the letter. "My dearest Blanche, I have seen Sir Patrick, and he has given me your message. I will set your mind at ease about me as soon as I can. But, before I say any thing else, let me entreat you, as the greatest favor you can do to your sister and your friend, not to enter into any disputes about me with Lady Lundie, and not to commit the imprudence—the useless imprudence, my love—of coming here." She stopped—the paper swam before her eyes. "My own darling!" she thought, "who could have foreseen that I should ever shrink from the thought of seeing *you?*" She sighed, and dipped the pen in the ink, and went on with the letter.

The sky darkened rapidly as the evening fell. The wind swept in fainter and fainter gusts across the dreary moor. Far and wide over the face of Nature the stillness was fast falling which tells of a coming storm.

---

## CHAPTER THE TWELFTH.

### ARNOLD.

MEANWHILE Arnold remained shut up in the head-waiter's pantry—chafing secretly at the position forced upon him.

He was, for the first time in his life, in hiding from another person, and that person a man. Twice—stung to it by the inevitable loss of self-respect which his situation occasioned—he had gone to the door, determined to face Sir Patrick boldly; and twice he had abandoned the idea, in mercy to Anne. It would have been impossible for him to set himself right with Blanche's guardian without betraying the unhappy woman whose secret he was bound in honor to keep. "I wish to Heaven I had never come here!" was the useless aspiration that escaped him, as he doggedly seated himself on the dresser to wait till Sir Patrick's departure set him free.

After an interval—not by any means the long interval which he had anticipated—his solitude was enlivened by the appearance of Father Bishopriggs.

"Well?" cried Arnold, jumping off the dresser, "is the coast clear?"

There were occasions when Mr. Bishopriggs became, on a sudden, unexpectedly hard of hearing. This was one of them.

"Hoo do ye find the paintry?" he asked, without paying the slightest attention to Arnold's question. "Snug and private? A Patmos in the weelderness, as ye may say!"

His one available eye, which had begun by looking at Arnold's face, dropped slowly downward, and fixed itself, in mute but eloquent expectation, on Arnold's waistcoat pocket.

"I understand!" said Arnold. "I promised to pay you for the Patmos—eh? There you are!"

Mr. Bishopriggs pocketed the money with a dreary smile and a sympathetic shake of the head. Other waiters would have returned thanks. The sage of Craig Fernie returned a few brief remarks instead. Admirable in many things, Father Bishopriggs was especially great at drawing a moral. He drew a moral on this occasion from his own gratuity.

"There I am—as ye say. Mercy presairve us! ye need the siller at every turn, when there's a woman at yer heels. It's an awfu' reflection— ye canna hae any thing to do wi' the sex they ca' the opposite sex without its being an expense to ye. There's this young leddy o' yours, I doot she'll ha' been an expense to ye from the first. When you were coortin' her, ye did it, I'll go bail, wi' the open hand. Presents and keep-sakes, flowers and jewelery, and little dogues. Sair expenses all of them!"

"Hang your reflections! Has Sir Patrick left the inn?"

The reflections of Mr. Bishopriggs declined to be disposed of in any thing approaching to a summary way. On they flowed from their parent source, as slowly and as smoothly as ever!

"Noo ye're married to her, there's her bonnets and goons and under-clothin'—her ribbons, laces, furbelows, and fallals. A sair expense again!"

"What is the expense of cutting your reflections short, Mr. Bishopriggs?"

"Thirdly, and lastly, if ye canna agree wi' her as time gaes on—if there's incompaitibeelity of temper betwixt ye—in short, if ye want a wee bit separation, hech, Sirs! ye pet yer hand in yer poaket, and come to an aimicable understandin' wi' her in that way. Or, maybe she takes ye into Court, and pets *her* hand in *your* poaket, and comes to a hoastile understandin' wi' ye there. Show me a woman—and I'll show ye a man not far off wha' has mair expenses on his back than he ever bairgained for." Arnold's patience would last no longer—he turned to the door. Mr. Bishopriggs, with equal alacrity on his side, turned to the matter in hand. "Yes, Sir! The room is e'en clear o' Sir Paitrick, and the leddy's alane, and waitin' for ye."

In a moment more Arnold was back in the sitting-room.

"Well?" he asked, anxiously. "What is it? Bad news from Lady Lundie's?"

Anne closed and directed the letter to Blanche, which she had just completed. "No," she replied. "Nothing to interest *you.*"

"What did Sir Patrick want?"

"Only to warn me. They have found out at Windygates that I am here."

"That's awkward, isn't it?"

"Not in the least. I can manage perfectly; I have nothing to fear. Don't think of *me*—think of yourself."

"I am not suspected, am I?"

"Thank heaven—no! But there is no knowing what may happen if you stay here. Ring the bell at once, and ask the waiter about the trains."

Struck by the unusual obscurity of the sky at that hour of the evening, Arnold went to the window. The rain had come—and was falling heavily. The view on the moor was fast disappearing in mist and darkness.

"Pleasant weather to travel in!" he said.

"The railway!" Anne exclaimed, impatiently. "It's getting late. See about the railway!"

Arnold walked to the fire-place to ring the bell. The railway time-table hanging over it met his eye.

"Here's the information I want," he said to Anne; "if I only knew how to get at it. 'Down'—'Up'—'A.M.'—'P.M.' What a cursed confusion! I believe they do it on purpose."

Anne joined him at the fire-place.

"I understand it—I'll help you. Did you say it was the up train you wanted?"

"Yes."

"What is the name of the station you stop at?"

Arnold told her. She followed the intricate net-work of lines and figures with her finger—suddenly stopped—looked again to make sure—and turned from the time-table with a face of blank despair. The last train for the day had gone an hour since.

In the silence which followed that discovery, a first flash of lightning passed across the window, and the low roll of thunder sounded the outbreak of the storm.

"What's to be done now?" asked Arnold.

In the face of the storm, Anne answered without hesitation, "You must take a carriage, and drive."

"Drive? They told me it was three-and-twenty miles, by railway, from the station to my place—let alone the distance from this inn to the station."

"What does the distance matter? Mr. Brinkworth, you can't possibly stay here!"

A second flash of lightning crossed the window; the roll of the thunder came nearer. Even Arnold's good temper began to be a little ruffled by Anne's determination to get rid of him. He sat down with the air of a man who had made up his mind not to leave the house.

"Do you hear that?" he asked, as the sound of the thunder died away grandly, and the hard pattering of the rain on the window became audible once more. "If I ordered horses, do you think they would let me have them, in such weather as this? And, if they did, do you suppose the horses could face it on the moor? No, no, Miss Silvester—I am sorry to be in the way; but the train has gone, and the night and the storm have come. I have no choice but to stay here!"

Anne still maintained her own view, but less resolutely than before. "After what you have told the landlady," she said, "think of the embarrassment, the cruel embarrassment of our position, if you stop at the inn till to-morrow morning!"

"Is that all?" returned Arnold.

Anne looked up at him, quickly and angrily. No! he was quite unconscious of having said any thing that could offend her. His rough masculine sense broke its way unconsciously through all the little feminine subtleties and delicacies of his companion, and looked the position practically in the face for what it was worth, and no more. "Where's the embarrassment?" he asked, pointing to the bedroom door. "There's your room, all ready for you. And here's the sofa, in this room, all ready for me. If you had seen the places I have slept in at sea—!"

She interrupted him, without ceremony. The places he had slept in, at sea, were of no earthly importance. The one question to consider, was the place he was to sleep in that night.

"If you must stay," she rejoined, "can't you get a room in some other part of the house?"

But one last mistake in dealing with her, in her present nervous condition, was left to make—and the innocent Arnold made it. "In some other part of the house?" he repeated, jestingly. "The landlady would be scandalized. Mr. Bishopriggs would never allow it!"

She rose, and stamped her foot impatiently on the floor. "Don't joke!" she exclaimed. "This is no laughing matter." She paced the room excitedly. "I don't like it! I don't like it!"

Arnold looked after her, with a stare of boyish wonder.

"What puts you out so?" he asked. "Is it the storm?"

She threw herself on the sofa again. "Yes," she said, shortly. "It's the storm."

Arnold's inexhaustible good-nature was at once roused to activity again.

"Shall we have the candles," he suggested, "and shut the weather out?" She turned irritably on the sofa, without replying. "I'll promise to go away the first thing in the morning!" he went on. "Do try and take it easy—and don't be angry with me. Come! come! you wouldn't turn a dog out, Miss Silvester, on such a night as this!"

He was irresistible. The most sensitive woman breathing could not have accused him of failing toward her in any single essential of consideration and respect. He wanted tact, poor fellow—but who could expect him to have learned that always superficial (and sometimes dangerous) accomplishment, in the life he had led at sea? At the sight of his honest, pleading face, Anne recovered possession of her gentler and sweeter self. She made her excuses for her irritability with a grace that enchanted him. "We'll have a pleasant evening of it yet!" cried Arnold, in his hearty way—and rang the bell.

The bell was hung outside the door of that Patmos in the wilderness—otherwise known as the head-waiter's pantry. Mr. Bishopriggs (employing his brief leisure in the seclusion of his own apartment) had just mixed a glass of the hot and comforting liquor called "toddy" in the language of North Britain, and was just lifting it to his lips, when the summons from Arnold invited him to leave his grog.

"Haud yer screechin' tongue!" cried Mr. Bishopriggs, addressing the bell through the door. "Ye're waur than a woman when ye aince begin!"

The bell—like the woman—went on again. Mr. Bishopriggs, equally pertinacious, went on with his toddy.

"Ay! ay! ye may e'en ring yer heart out—but ye won't part a Scotchman from his glass. It's maybe the end of their dinner they'll be wantin'. Sir Paitrick cam' in at the fair beginning of it, and spoilt the collops, like the dour deevil he is!" The bell rang for the third time. "Ay! ay! ring awa'! I doot yon young gentleman's little better than a belly-god—there's a scandalous haste to comfort the carnal part o' him in a' this ringin'! He knows naething o' wine," added Mr. Bishopriggs, on whose mind Arnold's discovery of the watered sherry still dwelt unpleasantly.

The lightning quickened, and lit the sitting-room horribly with its lurid glare; the thunder rolled nearer and nearer over the black gulf of the moor. Arnold had just raised his hand to ring for the fourth time, when the inevitable knock was heard at the door. It was useless to say "come in." The immutable laws of Bishopriggs had decided that a second knock was necessary. Storm or no storm, the second knock came—and then, and not till then, the sage appeared, with the dish of untasted "collops" in his hand.

"Candles!" said Arnold.

Mr. Bishopriggs set the "collops" (in the language of England, minced meat) upon the table, lit the candles on the mantle-piece, faced about, with the fire of recent toddy flaming in his nose, and waited for further orders, before he went back to his second glass. Anne declined to return to the dinner. Arnold ordered Mr. Bishopriggs to close the shutters, and sat down to dine by himself.

"It looks greasy, and smells greasy," he said to Anne, turning over the collops with a spoon. "I won't be ten minutes dining. Will you have some tea?"

Anne declined again.

Arnold tried her once more. "What shall we do to get through the evening?"

"Do what you like," she answered, resignedly.

Arnold's mind was suddenly illuminated by an idea.

"I have got it!" he exclaimed. "We'll kill the time as our cabin-passengers used to kill it at sea." He looked over his shoulder at Mr. Bishopriggs. "Waiter! bring a pack of cards."

"What's that ye're wantin'?" asked Mr. Bishopriggs, doubting the evidence of his own senses.

"A pack of cards," repeated Arnold.

"Cairds?" echoed Mr. Bishopriggs. "A pack o' cairds? The deevil's allegories in the deevil's own colors—red and black! I wunna execute yer order. For yer ain saul's sake, I wunna do it. Ha' ye lived to your time o' life, and are ye no' awakened yet to the awfu' seenfulness o' gamblin' wi' the cairds?"

"Just as you please," returned Arnold. "You will find me awakened—when I go away—to the awful folly of feeing a waiter."

"Does that mean that ye're bent on the cairds?" asked Mr. Bishopriggs, suddenly betraying signs of worldly anxiety in his look and manner.

"Yes—that means I am bent on the cards."

"I tak' up my testimony against 'em—but I'm no' telling ye that I canna lay my hand on 'em if I like. What do they say in my country? 'Him that will to Coupar, maun to Coupar.' And what do they say in your country? 'Needs must when the deevil drives.'" With that excellent reason for turning his back on his own principles, Mr. Bishopriggs shuffled out of the room to fetch the cards.

The dresser-drawer in the pantry contained a choice selection of miscellaneous objects—a pack of cards being among them. In searching for the cards, the wary hand of the head-waiter came in contact with a morsel of crumpled-up paper. He drew it out, and recognized the letter which he had picked up in the sitting-room some hours since.

"Ay! ay! I'll do weel, I trow, to look at this while my mind's runnin' on it," said Mr. Bishopriggs. "The cairds may e'en find their way to the parlor by other hands than mine."

He forthwith sent the cards to Arnold by his second in command, closed the pantry door, and carefully smoothed out the crumpled sheet of paper on which the two letters were written. This done, he trimmed his candle, and began with the letter in ink, which occupied the first three pages of the sheet of note-paper.

It ran thus:

"Windygates House, *August* 12, 1868.

"Geoffrey Delamayn,—I have waited in the hope that you would ride over from your brother's place, and see me—and I have waited in vain. Your conduct to me is cruelty itself; I will bear it no longer. Consider! in your own interests, consider—before you drive the miserable woman who has trusted you to despair. You have promised me marriage by all that is sacred. I claim your promise. I insist on nothing less than to be what you vowed I should be—what I have waited all this weary time to be—what I *am*, in the sight of Heaven, your wedded wife. Lady Lundie gives a lawn-party here on the 14th. I know you have been asked. I expect you to accept her invitation. If I don't see you, I won't answer for what may happen. My mind is made up to endure this suspense no longer. Oh, Geoffrey, remember the past! Be faithful—be just—to your loving wife,

"Anne Silvester."

Mr. Bishopriggs paused. His commentary on the correspondence, so far, was simple enough. "Hot words (in ink) from the leddy to the gentleman!" He ran his eye over the second letter, on the fourth page of the paper, and added, cynically, "A trifle caulder (in pencil) from the gentleman to the leddy! The way o' the warld, Sirs! From the time o' Adam downwards, the way o' the warld!"

The second letter ran thus:

"Dear Anne,—Just called to London to my father. They have telegraphed him in a bad way. Stop where you are, and I will write you. Trust the bearer. Upon my soul, I'll keep my promise. Your loving husband that is to be,

"Geoffrey Delamayn.

"Windygates House, *Augt.* 14, 4 p.m.

"In a mortal hurry. Train starts at 4.30."

There it ended!

"Who are the pairties in the parlor? Is ane o' them 'Silvester?' and t'other 'Delamayn?'" pondered Mr. Bishopriggs, slowly folding the letter up again in its original form. "Hech, Sirs! what, being intairpreted, may a' this mean?"

He mixed himself a second glass of toddy, as an aid to reflection, and sat sipping the liquor, and twisting and turning the letter in his gouty fingers. It was not easy to see his way to the true connection between the lady and gentleman in the parlor and the two letters now in his own possession. They might be themselves the writers of the letters, or they might be only friends of the writers. Who was to decide?

In the first case, the lady's object would appear to have been as good as gained; for the two had certainly asserted themselves to be man and wife, in his own presence, and in the presence of the landlady. In the second case, the correspondence so carelessly thrown aside might, for all a stranger knew to the contrary, prove to be of some importance in the future. Acting on this latter view, Mr. Bishopriggs—whose past experience as "a bit clerk body," in Sir Patrick's chambers, had made a man of business of him—produced his pen and ink, and indorsed the letter with a brief dated statement of the circumstances under which he had found it. "I'll do weel to keep the Doecument," he thought to himself. "Wha knows but there'll be a reward offered for it ane o' these days? Eh! eh! there may be the warth o' a fi' pun' note in this, to a puir lad like me!"

With that comforting reflection, he drew out a battered tin cash-box from the inner recesses of the drawer, and locked up the stolen correspondence to bide its time.

The storm rose higher and higher as the evening advanced.

In the sitting-room, the state of affairs, perpetually changing, now presented itself under another new aspect.

Arnold had finished his dinner, and had sent it away. He had next drawn a side-table up to the sofa on which Anne lay—had shuffled the pack of cards—and was now using all his powers of persuasion to induce her to try one game at *Ecarté* with him, by way of diverting her attention from the tumult of the storm. In sheer weariness, she gave up contesting the matter; and, raising herself languidly on the sofa, said she would try to play. "Nothing can make matters worse than they are," she thought, despairingly, as Arnold dealt the cards for her. "Nothing can justify my inflicting my own wretchedness on this kind-hearted boy!"

Two worse players never probably sat down to a game. Anne's attention perpetually wandered; and Anne's companion was, in all human probability, the most incapable card-player in Europe.

Anne turned up the trump—the nine of Diamonds. Arnold looked at his hand—and "proposed." Anne declined to change the cards. Arnold announced, with undiminished good-humor, that he saw his way clearly, now, to losing the game, and then played his first card—the Queen of Trumps!

Anne took it with the King, and forgot to declare the King. She played the ten of Trumps. Arnold unexpectedly discovered the eight of Trumps in his hand. "What a pity!" he said, as he played it. "Hullo! you haven't marked the King! I'll do it for you. That's two—no, three—to you. I said I should lose the game. Couldn't be expected to do any thing (could I?) with such a hand as mine. I've lost every thing, now I've lost my trumps. You to play."

Anne looked at her hand. At the same moment the lightning flashed into the room through the ill-closed shutters; the roar of the thunder burst over the house, and shook it to its foundation. The screaming of some hysterical female tourist, and the barking of a dog, rose shrill from the upper floor of the inn. Anne's nerves could support it no longer. She flung her cards on the table, and sprang to her feet.

"I can play no more," she said. "Forgive me—I am quite unequal to it. My head burns! my heart stifles me!"

She began to pace the room again. Aggravated by the effect of the storm on her nerves, her first vague distrust of the false position into which she and Arnold had allowed themselves to drift had strengthened, by this time, into a downright horror of their situation which was not to be endured. Nothing could justify such a risk as the risk they were now running! They had dined together like married people—and there they were, at that moment, shut in together, and passing the evening like man and wife!

"Oh, Mr. Brinkworth!" she pleaded. "Think —for Blanche's sake, think—is there no way out of this?"

Arnold was quietly collecting the scattered cards.

"Blanche, again?" he said, with the most exasperating composure. "I wonder how she feels, in this storm?"

In Anne's excited state, the reply almost maddened her. She turned from Arnold, and hurried to the door.

"I don't care!" she cried, wildly. "I won't let this deception go on. "I'll do what I ought to have done before. Come what may of it, I'll tell the landlady the truth!"

She had opened the door, and was on the point of stepping into the passage—when she stopped, and started violently. Was it possible, in that dreadful weather, that she had actually heard the sound of carriage wheels on the strip of paved road outside the inn?

Yes! others had heard the sound too. The hobbling figure of Mr. Bishopriggs passed her in the passage, making for the house door. The hard voice of the landlady rang through the inn, ejaculating astonishment in broad Scotch. Anne closed the sitting-room door again, and turned to Arnold—who had risen, in surprise, to his feet.

"Travelers!" she exclaimed. "At this time!"

"And in this weather!" added Arnold.

"*Can* it be Geoffrey?" she asked—going back to the old vain delusion that he might yet feel for her, and return.

Arnold shook his head. "Not Geoffrey. Whoever else it may be—not Geoffrey!"

Mrs. Inchbare suddenly entered the room— with her cap-ribbons flying, her eyes staring, and her bones looking harder than ever.

"Eh, mistress!" she said to Anne. "Wha do ye think has driven here to see ye, from Windygates Hoose, and been owertaken in the storm?"

Anne was speechless. Arnold put the question: "Who is it?"

"Wha is't?" repeated Mrs. Inchbare. "It's joost the bonny young leddy—Miss Blanche hersel'."

An irrepressible cry of horror burst from Anne. The landlady set it down to the lightning, which flashed into the room again at the same moment.

"Eh, mistress! ye'll find Miss Blanche a bit baulder than to skirl at a flash o' lightning, that gait! Here she is, the bonny birdie!" exclaimed Mrs. Inchbare, deferentially backing out into the passage again.

Blanche's voice reached them, calling for Anne.

Anne caught Arnold by the hand and wrung it hard. "Go!" she whispered. The next instant she was at the mantle-piece, and had blown out both the candles.

Another flash of lightning came through the darkness, and showed Blanche's figure standing at the door.

---

## CHAPTER THE THIRTEENTH.

### BLANCHE.

MRS. INCHBARE was the first person who acted in the emergency. She called for lights; and sternly rebuked the house-maid, who brought them, for not having closed the house door. "Ye feckless ne'er-do-weel!" cried the landlady; "the wind's blawn the candles oot."

The woman declared (with perfect truth) that the door had been closed. An awkward dispute might have ensued if Blanche had not diverted Mrs. Inchbare's attention to herself. The appearance of the lights disclosed her, wet through, with her arms round Anne's neck. Mrs. Inchbare digressed at once to the pressing question of changing the young lady's clothes, and gave Anne the opportunity of looking round her, unobserved. Arnold had made his escape before the candles had been brought in.

In the mean time Blanche's attention was absorbed in her own dripping skirts.

"Good gracious! I'm absolutely distilling rain from every part of me. And I'm making you, Anne, as wet as I am! Lend me some dry things. You can't? Mrs. Inchbare, what does your experience suggest? Which had I better do? Go to bed while my clothes are being dried? or borrow from your wardrobe—though you *are* a head and shoulders taller than I am?"

Mrs. Inchbare instantly bustled out to fetch the choicest garments that her wardrobe could produce. The moment the door had closed on her Blanche looked round the room in her turn. The rights of affection having been already asserted, the claims of curiosity naturally pressed for satisfaction next.

"Somebody passed me in the dark," she whispered. "Was it your husband? I'm dying to be introduced to him. And, oh my dear! what *is* your married name?"

Anne answered, coldly, "Wait a little. I can't speak about it yet."

"Are you ill?" asked Blanche.

"I am a little nervous."

"Has any thing unpleasant happened between you and my uncle? You have seen him, haven't you?"

"Yes."

"Did he give you my message?"

"He gave me your message.—Blanche! you promised him to stay at Windygates. Why, in the name of heaven, did you come here to-night?"

"If you were half as fond of me as I am of you," returned Blanche, "you wouldn't ask that. I tried hard to keep my promise, but I couldn't do it. It was all very well, while my uncle was laying down the law—with Lady Lundie in a rage, and the dogs barking, and the doors banging, and all that. The excitement kept me up. But when my uncle had gone, and the dreadful gray, quiet, rainy evening came, and it had all calmed down again, there was no bearing it. The house—without you—was like a tomb. If

I had had Arnold with me I might have done very well. But I was all by myself. Think of that! Not a soul to speak to! There wasn't a horrible thing that could possibly happen to you that I didn't fancy was going to happen. I went into your empty room and looked at your things. *That* settled it, my darling! I rushed down stairs—carried away, positively carried away, by an Impulse beyond human resistance. How could I help it? I ask any reasonable person how could I help it? I ran to the stables and found Jacob. Impulse—all impulse! I said, 'Get the pony-chaise—I must have a drive—I don't care if it rains—you come with me.' All in a breath, and all impulse! Jacob behaved like an angel. He said, 'All right, miss.' I am perfectly certain Jacob would die for me if I asked him. He is drinking hot grog at this moment, to prevent him from catching cold, by my express orders. He had the pony-chaise out in two minutes; and off we went. Lady Lundie, my dear, prostrate in her own room—too much sal volatile. I hate her. The rain got worse. I didn't mind it. Jacob didn't mind it. The pony didn't mind it. They had both caught my impulse—especially the pony. It didn't come on to thunder till some time afterward; and then we were nearer Craig Fernie than Windygates—to say nothing of your being at one place and not at the other. The lightning was quite awful on the moor. If I had had one of the horses, he would have been frightened. The pony shook his darling little head, and dashed through it. He is to have beer. A mash with beer in it—by my express orders. When he has done we'll borrow a lantern, and go into the stable, and kiss him. In the mean time, my dear, here I am—wet through in a thunderstorm, which doesn't in the least matter—and determined to satisfy my own mind about you, which matters a great deal, and must and shall be done before I rest to-night!"

She turned Anne, by main force, as she spoke, toward the light of the candles.

Her tone changed the moment she looked at Anne's face.

"I knew it!" she said. "You would never have kept the most interesting event in your life a secret from *me*—you would never have written me such a cold formal letter as the letter you left in your room—if there had not been something wrong. I said so at the time. I know it now! Why has your husband forced you to leave Windygates at a moment's notice? Why does he slip out of the room in the dark, as if he was afraid of being seen? Anne! Anne! what has come to you? Why do you receive me in this way?"

At that critical moment Mrs. Inchbare reappeared, with the choicest selection of wearing apparel which her wardrobe could furnish. Anne hailed the welcome interruption. She took the candles, and led the way into the bedroom immediately.

"Change your wet clothes first," she said. "We can talk after that."

The bedroom door had hardly been closed a minute before there was a tap at it. Signing to Mrs. Inchbare not to interrupt the services she was rendering to Blanche, Anne passed quickly into the sitting-room, and closed the door behind her. To her infinite relief, she

"THE PONY SHOOK HIS DARLING LITTLE HEAD, AND DASHED THROUGH IT."

only found herself face to face with the discreet Mr. Bishopriggs.

"What do you want?" she asked.

The eye of Mr. Bishopriggs announced, by a wink, that his mission was of a confidential nature. The hand of Mr. Bishopriggs wavered; the breath of Mr. Bishopriggs exhaled a spirituous fume. He slowly produced a slip of paper, with some lines of writing on it.

"From ye ken who," he explained, jocosely. "A bit love-letter, I trow, from him that's dear to ye. Eh! he's an awfu' reprobate is him that's dear to ye. Miss, in the bedchamber there, will nae doot be the one he's jilted for *you?* I see it all—ye can't blind Me—I ha' been a frail person my ain self, in my time. Hech! he's safe and sound, is the reprobate. I ha' lookit after a' his little creature-comforts—I'm joost a fether to him, as well as a fether to you. Trust Bishopriggs—when puir human nature wants a bit pat on the back, trust Bishopriggs."

While the sage was speaking these comfortable words, Anne was reading the lines traced on the paper. They were signed by Arnold; and they ran thus:

"I am in the smoking-room of the inn. It rests with you to say whether I must stop there. I don't believe Blanche would be jealous. If I knew how to explain my being at the inn without betraying the confidence which you and Geoffrey have placed in me, I wouldn't be away from her another moment. It does grate on me so! At the same time, I don't want to make your position harder than it is. Think of yourself first. I leave it in your hands. You have

only to say, Wait, by the bearer—and I shall understand that I am to stay where I am till I hear from you again."

Anne looked up from the message.

"Ask him to wait," she said; "and I will send word to him again."

"Wi' mony loves and kisses," suggested Mr. Bishopriggs, as a necessary supplement to the message. "Eh! it comes as easy as A. B. C. to a man o' my experience. Ye can ha' nae better gae-between than yer puir servant to command, Sawmuel Bishopriggs. I understand ye baith pairfeckly." He laid his forefinger along his flaming nose, and withdrew.

Without allowing herself to hesitate for an instant, Anne opened the bedroom door—with the resolution of relieving Arnold from the new sacrifice imposed on him by owning the truth.

"Is that you?" asked Blanche.

At the sound of her voice, Anne started back guiltily. "I'll be with you in a moment," she answered, and closed the door again between them.

No! it was not to be done. Something in Blanche's trivial question—or something, perhaps, in the sight of Blanche's face—roused the warning instinct in Anne, which silenced her on the very brink of the disclosure. At the last moment, the iron chain of circumstances made itself felt, binding her without mercy to the hateful, the degrading deceit. Could she own the truth, about Geoffrey and herself, to Blanche? and, without owning it, could she explain and justify Arnold's conduct in joining her privately at Craig Fernie? A shameful confession made to an innocent girl; a risk of fatally shaking

Arnold's place in Blanche's estimation; a scandal at the inn, in the disgrace of which the others would be involved with herself—this was the price at which she must speak, if she followed her first impulse, and said, in so many words, "Arnold is here."

It was not to be thought of. Cost what it might in present wretchedness — end how it might, if the deception was discovered in the future—Blanche must be kept in ignorance of the truth; Arnold must be kept in hiding until she had gone.

Anne opened the door for the second time, and went in.

The business of the toilet was standing still. Blanche was in confidential communication with Mrs. Inchbare. At the moment when Anne entered the room she was eagerly questioning the landlady about her friend's "invisible husband"—she was just saying, "Do tell me! what is he like?"

The capacity for accurate observation is a capacity so uncommon, and is so seldom associated, even where it does exist, with the equally rare gift of accurately describing the thing or the person observed, that Anne's dread of the consequences if Mrs. Inchbare was allowed time to comply with Blanche's request, was, in all probability, a dread misplaced. Right or wrong, however, the alarm that she felt hurried her into taking measures for dismissing the landlady on the spot. "We mustn't keep you from your occupations any longer," she said to Mrs. Inchbare. "I will give Miss Lundie all the help she needs."

Barred from advancing in one direction, Blanche's curiosity turned back, and tried in another. She boldly addressed herself to Anne.

"I *must* know something about him," she said. "Is he shy before strangers? I heard you whispering with him on the other side of the door. Are you jealous, Anne? Are you afraid I shall fascinate him in this dress?"

Blanche, in Mrs. Inchbare's best gown—an ancient and high-waisted silk garment, of the hue called "bottle-green," pinned up in front, and trailing far behind her—with a short, orange-colored shawl over her shoulders, and a towel tied turban fashion round her head, to dry her wet hair, looked at once the strangest and the prettiest human anomaly that ever was seen. "For heaven's sake," she said, gayly, "don't tell your husband I am in Mrs. Inchbare's clothes! I want to appear suddenly, without a word to warn him of what a figure I am! I should have nothing left to wish for in this world," she added, "if Arnold could only see me now!"

Looking in the glass, she noticed Anne's face reflected behind her, and started at the sight of it.

"What *is* the matter?" she asked. "Your face frightens me."

It was useless to prolong the pain of the inevitable misunderstanding between them. The one course to take was to silence all further inquiries then and there. Strongly as she felt this, Anne's inbred loyalty to Blanche still shrank from deceiving her to her face. "I might write it," she thought. "I can't say it, with Arnold Brinkworth in the same house with her!" Write it? As she reconsidered the word, a sudden idea struck her. She opened the bedroom door, and led the way back into the sitting-room.

"Gone again!" exclaimed Blanche, looking uneasily round the empty room. "Anne! there's something so strange in all this, that I neither can, nor will, put up with your silence any longer. It's not just, it's not kind, to shut me out of your confidence, after we have lived together like sisters all our lives!"

Anne sighed bitterly, and kissed her on the forehead. "You shall know all I *can* tell you —all I *dare* tell you," she said, gently. "Don't reproach me. It hurts me more than you think."

She turned away to the side-table, and came back with a letter in her hand. "Read that," she said, and handed it to Blanche.

Blanche saw her own name, on the address, in the handwriting of Anne.

"What does this mean?" she asked.

"I wrote to you, after Sir Patrick had left me," Anne replied. "I meant you to have received my letter to-morrow, in time to prevent any little imprudence into which your anxiety might hurry you. All that I *can* say to you is said there. Spare me the distress of speaking. Read it, Blanche."

Blanche still held the letter, unopened.

"A letter from you to me! when we are both together, and both alone in the same room! It's worse than formal, Anne! It's as if there was a quarrel between us. Why should it distress you to speak to me?"

Anne's eyes dropped to the ground. She pointed to the letter for the second time.

Blanche broke the seal.

She passed rapidly over the opening sentences, and devoted all her attention to the second paragraph.

"And now, my love, you will expect me to atone for the surprise and distress that I have caused you, by explaining what my situation really is, and by telling you all my plans for the future. Dearest Blanche! don't think me untrue to the affection we bear toward each other —don't think there is any change in my heart toward you—believe only that I am a very unhappy woman, and that I am in a position which forces me, against my own will, to be silent about myself. Silent even to you, the sister of my love —the one person in the world who is dearest to me! A time may come when I shall be able to open my heart to you. Oh, what good it will do me! what a relief it will be! For the present, I must be silent. For the present, we must be parted. God knows what it costs me to write this. I think of the dear old days that are gone; I remember how I promised your mother to be a sister to you, when her kind eyes looked at me, for the last time—*your* mother, who was an angel from heaven to *mine!* All this comes back on me now, and breaks my heart. But it must be! my own Blanche, for the present, it must be! I will write often—I will think of you, my darling, night and day, till a happier future unites us again. God bless *you,* my dear one! And God help *me!*"

Blanche silently crossed the room to the sofa on which Anne was sitting, and stood there for a moment, looking at her. She sat down, and laid her head on Anne's shoulder. Sorrowfully and quietly, she put the letter into her bosom— and took Anne's hand, and kissed it.

"All my questions are answered, dear. I will wait your time."

It was simply, sweetly, generously said.

Anne burst into tears.

\* \* \* \* \* \*

The rain still fell, but the storm was dying away.

Blanche left the sofa, and, going to the window, opened the shutters to look out at the night. She suddenly came back to Anne.

"I see lights," she said—"the lights of a carriage coming up out of the darkness of the moor. They are sending after me, from Windygates. Go into the bedroom. It's just possible Lady Lundie may have come for me herself."

The ordinary relations of the two toward each other were completely reversed. Anne was like a child in Blanche's hands. She rose, and withdrew.

Left alone, Blanche took the letter out of her bosom, and read it again, in the interval of waiting for the carriage.

The second reading confirmed her in a resolution which she had privately taken, while she had been sitting by Anne on the sofa—a resolution destined to lead to far more serious results in the future than any previsions of hers could anticipate. Sir Patrick was the one person she knew on whose discretion and experience she could implicitly rely. She determined, in Anne's own interests, to take her uncle into her confidence, and to tell him all that had happened at the inn. "I'll first make him forgive me," thought Blanche. "And then I'll see if he thinks as I do, when I tell him about Anne."

The carriage drew up at the door; and Mrs. Inchbare showed in—not Lady Lundie, but Lady Lundie's maid.

The woman's account of what had happened at Windygates was simple enough. Lady Lundie had, as a matter of course, placed the right interpretation on Blanche's abrupt departure in the pony-chaise, and had ordered the carriage, with the firm determination of following her step-daughter herself. But the agitations and anxieties of the day had proved too much for her. She had been seized by one of the attacks of giddiness to which she was always subject after excessive mental irritation; and, eager as she was (on more accounts than one) to go to the inn herself, she had been compelled, in Sir Patrick's absence, to commit the pursuit of Blanche to her own maid, in whose age and good sense she could place every confidence. The woman —seeing the state of the weather—had thoughtfully brought a box with her, containing a change of wearing apparel. In offering it to Blanche, she added, with all due respect, that she had full powers from her mistress to go on, if necessary, to the shooting-cottage, and to place the matter in Sir Patrick's hands. This said, she left it to her young lady to decide for herself, whether she would return to Windygates, under present circumstances, or not.

Blanche took the box from the woman's hands, and joined Anne in the bedroom, to dress herself for the drive home.

"I am going back to a good scolding," she said. "But a scolding is no novelty in my experience of Lady Lundie. I'm not uneasy about that, Anne—I'm uneasy about you. Can I be sure of one thing—do you stay here for the present?"

The worst that could happen at the inn *had* happened. Nothing was to be gained now—and every thing might be lost—by leaving the place at which Geoffrey had promised to write to her. Anne answered that she proposed remaining at the inn for the present.

"You promise to write to me?"

"Yes."

"If there is any thing I can do for you—?"

"There is nothing, my love."

"There may be. If you want to see me, we can meet at Windygates without being discovered. Come at luncheon-time—go round by the shrubbery—and step in at the library window. You know as well as I do there is nobody in the library at that hour. Don't say it's impossible—you don't know what may happen. I shall wait ten minutes every day on the chance of seeing you. That's settled—and it's settled that you write. Before I go, darling, is there any thing else we can think of for the future?"

At those words Anne suddenly shook off the depression that weighed on her. She caught Blanche in her arms; she held Blanche to her bosom with a fierce energy. "Will you always be to me, in the future, what you are now?" she asked, abruptly. "Or is the time coming when you will hate me?" She prevented any reply by a kiss—and pushed Blanche toward the door. "We have had a happy time together in the years that are gone," she said, with a farewell wave of her hand. "Thank God for that! And never mind the rest."

She threw open the bedroom door, and called to the maid, in the sitting-room. "Miss Lundie is waiting for you." Blanche pressed her hand, and left her.

Anne waited a while in the bedroom, listening to the sound made by the departure of the carriage from the inn door. Little by little, the tramp of the horses and the noise of the rolling wheels lessened and lessened. When the last faint sounds were lost in silence she stood for a moment thinking—then, rousing herself on a sudden, hurried into the sitting-room, and rang the bell.

"I shall go mad," she said to herself, "if I stay here alone."

Even Mr. Bishopriggs felt the necessity of being silent when he stood face to face with her on answering the bell.

"I want to speak to him. Send him here instantly."

Mr. Bishopriggs understood her, and withdrew.

Arnold came in.

"Has she gone?" were the first words he said.

"She has gone. She won't suspect you when you see her again. I have told her nothing. Don't ask me for my reasons!"

"I have no wish to ask you."

"Be angry with me, if you like!"

"I have no wish to be angry with you."

He spoke and looked like an altered man. Quietly seating himself at the table, he rested his head on his hand—and so remained silent. Anne was taken completely by surprise. She drew near, and looked at him curiously. Let a woman's mood be what it may, it is certain to feel the influence of any change for which she is unprepared in the manner of a man—when that man interests her. The cause of this is not to be found in the variableness of her humor. It is far more probably to be traced to the noble abnegation of Self, which is one of the grandest—and to the credit of woman be it said—one of the commonest virtues of the sex. Little by little, the sweet feminine charm of Anne's face came softly and sadly back. The inbred nobility of the woman's nature answered the call which the man had unconsciously made on it. She touched Arnold on the shoulder.

"This has been hard on *you*," she said. "And I am to blame for it. Try and forgive me, Mr. Brinkworth. I am sincerely sorry. I wish with all my heart I could comfort you!"

"Thank you, Miss Silvester. It was not a very pleasant feeling, to be hiding from Blanche as if I was afraid of her—and it's set me thinking, I suppose, for the first time in my life. Never mind. It's all over now. Can I do any thing for you?"

"What do you propose doing to-night?"

"What I have proposed doing all along—my duty by Geoffrey. I have promised him to see you through your difficulties here, and to provide for your safety till he comes back. I can only make sure of doing that by keeping up appearances, and staying in the sitting-room to-night. When we next meet it will be under pleasanter circumstances, I hope. I shall always be glad to think that I was of some service to you. In the mean time I shall be most likely away to-morrow morning before you are up."

Anne held out her hand to take leave. Nothing could undo what had been done. The time for warning and remonstrance had passed away.

"You have not befriended an ungrateful woman," she said. "The day may yet come, Mr. Brinkworth, when I shall prove it."

"I hope not, Miss Silvester. Good-by, and good luck!"

She withdrew into her own room. Arnold locked the sitting-room door, and stretched himself on the sofa for the night.

*    *    *    *    *    *

The morning was bright, the air was delicious after the storm.

Arnold had gone, as he had promised, before Anne was out of her room. It was understood at the inn that important business had unexpectedly called him south. Mr. Bishopriggs had been presented with a handsome gratuity; and Mrs. Inchbare had been informed that the rooms were taken for a week certain.

In every quarter but one the march of events had now, to all appearance, fallen back into a quiet course. Arnold was on his way to his estate; Blanche was safe at Windygates; Anne's residence at the inn was assured for a week to come. The one present doubt was the doubt which hung over Geoffrey's movements. The one event still involved in darkness turned on the question of life or death waiting for solution in London —otherwise, the question of Lord Holchester's health. Taken by itself, the alternative, either way, was plain enough. If my lord lived—Geoffrey would be free to come back, and marry her privately in Scotland. If my lord died—Geoffrey would be free to send for her, and marry her publicly in London. But could Geoffrey be relied on?

Anne went out on to the terrace-ground in front of the inn. The cool morning breeze blew steadily. Towering white clouds sailed in grand procession over the heavens, now obscuring, and now revealing the sun. Yellow light and purple shadow chased each other over the broad brown surface of the moor—even as hope and fear chased each other over Anne's mind, brooding on what might come to her with the coming time.

She turned away, weary of questioning the impenetrable future, and went back to the inn.

Crossing the hall she looked at the clock. It was past the hour when the train from Perthshire was due in London. Geoffrey and his brother were, at that moment, on their way to Lord Holchester's house.

---

### THIRD SCENE.—LONDON.

## CHAPTER THE FOURTEENTH.

#### GEOFFREY AS A LETTER-WRITER.

LORD HOLCHESTER'S servants—with the butler at their head—were on the look-out for Mr. Julius Delamayn's arrival from Scotland. The appearance of the two brothers together took the whole domestic establishment by surprise. All inquiries were addressed to the butler by Julius; Geoffrey standing by, and taking no other than a listener's part in the proceedings.

"Is my father alive?"

"His lordship, I am rejoiced to say, has astonished the doctors, Sir. He rallied last night in the most wonderful way. If things go on for the next eight-and-forty hours as they are going now, my lord's recovery is considered certain."

"What was the illness?"

"A paralytic stroke, Sir. When her ladyship telegraphed to you in Scotland the doctors had given his lordship up."

"Is my mother at home?"

"Her ladyship is at home to *you*, Sir."

The butler laid a special emphasis on the personal pronoun. Julius turned to his brother. The change for the better in the state of Lord Holchester's health made Geoffrey's position, at that moment, an embarrassing one. He had been positively forbidden to enter the house. His one excuse for setting that prohibitory sentence at defiance rested on the assumption that his father was actually dying. As matters now stood, Lord Holchester's order remained in full force. The under-servants in the hall (charged to obey that order as they valued their places) looked from "Mr. Geoffrey" to the butler. The butler looked from "Mr. Geoffrey" to "Mr. Julius." Julius looked at his brother. There was an awkward pause. The position of the second son was the position of a wild beast in the house —a creature to be got rid of, without risk to yourself, if you only knew how.

Geoffrey spoke, and solved the problem.

"Open the door, one of you fellows," he said to the footmen. "I'm off."

"Wait a minute," interposed his brother. "It will be a sad disappointment to my mother to know that you have been here, and gone away again without seeing her. These are no ordinary circumstances, Geoffrey. Come up stairs with me—I'll take it on myself."

"I'm blessed if I take it on *my*self!" returned Geoffrey. "Open the door!"

"Wait here, at any rate," pleaded Julius, "till I can send you down a message."

"Send your message to Nagle's Hotel. I'm at home at Nagle's—I'm not at home here."

At that point the discussion was interrupted by the appearance of a little terrier in the hall. Seeing strangers, the dog began to bark. Perfect tranquillity in the house had been absolutely insisted on by the doctors; and the servants, all trying together to catch the animal and quiet him, simply aggravated the noise he was making. Geoffrey solved this problem also in his own decisive way. He swung round as the dog was passing him, and kicked it with his heavy boot. The little creature fell on the spot, whining piteously. "My lady's pet dog!" exclaimed the butler. "You've broken its ribs, Sir." "I've broken it of barking, you mean," retorted Geoffrey. "Ribs be hanged!" He turned to his brother. "That settles it," he said, jocosely. "I'd better defer the pleasure of calling on dear mamma till the next opportunity. Ta-ta, Julius. You know where to find me. Come, and dine. We'll give you a steak at Nagle's that will make a man of you."

He went out. The tall footmen eyed his lordship's second son with unaffected respect. They had seen him, in public, at the annual festival of the Christian-Pugilistic-Association, with "the gloves" on. He could have beaten the biggest man in the hall within an inch of his life in three minutes. The porter bowed as he threw open the door. The whole interest and attention of the domestic establishment then present was concentrated on Geoffrey. Julius went up stairs to his mother without attracting the slightest notice.

The month was August. The streets were empty. The vilest breeze that blows—a hot east wind in London—was the breeze abroad on that day. Even Geoffrey appeared to feel the influence of the weather as the cab carried him from his father's door to the hotel. He took off his hat, and unbuttoned his waistcoat, and lit his everlasting pipe, and growled and grumbled between his teeth in the intervals of smoking. Was it only the hot wind that wrung from him these demonstrations of discomfort? Or was there some secret anxiety in his mind which assisted the depressing influences of the day? There was a secret anxiety in his mind. And the name of it was—Anne.

As things actually were at that moment, what course was he to take with the unhappy woman who was waiting to hear from him at the Scotch inn?

To write? or not to write? That was the question with Geoffrey.

The preliminary difficulty, relating to addressing a letter to Anne at the inn, had been already provided for. She had decided—if it proved necessary to give her name, before Geoffrey joined her—to call herself Mrs., instead of Miss, Silvester. A letter addressed to "Mrs. Silvester" might be trusted to find its way to her, without causing any embarrassment. The doubt was not here. The doubt lay, as usual, between two alternatives. Which course would it be wisest to take?—to inform Anne, by that day's post, that an interval of forty-eight hours must elapse before his father's recovery could be considered certain? Or to wait till the interval was over, and be guided by the result? Considering the alternatives in the cab, he decided that the wise course was to temporize with Anne, by reporting matters as they then stood.

Arrived at the hotel, he sat down to write the letter—doubted—and tore it up—doubted again—and began again—doubted once more—and tore up the second letter—rose to his feet—and owned to himself (in unprintable language) that he couldn't for the life of him decide which was safest—to write or to wait.

In this difficulty, his healthy physical instincts sent him to healthy physical remedies for relief. "My mind's in a muddle," said Geoffrey. "I'll try a bath."

It was an elaborate bath, proceeding through many rooms, and combining many postures and applications. He steamed. He plunged. He simmered. He stood under a pipe, and received a cataract of cold water on his head. He was laid on his back; he was laid on his stomach; he was respectfully pounded and kneaded, from head to foot, by the knuckles of accomplished practitioners. He came out of it all, sleek, clear, rosy, beautiful. He returned to the hotel, and took up the writing materials—and behold the intolerable indecision seized him again, declining to be washed out! This time he laid it all to Anne. "That infernal woman will be the ruin of me," said Geoffrey, taking up his hat. "I must try the dumb-bells."

The pursuit of the new remedy for stimulating a sluggish brain took him to a public house, kept by the professional pedestrian who had the honor of training him when he contended at Athletic Sports.

"A private room and the dumb-bells!" cried Geoffrey. "The heaviest you have got."

He stripped himself of his upper clothing, and set to work, with the heavy weights in each hand, waving them up and down, and backward and forward, in every attainable variety of movement, till his magnificent muscles seemed on the point of starting through his sleek skin. Little by little his animal spirits roused themselves. The strong exertion intoxicated the strong man. In sheer excitement he swore cheerfully—invoking thunder and lightning, explosion and blood, in return for the compliments profusely paid to him by the pedestrian and the pedestrian's son. "Pen, ink, and paper!" he roared, when he could use the dumb-bells no longer. "My mind's made up; I'll write, and have done with it!" He sat down to his writing on the spot; he actually finished the letter; another minute would have dispatched it to the post—and, in that minute, the maddening indecision took possession of him once more. He opened the letter again, read it over again, and tore it up again. "I'm out of my mind!" cried Geoffrey, fixing his big bewildered blue eyes fiercely on the professor who trained him. "Thunder and lightning! Explosion and blood! Send for Crouch."

Crouch (known and respected wherever English manhood is known and respected) was a retired prize-fighter. He appeared with the third and last remedy for clearing the mind known to the Honorable Geoffrey Delamayn—namely, two pair of boxing-gloves in a carpet-bag.

The gentleman and the prize-fighter put on the gloves, and faced each other in the classically-correct posture of pugilistic defense. "None of your play, mind!" growled Geoffrey. "Fight, you beggar, as if you were in the Ring again, with orders to win." No man knew better than the great and terrible Crouch what real fighting meant, and what heavy blows might be given even with such apparently harmless weapons as stuffed and padded gloves. He pretended, and only pretended, to comply with his patron's request. Geoffrey rewarded him for his polite forbearance by knocking him down. The great and terrible rose with unruffled composure. "Well hit, Sir!" he said. "Try it with the other hand now." Geoffrey's temper was not under similar control. Invoking everlasting destruction on the frequently-blackened eyes of Crouch, he threatened instant withdrawal of his patronage and support unless the polite pugilist hit, then and there, as hard as he could. The hero of a hundred fights quailed at the dreadful prospect. "I've got a family to support," remarked Crouch. "If you *will* have it, Sir—there it is!" The fall of Geoffrey followed, and shook the house. He was on his legs again in an instant—not satisfied even yet. "None of your body-hitting!" he roared. "Stick to my head. Thunder and lightning! explosion and blood! Knock it out of me! Stick to the head!" Obedient Crouch stuck to the head. The two gave and took blows which would have stunned—possibly have killed—any civilized member of the community. Now on one side of his patron's iron skull, and now on the other, the hammering of the prizefighter's gloves fell, thump upon thump, horrible to hear—until even Geoffrey himself had had enough of it. "Thank you, Crouch," he said, speaking civilly to the man for the first time. "That will do. I feel nice and clear again." He shook his head two or three times; he was rubbed down like a horse by the professional runner; he drank a mighty draught of malt liquor; he recovered his good-humor as if by magic. "Want the pen and ink, Sir?" inquired his pedestrian host. "Not I!" answered Geoffrey. "The muddle's out of me now. Pen and ink be hanged! I shall look up some of our fellows, and go to the play." He left the public house in the happiest condition of mental calm. Inspired by the stimulant application of Crouch's gloves, his torpid cunning had been shaken up into excellent working order at last. Write to Anne? Who but a fool would write to such a woman as that until he was forced to it? Wait and see what the chances of the next eight-and-forty hours might bring forth, and then write to her, or desert her, as the event might decide. It lay in a nut-shell, if you could only see it. Thanks to Crouch, he did see it—and so away, in a pleasant temper for a dinner with "our fellows" and an evening at the play!

---

## CHAPTER THE FIFTEENTH.

### GEOFFREY IN THE MARRIAGE MARKET.

THE interval of eight-and-forty hours passed—without the occurrence of any personal communication between the two brothers in that time.

Julius, remaining at his father's house, sent brief written bulletins of Lord Holchester's health to his brother at the hotel. The first bulletin said, "Going on well. Doctors satisfied." The second was firmer in tone. "Going on excellently. Doctors very sanguine." The third was the most explicit of all. "I am to see my father in an hour from this. The doctors answer for his recovery. Depend on my putting in a good word for you, if I can; and wait to hear from me further at the hotel."

Geoffrey's face darkened as he read the third bulletin. He called once more for the hated writing materials. There could be no doubt now as to the necessity of communicating with Anne. Lord Holchester's recovery had put him back again in the same critical position which he had occupied at Windygates. To keep Anne from committing some final act of despair, which would connect him with a public scandal, and ruin him so far as his expectations from his father were concerned, was, once more, the only safe policy that Geoffrey could pursue. His letter began and ended in twenty words:

"DEAR ANNE,—Have only just heard that my father is turning the corner. Stay where you are. Will write again."

Having dispatched this Spartan composition by the post, Geoffrey lit his pipe, and waited the event of the interview between Lord Holchester and his eldest son.

Julius found his father alarmingly altered in personal appearance, but in full possession of his faculties nevertheless. Unable to return the pressure of his son's hand—unable even to turn in the bed without help—the hard eye of the old lawyer was as keen, the hard mind of the old lawyer was as clear, as ever. His grand ambition was to see Julius in Parliament. Julius was offering himself for election in Perthshire, by his father's express desire, at that moment. Lord Holchester entered eagerly into politics before his eldest son had been two minutes by his bedside.

"Much obliged, Julius, for your congratulations. Men of my sort are not easily killed. (Look at Brougham and Lyndhurst!) You won't be called to the Upper House yet. You will begin in the House of Commons—precisely as I wished. What are your prospects with the constituency? Tell me exactly how you stand, and where I can be of use to you."

"Surely, Sir, you are hardly recovered enough to enter on matters of business yet?"

"I am quite recovered enough. I want some present interest to occupy me. My thoughts are beginning to drift back to past times, and to things which are better forgotten." A sudden contraction crossed his livid face. He looked hard at his son, and entered abruptly on a new question. "Julius!" he resumed, "have you ever heard of a young woman named Anne Silvester?"

Julius answered in the negative. He and his wife had exchanged cards with Lady Lundie, and had excused themselves from accepting her invitation to the lawn-party. With the exception of Blanche, they were both quite ignorant of the persons who composed the family circle at Windygates.

"Make a memorandum of the name," Lord Holchester went on. "Anne Silvester. Her father and mother are dead. I knew her father in former times. Her mother was ill-used. It

"MEN OF MY SORT ARE NOT EASILY KILLED."

was a bad business. I have been thinking of it again, for the first time for many years. If the girl is alive and about the world she may remember our family name. Help her, Julius, if she ever wants help, and applies to you." The painful contraction passed across his face once more. Were his thoughts taking him back to the memorable summer evening at the Hampstead villa? Did he see the deserted woman swooning at his feet again? "About your election?" he asked, impatiently. "My mind is not used to be idle. Give it something to do."

Julius stated his position as plainly and as briefly as he could. The father found nothing to object to in the report—except the son's absence from the field of action. He blamed Lady Holchester for summoning Julius to London. He was annoyed at his son's being there, at the bedside, when he ought to have been addressing the electors. "It's inconvenient, Julius," he said, petulantly. "Don't you see it yourself?"

Having previously arranged with his mother to take the first opportunity that offered of risking a reference to Geoffrey, Julius decided to "see it" in a light for which his father was not prepared. The opportunity was before him. He took it on the spot.

"It is no inconvenience to me, Sir," he replied, "and it is no inconvenience to my brother either. Geoffrey was anxious about you too. Geoffrey has come to London with me."

Lord Holchester looked at his eldest son with a grimly-satirical expression of surprise.

"Have I not already told you," he rejoined, "that my mind is not affected by my illness? Geoffrey anxious about me! Anxiety is one of the civilized emotions. Man in his savage state is incapable of feeling it."

"My brother is not a savage, Sir."

"His stomach is generally full, and his skin is covered with linen and cloth, instead of red ochre and oil. So far, certainly, your brother is civilized. In all other respects your brother is a savage."

"I know what you mean, Sir. But there is something to be said for Geoffrey's way of life. He cultivates his courage and his strength. Courage and strength are fine qualities, surely, in their way?"

"Excellent qualities, as far as they go. If you want to know how far that is, challenge Geoffrey to write a sentence of decent English, and see if his courage doesn't fail him there. Give him his books to read for his degree, and, strong as he is, he will be taken ill at the sight of them. You wish me to see your brother. Nothing will induce me to see him, until his way of life (as you call it) is altered altogether. I have but one hope of its ever being altered now. It is barely possible that the influence of a sensible woman—possessed of such advantages of birth and fortune as may compel respect, even from a savage—might produce its effect on Geoffrey. If he wishes to find his way back into this house, let him find his way back into good society first, and bring me a daughter-in-law to plead his cause for him—whom his mother and I can respect and receive. When that happens, I shall begin to have some belief in Geoffrey. Until it does happen, don't introduce your brother into any future conversations which you may have with Me. To return to your election. I have some advice to give you before you go back. You will do well to go back to-night. Lift me up on the pillow. I shall speak more easily with my head high."

His son lifted him on the pillows, and once more entreated him to spare himself.

It was useless. No remonstrances shook the iron resolution of the man who had hewed his way through the rank and file of political humanity to his own high place apart from the rest. Helpless, ghastly, snatched out of the very jaws of Death, there he lay, steadily distilling the clear common-sense which had won him all his worldly rewards into the mind of his son. Not a hint was missed, not a caution was forgotten, that could guide Julius safely through the miry political ways which he had trodden so safely and so dextrously himself. An hour more had passed before the impenetrable old man closed his weary eyes, and consented to take his nourishment and compose himself to rest. His last words, rendered barely articulate by exhaustion, still sang the praises of party manœuvres and political strife. "It's a grand career! I miss the House of Commons, Julius, as I miss nothing else!"

Left free to pursue his own thoughts, and to guide his own movements, Julius went straight from Lord Holchester's bedside to Lady Holchester's boudoir.

"Has your father said any thing about Geoffrey?" was his mother's first question as soon as he entered the room.

"My father gives Geoffrey a last chance, if Geoffrey will only take it."

Lady Holchester's face clouded. "I know," she said, with a look of disappointment. "His last chance is to read for his degree. Hopeless, my dear. Quite hopeless! If it had only been something easier than that; something that rested with me—"

"It does rest with you," interposed Julius. "My dear mother!—can you believe it?—Geoffrey's last chance is (in one word) Marriage!"

"Oh, Julius! it's too good to be true!"

Julius repeated his father's own words. Lady Holchester looked twenty years younger as she listened. When he had done she rang the bell. "No matter who calls," she said to the servant, "I am not at home." She turned to Julius, kissed him, and made a place for him on the sofa by her side. "Geoffrey shall take *that* chance," she said, gayly—"I will answer for it! I have three women in my mind, any one of whom would suit him. Sit down, my dear, and let us consider carefully which of the three will be most likely to attract Geoffrey, and to come up to your father's standard of what his daughter-in-law ought to be. When we have decided, don't trust to writing. Go yourself and see Geoffrey at his hotel."

Mother and son entered on their consultation —and innocently sowed the seeds of a terrible harvest to come.

---

## CHAPTER THE SIXTEENTH.

### GEOFFREY AS A PUBLIC CHARACTER.

TIME had advanced to after noon before the selection of Geoffrey's future wife was accomplished, and before the instructions of Geoffrey's brother were complete enough to justify the opening of the matrimonial negotiation at Nagle's Hotel.

"Don't leave him till you have got his prom-ise," were Lady Holchester's last words when her son started on his mission.

"If Geoffrey doesn't jump at what I am going to offer him," was the son's reply, "I shall agree with my father that the case is hopeless; and I shall end, like my father, in giving Geoffrey up."

This was strong language for Julius to use. It was not easy to rouse the disciplined and equable temperament of Lord Holchester's eldest son. No two men were ever more thoroughly unlike each other than these two brothers. It is melancholy to acknowledge it of the blood-relation of a "stroke oar," but it must be owned, in the interests of truth, that Julius cultivated his intelligence. This degenerate Briton could digest books—and couldn't digest beer. Could learn languages—and couldn't learn to row. Practiced the foreign vice of perfecting himself in the art of playing on a musical instrument — and couldn't learn the English virtue of knowing a good horse when he saw him. Got through life (Heaven only knows how!) without either a biceps or a betting-book. Had openly acknowledged, in English society, that he didn't think the barking of a pack of hounds the finest music in the world. Could go to foreign parts, and see a mountain which nobody had ever got to the top of yet—and didn't instantly feel his honor as an Englishman involved in getting to the top of it himself. Such people may, and do, exist among the inferior races of the Continent. Let us thank Heaven, Sir, that England never has been, and never will be, the right place for them!

Arrived at Nagle's Hotel, and finding nobody to inquire of in the hall, Julius applied to the young lady who sat behind the window of "the bar." The young lady was reading something so deeply interesting in the evening newspaper that she never even heard him. Julius went into the coffee-room.

The waiter, in his corner, was absorbed over a second newspaper. Three gentlemen, at three different tables, were absorbed in a third, fourth, and fifth newspaper. They all alike went on with their reading without noticing the entrance of the stranger. Julius ventured on disturbing the waiter by asking for Mr. Geoffrey Delamayn. At the sound of that illustrious name the waiter looked up with a start. "Are you Mr. Delamayn's brother, Sir?"

"Yes."

The three gentlemen at the tables looked up with a start. The light of Geoffrey's celebrity fell, reflected, on Geoffrey's brother, and made a public character of him.

"You'll find Mr. Geoffrey, Sir," said the waiter, in a flurried, excited manner, "at the Cock and Bottle, Putney."

"I expected to find him here. I had an appointment with him at this hotel."

The waiter opened his eyes on Julius with an expression of blank astonishment. "Haven't you heard the news, Sir?"

"No."

"God bless my soul!" exclaimed the waiter —and offered the newspaper.

"God bless my soul!" exclaimed the three gentlemen—and offered the three newspapers.

"What is it?" asked Julius.

"What is it?" repeated the waiter, in a hollow voice. "The most dreadful thing that's happened in my time. It's all up, Sir, with the Great Foot-Race at Fulham. Tinkler has gone stale."

The three gentlemen dropped solemnly back into their three chairs, and repeated the dreadful intelligence, in chorus—"Tinkler has gone stale."

A man who stands face to face with a great national disaster, and who doesn't understand it, is a man who will do wisely to hold his tongue, and enlighten his mind without asking other people to help him. Julius accepted the waiter's newspaper, and sat down to make (if possible) two discoveries: First, as to whether "Tinkler" did, or did not, mean a man. Second, as to what particular form of human affliction you implied when you described that man as "gone stale."

There was no difficulty in finding the news. It was printed in the largest type, and was followed by a personal statement of the facts, taken one way—which was followed, in its turn, by another personal statement of the facts, taken in another way. More particulars, and further personal statements, were promised in later editions. The royal salute of British journalism thundered the announcement of Tinkler's staleness before a people prostrate on the national betting-book.

Divested of exaggeration, the facts were few enough and simple enough. A famous Athletic Association of the North had challenged a famous Athletic Association of the South. The usual "Sports" were to take place—such as running, jumping, "putting" the hammer, throwing cricket-balls, and the like—and the whole was to wind up with a Foot-Race of unexampled length and difficulty in the annals of human achievement between the two best men on either side. "Tinkler" was the best man on the side of the South. "Tinkler" was backed in innumerable betting-books to win. And Tinkler's lungs had suddenly given way under stress of training! A prospect of witnessing a prodigious achievement in foot-racing, and (more important still) a prospect of winning and losing large sums of money, was suddenly withdrawn from the eyes of the British people. The "South" could produce no second opponent worthy of the North out of its own associated resources. Surveying the athletic world in general, but one man existed who might possibly replace "Tinkler"—and it was doubtful, in the last degree, whether he would consent to come forward under the circumstances. The name of that man—Julius read it with horror—was Geoffrey Delamayn.

Profound silence reigned in the coffee-room. Julius laid down the newspaper, and looked about him. The waiter was busy, in his corner, with a pencil and a betting-book. The three gentlemen were busy, at the three tables, with pencils and betting-books.

"Try and persuade him!" said the waiter, piteously, as Delamayn's brother rose to leave the room.

"Try and persuade him!" echoed the three gentlemen, as Delamayn's brother opened the door and went out.

Julius called a cab, and told the driver (busy with a pencil and a betting-book) to go to the Cock and Bottle, Putney. The man brightened into a new being at the prospect. No need to hurry him; he drove, unasked, at the top of his horse's speed.

As the cab drew near to its destination the signs of a great national excitement appeared, and multiplied. The lips of a people pronounced, with a grand unanimity, the name of "Tinkler." The heart of a people hung suspended (mostly in the public houses) on the chances for and against the possibility of replacing "Tinkler" by another man. The scene in front of the inn was impressive in the highest degree. Even the London blackguard stood awed and quiet in the presence of the national calamity. Even the irrepressible man with the apron, who always turns up to sell nuts and sweetmeats in a crowd, plied his trade in silence, and found few indeed (to the credit of the nation be it spoken) who had the heart to crack a nut at such a time as this. The police were on the spot, in large numbers, and in mute sympathy with the people, touching to see. Julius, on being stopped at the door, mentioned his name—and received an ovation! His brother! oh, heavens, his brother! The people closed round him, the people shook hands with him, the people invoked blessings on his head. Julius was half suffocated, when the police rescued him, and landed him safe in the privileged haven on the inner side of the public house door. A deafening tumult broke out, as he entered, from the regions above stairs. A distant voice screamed, "Mind yourselves!" A hatless shouting man tore down through the people congregated on the stairs. "Hooray! Hooray! He's promised to do it! He's entered for the race!" Hundreds on hundreds of voices took up the cry. A roar of cheering burst from the people outside. Reporters for the newspapers raced, in frantic procession, out of the inn, and rushed into cabs to put the news in print. The hand of the landlord, leading Julius carefully up stairs by the arm, trembled with excitement. "His brother, gentlemen! his brother!" At those magic words a lane was made through the throng. At those magic words the closed door of the council-chamber flew open; and Julius found himself among the Athletes of his native country, in full parliament assembled. Is any description of them needed? The description of Geoffrey applies to them all. The manhood and muscle of England resemble the wool and mutton of England, in this respect, that there is about as much variety in a flock of athletes as in a flock of sheep. Julius looked about him, and saw the same man in the same dress, with the same health, strength, tone, tastes, habits, conversation, and pursuits, repeated infinitely in every part of the room. The din was deafening; the enthusiasm (to an uninitiated stranger) something at once hideous and terrifying to behold. Geoffrey had been lifted bodily on to the table, in his chair, so as to be visible to the whole room. They sang round him, they danced round him, they cheered round him, they swore round him. He was hailed, in maudlin terms of endearment, by grateful giants with tears in their eyes. "Dear old man!" "Glorious, noble, splendid, beautiful fellow!" They hugged him. They patted him on the back. They wrung his hands. They prodded and punched his muscles. They embraced the noble legs that were going to run the unexampled race. At the opposite end of the room, where it was physically impossible to get near the hero, the enthusiasm vented itself in feats of strength and acts of destruction. Hercules I. cleared a space with his elbows, and laid down—and Hercules II. took him up in his teeth. Hercules III. seized the poker from the fire-place, and broke it on his arm. Hercules IV. followed with the tongs, and shattered them on his neck. The smashing of the furniture and the pulling down of the house seemed likely to succeed—when Geoffrey's eye lighted by accident on Julius, and Geoffrey's voice, calling fiercely for his brother, hushed the wild assembly into sudden attention, and turned the fiery enthusiasm into a new course. Hooray for his brother! One, two, three—and up with his brother on our shoulders! Four, five, six—and on with his brother, over our heads, to the other end of the room! See, boys —see! the hero has got him by the collar! the hero has lifted him on the table! The hero, heated red-hot with his own triumph, welcomes the poor little snob cheerfully, with a volley of oaths. "Thunder and lightning! Explosion and blood! What's up now, Julius? What's up now?"

Julius recovered his breath, and arranged his coat. The quiet little man, who had just muscle enough to lift a Dictionary from the shelf, and just training enough to play the fiddle, so far from being daunted by the rough reception accorded to him, appeared to feel no other sentiment in relation to it than a sentiment of unmitigated contempt.

"You're not frightened, are you?" said Geoffrey. "Our fellows are a roughish lot, but they mean well."

"I am not frightened," answered Julius. "I am only wondering—when the Schools and Universities of England turn out such a set of ruffians as these—how long the Schools and Universities of England will last."

"Mind what you are about, Julius! They'll cart you out of window if they hear you."

"They will only confirm my opinion of them, Geoffrey, if they do."

Here, the assembly, seeing but not hearing the colloquy between the two brothers, became uneasy on the subject of the coming race. A roar of voices summoned Geoffrey to announce it, if there was any thing wrong. Having pacified the meeting, Geoffrey turned again to his brother, and asked him, in no amiable mood, what the devil he wanted there?

"I want to tell you something, before I go back to Scotland," answered Julius. "My father is willing to give you a last chance. If you don't take it, my doors are closed against you as well as his."

Nothing is more remarkable, in its way, than the sound common-sense and admirable self-restraint exhibited by the youth of the present time, when confronted by an emergency in which their own interests are concerned. Instead of resenting the tone which his brother had taken with him, Geoffrey instantly descended from the pedestal of glory on which he stood, and placed himself without a struggle in the hands which vicariously held his destiny — otherwise, the hands which vicariously held the purse. In five minutes more the meeting had been dismissed, with all needful assurances relating to Geoffrey's share in the coming Sports—and the

two brothers were closeted together in one of the private rooms of the inn.

"Out with it!" said Geoffrey. "And don't be long about it."

"I won't be five minutes," replied Julius. "I go back to-night by the mail-train; and I have a great deal to do in the mean time. Here it is, in plain words: My father consents to see you again, if you choose to settle in life—with his approval. And my mother has discovered where you may find a wife. Birth, beauty, and money are all offered to you. Take them—and you recover your position as Lord Holchester's son. Refuse them—and you go to ruin your own way."

Geoffrey's reception of the news from home was not of the most reassuring kind. Instead of answering he struck his fist furiously on the table, and cursed with all his heart some absent woman unnamed.

"I have nothing to do with any degrading connection which you may have formed," Julius went on. "I have only to put the matter before you exactly as it stands, and to leave you to decide for yourself. The lady in question was formerly Miss Newenden—a descendant of one of the oldest families in England. She is now Mrs. Glenarm—the young widow (and the childless widow) of the great iron-master of that name. Birth and fortune—she unites both. Her income is a clear ten thousand a year. My father can, and will, make it fifteen thousand, if you are lucky enough to persuade her to marry you. My mother answers for her personal qualities. And my wife has met her at our house in London. She is now, as I hear, staying with some friends in Scotland; and when I get back I will take care that an invitation is sent to her to pay her next visit at my house. It remains, of course, to be seen whether you are fortunate enough to produce a favorable impression on her. In the mean time you will be doing every thing that my father can ask of you, if you make the attempt."

Geoffrey impatiently dismissed that part of the question from all consideration.

"If she don't cotton to a man who's going to run in the Great Race at Fulham," he said, "there are plenty as good as she is who will! That's not the difficulty. Bother that!"

"I tell you again, I have nothing to do with your difficulties," Julius resumed. "Take the rest of the day to consider what I have said to you. If you decide to accept the proposal, I shall expect you to prove you are in earnest by meeting me at the station to-night. We will travel back to Scotland together. You will complete your interrupted visit at Lady Lundie's (it is important, in my interests, that you should treat a person of her position in the county with all due respect); and my wife will make the necessary arrangements with Mrs. Glenarm, in anticipation of your return to our house. There is nothing more to be said, and no further necessity for my staying here. If you join me at the station to-night, your sister-in-law and I will do all we can to help you. If I travel back to Scotland alone, don't trouble yourself to follow—I have done with you." He shook hands with his brother, and went out.

Left alone, Geoffrey lit his pipe and sent for the landlord.

"Get me a boat. I shall scull myself up the river for an hour or two. And put in some towels. I may take a swim."

The landlord received the order—with a caution addressed to his illustrious guest.

"Don't show yourself in front of the house, Sir! If you let the people see you, they're in such a state of excitement, the police won't answer for keeping them in order."

"All right. I'll go out by the back way."

He took a turn up and down the room. What were the difficulties to be overcome before he could profit by the golden prospect which his brother had offered to him? The Sports? No! The committee had promised to defer the day, if he wished it—and a month's training, in his physical condition, would be amply enough for him. Had he any personal objection to trying his luck with Mrs. Glenarm? Not he! Any woman would do—provided his father was satisfied, and the money was all right. The obstacle which was really in his way was the obstacle of the woman whom he had ruined. Anne! The one insuperable difficulty was the difficulty of dealing with Anne.

"We'll see how it looks," he said to himself, "after a pull up the river!"

The landlord and the police inspector smuggled him out by the back way unknown to the expectant populace in front. The two men stood on the river-bank admiring him, as he pulled away from them, with his long, powerful, easy, beautiful stroke.

"That's what I call the pride and flower of England!" said the inspector. "Has the betting on him begun?"

"Six to four," said the landlord, "and no takers."

Julius went early to the station that night. His mother was very anxious. "Don't let Geoffrey find an excuse in your example," she said, "if he is late."

The first person whom Julius saw on getting out of the carriage was Geoffrey—with his ticket taken, and his portmanteau in charge of the guard.

---

FOURTH SCENE.—WINDYGATES.

## CHAPTER THE SEVENTEENTH.

### NEAR IT.

THE Library at Windygates was the largest and the handsomest room in the house. The two grand divisions under which Literature is usually arranged in these days occupied the customary places in it. On the shelves which ran round the walls were the books which humanity in general respects—and does not read. On the tables distributed over the floor were the books which humanity in general reads—and does not respect. In the first class, the works of the wise ancients; and the Histories, Biographies, and Essays of writers of more modern times—otherwise the Solid Literature, which is universally respected, and occasionally read. In the second class, the Novels of our own day—otherwise the Light Literature, which is universally read, and occasionally respected. At Windygates, as elsewhere, we believed History to be high literature, because it assumed to be true to Author-

ities (of which we knew little)—and Fiction to be low literature, because it attempted to be true to Nature (of which we knew less). At Windygates, as elsewhere, we were always more or less satisfied with ourselves, if we were publicly discovered consulting our History—and more or less ashamed of ourselves, if we were publicly discovered devouring our Fiction. An architectural peculiarity in the original arrangement of the library favored the development of this common and curious form of human stupidity. While a row of luxurious arm-chairs, in the main thoroughfare of the room, invited the reader of solid literature to reveal himself in the act of cultivating a virtue, a row of snug little curtained recesses, opening at intervals out of one of the walls, enabled the reader of light literature to conceal himself in the act of indulging a vice. For the rest, all the minor accessories of this spacious and tranquil place were as plentiful and as well chosen as the heart could desire. And solid literature and light literature, and great writers and small, were all bounteously illuminated alike by a fine broad flow of the light of heaven, pouring into the room through windows that opened to the floor.

It was the fourth day from the day of Lady Lundie's garden-party, and it wanted an hour or more of the time at which the luncheon-bell usually rang.

The guests at Windygates were most of them in the garden, enjoying the morning sunshine, after a prevalent mist and rain for some days past. Two gentlemen (exceptions to the general rule) were alone in the library. They were the two last gentlemen in the world who could possibly be supposed to have any legitimate motive for meeting each other in a place of literary seclusion. One was Arnold Brinkworth, and the other was Geoffrey Delamayn.

They had arrived together at Windygates that morning. Geoffrey had traveled from London with his brother by the train of the previous night. Arnold, delayed in getting away at his own time, from his own property, by ceremonies incidental to his position which were not to be abridged without giving offense to many worthy people—had caught the passing train early that morning at the station nearest to him, and had returned to Lady Lundie's, as he had left Lady Lundie's, in company with his friend.

After a short preliminary interview with Blanche, Arnold had rejoined Geoffrey in the safe retirement of the library, to say what was still left to be said between them on the subject of Anne. Having completed his report of events at Craig Fernie, he was now naturally waiting to hear what Geoffrey had to say on his side. To Arnold's astonishment, Geoffrey coolly turned away to leave the library without uttering a word.

Arnold stopped him without ceremony.

"Not quite so fast, Geoffrey," he said. "I have an interest in Miss Silvester's welfare as well as in yours. Now you are back again in Scotland, what are you going to do?"

If Geoffrey had told the truth, he must have stated his position much as follows:

He had necessarily decided on deserting Anne when he had decided on joining his brother on the journey back. But he had advanced no further than this. How he was to abandon the woman who had trusted him, without seeing his own dastardly conduct dragged into the light of day, was more than he yet knew. A vague idea of at once pacifying and deluding Anne, by a marriage which should be no marriage at all, had crossed his mind on the journey. He had asked himself whether a trap of that sort might not be easily set in a country notorious for the looseness of its marriage laws—if a man only knew how? And he had thought it likely that his well-informed brother, who lived in Scotland, might be tricked into innocently telling him what he wanted to know. He had turned the conversation to the subject of Scotch marriages in general by way of trying the experiment. Julius had not studied the question; Julius knew nothing about it; and there the experiment had come to an end. As the necessary result of the check thus encountered, he was now in Scotland with absolutely nothing to trust to as a means of effecting his release but the chapter of accidents, aided by his own resolution to marry Mrs. Glenarm. Such was his position, and such should have been the substance of his reply when he was confronted by Arnold's question, and plainly asked what he meant to do.

"The right thing," he answered, unblushingly. "And no mistake about it."

"I'm glad to hear you see your way so plainly," returned Arnold. "In your place, I should have been all abroad. I was wondering, only the other day, whether you would end, as I should have ended, in consulting Sir Patrick."

Geoffrey eyed him sharply.

"Consult Sir Patrick?" he repeated. "Why would you have done that?"

"I shouldn't have known how to set about marrying her," replied Arnold. "And—being in Scotland—I should have applied to Sir Patrick (without mentioning names, of course), because he would be sure to know all about it."

"Suppose I don't see my way quite so plainly as you think," said Geoffrey. "Would you advise me—"

"To consult Sir Patrick? Certainly! He has passed his life in the practice of the Scotch law. Didn't you know that?"

"No."

"Then take my advice—and consult him. You needn't mention names. You can say it's the case of a friend."

The idea was a new one and a good one. Geoffrey looked longingly toward the door. Eager to make Sir Patrick his innocent accomplice on the spot, he made a second attempt to leave the library; and made it for the second time in vain. Arnold had more unwelcome inquiries to make, and more advice to give unasked.

"How have you arranged about meeting Miss Silvester?" he went on. "You can't go to the hotel in the character of her husband. I have prevented that. Where else are you to meet her? She is all alone; she must be weary of waiting, poor thing. Can you manage matters so as to see her to-day?"

After staring hard at Arnold while he was speaking, Geoffrey burst out laughing when he had done. A disinterested anxiety for the welfare of another person was one of those refinements of feeling which a muscular education had not fitted him to understand.

"I say, old boy," he burst out, "you seem to take an extraordinary interest in Miss Silvester! You haven't fallen in love with her yourself—have you?"

"Come! come!" said Arnold, seriously. "Neither she nor I deserve to be sneered at, in that way. I have made a sacrifice to your interests, Geoffrey—and so has she."

Geoffrey's face became serious again. His secret was in Arnold's hands; and his estimate of Arnold's character was founded, unconsciously, on his experience of himself. "All right," he said, by way of timely apology and concession. "I was only joking."

"As much joking as you please, when you have married her," replied Arnold. "It seems serious enough, to my mind, till then." He stopped—considered—and laid his hand very earnestly on Geoffrey's arm. "Mind!" he resumed. "You are not to breathe a word to any living soul, of my having been near the inn!"

"I've promised to hold my tongue, once already. What do you want more?"

"I am anxious, Geoffrey. I was at Craig Fernie, remember, when Blanche came there! She has been telling me all that happened, poor darling, in the firm persuasion that I was miles off at the time. I swear I couldn't look her in the face! What would she think of me, if she knew the truth? Pray be careful! pray be careful!"

Geoffrey's patience began to fail him.

"We had all this out," he said, "on the way here from the station. What's the good of going over the ground again?"

"You're quite right," said Arnold, good-humoredly. "The fact is—I'm out of sorts, this morning. My mind misgives me—I don't know why."

"Mind?" repeated Geoffrey, in high contempt. "It's flesh—that's what's the matter with you. You're nigh on a stone over your right weight. Mind be hanged! A man in healthy training don't know that he has got a mind. Take a turn with the dumb-bells, and a run up hill with a great-coat on. Sweat it off, Arnold! Sweat it off!"

With that excellent advice, he turned to leave the room for the third time. Fate appeared to have determined to keep him imprisoned in the library, that morning. On this occasion, it was a servant who got in the way—a servant, with a letter and a message. "The man waits for an answer."

Geoffrey looked at the letter. It was in his brother's handwriting. He had left Julius at the junction about three hours since. What could Julius possibly have to say to him now?

He opened the letter. Julius had to announce that Fortune was favoring them already. He had heard news of Mrs. Glenarm, as soon as he reached home. She had called on his wife, during his absence in London—she had been invited to the house—and she had promised to accept the invitation early in the week. "Early in the week," Julius wrote, "may mean to-morrow. Make your apologies to Lady Lundie; and take care not to offend her. Say that family reasons, which you hope soon to have the pleasure of confiding to her, oblige you to appeal once more to her indulgence—and come to-morrow, and help us to receive Mrs. Glenarm."

Even Geoffrey was startled, when he found

himself met by a sudden necessity for acting on his own decision. Anne knew where his brother lived. Suppose Anne (not knowing where else to find him) appeared at his brother's house, and claimed him in the presence of Mrs. Glenarm? He gave orders to have the messenger kept waiting, and said he would send back a written reply.

"From Craig Fernie?" asked Arnold, pointing to the letter in his friend's hand.

Geoffrey looked up with a frown. He had just opened his lips to answer that ill-timed reference to Anne, in no very friendly terms, when a voice, calling to Arnold from the lawn outside, announced the appearance of a third person in the library, and warned the two gentlemen that their private interview was at an end.

---

## CHAPTER THE EIGHTEENTH.

### NEARER STILL.

BLANCHE stepped lightly into the room, through one of the open French windows.

"What are you doing here?" she said to Arnold.

"Nothing. I was just going to look for you in the garden."

"The garden is insufferable, this morning." Saying those words, she fanned herself with her handkerchief, and noticed Geoffrey's presence in the room with a look of very thinly-concealed annoyance at the discovery. "Wait till I am married!" she thought. "Mr. Delamayn will be cleverer than I take him to be, if he gets much of his friend's company then!"

"A trifle too hot—eh?" said Geoffrey, seeing her eyes fixed on him, and supposing that he was expected to say something.

Having performed that duty, he walked away without waiting for a reply; and seated himself, with his letter, at one of the writing-tables in the library.

"Sir Patrick is quite right about the young men of the present day," said Blanche, turning to Arnold. "Here is this one asks me a question, and doesn't wait for an answer. There are three more of them, out in the garden, who have been talking of nothing, for the last hour, but the pedigrees of horses and the muscles of men. When we are married, Arnold, don't present any of your male friends to me, unless they have turned fifty. What shall we do till luncheon-time? It's cool and quiet in here among the books. I want a mild excitement—and I have got absolutely nothing to do. Suppose you read me some poetry?"

"While he is here?" asked Arnold, pointing to the personified antithesis of poetry—otherwise to Geoffrey, seated with his back to them at the farther end of the library.

"Pooh!" said Blanche. "There's only an animal in the room. We needn't mind him!"

"I say!" exclaimed Arnold. "You're as bitter, this morning, as Sir Patrick himself. What will you say to Me when we are married, if you talk in that way of my friend?"

Blanche stole her hand into Arnold's hand, and gave it a little significant squeeze. "I shall always be nice to you," she whispered—with a look that contained a host of pretty promises in

itself. Arnold returned the look (Geoffrey was unquestionably in the way!). Their eyes met tenderly (why couldn't the great awkward brute write his letters somewhere else?). With a faint little sigh, Blanche dropped resignedly into one of the comfortable arm-chairs—and asked once more for "some poetry," in a voice that faltered softly, and with a color that was brighter than usual.

"Whose poetry am I to read?" inquired Arnold.

"Any body's," said Blanche. "This is another of my Impulses. I am dying for some poetry. I don't know whose poetry. And I don't know why."

Arnold went straight to the nearest book-shelf, and took down the first volume that his hand lighted on—a solid quarto, bound in sober brown.

"Well?" asked Blanche. "What have you found?"

Arnold opened the volume, and conscientiously read the title exactly as it stood:

"Paradise Lost. A Poem. By John Milton."

"I have never read Milton," said Blanche. "Have you?"

"No."

"Another instance of sympathy between us. No educated person ought to be ignorant of Milton. Let us be educated persons. Please begin."

"At the beginning?"

"Of course! Stop! You musn't sit all that way off—you must sit where I can look at you. My attention wanders if I don't look at people while they read."

Arnold took a stool at Blanche's feet, and opened the "First Book" of Paradise Lost. His "system" as a reader of blank verse was simplicity itself. In poetry we are some of us (as many living poets can testify) all for sound; and some of us (as few living poets can testify) all for sense. Arnold was for sound. He ended every line inexorably with a full stop; and he got on to his full stop as fast as the inevitable impediment of the words would let him. He began:

> "Of Man's first disobedience and the fruit.
> Of that forbidden tree whose mortal taste.
> Brought death into the world and all our woe.
> With loss of Eden till one greater Man.
> Restore us and regain the blissful seat.
> Sing heavenly Muse—"

"Beautiful!" said Blanche. "What a shame it seems to have had Milton all this time in the library and never to have read him yet! We will have Mornings with Milton, Arnold. He seems long; but we are both young, and we may live to get to the end of him. Do you know, dear, now I look at you again, you don't seem to have come back to Windygates in good spirits."

"Don't I? I can't account for it."

"I can. It's sympathy with Me. I am out of spirits too."

"You!"

"Yes. After what I saw at Craig Fernie, I grow more and more uneasy about Anne. You will understand that, I am sure, after what I told you this morning?"

Arnold looked back, in a violent hurry, from Blanche to Milton. That renewed reference to events at Craig Fernie was a renewed reproach to him for his conduct at the inn. He attempted to silence her by pointing to Geoffrey.

"ARNOLD TOOK A STOOL AT BLANCHE'S FEET, AND OPENED THE 'FIRST BOOK' OF
PARADISE LOST."

"Don't forget," he whispered, "that there is somebody in the room besides ourselves."

Blanche shrugged her shoulders contemptuously.

"What does *he* matter?" she asked. "What does *he* know or care about Anne?"

There was only one other chance of diverting her from the delicate subject. Arnold went on reading headlong, two lines in advance of the place at which he had left off, with more sound and less sense than ever:

"In the beginning how the heavens and earth.
Rose out of Chaos or if Sion hill—"

At "Sion hill," Blanche interrupted him again.

"Do wait a little, Arnold. I can't have Milton crammed down my throat in that way. Besides I had something to say. Did I tell you that I consulted my uncle about Anne? I don't think I did. I caught him alone in this very room. I told him all I have told you. I showed him Anne's letter. And I said, 'What do you think?' He took a little time (and a great deal of snuff) before he would say what he thought. When he did speak, he told me I might quite possibly be right in suspecting Anne's husband to be a very abominable person. His keeping himself out of my way was (just as I thought) a suspicious circumstance, to begin with. And then there was the sudden extinguishing of the candles, when I first went in. I thought (and Mrs. Inchbare thought) it was done by the wind. Sir Patrick suspects it was done by the horrid man himself, to prevent me from seeing him when I entered the room. I am firmly persuaded Sir Patrick is right. What do *you* think?"

"I think we had better go on," said Arnold, with his head down over his book. "We seem to be forgetting Milton."

"How you do worry about Milton! That last bit wasn't as interesting as the other. Is there any love in Paradise Lost?"

"Perhaps we may find some if we go on."

"Very well, then. Go on. And be quick about it."

Arnold was *so* quick about it that he lost his place. Instead of going on he went back. He read once more:

"In the beginning how the heavens and earth.
Rose out of Chaos or if Sion hill—"

"You read that before," said Blanche.

"I think not."

"I'm sure you did. When you said 'Sion hill' I recollect I thought of the Methodists directly. I couldn't have thought of the Methodists if you hadn't said 'Sion hill.' It stands to reason."

"I'll try the next page," said Arnold. "I can't have read that before—for I haven't turned over yet."

Blanche threw herself back in her chair, and flung her handkerchief resignedly over her face. "The flies," she explained. "I'm not going to sleep. Try the next page. Oh, dear me, try the next page!"

Arnold proceeded:

"Say first for heaven hides nothing from thy view.
Nor the deep tract of hell say first what cause.
Moved our grand parents in that happy state—"

Blanche suddenly threw the handkerchief off again, and sat bolt upright in her chair. "Shut it up," she cried. "I can't bear any more. Leave off, Arnold—leave off!"

"What's the matter now?"

"'That happy state,'" said Blanche. "What does 'that happy state' mean? Marriage, of course! And marriage reminds me of Anne. I won't have any more. Paradise Lost is painful. Shut it up. Well, my next question to Sir Patrick was, of course, to know what he thought Anne's husband had done. The wretch had behaved infamously to her in some way. In what way? Was it any thing to do with her marriage? My uncle considered again. He thought it quite possible. Private marriages were dangerous things (he said)—especially in Scotland. He asked me if they had been married in Scotland. I couldn't tell him—I only said, 'Suppose they were? What then?' 'It's barely possible, in that case,' says Sir Patrick, 'that Miss Silvester may be feeling uneasy about her marriage. She may even have reason—or may think she has reason—to doubt whether it is a marriage at all.'"

Arnold started, and looked round at Geoffrey still sitting at the writing-table with his back turned on them. Utterly as Blanche and Sir Patrick were mistaken in their estimate of Anne's position at Craig Fernie, they had drifted, nevertheless, into discussing the very question in which Geoffrey and Miss Silvester were interested — the question of marriage in Scotland. It was impossible in Blanche's presence to tell Geoffrey that he might do well to listen to Sir Patrick's opinion, even at second-hand. Perhaps the words had found their way to him? perhaps he was listening already, of his own accord?

(He *was* listening. Blanche's last words had found their way to him, while he was pondering over his half-finished letter to his brother. He waited to hear more—without moving, and with the pen suspended in his hand.)

Blanche proceeded, absently winding her fingers in and out of Arnold's hair as he sat at her feet:

"It flashed on me instantly that Sir Patrick had discovered the truth. Of course I told him so. He laughed, and said I mustn't jump at conclusions. We were guessing quite in the dark; and all the distressing things I had noticed at the inn might admit of some totally different explanation. He would have gone on splitting straws in that provoking way the whole morning if I hadn't stopped him. I was strictly logical. I said *I* had seen Anne, and *he* hadn't —and that made all the difference. I said, 'Every thing that puzzled and frightened me in the poor darling is accounted for now. The law must, and shall, reach that man, uncle—and I'll pay for it!' I was so much in earnest that I believe I cried a little. What do you think the dear old man did? He took me on his knee and gave me a kiss; and he said, in the nicest way, that he would adopt my view, for the present, if I would promise not to cry any more; and—wait! the cream of it is to come!—that he would put the view in quite a new light to me as soon as I was composed again. You may imagine how soon I dried my eyes, and what a picture of composure I presented in the course of half a minute. 'Let us take it for granted,' says Sir Patrick, 'that this man unknown has really tried to deceive Miss Silvester, as you and I suppose. I can tell you one thing: it's as likely as not that, in trying to overreach *her*, he may (with-

out in the least suspecting it) have ended in overreaching himself.'"

(Geoffrey held his breath. The pen dropped unheeded from his fingers. It was coming! The light that his brother couldn't throw on the subject was dawning on it at last!)

Blanche resumed:

"I was so interested, and it made such a tremendous impression on me, that I haven't forgotten a word. 'I mustn't make that poor little head of yours ache with Scotch law,' my uncle said; 'I must put it plainly. There are marriages allowed in Scotland, Blanche, which are called Irregular Marriages—and very abominable things they are. But they have this accidental merit in the present case. It is extremely difficult for a man to pretend to marry in Scotland, and not really to do it. And it is, on the other hand, extremely easy for a man to drift into marrying in Scotland without feeling the slightest suspicion of having done it himself.' That was exactly what he said, Arnold. When *we* are married, it sha'n't be in Scotland!"

(Geoffrey's ruddy color paled. If this was true, he might be caught himself in the trap which he had schemed to set for Anne! Blanche went on with her narrative. He waited and listened.)

"My uncle asked me if I understood him so far. It was as plain as the sun at noonday, of course I understood him! 'Very well, then —now for the application!' says Sir Patrick. 'Once more supposing our guess to be the right one, Miss Silvester may be making herself very unhappy without any real cause. If this invisible man at Craig Fernie has actually meddled, I won't say with marrying her, but only with pretending to make her his wife, and if he has attempted it in Scotland, the chances are nine to one (though *he* may not believe it, and though *she* may not believe it) that he has really married her, after all.' My uncle's own words again! Quite needless to say that, half an hour after they were out of his lips, I had sent them to Craig Fernie in a letter to Anne!"

(Geoffrey's stolidly-staring eyes suddenly brightened. A light of the devil's own striking illuminated him. An idea of the devil's own bringing entered his mind. He looked stealthily round at the man whose life he had saved—at the man who had devotedly served him in return. A hideous cunning leered at his mouth and peeped out of his eyes. "Arnold Brinkworth pretended to be married to her at the inn. By the lord Harry! that's a way out of it that never struck me before!" With that thought in his heart he turned back again to his half-finished letter to Julius. For once in his life he was strongly, fiercely agitated. For once in his life he was daunted—and that by his Own Thought! He had written to Julius under a strong sense of the necessity of gaining time to delude Anne into leaving Scotland before he ventured on paying his addresses to Mrs. Glenarm. His letter contained a string of clumsy excuses, intended to delay his return to his brother's house. "No," he said to himself, as he read it again. "Whatever else may do—*this* won't!" He looked round once more at Arnold, and slowly tore the letter into fragments as he looked.)

In the mean time Blanche had not done yet. "No," she said, when Arnold proposed an adjournment to the garden; "I have something more to say, and you are interested in it, this time." Arnold resigned himself to listen, and, worse still, to answer, if there was no help for it, in the character of an innocent stranger who had never been near the Craig Fernie inn.

"Well," Blanche resumed, "and what do you think has come of my letter to Anne?"

"I'm sure I don't know."

"Nothing has come of it!"

"Indeed?"

"Absolutely nothing! I know she received the letter yesterday morning. I ought to have had the answer to-day at breakfast."

"Perhaps she thought it didn't require an answer."

"She couldn't have thought that, for reasons that I know of. Besides, in my letter yesterday, I implored her to tell me (if it was one line only) whether, in guessing at what her trouble was, Sir Patrick and I had not guessed right. And here is the day getting on, and no answer! What am I to conclude?"

"I really can't say!"

"Is it possible, Arnold, that we have *not* guessed right, after all? Is the wickedness of that man who blew the candles out wickedness beyond our discovering? The doubt is so dreadful that I have made up my mind not to bear it after to-day. I count on your sympathy and assistance when to-morrow comes!"

Arnold's heart sank. Some new complication was evidently gathering round him. He waited in silence to hear the worst. Blanche bent forward, and whispered to him.

"This is a secret," she said. "If that creature at the writing-table has ears for any thing but rowing and racing, he mustn't hear this! Anne may come to me privately to-day while you are all at luncheon. If she doesn't come, and if I don't hear from her, then the mystery of her silence must be cleared up; and You must do it!"

"I!"

"Don't make difficulties! If you can't find your way to Craig Fernie, I can help you. As for Anne, you know what a charming person she is, and you know she will receive you perfectly, for my sake. I must and will have some news of her. I can't break the laws of the household a second time. Sir Patrick sympathizes, but he won't stir. Lady Lundie is a bitter enemy. The servants are threatened with the loss of their places if any one of them goes near Anne. There is nobody but you. And to Anne you go to-morrow, if I don't see her or hear from her to-day!"

This to the man who had passed as Anne's husband at the inn, and who had been forced into the most intimate knowledge of Anne's miserable secret! Arnold rose to put Milton away, with the composure of sheer despair. Any other secret he might, in the last resort, have confided to the discretion of a third person. But a woman's secret—with a woman's reputation depending on his keeping it—was not to be confided to any body, under any stress of circumstances whatever. "If Geoffrey doesn't get me out of *this*," he thought, "I shall have no choice but to leave Windygates to-morrow."

As he replaced the book on the shelf, Lady Lundie entered the library from the garden.

"What are you doing here?" she said to her step-daughter.

"Improving my mind," replied Blanche. "Mr. Brinkworth and I have been reading Milton."

"Can you condescend so far, after reading Milton all the morning, as to help me with the invitations for the dinner next week?"

"If *you* can condescend, Lady Lundie, after feeding the poultry all the morning, I must be humility itself after only reading Milton!"

With that little interchange of the acid amenities of feminine intercourse, step-mother and step-daughter withdrew to a writing-table, to put the virtue of hospitality in practice together.

Arnold joined his friend at the other end of the library.

Geoffrey was sitting with his elbows on the desk, and his clenched fists dug into his cheeks. Great drops of perspiration stood on his forehead, and the fragments of a torn letter lay scattered all round him. He exhibited symptoms of nervous sensibility for the first time in his life—he started when Arnold spoke to him.

"What's the matter, Geoffrey?"

"A letter to answer. And I don't know how."

"From Miss Silvester?" asked Arnold, dropping his voice so as to prevent the ladies at the other end of the room from hearing him.

"No," answered Geoffrey, in a lower voice still.

"Have you heard what Blanche has been saying to me about Miss Silvester?"

"Some of it."

"Did you hear Blanche say that she meant to send me to Craig Fernie to-morrow, if she failed to get news from Miss Silvester to-day?"

"No."

"Then you know it now. That is what Blanche has just said to me."

"Well?"

"Well—there's a limit to what a man can expect even from his best friend. I hope you won't ask me to be Blanche's messenger to-morrow. I can't, and won't, go back to the inn as things are now."

"You have had enough of it—eh?"

"I have had enough of distressing Miss Silvester, and more than enough of deceiving Blanche."

"What do you mean by 'distressing Miss Silvester?'"

"She doesn't take the same easy view that you and I do, Geoffrey, of my passing her off on the people of the inn as my wife."

Geoffrey absently took up a paper-knife. Still with his head down, he began shaving off the topmost layer of paper from the blotting-pad under his hand. Still with his head down, he abruptly broke the silence in a whisper.

"I say!"

"Yes?"

"How did you manage to pass her off as your wife?"

"I told you how, as we were driving from the station here."

"I was thinking of something else. Tell me again."

Arnold told him once more what had happened at the inn. Geoffrey listened, without making any remark. He balanced the paper-knife vacantly on one of his fingers. He was strangely sluggish and strangely silent.

"All *that* is done and ended," said Arnold, shaking him by the shoulder. "It rests with you now to get me out of the difficulty I'm placed in with Blanche. Things must be settled with Miss Silvester to-day."

"Things *shall* be settled."

"Shall be? What are you waiting for?"

"I'm waiting to do what you told me."

"What I told you?"

"Didn't you tell me to consult Sir Patrick before I married her?"

"To be sure! so I did."

"Well—I am waiting for a chance with Sir Patrick."

"And then?"

"And then—" He looked at Arnold for the first time. "Then," he said, "you may consider it settled."

"The marriage?"

He suddenly looked down again at the blotting-pad. "Yes—the marriage."

Arnold offered his hand in congratulation. Geoffrey never noticed it. His eyes were off the blotting-pad again. He was looking out of the window near him.

"Don't I hear voices outside?" he asked.

"I believe our friends are in the garden," said Arnold. "Sir Patrick may be among them. I'll go and see."

The instant his back was turned Geoffrey snatched up a sheet of note-paper. "Before I forget it!" he said to himself. He wrote the word "Memorandum" at the top of the page, and added these lines beneath it:

"He asked for her by the name of his wife at the door. He said, at dinner, before the landlady and the waiter, 'I take these rooms for my wife.' He made *her* say he was her husband at the same time. After that he stopped all night. What do the lawyers call this in Scotland?—(Query: a marriage?)"

After folding up the paper he hesitated for a moment. "No!" he thought. "It won't do to trust to what Miss Lundie said about it. I can't be certain till I have consulted Sir Patrick himself."

He put the paper away in his pocket, and wiped the heavy perspiration from his forehead. He was pale—for *him*, strikingly pale—when Arnold came back.

"Anything wrong, Geoffrey?—you're as white as ashes."

"It's the heat. Where's Sir Patrick?"

"You may see for yourself."

Arnold pointed to the window. Sir Patrick was crossing the lawn, on his way to the library, with a newspaper in his hand; and the guests at Windygates were accompanying him. Sir Patrick was smiling, and saying nothing. The guests were talking excitedly at the tops of their voices. There had apparently been a collision of some kind between the old school and the new. Arnold directed Geoffrey's attention to the state of affairs on the lawn.

"How are you to consult Sir Patrick with all those people about him?"

"I'll consult Sir Patrick, if I take him by the scruff of the neck and carry him into the next county!" He rose to his feet as he spoke those words, and emphasized them under his breath with an oath.

Sir Patrick entered the library, with the guests at his heels.

# CHAPTER THE NINETEENTH.

## CLOSE ON IT.

THE object of the invasion of the library by the party in the garden appeared to be twofold. Sir Patrick had entered the room to restore the newspaper to the place from which he had taken it. The guests, to the number of five, had followed him, to appeal in a body to Geoffrey Delamayn. Between these two apparently dissimilar motives there was a connection, not visible on the surface, which was now to assert itself.

Of the five guests, two were middle-aged gentlemen belonging to that large, but indistinct, division of the human family whom the hand of Nature has painted in unobtrusive neutral tint. They had absorbed the ideas of their time with such receptive capacity as they possessed; and they occupied much the same place in society which the chorus in an opera occupies on the stage. They echoed the prevalent sentiment of the moment; and they gave the solo-talker time to fetch his breath.

The three remaining guests were on the right side of thirty. All profoundly versed in horse-racing, in athletic sports, in pipes, beer, billiards, and betting. All profoundly ignorant of every thing else under the sun. All gentlemen by birth, and all marked as such by the stamp of "a University education." They may be personally described as faint reflections of Geoffrey; and they may be numerically distinguished (in the absence of all other distinction) as One, Two, and Three.

Sir Patrick laid the newspaper on the table, and placed himself in one of the comfortable arm-chairs. He was instantly assailed, in his domestic capacity, by his irrepressible sister-in-law. Lady Lundie dispatched Blanche to him with the list of her guests at the dinner. "For your uncle's approval, my dear, as head of the family."

While Sir Patrick was looking over the list, and while Arnold was making his way to Blanche, at the back of her uncle's chair, One, Two, and Three—with the Chorus in attendance on them—descended in a body on Geoffrey, at the other end of the room, and appealed in rapid succession to his superior authority, as follows:

"I say, Delamayn. We want You. Here is Sir Patrick running a regular Muck at us. Calls us aboriginal Britons. Tells us we ain't educated. Doubts if we could read, write, and cipher, if he tried us. Swears he's sick of fellows showing their arms and legs, and seeing which fellow's hardest, and who's got three belts of muscle across his wind, and who hasn't, and the like of that. Says a most infernal thing of a chap. Says—because a chap likes a healthy out-of-door life, and trains for rowing and running, and the rest of it, and don't see his way to stewing over his books—*therefore* he's safe to commit all the crimes in the calendar, murder included. Saw your name down in the newspaper for the Foot-Race; and said, when we asked him if he'd taken the odds, he'd lay any odds we liked against you in the other Race at the University—meaning, old boy, your Degree. Nasty, that about the Degree—in the opinion of Number One. Bad taste in Sir Patrick to rake up what we never mention among ourselves—in the opinion of Number Two. Un-English to sneer at a man in that way behind his back—in the opinion of Number Three. Bring him to book, Delamayn. Your name's in the papers; he can't ride rough-shod over You."

The two choral gentlemen agreed (in the minor key) with the general opinion. "Sir Patrick's views are certainly extreme, Smith?" "I think, Jones, it's desirable to hear Mr. Delamayn on the other side."

Geoffrey looked from one to the other of his admirers with an expression on his face which was quite new to them, and with something in his manner which puzzled them all.

"You can't argue with Sir Patrick yourselves," he said, "and you want me to do it?"

One, Two, Three, and the Chorus all answered, "Yes."

"I won't do it."

One, Two, Three, and the Chorus all asked, "Why?"

"Because," answered Geoffrey, "you're all wrong. And Sir Patrick's right."

Not astonishment only, but downright stupefaction, struck the deputation from the garden speechless.

Without saying a word more to any of the persons standing near him, Geoffrey walked straight up to Sir Patrick's arm-chair, and personally addressed him. The satellites followed, and listened (as well they might) in wonder.

"You will lay any odds, Sir," said Geoffrey, "against me taking my Degree? You're quite right. I sha'n't take my Degree. You doubt whether I, or any of those fellows behind me, could read, write, and cipher correctly if you tried us. You're right again—we couldn't. You say you don't know why men like Me, and men like Them, may not begin with rowing and running, and the like of that, and end in committing all the crimes in the calendar: murder included. Well! you may be right again there. Who's to know what may happen to him? or what he may not end in doing before he dies? It may be Another, or it may be Me. How do I know? and how do you?" He suddenly turned on the deputation, standing thunder-struck behind him. "If you want to know what I think, there it is for you, in plain words."

There was something, not only in the shamelessness of the declaration itself, but in the fierce pleasure that the speaker seemed to feel in making it, which struck the circle of listeners, Sir Patrick included, with a momentary chill.

In the midst of the silence a sixth guest appeared on the lawn, and stepped into the library—a silent, resolute, unassuming, elderly man, who had arrived the day before on a visit to Windygates, and who was well known, in and out of London, as one of the first consulting surgeons of his time.

"A discussion going on?" he asked. "Am I in the way?"

"There's no discussion—we are all agreed," cried Geoffrey, answering boisterously for the rest. "The more the merrier, Sir!"

After a glance at Geoffrey, the surgeon suddenly checked himself on the point of advancing to the inner part of the room, and remained standing at the window.

"I beg your pardon," said Sir Patrick, addressing himself to Geoffrey, with a grave dignity which was quite new in Arnold's experience of him. "We are *not* all agreed. I decline, Mr. Delamayn, to allow you to connect me with such an expression of feeling on your part as we have just heard. The language you have used leaves me no alternative but to meet your statement of what you suppose me to have said by my statement of what I really did say. It is not my fault if the discussion in the garden is revived before another audience in this room—it is yours."

He looked as he spoke to Arnold and Blanche, and from them to the surgeon standing at the window.

The surgeon had found an occupation for himself which completely isolated him among the rest of the guests. Keeping his own face in shadow, he was studying Geoffrey's face, in the full flood of light that fell on it, with a steady attention which must have been generally remarked, if all eyes had not been turned toward Sir Patrick at the time.

It was not an easy face to investigate at that moment.

While Sir Patrick had been speaking Geoffrey had seated himself near the window, doggedly impenetrable to the reproof of which he was the object. In his impatience to consult the one authority competent to decide the question of Arnold's position toward Anne, he had sided with Sir Patrick, as a means of ridding himself of the unwelcome presence of his friends—and he had defeated his own purpose, thanks to his own brutish incapability of bridling himself in the pursuit of it. Whether he was now discouraged under these circumstances, or whether he was simply resigned to bide his time till his time came, it was impossible, judging by outward appearances, to say. With a heavy dropping at the corners of his mouth, with a stolid indifference staring dull in his eyes, there he sat, a man forearmed, in his own obstinate neutrality, against all temptation to engage in the conflict of opinions that was to come.

Sir Patrick took up the newspaper which he had brought in from the garden, and looked once more to see if the surgeon was attending to him.

No! The surgeon's attention was absorbed in his own subject. There he was in the same position, with his mind still hard at work on something in Geoffrey which at once interested and puzzled it! "That man," he was thinking to himself, "has come here this morning after traveling from London all night. Does any ordinary fatigue explain what I see in his face? No!"

"Our little discussion in the garden," resumed Sir Patrick, answering Blanche's inquiring look as she bent over him, "began, my dear, in a paragraph here announcing Mr. Delamayn's forthcoming appearance in a foot-race in the neighborhood of London. I hold very unpopular opinions as to the athletic displays which are so much in vogue in England just now. And it is possible that I may have expressed those opinions a little too strongly, in the heat of discussion, with gentlemen who are opposed to me—I don't doubt, conscientiously opposed—on this question."

A low groan of protest rose from One, Two, and Three, in return for the little compliment which Sir Patrick had paid to them. "How about rowing and running ending in the Old Bailey and the gallows? You said that, Sir—you know you did!"

"SIR PATRICK TOOK UP THE NEWSPAPER."

The two choral gentlemen looked at each other, and agreed with the prevalent sentiment. "It came to that, I think, Smith." "Yes, Jones, it certainly came to that."

The only two men who still cared nothing about it were Geoffrey and the surgeon. There sat the first, stolidly neutral—indifferent alike to the attack and the defense. There stood the second, pursuing his investigation — with the growing interest in it of a man who was beginning to see his way to the end.

"Hear my defense, gentlemen," continued Sir Patrick, as courteously as ever. "You belong, remember, to a nation which especially claims to practice the rules of fair play. I must beg to remind you of what I said in the garden. I started with a concession. I admitted—as every person of the smallest sense must admit—that a man will, in the great majority of cases, be all the fitter for mental exercise if he wisely combines physical exercise along with it. The whole question between the two is a question of proportion and degree; and my complaint of the present time is that the present time doesn't see it. Popular opinion in England seems to me to be, not only getting to consider the cultivation of the muscles as of equal importance with the cultivation of the mind, but to be actually extending — in practice, if not in theory — to the absurd and dangerous length of putting bodily training in the first place of importance, and mental training in the second. To take a case in point: I can discover no enthusiasm in the nation any thing like so genuine and any thing like so general as the enthusiasm excited by your University boat-race. Again: I see this Athletic Education of yours made a matter of public celebration in schools and colleges; and I ask any unprejudiced witness to tell me which excites most popular enthusiasm, and which gets the most prominent place in the public journals— the exhibition, indoors (on Prize-day), of what the boys can do with their minds? or the exhibition, out of doors (on Sports-day), of what the boys can do with their bodies? You know perfectly well which performance excites the loudest cheers, which occupies the prominent place in the newspapers, and which, as a necessary consequence, confers the highest social honors on the hero of the day."

Another murmur from One, Two, and Three. "We have nothing to say to that, Sir; have it all your own way, so far."

Another ratification of agreement with the prevalent opinion between Smith and Jones.

"Very good," pursued Sir Patrick. "We are all of one mind as to which way the public feeling sets. If it is a feeling to be respected and encouraged, show me the national advantage which has resulted from it. Where is the influence of this modern outburst of manly enthusiasm on the serious concerns of life? and how has it improved the character of the people at large? Are we any of us individually readier than we ever were to sacrifice our own little private interests to the public good? Are we dealing with the serious social questions of our time in a conspicuously determined, downright, and definite way? Are we becoming a visibly and indisputably purer people in our code of commercial morals? Is there a healthier and higher tone in those public amusements which faithfully reflect in all countries the public taste? Produce me affirmative answers to these questions, which rest on solid proof, and I'll accept the present mania for athletic sports as something better than an outbreak of our insular boastfulness and our insular barbarity in a new form."

"Question! question!" in a general cry, from One, Two, and Three.

"Question! question!" in meek reverberation, from Smith and Jones.

"That *is* the question," rejoined Sir Patrick. "You admit the existence of the public feeling; and I ask, what good does it do?"

"What harm does it do?" from One, Two, and Three.

"Hear! hear!" from Smith and Jones.

"That's a fair challenge," replied Sir Patrick. "I am bound to meet you on that new ground. I won't point, gentlemen, by way of answer, to the coarseness which I can see growing on our national manners, or to the deterioration which appears to me to be spreading more and more widely in our national tastes. You may tell me with perfect truth that I am too old a man to be a fair judge of manners and tastes which have got beyond my standards. We will try the issue, as it now stands between us, on its abstract merits only. I assert that a state of public feeling which does practically place physical training, in its estimation, above moral and mental training, is a positively bad and dangerous state of feeling in this, that it encourages the inbred reluctance in humanity to submit to the demands which moral and mental cultivation must inevitably make on it. Which am I, as a boy, naturally most ready to do—to try how high I can jump? or to try how much I can learn? Which training comes easiest to me as a young man? The training which teaches me to handle an oar? or the training which teaches me to return good for evil, and to love my neighbor as myself? Of those two experiments, of those two trainings, which ought society in England to meet with the warmest encouragement? And which does society in England practically encourage, as a matter of fact?"

"What did you say yourself just now?" from One, Two, and Three.

"Remarkably well put!" from Smith and Jones.

"I said," admitted Sir Patrick, "that a man will go all the better to his books for his healthy physical exercise. And I say that again—provided the physical exercise be restrained within fit limits. But when public feeling enters into the question, and directly exalts the bodily exercises above the books—then I say public feeling is in a dangerous extreme. The bodily exercises, in that case, will be uppermost in the youth's thoughts, will have the strongest hold on his interest, will take the lion's share of his time, and will, by those means—barring the few purely exceptional instances—slowly and surely end in leaving him, to all good moral and mental purpose, certainly an uncultivated, and, possibly, a dangerous man."

A cry from the camp of the adversaries: "He's got to it at last! A man who leads an out-of-door life, and uses the strength that God has given to him, is a dangerous man. Did any body ever hear the like of that?"

Cry reverberated, with variations, by the two human echoes: "No! Nobody ever heard the like of that!"

"Clear your minds of cant, gentlemen," answered Sir Patrick. "The agricultural laborer leads an out-of-door life, and uses the strength that God has given to him. The sailor in the merchant service does the same. Both are an uncultivated, a shamefully uncultivated, class—and see the result! Look at the Map of Crime, and you will find the most hideous offenses in the calendar, committed — not in the towns, where the average man doesn't lead an out-of-door life, doesn't as a rule, use his strength, but *is*, as a rule, comparatively cultivated—not in the towns, but in the agricultural districts. As for the English sailor—except when the Royal Navy catches and cultivates him—ask Mr. Brinkworth, who has served in the merchant navy, what sort of specimen of the moral influence of out-of-door life and muscular cultivation *he* is."

"In nine cases out of ten," said Arnold, "he is as idle and vicious a ruffian as walks the earth."

Another cry from the Opposition: "Are *we* agricultural laborers? Are *we* sailors in the merchant service?"

A smart reverberation from the human echoes: "Smith! am I a laborer?" "Jones! am I a sailor?"

"Pray let us not be personal, gentlemen," said Sir Patrick. "I am speaking generally; and I can only meet extreme objections by pushing my argument to extreme limits. The laborer and the sailor have served my purpose. If the laborer and the sailor offend you, by all means let them walk off the stage! I hold to the position which I advanced just now. A man may be well born, well off, well dressed, well fed—but if he is an uncultivated man, he is (in spite of all those advantages) a man with special capacities for evil in him, on that very account. Don't mistake me! I am far from saying that the present rage for exclusively muscular accomplishments must lead inevitably downward to the lowest deep of depravity. Fortunately for society, all special depravity is more or less certainly the result, in the first instance, of special temptation. The ordinary mass of us, thank God, pass through life without being exposed to other than ordinary temptations. Thousands of the young gentlemen, devoted to the favorite pursuits of the present time, will get through existence with no worse consequences to themselves than a coarse tone of mind and manners, and a lamentable incapability of feeling any of those higher and gentler influences which sweeten and purify the lives of more cultivated men. But take the other case (which may occur to any body), the case of a special temptation trying a modern young man of your prosperous class and of mine. And let me beg Mr. Delamayn to honor with his attention what I have now to say, because it refers to the opinion which I did really express—as distinguished from the opinion which he affects to agree with, and which I never advanced."

Geoffrey's indifference showed no signs of giving way. "Go on!" he said—and still sat looking straight before him, with heavy eyes, which noticed nothing, and expressed nothing.

"Take the example which we have now in view," pursued Sir Patrick—"the example of an average young gentleman of our time, blest with every advantage that physical cultivation can bestow on him. Let this man be tried by a temptation which insidiously calls into action, in his own interests, the savage instincts latent in humanity—the instincts of self-seeking and cruelty which are at the bottom of all crime. Let this man be placed toward some other person, guiltless of injuring him, in a position which demands one of two sacrifices: the sacrifice of the other person, or the sacrifice of his own interests and his own desires. His neighbor's happiness, or his neighbor's life, stands, let us say, between him and the attainment of something that he wants. He can wreck the happiness, or strike down the life, without, to his knowledge, any fear of suffering for it himself. What is to prevent him, being the man he is, from going straight to his end, on those conditions? Will the skill in rowing, the swiftness in running, the admirable capacity and endurance in other physical exercises, which he has attained, by a strenuous cultivation in this kind that has excluded any similarly strenuous cultivation in other kinds—will these physical attainments help him to win a purely moral victory over his own selfishness and his own cruelty? They won't even help him to see that it *is* selfishness, and that it *is* cruelty. The essential principle of his rowing and racing (a harmless principle enough, if you can be sure of applying it to rowing and racing only) has taught him to take every advantage of another man that his superior strength and superior cunning can suggest. There has been nothing in his training to soften the barbarous hardness in his heart, and to enlighten the barbarous darkness in his mind. Temptation finds this man defenseless, when temptation passes his way. I don't care who he is, or how high he stands accidentally in the social scale—he is, to all moral intents and purposes, an Animal, and nothing more. If my happiness stands in his way—and if he can do it with impunity to himself—he will trample down my happiness. If my life happens to be the next obstacle he encounters—and if he can do it with impunity to himself—he will trample down my life. Not, Mr. Delamayn, in the character of a victim to irresistible fatality, or to blind chance; but in the character of a man who has sown the seed, and reaps the harvest. That, Sir, is the case which I put as an extreme case only, when this discussion began. As an extreme case only—but as a perfectly possible case, at the same time—I restate it now."

Before the advocates of the other side of the question could open their lips to reply, Geoffrey suddenly flung off his indifference, and started to his feet.

"Stop!" he cried, threatening the others, in his fierce impatience to answer for himself, with his clenched fist.

There was a general silence.

Geoffrey turned and looked at Sir Patrick, as if Sir Patrick had personally insulted him.

"Who is this anonymous man, who finds his way to his own ends, and pities nobody and sticks at nothing?" he asked. "Give him a name!"

"I am quoting an example," said Sir Patrick. "I am not attacking a man."

"What right have you," cried Geoffrey—utterly forgetful, in the strange exasperation that had seized on him, of the interest that he had in controlling himself before Sir Patrick—"what right have you to pick out an example of a row-ing man who is an infernal scoundrel—when it's quite as likely that a rowing man may be a good fellow: ay! and a better fellow, if you come to that, than ever stood in your shoes!"

"If the one case is quite as likely to occur as the other (which I readily admit)," answered Sir Patrick, "I have surely a right to choose which case I please for illustration. (Wait, Mr. Delamayn! These are the last words I have to say, and I mean to say them.) I have taken the example—not of a specially depraved man, as you erroneously suppose—but of an average man, with his average share of the mean, cruel, and dangerous qualities, which are part and parcel of unreformed human nature—as your religion tells you, and as you may see for yourself, if you choose to look at your untaught fellow-creatures any where. I suppose that man to be tried by a temptation to wickedness, out of the common; and I show, to the best of my ability, how completely the moral and mental neglect of himself, which the present material tone of public feeling in England has tacitly encouraged, leaves him at the mercy of all the worst instincts in his nature; and how surely, under those conditions, he *must* go down (gentleman as he is) step by step—as the lowest vagabond in the streets goes down under *his* special temptation—from the beginning in ignorance to the end in crime. If you deny my right to take such an example as that, in illustration of the views I advocate, you must either deny that a special temptation to wickedness can assail a man in the position of a gentleman; or you must assert that gentlemen who are naturally superior to all temptation are the only gentlemen who devote themselves to athletic pursuits. There is my defense. In stating my case, I have spoken out of my own sincere respect for the interests of virtue and of learning: out of my own sincere admiration for those young men among us who are resisting the contagion of barbarism about them. In *their* future is the future hope of England. I have done."

Angrily ready with a violent personal reply, Geoffrey found himself checked, in his turn, by another person with something to say, and with a resolution to say it at that particular moment.

For some little time past the surgeon had discontinued his steady investigation of Geoffrey's face, and had given all his attention to the discussion, with the air of a man whose self-imposed task had come to an end. As the last sentence fell from the last speaker's lips, he interposed so quickly and so skillfully between Geoffrey and Sir Patrick, that Geoffrey himself was taken by surprise.

"There is something still wanting to make Sir Patrick's statement of the case complete," he said. "I think I can supply it, from the result of my own professional experience. Before I say what I have to say, Mr. Delamayn will perhaps excuse me, if I venture on giving him a caution to control himself."

"Are *you* going to make a dead set at me, too?" inquired Geoffrey.

"I am recommending you to keep your temper—nothing more. There are plenty of men who can fly into a passion without doing themselves any particular harm. You are not one of them."

"What do you mean?"

"I don't think the state of your health, Mr. Delamayn, is quite so satisfactory as you may be disposed to consider it yourself."

Geoffrey turned to his admirers and adherents with a roar of derisive laughter. The admirers and adherents all echoed him together. Arnold and Blanche smiled at each other. Even Sir Patrick looked as if he could hardly credit the evidence of his own ears. There stood the modern Hercules, self-vindicated as a Hercules, before all eyes that looked at him. And there, opposite, stood a man whom he could have killed with one blow of his fist, telling him, in serious earnest, that he was not in perfect health!

"You are a rare fellow!" said Geoffrey, half in jest and half in anger. "What's the matter with me?"

"I have undertaken to give you, what I believe to be, a necessary caution," answered the surgeon. "I have *not* undertaken to tell you what I think is the matter with you. That may be a question for consideration some little time hence. In the mean while, I should like to put my impression about you to the test. Have you any objection to answer a question on a matter of no particular importance relating to yourself?"

"Let's hear the question first."

"I have noticed something in your behavior while Sir Patrick was speaking. You are as much interested in opposing his views as any of those gentlemen about you. I don't understand your sitting in silence, and leaving it entirely to the others to put the case on your side —until Sir Patrick said something which happened to irritate you. Had you, all the time before that, no answer ready in your own mind?"

"I had as good answers in my mind as any that have been made here to-day."

"And yet you didn't give them?"

"No; I didn't give them."

"Perhaps you felt—though you knew your objections to be good ones—that it was hardly worth while to take the trouble of putting them into words? In short, you let your friends answer for you, rather than make the effort of answering for yourself?"

Geoffrey looked at his medical adviser with a sudden curiosity and a sudden distrust.

"I say," he asked, "how do you come to know what's going on in my mind—without my telling you of it?"

"It is my business to find out what is going on in people's bodies—and to do that it is sometimes necessary for me to find out (if I can) what is going on in their minds. If I have rightly interpreted what was going on in *your* mind, there is no need for me to press my question. You have answered it already."

He turned to Sir Patrick next.

"There is a side to this subject," he said, "which you have not touched on yet. There is a Physical objection to the present rage for muscular exercises of all sorts, which is quite as strong, in its way, as the Moral objection. You have stated the consequences as they *may* affect the mind. I can state the consequences as they *do* affect the body."

"From your own experience?"

"From my own experience. I can tell you, as a medical man, that a proportion, and not by any means a small one, of the young men who are now putting themselves to violent athletic tests of their strength and endurance, are taking that course to the serious and permanent injury of their own health. The public who attend rowing-matches, foot-races, and other exhibitions of that sort, see nothing but the successful results of muscular training. Fathers and mothers at home see the failures. There are households in England—miserable households, to be counted, Sir Patrick, by more than ones and twos—in which there are young men who have to thank the strain laid on their constitutions by the popular physical displays of the present time, for being broken men, and invalided men, for the rest of their lives."

"Do you hear that?" said Sir Patrick, looking at Geoffrey.

Geoffrey carelessly nodded his head. His irritation had had time to subside: the stolid indifference had got possession of him again. He had resumed his chair—he sat, with outstretched legs, staring stupidly at the pattern on the carpet. "What does it matter to Me?" was the sentiment expressed all over him, from head to foot.

The surgeon went on.

"I can see no remedy for this sad state of things," he said, "as long as the public feeling remains what the public feeling is now. A fine healthy-looking young man, with a superb muscular development, longs (naturally enough) to distinguish himself like others. The training-authorities at his college, or elsewhere, take him in hand (naturally enough again) on the strength of outward appearances. And whether they have been right or wrong in choosing him is more than they can say, until the experiment has been tried, and the mischief has been, in many cases, irretrievably done. How many of them are aware of the important physiological truth, that the muscular power of a man is no fair guarantee of his vital power? How many of them know that we all have (as a great French writer puts it) two lives in us—the surface life of the muscles, and the inner life of the heart, lungs, and brain? Even if they did know this—even with medical men to help them—it would be in the last degree doubtful, in most cases, whether any previous examination would result in any reliable discovery of the vital fitness of the man to undergo the stress of muscular exertion laid on him. Apply to any of my brethren; and they will tell you, as the result of their own professional observation, that I am, in no sense, overstating this serious evil, or exaggerating the deplorable and dangerous consequences to which it leads. I have a patient at this moment, who is a young man of twenty, and who possesses one of the finest muscular developments I ever saw in my life. If that young man had consulted me, before he followed the example of the other young men about him, I can not honestly say that I could have foreseen the results. As things are, after going through a certain amount of muscular training, after performing a certain number of muscular feats, he suddenly fainted one day, to the astonishment of his family and friends. I was called in, and I have watched the case since. He will probably live, but he will never recover. I am obliged to take precautions with this youth of twenty which I should take with an old man of eighty. He is big enough and muscular enough to sit to a painter as a model for Samson—and only last week I saw him swoon away like a young girl, in his mother's arms."

"Name!" cried Geoffrey's admirers, still fighting the battle on their side, in the absence of any encouragement from Geoffrey himself.

"I am not in the habit of mentioning my patients' names," replied the surgeon. "But if you insist on my producing an example of a man broken by athletic exercises, I can do it."

"Do it! Who is he?"

"You all know him perfectly well."

"Is he in the doctor's hands?"

"Not yet."

"Where is he?"

"There?"

In a pause of breathless silence—with the eyes of every person in the room eagerly fastened on him—the surgeon lifted his hand and pointed to Geoffrey Delamayn.

---

## CHAPTER THE TWENTIETH.

### TOUCHING IT.

As soon as the general stupefaction was allayed, the general incredulity asserted itself as a matter of course.

The man who first declared that "seeing" was "believing" laid his finger (whether he knew it himself or not) on one of the fundamental follies of humanity. The easiest of all evidence to receive is the evidence that requires no other judgment to decide on it than the judgment of the eye—and it will be, on that account, the evidence which humanity is most ready to credit, as long as humanity lasts. The eyes of every body looked at Geoffrey; and the judgment of every body decided, on the evidence there visible, that the surgeon must be wrong. Lady Lundie herself (disturbed over her dinner invitations) led the general protest. "Mr. Delamayn in broken health!" she exclaimed, appealing to the better sense of her eminent medical guest. "Really, now, you can't expect us to believe that!"

Stung into action for the second time by the startling assertion of which he had been made the subject, Geoffrey rose, and looked the surgeon, steadily and insolently, straight in the face.

"Do you mean what you say?" he asked.

"Yes."

"You point me out before all these people—"

"One moment, Mr. Delamayn. I admit that I may have been wrong in directing the general attention to you. You have a right to complain of my having answered too publicly the public challenge offered to me by your friends. I apologize for having done that. But I don't retract a single word of what I have said on the subject of your health."

"You stick to it that I'm a broken-down man?"

"I do."

"I wish you were twenty years younger, Sir?"

"Why?"

"I'd ask you to step out on the lawn there; and I'd show you whether I'm a broken-down man or not."

Lady Lundie looked at her brother-in-law. Sir Patrick instantly interfered.

"Mr. Delamayn," he said, "you were invited here in the character of a gentleman, and you are a guest in a lady's house."

"No! no!" said the surgeon, good-humoredly. "Mr. Delamayn is using a strong argument, Sir Patrick—and that is all. If I *were* twenty years younger," he went on, addressing himself to Geoffrey, "and if I *did* step out on the lawn with you, the result wouldn't affect the question between us in the least. I don't say that the violent bodily exercises in which you are famous have damaged your muscular power. I assert that they have damaged your vital power. In what particular way they have affected it I don't consider myself bound to tell you. I simply give you a warning, as a matter of common humanity. You will do well to be content with the success you have already achieved in the field of athletic pursuits, and to alter your mode of life for the future. Accept my excuses, once more, for having said this publicly instead of privately —and don't forget my warning."

He turned to move away to another part of the room. Geoffrey fairly forced him to return to the subject.

"Wait a bit," he said. "You have had your innings. My turn now. I can't give it words as you do; but I can come to the point. And, by the Lord, I'll fix you to it! In ten days or a fortnight from this I'm going into training for the Foot-Race at Fulham. Do you say I shall break down?"

"You will probably get through your training."

"Shall I get through the race?"

"You may *possibly* get through the race. But if you do—"

"If I do?"

"You will never run another."

"And never row in another match?"

"Never."

"I have been asked to row in the Race, next spring; and I have said I will. Do you tell me, in so many words, that I sha'n't be able to do it?"

"Yes—in so many words."

"Positively?"

"Positively."

"Back your opinion!" cried Geoffrey, tearing his betting-book out of his pocket. "I lay you an even hundred I'm in fit condition to row in the University Match next spring."

"I don't bet, Mr. Delamayn."

With that final reply the surgeon walked away to the other end of the library. Lady Lundie (taking Blanche in custody) withdrew, at the same time, to return to the serious business of her invitations for the dinner. Geoffrey turned defiantly, book in hand, to his college friends about him. The British blood was up; and the British resolution to bet, which successfully defies common decency and common-law from one end of the country to the other, was not to be trifled with.

"Come on!" cried Geoffrey. "Back the doctor, one of you!"

Sir Patrick rose in undisguised disgust, and followed the surgeon. One, Two, and Three, invited to business by their illustrious friend, shook their thick heads at him knowingly, and answered with one accord, in one eloquent word —"Gammon!"

"One of *you* back him!" persisted Geoffrey, appealing to the two choral gentlemen in the

"AN EVEN HUNDRED ON THE DOCTOR."

back-ground, with his temper fast rising to fever heat. The two choral gentlemen compared notes, as usual. "We weren't born yesterday, Smith?" "Not if we know it, Jones."

"Smith!" said Geoffrey, with a sudden assumption of politeness ominous of something unpleasant to come.

Smith said "Yes?"—with a smile.

"Jones!"

Jones said "Yes?" — with a reflection of Smith.

"You're a couple of infernal cads—and you haven't got a hundred pound between you!"

"Come! come!" said Arnold, interfering for the first time. "This is shameful, Geoffrey!"

"Why the"—(never mind what!)—"won't they any of them take the bet?"

"If you must be a fool," returned Arnold, a little irritably on his side, "and if nothing else will keep you quiet, I'll take the bet."

"An even hundred on the doctor!" cried Geoffrey. "Done with you!"

His highest aspirations were satisfied; his temper was in perfect order again. He entered the bet in his book; and made his excuses to Smith and Jones in the heartiest way. "No offense, old chaps! Shake hands!" The two choral gentlemen were enchanted with him. "The English aristocracy—eh, Smith?" "Blood and breeding—ah, Jones!"

As soon as he had spoken, Arnold's conscience reproached him: not for betting (who is ashamed of that form of gambling in England?), but for "backing the doctor." With the best intention toward his friend, he was speculating on the failure of his friend's health. He anxiously assured Geoffrey that no man in the room could be more heartily persuaded that the surgeon was wrong

than himself. "I don't cry off from the bet," he said. "But, my dear fellow, pray understand that I only take it to please you."

"Bother all that!" answered Geoffrey, with the steady eye to business, which was one of the choicest virtues in his character. "A bet's a bet—and hang your sentiment!" He drew Arnold by the arm out of ear-shot of the others. "I say!" he asked, anxiously. "Do you think I've set the old fogy's back up?"

"Do you mean Sir Patrick?"

Geoffrey nodded, and went on.

"I haven't put that little matter to him yet—about marrying in Scotland, you know. Suppose he cuts up rough with me if I try him now?" His eye wandered cunningly, as he put the question, to the farther end of the room. The surgeon was looking over a port-folio of prints. The ladies were still at work on their notes of invitation. Sir Patrick was alone at the book-shelves, immersed in a volume which he had just taken down.

"Make an apology," suggested Arnold. "Sir Patrick may be a little irritable and bitter; but he's a just man and a kind man. Say you were not guilty of any intentional disrespect toward him—and you will say enough."

"All right!"

Sir Patrick, deep in an old Venetian edition of The Decameron, found himself suddenly recalled from medieval Italy to modern England, by no less a person than Geoffrey Delamayn.

"What do you want?" he asked, coldly.

"I want to make an apology," said Geoffrey. "Let by-gones be by-gones—and that sort of thing. I wasn't guilty of any intentional disrespect toward you. Forgive and forget. Not half a bad motto, Sir—eh?"

It was clumsily expressed—but still it was an apology. Not even Geoffrey could appeal to Sir Patrick's courtesy and Sir Patrick's consideration in vain.

"Not a word more, Mr. Delamayn!" said the polite old man. "Accept my excuses for any thing which I may have said too sharply, on my side; and let us by all means forget the rest."

Having met the advance made to him, in those terms, he paused, expecting Geoffrey to leave him free to return to the Decameron. To his unutterable astonishment, Geoffrey suddenly stooped over him, and whispered in his ear, "I want a word in private with you."

Sir Patrick started back, as if Geoffrey had tried to bite him.

"I beg your pardon, Mr. Delamayn—what did you say?"

"Could you give me a word in private?"

Sir Patrick put back the Decameron; and bowed in freezing silence. The confidence of the Honorable Geoffrey Delamayn was the last confidence in the world into which he desired to be drawn. "This is the secret of the apology!" he thought. "What can he possibly want with Me?"

"It's about a friend of mine," pursued Geoffrey; leading the way toward one of the windows. "He's in a scrape, my friend is. And I want to ask your advice. It's strictly private, you know." There he came to a full stop—and looked to see what impression he had produced, so far.

Sir Patrick declined, either by word or gesture, to exhibit the slightest anxiety to hear a word more.

"Would you mind taking a turn in the garden?" asked Geoffrey.

Sir Patrick pointed to his lame foot. "I have had my allowance of walking this morning," he said. "Let my infirmity excuse me."

Geoffrey looked about him for a substitute for the garden, and led the way back again toward one of the convenient curtained recesses opening out of the inner wall of the library. "We shall be private enough here," he said.

Sir Patrick made a final effort to escape the proposed conference—an undisguised effort, this time.

"Pray forgive me, Mr. Delamayn. Are you quite sure that you apply to the right person, in applying to *me?*"

"You're a Scotch lawyer, ain't you?"

"Certainly."

"And you understand about Scotch marriages—eh?"

Sir Patrick's manner suddenly altered.

"Is *that* the subject you wish to consult me on?" he asked.

"It's not me. It's my friend."

"Your friend, then?"

"Yes. It's a scrape with a woman. Here, in Scotland. My friend don't know whether he's married to her or not."

"I am at your service, Mr. Delamayn."

To Geoffrey's relief—by no means unmixed with surprise—Sir Patrick not only showed no further reluctance to be consulted by him, but actually advanced to meet his wishes, by leading the way to the recess that was nearest to them. The quick brain of the old lawyer had put Geoffrey's application to him for assistance, and

Blanche's application to him for assistance, together; and had built its own theory on the basis thus obtained. "Do I see a connection between the present position of Blanche's governess, and the present position of Mr. Delamayn's 'friend?'" thought Sir Patrick. "Stranger extremes than *that* have met me in my experience. Something may come out of this."

The two strangely-assorted companions seated themselves, one on each side of a little table in the recess. Arnold and the other guests had idled out again on to the lawn. The surgeon with his prints, and the ladies with their invitations, were safely absorbed in a distant part of the library. The conference between the two men, so trifling in appearance, so terrible in its destined influence, not over Anne's future only, but over the future of Arnold and Blanche, was, to all practical purposes, a conference with closed doors.

"Now," said Sir Patrick, "what is the question?"

"The question," said Geoffrey, "is whether my friend is married to her or not?"

"Did he mean to marry her?"

"No."

"He being a single man, and she being a single woman, at the time? And both in Scotland?"

"Yes."

"Very well. Now tell me the circumstances."

Geoffrey hesitated. The art of stating circumstances implies the cultivation of a very rare gift—the gift of arranging ideas. No one was better acquainted with this truth than Sir Patrick. He was purposely puzzling Geoffrey at starting, under the firm conviction that his client had something to conceal from him. The one process that could be depended on for extracting the truth, under those circumstances, was the process of interrogation. If Geoffrey was submitted to it, at the outset, his cunning might take the alarm. Sir Patrick's object was to make the man himself invite interrogation. Geoffrey invited it forthwith, by attempting to state the circumstances, and by involving them in the usual confusion. Sir Patrick waited until he had thoroughly lost the thread of his narrative—and then played for the winning trick.

"Would it be easier to you if I asked a few questions?" he inquired, innocently.

"Much easier."

"I am quite at your service. Suppose we clear the ground to begin with? Are you at liberty to mention names?"

"No."

"Places?"

"No."

"Dates?"

"Do you want me to be particular?"

"Be as particular as you can."

"Will it do, if I say the present year?"

"Yes. Were your friend and the lady—at some time in the present year—traveling together in Scotland?"

"No."

"Living together in Scotland?"

"No."

"What *were* they doing together in Scotland?"

"Well—they were meeting each other at an inn."

"Oh? They were meeting each other at an inn. Which was first at the rendezvous?"

"The woman was first. Stop a bit! We are getting to it now." He produced from his pocket the written memorandum of Arnold's proceedings at Craig Fernie, which he had taken down from Arnold's own lips. "I've got a bit of note here," he went on. "Perhaps you'd like to have a look at it?"

Sir Patrick took the note—read it rapidly through to himself—then re-read it, sentence by sentence, to Geoffrey; using it as a text to speak from, in making further inquiries.

" 'He asked for her by the name of his wife, at the door,' " read Sir Patrick. "Meaning, I presume, the door of the inn? Had the lady previously given herself out as a married woman to the people of the inn?"

"Yes."

"How long had she been at the inn before the gentleman joined her?"

"Only an hour or so."

"Did she give a name?"

"I can't be quite sure—I should say not."

"Did the gentleman give a name?"

"No. I'm certain he didn't."

Sir Patrick returned to the memorandum.

" 'He said at dinner, before the landlady and the waiter, I take these rooms for my wife. He made her say he was her husband, at the same time.' Was that done jocosely, Mr. Delamayn—either by the lady or the gentleman?"

"No. It was done in downright earnest."

"You mean it was done to look like earnest, and so to deceive the landlady and the waiter?"

"Yes."

Sir Patrick returned to the memorandum.

" 'After that, he stopped all night.' Stopped in the rooms he had taken for himself and his wife?"

"Yes."

"And what happened the next day?"

"He went away. Wait a bit! Said he had business for an excuse."

"That is to say, he kept up the deception with the people of the inn? and left the lady behind him, in the character of his wife?"

"That's it."

"Did he go back to the inn?"

"No."

"How long did the lady stay there, after he had gone?"

"She staid—well, she staid a few days."

"And your friend has not seen her since?"

"No."

"Are your friend and the lady English or Scotch?"

"Both English."

"At the time when they met at the inn, had they either of them arrived in Scotland, from the place in which they were previously living, within a period of less than twenty-one days?"

Geoffrey hesitated. There could be no difficulty in answering for Anne. Lady Lundie and her domestic circle had occupied Windygates for a much longer period than three weeks before the date of the lawn-party. The question, as it affected Arnold, was the only question that required reflection. After searching his memory for details of the conversation which had taken place between them, when he and Arnold had met at the lawn-party, Geoffrey recalled a certain reference on the part of his friend to a performance at the Edinburgh theatre, which at once decided the question of time. Arnold had been necessarily detained in Edinburgh, before his arrival at Windygates, by legal business connected with his inheritance; and he, like Anne, had certainly been in Scotland, before they met at Craig Fernie, for a longer period than a period of three weeks. He accordingly informed Sir Patrick that the lady and gentleman had been in Scotland for more than twenty-one days—and then added a question on his own behalf: "Don't let me hurry you, Sir—but, shall you soon have done?"

"I shall have done, after two more questions," answered Sir Patrick. "Am I to understand that the lady claims, on the strength of the circumstances which you have mentioned to me, to be your friend's wife?"

Geoffrey made an affirmative reply. The readiest means of obtaining Sir Patrick's opinion was, in this case, to answer, Yes. In other words, to represent Anne (in the character of "the lady") as claiming to be married to Arnold (in the character of "his friend").

Having made this concession to circumstances, he was, at the same time, quite cunning enough to see that it was of vital importance to the purpose which he had in view, to confine himself strictly to this one perversion of the truth. There could be plainly no depending on the lawyer's opinion, unless that opinion was given on the facts exactly as they had occurred at the inn. To the facts he had, thus far, carefully adhered; and to the facts (with the one inevitable departure from them which had been just forced on him) he determined to adhere to the end.

"Did no letters pass between the lady and gentleman?" pursued Sir Patrick.

"None that I know of," answered Geoffrey, steadily returning to the truth.

"I have done, Mr. Delamayn."

"Well? and what's your opinion?"

"Before I give my opinion I am bound to preface it by a personal statement which you are not to take, if you please, as a statement of the law. You ask me to decide—on the facts with which you have supplied me—whether your friend is, according to the law of Scotland, married or not?"

Geoffrey nodded. "That's it!" he said, eagerly.

"My experience, Mr. Delamayn, is that any single man, in Scotland, may marry any single woman, at any time, and under any circumstances. In short, after thirty years' practice as a lawyer, I don't know what is not a marriage in Scotland."

"In plain English," said Geoffrey, "you mean she's his wife?"

In spite of his cunning; in spite of his self-command, his eyes brightened as he said those words. And the tone in which he spoke—though too carefully guarded to be a tone of triumph—was, to a fine ear, unmistakably a tone of relief.

Neither the look nor the tone was lost on Sir Patrick.

His first suspicion, when he sat down to the conference, had been the obvious suspicion that, in speaking of "his friend," Geoffrey was speaking of himself. But, like all lawyers, he habitually distrusted first impressions, his own included. His object, thus far, had been to solve the problem of Geoffrey's true position and Geoffrey's real motive. He had set the snare accordingly, and had caught his bird.

It was now plain to his mind—first, that this man who was consulting him, was, in all probability, really speaking of the case of another person : secondly, that he had an interest (of what nature it was impossible yet to say) in satisfying his own mind that "his friend" was, by the law of Scotland, indisputably a married man. Having penetrated to that extent the secret which Geoffrey was concealing from him, he abandoned the hope of making any further advance at that present sitting. The next question to clear up in the investigation, was the question of who the anonymous "lady" might be. And the next discovery to make was, whether "the lady" could, or could not, be identified with Anne Silvester. Pending the inevitable delay in reaching that result, the straight course was (in Sir Patrick's present state of uncertainty) the only course to follow in laying down the law. He at once took the question of the marriage in hand—with no concealment whatever, as to the legal bearings of it, from the client who was consulting him.

"Don't rush to conclusions, Mr. Delamayn," he said. "I have only told you what my general experience is thus far. My professional opinion on the special case of your friend has not been given yet."

Geoffrey's face clouded again. Sir Patrick carefully noted the new change in it.

"The law of Scotland," he went on, "so far as it relates to Irregular Marriages, is an outrage on common decency and common-sense. If you think my language in thus describing it too strong —I can refer you to the language of a judicial authority. Lord Deas delivered a recent judgment of marriage in Scotland, from the bench, in these words : 'Consent makes marriage. No form or ceremony, civil or religious; no notice before, or publication after; no cohabitation, no writing, no witnesses even, are essential to the constitution of this, the most important contract which two persons can enter into.'—There is a Scotch judge's own statement of the law that he administers! Observe, at the same time, if you please, that we make full legal provision in Scotland for contracts affecting the sale of houses and lands, horses and dogs. The only contract which we leave without safeguards or precautions of any sort is the contract that unites a man and a woman for life. As for the authority of parents, and the innocence of children, our law recognizes no claim on it either in the one case or in the other. A girl of twelve and a boy of fourteen have nothing to do but to cross the Border, and to be married—without the interposition of the slightest delay or restraint, and without the slightest attempt to inform their parents on the part of the Scotch law. As to the marriages of men and women, even the mere interchange of consent which, as you have just heard, makes them man and wife, is not required to be directly proved : it may be proved by inference. And, more even than that, whatever the law for its consistency may presume, men and women are, in point of fact, held to be married in Scotland where consent has never been interchanged, and where the parties do not even know that they are legally held to be married persons. Are you sufficiently confused about the law of Irregular Marriages in Scotland by this time, Mr. Delamayn? And have I said enough to justify the strong language I used when I undertook to describe it to you?"

"Who's that 'authority' you talked of just now?" inquired Geoffrey. "Couldn't I ask *him?*"

"You might find him flatly contradicted, if you did ask him, by another authority equally learned and equally eminent," answered Sir Patrick. "I am not joking—I am only stating facts. Have you heard of the Queen's Commission?"

"No."

"Then listen to this. In March, 'sixty-five, the Queen appointed a Commission to inquire into the Marriage-Laws of the United Kingdom. The Report of that Commission is published in London ; and is accessible to any body who chooses to pay the price of two or three shillings for it. One of the results of the inquiry was, the discovery that high authorities were of entirely contrary opinions on one of the vital questions of Scottish marriage-law. And the Commissioners, in announcing that fact, add that the question of which opinion is right is still disputed, and has never been made the subject of legal decision. Authorities are every where at variance throughout the Report. A haze of doubt and uncertainty hangs in Scotland over the most important contract of civilized life. If no other reason existed for reforming the Scotch marriage-law, there would be reason enough afforded by that one fact. An uncertain marriage-law is a national calamity."

"You can tell me what you think yourself about my friend's case—can't you?" said Geoffrey, still holding obstinately to the end that he had in view.

"Certainly. Now that I have given you due warning of the danger of implicitly relying on any individual opinion, I may give *my* opinion with a clear conscience. I say that there has *not* been a positive marriage in this case. There has been evidence in favor of possibly establishing a marriage—nothing more."

The distinction here was far too fine to be appreciated by Geoffrey's mind. He frowned heavily, in bewilderment and disgust.

"Not married!" he exclaimed, "when they said they were man and wife, before witnesses?"

"That is a common popular error," said Sir Patrick. "As I have already told you, witnesses are not legally necessary to make a marriage in Scotland. They are only valuable—as in this case—to help, at some future time, in proving a marriage that is in dispute."

Geoffrey caught at the last words.

"The landlady and the waiter *might* make it out to be a marriage, then?" he said.

"Yes. And, remember, if you choose to apply to one of my professional colleagues, he might possibly tell you they were married already. A state of the law which allows the interchange of matrimonial consent to be proved by inference leaves a wide door open to conjecture. Your friend refers to a certain lady, in so many words, as his wife. The lady refers to your friend, in so many words, as her husband. In the rooms which they have taken, as man and wife, they remain, as man and wife, till the next morning. Your friend goes away, without undeceiving any body. The lady stays at the inn, for some days after, in the character of his wife. And all these circumstances take place in the presence of competent witnesses. Logically—if not legally—there is apparently an inference of the interchange of matrimonial consent here. I stick to my own opinion, nevertheless. Evidence in proof of a marriage (I say)—nothing more."

While Sir Patrick had been speaking, Geoffrey had been considering with himself. By dint of hard thinking he had found his way to a decisive question on his side.

"Look here!" he said, dropping his heavy hand down on the table. "I want to bring you to book, Sir! Suppose my friend had another lady in his eye?"

"Yes?"

"As things are now—would you advise him to marry her?"

"As things are now—certainly not!"

Geoffrey got briskly on his legs, and closed the interview.

"That will do," he said, "for him and for me."

With those words he walked back, without ceremony, into the main thoroughfare of the room.

"I don't know who your friend is," thought Sir Patrick, looking after him. "But if your interest in the question of his marriage is an honest and a harmless interest, I know no more of human nature than the babe unborn!"

Immediately on leaving Sir Patrick, Geoffrey was encountered by one of the servants in search of him.

"I beg your pardon, Sir," began the man. "The groom from the Honorable Mr. Delamayn's—"

"Yes? The fellow who brought me a note from my brother this morning?"

"He's expected back, Sir — he's afraid he mustn't wait any longer."

"Come here, and I'll give you the answer for him."

He led the way to the writing-table, and referred to Julius's letter again. He ran his eye carelessly over it, until he reached the final lines: "Come to-morrow, and help us to receive Mrs. Glenarm." For a while he paused, with his eye fixed on that sentence; and with the happiness of three people—of Anne, who had loved him; of Arnold, who had served him; of Blanche, guiltless of injuring him—resting on the decision that guided his movements for the next day. After what had passed that morning between Arnold and Blanche, if he remained at Lady Lundie's, he had no alternative but to perform his promise to Anne. If he returned to his brother's house, he had no alternative but to desert Anne, on the infamous pretext that she was Arnold's wife.

He suddenly tossed the letter away from him on the table, and snatched a sheet of note-paper out of the writing-case. "Here goes for Mrs. Glenarm!" he said to himself; and wrote back to his brother, in one line: "Dear Julius, Expect me to-morrow. G. D." The impassible man-servant stood by while he wrote, looking at his magnificent breadth of chest, and thinking

what a glorious "staying-power" was there for the last terrible mile of the coming race.

"There you are!" he said, and handed his note to the man.

"All right, Geoffrey?" asked a friendly voice behind him.

He turned—and saw Arnold, anxious for news of the consultation with Sir Patrick.

"Yes," he said. "All right."

NOTE.—There are certain readers who feel a disposition to doubt Facts, when they meet with them in a work of fiction. Persons of this way of thinking may be profitably referred to the book which first suggested to me the idea of writing the present Novel. The book is the Report of the Royal Commissioners on The Laws of Marriage. Published by the Queen's Printers. For her Majesty's Stationery Office. (London, 1868.) What Sir Patrick says professionally of Scotch Marriages in this chapter is taken from this high authority. What the lawyer (in the Prologue) says professionally of Irish Marriages is also derived from the same source. It is needless to encumber these pages with quotations. But as a means of satisfying my readers that they may depend on me, I subjoin an extract from my list of references to the Report of the Marriage Commission, which any persons who may be so inclined can verify for themselves.

*Irish Marriages* (in the Prologue).—See Report, pages XII., XIII., XXIV.

*Irregular Marriages in Scotland.*—Statement of the law by Lord Deas. Report, page XVI.—Marriages of children of tender years. Examination of Mr. Muirhead by Lord Chelmsford (Question 689).—Interchange of consent, established by inference. Examination of Mr. Muirhead by the Lord Justice Clerk (Question 654).—Marriage where consent has never been interchanged. Observations of Lord Deas. Report, page XIX.—Contradiction of opinions between authorities. Report, pages XIX., XX.—Legal provision for the sale of horses and dogs. No legal provision for the marriage of men and women. Mr. Seeton's Remarks. Report, page XXX.—Conclusion of the Commissioners. In spite of the arguments advanced before them in favor of not interfering with Irregular Marriages in Scotland, the Commissioners declare their opinion that "Such marriages ought not to continue." (Report, page XXXIV.)

In reference to the arguments (alluded to above) in favor of allowing the present disgraceful state of things to continue, I find them resting mainly on these grounds: That Scotland doesn't like being interfered with by England (!). That Irregular Marriages cost nothing (!!). That they are diminishing in number, and may therefore be trusted, in course of time, to exhaust themselves (!!!). That they act, on certain occasions, in the capacity of a moral trap to catch a profligate man (!!!!). Such is the elevated point of view from which the Institution of Marriage is regarded by some of the most pious and learned men in Scotland. A legal enactment providing for the sale of your wife, when you have done with her, or of your husband, when you "really can't put up with him any longer," appears to be all that is wanting to render this North British estimate of the "Estate of Matrimony" practically complete. It is only fair to add that, of the witnesses giving evidence—oral and written—before the Commissioners, fully one-half regard the Irregular Marriages of Scotland from the Christian and the civilized point of view, and entirely agree with the authoritative conclusion already cited—that such marriages ought to be abolished.　　　　W. C.

---

## CHAPTER THE TWENTY-FIRST.

### DONE!

ARNOLD was a little surprised by the curt manner in which Geoffrey answered him.

"Has Sir Patrick said any thing unpleasant?" he asked.

"Sir Patrick has said just what I wanted him to say."

"No difficulty about the marriage?"

"None."

" No fear of Blanche—"

" She won't ask you to go to Craig Fernie—I'll answer for that!" He said the words with a strong emphasis on them, took his brother's letter from the table, snatched up his hat, and went out.

His friends, idling on the lawn, hailed him. He passed by them quickly without answering, without so much as a glance at them over his shoulder. Arriving at the rose-garden, he stopped and took out his pipe; then suddenly changed his mind, and turned back again by another path. There was no certainty, at that hour of the day, of his being left alone in the rose-garden. He had a fierce and hungry longing to be by himself; he felt as if he could have been the death of any body who came and spoke to him at that moment. With his head down and his brows knit heavily, he followed the path to see what it ended in. It ended in a wicket-gate which led into a kitchen-garden. Here he was well out of the way of interruption : there was nothing to attract visitors in the kitchen-garden. He went on to a walnut-tree planted in the middle of the inclosure, with a wooden bench and a broad strip of turf running round it. After first looking about him, he seated himself and lit his pipe.

" I wish it was done !" he said.

He sat, with his elbows on his knees, smoking and thinking. Before long the restlessness that had got possession of him forced him to his feet again. He rose, and paced round and round the strip of green-sward under the walnut-tree, like a wild beast in a cage.

What was the meaning of this disturbance in the inner man ? Now that he had committed himself to the betrayal of the friend who had trusted and served him, was he torn by remorse ?

He was no more torn by remorse than you are while your eye is passing over this sentence. He was simply in a raging fever of impatience to see himself safely landed at the end which he had in view.

Why should he feel remorse ? All remorse springs, more or less directly, from the action of two sentiments, which are neither of them inbred in the natural man. The first of these sentiments is the product of the respect which we learn to feel for ourselves. The second is the product of the respect which we learn to feel for others. In their highest manifestations, these two feelings exalt themselves, until the first becomes the love of God, and the second the love of Man. I have injured you, and I repent of it when it is done. Why should I repent of it if I have gained something by it for my own self, and if you can't make me feel it by injuring Me ? I repent of it, because there has been a sense put into me which tells me that I have sinned against Myself, and sinned against You. No such sense as that exists among the instincts of the natural man. And no such feelings as these troubled Geoffrey Delamayn ; for Geoffrey Delamayn was the natural man.

When the idea of his scheme had sprung to life in his mind, the novelty of it had startled him—the enormous daring of it, suddenly self-revealed, had daunted him. The signs of emotion which he had betrayed at the writing-table in the library were the signs of mere mental perturbation, and of nothing more.

That first vivid impression past, the idea had made itself familiar to him. He had become composed enough to see such difficulties as it involved, and such consequences as it implied. These had fretted him with a passing trouble; for these he plainly discerned. As for the cruelty and the treachery of the thing he meditated doing—that consideration never crossed the limits of his mental view. His position toward the man whose life he had preserved was the position of a dog. The " noble animal" who has saved you or me from drowning will fly at your throat or mine, under certain conditions, ten minutes afterward. Add to the dog's unreasoning instinct the calculating cunning of a man ; suppose yourself to be in a position to say of some trifling thing, " Curious! at such and such a time I happened to pick up such and such an object; and now it turns out to be of some use to me !"—and there you have an index to the state of Geoffrey's feeling toward his friend when he recalled the past or when he contemplated the future. When Arnold had spoken to him at the critical moment, Arnold had violently irritated him ; and that was all.

The same impenetrable insensibility, the same primitively natural condition of the moral being, prevented him from being troubled by the slightest sense of pity for Anne. " She's out of my way !" was his first thought. " She's provided for, without any trouble to Me !" was his second. He was not in the least uneasy about her. Not the slightest doubt crossed his mind that, when once she had realized her own situation, when once she saw herself placed between the two alternatives of facing her own ruin or of claiming Arnold as a last resource, she would claim Arnold. She would do it as a matter of course; because he would have done it in her place.

But he wanted it over. He was wild, as he paced round and round the walnut-tree, to hurry on the crisis and be done with it. Give me my freedom to go to the other woman, and to train for the foot-race—that's what I want. They injured ? Confusion to them both! It's I who am injured by them. They are the worst enemies I have! They stand in my way.

How to be rid of them ? There was the difficulty. He had made up his mind to be rid of them that day. How was he to begin ?

There was no picking a quarrel with Arnold, and so beginning with him. This course of proceeding, in Arnold's position toward Blanche, would lead to a scandal at the outset—a scandal which would stand in the way of his making the right impression on Mrs. Glenarm. The woman —lonely and friendless, with her sex and her position both against her if she tried to make a scandal of it—the woman was the one to begin with. Settle it at once and forever with Anne; and leave Arnold to hear of it and deal with it, sooner or later, no matter which.

How was he to break it to her before the day was out ?

By going to the inn and openly addressing her to her face as Mrs. Arnold Brinkworth ? No ! He had had enough, at Windygates, of meeting her face to face. The easy way was to write to her, and send the letter, by the first messenger he could find, to the inn. She might appear afterward at Windygates ; she might follow him to his brother's ; she might appeal to his father.

It didn't matter; he had got the whip-hand of her now. "You are a married woman." There was the one sufficient answer, which was strong enough to back him in denying any thing!

He made out the letter in his own mind. "Something like this would do," he thought, as he went round and round the walnut-tree: "You may be surprised not to have seen me. You have only yourself to thank for it. I know what took place between you and him at the inn. I have had a lawyer's advice. You are Arnold Brinkworth's wife. I wish you joy, and good-by forever." Address those lines: "To Mrs. Arnold Brinkworth;" instruct the messenger to leave the letter late that night, without waiting for an answer; start the first thing the next morning for his brother's house; and behold, it was done!

But even here there was an obstacle—one last exasperating obstacle—still in the way.

If she was known at the inn by any name at all, it was by the name of Mrs. Silvester. A letter addressed to "Mrs. Arnold Brinkworth" would probably not be taken in at the door; or if it was admitted, and if it was actually offered to her, she might decline to receive it, as a letter not addressed to herself. A man of readier mental resources would have seen that the name on the outside of the letter mattered little or nothing, so long as the contents were read by the person to whom they were addressed. But Geoffrey's was the order of mind which expresses disturbance by attaching importance to trifles. He attached an absurd importance to preserving absolute consistency in his letter, outside and in. If he declared her to be Arnold Brinkworth's wife, he must direct to her as Arnold Brinkworth's wife; or who could tell what the law might say, or what scrape he might not get himself into by a mere scratch of the pen! The more he thought of it, the more persuaded he felt of his own cleverness here, and the hotter and the angrier he grew.

There is a way out of every thing. And there was surely a way out of this, if he could only see it.

He failed to see it. After dealing with all the great difficulties, the small difficulty proved too much for him. It struck him that he might have been thinking too long about it—considering that he was not accustomed to thinking long about any thing. Besides, his head was getting giddy, with going mechanically round and round the tree. He irritably turned his back on the tree, and struck into another path: resolved to think of something else, and then to return to his difficulty, and see it with a new eye.

Leaving his thoughts free to wander where they liked, his thoughts naturally busied themselves with the next subject that was uppermost in his mind, the subject of the Foot-Race. In a week's time his arrangements ought to be made. Now, as to the training, first.

He decided on employing two trainers this time. One to travel to Scotland, and begin with him at his brother's house. The other to take him up, with a fresh eye to him, on his return to London. He turned over in his mind the performances of the formidable rival against whom he was to be matched. That other man was the swiftest runner of the two. The betting in Geoffrey's favor was betting which calculated on the unparalleled length of the race, and on Geoffrey's prodigious powers of endurance. How long he should "wait on" the man? Whereabouts it would be safe to "pick the man up?" How near the end to calculate the man's exhaustion to a nicety, and "put on the spurt," and pass him? These were nice points to decide. The deliberations of a pedestrian-privy-council would be required to help him under this heavy responsibility. What men could he trust? He could trust A. and B.—both of them authorities: both of them stanch. Query about C.? As an authority, unexceptionable; as a man, doubtful. The problem relating to C. brought him to a standstill—and declined to be solved, even then. Never mind! he could always take the advice of A. and B. In the mean time, devote C. to the infernal regions; and, thus dismissing him, try and think of something else. What else? Mrs. Glenarm? Oh, bother the women! one of them is the same as another. They all waddle when they run; and they all fill their stomachs before dinner with sloppy tea. That's the only difference between women and men—the rest is nothing but a weak imitation of Us. Devote the women to the infernal regions; and, so dismissing *them*, try and think of something else. Of what? Of something worth thinking of, this time—of filling another pipe.

He took out his tobacco-pouch; and suddenly suspended operations at the moment of opening it.

What was the object he saw, on the other side of a row of dwarf pear-trees, away to the right? A woman—evidently a servant by her dress—stooping down with her back to him, gathering something: herbs they looked like, as well as he could make them out at the distance.

What was that thing hanging by a string at the woman's side? A slate? Yes. What the deuce did she want with a slate at her side? He was in search of something to divert his mind—and here it was found. "Any thing will do for me," he thought. "Suppose I 'chaff' her a little about her slate?"

He called to the woman across the pear-trees. "Hullo!"

The woman raised herself, and advanced toward him slowly—looking at him, as she came on, with the sunken eyes, the sorrow-stricken face, the stony tranquillity of Hester Dethridge.

Geoffrey was staggered. He had not bargained for exchanging the dullest producible vulgarities of human speech (called in the language of slang, "Chaff") with such a woman as this.

"What's that slate for?" he asked, not knowing what else to say, to begin with.

The woman lifted her hand to her lips—touched them—and shook her head.

"Dumb?"

The woman bowed her head.

"Who are you?"

The woman wrote on her slate, and handed it to him over the pear-trees. He read:—"I am the cook."

"Well, cook, were you born dumb?"

The woman shook her head.

"What struck you dumb?"

The woman wrote on her slate:—"A blow."

"Who gave you the blow?"

She shook her head.

"Won't you tell me?"

She shook her head again.

Her eyes had rested on his face while he was questioning her; staring at him, cold, dull, and changeless as the eyes of a corpse. Firm as his nerves were—dense as he was, on all ordinary occasions, to any thing in the shape of an imaginative impression—the eyes of the dumb cook slowly penetrated him with a stealthy inner chill. Something crept at the marrow of his back, and shuddered under the roots of his hair. He felt a sudden impulse to get away from her. It was simple enough; he had only to say good-morning, and go on. He did say good-morning—but he never moved. He put his hand into his pocket, and offered her some money, as a way of making *her* go. She stretched out her hand across the pear-trees to take it—and stopped abruptly, with her arm suspended in the air. A sinister change passed over the deathlike tranquillity of her face. Her closed lips slowly dropped apart. Her dull eyes slowly dilated; looked away, sideways, from *his* eyes; stopped again; and stared, rigid and glittering, over his shoulder—stared as if they saw a sight of horror behind him. "What the devil are you looking at?" he asked—and turned round quickly, with a start. There was neither person nor thing to be seen behind him. He turned back again to the woman. The woman had left him, under the influence of some sudden panic. She was hurrying away from him—running, old as she was—flying the sight of him, as if the sight of him was the pestilence.

"Mad!" he thought—and turned his back on the sight of her.

He found himself (hardly knowing how he had got there) under the walnut-tree once more. In a few minutes his hardy nerves had recovered themselves—he could laugh over the remembrance of the strange impression that had been produced on him. "Frightened for the first time in my life," he thought—"and that by an old woman! It's time I went into training again, when things have come to this!"

He looked at his watch. It was close on the luncheon hour up at the house; and he had not decided yet what to do about his letter to Anne. He resolved to decide, then and there.

The woman—the dumb woman, with the stony face and the horrid eyes — reappeared in his thoughts, and got in the way of his decision. Pooh! some crazed old servant, who might once have been cook; who was kept out of charity now. Nothing more important than that. No more of her! no more of her!

He laid himself down on the grass, and gave his mind to the serious question. How to address Anne as "Mrs. Arnold Brinkworth?" and how to make sure of her receiving the letter?

The dumb old woman got in his way again.

He closed his eyes impatiently, and tried to shut her out in a darkness of his own making.

The woman showed herself through the darkness. He saw her, as if he had just asked her a question, writing on her slate. What she wrote he failed to make out. It was all over in an instant. He started up, with a feeling of astonishment at himself—and, at the same moment, his brain cleared with the suddenness of a flash of light. He saw his way, without a conscious effort on his own part, through the difficulty that had troubled him. Two envelopes, of course: an inner one, unsealed, and addressed to "Mrs. Arnold Brinkworth;" an outer one, sealed, and addressed to "Mrs. Silvester:" and there was the problem solved! Surely the simplest problem that had ever puzzled a stupid head.

Why had he not seen it before? Impossible to say.

How came he to have seen it now?

The dumb old woman reappeared in his thoughts—as if the answer to the question lay in something connected with *her*.

He became alarmed about himself, for the first time in his life. Had this persistent impression, produced by nothing but a crazy old woman, any thing to do with the broken health which the surgeon had talked about? Was his head on the turn? Or had he smoked too much on an empty stomach, and gone too long (after traveling all night) without his customary drink of ale?

He left the garden to put that latter theory to the test forthwith. The betting would have gone dead against him if the public had seen him at that moment. He looked haggard and anxious —and with good reason too. His nervous system had suddenly forced itself on his notice, without the slightest previous introduction, and was saying (in an unknown tongue), Here I am!

Returning to the purely ornamental part of the grounds, Geoffrey encountered one of the footmen giving a message to one of the gardeners. He at once asked for the butler—as the only safe authority to consult in the present emergency.

Conducted to the butler's pantry, Geoffrey requested that functionary to produce a jug of his oldest ale, with appropriate solid nourishment in the shape of "a hunk of bread and cheese."

The butler stared. As a form of condescension among the upper classes this was quite new to him.

"Luncheon will be ready directly, Sir."

"What is there for lunch?"

The butler ran over an appetizing list of good dishes and rare wines.

"The devil take your kickshaws!" said Geoffrey. "Give me my old ale, and my hunk of bread and cheese."

"Where will you take them, Sir?"

"Here, to be sure! And the sooner the better."

The butler issued the necessary orders with all needful alacrity. He spread the simple refreshment demanded, before his distinguished guest, in a state of blank bewilderment. Here was a nobleman's son, and a public celebrity into the bargain, filling himself with bread and cheese and ale, in at once the most voracious and the most unpretending manner, at *his* table! The butler ventured on a little complimentary familiarity. He smiled, and touched the betting-book in his breast-pocket. "I've put six pound on you, Sir, for the Race." "All right, old boy! you shall win your money!" With those noble words the honorable gentleman clapped him on the back, and held out his tumbler for some more ale. The butler felt trebly an Englishman as he filled the foaming glass. Ah! foreign nations may have their revolutions! foreign aristocracies may tumble down! The British aristocracy lives in the hearts of the people, and lives forever!

"Another!" said Geoffrey, presenting his empty glass. "Here's luck!" He tossed off his liquor at a draught, and nodded to the butler, and went out.

Had the experiment succeeded? Had he proved his own theory about himself to be right? Not a doubt of it! An empty stomach, and a determination of tobacco to the head—these were the true causes of that strange state of mind into which he had fallen in the kitchen-garden. The dumb woman with the stony face vanished as if in a mist. He felt nothing now but a comfortable buzzing in his head, a genial warmth all over him, and an unlimited capacity for carrying any responsibility that could rest on mortal shoulders. Geoffrey was himself again.

He went round toward the library, to write his letter to Anne—and so have done with that, to begin with. The company had collected in the library waiting for the luncheon-bell. All were idly talking; and some would be certain, if he showed himself, to fasten on *him*. He turned back again, without showing himself. The only way of writing in peace and quietness would be to wait until they were all at luncheon, and then return to the library. The same opportunity would serve also for finding a messenger to take the letter, without exciting attention, and for going away afterward, unseen, on a long walk by himself. An absence of two or three hours would cast the necessary dust in Arnold's eyes; for it would be certainly interpreted by him as meaning absence at an interview with Anne.

He strolled idly through the grounds, farther and farther away from the house.

The talk in the library—aimless and empty enough, for the most part—was talk to the purpose, in one corner of the room, in which Sir Patrick and Blanche were sitting together.

"Uncle! I have been watching you for the last minute or two."

"At my age, Blanche, that is paying me a very pretty compliment."

"Do you know what I have seen?"

"You have seen an old gentleman in want of his lunch."

"I have seen an old gentleman with something on his mind. What is it?"

"Suppressed gout, my dear."

"That won't do! I am not to be put off in that way. Uncle! I want to know—"

"Stop there, Blanche! A young lady who says she 'wants to know,' expresses very dangerous sentiments. Eve 'wanted to know'—and see what it led to. Faust 'wanted to know'—and got into bad company, as the necessary result."

"You are feeling anxious about something," persisted Blanche. "And, what is more, Sir Patrick, you behaved in a most unaccountable manner a little while since."

"When?"

"When you went and hid yourself with Mr. Delamayn in that snug corner there. I saw you lead the way in, while I was at work on Lady Lundie's odious dinner-invitations."

"Oh! you call that being at work, do you? I wonder whether there was ever a woman yet who could give the whole of her mind to any earthly thing that she had to do?"

"Never mind the women! What subject in common could you and Mr. Delamayn possibly have to talk about? And why do I see a wrinkle between your eyebrows, now you have done with him?—a wrinkle which certainly wasn't there before you had that private conference together?"

Before answering, Sir Patrick considered whether he should take Blanche into his confidence or not. The attempt to identify Geoffrey's unnamed "lady," which he was determined to make, would no doubt lead him to Craig Fernie, and would no doubt end in obliging him to address himself to Anne. Blanche's intimate knowledge of her friend might unquestionably be made useful to him under these circumstances; and Blanche's discretion was to be trusted in any matter in which Miss Silvester's interests were concerned. On the other hand, caution was imperatively necessary, in the present imperfect state of his information—and caution, in Sir Patrick's mind, carried the day. He decided to wait and see what came first of his investigation at the inn.

"Mr. Delamayn consulted me on a dry point of law, in which a friend of his was interested," said Sir Patrick. "You have wasted your curiosity, my dear, on a subject totally unworthy of a lady's notice."

Blanche's penetration was not to be deceived on such easy terms as these. "Why not say at once that you won't tell me?" she rejoined. "*You* shutting yourself up with Mr. Delamayn to talk law! *You* looking absent and anxious about it afterward! I am a very unhappy girl!" said Blanche, with a little, bitter sigh. "There is something in me that seems to repel the people I love. Not a word in confidence can I get from Anne. And not a word in confidence can I get from you. And I do so long to sympathize! It's very hard. I think I shall go to Arnold."

Sir Patrick took his niece's hand.

"Stop a minute, Blanche. About Miss Silvester? Have you heard from her to-day?"

"No. I am more unhappy about her than words can say."

"Suppose somebody went to Craig Fernie and tried to find out the cause of Miss Silvester's silence? Would you believe that somebody sympathized with you then?"

Blanche's face flushed brightly with pleasure and surprise. She raised Sir Patrick's hand gratefully to her lips.

"Oh!" she exclaimed. "You don't mean that *you* would do that?"

"I am certainly the last person who ought to do it—seeing that you went to the inn in flat rebellion against my orders, and that I only forgave you, on your own promise of amendment, the other day. It is a miserably weak proceeding on the part of 'the head of the family' to be turning his back on his own principles, because his niece happens to be anxious and unhappy. Still (if you could lend me your little carriage), I *might* take a surly drive toward Craig Fernie, all by myself, and I *might* stumble against Miss Silvester—in case you have any thing to say."

"Any thing to say?" repeated Blanche. She put her arm round her uncle's neck, and whispered in his ear one of the most interminable messages that ever was sent from one human being to another. Sir Patrick listened, with a growing interest in the inquiry on which he was secretly bent. "The woman must have some noble qualities," he thought, "who can inspire such devotion as this."

While Blanche was whispering to her uncle, a second private conference—of the purely domestic sort—was taking place between Lady Lundie and the butler, in the hall outside the library door.

"I am sorry to say, my lady, Hester Dethridge has broken out again."

"What do you mean?"

"She was all right, my lady, when she went into the kitchen-garden, some time since. She's taken strange again, now she has come back. Wants the rest of the day to herself, your ladyship. Says she's overworked, with all the company in the house—and, I must say, does look like a person troubled and worn out in body and mind."

"Don't talk nonsense, Roberts! The woman is obstinate and idle and insolent. She is now in the house, as you know, under a month's notice to leave. If she doesn't choose to do her duty for that month I shall refuse to give her a character. Who is to cook the dinner to-day if I give Hester Dethridge leave to go out?"

"Any way, my lady, I am afraid the kitchen-maid will have to do her best to-day. Hester is very obstinate, when the fit takes her—as your ladyship says."

"If Hester Dethridge leaves the kitchen-maid to cook the dinner, Roberts, Hester Dethridge leaves my service to-day. I want no more words about it. If she persists in setting my orders at defiance, let her bring her account-book into the library, while we are at lunch, and lay it on my desk. I shall be back in the library after luncheon—and if I see the account-book I shall know what it means. In that case, you will receive my directions to settle with her and send her away. Ring the luncheon-bell."

The luncheon-bell rang. The guests all took the direction of the dining-room; Sir Patrick following, from the far end of the library, with Blanche on his arm. Arrived at the dining-room door, Blanche stopped, and asked her uncle to excuse her if she left him to go in by himself.

"I will be back directly," she said. "I have forgotten something up stairs."

Sir Patrick went in. The dining-room door closed; and Blanche returned alone to the library. Now on one pretense, and now on another, she had, for three days past, faithfully fulfilled the engagement she had made at Craig Fernie to wait ten minutes after luncheon-time in the library, on the chance of seeing Anne. On this, the fourth occasion, the faithful girl sat down alone in the great room, and waited with her eyes fixed on the lawn outside.

Five minutes passed, and nothing living appeared but the birds hopping about the grass.

In less than a minute more Blanche's quick ear caught the faint sound of a woman's dress brushing over the lawn. She ran to the nearest window, looked out, and clapped her hands with a cry of delight. There was the well-known figure, rapidly approaching her! Anne was true to their friendship—Anne had kept her engagement at last!

Blanche hurried out, and drew her into the library in triumph. "This makes amends, love, for every thing! You answer my letter in the best of all ways—you bring me your own dear self."

She placed Anne in a chair, and, lifting her veil, saw her plainly in the brilliant mid-day light.

The change in the whole woman was nothing less than dreadful to the loving eyes that rested on her. She looked years older than her real age. There was a dull calm in her face, a stagnant, stupefied submission to any thing, pitiable to see. Three days and nights of solitude and grief, three days and nights of unresting and unpartaken suspense, had crushed that sensitive nature, had frozen that warm heart. The animating spirit was gone—the mere shell of the woman lived and moved, a mockery of her former self.

"Oh, Anne! Anne! What *can* have happened to you? Are you frightened? There's not the least fear of any body disturbing us. They are all at luncheon, and the servants are at dinner. We have the room entirely to ourselves. My darling! you look so faint and strange! Let me get you something."

Anne drew Blanche's head down and kissed her. It was done in a dull, slow way—without a word, without a tear, without a sigh.

"You're tired—I'm sure you're tired. Have you walked here? You sha'n't go back on foot; I'll take care of that!"

Anne roused herself at those words. She spoke for the first time. The tone was lower than was natural to her; sadder than was natural to her—but the charm of her voice, the native gentleness and beauty of it, seemed to have survived the wreck of all besides.

"I don't go back, Blanche. I have left the inn."

"Left the inn? With your husband?"

She answered the first question—not the second.

"I can't go back," she said. "The inn is no place for me. A curse seems to follow me, Blanche, wherever I go. I am the cause of quarreling and wretchedness, without meaning it, God knows. The old man who is head-waiter at the inn has been kind to me, my dear, in his way, and he and the landlady had hard words together about it. A quarrel, a shocking, violent quarrel. He has lost his place in consequence. The woman, his mistress, lays all the blame of it to my door. She is a hard woman; and she has been harder than ever since Bishopriggs went away. I have missed a letter at the inn—I must have thrown it aside, I suppose, and forgotten it. I only know that I remembered about it, and couldn't find it last night. I told the landlady, and she fastened a quarrel on me almost before the words were out of my mouth. Asked me if I charged her with stealing my letter. Said things to me—I can't repeat them. I am not very well, and not able to deal with people of that sort. I thought it best to leave Craig Fernie this morning. I hope and pray I shall never see Craig Fernie again."

She told her little story with a total absence of emotion of any sort, and laid her head back wearily on the chair when it was done.

Blanche's eyes filled with tears at the sight of her.

"I won't tease you with questions, Anne," she said, gently. "Come up stairs and rest in my room. You're not fit to travel, love. I'll take care that nobody comes near us."

The stable-clock at Windygates struck the quarter to two. Anne raised herself in the chair with a start.

"What time was that?" she asked.

Blanche told her.

"I can't stay," she said. "I have come here to find something out, if I can. You won't ask me questions? Don't, Blanche, don't! for the sake of old times."

Blanche turned aside, heart-sick. "I will do nothing, dear, to annoy you," she said, and took Anne's hand, and hid the tears that were beginning to fall over her cheeks.

"I want to know something, Blanche. Will you tell me?"

"Yes. What is it?"

"Who are the gentlemen staying in the house?"

Blanche looked round at her again, in sudden astonishment and alarm. A vague fear seized her that Anne's mind had given way under the heavy weight of trouble laid on it. Anne persisted in pressing her strange request.

"Run over their names, Blanche. I have a reason for wishing to know who the gentlemen are who are staying in the house."

Blanche repeated the names of Lady Lundie's guests, leaving to the last the guests who had arrived last.

"Two more came back this morning," she went on. "Arnold Brinkworth and that hateful friend of his, Mr. Delamayn."

Anne's head sank back once more on the chair. She had found her way, without exciting suspicion of the truth, to the one discovery which she had come to Windygates to make. He was in Scotland again, and he had only arrived from London that morning. There was barely time for him to have communicated with Craig Fernie before she left the inn—he, too, who hated letter-writing! The circumstances were all in his favor: there was no reason, there was really and truly no reason, so far, to believe that he had deserted her. The heart of the unhappy woman bounded in her bosom, under the first ray of hope that had warmed it for four days past. Under that sudden revulsion of feeling, her weakened frame shook from head to foot. Her face flushed deep for a moment—then turned deadly pale again. Blanche, anxiously watching her, saw the serious necessity for giving some restorative to her instantly.

"I am going to get you some wine—you will faint, Anne, if you don't take something. I shall be back in a moment; and I can manage it without any body being the wiser."

She pushed Anne's chair close to the nearest open window—a window at the upper end of the library—and ran out.

Blanche had barely left the room, by the door that led into the hall, when Geoffrey entered it by one of the lower windows opening from the lawn.

With his mind absorbed in the letter that he was about to write, he slowly advanced up the room toward the nearest table. Anne, hearing the sound of footsteps, started, and looked round. Her failing strength rallied in an instant, under the sudden relief of seeing him again. She rose and advanced eagerly, with a faint tinge of color in her cheeks. He looked up. The two stood face to face together—alone.

"Geoffrey!"

He looked at her without answering—without advancing a step, on his side. There was an evil light in his eyes; his silence was the brute silence that threatens dumbly. He had made up his mind never to see her again, and she had entrapped him into an interview. He had made up his mind to write, and there she stood forcing him to speak. The sum of her offenses against him was now complete. If there had ever been the faintest hope of her raising even a passing pity in his heart, that hope would have been annihilated now.

She failed to understand the full meaning of his silence. She made her excuses, poor soul, for venturing back to Windygates—her excuses to the man whose purpose at that moment was to throw her helpless on the world.

"Pray forgive me for coming here," she said. "I have done nothing to compromise you, Geoffrey. Nobody but Blanche knows I am at Windygates. And I have contrived to make my inquiries about you without allowing her to suspect our secret." She stopped, and began to tremble. She saw something more in his face than she had read in it at first. "I got your letter," she went on, rallying her sinking courage. "I don't complain of its being so short: you don't like letter-writing, I know. But you promised I should hear from you again. And I have never heard. And oh, Geoffrey, it was so lonely at the inn!"

She stopped again, and supported herself by resting her hand on the table. The faintness was stealing back on her. She tried to go on again. It was useless—she could only look at him now.

"What do you want?" he asked, in the tone of a man who was putting an unimportant question to a total stranger.

A last gleam of her old energy flickered up in her face, like a dying flame.

"I am broken by what I have gone through," she said. "Don't insult me by making me remind you of your promise."

"What promise?"

"For shame, Geoffrey! for shame! Your promise to marry me."

"You claim my promise after what you have done at the inn?"

She steadied herself against the table with one hand, and put the other hand to her head. Her brain was giddy. The effort to think was too much for her. She said to herself, vacantly, "The inn? What did I do at the inn?"

"I have had a lawyer's advice, mind! I know what I am talking about."

She appeared not to have heard him. She repeated the words, "What did I do at the inn?" and gave it up in despair. Holding by the table, she came close to him and laid her hand on his arm.

"Do you refuse to marry me?" she asked.

He saw the vile opportunity, and said the vile words.

"You're married already to Arnold Brinkworth."

Without a cry to warn him, without an effort to save herself, she dropped senseless at his feet;

"HE TURNED AND FLED BY THE OPEN WINDOW."

as her mother had dropped at his father's feet in the by-gone time.

He disentangled himself from the folds of her dress. "Done!" he said, looking down at her as she lay on the floor.

As the word fell from his lips he was startled by a sound in the inner part of the house. One of the library doors had not been completely closed. Light footsteps were audible, advancing rapidly across the hall.

He turned and fled, leaving the library, as he had entered it, by the open window at the lower end of the room.

---

## CHAPTER THE TWENTY-SECOND.

### GONE.

BLANCHE came in, with a glass of wine in her hand, and saw the swooning woman on the floor.

She was alarmed, but not surprised, as she knelt by Anne, and raised her head. Her own previous observation of her friend necessarily prevented her from being at any loss to account for the fainting fit. The inevitable delay in getting the wine was—naturally to her mind—alone to blame for the result which now met her view. If she had been less ready in thus tracing the effect to the cause, she might have gone to the window to see if any thing had happened, out-of-doors, to frighten Anne — might have seen Geoffrey before he had time to turn the corner of the house—and, making that one discovery, might have altered the whole course of events, not in her coming life only, but in the coming lives of others. So do we shape our own desti-

nies, blindfold. So do we hold our poor little tenure of happiness at the capricious mercy of Chance. It is surely a blessed delusion which persuades us that we are the highest product of the great scheme of creation, and sets us doubting whether other planets are inhabited, because other planets are not surrounded by an atmosphere which *we* can breathe!

After trying such simple remedies as were within her reach, and trying them without success, Blanche became seriously alarmed. Anne lay, to all outward appearance, dead in her arms. She was on the point of calling for help —come what might of the discovery which would ensue—when the door from the hall opened once more, and Hester Dethridge entered the room.

The cook had accepted the alternative which her mistress's message had placed before her, if she insisted on having her own time at her own sole disposal for the rest of that day. Exactly as Lady Lundie had desired, she intimated her resolution to carry her point by placing her account-book on the desk in the library. It was only when this had been done that Blanche received any answer to her entreaties for help. Slowly and deliberately Hester Dethridge walked up to the spot where the young girl knelt with Anne's head on her bosom, and looked at the two without a trace of human emotion in her stern and stony face.

"Don't you see what's happened?" cried Blanche. "Are you alive or dead? Oh, Hester, I can't bring her to! Look at her! look at her!"

Hester Dethridge looked at her, and shook her head. Looked again, thought for a while, and wrote on her slate. Held out the slate over Anne's body, and showed what she had written:

"Who has done it?"

"You stupid creature!" said Blanche. "Nobody has done it."

The eyes of Hester Dethridge steadily read the worn white face, telling its own tale of sorrow mutely on Blanche's breast. The mind of Hester Dethridge steadily looked back at her own knowledge of her own miserable married life. She again returned to writing on her slate—again showed the written words to Blanche.

"Brought to it by a man. Let her be—and God will take her."

"You horrid unfeeling woman! how dare you write such an abominable thing!" With this natural outburst of indignation, Blanche looked back at Anne; and, daunted by the deathlike persistency of the swoon, appealed again to the mercy of the immovable woman who was looking down at her. "Oh, Hester! for Heaven's sake help me!"

The cook dropped her slate at her side, and bent her head gravely in sign that she submitted. She motioned to Blanche to loosen Anne's dress, and then—kneeling on one knee—took Anne to support her while it was being done.

The instant Hester Dethridge touched her, the swooning woman gave signs of life.

A faint shudder ran through her from head to foot—her eyelids trembled—half opened for a moment—and closed again. As they closed, a low sigh fluttered feebly from her lips.

Hester Dethridge put her back in Blanche's arms—considered a little with herself—returned to writing on her slate—and held out the written words once more:

"Shivered when I touched her. That means I have been walking over her grave."

Blanche turned from the sight of the slate, and from the sight of the woman, in horror. "You frighten me!" she said. "You will frighten her, if she sees you. I don't mean to offend you; but—leave us, please leave us."

Hester Dethridge accepted her dismissal, as she accepted every thing else. She bowed her head in sign that she understood—looked for the last time at Anne—dropped a stiff courtesy to her young mistress—and left the room.

An hour later the butler had paid her, and she had left the house.

Blanche breathed more freely when she found herself alone. She could feel the relief now of seeing Anne revive.

"Can you hear me, darling?" she whispered. "Can you let me leave you for a moment?"

Anne's eyes slowly opened and looked round her—in that torment and terror of reviving life which marks the awful protest of humanity against its recall to existence when mortal mercy has dared to wake it in the arms of Death.

Blanche rested Anne's head against the nearest chair, and ran to the table upon which she had placed the wine on entering the room.

After swallowing the first few drops Anne began to feel the effect of the stimulant. Blanche persisted in making her empty the glass, and refrained from asking or answering questions until her recovery under the influence of the wine was complete.

"You have overexerted yourself this morning," she said, as soon as it seemed safe to speak. "Nobody has seen you, darling—nothing has happened. Do you feel like yourself again?"

Anne made an attempt to rise and leave the library; Blanche placed her gently in the chair, and went on:

"There is not the least need to stir. We have another quarter of an hour to ourselves before any body is at all likely to disturb us. I have something to say, Anne—a little proposal to make. Will you listen to me?"

Anne took Blanche's hand, and pressed it gratefully to her lips. She made no other reply. Blanche proceeded:

"I won't ask any questions, my dear—I won't attempt to keep you here against your will—I won't even remind you of my letter yesterday. But I can't let you go, Anne, without having my mind made easy about you in some way. You will relieve all my anxiety, if you will do one thing—one easy thing, for my sake."

"What is it, Blanche?"

She put that question with her mind far away from the subject before her. Blanche was too eager in pursuit of her object to notice the absent tone, the purely mechanical manner, in which Anne had spoken to her.

"I want you to consult my uncle," she answered. "Sir Patrick is interested in you; Sir Patrick proposed to me this very day to go and see you at the inn. He is the wisest, the kindest, the dearest old man living—and you can trust him as you could trust nobody else. Will you take my uncle into your confidence, and be guided by his advice?"

With her mind still far away from the subject, Anne looked out absently at the lawn, and made no answer.

"Come!" said Blanche. "One word isn't much to say. Is it Yes or No?"

Still looking out on the lawn—still thinking of something else—Anne yielded, and said "Yes."

Blanche was enchanted. "How well I must have managed it!" she thought. "This is what my uncle means, when my uncle talks of 'putting it strongly.'"

She bent down over Anne, and gayly patted her on the shoulder.

"That's the wisest 'Yes,' darling, you ever said in your life. Wait here—and I'll go in to luncheon, or they will be sending to know what has become of me. Sir Patrick has kept my place for me, next to himself. I shall contrive to tell him what I want; and he will contrive (oh, the blessing of having to do with a clever man; there are so few of them!)—he will contrive to leave the table before the rest, without exciting any body's suspicions. Go away with him at once to the summer-house (we have been at the summer-house all the morning; nobody will go back to it now), and I will follow you as soon as I have satisfied Lady Lundie by eating some lunch. Nobody will be any the wiser but our three selves. In five minutes or less you may expect Sir Patrick. Let me go! We haven't a moment to lose!"

Anne held her back. Anne's attention was concentrated on her now.

"What is it?" she asked.

"Are you going on happily with Arnold, Blanche?"

"Arnold is nicer than ever, my dear."

"Is the day fixed for your marriage?"

"The day will be ages hence. Not till we are

back in town, at the end of the autumn. Let me go, Anne!"

"Give me a kiss, Blanche."

Blanche kissed her, and tried to release her hand. Anne held it as if she was drowning, as if her life depended on not letting it go.

"Will you always love me, Blanche, as you love me now?"

"How can you ask me!"

"*I* said Yes just now. *You* say Yes too."

Blanche said it. Anne's eyes fastened on her face, with one long, yearning look, and then Anne's hand suddenly dropped hers.

She ran out of the room, more agitated, more uneasy, than she liked to confess to herself. Never had she felt so certain of the urgent necessity of appealing to Sir Patrick's advice as she felt at that moment.

The guests were still safe at the luncheon-table when Blanche entered the dining-room.

Lady Lundie expressed the necessary surprise, in the properly graduated tone of reproof, at her step-daughter's want of punctuality. Blanche made her apologies with the most exemplary humility. She glided into her chair by her uncle's side, and took the first thing that was offered to her. Sir Patrick looked at his niece, and found himself in the company of a model young English Miss—and marveled inwardly what it might mean.

The talk, interrupted for the moment (topics, Politics and Sport—and then, when a change was wanted, Sport and Politics), was resumed again all round the table. Under cover of the conversation, and in the intervals of receiving the attentions of the gentlemen, Blanche whispered to Sir Patrick, "Don't start, uncle. Anne is in the library." (Polite Mr. Smith offered some ham. Gratefully declined.) "Pray, pray, pray go to her; she is waiting to see you—she is in dreadful trouble." (Gallant Mr. Jones proposed fruit tart and cream. Accepted with thanks.) "Take her to the summer-house: I'll follow you when I get the chance. And manage it at once, uncle, if you love me, or you will be too late."

Before Sir Patrick could whisper back a word in reply, Lady Lundie, cutting a cake of the richest Scottish composition, at the other end of the table, publicly proclaimed it to be her "own cake," and, as such, offered her brother-in-law a slice. The slice exhibited an eruption of plums and sweetmeats, overlaid by a perspiration of butter. It has been said that Sir Patrick had reached the age of seventy—it is, therefore, needless to add that he politely declined to commit an unprovoked outrage on his own stomach.

"My cake!" persisted Lady Lundie, elevating the horrible composition on a fork. "Won't that tempt you?"

Sir Patrick saw his way to slipping out of the room under cover of a compliment to his sister-in-law. He summoned his courtly smile, and laid his hand on his heart.

"A fallible mortal," he said, "is met by a temptation which he can not possibly resist. If he is a wise mortal, also, what does he do?"

"He eats some of My cake," said the prosaic Lady Lundie.

"No!" said Sir Patrick, with a look of unutterable devotion directed at his sister-in-law.

"He flies temptation, dear lady—as I do now." He bowed, and escaped, unsuspected, from the room.

Lady Lundie cast down her eyes, with an expression of virtuous indulgence for human frailty, and divided Sir Patrick's compliment modestly between herself and her cake.

Well aware that his own departure from the table would be followed in a few minutes by the rising of the lady of the house, Sir Patrick hurried to the library as fast as his lame foot would let him. Now that he was alone, his manner became anxious, and his face looked grave. He entered the room.

Not a sign of Anne Silvester was to be seen any where. The library was a perfect solitude.

"Gone!" said Sir Patrick. "This looks bad."

After a moment's reflection he went back into the hall to get his hat. It was possible that she might have been afraid of discovery if she staid in the library, and that she might have gone on to the summer-house by herself.

If she was not to not to be found in the summer-house, the quieting of Blanche's mind and the clearing up of her uncle's suspicions alike depended on discovering the place in which Miss Silvester had taken refuge. In this case time would be of importance, and the capacity of making the most of it would be a precious capacity at starting. Arriving rapidly at these conclusions, Sir Patrick rang the bell in the hall which communicated with the servants' offices, and summoned his own valet—a person of tried discretion and fidelity, nearly as old as himself.

"Get your hat, Duncan," he said, when the valet appeared, "and come out with me."

Master and servant set forth together silently, on their way through the grounds. Arrived within sight of the summer-house, Sir Patrick ordered Duncan to wait, and went on by himself.

There was not the least need for the precaution that he had taken. The summer-house was as empty as the library. He stepped out again and looked about him. Not a living creature was visible. Sir Patrick summoned his servant to join him.

"Go back to the stables, Duncan," he said, "and say that Miss Lundie lends me her pony-carriage to-day. Let it be got ready at once and kept in the stable-yard. I want to attract as little notice as possible. You are to go with me, and nobody else. Provide yourself with a railway time-table. Have you got any money?"

"Yes, Sir Patrick."

"Did you happen to see the governess (Miss Silvester) on the day when we came here—the day of the lawn-party?"

"I did, Sir Patrick."

"Should you know her again?"

"I thought her a very distinguished-looking person, Sir Patrick. I should certainly know her again."

"Have you any reason to think she noticed you?"

"She never even looked at me, Sir Patrick."

"Very good. Put a change of linen into your bag, Duncan—I may possibly want you to take a journey by railway. Wait for me in the stable-yard. This is a matter in which every thing is trusted to my discretion, and to yours."

"SHE CAME OUT AGAIN TO MEET HIM, WITH A LOOK OF BLANK DESPAIR."

"Thank you, Sir Patrick."

With that acknowledgment of the compliment which had been just paid to him, Duncan gravely went his way to the stables; and Duncan's master returned to the summer-house, to wait there until he was joined by Blanche.

Sir Patrick showed signs of failing patience during the interval of expectation through which he was now condemned to pass. He applied perpetually to the snuff-box in the knob of his cane. He fidgeted incessantly in and out of the summer-house. Anne's disappearance had placed a serious obstacle in the way of further discovery; and there was no attacking that obstacle, until precious time had been wasted in waiting to see Blanche.

At last she appeared in view, from the steps of the summer-house; breathless and eager, hastening to the place of meeting as fast as her feet would take her to it.

Sir Patrick considerately advanced, to spare her the shock of making the inevitable discovery. "Blanche," he said. "Try to prepare yourself, my dear, for a disappointment. I am alone."

"You don't mean that you have let her go?"

"My poor child! I have never seen her at all."

Blanche pushed by him, and ran into the summer-house. Sir Patrick followed her. She came out again to meet him, with a look of blank despair. "Oh, uncle! I did so truly pity her! And see how little pity she has for *me!*"

Sir Patrick put his arm round his niece, and softly patted the fair young head that dropped on his shoulder.

"Don't let us judge her harshly, my dear: we don't know what serious necessity may not plead her excuse. It is plain that she can trust nobody—and that she only consented to see me to get you out of the room and spare you the pain of parting. Compose yourself, Blanche. I don't despair of discovering where she has gone, if you will help me."

Blanche lifted her head, and dried her tears bravely.

"My father himself wasn't kinder to me than you are," she said. "Only tell me, uncle, what I can do!"

"I want to hear exactly what happened in the library," said Sir Patrick. "Forget nothing, my dear child, no matter how trifling it may be. Trifles are precious to us, and minutes are precious to us, now."

Blanche followed her instructions to the letter, her uncle listening with the closest attention. When she had completed her narrative, Sir Patrick suggested leaving the summer-house. "I have ordered your chaise," he said; "and I can tell you what I propose doing on our way to the stable-yard."

"Let me drive you, uncle!"

"Forgive me, my dear, for saying No to that. Your step-mother's suspicions are very easily excited—and you had better not be seen with me if my inquiries take me to the Craig Fernie inn. I promise, if you will remain here, to tell you every thing when I come back. Join the others in any plan they have for the afternoon—and you will prevent my absence from exciting any thing more than a passing remark. You will do as I tell you? That's a good girl! Now you shall hear how I propose to search for this poor lady, and how your little story has helped me."

He paused, considering with himself whether

he should begin by telling Blanche of his consultation with Geoffrey. Once more, he decided that question in the negative. Better to still defer taking her into his confidence until he had performed the errand of investigation on which he was now setting forth.

"What you have told me, Blanche, divides itself, in my mind, into two heads," began Sir Patrick. "There is what happened in the library before your own eyes; and there is what Miss Silvester told you had happened at the inn. As to the event in the library (in the first place), it is too late now to inquire whether that fainting-fit was the result, as you say, of mere exhaustion—or whether it was the result of something that occurred while you were out of the room."

"What could have happened while I was out of the room?"

"I know no more than you do, my dear. It is simply one of the possibilities in the case, and, as such, I notice it. To get on to what practically concerns us; if Miss Silvester is in delicate health it is impossible that she could get, unassisted, to any great distance from Windygates. She may have taken refuge in one of the cottages in our immediate neighborhood. Or she may have met with some passing vehicle from one of the farms on its way to the station, and may have asked the person driving to give her a seat in it. Or she may have walked as far as she can, and may have stopped to rest in some sheltered place, among the lanes to the south of this house."

"I'll inquire at the cottages, uncle, while you are gone."

"My dear child, there must be a dozen cottages, at least, within a circle of one mile from Windygates! Your inquiries would probably occupy you for the whole afternoon. I won't ask what Lady Lundie would think of your being away all that time by yourself. I will only remind you of two things. You would be making a public matter of an investigation which it is essential to pursue as privately as possible; and, even if you happened to hit on the right cottage, your inquiries would be completely baffled, and you would discover nothing."

"Why not?"

"I know the Scottish peasant better than you do, Blanche. In his intelligence and his sense of self-respect he is a very different being from the English peasant. He would receive you civilly, because you are a young lady; but he would let you see, at the same time, that he considered you had taken advantage of the difference between your position and his position to commit an intrusion. And if Miss Silvester had appealed, in confidence, to his hospitality, and if he had granted it, no power on earth would induce him to tell any person living that she was under his roof—without her express permission."

"But, uncle, if it's of no use making inquiries of any body, how are we to find her?"

"I don't say that nobody will answer our inquiries, my dear—I only say the peasantry won't answer them, if your friend has trusted herself to their protection. The way to find her is to look on, beyond what Miss Silvester may be doing at the present moment, to what Miss Silvester contemplates doing—let us say, before the day is out. We may assume, I think (after what has happened), that, as soon as she *can* leave this neighborhood, she assuredly *will* leave it. Do you agree, so far?"

"Yes! yes! Go on."

"Very well. She is a woman, and she is (to say the least of it) not strong. She can only leave this neighborhood either by hiring a vehicle or by traveling on the railway. I propose going first to the station. At the rate at which your pony gets over the ground, there is a fair chance, in spite of the time we have lost, of my being there as soon as she is—assuming that she leaves by the first train, up or down, that passes."

"There is a train in half an hour, uncle. She can never get there in time for that."

"She may be less exhausted than we think; or she may get a lift; or she may not be alone. How do we know but somebody may have been waiting in the lane—her husband, if there is such a person—to help her? No! I shall assume she is now on her way to the station; and I shall get there as fast as possible—"

"And stop her, if you find her there?"

"What I do, Blanche, must be left to my discretion. If I find her there, I must act for the best. If I don't find her there, I shall leave Duncan (who goes with me) on the watch for the remaining trains, until the last to-night. He knows Miss Silvester by sight, and he is sure that *she* has never noticed *him*. Whether she goes north or south, early or late, Duncan will have my orders to follow her. He is thoroughly to be relied on. If she takes the railway, I answer for it we shall know where she goes."

"How clever of you to think of Duncan!"

"Not in the least, my dear. Duncan is my factotum; and the course I am taking is the obvious course which would have occurred to any body. Let us get to the really difficult part of it now. Suppose she hires a carriage?"

"There are none to be had, except at the station."

"There are farmers about here; and farmers have light carts, or chaises, or something of the sort. It is in the last degree unlikely that they would consent to let her have them. Still, women break through difficulties which stop men. And this is a clever woman, Blanche—a woman, you may depend on it, who is bent on preventing you from tracing her. I confess I wish we had somebody we could trust lounging about where those two roads branch off from the road that leads to the railway. I must go in another direction; *I* can't do it."

"Arnold can do it!"

Sir Patrick looked a little doubtful. "Arnold is an excellent fellow," he said. "But can we trust to his discretion?"

"He is, next to you, the most perfectly discreet person I know," rejoined Blanche, in a very positive manner; "and, what is more, I have told him every thing about Anne, except what has happened to-day. I am afraid I shall tell him *that*, when I feel lonely and miserable, after you have gone. There is something in Arnold—I don't know what it is—that comforts me. Besides, do you think he would betray a secret that I gave him to keep? You don't know how devoted he is to me!"

"My dear Blanche, I am not the cherished object of his devotion; of course I don't know! You are the only authority on that point. I stand corrected. Let us have Arnold, by all means. Caution him to be careful; and send him out by himself, where the roads meet. We have now only one other place left in which there is a chance of finding a trace of her. I undertake to make the necessary investigation at the Craig Fernie inn."

"The Craig Fernie inn? Uncle! you have forgotten what I told you."

"Wait a little, my dear. Miss Silvester herself has left the inn, I grant you. But (if we should unhappily fail in finding her by any other means) Miss Silvester has left a trace to guide us at Craig Fernie. That trace must be picked up at once, in case of accidents. You don't seem to follow me? I am getting over the ground as fast as the pony gets over it. I have arrived at the second of those two heads into which your story divides itself in my mind. What did Miss Silvester tell you had happened at the inn?"

"She lost a letter at the inn."

"Exactly. She lost a letter at the inn; that is one event. And Bishopriggs, the waiter, has quarreled with Mrs. Inchbare, and has left his situation; that is another event. As to the letter first. It is either really lost, or it has been stolen. In either case, if we can lay our hands on it, there is at least a chance of its helping us to discover something. As to Bishopriggs, next—"

"You're not going to talk about the waiter, surely?"

"I am! Bishopriggs possesses two important merits. He is a link in my chain of reasoning; and he is an old friend of mine."

"A friend of yours?"

"We live in days, my dear, when one workman talks of another workman as 'that gentleman.' I march with the age, and feel bound to mention my clerk as my friend. A few years since Bishopriggs was employed in the clerks' room at my chambers. He is one of the most intelligent and most unscrupulous old vagabonds in Scotland; perfectly honest as to all average matters involving pounds, shillings, and pence; perfectly unprincipled in the pursuit of his own interests, where the violation of a trust lies on the boundary-line which marks the limit of the law. I made two unpleasant discoveries when I had him in my employment. I found that he had contrived to supply himself with a duplicate of my seal; and I had the strongest reason to suspect him of tampering with some papers belonging to two of my clients. He had done no actual mischief, so far; and I had no time to waste in making out the necessary case against him. He was dismissed from my service, as a man who was not to be trusted to respect any letters or papers that happened to pass through his hands."

"I see, uncle! I see!"

"Plain enough now—isn't it? If that missing letter of Miss Silvester's is a letter of no importance, I am inclined to believe that it is merely lost, and may be found again. If, on the other hand, there is any thing in it that could promise the most remote advantage to any person in possession of it, then, in the execrable slang of the day, I will lay any odds, Blanche, that Bishopriggs has got the letter!"

"And he has left the inn! How unfortunate!"

"Unfortunate as causing delay — nothing worse than that. Unless I am very much mistaken, Bishopriggs will come back to the inn. The old rascal (there is no denying it) is a most amusing person. He left a terrible blank when he left my clerks' room. Old customers at Craig Fernie (especially the English), in missing Bishopriggs, will, you may rely on it, miss one of the attractions of the inn. Mrs. Inchbare is not a woman to let her dignity stand in the way of her business. She and Bishopriggs will come together again, sooner or later, and make it up. When I have put certain questions to her, which may possibly lead to very important results, I shall leave a letter for Bishopriggs in Mrs. Inchbare's hands. The letter will tell him I have something for him to do, and will contain an address at which he can write to me. I shall hear of him, Blanche; and, if the letter is in his possession, I shall get it."

"Won't he be afraid—if he has stolen the letter—to tell you he has got it?"

"Very well put, my child. He might hesitate with other people. But I have my own way of dealing with him; and I know how to make him tell Me.—Enough of Bishopriggs till his time comes. There is one other point, in regard to Miss Silvester. I may have to describe her. How was she dressed when she came here? Remember, I am a man—and (if an Englishwoman's dress can be described in an Englishwoman's language) tell me, in English, what she had on."

"She wore a straw hat, with corn-flowers in it, and a white veil. Corn-flowers at one side, uncle, which is less common than corn-flowers in front. And she had on a light gray shawl. And a *Piqué*—"

"There you go with your French! Not a word more! A straw hat, with a white veil, and with corn-flowers at one side of the hat. And a light gray shawl. That's as much as the ordinary male mind can take in; and that will do. I have got my instructions, and saved precious time. So far—so good. Here we are at the end of our conference—in other words, at the gate of the stable-yard. You understand what you have to do while I am away?"

"I have to send Arnold to the cross-roads. And I have to behave (if I can) as if nothing had happened."

"Good child! Well put again! You have got what I call grasp of mind, Blanche. An invaluable faculty! You will govern the future domestic kingdom. Arnold will be nothing but a constitutional husband. Those are the only husbands who are thoroughly happy. You shall hear every thing, my love, when I come back. Got your bag, Duncan? Good. And the time-table? Good. You take the reins—I won't drive. I want to think. Driving is incompatible with intellectual exertion. A man puts his mind into his horse, and sinks to the level of that useful animal—as a necessary condition of getting to his destination without being upset. God bless you, Blanche! To the station, Duncan! to the station!"

———◆———

## CHAPTER THE TWENTY-THIRD.

### TRACED.

The chaise rattled out through the gates. The dogs barked furiously. Sir Patrick looked round, and waved his hand as he turned the corner of the road. Blanche was left alone in the yard.

She lingered a little, absently patting the dogs. They had especial claims on her sympathy at that moment; they, too, evidently thought it hard to be left behind at the house. After a while she roused herself. Sir Patrick had left the responsibility of superintending the cross-roads on her shoulders. There was something to be done yet before the arrangements for tracing Anne were complete. Blanche left the yard to do it.

On her way back to the house she met Arnold, dispatched by Lady Lundie in search of her.

The plan of occupation for the afternoon had been settled during Blanche's absence. Some demon had whispered to Lady Lundie to cultivate a taste for feudal antiquities, and to insist on spreading that taste among her guests. She had proposed an excursion to an old baronial castle among the hills—far to the westward (fortunately for Sir Patrick's chance of escaping discovery) of the hills at Craig Fernie. Some of the guests were to ride, and some to accompany their hostess in the open carriage. Looking right and left for proselytes, Lady Lundie had necessarily remarked the disappearance of certain members of her circle. Mr. Delamayn had vanished, nobody knew where. Sir Patrick and Blanche had followed his example. Her ladyship had observed, upon this, with some asperity, that if they were all to treat each other in that unceremonious manner, the sooner Windygates was turned into a Penitentiary, on the silent system, the fitter the house would be for the people who inhabited it. Under these circumstances, Arnold suggested that Blanche would do well to make her excuses as soon as possible at head-quarters, and accept the seat in the carriage which her step-mother wished her to take. "We are in for the feudal antiquities, Blanche; and we must help each other through as well as we can. If you will go in the carriage, I'll go too."

Blanche shook her head.

"There are serious reasons for *my* keeping up appearances," she said. "I shall go in the carriage. You mustn't go at all."

Arnold naturally looked a little surprised, and asked to be favored with an explanation.

Blanche took his arm and hugged it close. Now that Anne was lost, Arnold was more precious to her than ever. She literally hungered to hear at that moment, from his own lips, how fond he was of her. It mattered nothing that she was already perfectly satisfied on this point. It was so nice (after he had said it five hundred times already) to make him say it once more! "Suppose I had no explanation to give?" she said. "Would you stay behind by yourself to please *me?*"

"I would do any thing to please you!"

"Do you really love me as much as that?"

They were still in the yard; and the only witnesses present were the dogs. Arnold answered in the language without words—which is nevertheless the most expressive language in use, between men and women, all over the world.

"This is not doing my duty," said Blanche, penitently. "But, oh Arnold, I am so anxious and so miserable! And it *is* such a consolation to know that *you* won't turn your back on me too!"

With that preface she told him what had happened in the library. Even Blanche's estimate of her lover's capacity for sympathizing with her was more than realized by the effect which her narrative produced on Arnold. He was not merely surprised and sorry for her. His face showed plainly that he felt genuine concern and distress. He had never stood higher in Blanche's opinion than he stood at that moment.

"What is to be done?" he asked. "How does Sir Patrick propose to find her?"

Blanche repeated Sir Patrick's instructions relating to the cross-roads, and also to the serious necessity of pursuing the investigation in the strictest privacy. Arnold (relieved from all fear of being sent back to Craig Fernie) undertook to do every thing that was asked of him, and promised to keep the secret from every body.

They went back to the house, and met with an icy welcome from Lady Lundie. Her ladyship repeated her remark on the subject of turning Windygates into a Penitentiary for Blanche's benefit. She received Arnold's petition to be excused from going to see the castle with the barest civility. "Oh, take your walk, by all means! You may meet your friend, Mr. Delamayn—who appears to have such a passion for walking that he can't even wait till luncheon is over. As for Sir Patrick— Oh! Sir Patrick has borrowed the pony-carriage? and gone out driving by himself?—I'm sure I never meant to offend my brother-in-law when I offered him a slice of my poor little cake. Don't let me offend any body else. Dispose of your afternoon, Blanche, without the slightest reference to me. Nobody seems inclined to visit the ruins—the most interesting relic of feudal times in Perthshire, Mr. Brinkworth. It doesn't matter—oh, dear me, it doesn't matter! I can't force my guests to feel an intelligent curiosity on the subject of Scottish Antiquities. No! no! my dear Blanche!—it won't be the first time, or the last, that I have driven out alone. I don't at all object to being alone. 'My mind to me a kingdom is,' as the poet says." So Lady Lundie's outraged self-importance asserted its violated claims on human respect, until her distinguished medical guest came to the rescue and smoothed his hostess's ruffled plumes. The surgeon (he privately detested ruins) begged to go. Blanche begged to go. Smith and Jones (profoundly interested in feudal antiquities) said they would sit behind, in the "rumble"—rather than miss this unexpected treat. One, Two, and Three caught the infection, and volunteered to be the escort on horseback. Lady Lundie's celebrated "smile" (warranted to remain unaltered on her face for hours together) made its appearance once more. She issued her orders with the most charming amiability. "We'll take the guide-book," said her ladyship, with the eye to mean economy, which is only to be met with in very rich people, "and save a shilling to the man who shows the ruins." With that she went up stairs

"ARNOLD SAT DOWN ON THE SOFT HEATHER, AND LIT A CIGAR."

to array herself for the drive; and looked in the glass; and saw a perfectly virtuous, fascinating, and accomplished woman, facing her irresistibly in a new French bonnet!

At a private signal from Blanche, Arnold slipped out and repaired to his post, where the roads crossed the road that led to the railway.

There was a space of open heath on one side of him, and the stone-wall and gates of a farm-house inclosure on the other. Arnold sat down on the soft heather—and lit a cigar—and tried to see his way through the double mystery of Anne's appearance and Anne's flight.

He had interpreted his friend's absence exactly as his friend had anticipated: he could only assume that Geoffrey had gone to keep a private appointment with Anne. Miss Silvester's appearance at Windygates alone, and Miss Silvester's anxiety to hear the names of the gentlemen who were staying in the house, seemed, under these circumstances, to point to the plain conclusion that the two had, in some way, unfortunately missed each other. But what could be the motive of her flight? Whether she knew of some other place in which she might meet Geoffrey? or whether she had gone back to the inn? or whether she had acted under some sudden impulse of despair?—were questions which Arnold was necessarily quite incompetent to solve. There was no choice but to wait until an opportunity offered of reporting what had happened to Geoffrey himself.

After the lapse of half an hour, the sound of some approaching vehicle—the first sound of the sort that he had heard—attracted Arnold's attention. He started up, and saw the pony-chaise approaching him along the road from the station.

Sir Patrick, this time, was compelled to drive himself—Duncan was not with him. On discovering Arnold, he stopped the pony.

"So! so!" said the old gentleman. "You have heard all about it, I see? You understand that this is to be a secret from every body, till further notice? Very good. Has any thing happened since you have been here?"

"Nothing. Have you made any discoveries, Sir Patrick?"

"None. I got to the station before the train. No signs of Miss Silvester any where. I have left Duncan on the watch—with orders not to stir till the last train has passed to-night."

"I don't think she will turn up at the station," said Arnold. "I fancy she has gone back to Craig Fernie."

"Quite possible. I am now on my way to Craig Fernie, to make inquiries about her. I don't know how long I may be detained, or what it may lead to. If you see Blanche before I do, tell her I have instructed the station-master to let me know (if Miss Silvester does take the railway) what place she books for. Thanks to that arrangement, we sha'n't have to wait for news till Duncan can telegraph that he has seen her to her journey's end. In the mean time, you understand what you are wanted to do here?"

"Blanche has explained every thing to me."

"Stick to your post, and make good use of your eyes. You were accustomed to that, you know, when you were at sea. It's no great hardship to pass a few hours in this delicious summer air. I see you have contracted the vile modern habit of smoking—that will be occupation enough to amuse you, no doubt! Keep the roads in view; and, if she does come your way, don't attempt to stop her—you can't do that. Speak to her (quite innocently, mind!), by way of getting time enough to notice the face of the man who is driving her, and the name (if there is one) on his cart. Do that, and you will do enough. Pah! how that cigar poisons the air! What will have become of your stomach when you get to my age?"

"I sha'n't complain, Sir Patrick, if I can eat as good a dinner as you do."

"That reminds me! I met somebody I knew at the station. Hester Dethridge has left her place, and gone to London by the train. We may feed at Windygates—we have done with dining now. It has been a final quarrel this time between the mistress and the cook. I have given Hester my address in London, and told her to let me know before she decides on another place. A woman who *can't* talk, and a woman who *can* cook, is simply a woman who has arrived at absolute perfection. Such a treasure shall not go out of the family, if I can help it. Did you notice the Béchamel sauce at lunch? Pooh! a young man who smokes cigars doesn't know the difference between Béchamel sauce and melted butter. Good afternoon! good afternoon!"

He slackened the reins, and away he went to Craig Fernie. Counting by years, the pony was twenty, and the pony's driver was seventy. Counting by vivacity and spirit, two of the most youthful characters in Scotland had got together that afternoon in the same chaise.

An hour more wore itself slowly out; and nothing had passed Arnold on the cross-roads but a few stray foot-passengers, a heavy wagon, and a gig with an old woman in it. He rose again from the heather, weary of inaction, and resolved to walk backward and forward, within view of his post, for a change. At the second turn, when his face happened to be set toward the open heath, he noticed another foot-passenger—apparently a man—far away in the empty distance. Was the person coming toward him?

He advanced a little. The stranger was doubtless advancing too, so rapidly did his figure now reveal itself, beyond all doubt, as the figure of a man. A few minutes more, and Arnold fancied he recognized it. Yet a little longer, and he was quite sure. There was no mistaking the lithe strength and grace of *that* man, and the smooth easy swiftness with which he covered his ground. It was the hero of the coming foot-race. It was Geoffrey on his way back to Windygates House.

Arnold hurried forward to meet him. Geoffrey stood still, poising himself on his stick, and let the other come up.

"Have you heard what has happened at the house?" asked Arnold.

He instinctively checked the next question as it rose to his lips. There was a settled defiance in the expression of Geoffrey's face, which Arnold was quite at a loss to understand. He looked like a man who had made up his mind to confront any thing that could happen, and to contradict any body who spoke to him.

"Something seems to have annoyed you?" said Arnold.

"What's up at the house?" returned Geoffrey, with his loudest voice and his hardest look.

"Miss Silvester has been at the house."

"Who saw her?"

"Nobody but Blanche."

"Well?"

"Well, she was miserably weak and ill, so ill that she fainted, poor thing, in the library. Blanche brought her to."

"And what then?"

"We were all at lunch at the time. Blanche left the library, to speak privately to her uncle. When she went back Miss Silvester was gone, and nothing has been seen of her since."

"A row at the house?"

"Nobody knows of it at the house, except Blanche—"

"And you? And how many besides?"

"And Sir Patrick. Nobody else."

"Nobody else? Any thing more?"

Arnold remembered his promise to keep the investigation then on foot a secret from every body. Geoffrey's manner made him—unconsciously to himself—readier than he might otherwise have been to consider Geoffrey as included in the general prohibition.

"Nothing more," he answered.

Geoffrey dug the point of his stick deep into the soft, sandy ground. He looked at the stick, then suddenly pulled it out of the ground and looked at Arnold. "Good-afternoon!" he said, and went on his way again by himself.

Arnold followed, and stopped him. For a moment the two men looked at each other without a word passing on either side. Arnold spoke first.

"You're out of humor, Geoffrey. What has upset you in this way? Have you and Miss Silvester missed each other?"

Geoffrey was silent.

"Have you seen her since she left Windygates?"

No reply.

"Do you know where Miss Silvester is now?"

Still no reply. Still the same mutely-insolent defiance of look and manner. Arnold's dark color began to deepen.

"Why don't you answer me?" he said.

"Because I have had enough of it."

"Enough of what?"

"Enough of being worried about Miss Silvester. Miss Silvester's my business—not yours."

"Gently, Geoffrey! Don't forget that I have been mixed up in that business—without seeking it myself."

"There's no fear of my forgetting. You have cast it in my teeth often enough."

"Cast it in your teeth?"

"Yes! Am I never to hear the last of my obligation to you? The devil take the obligation! I'm sick of the sound of it."

There was a spirit in Arnold — not easily brought to the surface, through the overlying simplicity and good-humor of his ordinary character—which, once roused, was a spirit not readily quelled. Geoffrey had roused it at last.

"When you come to your senses," he said, "I'll remember old times — and receive your apology. Till you *do* come to your senses, go your way by yourself. I have no more to say to you."

Geoffrey set his teeth, and came one step nearer. Arnold's eyes met his, with a look which steadily and firmly challenged him—though he *was* the stronger man of the two—to force the quarrel a step further, if he dared. The one human virtue which Geoffrey respected and understood was the virtue of courage. And there it was before him—the undeniable courage of the weaker man. The callous scoundrel was touched on the one tender place in his whole being. He turned, and went on his way in silence.

Left by himself, Arnold's head dropped on his breast. The friend who had saved his life—the one friend he possessed, who was associated with his earliest and happiest remembrances of old days — had grossly insulted him: and had left him deliberately, without the slightest expression of regret. Arnold's affectionate nature—simple, loyal, clinging where it once fastened—was wounded to the quick. Geoffrey's fast-retreating figure, in the open view before him, became blurred and indistinct. He put his hand over his eyes, and hid, with a boyish shame, the hot tears that told of the heartache, and that honored the man who shed them.

He was still struggling with the emotion which had overpowered him, when something happened at the place where the roads met.

The four roads pointed as nearly as might be toward the four points of the compass. Arnold was now on the road to the eastward, having advanced in that direction to meet Geoffrey, between two and three hundred yards from the farm-house inclosure before which he had kept his watch. The road to the westward, curving away behind the farm, led to the nearest market-town. The road to the south was the way to the station. And the road to the north led back to Windygates House.

While Geoffrey was still fifty yards from the turning which would take him back to Windygates—while the tears were still standing thickly in Arnold's eyes—the gate of the farm inclosure opened. A light four-wheel chaise came out, with a man driving, and a woman sitting by his side. The woman was Anne Silvester, and the man was the owner of the farm.

Instead of taking the way which led to the station, the chaise pursued the westward road to the market-town. Proceeding in this direction, the backs of the persons in the vehicle were necessarily turned on Geoffrey, advancing behind them from the eastward. He just carelessly noticed the shabby little chaise, and then turned off north on his way to Windygates.

By the time Arnold was composed enough to look round him, the chaise had taken the curve in the road which wound behind the farm-house. He returned—faithful to the engagement which he had undertaken—to his post before the inclosure. The chaise was then a speck in the distance. In a minute more it was a speck out of sight.

So (to use Sir Patrick's phrase) had the woman broken through difficulties which would have stopped a man. So, in her sore need, had Anne Silvester won the sympathy which had given her a place, by the farmer's side, in the vehicle that took him on his own business to the market-town. And so, by a hair's-breadth, did she escape the treble risk of discovery which threatened her—from Geoffrey, on his way back; from Arnold, at his post; and from the valet, on the watch for her appearance at the station.

The afternoon wore on. The servants at Windygates, airing themselves in the grounds—

in the absence of their mistress and her guests—were disturbed, for the moment, by the unexpected return of one of "the gentlefolks." Mr Geoffrey Delamayn reappeared at the house, alone; went straight to the smoking-room; and calling for another supply of the old ale, settled himself in an arm-chair with the newspaper, and began to smoke.

He soon tired of reading, and fell into thinking of what had happened during the latter part of his walk.

The prospect before him had more than realized the most sanguine anticipations that he could have formed of it. He had braced himself—after what had happened in the library—to face the outbreak of a serious scandal, on his return to the house. And here—when he came back—was nothing to face! Here were three people (Sir Patrick, Arnold, and Blanche) who must at least know that Anne was in some serious trouble, keeping the secret as carefully as if they felt that his interests were at stake! And, more wonderful still, here was Anne herself—so far from raising a hue and cry after him—actually taking flight, without saying a word that could compromise him with any living soul!

What in the name of wonder did it mean? He did his best to find his way to an explanation of some sort; and he actually contrived to account for the silence of Blanche and her uncle, and Arnold. It was pretty clear that they must have all three combined to keep Lady Lundie in ignorance of her runaway governess's return to the house.

But the secret of Anne's silence completely baffled him.

He was simply incapable of conceiving that the horror of seeing herself set up as an obstacle to Blanche's marriage might have been vivid enough to overpower all sense of her own wrongs, and to hurry her away, resolute, in her ignorance of what else to do, never to return again, and never to let living eyes rest on her in the character of Arnold's wife. "It's clean beyond *my* making out," was the final conclusion at which Geoffrey arrived. "If it's her interest to hold her tongue, it's my interest to hold mine, and there's an end of it for the present!"

He put up his feet on a chair, and rested his magnificent muscles after his walk, and filled another pipe, in thorough contentment with himself. No interference to dread from Anne, no more awkward questions (on the terms they were on now) to come from Arnold. He looked back at the quarrel on the heath with a certain complacency—he did his friend justice; though they *had* disagreed. "Who would have thought the fellow had so much pluck in him!" he said to himself as he struck the match and lit his second pipe.

An hour more wore on; and Sir Patrick was the next person who returned.

He was thoughtful, but in no sense depressed. Judging by appearances, his errand to Craig Fernie had certainly not ended in disappointment. The old gentleman hummed his favorite little Scotch air—rather absently, perhaps—and took his pinch of snuff from the knob of his ivory cane much as usual. He went to the library bell and summoned a servant.

"Any body been here for me?"—"No, Sir Patrick."—"No letters?"—"No, Sir Patrick."—

"Very well. Come up stairs to my room, and help me on with my dressing-gown." The man helped him to his dressing-gown and slippers. "Is Miss Lundie at home?"—"No, Sir Patrick. They're all away with my lady on an excursion."—"Very good. Get me a cup of coffee; and wake me half an hour before dinner, in case I take a nap." The servant went out. Sir Patrick stretched himself on the sofa. "Ay! ay! a little aching in the back, and a certain stiffness in the legs. I dare say the pony feels just as I do. Age, I suppose, in both cases? Well! well! well! let's try and be young at heart. 'The rest' (as Pope says) 'is leather and prunella.'" He returned resignedly to his little Scotch air. The servant came in with the coffee. And then the room was quiet, except for the low humming of insects and the gentle rustling of the creepers at the window. For five minutes or so Sir Patrick sipped his coffee, and meditated—by no means in the character of a man who was depressed by any recent disappointment. In five minutes more he was asleep.

A little later, and the party returned from the ruins.

With the one exception of their lady-leader, the whole expedition was depressed—Smith and Jones, in particular, being quite speechless. Lady Lundie alone still met feudal antiquities with a cheerful front. She had cheated the man who showed the ruins of his shilling, and she was thoroughly well satisfied with herself. Her voice was flute-like in its melody, and the celebrated "smile" had never been in better order. "Deeply interesting!" said her ladyship, descending from the carriage with ponderous grace, and addressing herself to Geoffrey, lounging under the portico of the house. "You have had a loss, Mr. Delamayn. The next time you go out for a walk, give your hostess a word of warning, and you won't repent it." Blanche (looking very weary and anxious) questioned the servant, the moment she got in, about Arnold and her uncle. Sir Patrick was invisible up stairs. Mr. Brinkworth had not come back. It wanted only twenty minutes of dinner-time; and full evening-dress was insisted on at Windygates. Blanche, nevertheless, still lingered in the hall in the hope of seeing Arnold before she went up stairs. The hope was realized. As the clock struck the quarter he came in. And he, too, was out of spirits like the rest!

"Have you seen her?" asked Blanche.

"No," said Arnold, in the most perfect good faith. "The way she has escaped by is not the way by the cross-roads—I answer for that."

They separated to dress. When the party assembled again, in the library, before dinner, Blanche found her way, the moment he entered the room, to Sir Patrick's side.

"News, uncle! I'm dying for news."

"Good news, my dear—so far."

"You have found Anne?"

"Not exactly that."

"You have heard of her at Craig Fernie?"

"I have made some important discoveries at Craig Fernie, Blanche. Hush! here's your step-mother. Wait till after dinner, and you may hear more than I can tell you now. There may be news from the station between this and then."

The dinner was a wearisome ordeal to at least two other persons present besides Blanche. Ar-

nold, sitting opposite to Geoffrey, without exchanging a word with him, felt the altered relations between his former friend and himself very painfully. Sir Patrick, missing the skilled hand of Hester Dethridge in every dish that was offered to him, marked the dinner among the wasted opportunities of his life, and resented his sister-in-law's flow of spirits as something simply inhuman under present circumstances. Blanche followed Lady Lundie into the drawing-room in a state of burning impatience for the rising of the gentlemen from their wine. Her step-mother—mapping out a new antiquarian excursion for the next day, and finding Blanche's ears closed to her occasional remarks on baronial Scotland five hundred years since—lamented, with satirical emphasis, the absence of an intelligent companion of her own sex; and stretched her majestic figure on the sofa to wait until an audience worthy of her flowed in from the dining-room. Before very long—so soothing is the influence of an after-dinner view of feudal antiquities, taken through the medium of an approving conscience—Lady Lundie's eyes closed; and from Lady Lundie's nose there poured, at intervals, a sound, deep, like her ladyship's learning; regular, like her ladyship's habits—a sound associated with night-caps and bedrooms; evoked alike by Nature, the leveler, from high and low—the sound (oh, Truth, what enormities find publicity in thy name!)—the sound of a Snore.

Free to do as she pleased, Blanche left the echoes of the drawing-room in undisturbed enjoyment of Lady Lundie's audible repose.

She went into the library, and turned over the novels. Went out again, and looked across the hall at the dining-room door. Would the men never have done talking their politics and drinking their wine? She went up to her own room, and changed her ear-rings, and scolded her maid. Descended once more—and made an alarming discovery in a dark corner of the hall.

Two men were standing there, hat in hand, whispering to the butler. The butler, leaving them, went into the dining-room — came out again with Sir Patrick—and said to the two men, "Step this way, please." The two men came out into the light. Murdoch, the station-master; and Duncan, the valet! News of Anne!

"Oh, uncle, let me stay!" pleaded Blanche.

Sir Patrick hesitated. It was impossible to say—as matters stood at that moment—what distressing intelligence the two men might not have brought of the missing woman. Duncan's return, accompanied by the station-master, looked serious. Blanche instantly penetrated the secret of her uncle's hesitation. She turned pale, and caught him by the arm. "Don't send me away," she whispered. "I can bear any thing but suspense."

"Out with it!" said Sir Patrick, holding his niece's hand. "Is she found or not?"

"She's gone by the up-train," said the station-master. "And we know where."

Sir Patrick breathed freely; Blanche's color came back. In different ways, the relief to both of them was equally great.

"You had my orders to follow her," said Sir Patrick to Duncan. "Why have you come back?"

"Your man is not to blame, Sir," interposed

the station-master. "The lady took the train at Kirkandrew."

Sir Patrick started, and looked at the station-master. "Ay? ay? The next station—the market-town. Inexcusably stupid of me. I never thought of that."

"I took the liberty of telegraphing your description of the lady to Kirkandrew, Sir Patrick, in case of accidents."

"I stand corrected, Mr. Murdoch. Your head, in this matter, has been the sharper head of the two. Well?"

"There's the answer, Sir."

Sir Patrick and Blanche read the telegram together.

"Kirkandrew. Up train. 7.40 P.M. Lady as described. No luggage. Bag in her hand. Traveling alone. Ticket—second-class. Place—Edinburgh."

"Edinburgh!" repeated Blanche. "Oh, uncle! we shall lose her in a great place like that!"

"We shall find her, my dear; and you shall see how. Duncan, get me pen, ink, and paper. Mr. Murdoch, you are going back to the station, I suppose?"

"Yes, Sir Patrick."

"I will give you a telegram, to be sent at once to Edinburgh."

He wrote a carefully-worded telegraphic message, and addressed it to The Sheriff of Mid-Lothian.

"The Sheriff is an old friend of mine," he explained to his niece. "And he is now in Edinburgh. Long before the train gets to the terminus he will receive this personal description of Miss Silvester, with my request to have all her movements carefully watched till further notice. The police are entirely at his disposal; and the best men will be selected for the purpose. I have asked for an answer by telegraph. Keep a special messenger ready for it at the station, Mr. Murdoch. Thank you; good-evening. Duncan, get your supper, and make yourself comfortable. Blanche, my dear, go back to the drawing-room, and expect us in to tea immediately. You will know where your friend is before you go to bed to-night."

With those comforting words he returned to the gentlemen. In ten minutes more they all appeared in the drawing-room; and Lady Lundie (firmly persuaded that she had never closed her eyes) was back again in baronial Scotland five hundred years since.

Blanche, watching her opportunity, caught her uncle alone.

"Now for your promise," she said. "You have made some important discoveries at Craig Fernie. What are they?"

Sir Patrick's eye turned toward Geoffrey, dozing in an arm-chair in a corner of the room. He showed a certain disposition to trifle with the curiosity of his niece.

"After the discovery we have already made," he said, "can't you wait, my dear, till we get the telegram from Edinburgh?"

"That is just what it's impossible for me to do! The telegram won't come for hours yet. I want something to go on with in the mean time."

She seated herself on a sofa in the corner opposite Geoffrey, and pointed to the vacant place by her side.

Sir Patrick had promised—Sir Patrick had no choice but to keep his word. After another look at Geoffrey, he took the vacant place by his niece.

---

## CHAPTER THE TWENTY-FOURTH.

### BACKWARD.

"WELL?" whispered Blanche, taking her uncle confidentially by the arm.

"Well," said Sir Patrick, with a spark of his satirical humor flashing out at his niece, "I am going to do a very rash thing. I am going to place a serious trust in the hands of a girl of eighteen."

"The girl's hands will keep it, uncle—though she *is* only eighteen."

"I must run the risk, my dear; your intimate knowledge of Miss Silvester may be of the greatest assistance to me in the next step I take. You shall know all that I can tell you, but I must warn you first. I can only admit you into my confidence by startling you with a great surprise. Do you follow me, so far?"

"Yes! yes!"

"If you fail to control yourself, you place an obstacle in the way of my being of some future use to Miss Silvester. Remember that, and now prepare for the surprise. What did I tell you before dinner?"

"You said you had made discoveries at Craig Fernie. What have you found out?"

"I have found out that there is a certain person who is in full possession of the information which Miss Silvester has concealed from you and from me. The person is within our reach. The person is in this neighborhood. The person is in this room!"

He caught up Blanche's hand, resting on his arm, and pressed it significantly. She looked at him with the cry of surprise suspended on her lips—waited a little with her eyes fixed on Sir Patrick's face—struggled resolutely, and composed herself.

"Point the person out." She said the words with a self-possession which won her uncle's hearty approval. Blanche had done wonders for a girl in her teens.

"Look!" said Sir Patrick; "and tell me what you see."

"I see Lady Lundie, at the other end of the room, with the map of Perthshire and the Baronial Antiquities of Scotland on the table. And I see every body but you and me obliged to listen to her."

"Every body?"

Blanche looked carefully round the room, and noticed Geoffrey in the opposite corner; fast asleep by this time in his arm-chair.

"Uncle! you don't mean—?"

"There is the man."

"Mr. Delamayn—!"

"Mr. Delamayn knows every thing."

Blanche held mechanically by her uncle's arm, and looked at the sleeping man as if her eyes could never see enough of him.

"You saw me in the library in private consultation with Mr. Delamayn," resumed Sir Patrick. "I have to acknowledge, my dear, that you were quite right in thinking this a suspicious circumstance. And I am now to justify myself for having purposely kept you in the dark up to the present time."

With those introductory words, he briefly reverted to the earlier occurrences of the day, and then added, by way of commentary, a statement of the conclusions which events had suggested to his own mind.

The events, it may be remembered, were three in number. First, Geoffrey's private conference with Sir Patrick on the subject of Irregular Marriages in Scotland. Secondly, Anne Silvester's appearance at Windygates. Thirdly, Anne's flight.

The conclusions which had thereupon suggested themselves to Sir Patrick's mind were six in number.

First, that a connection of some sort might possibly exist between Geoffrey's acknowledged difficulty about his friend, and Miss Silvester's presumed difficulty about herself. Secondly, that Geoffrey had really put to Sir Patrick—not his own case—but the case of a friend. Thirdly, that Geoffrey had some interest (of no harmless kind) in establishing the fact of his friend's marriage. Fourthly, that Anne's anxiety (as described by Blanche) to hear the names of the gentlemen who were staying at Windygates, pointed, in all probability, to Geoffrey. Fifthly, that this last inference disturbed the second conclusion, and reopened the doubt whether Geoffrey had not been stating his own case, after all, under pretense of stating the case of a friend. Sixthly, that the one way of obtaining any enlightenment on this point, and on all the other points involved in mystery, was to go to Craig Fernie, and consult Mrs. Inchbare's experience during the period of Anne's residence at the inn. Sir Patrick's apology for keeping all this a secret from his niece followed. He had shrunk from agitating her on the subject until he could be sure of proving his conclusions to be true. The proof had been obtained; and he was now, therefore, ready to open his mind to Blanche without reserve.

"So much, my dear," proceeded Sir Patrick, "for those necessary explanations which are also the necessary nuisances of human intercourse. You now know as much as I did when I arrived at Craig Fernie—and you are, therefore, in a position to appreciate the value of my discoveries at the inn. Do you understand every thing, so far?"

"Perfectly!"

"Very good. I drove up to the inn; and—behold me closeted with Mrs. Inchbare in her own private parlor! (My reputation may or may not suffer, but Mrs. Inchbare's bones are above suspicion!) It was a long business, Blanche. A more sour-tempered, cunning, and distrustful witness I never examined in all my experience at the Bar. She would have upset the temper of any mortal man but a lawyer. We have such wonderful tempers in our profession; and we *can* be so aggravating when we like! In short, my dear, Mrs. Inchbare was a she-cat, and I was a he-cat—and I clawed the truth out of her at last. The result was well worth arriving at, as you shall see. Mr. Delamayn had described to me certain remarkable circumstances as taking place between a lady and a gentleman at an inn: the object of the parties being to pass themselves off at the time as man and wife. Every one of those circumstances, Blanche, occurred at Craig Fer-

nie, between a lady and a gentleman, on the day when Miss Silvester disappeared from this house. And—wait!—being pressed for her name, after the gentleman had left her behind him at the inn, the name the lady gave was, 'Mrs. Silvester.' What do you think of that?"

"Think! I'm bewildered—I can't realize it."

"It's a startling discovery, my dear child—there is no denying that. Shall I wait a little, and let you recover yourself?"

"No! no! Go on! The gentleman, uncle? The gentleman who was with Anne? Who is he? Not Mr. Delamayn?"

"Not Mr. Delamayn," said Sir Patrick. "If I have proved nothing else, I have proved that."

"What need was there to prove it? Mr. Delamayn went to London on the day of the lawn-party. And Arnold—"

"And Arnold went with him as far as the second station from this. Quite true! But how was I to know what Mr. Delamayn might have done after Arnold had left him? I could only make sure that he had not gone back privately to the inn, by getting the proof from Mrs. Inchbare."

"How did you get it?"

"I asked her to describe the gentleman who was with Miss Silvester. Mrs. Inchbare's description (vague as you will presently find it to be) completely exonerates that man," said Sir Patrick, pointing to Geoffrey still asleep in his chair. "*He* is not the person who passed Miss Silvester off as his wife at Craig Fernie. He spoke the truth when he described the case to me as the case of a friend."

"But who is the friend?" persisted Blanche. "That's what I want to know."

"That's what I want to know, too."

"Tell me exactly, uncle, what Mrs. Inchbare said. I have lived with Anne all my life. I *must* have seen the man somewhere."

"If you can identify him by Mrs. Inchbare's description," returned Sir Patrick, "you will be a great deal cleverer than I am. Here is the picture of the man, as painted by the landlady: Young; middle-sized; dark hair, eyes, and complexion; nice temper; pleasant way of speaking. Leave out 'young,' and the rest is the exact contrary of Mr. Delamayn. So far, Mrs. Inchbare guides us plainly enough. But how are we to apply her description to the right person? There must be, at the lowest computation, five hundred thousand men in England who are young, middle-sized, dark, nice-tempered, and pleasant spoken. One of the footmen here answers that description in every particular."

"And Arnold answers it," said Blanche—as a still stronger instance of the provoking vagueness of the description.

"And Arnold answers it," repeated Sir Patrick, quite agreeing with her.

They had barely said those words when Arnold himself appeared, approaching Sir Patrick with a pack of cards in his hand.

There—at the very moment when they had both guessed the truth, without feeling the slightest suspicion of it in their own minds—there stood Discovery, presenting itself unconsciously to eyes incapable of seeing it, in the person of the man who had passed Anne Silvester off as his wife at the Craig Fernie inn! The terrible caprice of Chance, the merciless irony of Circumstance, could go no further than this. The three had their feet on the brink of the precipice at that moment. And two of them were smiling at an odd coincidence; and one of them was shuffling a pack of cards!

"We have done with the Antiquities at last!" said Arnold; "and we are going to play at Whist. Sir Patrick, will you choose a card?"

"Too soon after dinner, my good fellow, for *me*. Play the first rubber, and then give me another chance. By-the-way," he added, "Miss Silvester has been traced to Kirkandrew. How is it that you never saw her go by?"

"She can't have gone my way, Sir Patrick, or I must have seen her."

Having justified himself in those terms, he was recalled to the other end of the room by the whist-party, impatient for the cards which he had in his hand.

"What were we talking of when he interrupted us?" said Sir Patrick to Blanche.

"Of the man, uncle, who was with Miss Silvester at the inn."

"It's useless to pursue that inquiry, my dear, with nothing better than Mrs. Inchbare's description to help us."

Blanche looked round at the sleeping Geoffrey.

"And *he* knows!" she said. "It's maddening, uncle, to look at the brute snoring in his chair!"

Sir Patrick held up a warning hand. Before a word more could be said between them they were silenced again by another interruption.

The whist-party comprised Lady Lundie and the surgeon, playing as partners against Smith and Jones. Arnold sat behind the surgeon, taking a lesson in the game. One, Two, and Three, thus left to their own devices, naturally thought of the billiard-table; and, detecting Geoffrey asleep in his corner, advanced to disturb his slumbers, under the all-sufficing apology of "Pool." Geoffrey roused himself, and rubbed his eyes, and said, drowsily, "All right." As he rose, he looked at the opposite corner in which Sir Patrick and his niece were sitting. Blanche's self-possession, resolutely as she struggled to preserve it, was not strong enough to keep her eyes from turning toward Geoffrey, with an expression that betrayed the reluctant interest that she now felt in him. He stopped, noticing something entirely new in the look with which the young lady was regarding him.

"Beg your pardon," said Geoffrey. "Do you wish to speak to me?"

Blanche's face flushed all over. Her uncle came to the rescue.

"Miss Lundie and I hope you have slept well, Mr. Delamayn," said Sir Patrick, jocosely. "That's all."

"Oh? That's all?" said Geoffrey, still looking at Blanche. "Beg your pardon again. Deuced long walk, and deuced heavy dinner. Natural consequence—a nap."

Sir Patrick eyed him closely. It was plain that he had been honestly puzzled at finding himself an object of special attention on Blanche's part. "See you in the billiard-room?" he said, carelessly, and followed his companions out of the room—as usual, without waiting for an answer."

"Mind what you are about," said Sir Patrick to his niece. "That man is quicker than he looks. We commit a serious mistake if we put him on his guard at starting."

"It sha'n't happen again, uncle," said Blanche. "But think of *his* being in Anne's confidence, and of *my* being shut out of it!"

"In his friend's confidence, you mean, my dear; and (if we only avoid awakening his suspicion) there is no knowing how soon he may say or do something which may show us who his friend is."

"But he is going back to his brother's to-morrow—he said so at dinner-time."

"So much the better. He will be out of the way of seeing strange things in a certain young lady's face. His brother's house is within easy reach of this; and I am his legal adviser. My experience tells me that he has not done consulting me yet—and that he will let out something more next time. So much for our chance of seeing the light through Mr. Delamayn—if we can't see it in any other way. And that is not our only chance, remember. I have something to tell you about Bishopriggs and the lost letter."

"Is it found?"

"No. I satisfied myself about that—I had it searched for, under my own eye. The letter is stolen, Blanche; and Bishopriggs has got it. I have left a line for him, in Mrs. Inchbare's care. The old rascal is missed already by the visitors at the inn, just as I told you he would be. His mistress is feeling the penalty of having been fool enough to vent her ill temper on her head-waiter. She lays the whole blame of the quarrel on Miss Silvester, of course. Bishopriggs neglected every body at the inn to wait on Miss Silvester. Bishopriggs was insolent on being remonstrated with, and Miss Silvester encouraged him—and so on. The result will be—now Miss Silvester has gone—that Bishopriggs will return to Craig Fernie before the autumn is over. We are sailing with wind and tide, my dear. Come, and learn to play whist."

He rose to join the card-players. Blanche detained him.

"You haven't told me one thing yet," she said. "Whoever the man may be, is Anne married to him?"

"Whoever the man may be," returned Sir Patrick, "he had better not attempt to marry any body else."

So the niece unconsciously put the question, and so the uncle unconsciously gave the answer, on which depended the whole happiness of Blanche's life to come. The "man!" How lightly they both talked of the "man!" Would nothing happen to rouse the faintest suspicion—in their minds or in Arnold's mind—that Arnold was the "man" himself?

"You mean that she *is* married?" said Blanche.

"I don't go as far as that."

"You mean that she is *not* married?"

"I don't go so far as *that*."

"Oh! the law!"

"Provoking, isn't it, my dear? I can tell you, professionally, that (in my opinion) she has grounds to go on if she claims to be the man's wife. That is what I meant by my answer; and, until we know more, that is all I can say."

"When shall we know more? When shall we get the telegram?"

"Not for some hours yet. Come, and learn to play whist."

"I think I would rather talk to Arnold, uncle, if you don't mind."

"By all means! But don't talk to him about what I have been telling you to-night. He and Mr. Delamayn are old associates, remember; and he might blunder into telling his friend what his friend had better not know. Sad (isn't it?) for me to be instilling these lessons of duplicity into the youthful mind. A wise person once said, 'The older a man gets the worse he gets.' That wise person, my dear, had me in his eye, and was perfectly right."

He mitigated the pain of that confession with a pinch of snuff, and went to the whist-table to wait until the end of the rubber gave him a place at the game.

---

## CHAPTER THE TWENTY-FIFTH.

### FORWARD.

BLANCHE found her lover as attentive as usual to her slightest wish, but not in his customary good spirits. He pleaded fatigue, after his long watch at the cross-roads, as an excuse for his depression. As long as there was any hope of a reconciliation with Geoffrey, he was unwilling to tell Blanche what had happened that afternoon. The hope grew fainter and fainter as the evening advanced. Arnold purposely suggested a visit to the billiard-room, and joined the game, with Blanche, to give Geoffrey an opportunity of saying the few gracious words which would have made them friends again. Geoffrey never spoke the words; he obstinately ignored Arnold's presence in the room.

At the card-table the whist went on interminably. Lady Lundie, Sir Patrick, and the surgeon, were all inveterate players, evenly matched. Smith and Jones (joining the game alternately) were aids to whist, exactly as they were aids to conversation. The same safe and modest mediocrity of style distinguished the proceedings of these two gentlemen in all the affairs of life.

The time wore on to midnight. They went to bed late and they rose late at Windygates House. Under that hospitable roof, no intrusive hints, in the shape of flat candlesticks exhibiting themselves with ostentatious virtue on side-tables, hurried the guest to his room; no vile bell rang him ruthlessly out of bed the next morning, and insisted on his breakfasting at a given hour. Life has surely hardships enough that are inevitable, without gratuitously adding the hardship of absolute government, administered by a clock?

It was a quarter past twelve when Lady Lundie rose blandly from the whist-table, and said that she supposed somebody must set the example of going to bed. Sir Patrick and Smith, the surgeon and Jones, agreed on a last rubber. Blanche vanished while her step-mother's eye was on her; and appeared again in the drawing-room, when Lady Lundie was safe in the hands of her maid. Nobody followed the example of the mistress of the house but Arnold. He left the billiard-room with the certainty that it was all over now between Geoffrey and himself. Not even the attraction of Blanche proved strong enough to detain him that night. He went his way to bed.

It was past one o'clock. The final rubber was at an end; the accounts were settled at the card-table; the surgeon had strolled into the billiard-room, and Smith and Jones had followed him, when Duncan came in, at last, with the telegram in his hand.

Blanche turned from the broad, calm autumn moonlight which had drawn her to the window, and looked over her uncle's shoulder while he opened the telegram.

She read the first line—and that was enough. The whole scaffolding of hope built round that morsel of paper fell to the ground in an instant. The train from Kirkandrew had reached Edinburgh at the usual time. Every passenger in it had passed under the eyes of the police; and nothing had been seen of any person who answered the description given of Anne!

Sir Patrick pointed to the two last sentences in the telegram: "Inquiries telegraphed to Falkirk. If with any result, you shall know."

"We must hope for the best, Blanche. They evidently suspect her of having got out at the junction of the two railways for the purpose of giving the telegraph the slip. There is no help for it. Go to bed, child—go to bed."

Blanche kissed her uncle in silence and went away. The bright young face was sad with the first hopeless sorrow which the old man had yet seen in it. His niece's parting look dwelt painfully on his mind when he was up in his room, with the faithful Duncan getting him ready for his bed.

"This is a bad business, Duncan. I don't like to say so to Miss Lundie; but I greatly fear the governess has baffled us."

"It seems likely, Sir Patrick. The poor young lady looks quite heart-broken about it."

"You noticed that too, did you? She has lived all her life, you see, with Miss Silvester; and there is a very strong attachment between them. I am uneasy about my niece, Duncan. I am afraid this disappointment will have a serious effect on her."

"She's young, Sir Patrick."

"Yes, my friend, she's young; but the young (when they are good for any thing) have warm hearts. Winter hasn't stolen on *them*, Duncan! And they feel keenly."

"I think there's reason to hope, Sir, that Miss Lundie may get over it more easily than you suppose."

"What reason, pray?"

"A person in my position can hardly venture to speak freely, Sir, on a delicate matter of this kind."

Sir Patrick's temper flashed out, half-seriously, half-whimsically, as usual.

"Is that a snap at Me, you old dog? If I am not your friend, as well as your master, who is? Am *I* in the habit of keeping any of my harmless fellow-creatures at a distance? I despise the cant of modern Liberalism; but it's not the less true that I have, all my life, protested against the inhuman separation of classes in England. We are, in that respect, brag as we may of our national virtue, the most unchristian people in the civilized world."

"I beg your pardon, Sir Patrick—"

"God help me! I'm talking politics at this time of night! It's your fault, Duncan. What do you mean by casting my station in my teeth, because I can't put my night-cap on comfortably till you have brushed my hair? I have a good mind to get up and brush yours. There! there! I'm uneasy about my niece—nervous irritability, my good fellow, that's all. Let's hear what you have to say about Miss Lundie. And go on with my hair. And don't be a humbug."

"I was about to remind you, Sir Patrick, that Miss Lundie has another interest in her life to turn to. If this matter of Miss Silvester ends badly—and I own it begins to look as if it would —I should hurry my niece's marriage, Sir, and see if *that* wouldn't console her."

Sir Patrick started under the gentle discipline of the hair-brush in Duncan's hand.

"That's very sensibly put," said the old gentleman. "Duncan! you are, what I call, a clear-minded man. Well worth thinking of, old Truepenny! If the worst comes to the worst, well worth thinking of!"

It was not the first time that Duncan's steady good sense had struck light, under the form of a new thought, in his master's mind. But never yet had he wrought such mischief as the mischief which he had innocently done now. He had sent Sir Patrick to bed with the fatal idea of hastening the marriage of Arnold and Blanche.

The situation of affairs at Windygates—now that Anne had apparently obliterated all trace of herself—was becoming serious. The one chance on which the discovery of Arnold's position depended, was the chance that accident might reveal the truth in the lapse of time. In this posture of circumstances, Sir Patrick now resolved —if nothing happened to relieve Blanche's anxiety in the course of the week—to advance the celebration of the marriage from the end of the autumn (as originally contemplated) to the first fortnight of the ensuing month. As dates then stood, the change led (so far as free scope for the development of accident was concerned) to this serious result. It abridged a lapse of three months into an interval of three weeks.

The next morning came; and Blanche marked it as a memorable morning, by committing an act of imprudence, which struck away one more of the chances of discovery that had existed, before the arrival of the Edinburgh telegram on the previous day.

She had passed a sleepless night; fevered in mind and body; thinking, hour after hour, of nothing but Anne. At sunrise she could endure it no longer. Her power to control herself was completely exhausted; her own impulses led her as they pleased. She got up, determined not to let Geoffrey leave the house without risking an effort to make him reveal what he knew about Anne. It was nothing less than downright treason to Sir Patrick to act on her own responsibility in this way. She knew it was wrong; she was heartily ashamed of herself for doing it. But the demon that possesses women with a recklessness all their own, at the critical moments of their lives, had got her—and she did it.

Geoffrey had arranged, overnight, to breakfast early, by himself, and to walk the ten miles to his brother's house; sending a servant to fetch his luggage later in the day.

He had got on his hat; he was standing in the hall, searching his pocket for his second self, the pipe—when Blanche suddenly appeared from the morning-room, and placed herself between him and the house door.

"Up early—eh?" said Geoffrey. "I'm off to my brother's."

She made no reply. He looked at her closer. The girl's eyes were trying to read his face, with an utter carelessness of concealment, which forbade (even to his mind) all unworthy interpretation of her motive for stopping him on his way out.

"Any commands for me?" he inquired.

This time she answered him. "I have something to ask you," she said.

He smiled graciously, and opened his tobacco-pouch. He was fresh and strong after his night's sleep—healthy and handsome and good-humored. The house-maids had had a peep at him that morning, and had wished—like Desdemona, with a difference—that "Heaven had made all three of them such a man."

"Well," he said, "what is it?"

She put her question, without a single word of preface—purposely to surprise him.

"Mr. Delamayn," she said, "do you know where Anne Silvester is this morning?"

He was filling his pipe as she spoke, and he dropped some of the tobacco on the floor. Instead of answering before he picked up the tobacco he answered after—in surly self-possession, and in one word—"No."

"Do you know nothing about her?"

He devoted himself doggedly to the filling of his pipe. "Nothing."

"On your word of honor, as a gentleman?"

"On my word of honor, as a gentleman."

He put back his tobacco-pouch in his pocket. His handsome face was as hard as stone. His clear blue eyes defied all the girls in England put together to see into *his* mind. "Have you done, Miss Lundie?" he asked, suddenly changing to a bantering politeness of tone and manner.

Blanche saw that it was hopeless—saw that she had compromised her own interests by her own headlong act. Sir Patrick's warning words came back reproachfully to her now when it was too late. "We commit a serious mistake if we put him on his guard at starting."

There was but one course to take now. "Yes," she said. "I have done."

"My turn now," rejoined Geoffrey. "You want to know where Miss Silvester is. Why do you ask Me?"

Blanche did all that could be done toward repairing the error that she had committed. She kept Geoffrey as far away as Geoffrey had kept *her* from the truth.

"I happen to know," she replied, "that Miss Silvester left the place at which she had been staying about the time when you went out walking yesterday. And I thought you might have seen her."

"Oh? That's the reason—is it?" said Geoffrey, with a smile.

The smile stung Blanche's sensitive temper to the quick. She made a final effort to control herself, before her indignation got the better of her.

"I have no more to say, Mr. Delamayn." With that reply she turned her back on him, and closed the door of the morning-room between them.

Geoffrey descended the house steps and lit his

"DO YOU KNOW WHERE ANNE SILVESTER IS THIS MORNING?"

pipe. He was not at the slightest loss, on this occasion, to account for what had happened. He assumed at once that Arnold had taken a mean revenge on him after his conduct of the day before, and had told the whole secret of his errand at Craig Fernie to Blanche. The thing would get next, no doubt, to Sir Patrick's ears; and Sir Patrick would thereupon be probably the first person who revealed to Arnold the position in which he had placed himself with Anne. All right! Sir Patrick would be an excellent witness to appeal to, when the scandal broke out, and when the time came for repudiating Anne's claim on him as the barefaced imposture of a woman who was married already to another man. He puffed away unconcernedly at his pipe, and started, at his swinging, steady pace, for his brother's house.

Blanche remained alone in the morning-room. The prospect of getting at the truth, by means of what Geoffrey might say on the next occasion when he consulted Sir Patrick, was a prospect that she herself had closed from that moment. She sat down in despair by the window. It commanded a view of the little side-terrace which had been Anne's favorite walk at Windygates. With weary eyes and aching heart the poor child looked at the familiar place; and asked herself, with the bitter repentance that comes too late, if she had destroyed the last chance of finding Anne!

She sat passively at the window, while the hours of the morning wore on, until the postman came. Before the servant could take the letter-bag she was in the hall to receive it. Was it possible to hope that the bag had brought tidings of Anne? She sorted the letters; and lighted suddenly on a letter to herself. It bore the Kirkandrew post-mark, and it was addressed to her in Anne's handwriting.

She tore the letter open, and read these lines:
"I have left you forever, Blanche. God bless and reward you! God make you a happy woman in all your life to come! Cruel as you will think me, love, I have never been so truly your sister as I am now. I can only tell you this—I can never tell you more. Forgive me, and forget me. Our lives are parted lives from this day."

Going down to breakfast about his usual hour, Sir Patrick missed Blanche, whom he was accustomed to see waiting for him at the table at that time. The room was empty; the other members of the household having all finished their morning meal. Sir Patrick disliked breakfasting alone. He sent Duncan with a message, to be given to Blanche's maid.

The maid appeared in due time. Miss Lundie was unable to leave her room. She sent a letter to her uncle, with her love—and begged he would read it.

Sir Patrick opened the letter and saw what Anne had written to Blanche.

He waited a little, reflecting, with evident pain and anxiety, on what he had read—then opened his own letters, and hurriedly looked at the signatures. There was nothing for him from his friend, the sheriff, at Edinburgh, and no communication from the railway, in the shape of a telegram. He had decided, overnight, on waiting till the end of the week before he interfered in the matter of Blanche's marriage. The events of the morning determined him on not waiting another day. Duncan returned to the breakfast-room to pour out his master's coffee. Sir Patrick sent him away again with a second message.

"Do you know where Lady Lundie is, Duncan?"

"Yes, Sir Patrick."

"My compliments to her ladyship. If she is not otherwise engaged, I shall be glad to speak to her privately in an hour's time."

---

## CHAPTER THE TWENTY-SIXTH.

### DROPPED.

SIR PATRICK made a bad breakfast. Blanche's absence fretted him, and Anne Silvester's letter puzzled him.

He read it, short as it was, a second time, and a third. If it meant any thing, it meant that the motive at the bottom of Anne's flight was to accomplish the sacrifice of herself to the happiness of Blanche. She had parted for life from his niece for his niece's sake! What did this mean? And how was it to be reconciled with Anne's position—as described to him by Mrs. Inchbare during his visit to Craig Fernie?

All Sir Patrick's ingenuity, and all Sir Patrick's experience, failed to find so much as the shadow of an answer to that question.

While he was still pondering over the letter, Arnold and the surgeon entered the breakfast-room together.

"Have you heard about Blanche?" asked Arnold, excitedly. "She is in no danger, Sir Patrick—the worst of it is over now."

The surgeon interposed before Sir Patrick could appeal to him.

"Mr. Brinkworth's interest in the young lady a little exaggerates the state of the case," he said. "I have seen her, at Lady Lundie's request; and I can assure you that there is not the slightest reason for any present alarm. Miss Lundie has had a nervous attack, which has yielded to the simplest domestic remedies. The only anxiety you need feel is connected with the management of her in the future. She is suffering from some mental distress, which it is not for me, but for her friends, to alleviate and remove. If you can turn her thoughts from the painful subject—whatever it may be—on which they are dwelling now, you will do all that needs to be done."

He took up a newspaper from the table, and strolled out into the garden, leaving Sir Patrick and Arnold together.

"You heard that?" said Sir Patrick.

"Is he right, do you think?" asked Arnold.

"Right? Do you suppose a man gets *his* reputation by making mistakes? You're one of the new generation, Master Arnold. You can all of you stare at a famous man; but you haven't an atom of respect for his fame. If Shakspeare came to life again, and talked of play-writing, the first pretentious nobody who sat opposite at dinner would differ with him as composedly as he might differ with you and me. Veneration is dead among us; the present age has buried it, without a stone to mark the place. So much for that! Let's get back to Blanche. I suppose you can guess what the painful subject is that's dwelling on her mind? Miss Silvester has baffled me, and baffled the Edinburgh police.

Blanche discovered that we had failed last night; and Blanche received that letter this morning."

He pushed Anne's letter across the breakfast-table.

Arnold read it, and handed it back without a word. Viewed by the new light in which he saw Geoffrey's character after the quarrel on the heath, the letter conveyed but one conclusion to his mind. Geoffrey had deserted her.

"Well?" said Sir Patrick. "Do you understand what it means?"

"I understand Blanche's wretchedness when she read it."

He said no more than that. It was plain that no information which he could afford—even if he had considered himself at liberty to give it—would be of the slightest use in assisting Sir Patrick to trace Miss Silvester, under present circumstances. There was—unhappily—no temptation to induce him to break the honorable silence which he had maintained thus far. And—more unfortunately still—assuming the temptation to present itself, Arnold's capacity to resist it had never been so strong a capacity as it was now.

To the two powerful motives which had hitherto tied his tongue—respect for Anne's reputation, and reluctance to reveal to Blanche the deception which he had been compelled to practice on her at the inn—to these two motives there was now added a third. The meanness of betraying the confidence which Geoffrey had reposed in him would be doubled meanness if he proved false to his trust after Geoffrey had personally insulted him. The paltry revenge which that false friend had unhesitatingly suspected him of taking was a revenge of which Arnold's nature was simply incapable. Never had his lips been more effectually sealed than at this moment—when his whole future depended on Sir Patrick's discovering the part that he had played in past events at Craig Fernie.

"Yes! yes!" resumed Sir Patrick, impatiently. "Blanche's distress is intelligible enough. But here is my niece apparently answerable for this unhappy woman's disappearance. Can you explain what my niece has got to do with it?"

"I! Blanche herself is completely mystified. How should *I* know?"

Answering in those terms, he spoke with perfect sincerity. Anne's vague distrust of the position in which they had innocently placed themselves at the inn had produced no corresponding effect on Arnold at the time. He had not regarded it; he had not even understood it. As a necessary result, not the faintest suspicion of the motive under which Anne was acting existed in his mind now.

Sir Patrick put the letter into his pocket-book, and abandoned all further attempt at interpreting the meaning of it in despair.

"Enough, and more than enough, of groping in the dark," he said. "One point is clear to me after what has happened up stairs this morning. We must accept the position in which Miss Silvester has placed us. I shall give up all further effort to trace her from this moment."

"Surely that will be a dreadful disappointment to Blanche, Sir Patrick?"

"I don't deny it. We must face that result."

"If you are sure there is nothing else to be done, I suppose we must."

"I am not sure of any thing of the sort, Master Arnold! There are two chances still left of throwing light on this matter, which are both of them independent of any thing that Miss Silvester can do to keep it in the dark."

"Then why not try them, Sir? It seems hard to drop Miss Silvester when she is in trouble."

"We can't help her against her own will," rejoined Sir Patrick. "And we can't run the risk, after that nervous attack this morning, of subjecting Blanche to any further suspense. I have thought of my niece's interests throughout this business; and if I now change my mind, and decline to agitate her by more experiments, ending (quite possibly) in more failures, it is because I am thinking of her interests still. I have no other motive. However numerous my weaknesses may be, ambition to distinguish myself as a detective policeman is not one of them. The case, from the police point of view, is by no means a lost case. I drop it, nevertheless, for Blanche's sake. Instead of encouraging her thoughts to dwell on this melancholy business, we must apply the remedy suggested by our medical friend."

"How is that to be done?" asked Arnold.

The sly twist of humor began to show itself in Sir Patrick's face.

"Has she nothing to think of in the future, which is a pleasanter subject of reflection than the loss of her friend?" he asked. "*You* are interested, my young gentleman, in the remedy that is to cure Blanche. *You* are one of the drugs in the moral prescription. Can you guess what it is?"

Arnold started to his feet, and brightened into a new being.

"Perhaps you object to be hurried?" said Sir Patrick.

"Object! If Blanche will only consent, I'll take her to church as soon as she comes down stairs!"

"Thank you!" said Sir Patrick, dryly. "Mr. Arnold Brinkworth, may you always be as ready to take Time by the forelock as you are now! Sit down again; and don't talk nonsense. It is just possible—if Blanche consents (as you say), and if we can hurry the lawyers—that you may be married in three weeks' or a month's time."

"What have the lawyers got to do with it?"

"My good fellow, this is not a marriage in a novel! This is the most unromantic affair of the sort that ever happened. Here are a young gentleman and a young lady, both rich people; both well matched in birth and character; one of age, and the other marrying with the full consent and approval of her guardian. What is the consequence of this purely prosaic state of things? Lawyers and settlements, of course!"

"Come into the library, Sir Patrick; and I'll soon settle the settlements! A bit of paper, and a dip of ink. 'I hereby give every blessed farthing I have got in the world to my dear Blanche.' Sign that; stick a wafer on at the side; clap your finger on the wafer; 'I deliver this as my act and deed;' and there it is—done!"

"Is it, really? You are a born legislator. You create and codify your own system all in a breath. Moses-Justinian-Mahomet, give me your arm! There is one atom of sense in what you have just said. 'Come into the library'— is a suggestion worth attending to. Do you

happen, among your other superfluities, to have such a thing as a lawyer about you?"

"I have got two. One in London, and one in Edinburgh."

"We will take the nearest of the two, because we are in a hurry. Who is the Edinburgh lawyer? Pringle of Pitt Street? Couldn't be a better man. Come and write to him. You have given me your abstract of a marriage settlement with the brevity of an ancient Roman. I scorn to be outdone by an amateur lawyer. Here is *my* abstract: You are just and generous to Blanche; Blanche is just and generous to you; and you both combine to be just and generous together to your children. There is a model settlement! and there are your instructions to Pringle of Pitt Street! Can you do it by yourself? No; of course you can't. Now don't be slovenly-minded! See the points in their order as they come. You are going to be married; you state to whom; you add that I am the lady's guardian; you give the name and address of my lawyer in Edinburgh; you write your instructions plainly in the fewest words, and leave details to your legal adviser; you refer the lawyers to each other; you request that the draft settlements be prepared as speedily as possible; and you give your address at this house. There are the heads. Can't you do it? Oh, the rising generation! Oh, the progress we are making in these enlightened modern times! There! there! you can marry Blanche, and make her happy, and increase the population—and all without knowing how to write the English language. One can only say with the learned Bevoriskius, looking out of his window at the illimitable loves of the sparrows, 'How merciful is Heaven to its creatures!' Take up the pen. I'll dictate! I'll dictate!"

Sir Patrick read the letter over, approved of it, and saw it safe in the box for the post. This done, he peremptorily forbade Arnold to speak to his niece on the subject of the marriage without his express permission. "There's somebody else's consent to be got," he said, "besides Blanche's consent and mine."

"Lady Lundie?"

"Lady Lundie. Strictly speaking, I am the only authority. But my sister-in-law is Blanche's step-mother, and she is appointed guardian in the event of my death. She has a right to be consulted—in courtesy, if not in law. Would you like to do it?"

Arnold's face fell. He looked at Sir Patrick in silent dismay.

"What! you can't even speak to such a perfectly pliable person as Lady Lundie? You may have been a very useful fellow at sea. A more helpless young man I never met with on shore. Get out with you into the garden among the other sparrows! Somebody must confront her ladyship. And if you won't—I must."

He pushed Arnold out of the library, and applied meditatively to the knob of his cane. His gayety disappeared, now that he was alone. His experience of Lady Lundie's character told him that, in attempting to win her approval to any scheme for hurrying Blanche's marriage, he was undertaking no easy task. "I suppose," mused Sir Patrick, thinking of his late brother—"I suppose poor Tom had some way of managing her. How did he do it, I wonder? If she had been the wife of a bricklayer, she is the sort of woman who would have been kept in perfect order by a vigorous and regular application of her husband's fist. But Tom wasn't a bricklayer. I wonder how Tom did it?" After a little hard thinking on this point Sir Patrick gave up the problem as beyond human solution. "It must be done," he concluded. "And my own mother-wit must help me to do it."

In that resigned frame of mind he knocked at the door of Lady Lundie's boudoir.

---

## CHAPTER THE TWENTY-SEVENTH.

### OUTWITTED.

Sir Patrick found his sister-in-law immersed in domestic business. Her ladyship's correspondence and visiting list; her ladyship's household bills and ledgers; her ladyship's Diary and Memorandum-book (bound in scarlet morocco); her ladyship's desk, envelope-case, match-box, and taper candlestick (all in ebony and silver); her ladyship herself, presiding over her responsibilities, and wielding her materials, equal to any calls of emergency, beautifully dressed in correct morning costume, blessed with perfect health both of the secretions and the principles; absolutely void of vice, and formidably full of virtue, presented, to every properly-constituted mind, the most imposing spectacle known to humanity—the British Matron on her throne, asking the world in general, When will you produce the like of Me?

"I am afraid I disturb you," said Sir Patrick.

"I am a perfectly idle person. Shall I look in a little later?"

Lady Lundie put her hand to her head, and smiled faintly.

"A little pressure *here*, Sir Patrick. Pray sit down. Duty finds me earnest; Duty finds me cheerful; Duty finds me accessible. From a poor, weak woman, Duty must expect no more. Now what is it?" (Her ladyship consulted her scarlet memorandum-book.) "I have got it here, under its proper head, distinguished by initial letters. P.—the poor. No. H.M.—heathen missions. No. V.T.A.—Visitors to arrive. No. P.I.P.—Here it is: private interview with Patrick. Will you forgive me the little harmless familiarity of omitting your title? Thank you! You are always so good. I am quite at your service when you like to begin. If it's any thing painful, pray don't hesitate. I am quite prepared."

With that intimation her ladyship threw herself back in her chair, with her elbows on the arms, and her fingers joined at the tips, as if she was receiving a deputation. "Yes?" she said, interrogatively. Sir Patrick paid a private tribute of pity to his late brother's memory, and entered on his business.

"We won't call it a painful matter," he began. "Let us say it's a matter of domestic anxiety. Blanche—"

Lady Lundie emitted a faint scream, and put her hand over her eyes.

"*Must* you?" cried her ladyship, in a tone of touching remonstrance. "Oh, Sir Patrick, *must* you?"

"Yes. I must."

Lady Lundie's magnificent eyes looked up at that hidden court of human appeal which is lodged in the ceiling. The hidden court looked down at Lady Lundie, and saw—Duty advertising itself in the largest capital letters.

"Go on, Sir Patrick. The motto of woman is Self-sacrifice. You sha'n't see how you distress me. Go on."

Sir Patrick went on impenetrably—without betraying the slightest expression of sympathy or surprise.

"I was about to refer to the nervous attack from which Blanche has suffered this morning," he said. "May I ask whether you have been informed of the cause to which the attack is attributable?"

"There!" exclaimed Lady Lundie, with a sudden bound in her chair, and a sudden development of vocal power to correspond. "The one thing I shrank from speaking of! the cruel, cruel, cruel behavior I was prepared to pass over! And Sir Patrick hints on it! Innocently—don't let me do an injustice—innocently hints on it!"

"Hints on what, my dear Madam?"

"Blanche's conduct to me this morning. Blanche's heartless secrecy. Blanche's undutiful silence. I repeat the words: Heartless secrecy. Undutiful silence."

"Allow me for one moment, Lady Lundie—"

"Allow *me*, Sir Patrick! Heaven knows how unwilling I am to speak of it. Heaven knows that not a word of reference to it escaped *my* lips. But you leave me no choice now. As mistress of the household, as a Christian woman, as the widow of your dear brother, as a mother to this misguided girl, I must state the facts. I know you mean well; I know you wish to spare me. Quite useless! I must state the facts."

Sir Patrick bowed, and submitted. (If he had only been a bricklayer! and if Lady Lundie had not been, what her ladyship unquestionably was, the strongest person of the two!)

"Permit me to draw a veil, for your sake," said Lady Lundie, "over the horrors—I can not, with the best wish to spare you, conscientiously call them by any other name—the horrors that took place up stairs. The moment I heard that Blanche was ill I was at my post. Duty will always find me ready, Sir Patrick, to my dying day. Shocking as the whole thing was, I presided calmly over the screams and sobs of my step-daughter. I closed my ears to the profane violence of her language. I set the necessary example, as an English gentlewoman at the head of her household. It was only when I distinctly heard the name of a person, never to be mentioned again in my family circle, issue (if I may use the expression) from Blanche's lips that I began to be really alarmed. I said to my maid: 'Hopkins, this is not Hysteria. This is a possession of the devil. Fetch the chloroform.'"

Chloroform, applied in the capacity of an exorcism, was entirely new to Sir Patrick. He preserved his gravity with considerable difficulty. Lady Lundie went on:

"Hopkins is an excellent person—but Hopkins has a tongue. She met our distinguished medical guest in the corridor, and told him. He was so good as to come to the door. I was shocked to trouble him to act in his professional capacity while he was a visitor, an honored visitor, in my house. Besides, I considered it more a case for a clergyman than for a medical man. However, there was no help for it after Hopkins's tongue. I requested our eminent friend to favor us with—I think the exact scientific term is—a Prognosis. He took the purely material view which was only to be expected from a person in his profession. He prognosed—*am* I right? Did he prognose? or did he diagnose? A habit of speaking correctly is *so* important, Sir Patrick! and I should be *so* grieved to mislead you!"

"Never mind, Lady Lundie! I have heard the medical report. Don't trouble yourself to repeat it."

"Don't trouble myself to repeat it?" echoed Lady Lundie—with her dignity up in arms at the bare prospect of finding her remarks abridged. "Ah, Sir Patrick! that little constitutional impatience of yours!—Oh, dear me! how often you must have given way to it, and how often you must have regretted it, in your time!"

"My dear lady! if you wish to repeat the report, why not say so, in plain words? Don't let me hurry you. Let us have the prognosis, by all means."

Lady Lundie shook her head compassionately, and smiled with angelic sadness. "Our little besetting sins!" she said. "What slaves we are to our little besetting sins! Take a turn in the room—do!"

Any ordinary man would have lost his temper. But the law (as Sir Patrick had told his niece) has a special temper of its own. Without exhibiting the smallest irritation, Sir Patrick dextrously applied his sister-in-law's blister to his sister-in-law herself.

"What an eye you have!" he said. "I *was* impatient. I *am* impatient. I am dying to know what Blanche said to you when she got better?"

The British Matron froze up into a matron of stone on the spot.

"Nothing!" answered her ladyship, with a vicious snap of her teeth, as if she had tried to bite the word before it escaped her.

"Nothing!" exclaimed Sir Patrick.

"Nothing," repeated Lady Lundie, with her most formidable emphasis of look and tone. "I applied all the remedies with my own hands; I cut her laces with my own scissors; I completely wetted her head through with cold water; I remained with her until she was quite exhausted; I took her in my arms, and folded her to my bosom; I sent every body out of the room; I said, 'Dear child, confide in me.' And how were my advances—my motherly advances—met? I have already told you. By heartless secrecy. By undutiful silence."

Sir Patrick pressed the blister a little closer to the skin. "She was probably afraid to speak," he said.

"Afraid? Oh!" cried Lady Lundie, distrusting the evidence of her own senses. "You can't have said that? I have evidently misapprehended you. You didn't really say, afraid?"

"I said she was probably afraid—"

"Stop! I can't be told to my face that I have failed to do my duty by Blanche. No, Sir Patrick! I can bear a great deal; but I can't bear that. After having been more than a mother to your dear brother's child; after having been an elder sister to Blanche; after having toiled—

I say *toiled*, Sir Patrick!—to cultivate her intelligence (with the sweet lines of the poet ever present to my memory: 'Delightful task to rear the tender mind, and teach the young idea how to shoot!'); after having done all I have done—a place in the carriage only yesterday, and a visit to the most interesting relic of feudal times in Perthshire—after having sacrificed all I have sacrificed, to be told that I have behaved in such a manner to Blanche as to frighten her when I ask her to confide in me, is a little too cruel. I have a sensitive—an unduly sensitive nature, dear Sir Patrick. Forgive me for wincing when I am wounded. Forgive me for feeling it when the wound is dealt me by a person whom I revere."

Her ladyship put her handkerchief to her eyes. Any other man would have taken off the blister. Sir Patrick pressed it harder than ever.

"You quite mistake me," he replied. "I meant that Blanche was afraid to tell you the true cause of her illness. The true cause is anxiety about Miss Silvester."

Lady Lundie emitted another scream—a loud scream this time—and closed her eyes in horror.

"I can run out of the house," cried her ladyship, wildly. "I can fly to the uttermost corners of the earth; but I can *not* hear that person's name mentioned! No, Sir Patrick! not in my presence! not in my room! not while I am mistress at Windygates House!"

"I am sorry to say any thing that is disagreeable to you, Lady Lundie. But the nature of my errand here obliges me to touch—as lightly as possible—on something which has happened in your house without your knowledge."

Lady Lundie suddenly opened her eyes, and became the picture of attention. A casual observer might have supposed her ladyship to be not wholly inaccessible to the vulgar emotion of curiosity.

"A visitor came to Windygates yesterday, while we were all at lunch," proceeded Sir Patrick. "She—"

Lady Lundie seized the scarlet memorandum-book, and stopped her brother-in-law, before he could get any further. Her ladyship's next words escaped her lips spasmodically, like words let at intervals out of a trap.

"I undertake—as a woman accustomed to self-restraint, Sir Patrick—I undertake to control myself, on one condition. I won't have the name mentioned. I won't have the sex mentioned. Say, 'The Person,' if you please. 'The Person,'" continued Lady Lundie, opening her memorandum-book and taking up her pen, "committed an audacious invasion of my premises yesterday?"

Sir Patrick bowed. Her ladyship made a note—a fiercely-penned note that scratched the paper viciously—and then proceeded to examine her brother-in-law, in the capacity of witness.

"What part of my house did 'The Person' invade? Be very careful, Sir Patrick! I propose to place myself under the protection of a justice of the peace; and this is a memorandum of my statement. The library—did I understand you to say? Just so—the library."

"Add," said Sir Patrick, with another pressure on the blister, "that The Person had an interview with Blanche in the library."

Lady Lundie's pen suddenly stuck in the paper, and scattered a little shower of ink-drops all round it. "The library," repeated her ladyship, in a voice suggestive of approaching suffocation. "I undertake to control myself, Sir Patrick! Any thing missing from the library?"

"Nothing missing, Lady Lundie, but The Person herself. She—"

"No, Sir Patrick! I won't have it! In the name of my own sex, I won't have it!"

"Pray pardon me—I forgot that 'she' was a prohibited pronoun on the present occasion. The Person has written a farewell letter to Blanche, and has gone nobody knows where. The distress produced by these events is alone answerable for what has happened to Blanche this morning. If you bear that in mind—and if you remember what your own opinion is of Miss Silvester—you will understand why Blanche hesitated to admit you into her confidence."

There he waited for a reply. Lady Lundie was too deeply absorbed in completing her memorandum to be conscious of his presence in the room.

"'Carriage to be at the door at two-thirty,'" said Lady Lundie, repeating the final words of the memorandum while she wrote them. "'Inquire for the nearest justice of the peace, and place the privacy of Windygates under the protection of the law.'—I beg your pardon!" exclaimed her ladyship, becoming conscious again of Sir Patrick's presence. "Have I missed any thing particularly painful? Pray mention it if I have!"

"You have missed nothing of the slightest importance," returned Sir Patrick. "I have placed you in possession of facts which you had a right to know; and we have now only to return to our medical friend's report on Blanche's health. You were about to favor me, I think, with the Prognosis?"

"Diagnosis!" said her ladyship, spitefully. "I had forgotten at the time—I remember now. Prognosis is entirely wrong."

"I sit corrected, Lady Lundie. Diagnosis."

"You have informed me, Sir Patrick, that you were already acquainted with the Diagnosis. It is quite needless for me to repeat it now."

"I was anxious to correct my own impression, my dear lady, by comparing it with yours."

"You are very good. You are a learned man. I am only a poor ignorant woman. Your impression can not possibly require correcting by mine."

"My impression, Lady Lundie, was that our friend recommended moral, rather than medical, treatment for Blanche. If we can turn her thoughts from the painful subject on which they are now dwelling, we shall do all that is needful. Those were his own words, as I remember them. Do you confirm me?"

"Can I presume to dispute with you, Sir Patrick? You are a master of refined irony, I know. I am afraid it's all thrown away on poor me."

(The law kept its wonderful temper! The law met the most exasperating of living women with a counter-power of defensive aggravation all its own!)

"I take that as confirming me, Lady Lundie. Thank you. Now, as to the method of carrying out our friend's advice. The method seems plain. All we can do to divert Blanche's mind is to turn Blanche's attention to some other sub-ject of reflection less painful than the subject which occupies her now. Do you agree, so far?"

"Why place the whole responsibility on my shoulders?" inquired Lady Lundie.

"Out of profound deference for your opinion," answered Sir Patrick. "Strictly speaking, no doubt, any serious responsibility rests with me. I am Blanche's guardian—"

"Thank God!" cried Lady Lundie, with a perfect explosion of pious fervor.

"I hear an outburst of devout thankfulness," remarked Sir Patrick. "Am I to take it as expressing—let me say—some little doubt, on your part, as to the prospect of managing Blanche successfully, under present circumstances?"

Lady Lundie's temper began to give way again—exactly as her brother-in-law had anticipated.

"You are to take it," she said, "as expressing my conviction that I saddled myself with the charge of an incorrigibly heartless, obstinate, and perverse girl, when I undertook the care of Blanche."

"Did you say 'incorrigibly?'"

"I said 'incorrigibly.'"

"If the case is as hopeless as that, my dear Madam—as Blanche's guardian, I ought to find means to relieve you of the charge of Blanche."

"Nobody shall relieve me of a duty that I have once undertaken!" retorted Lady Lundie. "Not if I die at my post!"

"Suppose it was consistent with your duty," pleaded Sir Patrick, "to be relieved at your post? Suppose it was in harmony with that 'self-sacrifice' which is 'the motto of women?'"

"I don't understand you, Sir Patrick. Be so good as to explain yourself."

Sir Patrick assumed a new character—the character of a hesitating man. He cast a look of respectful inquiry at his sister-in-law, sighed, and shook his head.

"No!" he said. "It would be asking too much. Even with your high standard of duty, it would be asking too much."

"Nothing which you can ask me in the name of duty is too much."

"No! no! Let me remind you. Human nature has its limits."

"A Christian gentlewoman's sense of duty knows no limits."

"Oh, surely yes!"

"Sir Patrick! after what I have just said, your perseverance in doubting me amounts to something like an insult!"

"Don't say that! Let me put a case. Let us suppose the future interests of another person to depend on your saying, Yes—when all your own most cherished ideas and opinions urge you to say, No. Do you really mean to tell me that you could trample your own convictions under foot, if it could be shown that the purely abstract consideration of duty was involved in the sacrifice?"

"Yes!" cried Lady Lundie, mounting the pedestal of her virtue on the spot. "Yes—without a moment's hesitation!"

"I sit corrected, Lady Lundie. You embolden me to proceed. Allow me to ask (after what I have just heard)—whether it is not your duty to act on advice given for Blanche's benefit, by one of the highest medical authorities in England?"

Her ladyship admitted that it was her duty;

"ADMIRABLE WOMAN—ADIEU!"

pending a more favorable opportunity for contradicting her brother-in-law.

"Very good," pursued Sir Patrick. "Assuming that Blanche is like most other human beings, and has some prospect of happiness to contemplate, if she could only be made to see it—are we not bound to make her see it, by our moral obligation to act on the medical advice?" He cast a courteously-persuasive look at her ladyship, and paused in the most innocent manner for a reply.

If Lady Lundie had not been bent—thanks to the irritation fomented by her brother-in-law—on disputing the ground with him, inch by inch, she must have seen signs, by this time, of the snare that was being set for her. As it was, she saw nothing but the opportunity of disparaging Blanche and contradicting Sir Patrick.

"If my step-daughter had any such prospect as you describe," she answered, "I should of course say, Yes. But Blanche's is an ill-regulated mind. An ill-regulated mind has no prospect of happiness."

"Pardon me," said Sir Patrick. "Blanche *has* a prospect of happiness. In other words, Blanche has a prospect of being married. And, what is more, Arnold Brinkworth is ready to marry her as soon as the settlements can be prepared."

Lady Lundie started in her chair—turned crimson with rage—and opened her lips to speak. Sir Patrick rose to his feet, and went on before she could utter a word.

"I beg to relieve you, Lady Lundie—by means which you have just acknowledged it to be your duty to accept—of all further charge of an incorrigible girl. As Blanche's guardian, I have the honor of proposing that her marriage be advanced to a day to be hereafter named in the first fortnight of the ensuing month."

In those words he closed the trap which he had set for his sister-in-law, and waited to see what came of it.

A thoroughly spiteful woman, thoroughly roused, is capable of subordinating every other consideration to the one imperative necessity of gratifying her spite. There was but one way now of turning the tables on Sir Patrick—and Lady Lundie took it. She hated him, at that moment, so intensely, that not even the assertion of her own obstinate will promised her more than a tame satisfaction, by comparison with the priceless enjoyment of beating her brother-in-law with his own weapons.

"My dear Sir Patrick!" she said, with a little silvery laugh, "you have wasted much precious time and many eloquent words in trying to entrap me into giving my consent, when you might have had it for the asking. I think the idea of hastening Blanche's marriage an excellent one. I am charmed to transfer the charge of such a person as my step-daughter to the unfortunate young man who is willing to take her off my hands. The less he sees of Blanche's character the more satisfied I shall feel of his performing his engagement to marry her. Pray hurry the lawyers, Sir Patrick, and let it be a week sooner rather than a week later, if you wish to please Me."

Her ladyship rose in her grandest proportions, and made a courtesy which was nothing less than a triumph of polite satire in dumb show. Sir Patrick answered by a profound bow and a smile which said, eloquently, "I believe every word of that charming answer. Admirable woman—adieu!"

So the one person in the family circle, whose opposition might have forced Sir Patrick to submit to a timely delay, was silenced by adroit management of the vices of her own character. So, in despite of herself, Lady Lundie was won over to the project for hurrying the marriage of Arnold and Blanche.

---

## CHAPTER THE TWENTY-EIGHTH.

### STIFLED.

It is the nature of Truth to struggle to the light. In more than one direction, the truth strove to pierce the overlying darkness, and to reveal itself to view, during the interval between the date of Sir Patrick's victory and the date of the wedding-day.

Signs of perturbation under the surface, suggestive of some hidden influence at work, were not wanting, as the time passed on. The one thing missing was the prophetic faculty that could read those signs aright at Windygates House.

On the very day when Sir Patrick's dextrous treatment of his sister-in-law had smoothed the way to the hastening of the marriage, an obstacle was raised to the new arrangement by no less a person than Blanche herself. She had sufficiently recovered, toward noon, to be able to receive Arnold in her own little sitting-room. It proved to be a very brief interview. A quarter of an hour later, Arnold appeared before Sir Patrick —while the old gentleman was sunning himself in the garden—with a face of blank despair. Blanche had indignantly declined even to think of such a thing as her marriage, at a time when she was heart-broken by the discovery that Anne had left her forever.

"You gave me leave to mention it, Sir Patrick —didn't you?" said Arnold.

Sir Patrick shifted round a little, so as to get the sun on his back, and admitted that he had given leave.

"If I had only known, I would rather have cut my tongue out than have said a word about it. What do you think she did? She burst out crying, and ordered me to leave the room."

It was a lovely morning—a cool breeze tempered the heat of the sun; the birds were singing; the garden wore its brightest look. Sir Patrick was supremely comfortable. The little wearisome vexations of this mortal life had retired to a respectful distance from him. He positively declined to invite them to come any nearer.

"Here is a world," said the old gentleman, getting the sun a little more broadly on his back, "which a merciful Creator has filled with lovely sights, harmonious sounds, delicious scents; and here are creatures with faculties expressly made for enjoyment of those sights, sounds, and scents —to say nothing of Love, Dinner, and Sleep, all thrown into the bargain. And these same creatures hate, starve, toss sleepless on their pillows, see nothing pleasant, hear nothing pleasant, smell nothing pleasant — cry bitter tears, say hard words, contract painful illnesses; wither, sink, age, die! What does it mean, Arnold? And how much longer is it all to go on?"

The fine connecting link between the blindness of Blanche to the advantage of being married, and the blindness of humanity to the advantage of being in existence, though sufficiently perceptible no doubt to venerable Philosophy ripening in the sun, was absolutely invisible to Arnold. He deliberately dropped the vast question opened by Sir Patrick; and, reverting to Blanche, asked what was to be done.

"What do you do with a fire, when you can't extinguish it?" said Sir Patrick. "You let it blaze till it goes out. What do you do with a woman when you can't pacify her? Let *her* blaze till she goes out."

Arnold failed to see the wisdom embodied in that excellent advice. "I thought you would have helped me to put things right with Blanche," he said.

"I *am* helping you. Let Blanche alone. Don't speak of the marriage again, the next time you see her. If she mentions it, beg her pardon, and tell her you won't press the question any more. I shall see her in an hour or two, and I shall take exactly the same tone myself. You have put the idea into her mind—leave it there to ripen. Give her distress about Miss Silvester nothing to feed on. Don't stimulate it by contradiction; don't rouse it to defend itself by disparagement of her lost friend. Leave Time to edge her gently nearer and nearer to the husband who is waiting for her—and take my word for it, Time will have her ready when the settlements are ready."

Toward the luncheon hour Sir Patrick saw Blanche, and put in practice the principle which he had laid down. She was perfectly tranquil before her uncle left her. A little later, Arnold was forgiven. A little later still, the old gentleman's sharp observation noted that his niece was unusually thoughtful, and that she looked at Arnold, from time to time, with an interest of a new kind—an interest which shyly hid itself from Arnold's view. Sir Patrick went up to dress for dinner, with a comfortable inner conviction that the difficulties which had beset him were settled at last. Sir Patrick had never been more mistaken in his life.

The business of the toilet was far advanced. Duncan had just placed the glass in a good light; and Duncan's master was at that turning-point in his daily life which consisted in attaining, or not attaining, absolute perfection in the tying of his white cravat—when some outer barbarian, ignorant of the first principles of dressing a gentleman's throat, presumed to knock at the bedroom door. Neither master nor servant moved or breathed until the integrity of the cravat was placed beyond the reach of accident. Then Sir Patrick cast the look of final criticism in the glass, and breathed again when he saw that it was done.

"A little labored in style, Duncan. But not bad, considering the interruption?"

"By no means, Sir Patrick."

"See who it is."

Duncan went to the door; and returned, to his master, with an excuse for the interruption, in the shape of a telegram!

Sir Patrick started at the sight of that unwelcome message. "Sign the receipt, Duncan," he said—and opened the envelope. Yes! Exactly as he had anticipated! News of Miss Silvester, on the very day when he had decided to abandon all further attempt at discovering her. The telegram ran thus:

"Message received from Falkirk this morning. Lady, as described, left the train at Falkirk last night. Went on, by the first train this morning, to Glasgow. Wait further instructions."

"Is the messenger to take any thing back, Sir Patrick?"

"No. I must consider what I am to do. If I find it necessary, I will send to the station. Here is news of Miss Silvester, Duncan," continued Sir Patrick, when the messenger had gone. "She has been traced to Glasgow."

"Glasgow is a large place, Sir Patrick."

"Yes. Even if they have telegraphed on and had her watched (which doesn't appear), she may escape us again at Glasgow. I am the last man in the world, I hope, to shrink from accepting my fair share of any responsibility. But I own I would have given something to have kept this telegram out of the house. It raises the most awkward question I have had to decide on for many a long day past. Help me on with my coat. I must think of it! I must think of it!"

Sir Patrick went down to dinner in no agreeable frame of mind. The unexpected recovery of the lost trace of Miss Silvester—there is no disguising it—seriously annoyed him.

The dinner-party that day, assembling punctually at the stroke of the bell, had to wait a quarter of an hour before the hostess came down stairs.

Lady Lundie's apology, when she entered the library, informed her guests that she had been detained by some neighbors who had called at an unusually late hour. Mr. and Mrs. Julius Delamayn, finding themselves near Windygates, had favored her with a visit, on their way home, and had left cards of invitation for a garden-party at their house.

Lady Lundie was charmed with her new acquaintances. They had included every body who was staying at Windygates in their invitation. They had been as pleasant and easy as old friends. Mrs. Delamayn had brought the kindest message from one of her guests—Mrs. Glenarm—to say that she remembered meeting Lady Lundie in London, in the time of the late Sir Thomas, and was anxious to improve the acquaintance. Mr. Julius Delamayn had given a most amusing account of his brother. Geoffrey had sent to London for a trainer; and the whole household was on the tip-toe of expectation to witness the magnificent spectacle of an athlete preparing himself for a foot-race. The ladies, with Mrs. Glenarm at their head, were hard at work, studying the profound and complicated question of human running—the muscles employed in it, the preparation required for it, the heroes eminent in it. The men had been all occupied that morning in assisting Geoffrey to measure a mile, for his exercising-ground, in a remote part of the park—where there was an empty cottage, which was to be fitted with all the necessary appliances for the reception of Geoffrey and his trainer. "You will see the last of my brother," Julius had said, "at the garden-party. After that he retires into athletic privacy, and has but one interest in life—the interest of watching the disappearance of his own superfluous flesh." Throughout the dinner Lady Lundie was in oppressively good spirits, singing the praises of her new friends. Sir Patrick, on the other hand,

had never been so silent within the memory of mortal man. He talked with an effort; and he listened with a greater effort still. To answer or not to answer the telegram in his pocket? To persist or not to persist in his resolution to leave Miss Silvester to go her own way? Those were the questions which insisted on coming round to him as regularly as the dishes themselves came round in the orderly progression of the dinner.

Blanche—who had not felt equal to taking her place at the table—appeared in the drawing-room afterward.

Sir Patrick came in to tea, with the gentlemen, still uncertain as to the right course to take in the matter of the telegram. One look at Blanche's sad face and Blanche's altered manner decided him. What would be the result if he roused new hopes by resuming the effort to trace Miss Silvester, and if he lost the trace a second time? He had only to look at his niece and to see. Could any consideration justify him in turning her mind back on the memory of the friend who had left her at the moment when it was just beginning to look forward for relief to the prospect of her marriage? Nothing could justify him; and nothing should induce him to do it.

Reasoning—soundly enough, from his own point of view—on that basis, Sir Patrick determined on sending no further instructions to his friend at Edinburgh. That night he warned Duncan to preserve the strictest silence as to the arrival of the telegram. He burned it, in case of accidents, with his own hand, in his own room.

Rising the next day and looking out of his window, Sir Patrick saw the two young people taking their morning walk at a moment when they happened to cross the open grassy space which separated the two shrubberies at Windygates. Arnold's arm was round Blanche's waist, and they were talking confidentially with their heads close together. "She is coming round already!" thought the old gentleman, as the two disappeared again in the second shrubbery from view. "Thank Heaven! things are running smoothly at last!"

Among the ornaments of Sir Patrick's bedroom there was a view (taken from above) of one of the Highland waterfalls. If he had looked at the picture when he turned away from his window, he might have remarked that a river which is running with its utmost smoothness at one moment may be a river which plunges into its most violent agitation at another; and he might have remembered, with certain misgivings, that the progress of a stream of water has been long since likened, with the universal consent of humanity, to the progress of the stream of life.

---

FIFTH SCENE.—GLASGOW.

## CHAPTER THE TWENTY-NINTH.

### ANNE AMONG THE LAWYERS.

On the day when Sir Patrick received the second of the two telegrams sent to him from Edinburgh, four respectable inhabitants of the City of Glasgow were startled by the appearance of an object of interest on the monotonous horizon of their daily lives.

The persons receiving this wholesome shock were—Mr. and Mrs. Karnegie of the Sheep's Head Hotel; and Mr. Camp, and Mr. Crum, attached as "Writers" to the honorable profession of the Law.

It was still early in the day when a lady arrived, in a cab from the railway, at the Sheep's Head Hotel. Her luggage consisted of a black box, and of a well-worn leather bag which she carried in her hand. The name on the box (recently written on a new luggage label, as the color of the ink and paper showed) was a very good name in its way, common to a very great number of ladies, both in Scotland and England. It was "Mrs. Graham."

Encountering the landlord at the entrance to the hotel, "Mrs. Graham" asked to be accommodated with a bedroom, and was transferred in due course to the chamber-maid on duty at the time. Returning to the little room behind the bar, in which the accounts were kept, Mr. Karnegie surprised his wife by moving more briskly, and looking much brighter than usual. Being questioned, Mr. Karnegie (who had cast the eye of a landlord on the black box in the passage) announced that one "Mrs. Graham" had just arrived, and was then and there to be booked as inhabiting Room Number Seventeen. Being informed (with considerable asperity of tone and manner) that this answer failed to account for the interest which appeared to have been inspired in him by a total stranger, Mr. Karnegie came to the point, and confessed that "Mrs. Graham" was one of the sweetest-looking women he had seen for many a long day, and that he feared she was very seriously out of health.

Upon that reply the eyes of Mrs. Karnegie developed in size, and the color of Mrs. Karnegie deepened in tint. She got up from her chair, and said that it might be just as well if she personally superintended the installation of "Mrs. Graham" in her room, and personally satisfied herself that "Mrs. Graham" was a fit inmate to be received at the Sheep's Head Hotel. Mr. Karnegie thereupon did what he always did— he agreed with his wife.

Mrs. Karnegie was absent for some little time. On her return her eyes had a certain tigerish cast in them when they rested on Mr. Karnegie. She ordered tea and some light refreshment to be taken to Number Seventeen. This done— without any visible provocation to account for the remark—she turned upon her husband, and said, "Mr. Karnegie, you are a fool." Mr. Karnegie asked, "Why, my dear?" Mrs. Karnegie snapped her fingers, and said, "*That* for her good looks! You don't know a good-looking woman when you see her." Mr. Karnegie agreed with his wife.

Nothing more was said until the waiter appeared at the bar with his tray. Mrs. Karnegie, having first waived the tray off, without instituting her customary investigation, sat down suddenly with a thump, and said to her husband (who had not uttered a word in the interval), "Don't talk to Me about her being out of health! *That* for her health! It's trouble on her mind."

Mr. Karnegie said, "Is it now?" Mrs. Karnegie replied, "When I have said, It is, I consider myself insulted if another person says, Is it?" Mr. Karnegie agreed with his wife.

There was another interval. Mrs. Karnegie added up a bill, with a face of disgust. Mr. Karnegie looked at her with a face of wonder. Mrs. Karnegie suddenly asked him why he wasted his looks on *her*, when he would have "Mrs. Graham" to look at before long. Mr. Karnegie, upon that, attempted to compromise the matter by looking, in the interim, at his own boots. Mrs. Karnegie wished to know whether, after twenty years of married life, she was considered to be not worth answering by her own husband. Treated with bare civility (she expected no more), she might have gone on to explain that "Mrs. Graham" was going out. She might also have been prevailed on to mention that "Mrs. Graham" had asked her a very remarkable question of a business nature, at the interview between them up stairs. As it was, Mrs. Karnegie's lips were sealed, and let Mr. Karnegie deny, if he dared, that he richly deserved it. Mr. Karnegie agreed with his wife.

In half an hour more, "Mrs. Graham" came down stairs; and a cab was sent for. Mr. Karnegie, in fear of the consequences if he did otherwise, kept in a corner. Mrs. Karnegie followed him into the corner, and asked him how he dared act in that way? Did he presume to think, after twenty years of married life, that his wife was jealous? "Go, you brute, and hand Mrs. Graham into the cab!"

Mr. Karnegie obeyed. He asked, at the cab window, to what part of Glasgow he should tell the driver to go. The reply informed him that the driver was to take "Mrs. Graham" to the office of Mr. Camp, the lawyer. Assuming "Mrs. Graham" to be a stranger in Glasgow, and remembering that Mr. Camp was Mr. Karnegie's lawyer, the inference appeared to be, that "Mrs. Graham's" remarkable question, addressed to the landlady, had related to legal business, and to the discovery of a trust-worthy person capable of transacting it for her.

Returning to the bar, Mr. Karnegie found his eldest daughter in charge of the books, the bills, and the waiters. Mrs. Karnegie had retired to her own room, justly indignant with her husband for his infamous conduct in handing "Mrs. Graham" into the cab before her own eyes. "It's the old story, Pa," remarked Miss Karnegie, with the most perfect composure. "Ma told you to do it, of course; and then Ma says you've insulted her before all the servants. I wonder how you bear it?" Mr. Karnegie looked at his boots, and answered, "I wonder, too, my dear." Miss Karnegie said, "You're not going to Ma, are you?" Mr. Karnegie looked up from his boots, and answered, "I must, my dear."

Mr. Camp sat in his private room, absorbed over his papers. Multitudinous as those documents were, they appeared to be not sufficiently numerous to satisfy Mr. Camp. He rang his bell, and ordered more.

The clerk appearing with a new pile of papers, appeared also with a message. A lady, recommended by Mrs. Karnegie, of the Sheep's Head, wished to consult Mr. Camp professionally. Mr. Camp looked at his watch, counting out precious time before him, in a little stand on the table, and said, "Show the lady in, in ten minutes."

In ten minutes the lady appeared. She took the client's chair and lifted her veil. The same

THE EFFECT OF MR. CAMP'S OPINION.

effect which had been produced on Mr. Karnegie was once more produced on Mr. Camp. For the first time, for many a long year past, he felt personally interested in a total stranger. It might have been something in her eyes, or it might have been something in her manner. Whatever it was, it took softly hold of him, and made him, to his own exceeding surprise, unmistakably anxious to hear what she had to say!

The lady announced—in a low sweet voice, touched with a quiet sadness—that her business related to a question of marriage (as marriage is understood by Scottish law), and that her own peace of mind, and the happiness of a person very dear to her, were concerned alike in the opinion which Mr. Camp might give when he had been placed in possession of the facts.

She then proceeded to state the facts, without mentioning names : relating in every particular precisely the same succession of events which Geoffrey Delamayn had already related to Sir Patrick Lundie—with this one difference, that she acknowledged herself to be the woman who was personally concerned in knowing whether, by Scottish law, she was now held to be a married woman or not.

Mr. Camp's opinion given upon this, after certain questions had been asked and answered, differed from Sir Patrick's opinion, as given at Windygates. He too quoted the language used by the eminent judge—Lord Deas,—but he drew an inference of his own from it. "In Scotland, consent makes marriage," he said ; "and consent may be proved by inference. I see a plain inference of matrimonial consent in the circumstances which you have related to me ; and I say you are a married woman."

The effect produced on the lady, when sentence was pronounced on her in those terms, was so distressing that Mr. Camp sent a message up stairs to his wife ; and Mrs. Camp appeared in her husband's private room, in business hours, for the first time in her life. When Mrs. Camp's services had in some degree restored the lady to herself, Mr. Camp followed with a word of professional comfort. He, like Sir Patrick, acknowledged the scandalous divergence of opinions produced by the confusion and uncertainty of the marriage-law of Scotland. He, like Sir Patrick, declared it to be quite possible that another lawyer might arrive at another conclusion. "Go," he said, giving her his card, with a line of writing on it, "to my colleague, Mr. Crum ; and say I sent you."

The lady gratefully thanked Mr. Camp and his wife, and went next to the office of Mr. Crum.

Mr. Crum was the older lawyer of the two, and the harder lawyer of the two ; but he, too, felt the influence which the charm that there was in this woman exercised, more or less, over every man who came in contact with her. He listened with a patience which was rare with him : he put his questions with a gentleness which was rarer still ; and when *he* was in possession of the circumstances—behold, *his* opinion flatly contradicted the opinion of Mr. Camp !

"No marriage, ma'am," he said, positively. "Evidence in favor of perhaps establishing a marriage, if you propose to claim the man. But that, as I understand it, is exactly what you don't wish to do."

The relief to the lady, on hearing this, almost overpowered her. For some minutes she was unable to speak. Mr. Crum did, what he had never done yet in all his experience as a lawyer. He patted a client on the shoulder; and, more extraordinary still, he gave a client permission to waste his time. "Wait, and compose yourself," said Mr. Crum—administering the law of humanity. The lady composed herself. "I must ask you some questions, ma'am," said Mr. Crum—administering the law of the land. The lady bowed, and waited for him to begin.

"I know, thus far, that you decline to claim the gentleman," said Mr. Crum. "I want to know now whether the gentleman is likely to claim *you*."

The answer to this was given in the most positive terms. The gentleman was not even aware of the position in which he stood. And, more yet, he was engaged to be married to the dearest friend whom the lady had in the world.

Mr. Crum opened his eyes—considered—and put another question as delicately as he could:

"Would it be painful to you to tell me how the gentleman came to occupy the awkward position in which he stands now?"

The lady acknowledged that it would be indescribably painful to her to answer that question.

Mr. Crum offered a suggestion under the form of an inquiry:

"Would it be painful to you to reveal the circumstances—in the interests of the gentleman's future prospects—to some discreet person (a legal person would be best) who is not, what I am, a stranger to you both?"

The lady declared herself willing to make any sacrifice, on those conditions—no matter how painful it might be—for her friend's sake.

Mr. Crum considered a little longer, and then delivered his word of advice:

"At the present stage of the affair," he said, "I need only tell you what is the first step that you ought to take under the circumstances. Inform the gentleman at once—either by word of mouth or by writing—of the position in which he stands; and authorize him to place the case in the hands of a person known to you both, who is competent to decide on what you are to do next. Do I understand that you know of such a person so qualified?"

The lady answered that she knew of such a person.

Mr. Crum asked if a day had been fixed for the gentleman's marriage.

The lady answered that she had made this inquiry herself on the last occasion when she had seen the gentleman's betrothed wife. The marriage was to take place, on a day to be hereafter chosen, at the end of the autumn.

"That," said Mr. Crum, "is a fortunate circumstance. You have time before you. Time is, here, of very great importance. Be careful not to waste it."

The lady said she would return to her hotel and write by that night's post, to warn the gentleman of the position in which he stood, and to authorize him to refer the matter to a competent and trust-worthy friend known to them both.

On rising to leave the room she was seized with giddiness, and with some sudden pang of pain, which turned her deadly pale and forced her to drop back into her chair. Mr. Crum had no wife; but he possessed a housekeeper—and he offered to send for her. The lady made a sign in the negative. She drank a little water, and conquered the pain. "I am sorry to have alarmed you," she said. "It's nothing—I am better now." Mr. Crum gave her his arm, and put her into the cab. She looked so pale and faint that he proposed sending his housekeeper with her. No: it was only five minutes' drive to the hotel. The lady thanked him—and went her way back by herself.

"The letter!" she said, when she was alone. "If I can only live long enough to write the letter!"

---

## CHAPTER THE THIRTIETH.

### ANNE IN THE NEWSPAPERS.

MRS. KARNEGIE was a woman of feeble intelligence and violent temper; prompt to take offense, and not, for the most part, easy to appease. But Mrs. Karnegie being—as we all are in our various degrees—a compound of many opposite qualities, possessed a character with more than one side to it, and had her human merits as well as her human faults. Seeds of sound good feeling were scattered away in the remoter corners of her nature, and only waited for the fertilizing occasion that was to help them to spring up. The occasion exerted that benign influence when the cab brought Mr. Crum's client back to the hotel. The face of the weary, heart-sick woman, as she slowly crossed the hall, roused all that was heartiest and best in Mrs. Karnegie's nature, and said to her, as if in words, "Jealous of this broken creature? Oh, wife and mother, is there no appeal to your common womanhood *here*?"

"I am afraid you have overtired yourself, ma'am. Let me send you something up stairs?"

"Send me pen, ink, and paper," was the answer. "I must write a letter. I must do it at once."

It was useless to remonstrate with her. She was ready to accept any thing proposed, provided the writing materials were supplied first. Mrs. Karnegie sent them up, and then compounded a certain mixture of eggs and hot wine, for which The Sheep's Head was famous, with her own hands. In five minutes or so it was ready—and Miss Karnegie was dispatched by her mother (who had other business on hand at the time) to take it up stairs.

After the lapse of a few moments a cry of alarm was heard from the upper landing. Mrs. Karnegie recognized her daughter's voice, and hastened to the bedroom floor.

"Oh, mamma! Look at her! look at her!"

The letter was on the table with the first lines written. The woman was on the sofa with her handkerchief twisted between her set teeth, and her tortured face terrible to look at. Mrs. Karnegie raised her a little, examined her closely—then suddenly changed color, and sent her daughter out of the room with directions to dispatch a messenger instantly for medical help.

Left alone with the sufferer, Mrs. Karnegie carried her to her bed. As she was laid down her left hand fell helpless over the side of the bed. Mrs. Karnegie suddenly checked the word of sympathy as it rose to her lips—suddenly lifted the hand, and looked, with a momentary sternness of scrutiny, at the third finger. There was a ring on it. Mrs. Karnegie's face softened on the instant: the word of pity that had been suspended the moment before passed her lips freely now. "Poor soul!" said the respectable landlady, taking appearances for granted. "Where's your husband, dear? Try and tell me."

The doctor made his appearance, and went up to the patient.

Time passed, and Mr. Karnegie and his daughter, carrying on the business of the hotel, received a message from up stairs which was ominous of something out of the common. The message gave the name and address of an experienced nurse—with the doctor's compliments, and would Mr. Karnegie have the kindness to send for her immediately.

The nurse was found and sent up stairs.

Time went on, and the business of the hotel went on, and it was getting to be late in the evening, when Mrs. Karnegie appeared at last in the parlor behind the bar. The landlady's face was grave; the landlady's manner was subdued. "Very, very ill," was the only reply she made to her daughter's inquiries. When she and her husband were together, a little later, she told the news from up stairs in greater detail. "A child born dead," said Mrs. Karnegie, in gentler tones than were customary with her. "And the mother dying, poor thing, so far as *I* can see."

A little later the doctor came down. Dead? No.—Likely to live? Impossible to say. The doctor returned twice in the course of the night. Both times he had but one answer. "Wait till to-morrow."

The next day came. She rallied a little. Toward the afternoon she began to speak. She expressed no surprise at seeing strangers by her bedside: her mind wandered. She passed again into insensibility. Then back to delirium once more. The doctor said, "This may last for weeks. Or it may end suddenly in death. It's time you did something toward finding her friends."

(Her friends! She had left the one friend she had forever!)

Mr. Camp was summoned to give his advice. The first thing he asked for was the unfinished letter.

It was blotted, it was illegible in more places than one. With pains and care they made out the address at the beginning, and here and there some fragments of the lines that followed. It began: "Dear Mr. Brinkworth." Then the writing got, little by little, worse and worse. To the eyes of the strangers who looked at it, it ran thus: "I should ill requite * * * Blanche's interests * * * For God's sake! * * * don't think of *me* * * *" There was a little more, but not so much as one word, in those last lines, was legible.

The names mentioned in the letter were reported by the doctor and the nurse to be also the names on her lips when she spoke in her wanderings. "Mr. Brinkworth" and "Blanche"—her mind ran incessantly on those two persons. The one intelligible thing that she mentioned in connection with them was the letter. She was perpetually trying, trying, trying to take that unfinished letter to the post; and she could never get there. Sometimes the post was across the sea. Sometimes it was at the top of an inaccessible mountain. Sometimes it was built in

by prodigious walls all round it. Sometimes a man stopped her cruelly at the moment when she was close at the post, and forced her back thousands of miles away from it. She once or twice mentioned this visionary man by his name. They made it out to be "Geoffrey."

Finding no clew to her identity either in the letter that she had tried to write or in the wild words that escaped her from time to time, it was decided to search her luggage, and to look at the clothes which she had worn when she arrived at the hotel.

Her black box sufficiently proclaimed itself as recently purchased. On opening it the address of a Glasgow trunk-maker was discovered inside. The linen was also new, and unmarked. The receipted shop-bill was found with it. The tradesmen, sent for in each case and questioned, referred to their books. It was proved that the box and the linen had both been purchased on the day when she appeared at the hotel.

Her black bag was opened next. A sum of between eighty and ninety pounds in Bank of England notes; a few simple articles belonging to the toilet; materials for needle-work; and a photographic portrait of a young lady, inscribed, "To Anne, from Blanche," were found in the bag—but no letters, and nothing whatever that could afford the slightest clew by which the owner could be traced. The pocket in her dress was searched next. It contained a purse, an empty card-case, and a new handkerchief unmarked.

Mr. Camp shook his head.

"A woman's luggage without any letters in it," he said, "suggests to my mind a woman who has a motive of her own for keeping her movements a secret. I suspect she has destroyed her letters, and emptied her card-case, with that view." Mrs. Karnegie's report, after examining the linen which the so-called "Mrs. Graham" had worn when she arrived at the inn, proved the soundness of the lawyer's opinion. In every case the marks had been cut out. Mrs. Karnegie began to doubt whether the ring which she had seen on the third finger of the lady's left hand had been placed there with the sanction of the law.

There was but one chance left of discovering—or rather of attempting to discover—her friends. Mr. Camp drew out an advertisement to be inserted in the Glasgow newspapers. If those newspapers happened to be seen by any member of her family, she would, in all probability, be claimed. In the contrary event there would be nothing for it but to wait for her recovery or her death—with the money belonging to her sealed up, and deposited in the landlord's strong-box.

The advertisement appeared. They waited for three days afterward, and nothing came of it. No change of importance occurred, during the same period, in the condition of the suffering woman. Mr. Camp looked in, toward evening, and said, "We have done our best. There is no help for it but to wait."

Far away in Perthshire that third evening was marked as a joyful occasion at Windygates House. Blanche had consented at last to listen to Arnold's entreaties, and had sanctioned the writing of a letter to London to order her wedding-dress.

SIXTH SCENE.—SWANHAVEN LODGE.

## CHAPTER THE THIRTY-FIRST

SEEDS OF THE FUTURE (FIRST SOWING).

"Not so large as Windygates. But—shall we say snug, Jones?"

"And comfortable, Smith. I quite agree with you."

Such was the judgment pronounced by the two choral gentlemen on Julius Delamayn's house in Scotland. It was, as usual with Smith and Jones, a sound judgment—as far as it went. Swanhaven Lodge was not half the size of Windygates; but it had been inhabited for two centuries when the foundations of Windygates were first laid—and it possessed the advantages, without inheriting the drawbacks, of its age. There is in an old house a friendly adaptation to the human character, as there is in an old hat a friendly adaptation to the human head. The visitor who left Swanhaven quitted it with something like a sense of leaving home. Among the few houses not our own which take a strong hold on our sympathies this was one. The ornamental grounds were far inferior in size and splendor to the grounds at Windygates. But the park was beautiful—less carefully laid out, but also less monotonous than an English park. The lake on the northern boundary of the estate, famous for its breed of swans, was one of the curiosities of the neighborhood; and the house had a history, associating it with more than one celebrated Scottish name, which had been written and illustrated by Julius Delamayn. Visitors to Swanhaven Lodge were invariably presented with a copy of the volume (privately printed). One in twenty read it. The rest were "charmed," and looked at the pictures.

The day was the last day of August, and the occasion was the garden-party given by Mr. and Mrs. Delamayn.

Smith and Jones—following, with the other guests at Windygates, in Lady Lundie's train—exchanged their opinions on the merits of the house, standing on a terrace at the back, near a flight of steps which led down into the garden. They formed the van-guard of the visitors, appearing by twos and threes from the reception rooms, and all bent on going to see the swans before the amusements of the day began. Julius Delamayn came out with the first detachment, recruited Smith and Jones, and other wandering bachelors, by the way, and set forth for the lake. An interval of a minute or two passed—and the terrace remained empty. Then two ladies—at the head of a second detachment of visitors—appeared under the old stone porch which sheltered the entrance on that side of the house. One of the ladies was a modest, pleasant little person, very simply dressed. The other was of the tall and formidable type of "fine women," clad in dazzling array. The first was Mrs. Julius Delamayn. The second was Lady Lundie.

"Exquisite!" cried her ladyship, surveying the old mullioned windows of the house, with their framing of creepers, and the grand stone buttresses projecting at intervals from the wall, each with its bright little circle of flowers blooming round the base. "I am really grieved that Sir Patrick should have missed this."

"I think you said, Lady Lundie, that Sir Pat-rick had been called to Edinburgh by family business?"

"Business, Mrs. Delamayn, which is any thing but agreeable to me, as one member of the family. It has altered all my arrangements for the autumn. My step-daughter is to be married next week."

"Is it so near as that? May I ask who the gentleman is?"

"Mr. Arnold Brinkworth."

"Surely I have some association with that name?"

"You have probably heard of him, Mrs. Delamayn, as the heir to Miss Brinkworth's Scotch property?"

"Exactly! Have you brought Mr. Brinkworth here to-day?"

"I bring his apologies, as well as Sir Patrick's. They went to Edinburgh together a day before yesterday. The lawyers engage to have the settlements ready in three or four days more, if a personal consultation can be managed. Some formal question, I believe, connected with title-deeds. Sir Patrick thought the safest way and the speediest way would be to take Mr. Brinkworth with him to Edinburgh—to get the business over to-day—and to wait until we join them, on our way south, to-morrow."

"You leave Windygates, in this lovely weather?"

"Most unwillingly! The truth is, Mrs. Delamayn, I am at my step-daughter's mercy. Her uncle has the authority, as her guardian—and the use he makes of it is to give her her own way in every thing. It was only on Friday last that she consented to let the day be fixed—and even then she made it a positive condition that the marriage was not to take place in Scotland. Pure willfulness! But what can I do? Sir Patrick submits; and Mr. Brinkworth submits. If I am to be present at the marriage I must follow their example. I feel it my duty to be present—and, as a matter of course, I sacrifice myself. We start for London to-morrow."

"Is Miss Lundie to be married in London at this time of year?"

"No. We only pass through, on our way to Sir Patrick's place in Kent—the place that came to him with the title; the place associated with the last days of my beloved husband. Another trial for *me!* The marriage is to be solemnized on the scene of my bereavement. My old wound is to be reopened on Monday next—simply because my step-daughter has taken a dislike to Windygates."

"This day week, then, is the day of the marriage?"

"Yes. This day week. There have been reasons for hurrying it which I need not trouble you with. No words can say how I wish it was over.—But, my dear Mrs. Delamayn, how thoughtless of me to assail *you* with my family worries! You are *so* sympathetic. That is my only excuse. Don't let me keep you from your guests. I could linger in this sweet place forever! Where is Mrs. Glenarm?"

"I really don't know. I missed her when we came out on the terrace. She will very likely join us at the lake. Do you care about seeing the lake, Lady Lundie?"

"I adore the beauties of Nature, Mrs. Delamayn—especially lakes!"

"We have something to show you besides; we have a breed of swans on the lake, peculiar to the place. My husband has gone on with some of our friends; and I believe we are expected to follow, as soon as the rest of the party—in charge of my sister—have seen the house."

"And what a house, Mrs. Delamayn! Historical associations in every corner of it! It is *such* a relief to my mind to take refuge in the past. When I am far away from this sweet place I shall people Swanhaven with its departed inmates, and share the joys and sorrows of centuries since."

As Lady Lundie announced, in these terms, her intention of adding to the population of the past, the last of the guests who had been roaming over the old house appeared under the porch. Among the members forming this final addition to the garden-party were Blanche, and a friend of her own age whom she had met at Swanhaven. The two girls lagged behind the rest, talking confidentially, arm in arm—the subject (it is surely needless to add?) being the coming marriage.

"But, dearest Blanche, why are you not to be married at Windygates?"

"I detest Windygates, Janet. I have the most miserable associations with the place. Don't ask me what they are! The effort of my life is not to think of them now. I long to see the last of Windygates. As for being married there, I have made it a condition that I am not to be married in Scotland at all."

"What has poor Scotland done to forfeit your good opinion, my dear?"

"Poor Scotland, Janet, is a place where people don't know whether they are married or not. I have heard all about it from my uncle. And I know somebody who has been a victim—an innocent victim—to a Scotch marriage."

"Absurd, Blanche! You are thinking of runaway matches, and making Scotland responsible for the difficulties of people who daren't own the truth!"

"I am not at all absurd. I am thinking of the dearest friend I have. If you only knew—"

"My dear! *I* am Scotch, remember! You can be married just as well—I really must insist on that—in Scotland as in England."

"I hate Scotland!"

"Blanche!"

"I never was so unhappy in my life as I have been in Scotland. I never want to see it again. I am determined to be married in England— from the dear old house where I used to live when I was a little girl. My uncle is quite willing. *He* understands me and feels for me."

"Is that as much as to say that *I* don't understand you and feel for you? Perhaps I had better relieve you of my company, Blanche?"

"If you are going to speak to me in that way, perhaps you had!"

"Am I to hear my native country run down and not to say a word in defense of it?"

"Oh! you Scotch people make such a fuss about your native country!"

"*We* Scotch people! you are of Scotch extraction yourself, and you ought to be ashamed to talk in that way. I wish you good-morning!"

"I wish you a better temper!"

A minute since the two young ladies had been like twin roses on one stalk. Now they parted with red cheeks and hostile sentiments and cutting words. How ardent is the warmth of youth! how unspeakably delicate the fragility of female friendship!

The flock of visitors followed Mrs. Delamayn to the shores of the lake. For a few minutes after the terrace was left a solitude. Then there appeared under the porch a single gentleman, lounging out with a flower in his mouth and his hands in his pockets. This was the strongest man at Swanhaven—otherwise, Geoffrey Delamayn.

After a moment a lady appeared behind him, walking softly, so as not to be heard. She was superbly dressed after the newest and the most costly Parisian design. The brooch on her bosom was a single diamond of resplendent water and great size. The fan in her hand was a master-piece of the finest Indian workmanship. She looked what she was, a person possessed of plenty of superfluous money, but not additionally blest with plenty of superfluous intelligence to correspond. This was the childless young widow of the great iron-master—otherwise, Mrs. Glenarm.

The rich woman tapped the strong man coquettishly on the shoulder with her fan. "Ah! you bad boy!" she said, with a slightly-labored archness of look and manner. "Have I found you at last!"

Geoffrey sauntered on to the terrace—keeping the lady behind him with a thoroughly savage superiority to all civilized submission to the sex— and looked at his watch.

"I said I'd come here when I'd got half an hour to myself," he mumbled, turning the flower carelessly between his teeth. "I've got half an hour, and here I am."

"Did you come for the sake of seeing the visitors, or did you come for the sake of seeing Me?"

Geoffrey smiled graciously, and gave the flower another turn in his teeth. "You. Of course."

The iron-master's widow took his arm, and looked up at him—as only a young woman would have dared to look up—with the searching summer light streaming in its full brilliancy on her face.

Reduced to the plain expression of what it is really worth, the average English idea of beauty in women may be summed up in three words—youth, health, plumpness. The more spiritual charm of intelligence and vivacity, the subtler attraction of delicacy of line and fitness of detail, are little looked for and seldom appreciated by the mass of men in this island. It is impossible otherwise to account for the extraordinary blindness of perception which (to give one instance only) makes nine Englishmen out of ten who visit France come back declaring that they have not seen a single pretty Frenchwoman, in or out of Paris, in the whole country. Our popular type of beauty proclaims itself, in its fullest material development, at every shop in which an illustrated periodical is sold. The same fleshy-faced girl, with the same inane smile, and with no other expression whatever, appears under every form of illustration, week after week, and month after month, all the year round. Those who wish to know what Mrs. Glenarm was like, have only to go out and stop at any bookseller's or news-vendor's shop, and there they will see her in the first illustration, with a young woman in it, which they discover in the window. The one noticeable peculiarity in Mrs. Glenarm's purely commonplace and purely material beauty, which would have struck an observant and a cultivated man, was the curious girlishness of her look and manner. No stranger speaking to this woman—who had been a wife at twenty, and who was now a widow at twenty-four—would ever have thought of addressing her otherwise than as "Miss."

"Is that the use you make of a flower when I give it to you?" she said to Geoffrey. "Mumbling it in your teeth, you wretch, as if you were a horse!"

"If you come to that," returned Geoffrey, "I'm more a horse than a man. I'm going to run in a race, and the public are betting on me. Haw! haw! Five to four."

"Five to four! I believe he thinks of nothing but betting. You great heavy creature, I can't move you. Don't you see I want to go like the rest of them to the lake? No! you're not to let go of my arm! You're to take me."

"Can't do it. Must be back with Perry in half an hour."

(Perry was the trainer from London. He had arrived sooner than he had been expected, and had entered on his functions three days since.)

"Don't talk to me about Perry! A little vulgar wretch. Put him off. You won't? Do you mean to say you are such a brute that you would rather be with Perry than be with me?"

"The betting's at five to four, my dear. And the race comes off in a month from this."

"Oh! go away to your beloved Perry! I hate you. I hope you'll lose the race. Stop in your cottage. Pray don't come back to the house. And—mind this!—don't presume to say 'my dear' to me again."

"It ain't presuming half far enough, is it? Wait a bit. Give me till the race is run—and then I'll presume to marry you."

"You! You will be as old as Methuselah, if you wait till I am your wife. I dare say Perry has got a sister. Suppose you ask him? She would be just the right person for you."

Geoffrey gave the flower another turn in his teeth, and looked as if he thought the idea worth considering.

"All right," he said. "Any thing to be agreeable to you. I'll ask Perry."

He turned away, as if he was going to do it at once. Mrs. Glenarm put out a little hand, ravishingly clothed in a blush-colored glove, and laid it on the athlete's mighty arm. She pinched those iron muscles (the pride and glory of England) gently. "What a man you are!" she said. "I never met with any body like you before!"

The whole secret of the power that Geoffrey had acquired over her was in those words.

They had been together at Swanhaven for little more than ten days; and in that time he had made the conquest of Mrs. Glenarm. On the day before the garden-party—in one of the leisure intervals allowed him by Perry—he had caught her alone, had taken her by the arm, and had asked her, in so many words, if she would marry him. Instances on record of women who have been wooed and won in ten days are—to speak it with all possible respect—not wanting. But an instance of a woman willing to have it known still remains to be discovered. The iron-master's widow exacted a promise of secrecy before she committed herself. When Geoffrey had pledged his word to hold his tongue in public until she gave him leave to speak, Mrs. Glenarm, without further hesitation, said Yes—having, be it observed, said No, in the course of the last two years, to at least half a dozen men who were Geoffrey's superiors in every conceivable respect, except personal comeliness and personal strength.

There is a reason for every thing; and there was a reason for this.

However persistently the epicene theorists of modern times may deny it, it is nevertheless a truth plainly visible in the whole past history of the sexes that the natural condition of a woman is to find her master in a man. Look in the face of any woman who is in no direct way dependent on a man; and, as certainly as you see the sun in a cloudless sky, you see a woman who is not happy. The want of a master is their great unknown want; the possession of a master is—unconsciously to themselves—the only possible completion of their lives. In ninety-nine cases out of a hundred this one primitive instinct is at the bottom of the otherwise inexplicable sacrifice, when we see a woman, of her own free will, throw herself away on a man who is unworthy of her. This one primitive instinct was at the bottom of the otherwise inexplicable facility of self-surrender exhibited by Mrs. Glenarm.

Up to the time of her meeting with Geoffrey, the young widow had gathered but one experience in her intercourse with the world—the experience of a chartered tyrant. In the brief six months of her married life with the man whose grand-daughter she might have been—and ought to have been—she had only to lift her finger to be obeyed. The doting old husband was the willing slave of the petulant young wife's slightest caprice. At a later period, when society offered its triple welcome to her birth, her beauty, and her wealth—go where she might, she found herself the object of the same prostrate admiration among the suitors who vied with each other in the rivalry for her hand. For the first time in her life she encountered a man with a will of his own when she met Geoffrey Delamayn at Swanhaven Lodge.

Geoffrey's occupation of the moment especially favored the conflict between the woman's assertion of her influence and the man's assertion of his will.

During the days that had intervened between his return to his brother's house and the arrival of the trainer Geoffrey had submitted himself to all needful preliminaries of the physical discipline which was to prepare him for the race. He knew, by previous experience, what exercise he ought to take, what hours he ought to keep, what temptations at the table he was bound to resist. Over and over again Mrs. Glenarm tried to lure him into committing infractions of his own discipline —and over and over again the influence with men which had never failed her before failed her now. Nothing she could say, nothing she could do, would move this man. Perry arrived; and Geoffrey's defiance of every attempted exercise of the charming feminine tyranny, to which every one else had bowed, grew more outrageous and more immovable than ever. Mrs. Glenarm became as jealous of Perry as if Perry had been a woman. She flew into passions; she burst into tears; she flirted with other men; she threatened to leave the house. All quite useless! Geoffrey never once missed an appointment with Perry; never once touched any thing to eat or drink that she could offer him, if Perry had forbidden it. No other human pursuit is so hostile to the influence of the sex as the pursuit of athletic sports. No men are so entirely beyond the reach of women as the men whose lives are passed in the cultivation of their own physical strength. Geoffrey resisted Mrs. Glenarm without the slightest effort. He casually extorted her admiration, and undesignedly forced her respect. She clung to him, as a hero; she recoiled from him, as a brute; she struggled with him, submitted to him, despised him, adored him, in a breath. And the clew to it all, confused and contradictory as it seemed, lay in one simple fact—Mrs. Glenarm had found her master.

"Take me to the lake, Geoffrey!" she said, with a little pleading pressure of the blush-colored hand.

Geoffrey looked at his watch. "Perry expects me in twenty minutes," he said.

"Perry again!"

"Yes."

Mrs. Glenarm raised her fan, in a sudden outburst of fury, and broke it with one smart blow on Geoffrey's face.

"There!" she cried, with a stamp of her foot. "My poor fan broken! You monster, all through you!"

Geoffrey coolly took the broken fan and put it in his pocket. "I'll write to London," he said, "and get you another. Come along! Kiss, and make it up."

He looked over each shoulder, to make sure that they were alone; then lifted her off the ground (she was no light weight), held her up in the air like a baby, and gave her a rough loud-sounding kiss on each cheek. "With kind compliments from yours truly!" he said—and burst out laughing, and put her down again.

"How dare you do that?" cried Mrs. Glenarm. "I shall claim Mrs. Delamayn's protection if I am to be insulted in this way! I will never forgive you, Sir!" As she said those indignant words she shot a look at him which flatly contradicted them. The next moment she was leaning on his arm, and was looking at him wonderingly, for the thousandth time, as an entire novelty in her experience of male human kind. "How rough you are, Geoffrey!" she said, softly. He smiled in recognition of that artless homage to the manly virtue of his character. She saw the smile, and instantly made another effort to dispute the hateful supremacy of Perry. "Put him off!" whispered the daughter of Eve, determined to lure Adam into taking a bite of the apple. "Come, Geoffrey, dear, never mind Perry, this once. Take me to the lake!"

Geoffrey looked at his watch. "Perry expects me in a quarter of an hour," he said.

Mrs. Glenarm's indignation assumed a new form. She burst out crying. Geoffrey surveyed her for a moment with a broad stare of surprise—and then took her by both arms, and shook her.

"Look here!" he said, impatiently. "Can you coach me through my training?"

"I would if I could!"

"That's nothing to do with it! Can you turn

me out, fit, on the day of the race? Yes? or No?"

"No."

"Then dry your eyes, and let Perry do it."

Mrs. Glenarm dried her eyes, and made another effort.

"I'm not fit to be seen," she said. "I'm so agitated, I don't know what to do. Come indoors, Geoffrey—and have a cup of tea."

Geoffrey shook his head. "Perry forbids tea," he said, "in the middle of the day."

"You brute!" cried Mrs. Glenarm.

"Do you want me to lose the race?" retorted Geoffrey.

"Yes!"

With that answer she left him at last, and ran back into the house.

Geoffrey took a turn on the terrace—considered a little—stopped—and looked at the porch under which the irate widow had disappeared from his view. "Ten thousand a year," he said, thinking of the matrimonial prospect which he was placing in peril. "And devilish well earned," he added, going into the house, under protest, to appease Mrs. Glenarm.

The offended lady was on a sofa, in the solitary drawing-room. Geoffrey sat down by her. She declined to look at him. "Don't be a fool!" said Geoffrey, in his most persuasive manner. Mrs. Glenarm put her handkerchief to her eyes. Geoffrey took it away again without ceremony. Mrs. Glenarm rose to leave the room. Geoffrey stopped her by main force. Mrs. Glenarm threatened to summon the servants. Geoffrey said, "All right! I don't care if the whole house knows I'm fond of you!" Mrs. Glenarm looked at the door, and whispered, "Hush! for Heaven's sake!" Geoffrey put her arm in his, and said, "Come along with me: I've got something to say to you." Mrs. Glenarm drew back, and shook her head. Geoffrey put his arm round her waist, and walked her out of the room, and out of the house—taking the direction, not of the terrace, but of a fir plantation on the opposite side of the grounds. Arrived among the trees, he stopped and held up a warning forefinger before the offended lady's face. "You're just the sort of woman I like," he said; "and there ain't a man living who's half as sweet on you as I am. You leave off bullying me about Perry, and I'll tell you what I'll do—I'll let you see me take a Sprint."

He drew back a step, and fixed his big blue eyes on her, with a look which said, "You are a highly-favored woman, if ever there was one yet!" Curiosity instantly took the leading place among the emotions of Mrs. Glenarm. "What's a Sprint, Geoffrey?" she asked.

"A short run, to try me at the top of my speed. There ain't another living soul in all England that I'd let see it but you. *Now* am I a brute?"

Mrs. Glenarm was conquered again, for the hundredth time at least. She said, softly, "Oh, Geoffrey, if you could only be always like this!" Her eyes lifted themselves admiringly to his. She took his arm again of her own accord, and pressed it with a loving clasp. Geoffrey prophetically felt the ten thousand a year in his pocket. "Do you really love me?" whispered Mrs. Glenarm. "Don't I!" answered the hero. The peace was made, and the two walked on again.

"YOU'RE JUST THE SORT OF WOMAN I LIKE."

They passed through the plantation, and came out on some open ground, rising and falling prettily, in little hillocks and hollows. The last of the hillocks sloped down into a smooth level plain, with a fringe of sheltering trees on its farther side—with a snug little stone cottage among the trees—and with a smart little man, walking up and down before the cottage, holding his hands behind him. The level plain was the hero's exercising ground; the cottage was the hero's retreat; and the smart little man was the hero's trainer.

If Mrs. Glenarm hated Perry, Perry (judging by appearances) was in no danger of loving Mrs. Glenarm. As Geoffrey approached with his companion, the trainer came to a stand-still, and stared silently at the lady. The lady, on her side, declined to observe that any such person as the trainer was then in existence, and present in bodily form on the scene.

"How about time?" said Geoffrey.

Perry consulted an elaborate watch, constructed to mark time to the fifth of a second, and answered Geoffrey, with his eye all the while on Mrs. Glenarm.

"You've got five minutes to spare."

"Show me where you run; I'm dying to see it!" said the eager widow, taking possession of Geoffrey's arm with both hands.

Geoffrey led her back to a place (marked by a sapling with a little flag attached to it) at some short distance from the cottage. She glided along by his side, with subtle undulations of movement which appeared to complete the exasperation of Perry. He waited until she was out of hearing—and then he invoked (let us say) the blasts of heaven on the fashionably-dressed head of Mrs. Glenarm.

"You take your place there," said Geoffrey, posting her by the sapling. "When I pass you—" He stopped, and surveyed her with a good-humored, masculine pity. "How the devil am I to make you understand it?" he went on. "Look here! when I pass you, it will be at what you would call (if I was a horse) full gallop. Hold your tongue—I haven't done yet. You're to look on after me as I leave you, to where the edge of the cottage wall cuts the trees. When you have lost sight of me behind the wall, you'll have seen me run my three hundred yards from this flag. You're in luck's way! Perry tries me at the long Sprint to-day. You understand you're to stop here? Very well then—let me go and get my toggery on."

"Sha'n't I see you again, Geoffrey?"

"Haven't I just told you that you'll see me run?"

"Yes—but after that?"

"After that, I'm sponged and rubbed down—and rest in the cottage."

"You'll come to us this evening?"

He nodded, and left her. The face of Perry looked unutterable things when he and Geoffrey met at the door of the cottage.

"I've got a question to ask you, Mr. Delamayn," said the trainer. "Do you want me? or don't you?"

"Of course I want you."

"What did I say when I first come here?" proceeded Perry, sternly. "I said, 'I won't have nobody a looking on at a man I'm training. These here ladies and gentlemen may all have made up their minds to see you. I've made up my mind not to have no lookers-on. I won't have you timed at your work by nobody but me. I won't have every blessed yard of ground you cover put in the noospapers. I won't have a living soul in the secret of what you can do, and what you can't, except our two selves.'—Did I say that, Mr. Delamayn? or didn't I?"

" All right!"

" Did I say it? or didn't I?"

" Of course you did!"

" Then don't you bring no more women here. It's clean against rules. And I won't have it."

Any other living creature adopting this tone of remonstrance would probably have had reason to repent it. But Geoffrey himself was afraid to show his temper in the presence of Perry. In view of the coming race, the first and foremost of British trainers was not to be trifled with, even by the first and foremost of British athletes.

" She won't come again," said Geoffrey. " She's going away from Swanhaven in two days' time."

" I've put every shilling I'm worth in the world on you," pursued Perry, relapsing into tenderness. " And I tell you I felt it! It cut me to the heart when I see you coming along with a woman at your heels. It's a fraud on his backers, I says to myself—that's what it is, a fraud on his backers!"

" Shut up!" said Geoffrey. " And come and help me to win your money." He kicked open the door of the cottage—and athlete and trainer disappeared from view.

After waiting a few minutes by the little flag, Mrs. Glenarm saw the two men approaching her from the cottage. Dressed in a close-fitting costume, light and elastic, adapting itself to every movement, and made to answer every purpose required by the exercise in which he was about to engage, Geoffrey's physical advantages showed themselves in their best and bravest aspect. His head sat proud and easy on his firm, white throat, bared to the air. The rising of his mighty chest, as he drew in deep draughts of the fragrant summer breeze ; the play of his lithe and supple loins; the easy, elastic stride of his straight and shapely legs, presented a triumph of physical manhood in its highest type. Mrs. Glenarm's eyes devoured him in silent admiration. He looked like a young god of mythology—like a statue animated with color and life. " Oh, Geoffrey!" she exclaimed, softly, as he went by. He neither answered, nor looked : he had other business on hand than listening to soft nonsense. He was gathering himself up for the effort; his lips were set; his fists were lightly clenched. Perry posted himself at his place, grim and silent, with the watch in his hand. Geoffrey walked on beyond the flag, so as to give himself start enough to reach his full speed as he passed it. " Now then!" said Perry. In an instant more, he flew by (to Mrs. Glenarm's excited imagination) like an arrow from a bow. His action was perfect. His speed, at its utmost rate of exertion, preserved its rare underlying elements of strength and steadiness. Less and less and less he grew to the eyes that followed his course ; still lightly flying over the ground, still firmly keeping the straight line. A moment more, and the runner vanished behind the wall of the cottage, and the stop-watch of the trainer returned to its place in his pocket.

In her eagerness to know the result, Mrs. Glenarm forgot her jealousy of Perry.

" How long has he been?" she asked.

" There's a good many besides you would be glad to know that," said Perry.

" Mr. Delamayn will tell me, you rude man!"

" That depends, ma'am, on whether I tell him."

With this reply, Perry hurried back to the cottage.

Not a word passed while the trainer was attending to his man, and while the man was recovering his breath. When Geoffrey had been carefully rubbed down, and clothed again in his ordinary garments, Perry pulled a comfortable easy-chair out of a corner. Geoffrey fell into the chair, rather than sat down in it. Perry started, and looked at him attentively.

" Well?" said Geoffrey. " How about the time? Long? short? or middling?"

" Very good time," said Perry.

" How long?"

" When did you say the lady was going, Mr. Delamayn?"

" In two days."

" Very well, Sir. I'll tell you 'how long' when the lady's gone."

Geoffrey made no attempt to insist on an immediate reply. He smiled faintly. After an interval of less than ten minutes he stretched out his legs and closed his eyes.

" Going to sleep?" said Perry.

Geoffrey opened his eyes with an effort. " No," he said. The word had hardly passed his lips before his eyes closed again.

" Hullo!" said Perry, watching him. " I don't like that."

He went closer to the chair. There was no doubt about it. The man was asleep.

Perry emitted a long whistle under his breath. He stooped and laid two of his fingers softly on Geoffrey's pulse. The beat was slow, heavy, and labored. It was unmistakably the pulse of an exhausted man.

The trainer changed color, and took a turn in the room. He opened a cupboard, and produced from it his diary of the preceding year. The entries relating to the last occasion on which he had prepared Geoffrey for a foot-race included the fullest details. He turned to the report of the first trial, at three hundred yards, full speed. The time was, by one or two seconds, not so good as the time on this occasion. But the result, afterward, was utterly different. There it was, in Perry's own words : " Pulse good. Man in high spirits. Ready, if I would have let him, to run it over again."

Perry looked round at the same man, a year afterward—utterly worn out, and fast asleep in the chair.

He fetched pen, ink, and paper out of the cupboard, and wrote two letters — both marked " Private." The first was to a medical man, a great authority among trainers. The second was to Perry's own agent in London, whom he knew he could trust. The letter pledged the agent to the strictest secrecy, and directed him to back Geoffrey's opponent in the Foot - Race for a sum equal to the sum which Perry had betted on Geoffrey himself. " If you have got any money of your own on him," the letter concluded, " do as I do.—and hold your tongue."

" Another of 'em gone stale!" said the trainer, looking round again at the sleeping man. " He'll lose the race."

## CHAPTER THE THIRTY-SECOND.

SEEDS OF THE FUTURE (SECOND SOWING).

AND what did the visitors say of the Swans?

They said, "Oh, what a number of them!"—which was all that was to be said by persons ignorant of the natural history of aquatic birds.

And what did the visitors say of the lake?

Some of them said, "How solemn!" Some of them said, "How romantic!" Some of them said nothing—but privately thought it a dismal scene.

Here again the popular sentiment struck the right note at starting. The lake was hidden in the centre of a fir wood. Except in the middle, where the sunlight reached them, the waters lay black under the sombre shadow of the trees. The one break in the plantation was at the farther end of the lake. The one sign of movement and life to be seen was the ghostly gliding of the swans on the dead-still surface of the water. It was solemn—as they said; it was romantic—as they said. It was dismal—as they thought. Pages of description could express no more. Let pages of description be absent, therefore, in this place.

Having satiated itself with the swans, having exhausted the lake, the general curiosity reverted to the break in the trees at the farther end—remarked a startlingly artificial object, intruding itself on the scene, in the shape of a large red curtain, which hung between two of the tallest firs, and closed the prospect beyond from view—requested an explanation of the curtain from Julius Delamayn—and received for answer that the mystery should be revealed on the arrival of his wife with the tardy remainder of the guests who had loitered about the house.

On the appearance of Mrs. Delamayn and the stragglers, the united party coasted the shore of the lake, and stood assembled in front of the curtain. Pointing to the silken cords, hanging at either side of it, Julius Delamayn picked out two little girls (children of his wife's sister), and sent them to the cords, with instructions to pull, and see what happened. The nieces of Julius pulled with the eager hands of children in the presence of a mystery—the curtains parted in the middle, and a cry of universal astonishment and delight saluted the scene revealed to view.

At the end of a broad avenue of firs a cool green glade spread its grassy carpet in the midst of the surrounding plantation. The ground at the farther end of the glade rose; and here, on the lower slopes, a bright little spring of water bubbled out between gray old granite rocks. Along the right-hand edge of the turf ran a row of tables, arrayed in spotless white, and covered with refreshments waiting for the guests. On the opposite side was a band of music, which burst into harmony at the moment when the curtains were drawn. Looking back through the avenue, the eye caught a distant glimpse of the lake, where the sunlight played on the water, and the plumage of the gliding swans flashed softly in brilliant white. Such was the charming surprise which Julius Delamayn had arranged for his friends. It was only at moments like these—or when he and his wife were playing Sonatas in the modest little music-room at Swanhaven—that Lord Holchester's eldest son was really happy. He secretly groaned over the du-

ties which his position as a landed gentleman imposed upon him; and he suffered under some of the highest privileges of his rank and station as under social martyrdom in its cruelest form.

"We'll dine first," said Julius, "and dance afterward. There is the programme!"

He led the way to the tables, with the two ladies nearest to him—utterly careless whether they were or were not among the ladies of the highest rank then present. To Lady Lundie's astonishment he took the first seat he came to, without appearing to care what place he occupied at his own feast. The guests, following his example, sat where they pleased, reckless of precedents and dignities. Mrs. Delamayn, feeling a special interest in a young lady who was shortly to be a bride, took Blanche's arm. Lady Lundie attached herself resolutely to her hostess on the other side. The three sat together. Mrs. Delamayn did her best to encourage Blanche to talk, and Blanche did her best to meet the advances made to her. The experiment succeeded but poorly on either side. Mrs. Delamayn gave it up in despair, and turned to Lady Lundie, with a strong suspicion that some unpleasant subject of reflection was preying privately on the bride's mind. The conclusion was soundly drawn. Blanche's little outbreak of temper with her friend on the terrace, and Blanche's present deficiency of gayety and spirit, were attributable to the same cause. She hid it from her uncle, she hid it from Arnold—but she was as anxious as ever, and as wretched as ever, about Anne; and she was still on the watch (no matter what Sir Patrick might say or do) to seize the first opportunity of renewing the search for her lost friend.

Meanwhile the eating, the drinking, and the talking went merrily on. The band played its liveliest melodies; the servants kept the glasses constantly filled: round all the tables gayety and freedom reigned supreme. The one conversation in progress, in which the talkers were not in social harmony with each other, was the conversation at Blanche's side, between her step-mother and Mrs. Delamayn.

Among Lady Lundie's other accomplishments the power of making disagreeable discoveries ranked high. At the dinner in the glade she had not failed to notice—what every body else had passed over—the absence at the festival of the hostess's brother-in-law; and more remarkable still, the disappearance of a lady who was actually one of the guests staying in the house: in plainer words, the disappearance of Mrs. Glenarm.

"Am I mistaken?" said her ladyship, lifting her eye-glass, and looking round the tables. "Surely there is a member of our party missing? I don't see Mr. Geoffrey Delamayn."

"Geoffrey promised to be here. But he is not particularly attentive, as you may have noticed, to keeping engagements of this sort. Every thing is sacrificed to his training. We only see him at rare intervals now."

With that reply Mrs. Delamayn attempted to change the subject. Lady Lundie lifted her eye-glass, and looked round the tables for the second time.

"Pardon me," persisted her ladyship—"but is it possible that I have discovered another absentee? I don't see Mrs. Glenarm. Yet surely she must be here! Mrs. Glenarm is not training for a foot-race. Do you see her? *I* don't."

"I missed her when we went out on the terrace, and I have not seen her since."

"Isn't it very odd, dear Mrs. Delamayn?"

"Our guests at Swanhaven, Lady Lundie, have perfect liberty to do as they please."

In those words Mrs. Delamayn (as she fondly imagined) dismissed the subject. But Lady Lundie's robust curiosity proved unassailable by even the broadest hint. Carried away, in all probability, by the infection of merriment about her, her ladyship displayed unexpected reserves of vivacity. The mind declines to realize it; but it is not the less true that this majestic woman actually simpered!

"Shall we put two and two together?" said Lady Lundie, with a ponderous playfulness wonderful to see. "Here, on the one hand, is Mr. Geoffrey Delamayn—a young single man. And here, on the other, is Mrs. Glenarm—a young widow. Rank on the side of the young single man; riches on the side of the young widow. And both mysteriously absent at the same time, from the same pleasant party. Ha, Mrs. Delamayn! should I guess wrong, if I guessed that *you* will have a marriage in the family, too, before long?"

Mrs. Delamayn looked a little annoyed. She had entered, with all her heart, into the conspiracy for making a match between Geoffrey and Mrs. Glenarm. But she was not prepared to own that the lady's facility had (in spite of all attempts to conceal it from discovery) made the conspiracy obviously successful in ten days' time.

"I am not in the secrets of the lady and gentleman whom you mention," she replied, dryly.

A heavy body is slow to acquire movement—and slow to abandon movement, when once acquired. The playfulness of Lady Lundie, being essentially heavy, followed the same rule. She still persisted in being as lively as ever.

"Oh, what a diplomatic answer!" exclaimed her ladyship. "I think I can interpret it, though, for all that. A little bird tells me that I shall see a Mrs. Geoffrey Delamayn in London, next season. And I, for one, shall not be surprised to find myself congratulating Mrs. Glenarm."

"If you persist in letting *your* imagination run away with you, Lady Lundie, I can't possibly help it. I can only request permission to keep the bridle on *mine*."

This time, even Lady Lundie understood that it would be wise to say no more. She smiled and nodded, in high private approval of her own extraordinary cleverness. If she had been asked at that moment who was the most brilliant Englishwoman living, she would have looked inward on herself—and would have seen, as in a glass brightly, Lady Lundie, of Windygates.

From the moment when the talk at her side entered on the subject of Geoffrey Delamayn and Mrs. Glenarm—and throughout the brief period during which it remained occupied with that topic—Blanche became conscious of a strong smell of some spirituous liquor; wafted down on her, as she fancied, from behind and from above. Finding the odor grow stronger and stronger, she looked round to see whether any special manufacture of grog was proceeding inexplicably at the back of her chair. The moment she moved her head, her attention was claimed by a pair of

tremulous gouty old hands, offering her a grouse pie, profusely sprinkled with truffles.

"Eh, my bonny Miss!" whispered a persuasive voice at her ear, "ye're joost stairving in a land o' plenty. Tak' my advice, and ye'll tak' the best thing at tebble—groose-poy, and trufflers."

Blanche looked up.

There he was—the man of the canny eye, the fatherly manner, and the mighty nose—Bishopriggs—preserved in spirits and ministering at the festival at Swanhaven Lodge!

Blanche had only seen him for a moment on the memorable night of the storm, when she had surprised Anne at the inn. But instants passed in the society of Bishopriggs were as good as hours spent in the company of inferior men. Blanche instantly recognized him; instantly called to mind Sir Patrick's conviction that he was in possession of Anne's lost letter; instantly rushed to the conclusion that, in discovering Bishopriggs, she had discovered a chance of tracing Anne. Her first impulse was to claim acquaintance with him on the spot. But the eyes of her neighbors were on her, warning her to wait. She took a little of the pie, and looked hard at Bishopriggs. That discreet man, showing no sign of recognition on his side, bowed respectfully, and went on round the table.

"I wonder whether he has got the letter about him?" thought Blanche.

He had not only got the letter about him—but, more than that, he was actually then on the look-out for the means of turning the letter to profitable pecuniary account.

The domestic establishment of Swanhaven Lodge included no formidable array of servants. When Mrs. Delamayn gave a large party, she depended for such additional assistance as was needed partly on the contributions of her friends, partly on the resources of the principal inn at Kirkandrew. Mr. Bishopriggs, serving at the time (in the absence of any better employment) as a supernumerary at the inn, made one among the waiters who could be spared to assist at the garden-party. The name of the gentleman by whom he was to be employed for the day had struck him, when he first heard it, as having a familiar sound. He had made his inquiries; and had then betaken himself, for additional information, to the letter which he had picked up from the parlor floor at Craig Fernie.

The sheet of note-paper, lost by Anne, contained, it may be remembered, two letters—one signed by herself; the other signed by Geoffrey —and both suggestive, to a stranger's eye, of relations between the writers which they were interested in concealing from the public view.

Thinking it just possible—if he kept his eyes and ears well open at Swanhaven—that he might improve his prospect of making a marketable commodity of the stolen correspondence, Mr. Bishopriggs had put the letter in his pocket when he left Kirkandrew. He had recognized Blanche, as a friend of the lady at the inn—and as a person who might perhaps be turned to account, in that capacity. And he had, moreover, heard every word of the conversation between Lady Lundie and Mrs. Delamayn on the subject of Geoffrey and Mrs. Glenarm. There were hours to be passed before the guests would retire, and before the waiters would be dismissed. The conviction was strong in the mind of Mr. Bishopriggs that he might find good reason yet for congratulating himself on the chance which had associated him with the festivities at Swanhaven Lodge.

It was still early in the afternoon when the gayety at the dinner-table began, in certain quarters, to show signs of wearing out.

The younger members of the party—especially the ladies—grew restless with the appearance of the dessert. One after another they looked longingly at the smooth level of elastic turf in the middle of the glade. One after another they beat time absently with their fingers to the waltz which the musicians happened to be playing at the moment. Noticing these symptoms, Mrs. Delamayn set the example of rising; and her husband sent a message to the band. In ten minutes more the first quadrille was in progress on the grass; the spectators were picturesquely grouped round, looking on; and the servants and waiters, no longer wanted, had retired out of sight, to a picnic of their own.

The last person to leave the deserted tables was the venerable Bishopriggs. He alone, of the men in attendance, had contrived to combine a sufficient appearance of waiting on the company with a clandestine attention to his own personal need of refreshment. Instead of hurrying away to the servants' dinner with the rest, he made the round of the tables, apparently clearing away the crumbs —actually, emptying the wine-glasses. Immersed in this occupation, he was startled by a lady's voice behind him, and, turning as quickly as he could, found himself face to face with Miss Lundie.

"I want some cold water," said Blanche. "Be so good as to get me some from the spring."

She pointed to the bubbling rivulet at the farther end of the glade.

Bishopriggs looked unaffectedly shocked.

"Lord's sake, miss," he exclaimed, "d'ye relly mean to offend yer stomach wi' cauld water —when there's wine to be had for the asking!"

Blanche gave him a look. Slowness of perception was not on the list of the failings of Bishopriggs. He took up a tumbler, winked with his one available eye, and led the way to the rivulet. There was nothing remarkable in the spectacle of a young lady who wanted a glass of spring-water, or of a waiter who was getting it for her. Nobody was surprised; and (with the band playing) nobody could by any chance overhear what might be said at the spring-side.

"Do you remember me at the inn on the night of the storm?" asked Blanche.

Mr. Bishopriggs had his reasons (carefully inclosed in his pocket-book) for not being too ready to commit himself with Blanche at starting.

"I'm no' saying I canna remember ye, miss. Whar's the man would mak' sic an answer as that to a bonny young leddy like you?"

By way of assisting his memory Blanche took out her purse. Bishopriggs became absorbed in the scenery. He looked at the running water with the eye of a man who thoroughly distrusted it, viewed as a beverage.

"There ye go," he said, addressing himself to the rivulet, "bubblin' to yer ain annihilation in the loch yonder! It's little I know that's gude aboot ye, in yer unconvairted state. Ye're a type o' human life, they say. I tak' up my testimony against that. Ye're a type o' naething at all till ye're heated wi' fire, and sweetened wi' sugar, and strengthened wi' whusky; and then ye're a type o' toddy—and human life (I grant it) has got something to say to ye in that capacity!"

"I have heard more about you, since I was at the inn," proceeded Blanche, "than you may suppose." (She opened her purse: Mr. Bishopriggs became the picture of attention.) "You were very, very kind to a lady who was staying at Craig Fernie," she went on, earnestly. "I know that you have lost your place at the inn, because you gave all your attention to that lady. She is my dearest friend, Mr. Bishopriggs. I want to thank you. I do thank you. Please accept what I have got here?"

All the girl's heart was in her eyes and in her voice as she emptied her purse into the gouty (and greedy) old hand of Bishopriggs.

A young lady with a well-filled purse (no matter how rich the young lady may be) is a combination not often witnessed in any country on the civilized earth. Either the money is always spent, or the money has been forgotten on the toilet-table at home. Blanche's purse contained a sovereign and some six or seven shillings in silver. As pocket-money for an heiress it was contemptible. But as a gratuity to Bishopriggs it was magnificent. The old rascal put the money into his pocket with one hand, and dashed away the tears of sensibility, which he had *not* shed, with the other.

"Cast yer bread on the waters," cried Mr. Bishopriggs, with his one eye raised devotionally to the sky, "and ye sall find it again after monny days! Hech! hech! didna I say when I first set eyes on that puir leddy, 'I feel like a fether to ye?' It's seemply mairvelous to see hoo a man's ain gude deeds find him oot in this lower warld o' ours. If ever I heard the voice o' naitural affection speaking in my ain breast," pursued Mr. Bishopriggs, with his eye fixed in uneasy expectation on Blanche, "it joost spak' trumpet-tongued when that winsome creature first lookit at me. Will it be she now that told ye of the wee bit sairvice I rendered to her in the time when I was in bondage at the hottle?"

"Yes—she told me herself."

"Might I mak' sae bauld as to ask whar' she may be at the present time?"

"I don't know, Mr. Bishopriggs. I am more miserable about it than I can say. She has gone away—and I don't know where."

"Ow! ow! that's bad. And the bit husband-creature danglin' at her petticoat's tail one day, and awa' wi' the sunrise next mornin'—have they baith taken leg-bail together?"

"I know nothing of him; I never saw him. You saw him. Tell me—what was he like?"

"Eh! he was joost a puir weak creature. Didn't know a glass o' good sherry-wine when he'd got it. Free wi' the siller—that's a' ye can say for him—free wi' the siller!"

Finding it impossible to extract from Mr. Bishopriggs any clearer description of the man who had been with Anne at the inn than this, Blanche approached the main object of the interview. Too anxious to waste time in circumlocution, she turned the conversation at once to the delicate and doubtful subject of the lost letter.

"There is something else that I want to say

to you," she resumed. "My friend had a loss while she was staying at the inn."

The clouds of doubt rolled off the mind of Mr. Bishopriggs. The lady's friend knew of the lost letter. And, better still, the lady's friend looked as if she wanted it!

"Ay! ay!" he said, with all due appearance of carelessness. "Like eneugh. From the mistress downward, they're a' kittle cattle at the inn since I've left 'em. What may it ha' been that she lost?"

"She lost a letter."

The look of uneasy expectation reappeared in the eye of Mr. Bishopriggs. It was a question —and a serious question,. from his point of view —whether any suspicion of theft was attached to the disappearance of the letter.

"When ye say 'lost,'" he asked, "d'ye mean stolen?"

Blanche was quite quick enough to see the necessity of quieting his mind on this point.

"Oh no!" she answered. "Not stolen. Only lost. Did you hear about it?"

"Wherefore suld *I* ha' heard aboot it?" He looked hard at Blanche—and detected a momentary hesitation in her face. "Tell me this, my young leddy," he went on, advancing warily nearer to the point. "When ye're speering for news o' your friend's lost letter—what sets ye on comin' to *me?*"

Those words were decisive. It is hardly too much to say that Blanche's future depended on Blanche's answer to that question.

If she could have produced the money; and if she had said, boldly, "You have got the letter, Mr. Bishopriggs: I pledge my word that no questions shall be asked, and I offer you ten pounds for it"—in all probability the bargain would have been struck; and the whole course of coming events would, in that case, have been altered. But she had no money left; and there were no friends, in the circle at Swanhaven, to whom she could apply, without being misinterpreted, for a loan of ten pounds, to be privately intrusted to her on the spot. Under stress of sheer necessity Blanche abandoned all hope of making any present appeal of a pecuniary nature to the confidence of Bishopriggs.

The one other way of attaining her object that she could see was to arm herself with the influence of Sir Patrick's name. A man, placed in her position, would have thought it mere madness to venture on such a risk as this. But Blanche—with one act of rashness already on her conscience—rushed, woman-like, straight to the commission of another. The same headlong eagerness to reach her end, which had hurried her into questioning Geoffrey before he left Windygates, now drove her, just as recklessly, into taking the management of Bishopriggs out of Sir Patrick's skilled and practiced hands. The starving sisterly love in her hungered for a trace of Anne. Her heart whispered, Risk it! And Blanche risked it on the spot.

"Sir Patrick set me on coming to you," she said.

The opening hand of Mr. Bishopriggs—ready to deliver the letter, and receive the reward—closed again instantly as she spoke those words.

"Sir Paitrick?" he repeated. "Ow! ow! ye've een tauld Sir Paitrick aboot it, have ye? There's a chiel wi' a lang head on his shouthers,

if ever there was ane yet! What might Sir Paitrick ha' said?"

Blanche noticed a change in his tone. Blanche was rigidly careful (when it was too late) to answer him in guarded terms.

"Sir Patrick thought you might have found the letter," she said, "and might not have remembered about it again until after you had left the inn."

Bishopriggs looked back into his own personal experience of his old master—and drew the correct conclusion that Sir Patrick's view of his connection with the disappearance of the letter was not the purely unsuspicious view reported by Blanche. "The dour auld deevil," he thought to himself, "knows me better than *that!*"

"Well?" asked Blanche, impatiently. "Is Sir Patrick right?"

"Richt?" rejoined Bishopriggs, briskly. "He's as far awa' from the truth as John o' Groat's House is from Jericho."

"You know nothing of the letter?"

"Deil a bit I know o' the letter. The first I ha' heard o' it is what I hear noo."

Blanche's heart sank within her. Had she defeated her own object, and cut the ground from under Sir Patrick's feet, for the second time? Surely not! There was unquestionably a chance, on this occasion, that the man might be prevailed upon to place the trust in her uncle which he was too cautious to confide to a stranger like herself. The one wise thing to do now was to pave the way for the exertion of Sir Patrick's superior influence, and Sir Patrick's superior skill. She resumed the conversation with that object in view.

"I am sorry to hear that Sir Patrick has guessed wrong," she resumed. "My friend was anxious to recover the letter when I last saw her; and I hoped to hear news of it from you. However, right or wrong, Sir Patrick has some reasons for wishing to see you—and I take the opportunity of telling you so. He has left a letter to wait for you at the Craig Fernie inn."

"I'm thinking the letter will ha' lang eneugh to wait, if it waits till I gae back for it to the hottle," remarked Bishopriggs.

"In that case," said Blanche, promptly, "you had better give me an address at which Sir Patrick can write to you. You wouldn't, I suppose, wish me to say that I had seen you here, and that you refused to communicate with him?"

"Never think it!" cried Bishopriggs, fervently. "If there's ain thing mair than anither that I'm carefu' to presairve intact, it's joost the respectful attention that I owe to Sir Paitrick. I'll make sae bauld, miss, as to chairge ye wi' that bit caird. I'm no' settled in ony place yet (mair's the pity at my time o' life!), but Sir Paitrick may hear o' me, when Sir Paitrick has need o' me, there." He handed a dirty little card to Blanche containing the name and address of a butcher in Edinburgh. "Sawmuel Bishopriggs," he went on, glibly. "Care o' Davie Dow, flesher; Cowgate; Embro. My Patmos in the weelderness, miss, for the time being."

Blanche received the address with a sense of unspeakable relief. If she had once more ventured on taking Sir Patrick's place, and once more failed in justifying her rashness by the results, she had at least gained some atoning advantage, this time, by opening a means of communication between her uncle and Bishopriggs.

"You will hear from Sir Patrick," she said, and nodded kindly, and returned to her place among the guests.

"I'll hear from Sir Paitrick, wull I?" repeated Bishopriggs, when he was left by himself. "Sir Paitrick will wark naething less than a meeracle if he finds Sawmuel Bishopriggs at the Cowgate, Embro!"

He laughed softly over his own cleverness; and withdrew to a lonely place in the plantation, in which he could consult the stolen correspondence without fear of being observed by any living creature. Once more the truth had tried to struggle into light, before the day of the marriage, and once more Blanche had innocently helped the darkness to keep it from view.

---

## CHAPTER THE THIRTY-THIRD.

### SEEDS OF THE FUTURE (THIRD SOWING).

AFTER a new and attentive reading of Anne's letter to Geoffrey, and of Geoffrey's letter to Anne, Bishopriggs laid down comfortably under a tree, and set himself the task of seeing his position plainly as it was at that moment.

The profitable disposal of the correspondence to Blanche was no longer among the possibilities involved in the case. As for treating with Sir Patrick, Bishopriggs determined to keep equally clear of the Cowgate, Edinburgh, and of Mrs. Inchbare's inn, so long as there was the faintest chance of his pushing his own interests in any other quarter. No person living would be capable of so certainly extracting the correspondence from him, on such ruinously cheap terms, as his old master. "I'll no' put myself under Sir Paitrick's thumb," thought Bishopriggs, "till I've gane my ain rounds among the lave o' them first."

Rendered into intelligible English, this resolution pledged him to hold no communication with Sir Patrick—until he had first tested his success in negotiating with other persons, who might be equally interested in getting possession of the correspondence, and more liberal in giving hush-money to the thief who had stolen it.

Who were the "other persons" at his disposal, under these circumstances?

He had only to recall the conversation which he had overheard between Lady Lundie and Mrs. Delamayn to arrive at the discovery of one person, to begin with, who was directly interested in getting possession of his own letter. Mr. Geoffrey Delamayn was in a fair way of being married to a lady named Mrs. Glenarm. And here was this same Mr. Geoffrey Delamayn in matrimonial correspondence, little more than a fortnight since, with another lady—who signed herself "Anne Silvester."

Whatever his position between the two women might be, his interest in possessing himself of the correspondence was plain beyond all doubt. It was equally clear that the first thing to be done by Bishopriggs was to find the means of obtaining a personal interview with him. If the interview led to nothing else, it would decide one important question which still remained to be solved. The lady whom Bishopriggs had waited on at Craig Fernie might well be "Anne Silvester." Was Mr. Geoffrey Delamayn, in that case, the

gentleman who had passed as her husband at the inn?

Bishopriggs rose to his gouty feet with all possible alacrity, and hobbled away to make the necessary inquiries, addressing himself, not to the men-servants at the dinner-table, who would be sure to insist on his joining them, but to the women-servants left in charge of the empty house.

He easily obtained the necessary directions for finding the cottage. But he was warned that Mr. Geoffrey Delamayn's trainer allowed nobody to see his patron at exercise, and that he would certainly be ordered off again the moment he appeared on the scene.

Bearing this caution in mind, Bishopriggs made a circuit, on reaching the open ground, so as to approach the cottage at the back, under shelter of the trees behind it. One look at Mr. Geoffrey Delamayn was all that he wanted in the first instance. They were welcome to order him off again, as long as he obtained that.

He was still hesitating at the outer line of the trees, when he heard a loud, imperative voice, calling from the front of the cottage, "Now, Mr. Geoffrey! Time's up!" Another voice answered, "All right!" and, after an interval, Geoffrey Delamayn appeared on the open ground, proceeding to the point from which he was accustomed to walk his measured mile.

Advancing a few steps to look at his man more closely, Bishopriggs was instantly detected by the quick eye of the trainer. "Hullo!" cried Perry, "what do you want here?" Bishopriggs opened his lips to make an excuse. "Who the devil are you?" roared Geoffrey. The trainer answered the question out of the resources of his own experience. "A spy, Sir—sent to time you at your work." Geoffrey lifted his mighty fist, and sprang forward a step. Perry held his patron back. "You can't do that, Sir," he said; "the man's too old. No fear of his turning up again—you've scared him out of his wits." The statement was strictly true. The terror of Bishopriggs at the sight of Geoffrey's fist restored to him the activity of his youth. He ran for the first time for twenty years; and only stopped to remember his infirmities, and to catch his breath, when he was out of sight of the cottage, among the trees.

He sat down to rest and recover himself, with the comforting inner conviction that, in one respect at least, he had gained his point. The furious savage, with the eyes that darted fire and the fist that threatened destruction, was a total stranger to him. In other words, *not* the man who had passed as the lady's husband at the inn.

At the same time it was equally certain that he *was* the man involved in the compromising correspondence which Bishopriggs possessed. To appeal, however, to his interest in obtaining the letter was entirely incompatible (after the recent exhibition of his fist) with the strong regard which Bishopriggs felt for his own personal security. There was no alternative now but to open negotiations with the one other person concerned in the matter (fortunately, on this occasion, a person of the gentler sex), who was actually within reach. Mrs. Glenarm was at Swanhaven. She had a direct interest in clearing up the question of a prior claim to Mr. Geoffrey Delamayn on the part of another woman. And

"GEOFFREY LIFTED HIS MIGHTY FIST, AND SPRANG FORWARD A STEP."

she could only do that by getting the correspondence into her own hands.

"Praise Providence for a' its mercies!" said Bishopriggs, getting on his feet again. "I've got twa strings, as they say, to my boo. I trow the woman's the canny string o' the twa—and we'll een try the twanging of her."

He set forth on his road back again, to search among the company at the lake for Mrs. Glenarm.

The dance had reached its climax of animation when Bishopriggs reappeared on the scene of his duties; and the ranks of the company had been recruited, in his absence, by the very person whom it was now his foremost object to approach.

Receiving, with supple submission, a reprimand for his prolonged absence from the chief of the servants, Bishopriggs—keeping his one observant eye carefully on the look-out—busied himself in promoting the circulation of ices and cool drinks.

While he was thus occupied, his attention was attracted by two persons who, in very different ways, stood out prominently as marked characters among the rank and file of the guests.

The first person was a vivacious, irascible old gentleman, who persisted in treating the undeniable fact of his age on the footing of a scandalous false report set afloat by Time. He was superbly strapped and padded. His hair, his teeth, and his complexion were triumphs of artificial youth. When he was not occupied among the youngest women present—which was very seldom —he attached himself exclusively to the youngest men. He insisted on joining every dance. Twice he measured his length upon the grass; but nothing daunted him. He was waltzing again, witn another young woman, at the next dance,

as if nothing had happened. Inquiring who this effervescent old gentleman might be, Bishopriggs discovered that he was a retired officer in the navy; commonly known (among his inferiors) as "The Tartar:" more formally described in society as Captain Newenden, the last male representative of one of the oldest families in England.

The second person, who appeared to occupy a position of distinction at the dance in the glade, was a lady.

To the eye of Bishopriggs, she was a miracle of beauty, with a small fortune for a poor man carried about her in silk, lace, and jewelry. No woman present was the object of such special attention among the men as this fascinating and priceless creature. She sat fanning herself with a matchless work of art (supposed to be a handkerchief) representing an island of cambric in the midst of an ocean of lace. She was surrounded by a little court of admirers, who fetched and carried at her slightest nod, like well-trained dogs. Sometimes they brought refreshments, which she had asked for, only to decline taking them when they came. Sometimes they brought information of what was going on among the dancers, which the lady had been eager to receive when they went away, and in which she had ceased to feel the smallest interest when they came back. Every body burst into ejaculations of distress when she was asked to account for her absence from the dinner, and answered, "My poor nerves." Every body said, "What should we have done without you!"—when she doubted if she had done wisely in joining the party at all. Inquiring who this favored lady might be, Bishopriggs discovered that she was the niece of the indomitable old gentleman who *would* dance—or, more plainly still, no less a person than his contemplated customer, Mrs. Glenarm.

With all his enormous assurance Bishopriggs was daunted when he found himself facing the question of what he was to do next.

To open negotiations with Mrs. Glenarm, under present circumstances, was, for a man in his position, simply impossible. But, apart from this, the prospect of profitably addressing himself to that lady in the future was, to say the least of it, beset with difficulties of no common kind.

Supposing the means of disclosing Geoffrey's position to her to be found—what would she do, when she received her warning? She would in all probability apply to one of two formidable men, both of whom were interested in the matter. If she went straight to the man accused of attempting to marry her, at a time when he was already engaged to another woman—Bishopriggs would find himself confronted with the owner of that terrible fist, which had justly terrified him even on a distant and cursory view. If, on the other hand, she placed her interests in the care of her uncle—Bishopriggs had only to look at the captain, and to calculate his chance of imposing terms on a man who owed Life a bill of more than sixty years' date, and who openly defied time to recover the debt.

With these serious obstacles standing in the way, what was to be done? The only alternative left was to approach Mrs. Glenarm under shelter of the dark.

Reaching this conclusion, Bishopriggs decided to ascertain from the servants what the lady's future movements might be; and, thus informed, to startle her by anonymous warnings, conveyed through the post, and claiming their answer through the advertising channel of a newspaper. Here was the certainty of alarming her, coupled with the certainty of safety to himself! Little did Mrs. Glenarm dream, when she capriciously stopped a servant going by with some glasses of lemonade, that the wretched old creature who offered the tray contemplated corresponding with her before the week was out, in the double character of her "Well-Wisher" and her "True Friend."

The evening advanced. The shadows lengthened. The waters of the lake grew pitchy black. The gliding of the ghostly swans became rare and more rare. The elders of the party thought of the drive home. The juniors (excepting Captain Newenden) began to flag at the dance. Little by little the comfortable attractions of the house — tea, coffee, and candle-light in snug rooms—resumed their influence. The guests abandoned the glade; and the fingers and lungs of the musicians rested at last.

Lady Lundie and her party were the first to send for the carriage and say farewell; the break-up of the household at Windygates on the next day, and the journey south, being sufficient apologies for setting the example of retreat. In an hour more the only visitors left were the guests staying at Swanhaven Lodge.

The company gone, the hired waiters from Kirkandrew were paid and dismissed.

On the journey back the silence of Bishopriggs created some surprise among his comrades. "I've got my ain concerns to think of," was the only answer he vouchsafed to the remonstrances addressed to him. The "concerns" alluded to, comprehended, among other changes of plan, his departure from Kirkandrew the next day—with a reference, in case of inquiries, to his convenient friend at the Cowgate, Edinburgh. His actual destination—to be kept a secret from every body —was Perth. The neighborhood of this town—as stated on the authority of her own maid—was the part of Scotland to which the rich widow contemplated removing when she left Swanhaven in two days' time. At Perth, Bishopriggs knew of more than one place in which he could get temporary employment—and at Perth he determined to make his first anonymous advances to Mrs. Glenarm.

The remainder of the evening passed quietly enough at the Lodge.

The guests were sleepy and dull after the excitement of the day. Mrs. Glenarm retired early. At eleven o'clock Julius Delamayn was the only person left up in the house. He was understood to be in his study, preparing an address to the electors, based on instructions sent from London by his father. He was actually occupied in the music-room—now that there was nobody to discover him—playing exercises softly on his beloved violin.

At the trainer's cottage a trifling incident occured, that night, which afforded materials for a note in Perry's professional diary.

Geoffrey had sustained the later trial of walking for a given time and distance, at his full speed, without showing any of those symptoms of exhaustion which had followed the more serious experiment of running, to which he had been subjected earlier in the day. Perry, honestly bent—though he had privately hedged his own bets—on doing his best to bring his man in good order to the post on the day of the race, had forbidden Geoffrey to pay his evening visit to the house, and had sent him to bed earlier than usual. The trainer was alone, looking over his own written rules, and considering what modifications he should introduce into the diet and exercises of the next day, when he was startled by a sound of groaning from the bedroom in which his patron lay asleep.

He went in, and found Geoffrey rolling to and fro on the pillow, with his face contorted, with his hands clenched, and with the perspiration standing thick on his forehead—suffering evidently under the nervous oppression produced by the phantom-terrors of a dream.

Perry spoke to him, and pulled him up in the bed. He woke with a scream. He stared at his trainer in vacant terror, and spoke to his trainer in wild words. "What are your horrid eyes looking at over my shoulder?" he cried out. "Go to the devil—and take your infernal slate with you!" Perry spoke to him once more. "You've been dreaming of somebody, Mr. Delamayn. What's to do about a slate?" Geoffrey looked eagerly round the room, and heaved a heavy breath of relief. "I could have sworn she was staring at me over the dwarf pear-trees," he said. "All right, I know where I am now." Perry (attributing the dream to nothing more important than a passing indigestion) administered some brandy and water, and left him to drop off again to sleep. He fretfully forbade the extinguishing of the light. "Afraid of the

"HE FOUND GEOFFREY ROLLING TO AND FRO ON HIS PILLOW."

dark?" said Perry, with a laugh. No. He was afraid of dreaming again of the dumb cook at Windygates House.

---

SEVENTH SCENE.—HAM FARM.

## CHAPTER THE THIRTY-FOURTH.

### THE NIGHT BEFORE.

The time was the night before the marriage. The place was Sir Patrick's house in Kent.

The lawyers had kept their word. The settlements had been forwarded, and had been signed two days since.

With the exception of the surgeon and one of the three young gentlemen from the University, who had engagements elsewhere, the visitors at Windygates had emigrated southward to be present at the marriage. Besides these gentlemen, there were some ladies among the guests invited by Sir Patrick—all of them family connections, and three of them appointed to the position of Blanche's bridemaids. Add one or two neighbors to be invited to the breakfast—and the wedding-party would be complete.

There was nothing architecturally remarkable about Sir Patrick's house. Ham Farm possessed neither the splendor of Windygates nor the picturesque antiquarian attraction of Swanhaven. It was a perfectly commonplace English country seat, surrounded by perfectly commonplace English scenery. Snug monotony welcomed you when you went in, and snug monotony met you again when you turned to the window and looked out.

The animation and variety wanting at Ham Farm were far from being supplied by the company in the house. It was remembered, at an after-period, that a duller wedding-party had never been assembled together.

Sir Patrick, having no early associations with the place, openly admitted that his residence in Kent preyed on his spirits, and that he would have infinitely preferred a room at the inn in the village. The effort to sustain his customary vivacity was not encouraged by persons and circumstances about him. Lady Lundie's fidelity to the memory of the late Sir Thomas, on the scene of his last illness and death, persisted in asserting itself, under an ostentation of concealment which tried even the trained temper of Sir Patrick himself. Blanche, still depressed by her private anxieties about Anne, was in no condition of mind to look gayly at the last memorable days of her maiden life. Arnold, sacrificed—by express stipulation on the part of Lady Lundie—to the prurient delicacy which forbids the bridegroom, before marriage, to sleep in the same house with the bride, found himself ruthlessly shut out from Sir Patrick's hospitality, and exiled every night to a bedroom at the inn. He accepted his solitary doom with a resignation which extended its sobering influence to his customary flow of spirits. As for the ladies, the elder among them existed in a state of chronic protest against Lady Lundie, and the younger were absorbed in the essentially serious occupation of considering and comparing their wedding-dresses. The two young gentlemen from the University performed prodigies of yawning, in the intervals of prodigies of billiard-playing. Smith said, in despair, "There's no making things pleasant in this house, Jones." And Jones sighed, and mildly agreed with him.

On the Sunday evening—which was the evening before the marriage—the dullness, as a matter of course, reached its climax.

But two of the occupations in which people may indulge on week days are regarded as harmless on Sunday by the obstinately anti-Christian tone of feeling which prevails in this matter among the Anglo-Saxon race. It is not sinful to wrangle in religious controversy; and it is not sinful to slumber over a religious book. The ladies at Ham Farm practiced the pious observance of the evening on this plan. The seniors of the sex wrangled in Sunday controversy; and the juniors of the sex slumbered over Sunday books. As for the men, it is unnecessary to say that the young ones smoked when they were not yawning, and yawned when they were not smoking. Sir Patrick staid in the library, sorting old letters and examining old accounts. Every person in the house felt the oppression of the senseless social prohibitions which they had imposed on themselves. And yet every person in the house would have been scandalized if the plain question had been put: You know this is a tyranny of your own making, you know you don't really believe in it, you know you don't really like it—why do you submit? The freest people on the civilized earth are the only people on the civilized earth who dare not face that question.

The evening dragged its slow length on; the welcome time drew nearer and nearer for oblivion in bed. Arnold was silently contemplating, for the last time, his customary prospects of banishment to the inn, when he became aware that Sir Patrick was making signs to him. He rose, and followed his host into the empty dining-room. Sir Patrick carefully closed the door. What did it mean?

It meant—so far as Arnold was concerned—that a private conversation was about to diversify the monotony of the long Sunday evening at Ham Farm.

"I have a word to say to you, Arnold," the old gentleman began, "before you become a married man. Do you remember the conversation at dinner yesterday, about the dancing-party at Swanhaven Lodge?"

"Yes."

"Do you remember what Lady Lundie said while the topic was on the table?"

"She told me, what I can't believe, that Geoffrey Delamayn was going to be married to Mrs. Glenarm."

"Exactly! I observed that you appeared to be startled by what my sister-in-law had said; and when you declared that appearances must certainly have misled her, you looked and spoke (to my mind) like a man animated by a strong feeling of indignation. Was I wrong in drawing that conclusion?"

"No, Sir Patrick. You were right."

"Have you any objection to tell me why you felt indignant?"

Arnold hesitated.

"You are probably at a loss to know what interest *I* can feel in the matter?"

Arnold admitted it with his customary frankness.

"In that case," rejoined Sir Patrick, "I had better go on at once with the matter in hand—leaving you to see for yourself the connection between what I am about to say, and the ques-

tion that I have just put. When I have done, you shall then reply to me or not, exactly as you think right. My dear boy, the subject on which I want to speak to you is—Miss Silvester."

Arnold started. Sir Patrick looked at him with a moment's attention, and went on:

"My niece has her faults of temper and her failings of judgment," he said. "But she has one atoning quality (among many others) which ought to make—and which I believe will make—the happiness of your married life. In the popular phrase, Blanche is as true as steel. Once her friend, always her friend. Do you see what I am coming to? She has said nothing about it, Arnold; but she has not yielded one inch in her resolution to reunite herself to Miss Silvester. One of the first questions you will have to determine, after to-morrow, will be the question of whether you do, or not, sanction your wife in attempting to communicate with her lost friend."

Arnold answered without the slightest reserve.

"I am heartily sorry for Blanche's lost friend, Sir Patrick. My wife will have my full approval if she tries to bring Miss Silvester back—and my best help too, if I can give it."

Those words were earnestly spoken. It was plain that they came from his heart.

"I think you are wrong," said Sir Patrick. "I, too, am sorry for Miss Silvester. But I am convinced that she has not left Blanche without a serious reason for it. And I believe you will be encouraging your wife in a hopeless effort, if you encourage her to persist in the search for her lost friend. However, it is your affair, and not mine. Do you wish me to offer you any facilities for tracing Miss Silvester which I may happen to possess?"

"If you *can* help us over any obstacles at starting, Sir Patrick, it will be a kindness to Blanche, and a kindness to me."

"Very good. I suppose you remember what I said to you, one morning, when we were talking of Miss Silvester at Windygates?"

"You said you had determined to let her go her own way."

"Quite right! On the evening of the day when I said that I received information that Miss Silvester had been traced to Glasgow. You won't require me to explain why I never mentioned this to you or to Blanche. In mentioning it now, I communicate to you the only positive information, on the subject of the missing woman, which I possess. There are two other chances of finding her (of a more speculative kind) which can only be tested by inducing two men (both equally difficult to deal with) to confess what they know. One of those two men is—a person named Bishopriggs, formerly waiter at the Craig Fernie inn."

Arnold started, and changed color. Sir Patrick (silently noticing him) stated the circumstances relating to Anne's lost letter, and to the conclusion in his own mind which pointed to Bishopriggs as the person in possession of it.

"I have to add," he proceeded, "that Blanche, unfortunately, found an opportunity of speaking to Bishopriggs at Swanhaven. When she and Lady Lundie joined us at Edinburgh she showed me privately a card which had been given to her by Bishopriggs. He had described it as the address at which he might be heard of—and Blanche entreated me, before we started for London, to put the reference to the test. I told her that she had committed a serious mistake in attempting to deal with Bishopriggs on her own responsibility; and I warned her of the result in which I was firmly persuaded the inquiry would end. She declined to believe that Bishopriggs had deceived her. I saw that she would take the matter into her own hands again unless I interfered; and I went to the place. Exactly as I had anticipated, the person to whom the card referred me had not heard of Bishopriggs for years, and knew nothing whatever about his present movements. Blanche had simply put him on his guard, and shown him the propriety of keeping out of the way. If you should ever meet with him in the future—say nothing to your wife, and communicate with me. I decline to assist you in searching for Miss Silvester; but I have no objection to assist in recovering a stolen letter from a thief. So much for Bishopriggs.—Now as to the other man."

"Who is he?"

"Your friend, Mr. Geoffrey Delamayn."

Arnold sprang to his feet in ungovernable surprise.

"I appear to astonish you," remarked Sir Patrick.

Arnold sat down again, and waited, in speechless suspense, to hear what was coming next.

"I have reason to know," said Sir Patrick, "that Mr. Delamayn is thoroughly well acquainted with the nature of Miss Silvester's present troubles. What his actual connection is with them, and how he came into possession of his information, I have not found out. My discovery begins and ends with the simple fact that he *has* the information."

"May I ask one question, Sir Patrick?"

"What is it?"

"How did you find out about Geoffrey Delamayn?"

"It would occupy a long time," answered Sir Patrick, "to tell you how—and it is not at all necessary to our purpose that you should know. My present obligation merely binds me to tell you—in strict confidence, mind!—that Miss Silvester's secrets are no secrets to Mr. Delamayn. I leave to your discretion the use you may make of that information. You are now entirely on a par with me in relation to your knowledge of the case of Miss Silvester. Let us return to the question which I asked you when we first came into the room. Do you see the connection, now, between that question, and what I have said since?"

Arnold was slow to see the connection. His mind was running on Sir Patrick's discovery. Little dreaming that he was indebted to Mrs. Inchbare's incomplete description of him for his own escape from detection, he was wondering how it had happened that *he* had remained unsuspected, while Geoffrey's position had been (in part at least) revealed to view.

"I asked you," resumed Sir Patrick, attempting to help him, "why the mere report that your friend was likely to marry Mrs. Glenarm roused your indignation, and you hesitated at giving an answer. Do you hesitate still?"

"It's not easy to give an answer, Sir Patrick."

"Let us put it in another way. I assume that your view of the report takes its rise in some knowledge, on your part, of Mr. Delamayn's private affairs, which the rest of us don't possess.—Is that conclusion correct?"

"Quite correct."

"Is what you know about Mr. Delamayn connected with any thing that you know about Miss Silvester?"

If Arnold had felt himself at liberty to answer that question, Sir Patrick's suspicions would have been aroused, and Sir Patrick's resolution would have forced a full disclosure from him before he left the house.

It was getting on to midnight. The first hour of the wedding-day was at hand, as the Truth made its final effort to struggle into light. The dark Phantoms of Trouble and Terror to come were waiting near them both at that moment. Arnold hesitated again—hesitated painfully. Sir Patrick paused for his answer. The clock in the hall struck the quarter to twelve.

"I can't tell you!" said Arnold.

"Is it a secret?"

"Yes."

"Committed to your honor?"

"Doubly committed to my honor."

"What do you mean?"

"I mean that Geoffrey and I have quarreled since he took me into his confidence. I am doubly bound to respect his confidence after that."

"Is the cause of your quarrel a secret also?"

"Yes."

Sir Patrick looked Arnold steadily in the face.

"I have felt an inveterate distrust of Mr. Delamayn from the first," he said. "Answer me this. Have you any reason to think—since we first talked about your friend in the summer-house at Windygates—that my opinion of him might have been the right one after all?"

"He has bitterly disappointed me," answered Arnold. "I can say no more."

"You have had very little experience of the world," proceeded Sir Patrick. "And you have just acknowledged that you have had reason to distrust your experience of your friend. Are you quite sure that you are acting wisely in keeping his secret from *me?* Are you quite sure that you will not repent the course you are taking to-night?" He laid a marked emphasis on those last words. "Think, Arnold," he added, kindly. "Think before you answer."

"I feel bound in honor to keep his secret," said Arnold. "No thinking can alter that."

Sir Patrick rose, and brought the interview to an end.

"There is nothing more to be said." With those words he gave Arnold his hand, and, pressing it cordially, wished him good-night.

Going out into the hall, Arnold found Blanche alone, looking at the barometer.

"The glass is at Set Fair, my darling," he whispered. "Good-night for the last time!"

He took her in his arms, and kissed her. At the moment when he released her Blanche slipped a little note into his hand.

"Read it," she whispered, "when you are alone at the inn."

So they parted on the eve of their wedding-day.

# CHAPTER THE THIRTY-FIFTH.

### THE DAY.

THE promise of the weather-glass was fulfilled. The sun shone on Blanche's marriage.

At nine in the morning the first of the proceedings of the day began. It was essentially of a clandestine nature. The bride and bridegroom evaded the restraints of lawful authority, and presumed to meet together privately, before they were married, in the conservatory at Ham Farm.

"You have read my letter, Arnold?"

"I have come here to answer it, Blanche. But why not have told me? Why write?"

"Because I put off telling you so long; and because I didn't know how you might take it; and for fifty other reasons. Never mind! I've made my confession. I haven't a single secret now which is not your secret too. There's time to say No, Arnold, if you think I ought to have no room in my heart for any body but you. My uncle tells me I am obstinate and wrong in refusing to give Anne up. If you agree with him, say the word, dear, before you make me your wife."

"Shall I tell you what I said to Sir Patrick last night?"

"About this?"

"Yes. The confession (as you call it) which you make in your pretty note, is the very thing that Sir Patrick spoke to me about in the dining-room before I went away. He told me your heart was set on finding Miss Silvester. And he asked me what I meant to do about it when we were married."

"And you said—?"

Arnold repeated his answer to Sir Patrick, with fervid embellishments of the original language, suitable to the emergency. Blanche's delight expressed itself in the form of two unblushing outrages on propriety, committed in close succession. She threw her arms round Arnold's neck; and she actually kissed him, three hours before the consent of State and Church sanctioned her in taking that proceeding. Let us shudder—but let us not blame her. These are the consequences of free institutions.

"Now," said Arnold, "it's my turn to take to pen and ink. I have a letter to write before we are married as well as you. Only there's this difference between us—I want you to help me."

"Who are you going to write to?"

"To my lawyer in Edinburgh. There will be no time unless I do it now. We start for Switzerland this afternoon—don't we?"

"Yes."

"Very well. I want to relieve your mind, my darling, before we go. Wouldn't you like to know—while we are away—that the right people are on the look-out for Miss Silvester? Sir Patrick has told me of the last place that she has been traced to—and my lawyer will set the right people at work. Come and help me to put it in the proper language, and the whole thing will be in train."

"Oh, Arnold! can I ever love you enough to reward you for this!"

"We shall see, Blanche—in Switzerland."

They audaciously penetrated, arm in arm, into Sir Patrick's own study—entirely at their disposal, as they well knew, at that hour of the morning. With Sir Patrick's pens and Sir Patrick's paper they produced a letter of instructions, de-liberately reopening the investigation which Sir Patrick's superior wisdom had closed. Neither pains nor money were to be spared by the lawyer in at once taking measures (beginning at Glasgow) to find Anne. The report of the result was to be addressed to Arnold, under cover to Sir Patrick at Ham Farm. By the time the letter was completed the morning had advanced to ten o'clock. Blanche left Arnold to array herself in her bridal splendor—after another outrage on propriety, and more consequences of free institutions.

The next proceedings were of a public and avowable nature, and strictly followed the customary precedents on such occasions.

Village nymphs strewed flowers on the path to the church door (and sent in the bill the same day). Village swains rang the joy-bells (and got drunk on their money the same evening). There was the proper and awful pause while the bridegroom was kept waiting at the church. There was the proper and pitiless staring of all the female spectators when the bride was led to the altar. There was the clergyman's preliminary look at the license—which meant official caution. And there was the clerk's preliminary look at the bridegroom—which meant official fees. All the women appeared to be in their natual element; and all the men appeared to be out of it.

Then the service began—rightly-considered, the most terrible, surely, of all mortal ceremonies—the service which binds two human beings, who know next to nothing of each other's natures, to risk the tremendous experiment of living together till death parts them—the service which says, in effect if not in words, Take your leap in the dark: we sanctify, but we don't insure, it!

The ceremony went on, without the slightest obstacle to mar its effect. There were no unforeseen interruptions. There were no ominous mistakes.

The last words were spoken, and the book was closed. They signed their names on the register; the husband was congratulated; the wife was embraced. They went back again to the house, with more flowers strewn at their feet. The wedding-breakfast was hurried; the wedding-speeches were curtailed: there was no time to be wasted, if the young couple were to catch the tidal train.

In an hour more the carriage had whirled them away to the station, and the guests had given them the farewell cheer from the steps of the house. Young, happy, fondly attached to each other, raised securely above all the sordid cares of life, what a golden future was theirs! Married with the sanction of the Family and the blessing of the Church—who could suppose that the time was coming, nevertheless, when the blighting question would fall on them, in the spring-time of their love: Are you Man and Wife?

---

# CHAPTER THE THIRTY-SIXTH.

### THE TRUTH AT LAST.

Two days after the marriage—on Wednesday, the ninth of September—a packet of letters, received at Windygates, was forwarded by Lady Lundie's steward to Ham Farm.

With one exception, the letters were all addressed either to Sir Patrick or to his sister-in-law. The one exception was directed to "Arnold Brinkworth, Esq., care of Lady Lundie, Windygates House, Perthshire"—and the envelope was specially protected by a seal.

Noticing that the post-mark was "Glasgow," Sir Patrick (to whom the letter had been delivered) looked with a certain distrust at the handwriting on the address. It was not known to him—but it was obviously the handwriting of a woman. Lady Lundie was sitting opposite to him at the table. He said, carelessly, "A letter for Arnold"—and pushed it across to her. Her ladyship took up the letter, and dropped it, the instant she looked at the handwriting, as if it had burned her fingers.

"The Person again!" exclaimed Lady Lundie. "The Person, presuming to address Arnold Brinkworth, at My house!"

"Miss Silvester?" asked Sir Patrick.

"No," said her ladyship, shutting her teeth with a snap. "The Person may insult me by addressing a letter to my care. But the Person's name shall not pollute my lips. Not even in your house, Sir Patrick. Not even to please *you.*"

Sir Patrick was sufficiently answered. After all that had happened—after her farewell letter to Blanche—here was Miss Silvester writing to Blanche's husband, of her own accord! It was unaccountable, to say the least of it. He took the letter back, and looked at it again. Lady Lundie's steward was a methodical man. He had indorsed each letter received at Windygates with the date of its delivery. The letter addressed to Arnold had been delivered on Monday, the seventh of September—on Arnold's wedding-day.

What did it mean?

It was pure waste of time to inquire. Sir Patrick rose to lock the letter up in one of the drawers of the writing-table behind him. Lady Lundie interfered (in the interest of morality).

"Sir Patrick!"

"Yes?"

"Don't you consider it your duty to open that letter?"

"My dear lady! what can you possibly be thinking of?"

The most virtuous of living women had her answer ready on the spot.

"I am thinking," said Lady Lundie, "of Arnold's moral welfare."

Sir Patrick smiled. On the long list of those respectable disguises under which we assert our own importance, or gratify our own love of meddling in our neighbor's affairs, a moral regard for the welfare of others figures in the foremost place, and stands deservedly as number one.

"We shall probably hear from Arnold in a day or two," said Sir Patrick, locking the letter up in the drawer. "He shall have it as soon as I know where to send it to him."

The next morning brought news of the bride and bridegroom.

They reported themselves to be too supremely happy to care where they lived, so long as they lived together. Every question but the question of Love was left in the competent hands of their courier. This sensible and trust-worthy man had decided that Paris was not to be thought of as a place of residence, by any sane human being, in the month of September. He had arranged that they were to leave for Baden—on their way to Switzerland—on the tenth. Letters were accordingly to be addressed to that place, until further notice. If the courier liked Baden, they would probably stay there for some time. If the courier took a fancy for the mountains, they would in that case go on to Switzerland. In the mean while nothing mattered to Arnold but Blanche—and nothing mattered to Blanche but Arnold.

Sir Patrick re-directed Anne Silvester's letter to Arnold, at the Poste Restante, Baden. A second letter, which had arrived that morning (addressed to Arnold in a legal handwriting, and bearing the post-mark of Edinburgh), was forwarded in the same way, and at the same time.

Two days later Ham Farm was deserted by the guests. Lady Lundie had gone back to Windygates. The rest had separated in their different directions. Sir Patrick, who also contemplated returning to Scotland, remained behind for a week—a solitary prisoner in his own country house. Accumulated arrears of business, with which it was impossible for his steward to deal single-handed, obliged him to remain at his estates in Kent for that time. To a man without a taste for partridge-shooting the ordeal was a trying one. Sir Patrick got through the day with the help of his business and his books. In the evening the rector of a neighboring parish drove over to dinner, and engaged his host at the noble but obsolete game of Piquet. They arranged to meet at each other's houses on alternate days. The rector was an admirable player; and Sir Patrick, though a born Presbyterian, blessed the Church of England from the bottom of his heart.

Three more days passed. Business at Ham Farm began to draw to an end. The time for Sir Patrick's journey to Scotland came nearer. The two partners at Piquet agreed to meet for a final game, on the next night, at the rector's house. But (let us take comfort in remembering it) our superiors in Church and State are as completely at the mercy of circumstances as the humblest and the poorest of us. That last game of Piquet between the baronet and the parson was never to be played.

On the afternoon of the fourth day Sir Patrick came in from a drive, and found a letter from Arnold waiting for him, which had been delivered by the second post.

Judged by externals only, it was a letter of an unusually perplexing—possibly also of an unusually interesting—kind. Arnold was one of the last persons in the world whom any of his friends would have suspected of being a lengthy correspondent. Here, nevertheless, was a letter from him, of three times the customary bulk and weight—and, apparently, of more than common importance, in the matter of news, besides. At the top of the envelope was marked "*Immediate.*" And at one side (also underlined) was the ominous word, "*Private.*"

"Nothing wrong, I hope?" thought Sir Patrick.

He opened the envelope.

Two inclosures fell out on the table. He looked at them for a moment. They were the two letters which he had forwarded to Baden.

The third letter remaining in his hand, and occupying a double sheet, was from Arnold himself. Sir Patrick read Arnold's letter first. It was dated " Baden," and it began as follows :

" My Dear Sir Patrick,—Don't be alarmed, if you can possibly help it. I am in a terrible mess."

Sir Patrick looked up for a moment from the letter. Given a young man who dates from " Baden," and declares himself to be in " a terrible mess," as representing the circumstances of the case—what is the interpretation to be placed on them? Sir Patrick drew the inevitable conclusion. Arnold had been gambling.

He shook his head, and went on with the letter.

" I must say, dreadful as it is, that I am not to blame—nor she either, poor thing."

Sir Patrick paused again. " She?" Blanche had apparently been gambling too? Nothing was wanting to complete the picture but an announcement in the next sentence, presenting the courier as carried away, in his turn, by the insatiate passion for play. Sir Patrick resumed :

" You can not, I am sure, expect *me* to have known the law. And as for poor Miss Silvester—"

" Miss Silvester?" What had Miss Silvester to do with it? And what could be the meaning of the reference to " the law?"

Sir Patrick had read the letter, thus far, standing up. A vague distrust stole over him at the appearance of Miss Silvester's name in connection with the lines which had preceded it. He felt nothing approaching to a clear prevision of what was to come. Some indescribable influence was at work in him, which shook his nerves, and made him feel the infirmities of his age (as it seemed) on a sudden. It went no further than that. He was obliged to sit down : he was obliged to wait a moment before he went on.

The letter proceeded, in these words :

" And, as for poor Miss Silvester, though she felt, as she reminds me, some misgivings—still, she never could have foreseen, being no lawyer either, how it was to end. I hardly know the best way to break it to you. I can't, and won't, believe it myself. But even if it should be true, I am quite sure you will find a way out of it for us. I will stick at nothing, and Miss Silvester (as you will see by her letter) will stick at nothing either, to set things right. Of course, I have not said one word to my darling Blanche, who is quite happy, and suspects nothing. All this, dear Sir Patrick, is very badly written, I am afraid, but it is meant to prepare you, and to put the best side on matters at starting. However, the truth must be told—and shame on the Scotch law is what *I* say. This it is, in short : Geoffrey Delamayn is even a greater scoundrel than you think him ; and I bitterly repent (as things have turned out) having held my tongue that night when you and I had our private talk at Ham Farm. You will think I am mixing two things up together. But I am not. Please to keep this about Geoffrey in your mind, and piece it together with what I have next to say. The worst is still to come. Miss Silvester's letter (inclosed) tells me this terrible thing. You must know that I went to her privately, as Geoffrey's messenger, on the day of the lawn-party at Windygates. Well—how it could have happened,

Heaven only knows—but there is reason to fear that I married her, without being aware of it myself, in August last, at the Craig Fernie inn."

The letter dropped from Sir Patrick's hand. He sank back in the chair, stunned for the moment, under the shock that had fallen on him.

He rallied, and rose bewildered to his feet. He took a turn in the room. He stopped, and summoned his will, and steadied himself by main force. He picked up the letter, and read the last sentence again. His face flushed. He was on the point of yielding himself to a useless outburst of anger against Arnold, when his better sense checked him at the last moment. " One fool in the family is enough," he said. " *My* business in this dreadful emergency is to keep my head clear for Blanche's sake."

He waited once more, to make sure of his own composure—and turned again to the letter, to see what the writer had to say for himself, in the way of explanation and excuse.

Arnold had plenty to say—with the drawback of not knowing how to say it. It was hard to decide which quality in his letter was most marked —the total absence of arrangement, or the total absence of reserve. Without beginning, middle, or end, he told the story of his fatal connection with the troubles of Anne Silvester, from the memorable day when Geoffrey Delamayn sent him to Craig Fernie, to the equally memorable night when Sir Patrick had tried vainly to make him open his lips at Ham Farm.

" I own I have behaved like a fool," the letter concluded, "in keeping Geoffrey Delamayn's secret for him—as things have turned out. But how could I tell upon him without compromising Miss Silvester? Read her letter, and you will see what she says, and how generously she releases me. It's no use saying I am sorry I wasn't more cautious. The mischief is done. I'll stick at nothing—as I have said before—to undo it. Only tell me what is the first step I am to take ; and, as long as it don't part me from Blanche, rely on my taking it. Waiting to hear from you, I remain, dear Sir Patrick, yours in great perplexity, Arnold Brinkworth."

Sir Patrick folded the letter, and looked at the two inclosures lying on the table. His eye was hard, his brow was frowning, as he put his hand to take up Anne's letter. The letter from Arnold's agent in Edinburgh lay nearer to him. As it happened, he took that first.

It was short enough, and clearly enough written, to invite a reading before he put it down again. The lawyer reported that he had made the necessary inquiries at Glasgow, with this result. Anne had been traced to The Sheep's Head Hotel. She had lain there utterly helpless, from illness, until the beginning of September. She had been advertised, without result, in the Glasgow newspapers. On the 5th of September she had sufficiently recovered to be able to leave the hotel. She had been seen at the railway station on the same day—but from that point all trace of her had been lost once more. The lawyer had accordingly stopped the proceedings, and now waited further instructions from his client.

This letter was not without its effect in encouraging Sir Patrick to suspend the harsh and hasty judgment of Anne, which any man, placed in his present situation, must have been inclined to form. Her illness claimed its small share of sympathy. Her friendless position—so plainly and so sadly revealed by the advertising in the newspapers—pleaded for merciful construction of faults committed, if faults there were. Gravely, but not angrily, Sir Patrick opened her letter —the letter that cast a doubt on his niece's marriage.

Thus Anne Silvester wrote:

"GLASGOW, *September* 5.

"DEAR MR. BRINKWORTH,—Nearly three weeks since I attempted to write to you from this place. I was seized by sudden illness while I was engaged over my letter; and from that time to this I have laid helpless in bed—very near, as they tell me, to death. I was strong enough to be dressed, and to sit up for a little while yesterday and the day before. To-day, I have made a better advance toward recovery. I can hold my pen and control my thoughts. The first use to which I put this improvement is to write these lines.

"I am going (so far as I know) to surprise— possibly to alarm—you. There is no escaping from it, for you or for me: it must be done.

"Thinking of how best to introduce what I am now obliged to say, I can find no better way than this. I must ask you to take your memory back to a day which we have both bitter reason to regret—the day when Geoffrey Delamayn sent you to see me at the inn at Craig Fernie.

"You may possibly not remember—it unhappily produced no impression on you at the time —that I felt, and expressed, more than once on that occasion, a very great dislike to your passing me off on the people of the inn as your wife. It was necessary to my being permitted to remain at Craig Fernie that you should do so. I knew this; but still I shrank from it. It was impossible for me to contradict you, without involving you in the painful consequences, and running the risk of making a scandal which might find its way to Blanche's ears. I knew this also; but still my conscience reproached me. It was a vague feeling. I was quite unaware of the actual danger in which you were placing yourself, or I would have spoken out, no matter what came of it. I had what is called a presentiment that you were not acting discreetly—nothing more. As I love and honor my mother's memory—as I trust in the mercy of God—this is the truth.

"You left the inn the next morning, and we have not met since.

"A few days after you went away my anxieties grew more than I could bear alone. I went secretly to Windygates, and had an interview with Blanche.

"She was absent for a few minutes from the room in which we had met. In that interval I saw Geoffrey Delamayn for the first time since I had left him at Lady Lundie's lawn-party. He treated me as if I was a stranger. He told me that he had found out all that had passed between us at the inn. He said he had taken a lawyer's opinion. Oh, Mr. Brinkworth! how can I break it to you? how can I write the words which repeat what he said to me next? It must be done. Cruel as it is, it must be done. He refused to my face to marry me. He said I was married already. He said I was your wife.

"Now you know why I have referred you to

what I felt (and confessed to feeling) when we were together at Craig Fernie. If you think hard thoughts, and say hard words of me, I can claim no right to blame you. I am innocent— and yet it is my fault.

"My head swims, and the foolish tears are rising in spite of me. I must leave off, and rest a little.

"I have been sitting at the window, and watching the people in the street as they go by. They are all strangers. But, somehow, the sight of them seems to rest my mind. The hum of the great city gives me heart, and helps me to go on.

"I can not trust myself to write of the man who has betrayed us both. Disgraced and broken as I am, there is something still left in me which lifts me above *him*. If he came repentant, at this moment, and offered me all that rank and wealth and worldly consideration can give, I would rather be what I am now than be his wife.

"Let me speak of you; and (for Blanche's sake) let me speak of myself.

"I ought, no doubt, to have waited to see you at Windygates, and to have told you at once of what had happened. But I was weak and ill; and the shock of hearing what I heard fell so heavily on me that I fainted. After I came to myself I was so horrified, when I thought of you and Blanche, that a sort of madness possessed me. I had but one idea—the idea of running away and hiding myself.

"My mind got clearer and quieter on the way to this place; and, arrived here, I did what I hope and believe was the best thing I could do. I consulted two lawyers. They differed in opinion as to whether we were married or not—according to the law which decides on such things in Scotland. The first said Yes. The second said No—but advised me to write immediately and tell you the position in which you stood. I attempted to write the same day, and fell ill as you know.

"Thank God, the delay that has happened is of no consequence. I asked Blanche, at Windygates, when you were to be married—and she told me not until the end of the autumn. It is only the fifth of September now. You have plenty of time before you. For all our sakes, make good use of it.

"What are you to do?

"Go at once to Sir Patrick Lundie, and show him this letter. Follow his advice—no matter how it may affect *me*. I should ill requite your kindness, I should be false indeed to the love I bear to Blanche, if I hesitated to brave any exposure that may now be necessary in your interests and in hers. You have been all that is generous, all that is delicate, all that is kind in this matter. You have kept my disgraceful secret—I am quite sure of it—with the fidelity of an honorable man who has had a woman's reputation placed in his charge. I release you, with my whole heart, dear Mr. Brinkworth, from your pledge. I entreat you, on my knees, to consider yourself free to reveal the truth. I will make any acknowledgment, on my side, that is needful under the circumstances—no matter how public it may be. Release yourself at any price; and then, and not till then, give back your regard

"I MUST LEAVE OFF, AND REST A LITTLE."

to the miserable woman who has laden you with the burden of her sorrow, and darkened your life for a moment with the shadow of her shame.

"Pray don't think there is any painful sacrifice involved in this. The quieting of my own mind is involved in it—and that is all.

"What has life left for *me*? Nothing but the barren necessity of living. When I think of the future now, my mind passes over the years that may be left to me in this world. Sometimes I dare to hope that the Divine Mercy of Christ—which once pleaded on earth for a woman like me—may plead, when death has taken me, for my spirit in Heaven. Sometimes I dare to hope that I may see my mother, and Blanche's mother, in the better world. Their hearts were bound together as the hearts of sisters while they were here; and they left to their children the legacy of their love. Oh, help me to say, if we meet again, that not in vain I promised to be a sister to Blanche! The debt I owe to her is the hereditary debt of my mother's gratitude. And what am I now? An obstacle in the way of the happiness of her life. Sacrifice me to that happiness, for God's sake! It is the one thing I have left to live for. Again and again I say it—I care nothing for myself. I have no right to be considered; I have no wish to be considered. Tell the whole truth about me, and call me to bear witness to it as publicly as you please!

"I have waited a little, once more, trying to think, before I close my letter, what there may be still left to write.

"I can not think of any thing left but the duty of informing you how you may find me, if you wish to write—or if it is thought necessary that we should meet again.

"One word before I tell you this.

"It is impossible for me to guess what you will do, or what you will be advised to do by others, when you get my letter. I don't even know that you may not already have heard of what your position is from Geoffrey Delamayn himself. In this event, or in the event of your thinking it desirable to take Blanche into your confidence, I venture to suggest that you should appoint some person whom you can trust to see me on your behalf—or, if you can not do this, that you should see me in the presence of a third person. The man who has not hesitated to betray us both, will not hesitate to misrepresent us in the vilest way, if he can do it in the future. For your own sake, let us be careful to give lying tongues no opportunity of assailing your place in Blanche's estimation. Don't act so as to risk putting yourself in a false position *again!* Don't let it be possible that a feeling unworthy of her should be roused in the loving and generous nature of your future wife!

"This written, I may now tell you how to communicate with me after I have left this place.

"You will find on the slip of paper inclosed the name and address of the second of the two lawyers whom I consulted in Glasgow. It is arranged between us that I am to inform him, by letter, of the next place to which I remove, and that he is to communicate the information either to you or to Sir Patrick Lundie, on your applying for it personally or by writing. I don't yet know myself where I may find refuge. Nothing is certain but that I can not, in my present state of weakness, travel far.

"If you wonder why I move at all until I am stronger, I can only give a reason which may appear fanciful and overstrained.

"I have been informed that I was advertised in the Glasgow newspapers during the time when I lay at this hotel, a stranger at the point of death. Trouble has perhaps made me morbidly suspicious. I am afraid of what may happen if I stay here, after my place of residence has been made publicly known. So, as soon as I can move, I go away in secret. It will be enough for me, if I can find rest and peace in some quiet place, in the country round Glasgow. You need feel no anxiety about my means of living. I have money enough for all that I need—and, if I get well again, I know how to earn my bread.

"I send no message to Blanche—I dare not till this is over. Wait till she is your happy wife; and then give her a kiss, and say it comes from Anne.

"Try and forgive me, dear Mr. Brinkworth. I have said all. Yours gratefully,
"ANNE SILVESTER."

Sir Patrick put the letter down with unfeigned respect for the woman who had written it.

Something of the personal influence which Anne exercised more or less over all the men with whom she came in contact seemed to communicate itself to the old lawyer through the medium of her letter. His thoughts perversely wandered away from the serious and pressing question of his niece's position into a region of purely speculative inquiry relating to Anne. What infatuation (he asked himself) had placed that noble creature at the mercy of such a man as Geoffrey Delamayn?

We have all, at one time or another in our lives, been perplexed as Sir Patrick was perplexed now.

If we know any thing by experience, we know that women cast themselves away impulsively on unworthy men, and that men ruin themselves headlong for unworthy women. We have the institution of Divorce actually among us, existing mainly because the two sexes are perpetually placing themselves in these anomalous relations toward each other. And yet, at every fresh instance which comes before us, we persist in being astonished to find that the man and the woman have not chosen each other on rational and producible grounds! We expect human passion to act on logical principles; and human fallibility—with love for its guide—to be above all danger of making a mistake! Ask the wisest among Anne Silvester's sex what they saw to rationally justify them in choosing the men to whom they have given their hearts and their lives, and you will be putting a question to those wise women which they never once thought of putting to themselves. Nay, more still. Look into your own experience, and say frankly, Could you justify your own excellent choice at the time when you irrevocably made it? Could you have put your reasons on paper when you first owned to yourself that you loved him? And would the reasons have borne critical inspection if you had?

Sir Patrick gave it up in despair. The interests of his niece were at stake. He wisely determined to rouse his mind by occupying himself with the practical necessities of the moment. It was essential to send an apology to the rector, in the first place, so as to leave the evening at his disposal for considering what preliminary course of conduct he should advise Arnold to pursue.

After writing a few lines of apology to his partner at Piquet—assigning family business as the excuse for breaking his engagement—Sir Patrick rang the bell. The faithful Duncan appeared, and saw at once in his master's face that something had happened.

"Send a man with this to the Rectory," said Sir Patrick. "I can't dine out to-day. I must have a chop at home."

"I am afraid, Sir Patrick—if I may be excused for remarking it—you have had some bad news?"

"The worst possible news, Duncan. I can't tell you about it now. Wait within hearing of the bell. In the mean time let nobody interrupt me. If the steward himself comes I can't see him."

After thinking it over carefully, Sir Patrick decided that there was no alternative but to send a message to Arnold and Blanche, summoning them back to England in the first place. The necessity of questioning Arnold, in the minutest detail, as to every thing that had happened between Anne Silvester and himself at the Craig Fernie inn, was the first and foremost necessity of the case.

At the same time it appeared to be desirable, for Blanche's sake, to keep her in ignorance, for the present at least, of what had happened. Sir Patrick met this difficulty with characteristic ingenuity and readiness of resource.

He wrote a telegram to Arnold, expressed in the following terms:

"Your letter and inclosures received. Return to Ham Farm as soon as you conveniently can. Keep the thing still a secret from Blanche. Tell her, as the reason for coming back, that the lost trace of Anne Silvester has been recovered, and that there may be reasons for her returning to England before any thing further can be done."

Duncan having been dispatched to the station with this message, Duncan's master proceeded to calculate the question of time.

Arnold would in all probability receive the telegram at Baden, on the next day, September the seventeenth. In three days more he and Blanche might be expected to reach Ham Farm. During the interval thus placed at his disposal Sir Patrick would have ample time in which to recover himself, and to see his way to acting for the best in the alarming emergency that now confronted him.

On the nineteenth Sir Patrick received a telegram informing him that he might expect to see the young couple late in the evening on the twentieth.

Late in the evening the sound of carriage-wheels was audible on the drive; and Sir Patrick, opening the door of his room, heard the familiar voices in the hall.

"Well!" cried Blanche, catching sight of him at the door, "is Anne found?"

"Not just yet, my dear."

"Is there news of her?"

"Yes."

"Am I in time to be of use?"

"In excellent time. You shall hear all about it to-morrow. Go and take off your traveling-things, and come down again to supper as soon as you can."

Blanche kissed him, and went on up stairs. She had, as her uncle thought in the glimpse he had caught of her, been improved by her marriage. It had quieted and steadied her. There were graces in her look and manner which Sir Patrick had not noticed before. Arnold, on his side, appeared to less advantage. He was restless and anxious; his position with Miss Silvester seemed to be preying on his mind. As soon as his young wife's back was turned, he appealed to Sir Patrick in an eager whisper.

"I hardly dare ask you what I have got it on my mind to say," he began. "I must bear it, if you are angry with me, Sir Patrick. But— only tell me one thing. Is there a way out of it for us? Have you thought of that?"

"I can not trust myself to speak of it clearly and composedly to-night," said Sir Patrick. "Be satisfied if I tell you that I have thought it all out—and wait for the rest till to-morrow."

Other persons concerned in the coming drama had had past difficulties to think out, and future movements to consider, during the interval occupied by Arnold and Blanche on their return journey to England. Between the seventeenth and the twentieth of September Geoffrey Delamayn had left Swanhaven, on the way to his new training quarters in the neighborhood in which the Foot-Race at Fulham was to be run. Between the same dates, also, Captain Newenden had taken the opportunity, while passing through London on his way south, to consult his solicitors. The object of the conference was to find means of discovering an anonymous letter-writer in Scotland, who had presumed to cause serious annoyance to Mrs. Glenarm.

Thus, by ones and twos, converging from widely distant quarters, they were now beginning to draw together, in the near neighborhood of the great city which was soon destined to assemble them all, for the first and the last time in this world, face to face.

## CHAPTER THE THIRTY-SEVENTH.

### THE WAY OUT.

BREAKFAST was just over. Blanche, seeing a pleasantly-idle morning before her, proposed to Arnold to take a stroll in the grounds.

The garden was bright with sunshine, and the bride was bright with good-humor. She caught her uncle's eye, looking at her admiringly, and paid him a little compliment in return. "You have no idea," she said, "how nice it is to be back at Ham Farm!"

"I am to understand then," rejoined Sir Patrick, "that I am forgiven for interrupting the honey-moon?"

"You are more than forgiven for interrupting it," said Blanche—"you are thanked. As a married woman," she proceeded, with the air of a matron of at least twenty years' standing, "I have been thinking the subject over; and I have arrived at the conclusion that a honey-moon which takes the form of a tour on the Continent, is one of our national abuses which stands in need of reform. When you are in love with each other (I consider a marriage without love to be no marriage at all), what do you want with the excitement of seeing strange places? Isn't it

excitement enough, and isn't it strange enough, to a newly-married woman to see such a total novelty as a husband? What is the most interesting object on the face of creation to a man in Arnold's position? The Alps? Certainly not! The most interesting object is the wife. And the proper time for a bridal tour is the time— say ten or a dozen years later—when you are beginning (not to get tired of each other; that's out of the question) but to get a little too well used to each other. Then take your tour to Switzerland—and you give the Alps a chance. A succession of honey-moon trips, in the autumn of married life—there is my proposal for an improvement on the present state of things! Come into the garden, Arnold; and let us calculate how long it will be before we get weary of each other, and want the beauties of nature to keep us company."

Arnold looked appealingly to Sir Patrick. Not a word had passed between them, as yet, on the serious subject of Anne Silvester's letter. Sir Patrick undertook the responsibility of making the necessary excuses to Blanche.

"Forgive me," he said, "if I ask leave to interfere with your monopoly of Arnold for a little while. I have something to say to him about his property in Scotland. Will you leave him with me, if I promise to release him as soon as possible?"

Blanche smiled graciously. "You shall have him as long as you like, uncle. There's your hat," she added, tossing it to her husband, gayly. "I brought it in for you when I got my own. You will find me on the lawn."

She nodded, and went out.

"Let me hear the worst at once, Sir Patrick," Arnold began. "Is it serious? Do you think I am to blame?"

"I will answer your last question first," said Sir Patrick. "Do I think you are to blame? Yes—in this way. You committed an act of unpardonable rashness when you consented to go, as Geoffrey Delamayn's messenger, to Miss Silvester at the inn. Having once placed yourself in that false position, you could hardly have acted, afterward, otherwise than you did. You could not be expected to know the Scotch law. And, as an honorable man, you were bound to keep a secret confided to you, in which the reputation of a woman was concerned. Your first and last error in this matter, was the fatal error of involving yourself in responsibilities which belonged exclusively to another man."

"The man had saved my life," pleaded Arnold—"and I believed I was giving service for service to my dearest friend."

"As to your other question," proceeded Sir Patrick. "Do I consider your position to be a serious one? Most assuredly, I do! So long as we are not absolutely certain that Blanche is your lawful wife, the position is more than serious: it is unendurable. I maintain the opinion, mind, out of which (thanks to your honorable silence) that scoundrel Delamayn contrived to cheat me. I told him, what I now tell you—that your sayings and doings at Craig Fernie, do not constitute a marriage, according to Scottish law. But," pursued Sir Patrick, holding up a warning forefinger at Arnold, "you have read it in Miss Silvester's letter, and you may now take it also as a result of my experience, that no individual opinion, in a matter of this kind, is to be relied on. Of two lawyers, consulted by Miss Silvester at Glasgow, one draws a directly opposite conclusion to mine, and decides that you and she *are* married. I believe him to be wrong; but, in our situation, we have no other choice than to boldly encounter the view of the case which he represents. In plain English, we must begin by looking the worst in the face."

Arnold twisted the traveling hat which Blanche had thrown to him, nervously, in both hands. "Supposing the worst comes to the worst," he asked, "what will happen?"

Sir Patrick shook his head.

"It is not easy to tell you," he said, "without entering into the legal aspect of the case. I shall only puzzle you if I do that. Suppose we look at the matter in its social bearings—I mean, as it may possibly affect you and Blanche, and your unborn children?"

Arnold gave the hat a tighter twist than ever. "I never thought of the children," he said, with a look of consternation.

"The children may present themselves," returned Sir Patrick, dryly, "for all that. Now listen. It may have occurred to your mind that the plain way out of our present dilemma is for you and Miss Silvester, respectively, to affirm what we know to be the truth—namely, that you never had the slightest intention of marrying each other. Beware of founding any hopes on any such remedy as that! If you reckon on it, you reckon without Geoffrey Delamayn. He is interested, remember, in proving you and Miss Silvester to be man and wife. Circumstances may arise—I won't waste time in guessing at what they may be—which will enable a third person to produce the landlady and the waiter at Craig Fernie in evidence against you—and to assert that your declaration and Miss Silvester's declaration are the result of collusion between you two. Don't start! Such things have happened before now. Miss Silvester is poor; and Blanche is rich. You may be made to stand in the awkward position of a man who is denying his marriage with a poor woman, in order to establish his marriage with an heiress: Miss Silvester presumably aiding the fraud, with two strong interests of her own as inducements—the interest of asserting her claim to be the wife of a man of rank, and the interest of earning her reward in money for resigning you to Blanche. There is a case which a scoundrel might set up —and with some appearance of truth too—in a court of justice!"

"Surely, the law wouldn't allow him to do that?"

"The law will argue any thing, with any body who will pay the law for the use of its brains and its time. Let that view of the matter alone now. Delamayn can set the case going, if he likes, without applying to any lawyer to help him. He has only to cause a report to reach Blanche's ears which publicly asserts that she is not your lawful wife. With her temper, do you suppose she would leave us a minute's peace till the matter was cleared up? Or take it the other way. Comfort yourself, if you will, with the idea that this affair will trouble nobody in the present. How are we to know it may not turn up in the future under circumstances which may place the legitimacy of your children in doubt?

We have a man to deal with who sticks at nothing. We have a state of the law which can only be described as one scandalous uncertainty from beginning to end. And we have two people (Bishopriggs and Mrs. Inchbare) who can, and will, speak to what took place between you and Anne Silvester at the inn. For Blanche's sake, and for the sake of your unborn children, we must face this matter on the spot—and settle it at once and forever. The question before us now is this. Shall we open the proceedings by communicating with Miss Silvester or not?"

At that important point in the conversation they were interrupted by the reappearance of Blanche. Had she, by any accident, heard what they had been saying?

No; it was the old story of most interruptions. Idleness that considers nothing, had come to look at Industry that bears every thing. It is a law of nature, apparently, that the people in this world who have nothing to do can not support the sight of an uninterrupted occupation in the hands of their neighbors. Blanche produced a new specimen from Arnold's collection of hats. "I have been thinking about it in the garden," she said, quite seriously. "Here is the brown one with the high crown. You look better in this than in the white one with the low crown. I have come to change them, that's all." She changed the hats with Arnold, and went on, without the faintest suspicion that she was in the way. "Wear the brown one when you come out—and come soon, dear. I won't stay an instant longer, uncle—I wouldn't interrupt you for the world." She kissed her hand to Sir Patrick, and smiled at her husband, and went out.

"What were we saying?" asked Arnold. "It's awkward to be interrupted in this way, isn't it?"

"If I know any thing of female human nature," returned Sir Patrick, composedly, "your wife will be in and out of the room, in that way, the whole morning. I give her ten minutes, Arnold, before she changes her mind again on the serious and weighty subject of the white hat and the brown. These little interruptions— otherwise quite charming—raised a doubt in my mind. Wouldn't it be wise (I ask myself), if we made a virtue of necessity, and took Blanche into the conversation? What do you say to calling her back and telling her the truth?"

Arnold started, and changed color.

"There are difficulties in the way," he said.

"My good fellow! at every step of this business there are difficulties in the way. Sooner or later, your wife must know what has happened. The time for telling her is, no doubt, a matter for your decision, not mine. All I say is this. Consider whether the disclosure won't come from you with a better grace, if you make it before you are fairly driven to the wall, and obliged to open your lips."

Arnold rose to his feet—took a turn in the room—sat down again—and looked at Sir Patrick, with the expression of a thoroughly bewildered and thoroughly helpless man.

"I don't know what to do," he said. "It beats me altogether. The truth is, Sir Patrick, I was fairly forced, at Craig Fernie, into deceiv-

"CHANGE AGAIN, DEAR."

ing Blanche—in what might seem to her a very unfeeling, and a very unpardonable way."

"That sounds awkward! What do you mean?"

"I'll try and tell you. You remember when you went to the inn to see Miss Silvester? Well, being there privately at the time, of course I was obliged to keep out of your way."

"I see! And, when Blanche came afterward, you were obliged to hide from Blanche, exactly as you had hidden from me?"

"Worse even than that! A day or two later, Blanche took me into her confidence. She spoke to me of her visit to the inn, as if I was a perfect stranger to the circumstances. She told me to my face, Sir Patrick, of the invisible man who had kept so strangely out of her way—without the faintest suspicion that I was the man. And I never opened my lips to set her right! I was obliged to be silent, or I must have betrayed Miss Silvester. What will Blanche think of me, if I tell her now? That's the question!"

Blanche's name had barely passed her husband's lips before Blanche herself verified Sir Patrick's prediction, by reappearing at the open French window, with the superseded white hat in her hand.

"Haven't you done yet!" she exclaimed. "I am shocked, uncle, to interrupt you again—but these horrid hats of Arnold's are beginning to weigh upon my mind. On reconsideration, I think the white hat with the low crown is the most becoming of the two. Change again, dear. Yes! the brown hat is hideous. There's a beggar at the gate. Before I go quite distracted, I shall give him the brown hat, and have done with the difficulty in that manner. Am I very much in the way of business? I'm afraid I must ap-

pear restless? Indeed, I *am* restless. I can't imagine what is the matter with me this morning."

"I can tell you," said Sir Patrick, in his gravest and dryest manner. "You are suffering, Blanche, from a malady which is exceedingly common among the young ladies of England. As a disease it is quite incurable—and the name of it is Nothing-to-Do."

Blanche dropped her uncle a smart little courtesy. "You might have told me I was in the way in fewer words than that." She whisked round, kicked the disgraced brown hat out into the veranda before her, and left the two gentlemen alone once more.

"Your position with your wife, Arnold," resumed Sir Patrick, returning gravely to the matter in hand, "is certainly a difficult one." He paused, thinking of the evening when he and Blanche had illustrated the vagueness of Mrs. Inchbare's description of the man at the inn, by citing Arnold himself as being one of the hundreds of innocent people who answered to it! "Perhaps," he added, "the situation is even more difficult than you suppose. It would have been certainly easier for *you*—and it would have looked more honorable in *her* estimation—if you had made the inevitable confession before your marriage. I am, in some degree, answerable for your not having done this—as well as for the far more serious dilemma with Miss Silvester in which you now stand. If I had not innocently hastened your marriage with Blanche, Miss Silvester's admirable letter would have reached us in ample time to prevent mischief. It's useless to dwell on that now. Cheer up, Arnold! I am bound to show you the way out of the labyrinth, no matter what the difficulties may be—and, please God, I will do it!"

He pointed to a table at the other end of the room, on which writing materials were placed. "I hate moving the moment I have had my breakfast," he said. "We won't go into the library. Bring me the pen and ink here."

"Are you going to write to Miss Silvester?"

"That is the question before us which we have not settled yet. Before I decide, I want to be in possession of the facts—down to the smallest detail of what took place between you and Miss Silvester at the inn. There is only one way of getting at those facts. I am going to examine you as if I had you before me in the witness-box in court."

With that preface, and with Arnold's letter from Baden in his hand as a brief to speak from, Sir Patrick put his questions in clear and endless succession; and Arnold patiently and faithfully answered them all.

The examination proceeded uninterruptedly until it had reached that point in the progress of events at which Anne had crushed Geoffrey Delamayn's letter in her hand, and had thrown it from her indignantly to the other end of the room. There, for the first time, Sir Patrick dipped his pen in the ink, apparently intending to take a note. "Be very careful here," he said; "I want to know every thing that you can tell me about that letter."

"The letter is lost," said Arnold.

"The letter has been stolen by Bishopriggs," returned Sir Patrick, "and is in the possession of Bishopriggs at this moment."

"Why, you know more about it than I do!" exclaimed Arnold.

"I sincerely hope not. I don't know what was inside the letter. Do you?"

"Yes. Part of it at least."

"Part of it?"

"There were two letters written, on the same sheet of paper," said Arnold. "One of them was written by Geoffrey Delamayn—and that is the one I know about."

Sir Patrick started. His face brightened ; he made a hasty note. "Go on!" he said, eagerly. "How came the letters to be written on the same sheet? Explain that!"

Arnold explained that Geoffrey, in the absence of any thing else to write his excuses on to Anne, had written to her on the fourth or blank page of a letter which had been addressed to him by Anne herself.

"Did you read that letter?" asked Sir Patrick.

"I might have read it if I had liked."

"And you didn't read it?"

"No."

"Why?"

"Out of delicacy."

Even Sir Patrick's carefully trained temper was not proof against this. "That is the most misplaced act of delicacy I ever heard of in my life!" cried the old gentleman, warmly. "Never mind! it's useless to regret it now. At any rate, you read Delamayn's answer to Miss Silvester's letter?"

"Yes—I did."

"Repeat it—as nearly as you can remember at this distance of time."

"It was so short," said Arnold, "that there is hardly any thing to repeat. As well as I remember, Geoffrey said he was called away to London by his father's illness. He told Miss Silvester to stop where she was ; and he referred her to me, as messenger. That's all I recollect of it now."

"Cudgel your brains, my good fellow! this is very important. Did he make no allusion to his engagement to marry Miss Silvester at Craig Fernie? Didn't he try to pacify her by an apology of some sort?"

The question roused Arnold's memory to make another effort.

"Yes," he answered. "Geoffrey said something about being true to his engagement, or keeping his promise, or words to that effect."

"You're sure of what you say now?"

"I am certain of it."

Sir Patrick made another note.

"Was the letter signed?" he asked, when he had done.

"Yes."

"And dated?"

"Yes." Arnold's memory made a second effort, after he had given his second affirmative answer. "Wait a little," he said. "I remember something else about the letter. It was not only dated. The time of day at which it was written was put as well."

"How came he to do that?"

"I suggested it. The letter was so short I felt ashamed to deliver it as it stood. I told him to put the time—so as to show her that he was obliged to write in a hurry. He put the time when the train started ; and (I think) the time when the letter was written as well."

"And you delivered that letter to Miss Silvester, with your own hand, as soon as you saw her at the inn?"

"I did."

Sir Patrick made a third note, and pushed the paper away from him with an air of supreme satisfaction.

"I always suspected that lost letter to be an important document," he said—"or Bishopriggs would never have stolen it. We must get possession of it, Arnold, at any sacrifice. The first thing to be done (exactly as I anticipated), is to write to the Glasgow lawyer, and find Miss Silvester."

"Wait a little!" cried a voice at the veranda. "Don't forget that I have come back from Baden to help you!"

Sir Patrick and Arnold both looked up. This time Blanche had heard the last words that had passed between them. She sat down at the table by Sir Patrick's side, and laid her hand caressingly on his shoulder.

"You are quite right, uncle," she said. "I am suffering this morning from the malady of having nothing to do. Are you going to write to Anne? Don't. Let me write instead."

Sir Patrick declined to resign the pen.

"The person who knows Miss Silvester's address," he said, "is a lawyer in Glasgow. I am going to write to the lawyer. When he sends us word where she is—then, Blanche, will be the time to employ your good offices, in winning back your friend."

He drew the writing materials once more within his reach, and, suspending the remainder of

Arnold's examination for the present, began his letter to Mr. Crum.

Blanche pleaded hard for an occupation of some sort. "Can nobody give me something to do?" she asked. "Glasgow is such a long way off, and waiting is such weary work. Don't sit there staring at me, Arnold! Can't you suggest something?"

Arnold, for once, displayed an unexpected readiness of resource.

"If you want to write," he said, "you owe Lady Lundie a letter. It's three days since you heard from her—and you haven't answered her yet."

Sir Patrick paused, and looked up quickly from his writing-desk.

"Lady Lundie?" he muttered, inquiringly.

"Yes," said Blanche. "It's quite true; I owe her a letter. And of course I ought to tell her we have come back to England. She will be finely provoked when she hears why!"

The prospect of provoking Lady Lundie seemed to rouse Blanche's dormant energies. She took a sheet of her uncle's note-paper, and began writing her answer then and there.

Sir Patrick completed his communication to the lawyer—after a look at Blanche, which expressed any thing rather than approval of her present employment. Having placed his completed note in the post-bag, he silently signed to Arnold to follow him into the garden. They went out together, leaving Blanche absorbed over her letter to her step-mother.

"Is my wife doing any thing wrong?" asked Arnold, who had noticed the look which Sir Patrick had cast on Blanche.

"Your wife is making mischief as fast as her fingers can spread it."

Arnold stared. "She must answer Lady Lundie's letter," he said.

"Unquestionably."

"And she must tell Lady Lundie we have come back."

"I don't deny it."

"Then what is the objection to her writing?"

Sir Patrick took a pinch of snuff—and pointed with his ivory cane to the bees humming busily about the flower-beds in the sunshine of the autumn morning.

"I'll show you the objection," he said. "Suppose Blanche told one of those inveterately intrusive insects that the honey in the flowers happens, through an unexpected accident, to have come to an end—do you think he would take the statement for granted? No. He would plunge head-foremost into the nearest flower, and investigate it for himself."

"Well?" said Arnold.

"Well—there is Blanche in the breakfast-room telling Lady Lundie that the bridal tour happens, through an unexpected accident, to have come to an end. Do you think Lady Lundie is the sort of person to take the statement for granted? Nothing of the sort! Lady Lundie, like the bee, will insist on investigating for herself. How it will end, if she discovers the truth—and what new complications she may not introduce into a matter which, Heaven knows, is complicated enough already—I leave you to imagine. *My* poor powers of prevision are not equal to it."

Before Arnold could answer, Blanche joined them from the breakfast-room.

"I've done it," she said. "It was an awkward letter to write—and it's a comfort to have it over."

"You have done it, my dear," remarked Sir Patrick, quietly. "And it may be a comfort. But it's not over."

"What do you mean?"

"I think, Blanche, we shall hear from your step-mother by return of post."

--------

## CHAPTER THE THIRTY-EIGHTH.

### THE NEWS FROM GLASGOW.

THE letters to Lady Lundie and to Mr. Crum having been dispatched on Monday, the return of the post might be looked for on Wednesday afternoon at Ham Farm.

Sir Patrick and Arnold held more than one private consultation, during the interval, on the delicate and difficult subject of admitting Blanche to a knowledge of what had happened. The wise elder advised; and the inexperienced junior listened. "Think of it," said Sir Patrick; "and do it." And Arnold thought of it—and left it undone.

Let those who feel inclined to blame him remember that he had only been married a fortnight. It is hard, surely, after but two weeks' possession of your wife, to appear before her in the character of an offender on trial—and to find that an angel of retribution has been thrown into the bargain by the liberal destiny which bestowed on you the woman whom you adore!

They were all three at home on the Wednesday afternoon, looking out for the postman. The correspondence delivered included (exactly as Sir Patrick had foreseen) a letter from Lady Lundie. Further investigation, on the far more interesting subject of the expected news from Glasgow, revealed—nothing. The lawyer had not answered Sir Patrick's inquiry by return of post.

"Is that a bad sign?" asked Blanche.

"It is a sign that something has happened," answered her uncle. "Mr. Crum is possibly expecting to receive some special information, and is waiting on the chance of being able to communicate it. We must hope, my dear, in to-morrow's post."

"Open Lady Lundie's letter in the mean time," said Blanche. "Are you sure it is for you—and not for me?"

There was no doubt about it. Her ladyship's reply was ominously addressed to her ladyship's brother-in-law. "I know what that means," said Blanche, eying her uncle eagerly while he was reading the letter. "If you mention Anne's name you insult my step-mother. I have mentioned it freely. Lady Lundie is mortally offended with me."

Rash judgment of youth! A lady who takes a dignified attitude, in a family emergency, is never mortally offended—she is only deeply grieved. Lady Lundie took a dignified attitude. "I well know," wrote this estimable and Christian woman, "that I have been all along regarded in the light of an intruder by the family connections of my late beloved husband. But I was hardly prepared to find myself entirely shut out from all domestic confidence, at a time when some serious domestic catastrophe has but too evidently taken place. I have no desire, dear Sir Patrick, to intrude. Feeling it, however, to be quite inconsistent with a due regard for my own position—after what has happened—to correspond with Blanche, I address myself to the head of the family, purely in the interests of propriety. Permit me to ask whether—under circumstances which appear to be serious enough to require the recall of my step-daughter and her husband from their wedding tour—you think it DECENT to keep the widow of the late Sir Thomas Lundie entirely in the dark? Pray consider this—not at all out of regard for Me!—but out of regard for your own position with Society. Curiosity is, as you know, foreign to my nature. But when this dreadful scandal (whatever it may be) comes out—which, dear Sir Patrick, it can not fail to do—what will the world think, when it asks for Lady Lundie's opinion, and hears that Lady Lundie knew nothing about it? Whichever way you may decide I shall take no offense. I may possibly be wounded—but that won't matter. My little round of duties will find me still earnest, still cheerful. And even if you shut me out, my best wishes will find their way, nevertheless, to Ham Farm. May I add—without encountering a sneer—that the prayers of a lonely woman are offered for the welfare of all?"

"Well?" said Blanche.

Sir Patrick folded up the letter, and put it in his pocket.

"You have your step-mother's best wishes, my dear." Having answered in those terms, he bowed to his niece with his best grace, and walked out of the room.

"Do I think it decent," he repeated to himself, as he closed the door, "to leave the widow of the late Sir Thomas Lundie in the dark? When a lady's temper is a little ruffled, I think it more than decent, I think it absolutely desirable, to let that lady have the last word." He went into the library, and dropped his sister-in-law's remonstrance into a box, labeled "Unanswered Letters." Having got rid of it in that way, he hummed his favorite little Scotch air—and put on his hat, and went out to sun himself in the garden.

Meanwhile, Blanche was not quite satisfied with Sir Patrick's reply. She appealed to her husband. "There is something wrong," she said—"and my uncle is hiding it from me."

Arnold could have desired no better opportunity than she had offered to him, in those words, for making the long-deferred disclosure to her of the truth. He lifted his eyes to Blanche's face. By an unhappy fatality she was looking charmingly that morning. How would she look if he told her the story of the hiding at the inn? Arnold was still in love with her—and Arnold said nothing.

The next day's post brought not only the anticipated letter from Mr. Crum, but an unexpected Glasgow newspaper as well.

This time Blanche had no reason to complain that her uncle kept his correspondence a secret from her. After reading the lawyer's letter, with an interest and agitation which showed that the contents had taken him by surprise, he handed it to Arnold and his niece. "Bad news there," he said. "We must share it together."

After acknowledging the receipt of Sir Patrick's letter of inquiry, Mr. Crum began by stating all that he knew of Miss Silvester's movements—dating from the time when she had left the Sheep's Head Hotel. About a fortnight since he had received a letter from her informing him that she had found a suitable place of residence in a village near Glasgow. Feeling a strong interest in Miss Silvester, Mr. Crum had visited her some few days afterward. He had satisfied himself that she was lodging with respectable people, and was as comfortably situated as circumstances would permit. For a week more he had heard nothing from the lady. At the expiration of that time he had received a letter from her, telling him that she had read something in a Glasgow newspaper, of that day's date, which seriously concerned herself, and which would oblige her to travel northward immediately as fast as her strength would permit. At a later period, when she would be more certain of her own movements, she engaged to write again, and let Mr. Crum know where he might communicate with her if necessary. In the mean time, she could only thank him for his kindness, and beg him to take care of any letters or messages which might be left for her. Since the receipt of this communication the lawyer had heard nothing further. He had waited for the morning's post in the hope of being able to report that he had received some further intelligence. The hope had not been realized. He had now stated all that he knew himself thus far—and he had forwarded a copy of the newspaper alluded to by Miss Silvester, on the chance that an examination of it by Sir Patrick might possibly lead to further discoveries. In conclusion, he pledged himself to write again the moment he had any information to send.

Blanche snatched up the newspaper, and opened it. "Let me look!" she said. "I can find what Anne saw here if any body can!"

She ran her eye eagerly over column after column and page after page—and dropped the newspaper on her lap with a gesture of despair.

"Nothing!" she exclaimed. "Nothing any where, that I can see, to interest Anne. Nothing to interest any body—except Lady Lundie," she went on, brushing the newspaper off her lap. "It turns out to be all true, Arnold, at Swanhaven. Geoffrey Delamayn is going to marry Mrs. Glenarm."

"What!" cried Arnold; the idea instantly flashing on him that this was the news which Anne had seen.

Sir Patrick gave him a warning look, and picked up the newspaper from the floor.

"I may as well run through it, Blanche, and make quite sure that you have missed nothing," he said.

The report to which Blanche had referred was among the paragraphs arranged under the heading of "Fashionable News." "A matrimonial alliance" (the Glasgow journal announced) "was in prospect between the Honorable Geoffrey Delamayn and the lovely and accomplished relict of the late Mathew Glenarm, Esq., formerly Miss Newenden." The marriage would, in all probability, "be solemnized in Scotland, before the end of the present autumn;" and the wedding breakfast, it was whispered, "would collect a large and fashionable party at Swanhaven Lodge."

Sir Patrick handed the newspaper silently to Arnold. It was plain to any one who knew Anne Silvester's story that those were the words which had found their fatal way to her in her place of rest. The inference that followed seemed to be hardly less clear. But one intelligible object, in the opinion of Sir Patrick, could be at the end of her journey to the north. The deserted woman had rallied the last relics of her old energy—and had devoted herself to the desperate purpose of stopping the marriage of Mrs. Glenarm.

Blanche was the first to break the silence.

"It seems like a fatality," she said. "Perpetual failure! Perpetual disappointment! Are Anne and I doomed never to meet again?"

She looked at her uncle. Sir Patrick showed none of his customary cheerfulness in the face of disaster.

"She has promised to write to Mr. Crum," he said. "And Mr. Crum has promised to let us know when he hears from her. That is the only prospect before us. We must accept it as resignedly as we can."

Blanche wandered out listlessly among the flowers in the conservatory. Sir Patrick made no secret of the impression produced upon him by Mr. Crum's letter, when he and Arnold were left alone.

"There is no denying," he said, "that matters have taken a very serious turn. My plans and calculations are all thrown out. It is impossible to foresee what new mischief may not come of it, if those two women meet; or what desperate act Delamayn may not commit, if he finds himself driven to the wall. As things are, I own frankly I don't know what to do next. A great light of the Presbyterian Church," he added, with a momentary outbreak of his whimsical humor, "once declared, in my hearing, that the invention of printing was nothing more or less than a proof of the intellectual activity of the Devil. Upon my honor, I feel for the first time in my life inclined to agree with him."

He mechanically took up the Glasgow journal, which Arnold had laid aside, while he spoke.

"What's this!" he exclaimed, as a name caught his eye in the first line of the newspaper at which he happened to look. "Mrs. Glenarm again! Are they turning the iron-master's widow into a public character?"

There the name of the widow was, unquestionably; figuring for the second time in type, in a letter of the gossiping sort, supplied by an "Occasional Correspondent," and distinguished by the title of "Sayings and Doings in the North." After tattling pleasantly of the prospects of the shooting season, of the fashions from Paris, of an accident to a tourist, and of a scandal in the Scottish Kirk, the writer proceeded to the narrative of a case of interest, relating to a marriage in the sphere known (in the language of footmen) as the sphere of "high life."

Considerable sensation (the correspondent announced) had been caused in Perth and its neighborhood, by the exposure of an anonymous attempt at extortion, of which a lady of distinction had lately been made the object. As her name had already been publicly mentioned in an application to the magistrates, there could be no

impropriety in stating that the lady in question was Mrs. Glenarm—whose approaching union with the Honorable Geoffrey Delamayn was alluded to in another column of the journal.

Mrs. Glenarm had, it appeared, received an anonymous letter, on the first day of her arrival as guest at the house of a friend, residing in the neighborhood of Perth. The letter warned her that there was an obstacle, of which she was herself probably not aware, in the way of her projected marriage with Mr. Geoffrey Delamayn. That gentleman had seriously compromised himself with another lady; and the lady would oppose his marriage to Mrs. Glenarm, with proof in writing to produce in support of her claim. The proof was contained in two letters exchanged between the parties, and signed by their names; and the correspondence was placed at Mrs. Glenarm's disposal, on two conditions, as follows:

First, that she should offer a sufficiently liberal price to induce the present possessor of the letters to part with them. Secondly, that she should consent to adopt such a method of paying the money as should satisfy the person that he was in no danger of finding himself brought within reach of the law. The answer to these two proposals was directed to be made through the medium of an advertisement in the local newspaper—distinguished by this address, "To a Friend in the Dark."

Certain turns of expression, and one or two mistakes in spelling, pointed to this insolent letter as being, in all probability, the production of a Scotchman, in the lower ranks of life. Mrs. Glenarm had at once shown it to her nearest relative, Captain Newenden. The captain had sought legal advice in Perth. It had been decided, after due consideration, to insert the advertisement demanded, and to take measures to entrap the writer of the letter into revealing himself—without, it is needless to add, allowing the fellow really to profit by his attempted act of extortion.

The cunning of the "Friend in the Dark" (whoever he might be) had, on trying the proposed experiment, proved to be more than a match for the lawyers. He had successfully eluded not only the snare first set for him, but others subsequently laid. A second, and a third, anonymous letter, one more impudent than the other, had been received by Mrs. Glenarm, assuring that lady and the friends who were acting for her, that they were only wasting time, and raising the price which would be asked for the correspondence, by the course they were taking. Captain Newenden had thereupon, in default of knowing what other course to pursue, appealed publicly to the city magistrates; and a reward had been offered, under the sanction of the municipal authorities, for the discovery of the man. This proceeding also having proved quite fruitless, it was understood that the captain had arranged, with the concurrence of his English solicitors, to place the matter in the hands of an experienced officer of the London police.

Here, so far as the newspaper correspondent was aware, the affair rested for the present.

It was only necessary to add, that Mrs. Glenarm had left the neighborhood of Perth, in order to escape further annoyance; and had placed herself under the protection of friends in another part of the county. Mr. Geoffrey Delamayn, whose fair fame had been assailed (it was needless, the correspondent added in parenthesis, to say how groundlessly), was understood to have expressed, not only the indignation natural under the circumstances, but also his extreme regret at not finding himself in a position to aid Captain Newenden's efforts to bring the anonymous slanderer to justice. The honorable gentleman was, as the sporting public were well aware, then in course of strict training for his forthcoming appearance at the Fulham Foot-Race. So important was it considered that his mind should not be harassed by annoyances, in his present responsible position, that his trainer and his principal backers had thought it desirable to hasten his removal to the neighborhood of Fulham—where the exercises which were to prepare him for the race were now being continued on the spot.

"The mystery seems to thicken," said Arnold.

"Quite the contrary," returned Sir Patrick, briskly. "The mystery is clearing fast—thanks to the Glasgow newspaper. I shall be spared the trouble of dealing with Bishopriggs for the stolen letter. Miss Silvester has gone to Perth, to recover her correspondence with Geoffrey Delamayn."

"Do you think she would recognize it," said Arnold, pointing to the newspaper, "in the account given of it here?"

"Certainly! And she could hardly fail, in my opinion, to get a step farther than that. Unless I am entirely mistaken, the authorship of the anonymous letters has not mystified *her.*"

"How could she guess at that?"

"In this way, as I think. Whatever she may have previously thought, she must suspect, by this time, that the missing correspondence has been stolen, and not lost. Now, there are only two persons whom she can think of, as probably guilty of the theft—Mrs. Inchbare or Bishopriggs. The newspaper description of the style of the anonymous letters declares it to be the style of a Scotchman in the lower ranks of life—in other words, points plainly to Bishopriggs. You see that? Very well. Now suppose she recovers the stolen property. What is likely to happen then? She will be more or less than woman if she doesn't make her way next, provided with her proofs in writing, to Mrs. Glenarm. She may innocently help, or she may innocently frustrate, the end we have in view—either way, our course is clear before us again. Our interest in communicating with Miss Silvester remains precisely the same interest that it was before we received the Glasgow newspaper. I propose to wait till Sunday, on the chance that Mr. Crum may write again. If we don't hear from him, I shall start for Scotland on Monday morning, and take my chance of finding my way to Miss Silvester, through Mrs. Glenarm."

"Leaving me behind?"

"Leaving you behind. Somebody must stay with Blanche. After having only been a fortnight married, must I remind you of that?"

"Don't you think Mr. Crum will write before Monday?"

"It will be such a fortunate circumstance for us, if he does write, that I don't venture to anticipate it."

"You are down on our luck, Sir."

"I detest slang, Arnold. But slang, I own, expresses my state of mind, in this instance, with an accuracy which almost reconciles me to the use of it—for once in a way."

"Every body's luck turns sooner or later," persisted Arnold. "I can't help thinking *our* luck is on the turn at last. Would you mind taking a bet, Sir Patrick?"

"Apply at the stables. I leave betting, as I leave cleaning the horses, to my groom."

With that crabbed answer he closed the conversation for the day.

The hours passed, and time brought the post again in due course—and the post decided in Arnold's favor! Sir Patrick's want of confidence in the favoring patronage of Fortune was practically rebuked by the arrival of a second letter from the Glasgow lawyer on the next day.

"I have the pleasure of announcing" (Mr. Crum wrote) "that I have heard from Miss Silvester, by the next postal delivery ensuing, after I had dispatched my letter to Ham Farm. She writes, very briefly, to inform me that she has decided on establishing her next place of residence in London. The reason assigned for taking this step—which she certainly did not contemplate when I last saw her—is, that she finds herself approaching the end of her pecuniary resources. Having already decided on adopting, as a means of living, the calling of a concert-singer, she has arranged to place her interests in the hands of an old friend of her late mother (who appears to have belonged also to the musical profession): a dramatic and musical agent long established in the metropolis, and well known to her as a trust-worthy and respectable man. She sends me the name and address of this person—a copy of which you will find on the inclosed slip of paper—in the event of my having occasion to write to her, before she is settled in London. This is the whole substance of her letter. I have only to add, that it does not contain the slightest allusion to the nature of the errand on which she left Glasgow."

Sir Patrick happened to be alone when he opened Mr. Crum's letter.

His first proceeding, after reading it, was to consult the railway time-table hanging in the hall. Having done this, he returned to the library—wrote a short note of inquiry, addressed to the musical agent—and rang the bell.

"Miss Silvester is expected in London, Duncan. I want a discreet person to communicate with her. You are the person."

Duncan bowed. Sir Patrick handed him the note.

"If you start at once you will be in time to catch the train. Go to that address, and inquire for Miss Silvester. If she has arrived, give her my compliments, and say I will have the honor of calling on her (on Mr. Brinkworth's behalf) at the earliest date which she may find it convenient to appoint. Be quick about it—and you will have time to get back before the last train. Have Mr. and Mrs. Brinkworth returned from their drive?"

"No, Sir Patrick."

Pending the return of Arnold and Blanche, Sir Patrick looked at Mr. Crum's letter for the second time.

He was not quite satisfied that the pecuniary motive was really the motive at the bottom of

Anne's journey south. Remembering that Geoffrey's trainers had removed him to the neighborhood of London, he was inclined to doubt whether some serious quarrel had not taken place between Anne and Mrs. Glenarm—and whether some direct appeal to Geoffrey himself might not be in contemplation as the result. In that event, Sir Patrick's advice and assistance would be placed, without scruple, at Miss Silvester's disposal. By asserting her claim, in opposition to the claim of Mrs. Glenarm, she was also asserting herself to be an unmarried woman, and was thus serving Blanche's interests as well as her own. "I owe it to Blanche to help her," thought Sir Patrick. "And I owe it to myself to bring Geoffrey Delamayn to a day of reckoning if I can."

The barking of the dogs in the yard announced the return of the carriage. Sir Patrick went out to meet Arnold and Blanche at the gate, and tell them the news.

Punctual to the time at which he was expected, the discreet Duncan reappeared with a note from the musical agent.

Miss Silvester had not yet reached London; but she was expected to arrive not later than Tuesday in the ensuing week. The agent had already been favored with her instructions to pay the strictest attention to any commands received from Sir Patrick Lundie. He would take care that Sir Patrick's message should be given to Miss Silvester as soon as she arrived.

At last, then, there was news to be relied on! At last there was a prospect of seeing her! Blanche was radiant with happiness. Arnold was in high spirits for the first time since his return from Baden.

Sir Patrick tried hard to catch the infection of gayety from his young friends; but, to his own surprise, not less than to theirs, the effort proved fruitless. With the tide of events turning decidedly in his favor—relieved of the necessity of taking a doubtful journey to Scotland; assured of obtaining his interview with Anne in a few days' time—he was out of spirits all through the evening.

"Still down on our luck!" exclaimed Arnold, as he and his host finished their last game of billiards, and parted for the night. "Surely, we couldn't wish for a more promising prospect than *our* prospect next week?"

Sir Patrick laid his hand on Arnold's shoulder.

"Let us look indulgently together," he said, in his whimsically grave way, "at the humiliating spectacle of an old man's folly. I feel, at this moment, Arnold, as if I would give every thing that I possess in the world to have passed over next week, and to be landed safely in the time beyond it."

"But why?"

"There is the folly! I can't tell why. With every reason to be in better spirits than usual, I am unaccountably, irrationally, invincibly depressed. What are we to conclude from that? Am I the object of a supernatural warning of misfortune to come? Or am I the object of a temporary derangement of the functions of the liver? There is the question. Who is to decide it? How contemptible is humanity, Arnold, rightly understood! Give me my candle, and let's hope it's the liver."

## CHAPTER THE THIRTY-NINTH.

### ANNE WINS A VICTORY.

On a certain evening in the month of September (at that period of the month when Arnold and Blanche were traveling back from Baden to Ham Farm) an ancient man—with one eye filmy and blind, and one eye moist and merry—sat alone in the pantry of the Harp of Scotland Inn, Perth, pounding the sugar softly in a glass of whisky-punch. He has hitherto been personally distinguished in these pages as the self-appointed father of Anne Silvester and the humble servant of Blanche at the dance at Swanhaven Lodge. He now dawns on the view in amicable relations with a third lady—and assumes the mystic character of Mrs. Glenarm's "Friend in the Dark."

Arriving in Perth the day after the festivities at Swanhaven, Bishopriggs proceeded to the Harp of Scotland—at which establishment for the reception of travelers he possessed the advantage of being known to the landlord as Mrs. Inchbare's right-hand man, and of standing high on the head-waiter's list of old and intimate friends.

Inquiring for the waiter first by the name of Thomas (otherwise Tammy) Pennyquick, Bishopriggs found his friend in sore distress of body and mind. Contending vainly against the disabling advances of rheumatism, Thomas Pennyquick ruefully contemplated the prospect of being laid up at home by a long illness—with a wife and children to support, and with the emoluments attached to his position passing into the pockets of the first stranger who could be found to occupy his place at the inn.

Hearing this doleful story, Bishopriggs cunningly saw his way to serving his own private interests by performing the part of Thomas Pennyquick's generous and devoted friend.

He forthwith offered to fill the place, without taking the emoluments, of the invalided head-waiter—on the understanding, as a matter of course, that the landlord consented to board and lodge him free of expense at the inn. The landlord having readily accepted this condition, Thomas Pennyquick retired to the bosom of his family. And there was Bishopriggs, doubly secured behind a respectable position and a virtuous action, against all likelihood of suspicion falling on him, as a stranger in Perth—in the event of his correspondence with Mrs. Glenarm being made the object of legal investigation on the part of her friends!

Having opened the campaign in this masterly manner, the same sagacious foresight had distinguished the operations of Bishopriggs throughout.

His correspondence with Mrs. Glenarm was invariably written with the left hand—the writing thus produced defying detection, in all cases, as bearing no resemblance of character whatever to writing produced by persons who habitually use the other hand. A no less far-sighted cunning distinguished his proceedings in answering the advertisements which the lawyers duly inserted in the newspaper. He appointed hours at which he was employed on business-errands for the inn, and places which lay on the way to those errands, for his meetings with Mrs. Glenarm's representatives: a pass-word being determined on, as usual in such cases, by exchanging which the persons concerned could discover each other. However carefully the lawyers might set the snare—whether they had their necessary "witness" disguised as an artist sketching in the neighborhood, or as an old woman selling fruit, or what not—the wary eye of Bishopriggs detected it. He left the pass-word unspoken; he went his way on his errand; he was followed on suspicion; and he was discovered to be only "a respectable person," charged with a message by the landlord of the Harp of Scotland Inn!

To a man intrenched behind such precautions as these, the chance of being detected might well be reckoned among the last of all the chances that could possibly happen.

Discovery was, nevertheless, advancing on Bishopriggs from a quarter which had not been included in his calculations. Anne Silvester was in Perth; forewarned by the newspaper (as Sir Patrick had guessed) that the letters offered to Mrs. Glenarm were the letters between Geoffrey and herself, which she had lost at Craig Fernie, and bent on clearing up the suspicion which pointed to Bishopriggs as the person who was trying to turn the correspondence to pecuniary account. The inquiries made for him, at Anne's request, as soon as she arrived in the town, openly described his name, and his former position as head-waiter at Craig Fernie—and thus led easily to the discovery of him, in his publicly avowed character of Thomas Pennyquick's devoted friend. Toward evening, on the day after she reached Perth, the news came to Anne that Bishopriggs was in service at the inn known as the Harp of Scotland. The landlord of the hotel at which she was staying inquired whether he should send a message for her. She answered, "No, I will take my message myself. All I want is a person to show me the way to the inn."

Secluded in the solitude of the head-waiter's pantry, Bishopriggs sat peacefully melting the sugar in his whisky-punch.

It was the hour of the evening at which a period of tranquillity generally occurred before what was called "the night-business" of the house began. Bishopriggs was accustomed to drink and meditate daily in this interval of repose. He tasted the punch, and smiled contentedly as he set down his glass. The prospect before him looked fairly enough. He had outwitted the lawyers in the preliminary negotiations thus far. All that was needful now was to wait till the terror of a public scandal (sustained by occasional letters from her "Friend in the Dark") had its due effect on Mrs. Glenarm, and hurried her into paying the purchase-money for the correspondence with her own hand. "Let it breed in the brain," he thought, "and the siller will soon come out o' the purse."

His reflections were interrupted by the appearance of a slovenly maid-servant, with a cotton handkerchief tied round her head, and an uncleaned sauce-pan in her hand.

"Eh, Maister Bishopriggs," cried the girl, "here's a braw young leddy speerin' for ye by yer ain name at the door."

"A leddy?" repeated Bishopriggs, with a look of virtuous disgust. "Ye donnert ne'er-do-weel, do you come to a decent, 'sponsible man like me, wi' sic a Cyprian overture as that? What d'ye tak' me for? Mark Antony that lost the world

for love (the mair fule he!)? or Don Jovanny that counted his concubines by hundreds, like the blessed Solomon himself? Awa' wi' ye to yer pots and pans; and bid the wandering Venus that sent ye go spin!"

Before the girl could answer she was gently pulled aside from the doorway, and Bishopriggs, thunder-struck, saw Anne Silvester standing in her place.

"You had better tell the servant I am no stranger to you," said Anne, looking toward the kitchen-maid, who stood in the passage staring at her in stolid amazement.

"My ain sister's child!" cried Bishopriggs, lying with his customary readiness. "Go yer ways, Maggie. The bonny lassie's my ain kith and kin. The tongue o' scandal, I trow, is naething to say against that.—Lord save us and guide us!" he added in another tone, as the girl closed the door on them, "what brings ye here?"

"I have something to say to you. I am not very well; I must wait a little first. Give me a chair."

Bishopriggs obeyed in silence. His one available eye rested on Anne, as he produced the chair, with an uneasy and suspicious attention. "I'm wanting to know one thing," he said. "By what meeraiculous means, young madam, do ye happen to ha' fund yer way to this inn?"

Anne told him how her inquiries had been made, and what the result had been, plainly and frankly. The clouded face of Bishopriggs began to clear again.

"Hech! hech!" he exclaimed, recovering all his native impudence, "I hae had occasion to remark already, to anither leddy than yersel', that it's seemply mairvelous hoo a man's ain gude deeds find him oot in this lower warld o' ours. I hae dune a gude deed by pure Tammy Pennyquick, and here's a' Pairth ringing wi' the report o' it; and Sawmuel Bishopriggs sae weel known that ony stranger has only to ask, and find him. Understand, I beseech ye, that it's no hand o' mine that pets this new feather in my cap. As a gude Calvinist, my saul's clear o' the smallest figment o' belief in Warks. When I look at my ain celebrity I joost ask, as the Psawmist asked before me, 'Why do the heathen rage, and the people imagine a vain thing?' It seems ye've something to say to me," he added, suddenly reverting to the object of Anne's visit. "Is it humanly possible that ye can ha' come a' the way to Pairth for naething but that?"

The expression of suspicion began to show itself again in his face. Concealing as she best might the disgust that he inspired in her, Anne stated her errand in the most direct manner, and in the fewest possible words.

"I have come here to ask you for something," she said.

"Ay? ay? What may it be ye're wanting of me?"

"I want the letter I lost at Craig Fernie."

Even the solidly-founded self-possession of Bishopriggs himself was shaken by the startling directness of that attack on it. His glib tongue was paralyzed for the moment. "I dinna ken what ye're drivin' at," he said, after an interval, with a sullen consciousness that he had been all but tricked into betraying himself.

The change in his manner convinced Anne

"'MY AIN SISTER'S CHILD!' CRIED BISHOPRIGGS."

that she had found in Bishopriggs the person of whom she was in search.

"You have got my letter," she said, sternly insisting on the truth. "And you are trying to turn it to a disgraceful use. I won't allow you to make a market of my private affairs. You have offered a letter of mine for sale to a stranger. I insist on your restoring it to me before I leave this room!"

Bishopriggs hesitated again. His first suspicion that Anne had been privately instructed by Mrs. Glenarm's lawyers returned to his mind as a suspicion confirmed. He felt the vast importance of making a cautious reply.

"I'll no' waste precious time," he said, after a moment's consideration with himself, "in brushing awa' the fawse breath o' scandal, when it passes my way. It blaws to nae purpose, my young leddy, when it blaws on an honest man like me. Fie for shame on ye for saying what ye've joost said—to me that was a fether to ye at Craig Fernie! Wha' set ye on to it? Will it be man or woman that's misca'ed me behind my back?"

Anne took the Glasgow newspaper from the pocket of her traveling cloak, and placed it before him, open at the paragraph which described the act of extortion attempted on Mrs. Glenarm.

"I have found there," she said, "all that I want to know."

"May a' the tribe o' editors, preenters, paper-makers, news-vendors, and the like, bleeze together in the pit o' Tophet!" With this devout aspiration—internally felt, not openly uttered—Bishopriggs put on his spectacles, and read the passage pointed out to him. "I see naething here touching the name o' Sawmuel Bishopriggs, or the matter o' ony loss ye may or may not ha'

had at Craig Fernie," he said, when he had done; still defending his position, with a resolution worthy of a better cause.

Anne's pride recoiled at the prospect of prolonging the discussion with him. She rose to her feet, and said her last words.

"I have learned enough by this time," she answered, "to know that the one argument that prevails with you is the argument of money. If money will spare me the hateful necessity of disputing with you—poor as I am, money you shall have. Be silent, if you please. You are personally interested in what I have to say next."

She opened her purse, and took a five-pound note from it.

"If you choose to own the truth, and produce the letter," she resumed, "I will give you this, as your reward for finding, and restoring to me, something that I had lost. If you persist in your present prevarication, I can, and will, make that sheet of note-paper you have stolen from me nothing but waste paper in your hands. You have threatened Mrs. Glenarm with my interference. Suppose I go to Mrs. Glenarm? Suppose I interfere before the week is out? Suppose I have other letters of Mr. Delamayn's in my possession, and produce them to speak for me? What has Mrs. Glenarm to purchase of you *then?* Answer me that!"

The color rose on her pale face. Her eyes, dim and weary when she entered the room, looked him brightly through and through in immeasurable contempt. "Answer me that!" she repeated, with a burst of her old energy which revealed the fire and passion of the woman's nature, not quenched even yet!

If Bishopriggs had a merit, it was a rare merit, as men go, of knowing when he was beaten.

If he had an accomplishment, it was the accomplishment of retiring defeated, with all the honors of war.

"Mercy presairve us!" he exclaimed, in the most innocent manner. "Is it even You Yersel' that writ the letter to the man ca'ed Jaffray Delamayn, and got the wee bit answer in pencil, on the blank page? Hoo, in Heeven's name, was I to know *that* was the letter ye were after when ye cam' in here? Diʋ ye ever tell me ye were Anne Silvester, at the hottle? Never ance! Was the puir feckless husband-creature ye had wi' ʋe at the inn, Jaffray Delamayn? Jaffray wad mak' twa o' him, as my ain eyes ha' seen. Gi' ye back yer letter? My certie! noo I know it *is* yer letter, I'll gi' it back wi' a' the pleasure in life!"

He opened his pocket-book, and took it out, with an alacrity worthy of the honestest man in Christendom — and (more wonderful still) he looked with a perfectly assumed expression of indifference at the five-pound note in Anne's hand.

"Hoot! toot!" he said, "I'm no' that clear in my mind that I'm free to tak' yer money. Eh, weel! weel! I'll een receive it, if ye like, as a bit Memento o' the time when I was o' some sma' sairvice to ye at the hottle. Ye'll no' mind," he added, suddenly returning to business, "writin' me joost a line—in the way o' receipt, ye ken —to clear me o' ony future suspicion in the matter o' the letter?"

Anne threw down the bank-note on the table near which they were standing, and snatched the letter from him.

"You need no receipt," she answered. "There shall be no letter to bear witness against you!"

She lifted her other hand to tear it in pieces. Bishopriggs caught her by both wrists, at the same moment, and held her fast.

"Bide a wee!" he said. "Ye don't get the letter, young madam, without the receipt. It may be a' the same to *you*, now ye've married the other man, whether Jaffray Delamayn ance promised ye fair in the by-gone time, or no. But, my certie! it's a matter o' some moment to *me*, that ye've chairged wi' stealin' the letter, and making a market o't, and Lord knows what besides, that I suld hae yer ain acknowledgment for it in black and white. Gi' me my bit receipt —and een do as ye will with yer letter after that!"

Anne's hold of the letter relaxed. She let Bishopriggs repossess himself of it as it dropped on the floor between them, without making an effort to prevent him.

"It may be a' the same to *you*, now ye've married the other man, whether Jaffray Delamayn ance promised ye fair in the by-gone time, or no." Those words presented Anne's position before her in a light in which she had not seen it yet. She had truly expressed the loathing that Geoffrey now inspired in her, when she had declared, in her letter to Arnold, that, even if he offered her marriage, in atonement for the past, she would rather be what she was than be his wife. It had never occurred to her, until this moment, that others would misinterpret the sensitive pride which had prompted the abandonment of her claim on the man who had ruined her. It had never been brought home to her until now, that if she left him contemptuously to go his own way, and sell himself to the first woman who had money enough to buy him, her conduct would sanction the false conclusion that she was power-

less to interfere, because she was married already to another man. The color that had risen in her face vanished, and left it deadly pale again. She began to see that the purpose of her journey to the north was not completed yet.

"I will give you your receipt," she said. "Tell me what to write, and it shall be written."

Bishopriggs dictated the receipt. She wrote and signed it. He put it in his pocket-book with the five-pound note, and handed her the letter in exchange.

"Tear it if ye will," he said. "It matters naething to *me*."

For a moment she hesitated. A sudden shuddering shook her from head to foot—the forewarning, it might be, of the influence which that letter, saved from destruction by a hair's-breadth, was destined to exercise on her life to come. She recovered herself, and folded her cloak closer to her, as if she had felt a passing chill.

"No," she said; "I will keep the letter."

She folded it and put it in the pocket of her dress. Then turned to go—and stopped at the door.

"One thing more," she added. "Do you know Mrs. Glenarm's present address?"

"Ye're no' reely going to Mistress Glenarm?"

"That is no concern of yours. You can answer my question or not, as you please."

"Eh, my leddy! yer temper's no' what it used to be in the auld times at the hottle. Aweel! aweel! ye ha' gi'en me yer money, and I'll een gi' ye back gude measure for it, on my side. Mistress Glenarm's awa' in private—incog, as they say—to Jaffray Delamayn's brither at Swanhaven Lodge. Ye may rely on the information, and it's no' that easy to come at either. They've keepit it a secret as they think frae a' the warld. Hech! hech! Tammy Pennyquick's youngest but twa is page-boy at the hoose where the leddy's been veesitin', on the outskirts o' Pairth. Keep a secret if ye can frae the pawky ears o' yer domestics in the servants' hall!—Eh! she's aff, without a word at parting!" he exclaimed, as Anne left him without ceremony in the middle of his dissertation on secrets and servants' halls. "I trow I ha' gaen out for wool, and come back shorn," he added, reflecting grimly on the disastrous overthrow of the promising speculation on which he had embarked. "My certie! there was naething left for't, when madam's fingers had grippit me, but to slip through them as cannily as I could. What's Jaffray's marrying, or no' marrying, to do wi' *her*?" he wondered, reverting to the question which Anne had put to him at parting. "And whar's the sense o' her errand, if she's reely bent on finding her way to Mistress Glenarm?"

Whatever the sense of her errand might be, Anne's next proceeding proved that she was really bent on it. After resting two days, she left Perth by the first train in the morning, for Swanhaven Lodge.

---

NINTH SCENE.—THE MUSIC-ROOM.

## CHAPTER THE FORTIETH.

### JULIUS MAKES MISCHIEF.

JULIUS DELAMAYN was alone; idly sauntering to and fro, with his violin in his hand, on the terrace at Swanhaven Lodge.

The first mellow light of evening was in the sky. It was the close of the day on which Anne Silvester had left Perth.

Some hours earlier, Julius had sacrificed himself to the duties of his political position—as made for him by his father. He had submitted to the dire necessity of delivering an oration to the electors, at a public meeting in the neighboring town of Kirkandrew. A detestable atmosphere to breathe; a disorderly audience to address; insolent opposition to conciliate; imbecile inquiries to answer; brutish interruptions to endure; greedy petitioners to pacify; and dirty hands to shake: these are the stages by which the aspiring English gentleman is compelled to travel on the journey which leads him from the modest obscurity of private life to the glorious publicity of the House of Commons. Julius paid the preliminary penalties of a political first appearance, as exacted by free institutions, with the necessary patience; and returned to the welcome shelter of home, more indifferent, if possible, to the attractions of Parliamentary distinction than when he set out. The discord of the roaring "people" (still echoing in his ears) had sharpened his customary sensibility to the poetry of sound, as composed by Mozart, and as interpreted by piano and violin. Possessing himself of his beloved instrument, he had gone out on the terrace to cool himself in the evening air, pending the arrival of the servant whom he had summoned by the music-room bell. The man appeared at the glass door which led into the room; and reported, in answer to his master's inquiry, that Mrs. Julius Delamayn was out paying visits, and was not expected to return for another hour at least.

Julius groaned in spirit. The finest music which Mozart has written for the violin associates that instrument with the piano. Without the wife to help him, the husband was mute. After an instant's consideration, Julius hit on an idea which promised, in some degree, to remedy the disaster of Mrs. Delamayn's absence from home.

"Has Mrs. Glenarm gone out, too?" he asked.

"No, Sir."

"My compliments. If Mrs. Glenarm has nothing else to do, will she be so kind as to come to me in the music-room?"

The servant went away with his message. Julius seated himself on one of the terrace-benches, and began to tune his violin.

Mrs. Glenarm—rightly reported by Bishopriggs as having privately taken refuge from her anonymous correspondent at Swanhaven Lodge—was, musically speaking, far from being an efficient substitute for Mrs. Delamayn. Julius possessed, in his wife, one of the few players on the piano-forte under whose subtle touch that shallow and soulless instrument becomes inspired with expression not its own, and produces music instead of noise. The fine organization which can work this miracle had not been bestowed on Mrs. Glenarm. She had been carefully taught; and she was to be trusted to play correctly—and that was all. Julius, hungry for music, and resigned to circumstances, asked for no more.

The servant returned with his answer. Mrs. Glenarm would join Mr. Delamayn in the music-room in ten minutes' time.

Julius rose, relieved, and resumed his sauntering walk; now playing little snatches of music; now stopping to look at the flowers on the terrace, with an eye that enjoyed their beauty, and a hand that fondled them with caressing touch. If Imperial Parliament had seen him at that moment, Imperial Parliament must have given notice of a question to his illustrious father: Is it possible, my lord, that *you* can have begotten such a Member as this?

After stopping for a moment to tighten one of the strings of his violin, Julius, raising his head from the instrument, was surprised to see a lady approaching him on the terrace. Advancing to meet her, and perceiving that she was a total stranger to him, he assumed that she was, in all probability, a visitor to his wife.

"Have I the honor of speaking to a friend of Mrs. Delamayn's?" he asked. "My wife is not at home, I am sorry to say."

"I am a stranger to Mrs. Delamayn," the lady answered. "The servant informed me that she had gone out; and that I should find Mr. Delamayn here."

Julius bowed—and waited to hear more.

"I must beg you to forgive my intrusion," the stranger went on. "My object is to ask permission to see a lady who is, I have been informed, a guest in your house."

The extraordinary formality of the request rather puzzled Julius.

"Do you mean Mrs. Glenarm?" he asked.

"Yes."

"Pray don't think any permission necessary. A friend of Mrs. Glenarm's may take her welcome for granted in this house."

"I am not a friend of Mrs. Glenarm. I am a total stranger to her."

This made the ceremonious request preferred by the lady a little more intelligible—but it left the lady's object in wishing to speak to Mrs. Glenarm still in the dark. Julius politely waited, until it pleased her to proceed further, and explain herself. The explanation did not appear to be an easy one to give. Her eyes dropped to the ground. She hesitated painfully.

"My name—if I mention it," she resumed, without looking up, "may possibly inform you—" She paused. Her color came and went. She hesitated again; struggled with her agitation, and controlled it. "I am Anne Silvester," she said, suddenly raising her pale face, and suddenly steadying her trembling voice.

Julius started, and looked at her in silent surprise.

The name was doubly known to him. Not long since, he had heard it from his father's lips, at his father's bedside. Lord Holchester had charged him, had earnestly charged him, to bear that name in mind, and to help the woman who bore it, if the woman ever applied to him in time to come. Again, he had heard the name, more lately, associated scandalously with the name of his brother. On the receipt of the first of the anonymous letters sent to her, Mrs. Glenarm had not only summoned Geoffrey himself to refute the aspersion cast upon him, but had forwarded a private copy of the letter to his relatives at Swanhaven. Geoffrey's defense had not entirely satisfied Julius that his brother was free from blame. As he now looked at Anne Silvester, the doubt returned upon him strengthened—almost confirmed. Was this woman—so modest, so gentle, so simply and unaffectedly refined—the shameless adventuress denounced by Geoffrey, as claiming him on the strength of a foolish flirtation; knowing herself, at the time, to be privately married to another man? Was this woman—with the voice of a lady, the look of a lady, the manner of a lady—in league (as Geoffrey had declared) with the illiterate vagabond who was attempting to extort money anonymously from Mrs. Glenarm? Impossible! Making every allowance for the proverbial deceitfulness of appearances, impossible!

"Your name has been mentioned to me," said Julius, answering her after a momentary pause. His instincts, as a gentleman, made him shrink from referring to the association of her name with the name of his brother. "My father mentioned you," he added, considerately explaining his knowledge of her in *that* way, "when I last saw him in London."

"Your father!" She came a step nearer, with a look of distrust as well as a look of astonishment in her face. "Your father is Lord Holchester—is he not?"

"Yes."

"What made him speak of *me*?"

"He was ill at the time," Julius answered. "And he had been thinking of events in his past life with which I am entirely unacquainted. He said he had known your father and mother. He desired me, if you were *ever* in want of any assistance, to place my services at your disposal. When he expressed that wish, he spoke very earnestly—he gave me the impression that there was a feeling of regret associated with the recollections on which he had been dwelling."

Slowly, and in silence, Anne drew back to the low wall of the terrace close by. She rested one hand on it to support herself. Julius had said words of terrible import without a suspicion of what he had done. Never until now had Anne Silvester known that the man who had betrayed her was the son of that other man whose discovery of the flaw in the marriage had ended in the betrayal of her mother before her. She felt the shock of the revelation with a chill of superstitious dread. Was the chain of a fatality wound invisibly round her? Turn which way she might, was she still going darkly on, in the track of her dead mother, to an appointed and hereditary doom? Present things passed from her view as the awful doubt cast its shadow over her mind. She lived again for a moment in the time when she was a child. She saw the face of her mother once more, with the wan despair on it of the bygone days when the title of wife was denied her, and the social prospect was closed forever.

Julius approached, and roused her.

"Can I get you any thing?" he asked. "You are looking very ill. I hope I have said nothing to distress you?"

The question failed to attract her attention. She put a question herself instead of answering it.

"Did you say you were quite ignorant of what your father was thinking of when he spoke to you about me?"

"Quite ignorant."

"Is your brother likely to know more about it than you do?"

"Certainly not."

She paused, absorbed once more in her own thoughts. Startled, on the memorable day when they had first met, by Geoffrey's family name, she had put the question to him whether there had not been some acquaintance between their parents in the past time. Deceiving her in all else, he had not deceived in this. He had spoken in good faith, when he had declared that he had never heard her father or her mother mentioned at home.

The curiosity of Julius was aroused. He attempted to lead her on into saying more.

"You appear to know what my father was thinking of when he spoke to me," he resumed. "May I ask—"

She interrupted him with a gesture of entreaty.

"Pray don't ask! It's past and over—it can have no interest for you—it has nothing to do with my errand here. I must return," she went on, hurriedly, "to my object in trespassing on your kindness. Have you heard me mentioned, Mr. Delamayn, by another member of your family besides your father?"

Julius had not anticipated that she would approach, of her own accord, the painful subject on which he had himself forborne to touch. He was a little disappointed. He had expected more delicacy of feeling from her than she had shown.

"Is it necessary," he asked, coldly, "to enter on that?"

The blood rose again in Anne's cheeks.

"If it had not been necessary," she answered, "do you think I could have forced myself to mention it to *you*? Let me remind you that I am here on sufferance. If I don't speak plainly (no matter at what sacrifice to my own feelings), I make my situation more embarrassing than it is already. I have something to tell Mrs. Glenarm relating to the anonymous letters which she has lately received. And I have a word to say to her, next, about her contemplated marriage. Before you allow me to do this, you ought to know who I am. (I have owned it.) You ought to have heard the worst that can be said of my conduct. (Your face tells me you have heard the worst.) After the forbearance you have shown to me, as a perfect stranger, I will not commit the meanness of taking you by surprise. Perhaps, Mr. Delamayn, you understand, *now*, why I felt myself obliged to refer to your brother. Will you trust me with permission to speak to Mrs. Glenarm?"

It was simply and modestly said—with an unaffected and touching resignation of look and manner. Julius gave her back the respect and the sympathy which, for a moment, he had unjustly withheld from her.

"You have placed a confidence in me," he said, "which most persons in your situation would have withheld. I feel bound, in return, to place confidence in you. I will take it for granted that your motive in this matter is one which it is my duty to respect. It will be for Mrs. Glenarm to say whether she wishes the interview to take place or not. All that I can do is to leave you free to propose it to her. You *are* free."

As he spoke the sound of the piano reached them from the music-room. Julius pointed to the glass door which opened on to the terrace.

"You have only to go in by that door," he said, "and you will find Mrs. Glenarm alone."

Anne bowed, and left him. Arrived at the

short flight of steps which led up to the door, she paused to collect her thoughts before she went in.

A sudden reluctance to go on and enter the room took possession of her, as she waited with her foot on the lower step. The report of Mrs. Glenarm's contemplated marriage had produced no such effect on her as Sir Patrick had supposed: it had found no love for Geoffrey left to wound, no latent jealousy only waiting to be inflamed. Her object in taking the journey to Perth was completed when her correspondence with Geoffrey was in her own hands again. The change of purpose which had brought her to Swanhaven was due entirely to the new view of her position toward Mrs. Glenarm which the coarse common-sense of Bishopriggs had first suggested to her. If she failed to protest against Mrs. Glenarm's marriage, in the interests of the reparation which Geoffrey owed to her, her conduct would only confirm Geoffrey's audacious assertion that she was a married woman already. For her own sake she might still have hesitated to move in the matter. But Blanche's interests were concerned as well as her own; and, for Blanche's sake, she had resolved on making the journey to Swanhaven Lodge.

At the same time, feeling toward Geoffrey as she felt now—conscious as she was of not really desiring the reparation on which she was about to insist—it was essential to the preservation of her own self-respect that she should have some purpose in view which could justify her to her own conscience in assuming the character of Mrs. Glenarm's rival.

She had only to call to mind the critical situation of Blanche—and to see her purpose before her plainly. Assuming that she could open the coming interview by peaceably proving that her claim on Geoffrey was beyond dispute, she might then, without fear of misconception, take the tone of a friend instead of an enemy, and might, with the best grace, assure Mrs. Glenarm that she had no rivalry to dread, on the one easy condition that she engaged to make Geoffrey repair the evil that he had done. "Marry him without a word against it to dread from *me*—so long as he unsays the words and undoes the deeds which have thrown a doubt on the marriage of Arnold and Blanche." If she could but bring the interview to this end—there was the way found of extricating Arnold, by her own exertions, from the false position in which she had innocently placed him toward his wife! Such was the object before her, as she now stood on the brink of her interview with Mrs. Glenarm.

Up to this moment, she had firmly believed in her capacity to realize her own visionary project. It was only when she had her foot on the step that a doubt of the success of the coming experiment crossed her mind. For the first time, she saw the weak point in her own reasoning. For the first time, she felt how much she had blindly taken for granted, in assuming that Mrs. Glenarm would have sufficient sense of justice and sufficient command of temper to hear her patiently. All her hopes of success rested on her own favorable estimate of a woman who was a total stranger to her! What if the first words exchanged between them proved the estimate to be wrong?

It was too late to pause and reconsider the position. Julius Delamayn had noticed her hesitation, and was advancing toward her from the end of the terrace. There was no help for it but to master her own irresolution, and to run the risk boldly. "Come what may, I have gone too far to stop *here*." With that desperate resolution to animate her, she opened the glass door at the top of the steps, and went into the room.

Mrs. Glenarm rose from the piano. The two women—one so richly, the other so plainly dressed; one with her beauty in its full bloom, the other worn and blighted; one with society at her feet, the other an outcast living under the bleak shadow of reproach—the two women stood face to face, and exchanged the cold courtesies of salute between strangers, in silence.

The first to meet the trivial necessities of the situation was Mrs. Glenarm. She good-humoredly put an end to the embarrassment—which the shy visitor appeared to feel acutely—by speaking first.

"I am afraid the servants have not told you?" she said. "Mrs. Delamayn has gone out."

"I beg your pardon—I have not called to see Mrs. Delamayn."

Mrs. Glenarm looked a little surprised. She went on, however, as amiably as before.

"Mr. Delamayn, perhaps?" she suggested. "I expect him here every moment."

Anne explained again. "I have just parted from Mr. Delamayn." Mrs. Glenarm opened her eyes in astonishment. Anne proceeded. "I have come here, if you will excuse the intrusion—"

She hesitated—at a loss how to end the sentence. Mrs. Glenarm, beginning by this time to feel a strong curiosity as to what might be coming next, advanced to the rescue once more.

"Pray don't apologize," she said. "I think I understand that you are so good as to have come to see *me*. You look tired. Won't you take a chair?"

Anne could stand no longer. She took the offered chair. Mrs. Glenarm resumed her place on the music-stool, and ran her fingers idly over the keys of the piano. "Where did you see Mr. Delamayn?" she went on. "The most irresponsible of men, except when he has got his fiddle in his hand! Is he coming in soon? Are we going to have any music? Have you come to play with us? Mr. Delamayn is a perfect fanatic in music, isn't he? Why isn't he here to introduce us? I suppose you like the classical style, too? Did you know that I was in the music-room? Might I ask your name?"

Frivolous as they were, Mrs. Glenarm's questions were not without their use. They gave Anne time to summon her resolution, and to feel the necessity of explaining herself.

"I am speaking, I believe, to Mrs. Glenarm?" she began.

The good-humored widow smiled and bowed graciously.

"I have come here, Mrs. Glenarm—by Mr. Delamayn's permission—to ask leave to speak to you on a matter in which you are interested."

Mrs. Glenarm's many-ringed fingers paused over the keys of the piano. Mrs. Glenarm's plump face turned on the stranger with a dawning expression of surprise.

"Indeed? I am interested in so many matters. May I ask what *this* matter is?"

The flippant tone of the speaker jarred on Anne. If Mrs. Glenarm's nature was as shallow as it appeared to be on the surface, there was little hope of any sympathy establishing itself between them.

"I wished to speak to you," she answered, "about something that happened while you were paying a visit in the neighborhood of Perth."

The dawning surprise in Mrs. Glenarm's face became intensified into an expression of distrust. Her hearty manner vanished under a veil of conventional civility, drawn over it suddenly. She looked at Anne. "Never at the best of times a beauty," she thought. "Wretchedly out of health now. Dressed like a servant, and looking like a lady. What *does* it mean?"

The last doubt was not to be borne in silence by a person of Mrs. Glenarm's temperament. She addressed herself to the solution of it with the most unblushing directness—dextrously excused by the most winning frankness of manner.

"Pardon me," she said. "My memory for faces is a bad one; and I don't think you heard me just now, when I asked for your name. Have we ever met before?"

"Never."

"And yet—if I understand what you are referring to—you wish to speak to me about something which is only interesting to myself and my most intimate friends."

"You understand me quite correctly," said Anne. "I wish to speak to you about some anonymous letters—"

"For the third time, will you permit me to ask for your name?"

"You shall hear it directly—if you will first allow me to finish what I wanted to say. I wish —if I can—to persuade you that I come here as a friend, before I mention my name. You will, I am sure, not be very sorry to hear that you need dread no further annoyance—"

"Pardon me once more," said Mrs. Glenarm, interposing for the second time. "I am at a loss to know to what I am to attribute this kind interest in my affairs on the part of a total stranger."

This time, her tone was more than politely cold—it was politely impertinent. Mrs. Glenarm had lived all her life in good society, and was a perfect mistress of the subtleties of refined insolence in her intercourse with those who incurred her displeasure.

Anne's sensitive nature felt the wound—but Anne's patient courage submitted. She put away from her the insolence which had tried to sting, and went on, gently and firmly, as if nothing had happened.

"The person who wrote to you anonymously," she said, "alluded to a correspondence. He is no longer in possession of it. The correspondence has passed into hands which may be trusted to respect it. It will be put to no base use in the future—I answer for that."

"You answer for that?" repeated Mrs. Glenarm. She suddenly leaned forward over the piano, and fixed her eyes in unconcealed scrutiny on Anne's face. The violent temper, so often found in combination with the weak nature, began to show itself in her rising color, and her lowering brow. "How do *you* know what the person wrote?" she asked. "How do *you* know that the correspondence has passed into other hands? Who are you?" Before Anne could answer her, she sprang to her feet, electrified by a new idea. "The man who wrote to me spoke of something else besides a correspondence. He spoke of a woman. I have found you out!" she exclaimed, with a burst of jealous fury. "*You* are the woman!"

Anne rose on her side, still in firm possession of her self-control.

"Mrs. Glenarm," she said, calmly, "I warn —no, I entreat you—not to take that tone with me. Compose yourself; and I promise to satisfy you that you are more interested than you are willing to believe in what I have still to say. Pray bear with me for a little longer. I admit that you have guessed right. I own that I am the miserable woman who has been ruined and deserted by Geoffrey Delamayn."

"It's false!" cried Mrs. Glenarm. "You wretch! Do you come to *me* with your trumped-up story? What does Julius Delamayn mean by exposing me to this?" Her indignation at finding herself in the same room with Anne broke its way through, not the restraints only, but the common decencies of politeness. "I'll ring for the servants!" she said. "I'll have you turned out of the house."

She tried to cross the fire-place to ring the bell. Anne, who was standing nearest to it, stepped forward at the same moment. Without saying a word, she motioned with her hand to the other woman to stand back. There was a pause. The two waited, with their eyes steadily fixed on one another—each with her resolution laid bare to the other's view. In a moment more, the finer nature prevailed. Mrs. Glenarm drew back a step in silence.

"Listen to me," said Anne.

"Listen to you?" repeated Mrs. Glenarm. "You have no right to be in this house. You have no right to force yourself in here. Leave the room!"

Anne's patience—so firmly and admirably preserved thus far—began to fail her at last.

"Take care, Mrs. Glenarm!" she said, still struggling with herself. "I am not naturally a patient woman. Trouble has done much to tame my temper—but endurance has its limits. You have reached the limits of mine. I have a claim to be heard—and after what you have said to me, I *will* be heard!"

"You have no claim! You shameless woman, you are married already. I know the man's name. Arnold Brinkworth."

"Did Geoffrey Delamayn tell you that?"

"I decline to answer a woman who speaks of Mr. Geoffrey Delamayn in that familiar way."

Anne advanced a step nearer.

"Did Geoffrey Delamayn tell you that?" she repeated.

There was a light in her eyes, there was a ring in her voice, which showed that she was roused at last. Mrs. Glenarm answered her, this time.

"He did tell me."

"He lied!"

"He did *not!* He knew. I believe *him.* I don't believe *you.*"

"If he told you that I was any thing but a single woman—if he told you that Arnold Brink-

"FOR AN INSTANT THEY FACED EACH OTHER."

worth was married to any body but Miss Lundie of Windygates—I say again he lied!"

"I say again—I believe *him*, and not *you*."

"You believe I am Arnold Brinkworth's wife?"

"I am certain of it."

"You tell me that to my face?"

"I tell you to your face—you *may* have been Geoffrey Delamayn's mistress; you *are* Arnold Brinkworth's wife."

At those words the long-restrained anger leaped up in Anne—all the more hotly for having been hitherto so steadily controlled. In one breathless moment the whirlwind of her indignation swept away, not only all remembrance of the purpose which had brought her to Swanhaven, but all sense even of the unpardonable wrong which she had suffered at Geoffrey's hands. If he had been there, at that moment, and had offered to redeem his pledge, she would have consented to marry him, while Mrs. Glenarm's eye was on her—no matter whether she destroyed herself in her first cool moment afterward or not. The small sting had planted itself at last in the great nature. The noblest woman is only a woman, after all!

"I forbid your marriage to Geoffrey Delamayn! I insist on his performing the promise he gave me, to make me his wife! I have got it here in his own words, in his own writing. On his soul, he swears it to me—he will redeem his pledge. His mistress, did you say? His wife, Mrs. Glenarm, before the week is out!"

In those wild words she cast back the taunt —with the letter held in triumph in her hand.

Daunted for the moment by the doubt now literally forced on her, that Anne might really have the claim on Geoffrey which she advanced,

Mrs. Glenarm answered nevertheless with the obstinacy of a woman brought to bay—with a resolution not to be convinced by conviction itself.

"I won't give him up!" she cried. "Your letter is a forgery. You have no proof. I won't, I won't, I won't give him up!" she repeated, with the impotent iteration of an angry child.

Anne pointed disdainfully to the letter that she held. "Here is his pledged and written word," she said. "While I live, you will never be his wife."

"I shall be his wife the day after the race. I am going to him in London—to warn him against You!"

"You will find me in London, before you— with this in my hand. Do you know his writing?"

She held up the letter, open. Mrs. Glenarm's hand flew out with the stealthy rapidity of a cat's paw, to seize and destroy it. Quick as she was, her rival was quicker still. For an instant they faced each other breathless—one with the letter held behind her; one with her hand still stretched out.

At the same moment—before a word more had passed between them—the glass door opened; and Julius Delamayn appeared in the room.

He addressed himself to Anne.

"We decided, on the terrace," he said, quietly, "that you should speak to Mrs. Glenarm, if Mrs. Glenarm wished it. Do you think it desirable that the interview should be continued any longer?"

Anne's head drooped on her breast. The fiery anger in her was quenched in an instant.

"I have been cruelly provoked, Mr. Delamayn," she answered. "But I have no right to plead that." She looked up at him for a moment. The hot tears of shame gathered in her eyes, and fell slowly over her cheeks. She bent her head again, and hid them from him. "The only atonement I can make," she said, "is to ask your pardon, and to leave the house."

In silence, she turned away to the door. In silence, Julius Delamayn paid her the trifling courtesy of opening it for her. She went out.

Mrs. Glenarm's indignation—suspended for the moment—transferred itself to Julius.

"If I have been entrapped into seeing that woman, with your approval," she said, haughtily, "I owe it to myself, Mr. Delamayn, to follow her example, and to leave your house."

"I authorized her to ask you for an interview, Mrs. Glenarm. If she has presumed on the permission that I gave her, I sincerely regret it, and I beg you to accept my apologies. At the same time, I may venture to add, in defense of my conduct, that I thought her—and think her still—a woman to be pitied more than to be blamed."

"To be pitied—did you say?" asked Mrs. Glenarm, doubtful whether her ears had not deceived her.

"To be pitied," repeated Julius.

"You may find it convenient, Mr. Delamayn, to forget what your brother has told us about that person. I happen to remember it."

"So do I, Mrs. Glenarm. But, with my experience of Geoffrey—" He hesitated, and ran his fingers nervously over the strings of his violin.

"You don't believe him?" said Mrs. Glenarm.

Julius declined to admit that he doubted his brother's word, to the lady who was about to become his brother's wife.

"I don't quite go that length," he said. "I find it difficult to reconcile what Geoffrey has told us, with Miss Silvester's manner and appearance—"

"Her appearance!" cried Mrs. Glenarm, in a transport of astonishment and disgust. "Her appearance! Oh, the men! I beg your pardon—I ought to have remembered that there is no accounting for tastes. Go on—pray go on!"

"Shall we compose ourselves with a little music?" suggested Julius.

"I particularly request you will go on," answered Mrs. Glenarm, emphatically. "You find it 'impossible to reconcile'—"

"I said 'difficult.'"

"Oh, very well. Difficult to reconcile what Geoffrey told us, with Miss Silvester's manner and appearance. What next? You had something else to say, when I was so rude as to interrupt you. What was it?"

"Only this," said Julius. "I don't find it easy to understand Sir Patrick Lundie's conduct in permitting Mr. Brinkworth to commit bigamy with his niece."

"Wait a minute! The marriage of that horrible woman to Mr. Brinkworth was a private marriage. Of course, Sir Patrick knew nothing about it!"

Julius owned that this might be possible, and made a second attempt to lead the angry lady back to the piano. Useless, once more! Though she shrank from confessing it to herself, Mrs. Glenarm's belief in the genuineness of her lover's defense had been shaken. The tone taken by Julius—moderate as it was—revived the first startling suspicion of the credibility of Geoffrey's statement which Anne's language and conduct had forced on Mrs. Glenarm. She dropped into the nearest chair, and put her handkerchief to her eyes. "You always hated poor Geoffrey," she said, with a burst of tears. "And now you're defaming him to me!"

Julius managed her admirably. On the point of answering her seriously, he checked himself. "I always hated poor Geoffrey," he repeated, with a smile. "You ought to be the last person to say that, Mrs. Glenarm! I brought him all the way from London expressly to introduce him to you."

"Then I wish you had left him in London!" retorted Mrs. Glenarm, shifting suddenly from tears to temper. "I was a happy woman before I met your brother. I can't give him up!" she burst out, shifting back again from temper to tears. "I don't care if he has deceived me. I won't let another woman have him! I will be his wife!" She threw herself theatrically on her knees before Julius. "Oh, do help me to find out the truth!" she said. "Oh, Julius, pity me! I am so fond of him!"

There was genuine distress in her face, there was true feeling in her voice. Who would have believed that there were reserves of merciless insolence and heartless cruelty in this woman—and that they had been lavishly poured out on a fallen sister not five minutes since?

"I will do all I can," said Julius, raising her. "Let us talk of it when you are more composed. Try a little music," he repeated, "just to quiet your nerves."

"Would you like me to play?" asked Mrs. Glenarm, becoming a model of feminine docility at a moment's notice.

Julius opened the Sonatas of Mozart, and shouldered his violin.

"Let's try the Fifteenth," he said, placing Mrs. Glenarm at the piano. "We will begin with the Adagio. If ever there was divine music written by mortal man, there it is!"

They began. At the third bar Mrs. Glenarm dropped a note—and the bow of Julius paused shuddering on the strings.

"I can't play!" she said. "I am so agitated; I am so anxious. How am I to find out whether that wretch is really married or not? Who can I ask? I can't go to Geoffrey in London—the trainers won't let me see him. I can't appeal to Mr. Brinkworth himself—I am not even acquainted with him. Who else is there? Do think, and tell me!"

There was but one chance of making her return to the Adagio—the chance of hitting on a suggestion which would satisfy and quiet her. Julius laid his violin on the piano, and considered the question before him carefully.

"There are the witnesses," he said. "If Geoffrey's story is to be depended on, the landlady and the waiter at the inn can speak to the facts."

"Low people!" objected Mrs. Glenarm. "People I don't know. People who might take advantage of my situation, and be insolent to me."

Julius considered once more; and made another suggestion. With the fatal ingenuity of innocence, he hit on the idea of referring Mrs. Glenarm to no less a person than Lady Lundie herself!

"There is our good friend at Windygates," he said. "Some whisper of the matter may have reached Lady Lundie's ears. It may be a little awkward to call on her (if she *has* heard any thing) at the time of a serious family disaster. You are the best judge of that, however. All I can do is to throw out the notion. Windygates isn't very far off—and something might come of it. What do you think?"

Something might come of it! Let it be remembered that Lady Lundie had been left entirely in the dark—that she had written to Sir Patrick in a tone which plainly showed that her self-esteem was wounded and her suspicion roused—and that her first intimation of the serious dilemma in which Arnold Brinkworth stood was now likely, thanks to Julius Delamayn, to reach her from the lips of a mere acquaintance. Let this be remembered; and then let the estimate be formed of what might come of it—not at Windygates only, but also at Ham Farm!

"What do you think?" asked Julius.

Mrs. Glenarm was enchanted. "The very person to go to!" she said. "If I am not let in I can easily write—and explain my object as an apology. Lady Lundie is so right-minded, so sympathetic. If she sees no one else—I have only to confide my anxieties to her, and I am sure she will see me. You will lend me a carriage, won't you? I'll go to Windygates to-morrow."

Julius took his violin off the piano.

"Don't think me very troublesome," he said, coaxingly. "Between this and to-morrow we have nothing to do. And it is *such* music, if you once get into the swing of it! Would you mind trying again?"

Mrs. Glenarm was willing to do any thing to prove her gratitude, after the invaluable hint which she had just received. At the second trial the fair pianist's eye and hand were in perfect harmony. The lovely melody which the Adagio of Mozart's Fifteenth Sonata has given to violin and piano flowed smoothly at last—and Julius Delamayn soared to the seventh heaven of musical delight.

The next day Mrs. Glenarm and Mrs. Delamayn went together to Windygates House.

----

TENTH SCENE.—THE BEDROOM.

## CHAPTER THE FORTY-FIRST.

### LADY LUNDIE DOES HER DUTY.

THE scene opens on a bedroom—and discloses, in broad daylight, a lady in bed.

Persons with an irritable sense of propriety, whose self-appointed duty it is to be always crying out, are warned to pause before they cry out on this occasion. The lady now presented to view being no less a person than Lady Lundie herself, it follows, as a matter of course, that the utmost demands of propriety are, by the mere assertion of that fact, abundantly and indisputably satisfied. To say that any thing short of direct moral advantage could, by any possibility, accrue to any living creature by the presentation of her ladyship in a horizontal, instead of a perpendicular position, is to assert that Virtue is a question of posture, and that Respectability

ceases to assert itself when it ceases to appear in morning or evening dress. Will any body be bold enough to say that? Let nobody cry out, then, on the present occasion.

Lady Lundie was in bed.

Her ladyship had received Blanche's written announcement of the sudden stoppage of the bridal tour; and had penned the answer to Sir Patrick—the receipt of which at Ham Farm has been already described. This done, Lady Lundie felt it due to herself to take a becoming position in her own house, pending the possible arrival of Sir Patrick's reply. What does a right-minded woman do, when she has reason to believe that she is cruelly distrusted by the members of her own family? A right-minded woman feels it so acutely that she falls ill. Lady Lundie fell ill accordingly.

The case being a serious one, a medical practitioner of the highest grade in the profession was required to treat it. A physician from the neighboring town of Kirkandrew was called in.

The physician came in a carriage and pair, with the necessary bald head, and the indispensable white cravat. He felt her ladyship's pulse, and put a few gentle questions. He turned his back solemnly, as only a great doctor can, on his own positive internal conviction that his patient had nothing whatever the matter with her. He said, with every appearance of believing in himself, "Nerves, Lady Lundie. Repose in bed is essentially necessary. I will write a prescription." He prescribed, with perfect gravity: Aromatic Spirits of Ammonia—15 drops. Spirits of Red Lavender—10 drops. Syrup of Orange Peel—2 drams. Camphor Julep—1 ounce. When he had written, Misce fiat Haustus (instead of Mix a Draught)—when he had added, Ter die Sumendus (instead of To be taken Three times a day)—and when he had certified to his own Latin, by putting his initials at the end, he had only to make his bow; to slip two guineas into his pocket; and to go his way, with an approving professional conscience, in the character of a physician who had done his duty.

Lady Lundie was in bed. The visible part of her ladyship was perfectly attired, with a view to the occasion. A fillet of superb white lace encircled her head. She wore an adorable invalid jacket of white cambric, trimmed with lace and pink ribbons. The rest was—bed-clothes. On a table at her side stood the Red Lavender Draught—in color soothing to the eye; in flavor not unpleasant to the taste. A book of devotional character was near it. The domestic ledgers, and the kitchen report for the day, were ranged modestly behind the devout book. (Not even her ladyship's nerves, observe, were permitted to interfere with her ladyship's duty.) A fan, a smelling-bottle, and a handkerchief lay within reach on the counterpane. The spacious room was partially darkened. One of the lower windows was open, affording her ladyship the necessary cubic supply of air. The late Sir Thomas looked at his widow, in effigy, from the wall opposite the end of the bed. Not a chair was out of its place; not a vestige of wearing apparel dared to show itself outside the sacred limits of the wardrobe and the drawers. The sparkling treasures of the toilet-table glittered in the dim distance. The jugs and basins were of a rare

"HER LADYSHIP'S EYES WERE CLOSED."

and creamy white; spotless and beautiful to see. Look where you might, you saw a perfect room. Then look at the bed—and you saw a perfect woman, and completed the picture.

It was the day after Anne's appearance at Swanhaven—toward the end of the afternoon.

Lady Lundie's own maid opened the door noiselessly, and stole on tip-toe to the bedside. Her ladyship's eyes were closed. Her ladyship suddenly opened them.

"Not asleep, Hopkins. Suffering. What is it?"

Hopkins laid two cards on the counterpane. "Mrs. Delamayn, my lady—and Mrs. Glenarm."

"They were told I was ill, of course?"

"Yes, my lady. Mrs. Glenarm sent for me. She went into the library, and wrote this note." Hopkins produced the note, neatly folded in three-cornered form.

"Have they gone?"

"No, my lady. Mrs. Glenarm told me Yes or No would do for answer, if you could only have the goodness to read this."

"Thoughtless of Mrs. Glenarm—at a time when the doctor insists on perfect repose," said Lady Lundie. "It doesn't matter. One sacrifice more or less is of very little consequence."

She fortified herself by an application of the smelling-bottle, and opened the note. It ran thus:

"So grieved, dear Lady Lundie, to hear that you are a prisoner in your room! I had taken the opportunity of calling with Mrs. Delamayn, in the hope that I might be able to ask you a question. Will your inexhaustible kindness forgive me if I ask it in writing? Have you had any unexpected news of Mr. Arnold Brinkworth lately? I mean, have you heard any thing about him, which has taken you very much by surprise? I have a serious reason for asking this. I will tell you what it is, the moment you are able to see me. Until then, one word of answer is all I expect. Send word down—Yes, or No. A thousand apologies—and pray get better soon!"

The singular question contained in this note suggested one of two inferences to Lady Lundie's mind. Either Mrs. Glenarm had heard a report of the unexpected return of the married couple to England—or she was in the far more interesting and important position of possessing a clew to the secret of what was going on under the surface at Ham Farm. The phrase used in the note, "I have a serious reason for asking this," appeared to favor the latter of the two interpretations. Impossible as it seemed to be that Mrs. Glenarm could know something about Arnold of which Lady Lundie was in absolute ignorance, her ladyship's curiosity (already powerfully excited by Blanche's mysterious letter) was only to be quieted by obtaining the necessary explanation forthwith, at a personal interview.

"Hopkins," she said, "I must see Mrs. Glenarm."

Hopkins respectfully held up her hands in horror. Company in the bedroom in the present state of her ladyship's health!

"A matter of duty is involved in this, Hopkins. Give me the glass."

Hopkins produced an elegant little hand-mirror. Lady Lundie carefully surveyed herself in it down to the margin of the bed-clothes. Above criticism in every respect? Yes—even when the critic was a woman.

"Show Mrs. Glenarm up here."

In a minute or two more the iron-master's widow fluttered into the room—a little over-dressed as usual; and a little profuse in expressions of gratitude for her ladyship's kindness, and of anxiety about her ladyship's health. Lady Lundie endured it as long as she could—then stopped it with a gesture of polite remonstrance, and came to the point.

"Now, my dear—about this question in your note? Is it possible you have heard already that Arnold Brinkworth and his wife have come back from Baden?" Mrs. Glenarm opened her eyes in astonishment. Lady Lundie put it more plainly. "They were to have gone on to Switzerland, you know, for their wedding tour, and they suddenly altered their minds, and came back to England on Sunday last."

"Dear Lady Lundie, it's not that! Have you heard nothing about Mr. Brinkworth except what you have just told me?"

"Nothing."

There was a pause. Mrs. Glenarm toyed hesitatingly with her parasol. Lady Lundie leaned forward in the bed, and looked at her attentively.

"What have *you* heard about him?" she asked.

Mrs. Glenarm was embarrassed. "It's so difficult to say," she began.

"I can bear any thing but suspense," said Lady Lundie. "Tell me the worst."

Mrs. Glenarm decided to risk it. "Have you never heard," she asked, "that Mr. Brinkworth might possibly have committed himself with another lady before he married Miss Lundie?"

Her ladyship first closed her eyes in horror, and then searched blindly on the counterpane for the smelling-bottle. Mrs. Glenarm gave it to her, and waited to see how the invalid bore it before she said any more.

"There are things one *must* hear," remarked Lady Lundie. "I see an act of duty involved in this. No words can describe how you astonish me. Who told you?"

"Mr. Geoffrey Delamayn told me."

Her ladyship applied for the second time to the smelling-bottle. "Arnold Brinkworth's most intimate friend!" she exclaimed. "He ought to know if any body does. This is dreadful. Why should Mr. Geoffrey Delamayn tell *you?*"

"I am going to marry him," answered Mrs. Glenarm. "That is my excuse, dear Lady Lundie, for troubling you in this matter."

Lady Lundie partially opened her eyes in a state of faint bewilderment. "I don't understand," she said. "For Heaven's sake explain yourself!"

"Haven't you heard about the anonymous letters?" asked Mrs. Glenarm.

Yes. Lady Lundie had heard about the letters. But only what the public in general had heard. The name of the lady in the background not mentioned; and Mr. Geoffrey Delamayn assumed to be as innocent as the babe unborn. Any mistake in that assumption? "Give me your hand, my poor dear, and confide it all to *me!*"

"He is not quite innocent," said Mrs. Glenarm. "He owned to a foolish flirtation—all *her* doing, no doubt. Of course, I insisted on a distinct explanation. Had she really any claim on

him? Not the shadow of a claim. I felt that I only had his word for that—and I told him so. He said he could prove it—he said he knew her to be privately married already. Her husband had disowned and deserted her; she was at the end of her resources; she was desperate enough to attempt any thing. I thought it all very suspicious—until Geoffrey mentioned the man's name. *That* certainly proved that he had cast off his wife; for I myself knew that he had lately married another person."

Lady Lundie suddenly started up from her pillow—honestly agitated; genuinely alarmed by this time.

"Mr. Delamayn told you the man's name?" she said, breathlessly.

"Yes."

"Do I know it?"

"Don't ask me!"

Lady Lundie fell back on the pillow.

Mrs. Glenarm rose to ring for help. Before she could touch the bell, her ladyship had rallied again.

"Stop!" she cried. "I can confirm it! It's true, Mrs. Glenarm! it's true! Open the silver box on the toilet-table—you will find the key in it. Bring me the top letter. Here! Look at it. I got this from Blanche. Why have they suddenly given up their bridal tour? Why have they gone back to Sir Patrick at Ham Farm? Why have they put me off with an infamous subterfuge to account for it? I felt sure something dreadful had happened. Now I know what it is!" She sank back again, with closed eyes, and repeated the words, in a fierce whisper, to herself. "Now I know what it is!"

Mrs. Glenarm read the letter. The reason given for the suspiciously-sudden return of the bride and bridegroom was palpably a subterfuge—and, more remarkable still, the name of Anne Silvester was connected with it. Mrs. Glenarm became strongly agitated on her side.

"This *is* a confirmation," she said. "Mr. Brinkworth has been found out—the woman *is* married to him—Geoffrey is free. Oh, my dear friend, what a load of anxiety you have taken off my mind! That vile wretch—"

Lady Lundie suddenly opened her eyes.

"Do you mean," she asked, "the woman who is at the bottom of all the mischief?"

"Yes. I saw her yesterday. She forced herself in at Swanhaven. She called him Geoffrey Delamayn. She declared herself a single woman. She claimed him before my face in the most audacious manner. She shook my faith, Lady Lundie—she shook my faith in Geoffrey!"

"Who is she?"

"Who?" echoed Mrs. Glenarm. "Don't you even know that? Why her name is repeated half a dozen times in this letter!"

Lady Lundie uttered a scream that rang through the room. Mrs. Glenarm started to her feet. The maid appeared at the door in terror. Her ladyship motioned to the woman to withdraw again instantly, and then pointed to Mrs. Glenarm's chair.

"Sit down," she said. "Let me have a minute or two of quiet. I want nothing more."

The silence in the room was unbroken until Lady Lundie spoke again. She asked for Blanche's letter. After reading it carefully, she laid it aside, and fell for a while into deep thought.

"I have done Blanche an injustice!" she exclaimed. "My poor Blanche!"

"You think she knows nothing about it?"

"I am certain of it! You forget, Mrs. Glenarm, that this horrible discovery casts a doubt on my step-daughter's marriage. Do you think, if she knew the truth, she would write of a wretch who has mortally injured her as she writes here? They have put her off with the excuse that she innocently sends to me. I see it as plainly as I see you! Mr. Brinkworth and Sir Patrick are in league to keep us both in the dark. Dear child! I owe her an atonement. If nobody else opens her eyes, I will do it. Sir Patrick shall find that Blanche has a friend in Me!"

A smile—the dangerous smile of an inveterately vindictive woman thoroughly roused—showed itself with a furtive suddenness on her face. Mrs. Glenarm was a little startled. Lady Lundie below the surface—as distinguished from Lady Lundie *on* the surface—was not a pleasant object to contemplate.

"Pray try to compose yourself," said Mrs. Glenarm. "Dear Lady Lundie, you frighten me!"

The bland surface of her ladyship appeared smoothly once more; drawn back, as it were, over the hidden inner self, which it had left for the moment exposed to view.

"Forgive me for feeling it!" she said, with the patient sweetness which so eminently distinguished her in times of trial. "It falls a little heavily on a poor sick woman—innocent of all suspicion, and insulted by the most heartless neglect. Don't let me distress you. I shall rally, my dear; I shall rally! In this dreadful calamity—this abyss of crime and misery and deceit—I have no one to depend on but myself. For Blanche's sake, the whole thing must be cleared up—probed, my dear, probed to the depths. Blanche must take a position that is worthy of her. Blanche must insist on her rights, under My protection. Never mind what I suffer, or what I sacrifice. There is a work of justice for poor weak Me to do. It shall be done!" said her ladyship, fanning herself with an aspect of illimitable resolution. "It shall be done!"

"But, Lady Lundie, what can you do? They are all away in the south. And as for that abominable woman—"

Lady Lundie touched Mrs. Glenarm on the shoulder with her fan.

"I have my surprise in store, dear friend, as well as you. That abominable woman was employed as Blanche's governess in this house. Wait! that is not all. She left us suddenly—ran away—on the pretense of being privately married. I know where she went. I can trace what she did. I can find out who was with her. I can follow Mr. Brinkworth's proceedings, behind Mr. Brinkworth's back. I can search out the truth, without depending on people compromised in this black business, whose interest it is to deceive me. And I will do it to-day!" She closed the fan with a sharp snap of triumph, and settled herself on the pillow in placid enjoyment of her dear friend's surprise.

Mrs. Glenarm drew confidentially closer to the bedside. "How can you manage it?" she asked, eagerly. "Don't think me curious. I have my interest, too, in getting at the truth. Don't leave me out of it, pray!"

"Can you come back to-morrow, at this time?"

"Yes! yes!"

"Come, then—and you shall know."

"Can I be of any use?"

"Not at present."

"Can my uncle be of any use?"

"Do you know where to communicate with Captain Newenden?"

"Yes—he is staying with some friends in Sussex."

"We may possibly want his assistance. I can't tell yet. Don't keep Mrs. Delamayn waiting any longer, my dear. I shall expect you to-morrow."

They exchanged an affectionate embrace. Lady Lundie was left alone.

Her ladyship resigned herself to meditation, with frowning brow and close-shut lips. She looked her full age, and a year or two more, as she lay thinking, with her head on her hand, and her elbow on the pillow. After committing herself to the physician (and to the red lavender draught), the commonest regard for consistency made it necessary that she should keep her bed for that day. And yet it was essential that the proposed inquiries should be instantly set on foot. On the one hand, the problem was not an easy one to solve; on the other, her ladyship was not an easy one to beat. How to send for the landlady at Craig Fernie, without exciting any special suspicion or remark—was the question before her. In less than five minutes she had looked back into her memory of current events at Windygates—and had solved it.

Her first proceeding was to ring the bell for her maid.

"I am afraid I frightened you, Hopkins. The state of my nerves. Mrs. Glenarm was a little sudden with some news that surprised me. I am better now—and able to attend to the household matters. There is a mistake in the butcher's account. Send the cook here."

She took up the domestic ledger and the kitchen report; corrected the butcher; cautioned the cook; and disposed of all arrears of domestic business before Hopkins was summoned again. Having, in this way, dextrously prevented the woman from connecting any thing that her mistress said or did, after Mrs. Glenarm's departure, with any thing that might have passed during Mrs. Glenarm's visit, Lady Lundie felt herself at liberty to pave the way for the investigation on which she was determined to enter before she slept that night.

"So much for the indoor arrangements," she said. "You must be my prime minister, Hopkins, while I lie helpless here. Is there any thing wanted by the people out of doors? The coachman? The gardener?"

"I have just seen the gardener, my lady. He came with last week's accounts. I told him he couldn't see your ladyship to-day."

"Quite right. Had he any report to make?"

"No, my lady."

"Surely, there was something I wanted to say to him—or to somebody else? My memorandum-book, Hopkins. In the basket, on that chair. Why wasn't the basket placed by my bedside?"

Hopkins brought the memorandum-book. Lady Lundie consulted it (without the slightest necessity), with the same masterly gravity exhibited by the doctor when he wrote her prescription (without the slightest necessity also).

"Here it is," she said, recovering the lost remembrance. "Not the gardener, but the gardener's wife. A memorandum to speak to her about Mrs. Inchbare. Observe, Hopkins, the association of ideas. Mrs. Inchbare is associated with the poultry; the poultry are associated with the gardener's wife; the gardener's wife is associated with the gardener—and so the gardener gets into my head. Do you see it? I am always trying to improve your mind. You do see it? Very well. Now about Mrs. Inchbare? Has she been here again?"

"No, my lady."

"I am not at all sure, Hopkins, that I was right in declining to consider the message Mrs. Inchbare sent to me about the poultry. Why shouldn't she offer to take any fowls that I can spare off my hands? She is a respectable woman; and it is important to me to live on good terms with all my neighbors, great and small. Has she got a poultry-yard of her own at Craig Fernie?"

"Yes, my lady. And beautifully kept, I am told."

"I really don't see—on reflection, Hopkins—why I should hesitate to deal with Mrs. Inchbare. (I don't think it beneath me to sell the game killed on my estate to the poulterer.) What was it she wanted to buy? Some of my black Spanish fowls?"

"Yes, my lady. Your ladyship's black Spaniards are famous all round the neighborhood. Nobody has got the breed. And Mrs. Inchbare—"

"Wants to share the distinction of having the breed with me," said Lady Lundie. "I won't appear ungracious. I will see her myself, as soon as I am a little better, and tell her that I have changed my mind. Send one of the men to Craig Fernie with a message. I can't keep a trifling matter of this sort in my memory—send him at once, or I may forget it. He is to say I am willing to see Mrs. Inchbare, about the fowls, the first time she finds it convenient to come this way."

"I am afraid, my lady—Mrs. Inchbare's heart is so set on the black Spaniards—she will find it convenient to come this way at once as fast as her feet can carry her."

"In that case, you must take her to the gardener's wife. Say she is to have some eggs—on condition, of course, of paying the price for them. If she does come, mind I hear of it."

Hopkins withdrew. Hopkins's mistress reclined on her comfortable pillows, and fanned herself gently. The vindictive smile reappeared on her face. "I fancy I shall be well enough to see Mrs. Inchbare," she thought to herself. "And it is just possible that the conversation may get beyond the relative merits of her poultry-yard and mine."

A lapse of little more than two hours proved Hopkins's estimate of the latent enthusiasm in Mrs. Inchbare's character to have been correctly formed. The eager landlady appeared at Windygates on the heels of the returning servant. Among the long list of human weaknesses, a passion for poultry seems to have its practical advantages (in the shape of eggs) as compared with the more occult frenzies for collecting snuff-boxes and fiddles, and amassing autographs and old postage-stamps. When the mistress of Craig Fernie was duly announced to the mistress of Windygates, Lady Lundie developed a sense of humor for the first time in her life. Her ladyship was feebly merry (the result, no doubt, of the exhilarating properties of the red lavender draught) on the subject of Mrs. Inchbare and the Spanish fowls.

"Most ridiculous, Hopkins! This poor woman must be suffering from a determination of poultry to the brain. Ill as I am, I should have thought that nothing could amuse me. But, really, this good creature starting up, and rushing here, as you say, as fast as her feet can carry her—it's impossible to resist it! I positively think I must see Mrs. Inchbare. With my active habits, this imprisonment to my room is dreadful. I can neither sleep nor read. Any thing, Hopkins, to divert my mind from myself. It's easy to get rid of her if she is too much for me. Send her up."

Mrs. Inchbare made her appearance, courtesying deferentially; amazed at the condescension which admitted her within the hallowed precincts of Lady Lundie's room.

"Take a chair," said her ladyship, graciously. "I am suffering from illness, as you perceive."

"My certie! sick or well, yer leddyship's a braw sight to see!" returned Mrs. Inchbare, profoundly impressed by the elegant costume which illness assumes when illness appears in the regions of high life.

"I am far from being in a fit state to receive any body," proceeded Lady Lundie. "But I had a motive for wishing to speak to you when you next came to my house. I failed to treat a proposal you made to me, a short time since, in a friendly and neighborly way. I beg you to understand that I regret having forgotten the consideration due from a person in my position to a person in yours. I am obliged to say this under very unusual circumstances," added her ladyship, with a glance round her magnificent bedroom, "through your unexpected promptitude in favoring me with a call. You have lost no time, Mrs. Inchbare, in profiting by the message which I had the pleasure of sending to you."

"Eh, my leddy, I wasna' that sure (yer leddyship having ance changed yer mind) but that ye might e'en change again if I failed to strike, as they say, while the iron's het. I crave yer pardon, I'm sure, if I ha' been ower hasty. The pride o' my hairt's in my powltry—and the 'black Spaniards' (as they ca' them) are a sair temptation to me to break the tenth commandment, sae lang as they're a' in yer leddyship's possession, and nane o' them in mine."

"I am shocked to hear that I have been the innocent cause of your falling into temptation, Mrs. Inchbare! Make your proposal—and I shall be happy to meet it, if I can."

"I must e'en be content wi' what yer leddyship will condescend on. A haitch o' eggs if I can come by naething else."

"There is something else you would prefer to a hatch of eggs?"

"I wad prefer," said Mrs. Inchbare, modestly, "a cock and twa pullets."

"Open the case on the table behind you," said Lady Lundie, "and you will find some writing-paper inside. Give me a sheet of it—and the pencil out of the tray."

Eagerly watched by Mrs. Inchbare, she wrote an order to the poultry-woman, and held it out with a gracious smile.

"Take that to the gardener's wife. If you agree with her about the price, you can have the cock and the two pullets."

Mrs. Inchbare opened her lips—no doubt to express the utmost extremity of human gratitude. Before she had said three words, Lady Lundie's impatience to reach the end which she had kept in view from the time when Mrs. Glenarm had left the house burst the bounds which had successfully restrained it thus far. Stopping the landlady without ceremony, she fairly forced the conversation to the subject of Anne Silvester's proceedings at the Craig Fernie inn.

"How are you getting on at the hotel, Mrs. Inchbare? Plenty of tourists, I suppose, at this time of year?"

"Full, my leddy (praise Providence), frae the basement to the ceiling."

"You had a visitor, I think, some time since of whom I know something? A person—" She paused, and put a strong constraint on herself. There was no alternative but to yield to the hard necessity of making her inquiry intelligible. "A lady," she added, "who came to you about the middle of last month."

"Could yer leddyship condescend on her name?"

Lady Lundie put a still stronger constraint on herself. "Silvester," she said, sharply.

"Presairve us a'!" cried Mrs. Inchbare. "It will never be the same that cam' driftin' in by hersel'—wi' a bit bag in her hand, and a husband left daidling an hour or mair on the road behind her?"

"I have no doubt it is the same."

"Will she be a freend o' yer leddyship's?" asked Mrs. Inchbare, feeling her ground cautiously.

"Certainly not!" said Lady Lundie. "I felt a passing curiosity about her—nothing more."

Mrs. Inchbare looked relieved. "To tell ye truth, my leddy, there was nae love lost between us. She had a maisterfu' temper o' her ain—and I was weel pleased when I'd seen the last of her."

"I can quite understand that, Mrs. Inchbare—I know something of her temper myself. Did I understand you to say that she came to your hotel alone, and that her husband joined her shortly afterward?"

"E'en sae, yer leddyship. I was no' free to gi' her house-room in the hottle till her husband daidled in at her heels and answered for her."

"I fancy I must have seen her husband," said Lady Lundie. "What sort of a man was he?"

Mrs. Inchbare replied in much the same words which she had used in answering the similar question put by Sir Patrick.

"Eh! he was ower young for the like o' her. A pratty man, my leddy—betwixt tall and short; wi' bonny brown eyes and cheeks, and fine coal-blaik hair. A nice douce-spoken lad. I hae naething to say against him—except that he cam' late one day, and took leg-bail betimes the next morning, and left madam behind, a load on my hands."

The answer produced precisely the same effect on Lady Lundie which it had produced on Sir Patrick. She, also, felt that it was too vaguely like too many young men of no uncommon humor and complexion to be relied on. But her ladyship possessed one immense advantage over her brother-in-law in attempting to arrive at the truth. *She* suspected Arnold—and it was possible, in her case, to assist Mrs. Inchbare's memory by hints contributed from her own superior resources of experience and observation.

"Had he any thing about him of the look and way of a sailor?" she asked. "And did you notice, when you spoke to him, that he had a habit of playing with a locket on his watch-chain?"

"There he is, het aff to a T!" cried Mrs. Inchbare. "Yer leddyship's weel acquented wi' him—there's nae doot o' that."

"I thought I had seen him," said Lady Lundie. "A modest, well-behaved young man, Mrs. Inchbare, as you say. Don't let me keep you any longer from the poultry-yard. I am transgressing the doctor's orders in seeing any body. We quite understand each other now, don't we? Very glad to have seen you. Good-evening."

So she dismissed Mrs. Inchbare, when Mrs. Inchbare had served her purpose.

Most women, in her position, would have been content with the information which she had now obtained. But Lady Lundie—having a man like Sir Patrick to deal with—determined to be doubly sure of her facts before she ventured on interfering at Ham Farm. She had learned from Mrs. Inchbare that the so-called husband of Anne Silvester had joined her at Craig Fernie on the day when she arrived at the inn, and had left her again the next morning. Anne had made her escape from Windygates on the occasion of the lawn-party—that is to say, on the fourteenth of August. On the same day Arnold Brinkworth had taken his departure for the purpose of visiting the Scotch property left to him by his aunt. If Mrs. Inchbare was to be depended on, he must have gone to Craig Fernie instead of going to his appointed destination—and must, therefore, have arrived to visit his house and lands one day later than the day which he had originally set apart for that purpose. If this fact could be proved, the testimony of a disinterested witness, the case against Arnold would be strengthened tenfold; and Lady Lundie might act on her discovery with something like a certainty that her information was to be relied on.

After a little consideration she decided on sending a messenger with a note of inquiry addressed to Arnold's steward. The apology she invented to excuse and account for the strangeness of the proposed question, referred it to a little family discussion as to the exact date of Arnold's arrival at his estate, and to a friendly wager in which the difference of opinion had ended. If the steward could state whether his employer had arrived on the fourteenth or on the fifteenth of August, that was all that would be wanted to decide the question in dispute.

Having written in those terms, Lady Lundie gave the necessary directions for having the note delivered at the earliest possible hour on the next morning; the messenger being ordered to make his way back to Windygates by the first return train on the same day.

This arranged, her ladyship was free to refresh herself with another dose of the red lavender draught, and to sleep the sleep of the just, who close their eyes with the composing conviction that they have done their duty.

The events of the next day at Windygates succeeded each other in due course, as follows:

The post arrived, and brought no reply from Sir Patrick. Lady Lundie entered that incident on her mental register of debts owed by her brother-in-law—to be paid, with interest, when the day of reckoning came.

Next in order occurred the return of the messenger with the steward's answer.

He had referred to his Diary; and he had discovered that Mr. Brinkworth had written beforehand to announce his arrival at his estate for the fourteenth of August—but that he had not actually appeared until the fifteenth. The one discovery needed to substantiate Mrs. Inchbare's evidence being now in Lady Lundie's possession, she decided to allow another day to pass—on the chance that Sir Patrick might alter his mind, and write to her. If no letter arrived, and if nothing more was received from Blanche, she resolved to leave Windygates by the next morning's train, and to try the bold experiment of personal interference at Ham Farm.

The third in the succession of events was the appearance of the doctor to pay his professional visit.

A severe shock awaited him. He found his patient cured by the draught! It was contrary to all rule and precedent; it savored of quackery—the red lavender had no business to do what the red lavender had done—but there she was, nevertheless, up and dressed, and contemplating a journey to London on the next day but one. "An act of duty, doctor, is involved in this—whatever the sacrifice, I must go!" No other explanation could be obtained. The patient was plainly determined—nothing remained for the physician but to retreat with unimpaired dignity, and a paid fee. He did it. "Our art," he explained to Lady Lundie in confidence, "is nothing, after all, but a choice between alternatives. For instance. I see you—not cured, as you think—but sustained by abnormal excitement. I have to ask which is the least of the two evils—to risk letting you travel, or to irritate you by keeping you at home. With your constitution, we must risk the journey. Be careful to keep the window of the carriage up on the side on which the wind blows. Let the extremities be moderately warm, and the mind easy—and pray don't omit to provide yourself with a second bottle of the Mixture before you start." He made his bow, as before—he slipped two guineas into his pocket, as before—and he went his way, as before, with an approving conscience, in the character of a physician who had done his duty. (What an enviable profession is Medicine! And why don't we all belong to it?)

The last of the events was the arrival of Mrs. Glenarm.

"Well?" she began, eagerly, "what news?"

The narrative of her ladyship's discoveries—recited at full length; and the announcement of her ladyship's resolution—declared in the most uncompromising terms—raised Mrs. Glenarm's excitement to the highest pitch.

"You go to town on Saturday?" she said.

"I will go with you. Ever since that woman declared she should be in London before me, I have been dying to hasten my journey—and it is such an opportunity to go with you! I can easily manage it. My uncle and I were to have met in London, early next week, for the foot-race. I have only to write and tell him of my change of plans.—By-the-by, talking of my uncle, I have heard, since I saw you, from the lawyers at Perth."

"More anonymous letters?"

"One more—received by the lawyers this time. My unknown correspondent has written to them to withdraw his proposal, and to announce that he has left Perth. The lawyers recommended me to stop my uncle from spending money uselessly in employing the London police. I have forwarded their letter to the captain; and he will probably be in town to see his solicitors as soon as I get there with you. So much for what *I* have done in this matter. Dear Lady Lundie—when we are at our journey's end, what do *you* mean to do?"

"My course is plain," answered her ladyship, calmly. "Sir Patrick will hear from me, on Sunday morning next, at Ham Farm."

"Telling him what you have found out?"

"Certainly not! Telling him that I find myself called to London by business, and that I propose paying him a short visit on Monday next."

"Of course, he must receive you?"

"I think there is no doubt of that. Even *his* hatred of his brother's widow can hardly go to the length—after leaving my letter unanswered—of closing his doors against me next."

"How will you manage it when you get there?"

"When I get there, my dear, I shall be breathing an atmosphere of treachery and deceit; and, for my poor child's sake (abhorrent as all dissimulation is to me), I must be careful what I do. Not a word will escape my lips until I have first seen Blanche in private. However painful it may be, I shall not shrink from my duty, if my duty compels me to open her eyes to the truth. Sir Patrick and Mr. Brinkworth will have somebody else besides an inexperienced young creature to deal with on Monday next. I shall be there."

With that formidable announcement, Lady Lundie closed the conversation; and Mrs. Glenarm rose to take her leave.

"We meet at the Junction, dear Lady Lundie?"

"At the Junction, on Saturday."

---

ELEVENTH SCENE.—SIR PATRICK'S HOUSE.

## CHAPTER THE FORTY-SECOND.

### THE SMOKING-ROOM WINDOW.

"I CAN'T believe it! I won't believe it! You're trying to part me from my husband—you're trying to set me against my dearest friend. It's infamous. It's horrible. What have I done to you? Oh, my head! my head! Are you trying to drive me mad?"

Pale and wild; her hands twisted in her hair; her feet hurrying her aimlessly to and fro in the room — so Blanche answered her step-mother, when the object of Lady Lundie's pilgrimage had been accomplished, and the cruel truth had been plainly told.

Her ladyship sat, superbly composed, looking out through the window at the placid landscape of woods and fields which surrounded Ham Farm.

"I was prepared for this outbreak," she said, sadly. "These wild words relieve your over-burdened heart, my poor child. I can wait, Blanche—I can wait!"

Blanche stopped, and confronted Lady Lundie.

"You and I never liked each other," she said. "I wrote you a pert letter from this place. I have always taken Anne's part against you. I have shown you plainly—rudely, I dare say—that I was glad to be married and get away from you. This is not your revenge, is it?"

"Oh, Blanche, Blanche, what thoughts to think! what words to say! I can only pray for you."

"I am mad, Lady Lundie. You bear with mad people. Bear with me. I have been hard-ly more than a fortnight married. I love *him*—I love *her*—with all my heart. Remember what you have told me about them. Remember! remember! remember!"

She reiterated the words with a low cry of pain. Her hands went up to her head again; and she returned restlessly to pacing this way and that in the room.

Lady Lundie tried the effect of a gentle re-monstrance. "For your own sake," she said, "don't persist in estranging yourself from me. In this dreadful trial, I am the only friend you have."

Blanche came back to her step-mother's chair; and looked at her steadily, in silence. Lady Lundie submitted to inspection—and bore it per-fectly.

"Look into my heart," she said. "Blanche! it bleeds for you!"

Blanche heard, without heeding. Her mind was painfully intent on its own thoughts. "You are a religious woman," she said, abruptly. "Will you swear on your Bible, that what you told me is true?"

"*My* Bible!" repeated Lady Lundie with sor-rowful emphasis. "Oh, my child! have *you* no part in that precious inheritance? Is it not *your* Bible, too?"

A momentary triumph showed itself in Blanche's face. "You daren't swear it!" she said. "That's enough for me!"

She turned away scornfully. Lady Lundie caught her by the hand, and drew her sharply back. The suffering saint disappeared, and the woman who was no longer to be trifled with took her place.

"There must be an end to this," she said. "You don't believe what I have told you. Have you courage enough to put it to the test?"

Blanche started, and released her hand. She trembled a little. There was a horrible certainty of conviction expressed in Lady Lundie's sudden change of manner.

"How?" she asked.

"You shall see. Tell me the truth, on your side, first. Where is Sir Patrick? Is he really out, as his servant told me?"

"Yes. He is out with the farm bailiff. You have taken us all by surprise. You wrote that we were to expect you by the next train."

"When does the next train arrive? It is eleven o'clock now."

"Between one and two."

"Sir Patrick will not be back till then?"

"Not till then."

"Where is Mr. Brinkworth?"

"My husband?"

"Your husband—if you like. Is he out, too?"

"He is in the smoking-room."

"Do you mean the long room, built out from the back of the house?"

"Yes."

"Come down stairs at once with me."

Blanche advanced a step—and drew back. "What do you want of me?" she asked, inspired by a sudden distrust.

Lady Lundie turned round, and looked at her impatiently.

"Can't you see yet," she said, sharply, "that your interest and my interest in this matter are one? What have I told you?"

"Don't repeat it!"

"I must repeat it! I have told you that Ar-nold Brinkworth was privately at Craig Fernie, with Miss Silvester, in the acknowledged char-acter of her husband—when we supposed him to be visiting the estate left him by his aunt. You refuse to believe it—and I am about to put it to the proof. Is it your interest or is it not, to know whether this man deserves the blind belief that you place in him?"

Blanche trembled from head to foot, and made no reply.

"I am going into the garden, to speak to Mr. Brinkworth through the smoking-room window," pursued her ladyship. "Have you the courage to come with me; to wait behind out of sight; and to hear what he says with his own lips? I am not afraid of putting it to that test. Are you?"

The tone in which she asked the question roused Blanche's spirit.

"If I believed him to be guilty," she said, res-olutely, "I should *not* have the courage. I be-lieve him to be innocent. Lead the way, Lady Lundie, as soon as you please."

They left the room—Blanche's own room at Ham Farm—and descended to the hall. Lady Lundie stopped, and consulted the railway time-table hanging near the house-door.

"There is a train to London at a quarter to twelve," she said. "How long does it take to walk to the station?"

"Why do you ask?"

"You will soon know. Answer my question."

"It's a walk of twenty minutes to the station."

Lady Lundie referred to her watch. "There will be just time," she said.

"Time for what?"

"Come into the garden."

With that answer, she led the way out.

The smoking-room projected at right angles from the wall of the house, in an oblong form—with a bow-window at the farther end, looking into the garden. Before she turned the corner, and showed herself within the range of view from the window, Lady Lundie looked back, and signed to Blanche to wait behind the angle of the wall. Blanche waited.

The next instant she heard the voices in con-versation through the open window. Arnold's voice was the first that spoke.

"HAVE YOU SEEN BLANCHE?"

"Lady Lundie! Why, we didn't expect you till luncheon time!"

Lady Lundie was ready with her answer.

"I was able to leave town earlier than I had anticipated. Don't put out your cigar; and don't move. I am not coming in."

The quick interchange of question and answer went on; every word being audible in the perfect stillness of the place. Arnold was the next to speak.

"Have you seen Blanche?"

"Blanche is getting ready to go out with me. We mean to have a walk together. I have many things to say to her. Before we go, I have something to say to *you*."

"Is it any thing very serious?"

"It is most serious."

"About me?"

"About you. I know where you went on the evening of my lawn-party at Windygates—you went to Craig Fernie."

"Good Heavens! how did you find out—?"

"I know whom you went to meet—Miss Silvester. I know what is said of you and of her—you are man and wife."

"Hush! don't speak so loud. Somebody may hear you!"

"What does it matter if they do? I am the only person whom you have kept out of the secret. You all of you know it here."

"Nothing of the sort! Blanche doesn't know it."

"What! Neither you nor Sir Patrick has told Blanche of the situation you stand in at this moment?"

"Not yet. Sir Patrick leaves it to me. I haven't been able to bring myself to do it. Don't say a word, I entreat you! I don't know how Blanche may interpret it. Her friend is expected in London to-morrow. I want to wait till Sir Patrick can bring them together. Her friend will break it to her better than I can. It's *my* notion. Sir Patrick thinks it a good one. Stop! you're not going away already?"

"She will be here to look for me if I stay any longer."

"One word! I want to know—"

"You shall know later in the day."

Her ladyship appeared again round the angle of the wall. The next words that passed were words spoken in a whisper.

"Are you satisfied now, Blanche?"

"Have you mercy enough left, Lady Lundie, to take me away from this house?"

"My dear child! Why else did I look at the time-table in the hall?"

---

## CHAPTER THE FORTY-THIRD.

### THE EXPLOSION.

ARNOLD's mind was far from easy when he was left by himself again in the smoking-room.

After wasting some time in vainly trying to guess at the source from which Lady Lundie had derived her information, he put on his hat, and took the direction which led to Blanche's favorite walk at Ham Farm. Without absolutely distrusting her ladyship's discretion, the idea had occurred to him that he would do well to join his wife and her step-mother. By making a third at the interview between them, he might prevent the conversation from assuming a perilously confidential turn.

The search for the ladies proved useless. They had not taken the direction in which he supposed them to have gone.

He returned to the smoking-room, and composed himself to wait for events as patiently as he might. In this passive position—with his thoughts still running on Lady Lundie—his memory reverted to a brief conversation between Sir Patrick and himself, occasioned, on the previous day, by her ladyship's announcement of her proposed visit to Ham Farm. Sir Patrick had at once expressed his conviction that his sister-in-law's journey south had some acknowledged purpose at the bottom of it.

"I am not at all sure, Arnold" (he had said), "that I have done wisely in leaving her letter unanswered. And I am strongly disposed to think that the safest course will be to take her into the secret when she comes to-morrow. We can't help the position in which we are placed. It was impossible (without admitting your wife to our confidence) to prevent Blanche from writing that unlucky letter to her—and, even if we had prevented it, she must have heard in other ways of your return to England. I don't doubt my own discretion, so far; and I don't doubt the convenience of keeping her in the dark, as a means of keeping her from meddling in this business of yours, until I have had time to set it right. But she may, by some unlucky accident, discover the truth for herself—and, in that case, I strongly distrust the influence which she might attempt to exercise on Blanche's mind."

Those were the words—and what had happened on the day after they had been spoken? Lady Lundie *had* discovered the truth; and she was, at that moment, alone somewhere with Blanche. Arnold took up his hat once more, and set forth on the search for the ladies in another direction.

The second expedition was as fruitless as the first. Nothing was to be seen, and nothing was to be heard, of Lady Lundie and Blanche.

Arnold's watch told him that it was not far from the time when Sir Patrick might be expected to return. In all probability, while he had been looking for them, the ladies had gone back by some other way to the house. He entered the rooms on the ground-floor, one after another. They were all empty. He went up stairs, and knocked at the door of Blanche's room. There was no answer. He opened the door and looked in. The room was empty, like the rooms down stairs. But, close to the entrance, there was a trifling circumstance to attract notice, in the shape of a note lying on the carpet. He picked it up, and saw that it was addressed to him in the handwriting of his wife.

He opened it. The note began, without the usual form of address, in these words:

"I know the abominable secret that you and my uncle have hidden from me. I know *your* infamy, and *her* infamy, and the position in which, thanks to you and to her, I now stand. Reproaches would be wasted words, addressed to such a man as you are. I write these lines to tell you that I have placed myself under my step-mother's protection in London. It is useless to attempt to follow me. Others will find out whether the ceremony of marriage which

you went through with me is binding on you or not. For myself, I know enough already. I have gone, never to come back, and never to let you see me again.—Blanche."

Hurrying headlong down the stairs with but one clear idea in his mind—the idea of instantly following his wife—Arnold encountered Sir Patrick, standing by a table in the hall, on which cards and notes left by visitors were usually placed, with an open letter in his hand. Seeing in an instant what had happened, he threw one of his arms round Arnold, and stopped him at the house-door.

"You are a man," he said, firmly. "Bear it like a man."

Arnold's head fell on the shoulder of his kind old friend. He burst into tears.

Sir Patrick let the irrepressible outbreak of grief have its way. In those first moments, silence was mercy. He said nothing. The letter which he had been reading (from Lady Lundie, it is needless to say), dropped unheeded at his feet.

Arnold lifted his head, and dashed away the tears.

"I am ashamed of myself," he said. "Let me go."

"Wrong, my poor fellow—doubly wrong!" returned Sir Patrick. "There is no shame in shedding such tears as those. And there is nothing to be done by leaving *me*."

"I must and will see her!"

"Read that," said Sir Patrick, pointing to the letter on the floor. "See your wife? Your wife is with the woman who has written those lines. Read them."

Arnold read them.

"DEAR SIR PATRICK,—If you had honored me with your confidence, I should have been happy to consult you before I interfered to rescue Blanche from the position in which Mr. Brinkworth has placed her. As it is, your late brother's child is under my protection at my house in London. If *you* attempt to exercise your authority, it must be by main force—I will submit to nothing less. If Mr. Brinkworth attempts to exercise *his* authority, he shall establish his right to do so (if he can) in a police-court.

"Very truly yours, JULIA LUNDIE."

Arnold's resolution was not to be shaken even by this. "What do I care," he burst out, hotly, "whether I am dragged through the streets by the police or not! I *will* see my wife. I *will* clear myself of the horrible suspicion she has about me. You have shown me your letter. Look at mine!"

Sir Patrick's clear sense saw the wild words that Blanche had written in their true light.

"Do you hold your wife responsible for that letter?" he asked. "I see her step-mother in every line of it. You descend to something unworthy of you, if you seriously defend yourself against *this!* You can't see it? You persist in holding to your own view? Write, then. You can't get to her—your letter may. No! When you leave this house, you leave it with me. I have conceded something, on my side, in allowing you to write. I insist on your conceding something, on your side, in return. Come into the library! I answer for setting things right between you and Blanche, if you will place your interests in my hands. Do you trust me or not?"

Arnold yielded. They went into the library together. Sir Patrick pointed to the writing-table. "Relieve your mind there," he said. "And let me find you a reasonable man again when I come back."

When he returned to the library the letter was written; and Arnold's mind was so far relieved—for the time at least.

"I shall take your letter to Blanche myself," said Sir Patrick, "by the train that leaves for London in half an hour's time."

"You will let me go with you?"

"Not to-day. I shall be back this evening to dinner. You shall hear all that has happened; and you shall accompany me to London to-morrow—if I find it necessary to make any lengthened stay there. Between this and then, after the shock that you have suffered, you will do well to be quiet here. Be satisfied with my assurance that Blanche shall have your letter. I will force my authority on her step-mother to that extent (if her step-mother resists) without scruple. The respect in which I hold the sex only lasts as long as the sex deserves it—and does not extend to Lady Lundie. There is no advantage that a man can take of a woman which I am not fully prepared to take of my sister-in-law."

With that characteristic farewell, he shook hands with Arnold, and departed for the station.

At seven o'clock the dinner was on the table. At seven o'clock Sir Patrick came down stairs to eat it, as perfectly dressed as usual, and as composed as if nothing had happened.

"She has got your letter," he whispered, as he took Arnold's arm, and led him into the dining-room.

"Did she say any thing?"

"Not a word."

"How did she look?"

"As she ought to look—sorry for what she has done."

The dinner began. As a matter of necessity, the subject of Sir Patrick's expedition was dropped while the servants were in the room—to be regularly taken up again by Arnold in the intervals between the courses. He began when the soup was taken away.

"I confess I had hoped to see Blanche come back with you!" he said, sadly enough.

"In other words," returned Sir Patrick, "you forgot the native obstinacy of the sex. Blanche is beginning to feel that she has been wrong. What is the necessary consequence? She naturally persists in being wrong. Let her alone, and leave your letter to have its effect. The serious difficulties in our way don't rest with Blanche. Content yourself with knowing that."

The fish came in, and Arnold was silenced—until his next opportunity came with the next interval in the course of the dinner.

"What are the difficulties?" he asked.

"The difficulties are my difficulties and yours," answered Sir Patrick. "My difficulty is, that I can't assert my authority, as guardian, if I assume my niece (as I do) to be a married woman. Your difficulty is, that you can't assert your authority as her husband, until it is distinctly proved that you and Miss Silvester are not man and wife.

Lady Lundie was perfectly aware that she would place us in that position, when she removed Blanche from this house. She has cross-examined Mrs. Inchbare; she has written to your steward for the date of your arrival at your estate; she has done every thing, calculated every thing, and foreseen every thing—except my excellent temper. The one mistake she has made, is in thinking she could get the better of *that*. No, my dear boy! My trump card is my temper. I keep it in my hand, Arnold—I keep it in my hand!"

The next course came in—and there was an end of the subject again. Sir Patrick enjoyed his mutton, and entered on a long and interesting narrative of the history of some rare white Burgundy on the table imported by himself. Arnold resolutely resumed the discussion with the departure of the mutton.

"It seems to be a dead lock," he said.

"No slang!" retorted Sir Patrick.

"For Heaven's sake, Sir, consider my anxiety, and tell me what you propose to do!"

"I propose to take you to London with me to-morrow, on this condition—that you promise me, on your word of honor, not to attempt to see your wife before Saturday next."

"I shall see her then?"

"If you give me your promise."

"I do! I do!"

The next course came in. Sir Patrick entered on the question of the merits of the partridge, viewed as an eatable bird. "By himself, Arnold—plainly roasted, and tested on his own merits—an overrated bird. Being too fond of shooting him in this country, we become too fond of eating him next. Properly understood, he is a vehicle for sauce and truffles—nothing more. Or no—that is hardly doing him justice. I am bound to add that he is honorably associated with the famous French receipt for cooking an olive. Do you know it?"

There was an end of the bird; there was an end of the jelly. Arnold got his next chance—and took it.

"What is to be done in London to-morrow?" he asked.

"To-morrow," answered Sir Patrick, "is a memorable day in our calendar. To-morrow is Tuesday—the day on which I am to see Miss Silvester."

Arnold set down the glass of wine which he was just raising to his lips.

"After what has happened," he said, "I can hardly bear to hear her name mentioned. Miss Silvester has parted me from my wife."

"Miss Silvester may atone for that, Arnold, by uniting you again."

"She has been the ruin of me so far."

"She may be the salvation of you yet."

The cheese came in; and Sir Patrick returned to the Art of Cookery.

"Do you know the receipt for cooking an olive, Arnold?"

"No."

"What *does* the new generation know? It knows how to row, how to shoot, how to play at cricket, and how to bet. When it has lost its muscle and lost its money—that is to say, when it has grown old—what a generation it will be! It doesn't matter: I sha'n't live to see it. Are you listening, Arnold?"

"Yes, Sir."

"How to cook an olive: Put an olive into a lark; put a lark into a quail; put a quail into a plover; put a plover into a partridge; put a partridge into a pheasant; put a pheasant into a turkey. Good. First, partially roast; then carefully stew—until all is thoroughly done down to the olive. Good again. Next, open the window. Throw out the turkey, the pheasant, the partridge, the plover, the quail, and the lark. *Then, eat the olive.* The dish is expensive, but (we have it on the highest authority) well worth the sacrifice. The quintessence of the flavor of six birds, concentrated in one olive. Grand idea! Try another glass of the white Burgundy, Arnold."

At last the servants left them—with the wine and dessert on the table.

"I have borne it as long as I can, Sir," said Arnold. "Add to all your kindness to me by telling me at once what happened at Lady Lundie's."

It was a chilly evening. A bright wood fire was burning in the room. Sir Patrick drew his chair to the fire.

"This is exactly what happened," he said. "I found company at Lady Lundie's, to begin with. Two perfect strangers to me. Captain Newenden, and his niece, Mrs. Glenarm. Lady Lundie offered to see me in another room; the two strangers offered to withdraw. I declined both proposals. First check to her ladyship! She has reckoned throughout, Arnold, on our being afraid to face public opinion. I showed her at starting that we were as ready to face it as she was. 'I always accept what the French call accomplished facts,' I said. 'You have brought matters to a crisis, Lady Lundie. So let it be. I have a word to say to my niece (in your presence, if you like); and I have another word to say to you afterward—without presuming to disturb your guests.' The guests sat down again (both naturally devoured by curiosity). Could her ladyship decently refuse me an interview with my own niece, while two witnesses were looking on? Impossible. I saw Blanche (Lady Lundie being present, it is needless to say) in the back drawing-room. I gave her your letter; I said a good word for you; I saw that she was sorry, though she wouldn't own it—and that was enough. We went back into the front drawing-room. I had not spoken five words on our side of the question before it appeared, to my astonishment and delight, that Captain Newenden was in the house on the very question that had brought me into the house—the question of you and Miss Silvester. My business, in the interests of *my* niece, was to deny your marriage to the lady. His business, in the interests of *his* niece, was to assert your marriage to the lady. To the unutterable disgust of the two women, we joined issue, in the most friendly manner, on the spot. 'Charmed to have the pleasure of meeting you, Captain Newenden.'—'Delighted to have the honor of making your acquaintance, Sir Patrick.'—'I think we can settle this in two minutes?'—'My own idea perfectly expressed.'—'State your position, Captain.'—'With the greatest pleasure. Here is my niece, Mrs. Glenarm, engaged to marry Mr. Geoffrey Delamayn. All very well, but there happens to be an obstacle—in the shape of a lady. Do I put it plainly?'—'You put it admirably, Captain; but for the loss to the British navy, you ought to have been a lawyer. Pray, go on.'—'You are too good, Sir Patrick. I resume. Mr. Delamayn asserts that this person in the back-ground has no claim on him, and backs his assertion by declaring that she is married already to Mr. Arnold Brinkworth. Lady Lundie and my niece assure me, on evidence which satisfies *them*, that the assertion is true. The evidence does not satisfy *me*. I hope, Sir Patrick, I don't strike you as being an excessively obstinate man?'—'My dear Sir, you impress me with the highest opinion of your capacity for sifting human testimony! May I ask, next, what course you mean to take?'—'The very thing I was going to mention, Sir Patrick! This is my course. I refuse to sanction my niece's engagement to Mr. Delamayn, until Mr. Delamayn has actually proved his statement by appeal to witnesses of the lady's marriage. He refers me to two witnesses; but declines acting at once in the matter for himself, on the ground that he is in training for a foot-race. I admit that that is an obstacle, and consent to arrange for bringing the two witnesses to London myself. By this post I have written to my lawyers in Perth to look the witnesses up; to offer them the necessary terms (at Mr. Delamayn's expense) for the use of their time; and to produce them by the end of the week. The foot-race is on Thursday next. Mr. Delamayn will be able to attend after that, and establish his own assertion by his own witnesses. What do you say, Sir Patrick, to Saturday next (with Lady Lundie's permission) in this room?'—There is the substance of the captain's statement. He is as old as I am, and is dressed to look like thirty; but a very pleasant fellow for all that. I struck my sister-in-law dumb by accepting the proposal without a moment's hesitation. Mrs. Glenarm and Lady Lundie looked at each other in mute amazement. Here was a difference about which two women would have mortally quarreled; and here were two men settling it in the friendliest possible manner. I wish you had seen Lady Lundie's face, when I declared myself deeply indebted to Captain Newenden for rendering any prolonged interview with her ladyship quite unnecessary. 'Thanks to the captain,' I said to her, in the most cordial manner, 'we have absolutely nothing to discuss. I shall catch the next train, and set Arnold Brinkworth's mind quite at ease.' To come back to serious things, I have engaged to produce you, in the presence of every body—your wife included—on Saturday next. I put a bold face on it before the others. But I am bound to tell *you* that it is by no means easy to say—situated as we are now—what the result of Saturday's inquiry will be. Every thing depends on the issue of my interview with Miss Silvester to-morrow. It is no exaggeration to say, Arnold, that your fate is in her hands."

"I wish to heaven I had never set eyes on her!" said Arnold.

"Lay the saddle on the right horse," returned Sir Patrick. "Wish you had never set eyes on Geoffrey Delamayn."

Arnold hung his head. Sir Patrick's sharp tongue had got the better of him once more.

TWELFTH SCENE.—DRURY LANE.

## CHAPTER THE FORTY-FOURTH.

### THE LETTER AND THE LAW.

The many-toned murmur of the current of London life—flowing through the murky channel of Drury Lane—found its muffled way from the front room to the back. Piles of old music lumbered the dusty floor. Stage masks and weapons, and portraits of singers and dancers, hung round the walls. An empty violin case in one corner faced a broken bust of Rossini in another. A frameless print, representing the Trial of Queen Caroline, was pasted over the fireplace. The chairs were genuine specimens of ancient carving in oak. The table was an equally excellent example of dirty modern deal. A small morsel of drugget was on the floor; and a large deposit of soot was on the ceiling. The scene thus presented, revealed itself in the back drawing-room of a house in Drury Lane, devoted to the transaction of musical and theatrical business of the humbler sort. It was late in the afternoon, on Michaelmas-day. Two persons were seated together in the room: they were Anne Silvester and Sir Patrick Lundie.

The opening conversation between them—comprising, on one side, the narrative of what had happened at Perth and at Swanhaven; and, on the other, a statement of the circumstances attending the separation of Arnold and Blanche—had come to an end. It rested with Sir Patrick to lead the way to the next topic. He looked at his companion, and hesitated.

"Do you feel strong enough to go on?" he asked. "If you would prefer to rest a little, pray say so."

"Thank you, Sir Patrick. I am more than ready, I am eager, to go on. No words can say how anxious I feel to be of some use to you, if I can. It rests entirely with your experience to show me how."

"I can only do that, Miss Silvester, by asking you without ceremony for all the information that I want. Had you any object in traveling to London, which you have not mentioned to me yet? I mean, of course, any object with which I have a claim (as Arnold Brinkworth's representative) to be acquainted?"

"I had an object, Sir Patrick. And I have failed to accomplish it."

"May I ask what it was?"

"It was to see Geoffrey Delamayn."

Sir Patrick started. "You have attempted to see *him!* When?"

"This morning."

"Why, you only arrived in London last night!"

"I only arrived," said Anne, "after waiting many days on the journey. I was obliged to rest at Edinburgh, and again at York—and I was afraid I had given Mrs. Glenarm time enough to get to Geoffrey Delamayn before me."

"Afraid?" repeated Sir Patrick. "I understood that you had no serious intention of disputing the scoundrel with Mrs. Glenarm. What motive could possibly have taken you *his* way?"

"The same motive which took me to Swanhaven."

"What! the idea that it rested with Delamayn to set things right? and that you might bribe

him to do it, by consenting to release him, so far as your claims were concerned?"

"Bear with my folly, Sir Patrick, as patiently as you can! I am always alone now; and I get into a habit of brooding over things. I have been brooding over the position in which my misfortunes have placed Mr. Brinkworth. I have been obstinate—unreasonably obstinate—in believing that I could prevail with Geoffrey Delamayn, after I had failed with Mrs. Glenarm. I am obstinate about it still. If he would only have heard me, my madness in going to Fulham might have had its excuse." She sighed bitterly, and said no more.

Sir Patrick took her hand.

"It *has* its excuse," he said, kindly. "Your motive is beyond reproach. Let me add—to quiet your mind—that, even if Delamayn had been willing to hear you, and had accepted the condition, the result would still have been the same. You are quite wrong in supposing that he has only to speak, and to set this matter right. It has passed entirely beyond his control. The mischief was done when Arnold Brinkworth spent those unlucky hours with you at Craig Fernie."

"Oh, Sir Patrick, if I had only known that, before I went to Fulham this morning!"

She shuddered as she said the words. Something was plainly associated with her visit to Geoffrey, the bare remembrance of which shook her nerves. What was it? Sir Patrick resolved to obtain an answer to that question, before he ventured on proceeding further with the main object of the interview.

"You have told me your reason for going to Fulham," he said. "But I have not heard what happened there."

Anne hesitated. "Is it necessary for me to trouble you about that?" she asked—with evident reluctance to enter on the subject.

"It is absolutely necessary," answered Sir Patrick, "because Delamayn is concerned in it."

Anne summoned her resolution, and entered on her narrative in these words:

"The person who carries on the business here discovered the address for me," she began. "I had some difficulty, however, in finding the house. It is little more than a cottage; and it is quite lost in a great garden, surrounded by high walls. I saw a carriage waiting. The coachman was walking his horses up and down —and he showed me the door. It was a high wooden door in the wall, with a grating in it. I rang the bell. A servant-girl opened the grating, and looked at me. She refused to let me in. Her mistress had ordered her to close the door on all strangers—especially strangers who were women. I contrived to pass some money to her through the grating, and asked to speak to her mistress. After waiting some time, I saw another face behind the bars—and it struck me that I recognized it. I suppose I was nervous. It startled me. I said, 'I think we know each other.' There was no answer. The door was suddenly opened—and who do you think stood before me?"

"Was it somebody I know?"

"Yes."

"Man? or woman?"

"It was Hester Dethridge."

"Hester Dethridge!"

"Yes. Dressed just as usual, and looking just as usual—with her slate hanging at her side."

"Astonishing! Where did I last see her? At the Windygates station, to be sure—going to London, after she had left my sister-in-law's service. Has she accepted another place—without letting me know first, as I told her?"

"She is living at Fulham."

"In service?"

"No. As mistress of her own house."

"What! Hester Dethridge in possession of a house of her own? Well! well! why shouldn't she have a rise in the world like other people? Did she let you in?"

"She stood for some time looking at me, in that dull strange way that she has. The servants at Windygates always said she was not in her right mind—and you will say, Sir Patrick, when you hear what happened, that the servants were not mistaken. She must be mad. I said, 'Don't you remember me?' She lifted her slate, and wrote, 'I remember you, in a dead swoon at Windygates House.' I was quite unaware that she had been present when I fainted in the library. The discovery startled me — or that dreadful, dead-cold look that she has in her eyes startled me—I don't know which. I couldn't speak to her just at first. She wrote on her slate again—the strangest question—in these words: 'I said, at the time, brought to it by a man. Did I say true?' If the question had been put in the usual way, by any body else, I should have considered it too insolent to be noticed. Can you understand my answering it, Sir Patrick? I can't understand it myself, now —and yet I did answer. She forced me to it with her stony eyes. I said 'yes.'"

"Did all this take place at the door?"

"At the door."

"When did she let you in?"

"The next thing she did was to let me in. She took me by the arm, in a rough way, and drew me inside the door, and shut it. My nerves are broken; my courage is gone. I crept with cold when she touched me. She dropped my arm. I stood like a child, waiting for what it pleased her to say or do next. She rested her two hands on her sides, and took a long look at me. She made a horrid dumb sound—not as if she was angry; more, if such a thing could be, as if she was satisfied—pleased even, I should have said, if it had been any body but Hester Dethridge. Do you understand it?"

"Not yet. Let me get nearer to understanding it by asking something before you go on. Did she show any attachment to you, when you were both at Windygates?"

"Not the least. She appeared to be incapable of attachment to me, or to any body."

"Did she write any more questions on her slate?"

"Yes. She wrote another question under what she had written just before. Her mind was still running on my fainting fit, and on the 'man' who had 'brought me to it.' She held up the slate; and the words were these: 'Tell me how he served you; did he knock you down?' Most people would have laughed at the question. I was startled by it. I told her, No. She shook her head as if she didn't believe me. She wrote

on her slate, 'We are loth to own it when they up with their fists and beat us—ain't we?' I said, 'You are quite wrong.' She went on obstinately with her writing. 'Who is the man?'—was her next question. I had control enough over myself to decline telling her that. She opened the door, and pointed to me to go out. I made a sign entreating her to wait a little. She went back, in her impenetrable way, to the writing on the slate—still about the 'man.' This time, the question was plainer still. She had evidently placed her own interpretation of my appearance at the house. She wrote, 'Is it the man who lodges here?' I saw that she would close the door on me if I didn't answer. My only chance with her was to own that she had guessed right. I said 'Yes. I want to see him.' She took me by the arm, as roughly as before—and led me into the house."

"I begin to understand her," said Sir Patrick. "I remember hearing, in my brother's time, that she had been brutally ill-used by her husband. The association of ideas, even in *her* confused brain, becomes plain, if you bear that in mind. What is her last remembrance of you? It is the remembrance of a fainting woman at Windygates."

"Yes."

"She makes you acknowledge that she has guessed right, in guessing that a man was, in some way, answerable for the condition in which she found you. A swoon produced by a shock inflicted on the mind, is a swoon that she doesn't understand. She looks back into her own experience, and associates it with the exercise of actual physical brutality on the part of the man. And she sees, in you, a reflection of her own sufferings and her own case. It's curious—to a student of human nature. And it explains, what is otherwise unintelligible—her overlooking her own instructions to the servant, and letting you into the house. What happened next?"

"She took me into a room, which I suppose was her own room. She made signs, offering me tea. It was done in the strangest way—without the least appearance of kindness. After what you have just said to me, I think I can in some degree interpret what was going on in her mind. I believe she felt a hard-hearted interest in seeing a woman whom she supposed to be as unfortunate as she had once been herself. I declined taking any tea, and tried to return to the subject of what I wanted in the house. She paid no heed to me. She pointed round the room; and then took me to a window, and pointed round the garden—and then made a sign indicating herself. 'My house; and my garden'—that was what she meant. There were four men in the garden—and Geoffrey Delamayn was one of them. I made another attempt to tell her that I wanted to speak to him. But, no! She had her own idea in her mind. After beckoning to me to leave the window, she led the way to the fire-place, and showed me a sheet of paper with writing on it, framed and placed under a glass, and hung on the wall. She seemed, I thought, to feel some kind of pride in her framed manuscript. At any rate, she insisted on my reading it. It was an extract from a will."

"The will under which she had inherited the house?"

"Yes. Her brother's will. It said, that he

regretted, on his death-bed, his estrangement from his only sister, dating from the time when she had married in defiance of his wishes and against his advice. As a proof of his sincere desire to be reconciled with her, before he died, and as some compensation for the sufferings that she had endured at the hands of her deceased husband, he left her an income of two hundred pounds a year, together with the use of his house and garden, for her lifetime. That, as well as I remember, was the substance of what it said."

"Creditable to her brother, and creditable to herself," said Sir Patrick. "Taking her odd character into consideration, I understand her liking it to be seen. What puzzles me, is her letting lodgings with an income of her own to live on."

"That was the very question which I put to her myself. I was obliged to be cautious, and to begin by asking about the lodgers first—the men being still visible out in the garden, to excuse the inquiry. The rooms to let in the house had (as I understood her) been taken by a person acting for Geoffrey Delamayn—his trainer, I presume. He had surprised Hester Dethridge by barely noticing the house, and showing the most extraordinary interest in the garden."

"That is quite intelligible, Miss Silvester. The garden you have described would be just the place he wanted for the exercises of his employer—plenty of space, and well secured from observation by the high walls all round. What next?"

"Next, I got to the question of why she should let her house in lodgings at all. When I asked her that, her face turned harder than ever. She answered me on her slate in these dismal words: 'I have not got a friend in the world. I dare not live alone.' There was her reason! Dreary and dreadful, Sir Patrick, was it not?"

"Dreary indeed! How did it end? Did you get into the garden?"

"Yes—at the second attempt. She seemed suddenly to change her mind; she opened the door for me herself. Passing the window of the room in which I had left her, I looked back. She had taken her place, at a table before the window, apparently watching for what might happen. There was something about her, as her eyes met mine (I can't say what), which made me feel uneasy at the time. Adopting your view, I am almost inclined to think now, horrid as the idea is, that she had the expectation of seeing me treated as *she* had been treated in former days. It was actually a relief to me—though I knew I was going to run a serious risk—to lose sight of her. As I got nearer to the men in the garden, I heard two of them talking very earnestly to Geoffrey Delamayn. The fourth person, an elderly gentleman, stood apart from the rest at some little distance. I kept as far as I could out of sight, waiting till the talk was over. It was impossible for me to help hearing it. The two men were trying to persuade Geoffrey Delamayn to speak to the elderly gentleman. They pointed to him as a famous medical man. They reiterated over and over again, that his opinion was well worth having—"

Sir Patrick interrupted her. "Did they mention his name?" he asked.

"Yes. They called him Mr. Speedwell."

"The man himself! This is even more interesting, Miss Silvester, than you suppose. I myself heard Mr. Speedwell warn Delamayn that he was in broken health, when we were visiting together at Windygates House last month. Did he do as the other men wished him? Did he speak to the surgeon?"

"No. He sulkily refused—he remembered what you remember. He said, 'See the man who told me I was broken down?—not I!' After confirming it with an oath, he turned away from the others. Unfortunately, he took the direction in which I was standing, and discovered me. The bare sight of me seemed to throw him instantly into a state of frenzy. He—it is impossible for me to repeat the language that he used: it is bad enough to have heard it. I believe, Sir Patrick, but for the two men, who ran up and laid hold of him, that Hester Dethridge would have seen what she expected to see. The change in him was so frightful—even to me, well as I thought I knew him in his fits of passion—I tremble when I think of it. One of the men who had restrained him was almost as brutal, in his way. He declared, in the foulest language, that if Delamayn had a fit, he would lose the race, and that I should be answerable for it. But for Mr. Speedwell, I don't know what I should have done. He came forward directly. 'This is no place either for you, or for me,' he said—and gave me his arm, and led me back to the house. Hester Dethridge met us in the passage, and lifted her hand to stop me. Mr. Speedwell asked her what she wanted. She looked at me, and then looked toward the garden, and made the motion of striking a blow with her clenched fist. For the first time in my experience of her—I hope it was my fancy—I thought I saw her smile. Mr. Speedwell took me out. 'They are well matched in that house,' he said. 'The woman is as complete a savage as the men.' The carriage which I had seen waiting at the door was his. He called it up, and politely offered me a place in it. I said I would only trespass on his kindness as far as to the railway station. While we were talking, Hester Dethridge followed us to the door. She made the same motion again with her clenched hand, and looked back toward the garden—and then looked at me, and nodded her head, as much as to say, 'He will do it yet!' No words can describe how glad I was to see the last of her. I hope and trust I shall never set eyes on her again!"

"Did you hear how Mr. Speedwell came to be at the house? Had he gone of his own accord? or had he been sent for?"

"He had been sent for. I ventured to speak to him about the persons whom I had seen in the garden. Mr. Speedwell explained every thing which I was not able of myself to understand, in the kindest manner. One of the two strange men in the garden was the trainer; the other was a doctor, whom the trainer was usually in the habit of consulting. It seems that the real reason for their bringing Geoffrey Delamayn away from Scotland when they did, was that the trainer was uneasy, and wanted to be near London for medical advice. The doctor, on being consulted, owned that he was at a loss to understand the symptoms which he was asked to treat. He had himself fetched the great surgeon to Fulham, that morning. Mr. Speedwell abstained

"HE GAVE ME HIS ARM, AND LED ME BACK TO THE HOUSE."

from mentioning that he had foreseen what would happen, at Windygates. All he said was, 'I had met Mr. Delamayn in society, and I felt interest enough in the case to pay him a visit—with what result, you have seen yourself.'"

"Did he tell you any thing about Delamayn's health?"

"He said that he had questioned the doctor on the way to Fulham, and that some of the patient's symptoms indicated serious mischief. What the symptoms were I did not hear. Mr. Speedwell only spoke of changes for the worse in him which a woman would be likely to understand. At one time, he would be so dull and heedless that nothing could rouse him. At another, he flew into the most terrible passions without any apparent cause. The trainer had found it almost impossible (in Scotland) to keep him to the right diet; and the doctor had only sanctioned taking the house at Fulham, after being first satisfied, not only of the convenience of the garden, but also that Hester Dethridge could be thoroughly trusted as a cook. With her help, they had placed him on an entirely new diet. But they had found an unexpected difficulty even in doing that. When the trainer took him to the new lodgings, it turned out that he had seen Hester Dethridge at Windygates, and had taken the strongest prejudice against her. On seeing her again at Fulham, he appeared to be absolutely terrified."

"Terrified? Why?"

"Nobody knows why. The trainer and the doctor together could only prevent his leaving the house, by threatening to throw up the responsibility of preparing him for the race, unless he instantly controlled himself, and behaved like a man instead of a child. Since that time, he has become reconciled, little by little, to his new abode—partly through Hester Dethridge's caution in keeping herself always out of his way; and partly through his own appreciation of the change in his diet, which Hester's skill in cookery has enabled the doctor to make. Mr. Speedwell mentioned some things which I have forgotten. I can only repeat, Sir Patrick, the result at which he has arrived in his own mind. Coming from a man of his authority, the opinion seems to me to be startling in the last degree. If Geoffrey Delamayn runs in the race on Thursday next, he will do it at the risk of his life."

"At the risk of dying on the ground?"

"Yes."

Sir Patrick's face became thoughtful. He waited a little before he spoke again.

"We have not wasted our time," he said, "in dwelling on what happened during your visit to Fulham. The possibility of this man's death suggests to my mind serious matter for consideration. It is very desirable, in the interests of my niece and her husband, that I should be able to foresee, if I can, how a fatal result of the race might affect the inquiry which is to be held on Saturday next. I believe you may be able to help me in this."

"You have only to tell me how, Sir Patrick."

"I may count on your being present on Saturday?"

"Certainly."

"You thoroughly understand that, in meeting Blanche, you will meet a person estranged from you, for the present—a friend and sister who has ceased (under Lady Lundie's influence mainly) to feel as a friend and sister toward you now?"

"I was not quite unprepared, Sir Patrick, to hear that Blanche had misjudged me. When I wrote my letter to Mr. Brinkworth, I warned him as delicately as I could, that his wife's jealousy might be very easily roused. You may rely on my self-restraint, no matter how hardly it may be tried. Nothing that Blanche can say or do will alter my grateful remembrance of the past. While I live, I love her. Let that assurance quiet any little anxiety that you may have felt as to my conduct—and tell me how I can serve those interests which I have at heart as well as you."

"You can serve them, Miss Silvester, in this way. You can make me acquainted with the position in which you stood toward Delamayn at the time when you went to the Craig Fernie inn."

"Put any questions to me that you think right, Sir Patrick."

"You mean that?"

"I mean it."

"I will begin by recalling something which you have already told me. Delamayn has promised you marriage—"

"Over and over again!"

"In words?"

"Yes."

"In writing?"

"Yes."

"Do you see what I am coming to?"

"Hardly yet."

"You referred, when we first met in this room, to a letter which you recovered from Bishopriggs, at Perth. I have ascertained from Arnold Brinkworth that the sheet of note-paper stolen from you contained two letters. One was written by you to Delamayn—the other was written by Delamayn to you. The substance of this last Arnold remembered. Your letter he had not read. It is of the utmost importance, Miss Silvester, to let me see that correspondence before we part to-day."

Anne made no answer. She sat with her clasped hands on her lap. Her eyes looked uneasily away from Sir Patrick's face, for the first time.

"Will it not be enough," she asked, after an interval, "if I tell you the substance of my letter, without showing it?"

"It will *not* be enough," returned Sir Patrick, in the plainest manner. "I hinted—if you remember—at the propriety of my seeing the letter, when you first mentioned it; and I observed that you purposely abstained from understanding me. I am grieved to put you, on this occasion, to a painful test. But if you *are* to help me at this serious crisis, I have shown you the way."

Anne rose from her chair, and answered by putting the letter into Sir Patrick's hands. "Remember what he has done, since I wrote that," she said. "And try to excuse me, if I own that I am ashamed to show it to you now."

With those words she walked aside to the window. She stood there, with her hand pressed on her breast, looking out absently on the murky London view of house-roof and chimney, while Sir Patrick opened the letter.

It is necessary to the right appreciation of events, that other eyes besides Sir Patrick's should follow the brief course of the correspondence in this place.

1. *From Anne Silvester to Geoffrey Delamayn.*

"WINDYGATES HOUSE, *August* 12, 1868.

"GEOFFREY DELAMAYN,—I have waited in the hope that you would ride over from your brother's place, and see me—and I have waited in vain. Your conduct to me is cruelty itself; I will bear it no longer. Consider! in your own interests, consider—before you drive the miserable woman who has trusted you to despair. You have promised me marriage by all that is sacred. I claim your promise. I insist on nothing less than to be what you vowed I should be—what I have waited all this weary time to be—what I *am*, in the sight of Heaven, your wedded wife. Lady Lundie gives a lawn-party here on the 14th. I know you have been asked. I expect you to accept her invitation. If I don't see you, I won't answer for what may happen. My mind is made up to endure this suspense no longer. Oh, Geoffrey, remember the past! Be faithful—be just—to your loving wife,

"ANNE SILVESTER."

2. *From Geoffrey Delamayn to Anne Silvester.*

"DEAR ANNE,—Just called to London to my father. They have telegraphed him in a bad way. Stop where you are, and I will write you. Trust the bearer. Upon my soul, I'll keep my promise. Your loving husband that is to be,

"GEOFFREY DELAMAYN.

"WINDYGATES HOUSE, *Augt.* 14, 4 P.M.

"In a mortal hurry. The train starts 4.30."

Sir Patrick read the correspondence with breathless attention to the end. At the last lines of the last letter he did what he had not done for twenty years past—he sprang to his feet at a bound, and he crossed a room without the help of his ivory cane.

Anne started; and turning round from the window, looked at him in silent surprise. He was under the influence of strong emotion; his face, his voice, his manner, all showed it.

"How long had you been in Scotland, when you wrote this?" He pointed to Anne's letter as he asked the question, putting it so eagerly that he stammered over the first words. "More than three weeks?" he added, with his bright black eyes fixed in absorbing interest on her face.

"Yes."

"Are you sure of that?"

"I am certain of it."

"You can refer to persons who have seen you?"

"Easily."

He turned the sheet of note-paper, and pointed to Geoffrey's penciled letter on the fourth page.

"How long had *he* been in Scotland, when he wrote this? More than three weeks, too?"

Anne considered for a moment.

"For God's sake, be careful!" said Sir Patrick. "You don't know what depends on this. If your memory is not clear about it, say so."

"My memory was confused for a moment. It is clear again now. He had been at his brother's in Perthshire three weeks before he wrote that. And before he went to Swanhaven, he spent three or four days in the valley of the Esk."

"Are you sure again?"

"Quite sure!"

" Do you know of any one who saw him in the valley of the Esk ?"

" I know of a person who took a note to him, from me."

" A person easily found ?"

" Quite easily."

Sir Patrick laid aside the letter, and seized in ungovernable agitation on both her hands.

" Listen to me," he said. "The whole conspiracy against Arnold Brinkworth and you falls to the ground before that correspondence. When you and he met at the inn—"

He paused, and looked at her. Her hands were beginning to tremble in his.

" When you and Arnold Brinkworth met at the inn," he resumed, " the law of Scotland had made you a married woman. On the day, and at the hour, when he wrote those lines at the back of your letter to him, you were *Geoffrey Delamayn's wedded wife !*"

He stopped, and looked at her again.

Without a word in reply, without the slightest movement in her from head to foot, she looked back at him. The blank stillness of horror was in her face. The deadly cold of horror was in her hands.

In silence, on his side, Sir Patrick drew back a step, with a faint reflection of *her* dismay in his face. Married—to the villain who had not hesitated to calumniate the woman whom he had ruined, and then to cast her helpless on the world. Married—to the traitor who had not shrunk from betraying Arnold's trust in him, and desolating Arnold's home. Married—to the ruffian who would have struck her that morning, if the hands of his own friends had not held him back. And Sir Patrick had never thought of it ! Absorbed in the one idea of Blanche's future, he had never thought of it, till that horror-stricken face looked at him, and said, Think of *my* future, too !

He came back to her. He took her cold hand once more in his.

" Forgive me," he said, " for thinking first of Blanche."

Blanche's name seemed to rouse her. The life came back to her face ; the tender brightness began to shine again in her eyes. He saw that he might venture to speak more plainly still : he went on.

" I see the dreadful sacrifice as *you* see it. I ask myself, have I any right, has Blanche any right—"

She stopped him by a faint pressure of his hand.

" Yes," she said, softly, " if Blanche's happiness depends on it."

---

THIRTEENTH SCENE.—FULHAM.

## CHAPTER THE FORTY-FIFTH.

### THE FOOT-RACE.

A SOLITARY foreigner, drifting about London, drifted toward Fulham on the day of the Foot-Race.

Little by little, he found himself involved in the current of a throng of impetuous English people, all flowing together toward one given point, and all decorated alike with colors of two prevailing hues—pink and yellow. He drifted along with the stream of passengers on the pavement (accompanied by a stream of carriages in the road) until they stopped with one accord at a gate —and paid admission-money to a man in office— and poured into a great open space of ground which looked like an uncultivated garden.

Arrived here, the foreign visitor opened his eyes in wonder at the scene revealed to view. He observed thousands of people assembled, composed almost exclusively of the middle and upper classes of society. They were congregated round a vast inclosure ; they were elevated on amphitheatrical wooden stands ; and they were perched on the roofs of horseless carriages, drawn up in rows. From this congregation there rose such a roar of eager voices as he had never heard yet from any assembled multitude in these islands. Predominating among the cries, he detected one everlasting question. It began with, " Who backs— ?" and it ended in the alternate pronouncing of two British names unintelligible to foreign ears. Seeing these extraordinary sights, and hearing these stirring sounds, he applied to a policeman on duty ; and said, in his best producible English, "If you please, Sir, what is this ?"

The policeman answered, "North against South—Sports."

The foreigner was informed, but not satisfied. He pointed all round the assembly with a circular sweep of his hand ; and said, " Why ?"

The policeman declined to waste words on a man who could ask such a question as that. He lifted a large purple forefinger, with a broad white nail at the end of it, and pointed gravely to a printed Bill, posted on the wall behind him. The drifting foreigner drifted to the Bill.

After reading it carefully, from top to bottom, he consulted a polite private individual near at hand, who proved to be far more communicative than the policeman. The result on his mind, as a person not thoroughly awakened to the enormous national importance of Athletic Sports, was much as follows :

The color of North is pink. The color of South is yellow. North produces fourteen pink men, and South produces thirteen yellow men. The meeting of pink and yellow is a solemnity. The solemnity takes its rise in an indomitable national passion for hardening the arms and legs, by throwing hammers and cricket-balls with the first, and running and jumping with the second. The object in view is to do this in public rivalry. The ends arrived at are (physically) an excessive development of the muscles, purchased at the expense of an excessive strain on the heart and the lungs—(morally), glory ; conferred at the moment by the public applause ; confirmed the next day by a report in the newspapers. Any person who presumes to see any physical evil involved in these exercises to the men who practice them, or any moral obstruction in the exhibition itself to those civilizing influences on which the true greatness of all nations depends, is a person without a biceps, who is simply incomprehensible. Muscular England develops itself, and takes no notice of him.

The foreigner mixed with the assembly, and looked more closely at the social spectacle around him.

He had met with these people before. He had seen them (for instance) at the theatre, and had observed their manners and customs with considerable curiosity and surprise. When the curtain was down, they were so little interested in what they had come to see, that they had hardly spirit enough to speak to each other between the acts. When the curtain was up, if the play made any appeal to their sympathy with any of the higher and nobler emotions of humanity, they received it as something wearisome, or sneered at it as something absurd. The public feeling of the countrymen of Shakspeare, so far as they represented it, recognized but two duties in the dramatist—the duty of making them laugh, and the duty of getting it over soon. The two great merits of a stage proprietor, in England (judging by the rare applause of his cultivated customers), consisted in spending plenty of money on his scenery, and in hiring plenty of brazen-faced women to exhibit their bosoms and their legs. Not at theatres only; but among other gatherings, in other places, the foreigner had noticed the same stolid languor where any effort was exacted from genteel English brains, and the same stupid contempt where any appeal was made to genteel English hearts. Preserve us from enjoying any thing but jokes and scandal! Preserve us from respecting any thing but rank and money! There were the social aspirations of these insular ladies and gentlemen, as expressed under other circumstances, and as betrayed amidst other scenes. Here, all was changed. Here was the strong feeling, the breathless interest, the hearty enthusiasm, not visible elsewhere. Here were the superb gentlemen who were too weary to speak, when an Art was addressing them, shouting themselves hoarse with burst on burst of genuine applause. Here were the fine ladies who yawned behind their fans, at the bare idea of being called on to think or to feel, waving their handkerchiefs in honest delight, and actually flushing with excitement through their powder and their paint. And all for what? All for running and jumping—all for throwing hammers and balls.

The foreigner looked at it, and tried, as a citizen of a civilized country, to understand it. He was still trying—when there occurred a pause in the performances.

Certain hurdles, which had served to exhibit the present satisfactory state of civilization (in jumping) among the upper classes, were removed. The privileged persons who had duties to perform within the inclosure, looked all round it; and disappeared one after another. A great hush of expectation pervaded the whole assembly. Something of no common interest and importance was evidently about to take place. On a sudden, the silence was broken by a roar of cheering from the mob in the road outside the grounds. People looked at each other excitedly, and said, "One of them has come." The silence prevailed again—and was a second time broken by another roar of applause. People nodded to each other with an air of relief and said, "Both of them have come." Then the great hush fell on the crowd once more; and all eyes looked toward one particular point of the ground, occupied by a little wooden pavilion, with the blinds down over the open windows, and the door closed.

The foreigner was deeply impressed by the silent expectation of the great throng about him.

He felt his own sympathies stirred, without knowing why. He believed himself to be on the point of understanding the English people.

Some ceremony of grave importance was evidently in preparation. Was a great orator going to address the assembly? Was a glorious anniversary to be commemorated? Was a religious service to be performed? He looked round him to apply for information once more. Two gentlemen—who contrasted favorably, so far as refinement of manner was concerned, with most of the spectators present—were slowly making their way, at that moment, through the crowd near him. He respectfully asked what national solemnity was now about to take place. They informed him that a pair of strong young men were going to run round the inclosure for a given number of turns, with the object of ascertaining which could run the fastest of the two.

The foreigner lifted his hands and eyes to heaven. Oh, multifarious Providence! who would have suspected that the infinite diversities of thy creation included such beings as these! With that aspiration, he turned his back on the race-course, and left the place.

On his way out of the grounds he had occasion to use his handkerchief, and found that it was gone. He felt next for his purse. His purse was missing too. When he was back again in his own country, intelligent inquiries were addressed to him on the subject of England. He had but one reply to give. "The whole nation is a mystery to me. Of all the English people I only understand the English thieves!"

In the mean time the two gentlemen, making their way through the crowd, reached a wicket-gate in the fence which surrounded the inclosure.

Presenting a written order to the policeman in charge of the gate, they were forthwith admitted within the sacred precincts. The closely packed spectators, regarding them with mixed feelings of envy and curiosity, wondered who they might be. Were they referees appointed to act at the coming race? or reporters for the newspapers? or commissioners of police? They were neither the one nor the other. They were only Mr. Speedwell, the surgeon, and Sir Patrick Lundie.

The two gentlemen walked into the centre of the inclosure, and looked round them.

The grass on which they were standing was girdled by a broad smooth path, composed of finely-sifted ashes and sand—and this again was surrounded by the fence and by the spectators ranked behind it. Above the lines thus formed rose on one side the amphitheatres with their tiers of crowded benches, and on the other the long rows of carriages with the sight-seers inside and out. The evening sun was shining brightly, the light and shade lay together in grand masses, the varied colors of objects blended softly one with the other. It was a splendid and an inspiriting scene.

Sir Patrick turned from the rows of eager faces all round him to his friend the surgeon.

"Is there one person to be found in this vast crowd," he asked, "who has come to see the race with the doubt in his mind which has brought us to see it?"

Mr. Speedwell shook his head. "Not one of them knows or cares what the struggle may cost the men who engage in it."

Sir Patrick looked round him again. "I almost wish I had not come to see it," he said. "If this wretched man—"

The surgeon interposed. "Don't dwell needlessly, Sir Patrick, on the gloomy view," he rejoined. "The opinion I have formed has, thus far, no positive grounds to rest on. I am guessing rightly, as I believe, but at the same time I am guessing in the dark. Appearances *may* have misled me. There may be reserves of vital force in Mr. Delamayn's constitution which I don't suspect. I am here to learn a lesson—not to see a prediction fulfilled. I know his health is broken, and I believe he is going to run this race at his own proper peril. Don't feel too sure beforehand of the event. The event may prove me to be wrong."

For the moment Sir Patrick dropped the subject. He was not in his usual spirits.

Since his interview with Anne had satisfied him that she was Geoffrey's lawful wife, the conviction had inevitably forced itself on his mind that the one possible chance for her in the future was the chance of Geoffrey's death. Horrible as it was to him, he had been possessed by that one idea—go where he might, do what he might, struggle as he might to force his thoughts in other directions. He looked round the broad ashen path on which the race was to be run, conscious that he had a secret interest in it which it was unutterably repugnant to him to feel. He tried to resume the conversation with his friend, and to lead it to other topics. The effort was useless. In despite of himself, he returned to the one fatal subject of the struggle that was now close at hand.

"How many times must they go round this inclosure," he inquired, "before the race is ended?"

Mr. Speedwell turned toward a gentleman who was approaching them at the moment. "Here is somebody coming who can tell us," he said.

"You know him?"

"He is one of my patients."

"Who is he?"

"After the two runners he is the most important personage on the ground. He is the final authority—the umpire of the race."

The person thus described was a middle-aged man, with a prematurely wrinkled face, with prematurely white hair, and with something of a military look about him—brief in speech, and quick in manner.

"The path measures four hundred and forty yards round," he said, when the surgeon had repeated Sir Patrick's question to him. "In plainer words, and not to put you to your arithmetic, once round it is a quarter of a mile. Each round is called a 'Lap.' The men must run sixteen Laps to finish the race. Not to put you to your arithmetic again, they must run four miles—the longest race of this kind which it is customary to attempt at Sports like these."

"Professional pedestrians exceed that limit, do they not?"

"Considerably—on certain occasions."

"Are they a long-lived race?"

"Far from it. They are exceptions when they live to be old men."

Mr. Speedwell looked at Sir Patrick. Sir Patrick put a question to the umpire.

"You have just told us," he said, "that the two young men who appear to-day are going to run the longest distance yet attempted in their experience. Is it generally thought, by persons who understand such things, that they are both fit to bear the exertion demanded of them?"

"You can judge for yourself, Sir. Here is one of them."

He pointed toward the pavilion. At the same moment there rose a mighty clapping of hands from the great throng of spectators. Fleetwood, champion of the North, decorated in his pink colors, descended the pavilion steps and walked into the arena.

Young, lithe, and elegant, with supple strength expressed in every movement of his limbs, with a bright smile on his resolute young face, the man of the north won the women's hearts at starting. The murmur of eager talk rose among them on all sides. The men were quieter—especially the men who understood the subject. It was a serious question with these experts whether Fleetwood was not "a little too fine." Superbly trained, it was admitted—but, possibly, a little *over*-trained for a four-mile race.

The northern hero was followed into the inclosure by his friends and backers, and by his trainer. This last carried a tin can in his hand. "Cold water," the umpire explained. "If he gets exhausted, his trainer will pick him up with a dash of it as he goes by."

A new burst of hand-clapping rattled all round the arena. Delamayn, champion of the South, decorated in his yellow colors, presented himself to the public view.

The immense hum of voices rose louder and louder as he walked into the centre of the great green space. Surprise at the extraordinary contrast between the two men was the prevalent emotion of the moment. Geoffrey was more than a head taller than his antagonist, and broader in full proportion. The women who had been charmed with the easy gait and confident smile of Fleetwood, were all more or less painfully impressed by the sullen strength of the southern man, as he passed before them slowly, with his head down and his brows knit, deaf to the applause showered on him, reckless of the eyes that looked at him; speaking to nobody; concentrated in himself; biding his time. He held the men who understood the subject breathless with interest. There it was! the famous "staying power" that was to endure in the last terrible half-mile of the race, when the nimble and jaunty Fleetwood was run off his legs. Whispers had been spread abroad hinting at something which had gone wrong with Delamayn in his training. And now that all eyes could judge him, his appearance suggested criticism in some quarters. It was exactly the opposite of the criticism passed on his antagonist. The doubt as to Delamayn was whether he had been sufficiently trained. Still the solid strength of the man, the slow, panther-like smoothness of his movements —and, above all, his great reputation in the world of muscle and sport—had their effect. The betting which, with occasional fluctuations, had held steadily in his favor thus far, held, now that he was publicly seen, steadily in his favor still. "Fleetwood for shorter distances, if you like; but Delamayn for a four-mile race."

"Do you think he sees us?" whispered Sir Patrick to the surgeon.

"He sees nobody."

"Can you judge of the condition he is in, at this distance?"

"He has twice the muscular strength of the other man. His trunk and limbs are magnificent. It is useless to ask me more than that about his condition. We are too far from him to see his face plainly."

The conversation among the audience began to flag again; and the silent expectation set in among them once more. One by one, the different persons officially connected with the race gathered together on the grass. The trainer Perry was among them, with his can of water in his hand, in anxious whispering conversation with his principal—giving him the last words of advice before the start. The trainer's doctor, leaving them together, came up to pay his respects to his illustrious colleague.

"How has he got on since I was at Fulham?" asked Mr. Speedwell.

"First-rate, Sir! It was one of his bad days when you saw him. He has done wonders in the last eight-and-forty hours."

"Is he going to win the race?"

Privately the doctor had done what Perry had done before him—he had backed Geoffrey's antagonist. Publicly he was true to his colors. He cast a disparaging look at Fleetwood—and answered Yes, without the slightest hesitation.

At that point, the conversation was suspended by a sudden movement in the inclosure. The runners were on their way to the starting-place. The moment of the race had come.

Shoulder to shoulder, the two men waited—each with his foot touching the mark. The firing of a pistol gave the signal for the start. At the instant when the report sounded they were off.

Fleetwood at once took the lead; Delamayn following, at from two to three yards behind him. In that order, they ran the first round, the second, and the third—both reserving their strength; both watched with breathless interest by every soul in the place. The trainers, with their cans in their hands, ran backward and forward over the grass, meeting their men at certain points, and eyeing them narrowly, in silence. The official persons stood together in a group; their eyes following the runners round and round with the closest attention. The trainer's doctor, still attached to his illustrious colleague, offered the necessary explanations to Mr. Speedwell and his friend.

"Nothing much to see for the first mile, Sir, except the 'style' of the two men."

"You mean they are not really exerting themselves yet?"

"No. Getting their wind, and feeling their legs. Pretty runner, Fleetwood—if you notice, Sir? Gets his legs a trifle better in front, and hardly lifts his heels quite so high as our man. His action's the best of the two; I grant that. But just look, as they come by, which keeps the straightest line. There's where Delamayn has him! It's a steadier, stronger, truer pace; and you'll see it tell when they're half-way through." So, for the first three rounds, the doctor expatiated on the two contrasted "styles"—in terms mercifully adapted to the comprehension of persons unacquainted with the language of the running ring.

At the fourth round—in other words, at the round which completed the first mile, the first change in the relative position of the runners occurred. Delamayn suddenly dashed to the front. Fleetwood smiled as the other passed him. Delamayn held the lead till they were half-way through the fifth round—when Fleetwood, at a hint from his trainer, forced the pace. He lightly passed Delamayn in an instant; and led again to the completion of the sixth round. At the opening of the seventh, Delamayn forced the pace on his side. For a few moments, they ran exactly abreast. Then Delamayn drew away inch by inch; and recovered the lead. The first burst of applause (led by the south) rang out, as the big man beat Fleetwood at his own tactics, and headed him at the critical moment when the race was nearly half run.

"It begins to look as if Delamayn *was* going to win!" said Sir Patrick.

The trainer's doctor forgot himself. Infected by the rising excitement of every body about him, he let out the truth.

"Wait a bit!" he said. "Fleetwood has got directions to let him pass—Fleetwood is waiting to see what he can do."

"Cunning, you see, Sir Patrick, is one of the elements in a manly sport," said Mr. Speedwell, quietly.

At the end of the seventh round, Fleetwood proved the doctor to be right. He shot past Delamayn like an arrow from a bow. At the end of the eight round, he was leading by two yards. Half the race had then been run. Time, ten minutes and thirty-three seconds.

Toward the end of the ninth round, the pace slackened a little; and Delamayn was in front again. He kept ahead, until the opening of the eleventh round. At that point, Fleetwood flung up one hand in the air with a gesture of triumph; and bounded past Delamayn with a shout of "Hooray for the North!" The shout was echoed by the spectators. In proportion as the exertion began to tell upon the men, so the excitement steadily rose among the people looking at them.

At the twelfth round, Fleetwood was leading by six yards. Cries of triumph rose among the adherents of the north, met by counter-cries of defiance from the south. At the next turn Delamayn resolutely lessened the distance between his antagonist and himself. At the opening of the fourteenth round, they were coming side by side. A few yards more, and Delamayn was in front again, amidst a roar of applause from the whole public voice. Yet a few yards further, and Fleetwood neared him; passed him; dropped behind again; led again; and was passed again at the end of the round. The excitement rose to its highest pitch, as the runners—gasping for breath; with dark-flushed faces, and heaving breasts—alternately passed and repassed each other. Oaths were heard now as well as cheers. Women turned pale, and men set their teeth, as the last round but one began.

At the opening of it, Delamayn was still in advance. Before six yards more had been covered, Fleetwood betrayed the purpose of his running in the previous round, and electrified the whole assembly, by dashing past his antagonist —for the first time in the race at the top of his speed. Every body present could see, now, that

"EVERY BODY WAITED, WITH THEIR EYES RIVETED ON THE SURGEON'S HAND."

Delamayn had been allowed to lead on sufferance—had been dextrously drawn on to put out his whole power—and had then, and not till then, been seriously deprived of the lead. He made another effort, with a desperate resolution that roused the public enthusiasm to frenzy. While the voices were roaring; while the hats and handkerchiefs were waving round the course; while the actual event of the race was, for one supreme moment, still in doubt—Mr. Speedwell caught Sir Patrick by the arm.

"Prepare yourself!" he whispered. "It's all over."

As the words passed his lips, Delamayn swerved on the path. His trainer dashed water over him. He rallied, and ran another step or two—swerved again—staggered—lifted his arm to his mouth with a hoarse cry of rage—fastened his own teeth in his flesh like a wild beast—and fell senseless on the course.

A Babel of sounds arose. The cries of alarm in some places, mingling with the shouts of triumph from the backers of Fleetwood in others— as their man ran lightly on to win the now uncontested race. Not the inclosure only, but the course itself was invaded by the crowd. In the midst of the tumult the fallen man was drawn on to the grass—with Mr. Speedwell and the trainer's doctor in attendance on him. At the terrible moment when the surgeon laid his hand on the heart, Fleetwood passed the spot—a passage being forced for him through the people by his friends and the police—running the sixteenth and last round of the race.

Had the beaten man fainted under it, or had he died under it? Every body waited, with their eyes riveted on the surgeon's hand.

The surgeon looked up from him, and called for water to throw over his face, for brandy to put into his mouth. He was coming to life again—he had survived the race. The last shout of applause which hailed Fleetwood's victory rang out as they lifted him from the ground to carry him to the pavilion. Sir Patrick (admitted at Mr. Speedwell's request) was the one stranger allowed to pass the door. At the moment when he was ascending the steps, some one touched his arm. It was Captain Newenden.

"Do the doctors answer for his life?" asked the captain. "I can't get my niece to leave the ground till she is satisfied of that."

Mr. Speedwell heard the question, and replied to it briefly from the top of the pavilion steps.

"For the present—yes," he said.

The captain thanked him, and disappeared.

They entered the pavilion. The necessary restorative measures were taken under Mr. Speedwell's directions. There the conquered athlete lay: outwardly an inert mass of strength, formidable to look at, even in its fall; inwardly, a weaker creature, in all that constitutes vital force, than the fly that buzzed on the window-pane. By slow degrees the fluttering life came back. The sun was setting; and the evening light was beginning to fail. Mr. Speedwell beckoned to Perry to follow him into an unoccupied corner of the room.

"In half an hour or less he will be well enough to be taken home. Where are his friends? He has a brother—hasn't he?"

"His brother's in Scotland, Sir."

"His father?"

Perry scratched his head. "From all I hear, Sir, he and his father don't agree."

Mr. Speedwell applied to Sir Patrick.

"Do you know any thing of his family affairs?"

"Very little. I believe what the man has told you to be the truth."

"Is his mother living?"

"Yes."

"I will write to her myself. In the mean time, somebody must take him home. He has plenty of friends here. Where are they?"

He looked out of the window as he spoke. A throng of people had gathered round the pavilion, waiting to hear the latest news. Mr. Speedwell directed Perry to go out and search among them for any friends of his employer whom he might know by sight. Perry hesitated, and scratched his head for the second time.

"What are you waiting for?" asked the surgeon, sharply. "You know his friends by sight, don't you?"

"I don't think I shall find them outside," said Perry.

"Why not?"

"They backed him heavily, Sir—and they have all lost."

Deaf to this unanswerable reason for the absence of friends, Mr. Speedwell insisted on sending Perry out to search among the persons who composed the crowd. The trainer returned with his report. "You were right, Sir. There are some of his friends outside. They want to see him."

"Let two or three of them in."

Three came in. They stared at him. They uttered brief expressions of pity in slang. They said to Mr. Speedwell, "We wanted to see him. What is it—eh?"

"It's a break-down in his health."

"Bad training?"

"Athletic Sports."

"Oh! Thank you. Good-evening."

Mr. Speedwell's answer drove them out like a flock of sheep before a dog. There was not even time to put the question to them as to who was to take him home.

"I'll look after him, Sir," said Perry. "You can trust me."

"I'll go too," added the trainer's doctor; "and see him littered down for the night."

(The only two men who had "hedged" their bets, by privately backing his opponent, were also the only two men who volunteered to take him home!)

They went back to the sofa on which he was lying. His bloodshot eyes were rolling heavily and vacantly about him, on the search for something. They rested on the doctor—and looked away again. They turned to Mr. Speedwell—and stopped, riveted on his face. The surgeon bent over him, and said, "What is it?"

He answered with a thick accent and laboring breath—uttering a word at a time: "Shall—I—die?"

"I hope not."

"Sure?"

"No."

He looked round him again. This time his eyes rested on the trainer. Perry came forward.

"What can I do for you, Sir?"

The reply came slowly as before. "My—coat—pocket."

"This one, Sir?"

"No."

"This?"

"Yes. Book."

The trainer felt in the pocket, and produced a betting-book.

"What's to be done with this, Sir?"

"Read."

The trainer held the book before him; open at the last two pages on which entries had been made. He rolled his head impatiently from side to side on the sofa pillow. It was plain that he was not yet sufficiently recovered to be able to read what he had written.

"Shall I read for you, Sir?"

"Yes."

The trainer read three entries, one after another, without result; they had all been honestly settled. At the fourth the prostrate man said, "Stop!" This was the first of the entries which still depended on a future event. It recorded the wager laid at Windygates, when Geoffrey had backed himself (in defiance of the surgeon's opinion) to row in the University boat-race next spring—and had forced Arnold Brinkworth to bet against him.

"Well, Sir? What's to be done about this?"

He collected his strength for the effort; and answered by a word at a time.

"Write—brother—Julius. Pay—Arnold—wins."

His lifted hand, solemnly emphasizing what he said, dropped at his side. He closed his eyes; and fell into a heavy stertorous sleep. Give him his due. Scoundrel as he was, give him his due. The awful moment, when his life was trembling in the balance, found him true to the last living faith left among the men of his tribe and time—the faith of the betting-book.

Sir Patrick and Mr. Speedwell quitted the race-ground together; Geoffrey having been previously removed to his lodgings hard by. They met Arnold Brinkworth at the gate. He had, by his own desire, kept out of view among the crowd; and he decided on walking back by himself. The separation from Blanche had changed him in all his habits. He asked but two favors during the interval which was to elapse before he saw his wife again—to be allowed to bear it in his own way, and to be left alone.

Relieved of the oppression which had kept him silent while the race was in progress, Sir Patrick put a question to the surgeon as they drove home, which had been in his mind from the moment when Geoffrey had lost the day.

"I hardly understand the anxiety you showed about Delamayn," he said, "when you found that he had only fainted under the fatigue. Was it something more than a common fainting fit?"

"It is useless to conceal it now," replied Mr. Speedwell. "He has had a narrow escape from a paralytic stroke."

"Was that what you dreaded when you spoke to him at Windygates?"

"That was what I saw in his face when I gave him the warning. I was right, so far. I was wrong in my estimate of the reserve of vital power left in him. When he dropped on the race-course, I firmly believed we should find him a dead man."

"Is it hereditary paralysis? His father's last illness was of that sort."

Mr. Speedwell smiled. "Hereditary paralysis?" he repeated. "Why the man is (naturally) a phenomenon of health and strength—in the prime of his life. Hereditary paralysis might have found him out thirty years hence. His rowing and his running, for the last four years, are alone answerable for what has happened to-day."

Sir Patrick ventured on a suggestion.

"Surely," he said, "with your name to compel attention to it, you ought to make this public—as a warning to others?"

"It would be quite useless. Delamayn is far from being the first man who has dropped at foot-racing, under the cruel stress laid on the vital organs. The public have a happy knack of forgetting these accidents. They would be quite satisfied when they found the other man (who happens to have got through it) produced as a sufficient answer to me."

Anne Silvester's future was still dwelling on Sir Patrick's mind. His next inquiry related to the serious subject of Geoffrey's prospect of recovery in the time to come.

"He will never recover," said Mr. Speedwell. "Paralysis is hanging over him. How long he may live it is impossible for me to say. Much depends on himself. In his condition, any new imprudence, any violent emotion, may kill him at a moment's notice."

"If no accident happens," said Sir Patrick, "will he be sufficiently himself again to leave his bed and go out?"

"Certainly."

"He has an appointment that I know of for Saturday next. Is it likely that he will be able to keep it?"

"Quite likely."

Sir Patrick said no more. Anne's face was before him again at the memorable moment when he had told her that she was Geoffrey's wife.

---

FOURTEENTH SCENE.—PORTLAND PLACE.

## CHAPTER THE FORTY-SIXTH.

### A SCOTCH MARRIAGE.

IT was Saturday, the third of October — the day on which the assertion of Arnold's marriage to Anne Silvester was to be put to the proof.

Toward two o'clock in the afternoon Blanche and her step-mother entered the drawing-room of Lady Lundie's town house in Portland Place.

Since the previous evening the weather had altered for the worse. The rain, which had set in from an early hour that morning, still fell. Viewed from the drawing-room windows, the desolation of Portland Place in the dead season wore its aspect of deepest gloom. The dreary opposite houses were all shut up; the black mud was inches deep in the roadway; the soot, floating in tiny black particles, mixed with the falling rain, and heightened the dirty obscurity of the rising mist. Foot-passengers and vehicles, succeeding each other at rare intervals, left great gaps of silence absolutely uninterrupted by sound. Even the grinders of organs were mute; and the wandering dogs of the street were too wet to bark. Looking back from the view out of Lady Lundie's state windows to the view in Lady Lun-

die's state room, the melancholy that reigned without was more than matched by the melancholy that reigned within. The house had been shut up for the season: it had not been considered necessary, during its mistress's brief visit, to disturb the existing state of things. Coverings of dim brown hue shrouded the furniture. The chandeliers hung invisible in enormous bags. The silent clocks hibernated under extinguishers dropped over them two months since. The tables, drawn up in corners—loaded with ornaments at other times—had nothing but pen, ink, and paper (suggestive of the coming proceedings) placed on them now. The smell of the house was musty; the voice of the house was still. One melancholy maid haunted the bedrooms up stairs, like a ghost. One melancholy man, appointed to admit the visitors, sat solitary in the lower regions—the last of the flunkies, mouldering in an extinct servants' hall. Not a word passed, in the drawing-room, between Lady Lundie and Blanche. Each waited the appearance of the persons concerned in the coming inquiry, absorbed in her own thoughts. Their situation at the moment was a solemn burlesque of the situation of two ladies who are giving an evening party, and who are waiting to receive their guests. Did neither of them see this? Or, seeing it, did they shrink from acknowledging it? In similar positions, who does not shrink? The occasions are many on which we have excellent reason to laugh when the tears are in our eyes; but only children are bold enough to follow the impulse. So strangely, in human existence, does the mockery of what is serious mingle with the serious reality itself, that nothing but our own self-respect preserves our gravity at some of the most important emergencies in our lives. The two ladies waited the coming ordeal together gravely, as became the occasion. The silent maid flitted noiseless up stairs. The silent man waited motionless in the lower regions. Outside, the street was a desert. Inside, the house was a tomb.

The church clock struck the hour. Two.

At the same moment the first of the persons concerned in the investigation arrived.

Lady Lundie waited composedly for the opening of the drawing-room door. Blanche started, and trembled. Was it Arnold? Was it Anne?

The door opened—and Blanche drew a breath of relief. The first arrival was only Lady Lundie's solicitor—invited to attend the proceedings on her ladyship's behalf. He was one of that large class of purely mechanical and perfectly mediocre persons connected with the practice of the law who will probably, in a more advanced state of science, be superseded by machinery. He made himself useful in altering the arrangement of the tables and chairs, so as to keep the contending parties effectually separated from each other. He also entreated Lady Lundie to bear in mind that he knew nothing of Scotch law, and that he was there in the capacity of friend only. This done, he sat down, and looked out with silent interest at the rain—as if it was an operation of Nature which he had never had an opportunity of inspecting before.

The next knock at the door heralded the arrival of a visitor of a totally different order. The melancholy man-servant announced Captain Newenden.

Possibly, in deference to the occasion, possibly, in defiance of the weather, the captain had taken another backward step toward the days of his youth. He was painted and padded, wigged and dressed, to represent the abstract idea of a male human being of five-and-twenty in robust health. There might have been a little stiffness in the region of the waist, and a slight want of firmness in the eyelid and the chin. Otherwise there was the fiction of five-and-twenty, founded in appearance on the fact of five-and-thirty—with the truth invisible behind it, counting seventy years! Wearing a flower in his button-hole, and carrying a jaunty little cane in his hand—brisk, rosy, smiling, perfumed—the captain's appearance brightened the dreary room. It was pleasantly suggestive of a morning visit from an idle young man. He appeared to be a little surprised to find Blanche present on the scene of approaching conflict. Lady Lundie thought it due to herself to explain. "My step-daughter is here in direct defiance of my entreaties and my advice. Persons may present themselves whom it is, in my opinion, improper she should see. Revelations will take place which no young woman, in her position, should hear. She insists on it, Captain Newenden—and I am obliged to submit."

The captain shrugged his shoulders, and showed his beautiful teeth.

Blanche was far too deeply interested in the coming ordeal to care to defend herself: she looked as if she had not even heard what her step-mother had said of her. The solicitor remained absorbed in the interesting view of the falling rain. Lady Lundie asked after Mrs. Glenarm. The captain, in reply, described his niece's anxiety as something—something—something, in short, only to be indicated by shaking his ambrosial curls and waving his jaunty cane. Mrs. Delamayn was staying with her until her uncle returned with the news. And where was Julius? Detained in Scotland by election business. And Lord and Lady Holchester? Lord and Lady Holchester knew nothing about it.

There was another knock at the door. Blanche's pale face turned paler still. Was it Arnold? Was it Anne? After a longer delay than usual, the servant announced Mr. Geoffrey Delamayn and Mr. Moy.

Geoffrey, slowly entering first, saluted the two ladies in silence, and noticed no one else. The London solicitor, withdrawing himself for a moment from the absorbing prospect of the rain, pointed to the places reserved for the new-comer and for the legal adviser whom he had brought with him. Geoffrey seated himself, without so much as a glance round the room. Leaning his elbows on his knees, he vacantly traced patterns on the carpet with his clumsy oaken walking-stick. Stolid indifference expressed itself in his lowering brow and his loosely-hanging mouth. The loss of the race, and the circumstances accompanying it, appeared to have made him duller than usual and heavier than usual—and that was all.

Captain Newenden, approaching to speak to him, stopped half-way, hesitated, thought better of it—and addressed himself to Mr. Moy.

Geoffrey's legal adviser—a Scotchman of the ruddy, ready, and convivial type—cordially met the advance. He announced, in reply to the captain's inquiry, that the witnesses (Mrs. Inchbare and Bishopriggs) were waiting below until they were wanted, in the housekeeper's room. Had there been any difficulty in finding them? Not the least. Mrs. Inchbare was, as a matter of course, at her hotel. Inquiries being set on foot for Bishopriggs, it appeared that he and the landlady had come to an understanding, and that he had returned to his old post of head-waiter at the inn. The captain and Mr. Moy kept up the conversation between them, thus begun, with unflagging ease and spirit. Theirs were the only voices heard in the trying interval that elapsed before the next knock was heard at the door.

At last it came. There could be no doubt now as to the persons who might next be expected to enter the room. Lady Lundie took her step-daughter firmly by the hand. She was not sure of what Blanche's first impulse might lead her to do. For the first time in her life, Blanche left her hand willingly in her step-mother's grasp.

The door opened, and they came in.

Sir Patrick Lundie entered first, with Anne Silvester on his arm. Arnold Brinkworth followed them.

Both Sir Patrick and Anne bowed in silence to the persons assembled. Lady Lundie ceremoniously returned her brother-in-law's salute—and pointedly abstained from noticing Anne's presence in the room. Blanche never looked up. Arnold advanced to her, with his hand held out. Lady Lundie rose, and motioned him back. "Not *yet*, Mr. Brinkworth!" she said, in her most quietly merciless manner. Arnold stood, heedless of her, looking at his wife. His wife lifted her eyes to his; the tears rose in them on the instant. Arnold's dark complexion turned ashy pale under the effort that it cost him to command himself. "I won't distress you," he said, gently—and turned back again to the table at which Sir Patrick and Anne were seated together apart from the rest. Sir Patrick took his hand, and pressed it in silent approval.

The one person who took no part, even as spectator, in the events that followed the appearance of Sir Patrick and his companions in the room—was Geoffrey. The only change visible in him was a change in the handling of his walking-stick. Instead of tracing patterns on the carpet, it beat a tattoo. For the rest, there he sat with his heavy head on his breast and his brawny arms on his knees—weary of it by anticipation before it had begun.

Sir Patrick broke the silence. He addressed himself to his sister-in-law.

"Lady Lundie, are all the persons present whom you expected to see here to-day?"

The gathered venom in Lady Lundie seized the opportunity of planting its first sting.

"All whom I expected are here," she answered. "And more than I expected," she added, with a look at Anne.

The look was not returned — was not even seen. From the moment when she had taken her place by Sir Patrick, Anne's eyes had rested on Blanche. They never moved—they never for an instant lost their tender sadness—when the woman who hated her spoke. All that was beautiful and true in that noble nature seemed to find its one sufficient encouragement in Blanche.

As she looked once more at the sister of the un-forgotten days of old, its native beauty of expression shone out again in her worn and weary face. Every man in the room (but Geoffrey) looked at her; and every man (but Geoffrey) felt for her.

Sir Patrick addressed a second question to his sister-in-law.

"Is there any one here to represent the interests of Mr. Geoffrey Delamayn?" he asked.

Lady Lundie referred Sir Patrick to Geoffrey himself. Without looking up, Geoffrey motioned with his big brown hand to Mr. Moy, sitting by his side.

Mr. Moy (holding the legal rank in Scotland which corresponds to the rank held by solicitors in England) rose and bowed to Sir Patrick, with the courtesy due to a man eminent in his time at the Scottish Bar.

"I represent Mr. Delamayn," he said. "I congratulate myself, Sir Patrick, on having your ability and experience to appeal to in the conduct of the pending inquiry."

Sir Patrick returned the compliment as well as the bow.

"It is I who should learn from you," he answered. "*I* have had time, Mr. Moy, to forget what I once knew."

Lady Lundie looked from one to the other with unconcealed impatience as these formal courtesies were exchanged between the lawyers. "Allow me to remind you, gentlemen, of the suspense that we are suffering at this end of the room," she said. "And permit me to ask when you propose to begin?"

Sir Patrick looked invitingly at Mr. Moy. Mr. Moy looked invitingly at Sir Patrick. More formal courtesies! a polite contest this time as to which of the two learned gentlemen should permit the other to speak first! Mr. Moy's modesty proving to be quite immovable, Sir Patrick ended it by opening the proceedings.

"I am here," he said, "to act on behalf of my friend, Mr. Arnold Brinkworth. I beg to present him to you, Mr. Moy, as the husband of my niece—to whom he was lawfully married on the seventh of September last, at the Church of Saint Margaret, in the parish of Hawley, Kent. I have a copy of the marriage certificate here—if you wish to look at it."

Mr. Moy's modesty declined to look at it.

"Quite needless, Sir Patrick! I admit that a marriage ceremony took place on the date named, between the persons named; but I contend that it was not a valid marriage. I say, on behalf of my client here present (Mr. Geoffrey Delamayn), that Arnold Brinkworth was married at a date prior to the seventh of September last—namely, on the fourteenth of August in this year, and at a place called Craig Fernie, in Scotland—to a lady named Anne Silvester, now living, and present among us (as I understand) at this moment."

Sir Patrick presented Anne. "This is the lady, Mr. Moy."

Mr. Moy bowed, and made a suggestion. "To save needless formalities, Sir Patrick, shall we take the question of identity as established on both sides?"

Sir Patrick agreed with his learned friend. Lady Lundie opened and shut her fan in undisguised impatience. The London solicitor was deeply interested. Captain Newenden, taking out his handkerchief, and using it as a screen, yawned behind it to his heart's content. Sir Patrick resumed.

"You assert the prior marriage," he said to his colleague. "It rests with you to begin."

Mr. Moy cast a preliminary look round him at the persons assembled.

"The object of our meeting here," he said, "is, if I am not mistaken, of a twofold nature. In the first place, it is thought desirable, by a person who has a special interest in the issue of this inquiry" (he glanced at the captain—the captain suddenly became attentive), "to put my client's assertion, relating to Mr. Brinkworth's marriage, to the proof. In the second place, we are all equally desirous—whatever difference of opinion may otherwise exist—to make this informal inquiry a means, if possible, of avoiding the painful publicity which would result from an appeal to a Court of Law."

At those words the gathered venom in Lady Lundie planted its second sting—under cover of a protest addressed to Mr. Moy.

"I beg to inform you, Sir, on behalf of my step-daughter," she said, "that we have nothing to dread from the widest publicity. We consent to be present at, what you call, 'this informal inquiry,' reserving our right to carry the matter beyond the four walls of this room. I am not referring now to Mr. Brinkworth's chance of clearing himself from an odious suspicion which rests upon him, and upon another Person present. That is an after-matter. The object immediately before us—so far as a woman can pretend to understand it—is to establish my step-daughter's right to call Mr. Brinkworth to account in the character of his wife. If the result, so far, fails to satisfy us in that particular, we shall not hesitate to appeal to a Court of Law." She leaned back in her chair, and opened her fan, and looked round her with the air of a woman who called society to witness that she had done her duty.

An expression of pain crossed Blanche's face while her step-mother was speaking. Lady Lundie took her hand for the second time. Blanche resolutely and pointedly withdrew it—Sir Patrick noticing the action with special interest. Before Mr. Moy could say a word in answer, Arnold centred the general attention on himself by suddenly interfering in the proceedings. Blanche looked at him. A bright flush of color appeared on her face—and left it again. Sir Patrick noted the change of color—and observed her more attentively than ever. Arnold's letter to his wife, with time to help it, had plainly shaken her ladyship's influence over Blanche.

"After what Lady Lundie has said, in my wife's presence," Arnold burst out, in his straightforward, boyish way, "I think I ought to be allowed to say a word on my side. I only want to explain how it was I came to go to Craig Fernie at all—and I challenge Mr. Geoffrey Delamayn to deny it, if he can."

His voice rose at the last words, and his eyes brightened with indignation as he looked at Geoffrey.

Mr. Moy appealed to his learned friend.

"With submission, Sir Patrick, to your better judgment," he said, "this young gentleman's

"ARNOLD STERNLY ADDRESSED HIMSELF TO GEOFFREY."

proposal seems to be a little out of place at the present stage of the proceedings."

"Pardon me," answered Sir Patrick. "You have yourself described the proceedings as representing an informal inquiry. An informal proposal—with submission to *your* better judgment, Mr. Moy—is hardly out of place, under those circumstances, is it?"

Mr. Moy's inexhaustible modesty gave way, without a struggle. The answer which he received had the effect of puzzling him at the outset of the investigation. A man of Sir Patrick's experience must have known that Arnold's mere assertion of his own innocence could be productive of nothing but useless delay in the proceedings. And yet he sanctioned that delay. Was he privately on the watch for any accidental circumstance which might help him to better a case that he knew to be a bad one?

Permitted to speak, Arnold spoke. The unmistakable accent of truth was in every word that he uttered. He gave a fairly coherent account of events, from the time when Geoffrey had claimed his assistance at the lawn-party to the time when he found himself at the door of the inn at Craig Fernie. There Sir Patrick interfered, and closed his lips. He asked leave to appeal to Geoffrey to confirm him. Sir Patrick amazed Mr. Moy by sanctioning this irregularity also. Arnold sternly addressed himself to Geoffrey.

"Do you deny that what I have said is true?" he asked.

Mr. Moy did his duty by his client. "You are not bound to answer," he said, "unless you wish it yourself."

Geoffrey slowly lifted his heavy head, and confronted the man whom he had betrayed.

"I deny every word of it," he answered—with a stolid defiance of tone and manner.

"Have we had enough of assertion and counter-assertion, Sir Patrick, by this time?" asked Mr. Moy, with undiminished politeness.

After first forcing Arnold—with some little difficulty—to control himself, Sir Patrick raised Mr. Moy's astonishment to the culminating point. For reasons of his own, he determined to strengthen the favorable impression which Arnold's statement had plainly produced on his wife before the inquiry proceeded a step farther.

"I must throw myself on your indulgence, Mr. Moy," he said. "I have not had enough of assertion and counter-assertion, even yet."

Mr. Moy leaned back in his chair, with a mixed expression of bewilderment and resignation. Either his colleague's intellect was in a failing state—or his colleague had some purpose in view which had not openly asserted itself yet. He began to suspect that the right reading of the riddle was involved in the latter of those two alternatives. Instead of entering any fresh protest, he wisely waited and watched.

Sir Patrick went on unblushingly from one irregularity to another.

"I request Mr. Moy's permission to revert to the alleged marriage, on the fourteenth of August, at Craig Fernie," he said. "Arnold Brinkworth! answer for yourself, in the presence of the persons here assembled. In all that you said, and all that you did, while you were at the inn, were you not solely influenced by the wish to make Miss Silvester's position as little painful to her as possible, and by anxiety to carry out the instructions given to you by Mr. Geoffrey Delamayn? Is that the whole truth?"

"That is the whole truth, Sir Patrick."

"On the day when you went to Craig Fernie, had you not, a few hours previously, applied for my permission to marry my niece?"

"I applied for your permission, Sir Patrick; and you gave it me."

"From the moment when you entered the inn to the moment when you left it, were you absolutely innocent of the slightest intention to marry Miss Silvester?"

"No such thing as the thought of marrying Miss Silvester ever entered my head."

"And this you say, on your word of honor as a gentleman?"

"On my word of honor as a gentleman."

Sir Patrick turned to Anne.

"Was it a matter of necessity, Miss Silvester, that you should appear in the assumed character of a married woman—on the fourteenth of August last, at the Craig Fernie inn?"

Anne looked away from Blanche for the first time. She replied to Sir Patrick quietly, readily, firmly—Blanche looking at her, and listening to her with eager interest.

"I went to the inn alone, Sir Patrick. The landlady refused, in the plainest terms, to let me stay there, unless she was first satisfied that I was a married woman."

"Which of the two gentlemen did you expect to join you at the inn—Mr. Arnold Brinkworth, or Mr. Geoffrey Delamayn?"

"Mr. Geoffrey Delamayn."

"When Mr. Arnold Brinkworth came in his place, and said what was necessary to satisfy the scruples of the landlady, you understood that he was acting in your interests, from motives of kindness only, and under the instructions of Mr. Geoffrey Delamayn?"

"I understood that; and I objected as strongly as I could to Mr. Brinkworth placing himself in a false position on my account."

"Did your objection proceed from any knowledge of the Scottish law of marriage, and of the position in which the peculiarities of that law might place Mr. Brinkworth?"

"I had no knowledge of the Scottish law. I had a vague dislike and dread of the deception which Mr. Brinkworth was practicing on the people of the inn. And I feared that it might lead to some possible misinterpretation of me on the part of a person whom I dearly loved."

"That person being my niece?"

"Yes."

"You appealed to Mr. Brinkworth (knowing of his attachment to my niece), in her name, and for her sake, to leave you to shift for yourself?"

"I did."

"As a gentleman who had given his promise to help and protect a lady, in the absence of the person whom she had depended on to join her, he refused to leave you to shift for yourself?"

"Unhappily, he refused on that account."

"From first to last, you were absolutely innocent of the slightest intention to marry Mr. Brinkworth?"

"I answer, Sir Patrick, as Mr. Brinkworth has answered. No such thing as the thought of marrying him ever entered my head."

"And this you say, on your oath as a Christian woman?"

"On my oath as a Christian woman."

Sir Patrick looked round at Blanche. Her face was hidden in her hands. Her step-mother was vainly appealing to her to compose herself.

In the moment of silence that followed, Mr. Moy interfered in the interests of his client.

"I waive my claim, Sir Patrick, to put any questions on my side. I merely desire to remind you, and to remind the company present, that all that we have just heard is mere assertion—on the part of two persons strongly interested in extricating themselves from a position which fatally compromises them both. The marriage which they deny I am now waiting to prove—not by assertion, on my side, but by appeal to competent witnesses."

After a brief consultation with her own solicitor, Lady Lundie followed Mr. Moy, in stronger language still.

"I wish you to understand, Sir Patrick, before you proceed any farther, that I shall remove my step-daughter from the room if any more attempts are made to harrow her feelings and mislead her judgment. I want words to express my sense of this most cruel and unfair way of conducting the inquiry."

The London lawyer followed, stating his professional approval of his client's view. "As her ladyship's legal adviser," he said, "I support the protest which her ladyship has just made."

Even Captain Newenden agreed in the general disapproval of Sir Patrick's conduct. "Hear, hear!" said the captain, when the lawyer had spoken. "Quite right. I must say, quite right."

Apparently impenetrable to all due sense of his position, Sir Patrick addressed himself to Mr. Moy, as if nothing had happened.

"Do you wish to produce your witnesses at once?" he asked. "I have not the least objection to meet your views—on the understanding that I am permitted to return to the proceedings as interrupted at this point."

Mr. Moy considered. The adversary (there could be no doubt of it by this time) had something in reserve—and the adversary had not yet shown his hand. It was more immediately important to lead him into doing this than to insist on rights and privileges of the purely formal sort. Nothing could shake the strength of the position which Mr. Moy occupied. The longer Sir Patrick's irregularities delayed the proceedings, the more irresistibly the plain facts of the case would assert themselves—with all the force of contrast—out of the mouths of the witnesses who were in attendance down stairs. He determined to wait.

"Reserving my right of objection, Sir Patrick," he answered, "I beg you to go on."

To the surprise of every body, Sir Patrick addressed himself directly to Blanche—quoting the language in which Lady Lundie had spoken to him, with perfect composure of tone and manner.

"You know me well enough, my dear," he said, "to be assured that I am incapable of willingly harrowing your feelings or misleading your judgment. I have a question to ask you, which you can answer or not, entirely as you please."

Before he could put the question there was a momentary contest between Lady Lundie and her legal adviser. Silencing her ladyship (not without difficulty), the London lawyer interposed.

He also begged leave to reserve the right of objection, so far as *his* client was concerned.

Sir Patrick assented by a sign, and proceeded to put his question to Blanche.

"You have heard what Arnold Brinkworth has said, and what Miss Silvester has said," he resumed. "The husband who loves you, and the sisterly friend who loves you, have each made a solemn declaration. Recall your past experience of both of them; remember what they have just said; and now tell me—do you believe they have spoken falsely?"

Blanche answered on the instant.

"I believe, uncle, they have spoken the truth!"

Both the lawyers registered their objections. Lady Lundie made another attempt to speak, and was stopped once more—this time by Mr. Moy as well as by her own adviser. Sir Patrick went on.

"Do you feel any doubt as to the entire propriety of your husband's conduct and your friend's conduct, now you have seen them and heard them, face to face?"

Blanche answered again, with the same absence of reserve.

"I ask them to forgive me," she said. "I believe I have done them both a great wrong."

She looked at her husband first—then at Anne. Arnold attempted to leave his chair. Sir Patrick firmly restrained him. "Wait!" he whispered. "You don't know what is coming." Having said that, he turned toward Anne. Blanche's look had gone to the heart of the faithful woman who loved her. Anne's face was turned away—the tears were forcing themselves through the worn weak hands that tried vainly to hide them.

The formal objections of the lawyers were registered once more. Sir Patrick addressed himself to his niece for the last time.

"You believe what Arnold Brinkworth has said; you believe what Miss Silvester has said. You know that not even the thought of marriage was in the mind of either of them, at the inn. You know—whatever else may happen in the future—that there is not the most remote possibility of either of them consenting to acknowledge that they ever have been, or ever can be, Man and Wife. Is that enough for you? Are you willing, before this inquiry proceeds any farther, to take your husband's hand; to return to your husband's protection; and to leave the rest to me—satisfied with my assurance that, on the facts as they happened, not even the Scotch Law can prove the monstrous assertion of the marriage at Craig Fernie to be true?"

Lady Lundie rose. Both the lawyers rose. Arnold sat lost in astonishment. Geoffrey himself—brutishly careless thus far of all that had passed—lifted his head with a sudden start. In the midst of the profound impression thus produced, Blanche, on whose decision the whole future course of the inquiry now turned, answered in these words:

"I hope you will not think me ungrateful, uncle. I am sure that Arnold has not, knowingly, done me any wrong. But I can't go back to him until I am first *certain* that I am his wife."

Lady Lundie embraced her step-daughter, with a sudden outburst of affection. "My dear child!" exclaimed her ladyship, fervently. "Well done, my own dear child!"

Sir Patrick's head dropped on his breast. "Oh, Blanche! Blanche!" Arnold heard him whisper to himself; "if you only knew what you are forcing me to!"

Mr. Moy put in his word, on Blanche's side of the question.

"I must most respectfully express my approval also of the course which the young lady has taken," he said. "A more dangerous compromise than the compromise which we have just heard suggested it is difficult to imagine. With all deference to Sir Patrick Lundie, his opinion of the impossibility of proving the marriage at Craig Fernie remains to be confirmed as the right one. My own professional opinion is opposed to it. The opinion of another Scottish lawyer (in Glasgow) is, to my certain knowledge, opposed to it. If the young lady had not acted with a wisdom and courage which do her honor, she might have lived to see the day when her reputation would have been destroyed, and her children declared illegitimate. Who is to say that circumstances may not happen in the future which may force Mr. Brinkworth or Miss Silvester—one or the other—to assert the very marriage which they repudiate now? Who is to say that interested relatives (property being concerned here) may not, in the lapse of years, discover motives of their own for questioning the asserted marriage in Kent? I acknowledge that I envy the immense self-confidence which emboldens Sir Patrick to venture, what he is willing to venture upon his own individual opinion on an undecided point of law."

He sat down amidst a murmur of approval, and cast a slyly-expectant look at his defeated adversary. "If *that* doesn't irritate him into showing his hand," thought Mr. Moy, "nothing will!"

Sir Patrick slowly raised his head. There was no irritation—there was only distress in his face —when he spoke next.

"I don't propose, Mr. Moy, to argue the point with you," he said, gently. "I can understand that my conduct must necessarily appear strange and even blameworthy, not in your eyes only, but in the eyes of others. My young friend here will tell you" (he looked toward Arnold) "that the view which you express as to the future peril involved in this case was once the view in my mind too, and that in what I have done thus far I have acted in direct contradiction to advice which I myself gave at no very distant period. Excuse me, if you please, from entering (for the present at least) into the motive which has influenced me from the time when I entered this room. My position is one of unexampled responsibility and of indescribable distress. May I appeal to that statement to stand as my excuse, if I plead for a last extension of indulgence toward the last irregularity of which I shall be guilty, in connection with these proceedings?"

Lady Lundie alone resisted the unaffected and touching dignity with which those words were spoken.

"We have had enough of irregularity," she said, sternly. "I, for one, object to more."

Sir Patrick waited patiently for Mr. Moy's reply. The Scotch lawyer and the English lawyer looked at each other—and understood each other. Mr. Moy answered for both.

"We don't presume to restrain you, Sir Patrick, by other limits than those which, as a gentleman, you impose on yourself. Subject," added the cautious Scotchman, "to the right of objection which we have already reserved."

"Do you object to my speaking to your client?" asked Sir Patrick.

"To Mr. Geoffrey Delamayn?"

"Yes."

All eyes turned on Geoffrey. He was sitting half asleep, as it seemed—with his heavy hands hanging listlessly over his knees, and his chin resting on the hooked handle of his stick.

Looking toward Anne, when Sir Patrick pronounced Geoffrey's name, Mr. Moy saw a change in her. She withdrew her hands from her face, and turned suddenly toward her legal adviser. Was she in the secret of the carefully concealed object at which his opponent had been aiming from the first? Mr. Moy decided to put that doubt to the test. He invited Sir Patrick, by a gesture, to proceed. Sir Patrick addressed himself to Geoffrey.

"You are seriously interested in this inquiry," he said; "and you have taken no part in it yet. Take a part in it now. Look at this lady."

Geoffrey never moved.

"I've seen enough of her already," he said, brutally.

"You may well be ashamed to look at her," said Sir Patrick, quietly. "But you might have acknowledged it in fitter words. Carry your memory back to the fourteenth of August. Do you deny that you promised to marry Miss Silvester privately at the Craig Fernie inn?"

"I object to that question," said Mr. Moy. "My client is under no sort of obligation to answer it."

Geoffrey's rising temper—ready to resent any thing—resented his adviser's interference. "I shall answer if I like," he retorted, insolently. He looked up for a moment at Sir Patrick, without moving his chin from the hook of his stick. Then he looked down again. "I do deny it," he said.

"You deny that you have promised to marry Miss Silvester?"

"Yes."

"I asked you just now to look at her—"

"And I told you I had seen enough of her already."

"Look at *me*. In my presence, and in the presence of the other persons here, do you deny that you owe this lady, by your own solemn engagement, the reparation of marriage?"

He suddenly lifted his head. His eyes, after resting for an instant only on Sir Patrick, turned, little by little; and, brightening slowly, fixed themselves with a hideous, tigerish glare on Anne's face. "I know what I owe her," he said.

The devouring hatred of his look was matched by the ferocious vindictiveness of his tone, as he spoke those words. It was horrible to see him; it was horrible to hear him. Mr. Moy said to him, in a whisper, "Control yourself, or I will throw up your case."

Without answering—without even listening—he lifted one of his hands, and looked at it vacantly. He whispered something to himself; and counted out what he was whispering slowly; in divisions of his own, on three of his fingers in succession. He fixed his eyes again on Anne, with the same devouring hatred in their look,

and spoke (this time directly addressing himself to her) with the same ferocious vindictiveness in his tone. "But for you, I should be married to Mrs. Glenarm. But for you, I should be friends with my father. But for you, I should have won the race. I know what I owe you." His loosely hanging hands stealthily clenched themselves. His head sank again on his broad breast. He said no more.

Not a soul moved—not a word was spoken. The same common horror held them all speechless. Anne's eyes turned once more on Blanche. Anne's courage upheld her, even at that moment.

Sir Patrick rose. The strong emotion which he had suppressed thus far, showed itself plainly in his face—uttered itself plainly in his voice.

"Come into the next room," he said to Anne. "I must speak to you instantly!"

Without noticing the astonishment that he caused; without paying the smallest attention to the remonstrances addressed to him by his sister-in-law and by the Scotch lawyer, he took Anne by the arm—opened the folding-doors at one end of the room—entered the room beyond with her —and closed the doors again.

Lady Lundie appealed to her legal adviser. Blanche rose—advanced a few steps—and stood in breathless suspense, looking at the folding-doors. Arnold advanced a step, to speak to his wife. The captain approached Mr. Moy.

"What does this mean?" he asked.

Mr. Moy answered, in strong agitation on his side.

"It means that I have not been properly instructed. Sir Patrick Lundie has some evidence in his possession that seriously compromises Mr. Delamayn's case. He has shrunk from producing it hitherto—he finds himself forced to produce it now. How is it," asked the lawyer, turning sternly on his client, "that you have left me in the dark?"

"I know nothing about it," answered Geoffrey, without lifting his head.

Lady Lundie signed to Blanche to stand aside, and advanced toward the folding-doors. Mr. Moy stopped her.

"I advise your ladyship to be patient. Interference is useless there."

"Am I not to interfere, Sir, in my own house?"

"Unless I am entirely mistaken, madam, the end of the proceedings in your house is at hand. You will damage your own interests by interfering. Let us know what we are about at last. Let the end come."

Lady Lundie yielded, and returned to her place. They all waited in silence for the opening of the doors.

Sir Patrick Lundie and Anne Silvester were alone in the room.

He took from the breast-pocket of his coat the sheet of note-paper which contained Anne's letter, and Geoffrey's reply. His hand trembled as he held it; his voice faltered as he spoke.

"I have done all that can be done," he said. "I have left nothing untried, to prevent the necessity of producing this."

"I feel your kindness gratefully, Sir Patrick. You must produce it now."

The woman's calmness presented a strange and touching contrast to the man's emotion. There

"SHE WAITED FOR HIM, WITH HER HAND ON THE LOCK."

was no shrinking in her face, there was no unsteadiness in her voice as she answered him. He took her hand. Twice he attempted to speak; and twice his own agitation overpowered him. He offered the letter to her in silence.

In silence, on her side, she put the letter away from her, wondering what he meant.

"Take it back," he said. "I can't produce it! I daren't produce it! After what my own eyes have seen, after what my own ears have heard, in the next room—as God is my witness, I daren't ask you to declare yourself Geoffrey Delamayn's wife!"

She answered him in one word.

"Blanche!"

He shook his head impatiently. "Not even in Blanche's interests! Not even for Blanche's sake! If there is any risk, it is a risk I am ready to run. I hold to my own opinion. I believe my own view to be right. Let it come to an appeal to the law! I will fight the case, and win it."

"Are you *sure* of winning it, Sir Patrick?"

Instead of replying, he pressed the letter on her. "Destroy it," he whispered. "And rely on my silence."

She took the letter from him.

"Destroy it," he repeated. "They may open the doors. They may come in at any moment, and see it in your hand."

"I have something to ask you, Sir Patrick, before I destroy it. Blanche refuses to go back to her husband, unless she returns with the certain assurance of being really his wife. If I produce this letter, she may go back to him to-day. If I declare myself Geoffrey Delamayn's wife, I clear Arnold Brinkworth, at once and forever, of all suspicion of being married to me. Can

you as certainly and effectually clear him in any other way? Answer me that, as a man of honor speaking to a woman who implicitly trusts him!"

She looked him full in the face. His eyes dropped before hers—he made no reply.

"I am answered," she said.

With those words, she passed him, and laid her hand on the door.

He checked her. The tears rose in his eyes as he drew her gently back into the room.

"Why should we wait?" she asked.

"Wait," he answered, "as a favor to *me*."

She seated herself calmly in the nearest chair, and rested her head on her hand, thinking.

He bent over her, and roused her, impatiently, almost angrily. The steady resolution in her face was terrible to him, when he thought of the man in the next room.

"Take time to consider," he pleaded. "Don't be led away by your own impulse. Don't act under a false excitement. Nothing binds you to this dreadful sacrifice of yourself."

"Excitement! Sacrifice!" She smiled sadly as she repeated the words. "Do you know, Sir Patrick, what I was thinking of a moment since? Only of old times, when I was a little girl. I saw the sad side of life sooner than most children see it. My mother was cruelly deserted. The hard marriage laws of this country were harder on her than on me. She died broken-hearted. But one friend comforted her at the last moment, and promised to be a mother to her child. I can't remember one unhappy day in all the after-time when I lived with that faithful woman and her little daughter—till the day that parted us. She went away with her husband; and I and the little daughter were left behind. She said her last words to me. Her heart was sinking under the dread of coming death. 'I promised your mother that you should be like my own child to me, and it quieted her mind. Quiet *my* mind, Anne, before I go. Whatever happens in years to come—promise me to be always what you are now, a sister to Blanche.' Where is the false excitement, Sir Patrick, in old remembrances like these? And how can there be a sacrifice in any thing that I do for Blanche?"

She rose, and offered him her hand. Sir Patrick lifted it to his lips in silence.

"Come!" she said. "For both our sakes, let us not prolong this."

He turned aside his head. It was no moment to let her see that she had completely unmanned him. She waited for him, with her hand on the lock. He rallied his courage—he forced himself to face the horror of the situation calmly. She opened the door, and led the way back into the other room.

Not a word was spoken by any of the persons present, as the two returned to their places. The noise of a carriage passing in the street was painfully audible. The chance banging of a door in the lower regions of the house made every one start.

Anne's sweet voice broke the dreary silence.

"Must I speak for myself, Sir Patrick? Or will you (I ask it as a last and greatest favor) speak for me?"

"You insist on appealing to the letter in your hand?"

"I am resolved to appeal to it."

"Will nothing induce you to defer the close of this inquiry—so far as you are concerned—for four-and-twenty hours?"

"Either you or I, Sir Patrick, must say what is to be said, and do what is to be done, before we leave this room."

"Give me the letter."

She gave it to him. Mr. Moy whispered to his client, "Do you know what that is?" Geoffrey shook his head. "Do you really remember nothing about it?" Geoffrey answered in one surly word, "Nothing!"

Sir Patrick addressed himself to the assembled company.

"I have to ask your pardon," he said, "for abruptly leaving the room, and for obliging Miss Silvester to leave it with me. Every body present, except that man" (he pointed to Geoffrey), "will, I believe, understand and forgive me, now that I am forced to make my conduct the subject of the plainest and the fullest explanation. I shall address that explanation, for reasons which will presently appear, to my niece."

Blanche started. "To me!" she exclaimed.

"To you," Sir Patrick answered.

Blanche turned toward Arnold, daunted by a vague sense of something serious to come. The letter that she had received from her husband on her departure from Ham Farm had necessarily alluded to relations between Geoffrey and Anne, of which Blanche had been previously ignorant. Was any reference coming to those relations? Was there something yet to be disclosed which Arnold's letter had not prepared her to hear?

Sir Patrick resumed.

"A short time since," he said to Blanche, "I proposed to you to return to your husband's protection—and to leave the termination of this matter in my hands. You have refused to go back to him until you are first certainly assured that you are his wife. Thanks to a sacrifice to your interests and your happiness, on Miss Silvester's part—which I tell you frankly I have done my utmost to prevent—I am in a position to prove positively that Arnold Brinkworth was a single man when he married you from my house in Kent."

Mr. Moy's experience forewarned him of what was coming. He pointed to the letter in Sir Patrick's hand.

"Do you claim on a promise of marriage?" he asked.

Sir Patrick rejoined by putting a question on his side.

"Do you remember the famous decision at Doctors' Commons, which established the marriage of Captain Dalrymple and Miss Gordon?"

Mr. Moy was answered. "I understand you, Sir Patrick," he said. After a moment's pause, he addressed his next words to Anne. "And, from the bottom of my heart, madam, I respect *you.*"

It was said with a fervent sincerity of tone which wrought the interest of the other persons, who were still waiting for enlightenment, to the highest pitch. Lady Lundie and Captain Newenden whispered to each other anxiously. Arnold turned pale. Blanche burst into tears.

Sir Patrick turned once more to his niece.

"Some little time since," he said, "I had occasion to speak to you of the scandalous uncertainty of the marriage laws of Scotland. But for that uncertainty (entirely without parallel in any other civilized country in Europe), Arnold Brinkworth would never have occupied the position in which he stands here to-day—and these proceedings would never have taken place. Bear that fact in mind. It is not only answerable for the mischief that has been already done, but for the far more serious evil which is still to come."

Mr. Moy took a note. Sir Patrick went on.

"Loose and reckless as the Scotch law is, there happens, however, to be one case in which the action of it has been confirmed and settled by the English Courts. A written promise of marriage exchanged between a man and woman, in Scotland, marries that man and woman by Scotch law. An English Court of Justice (sitting in judgment on the case I have just mentioned to Mr. Moy) has pronounced that law to be good—and the decision has since been confirmed by the supreme authority of the House of Lords. Where the persons therefore—living in Scotland at the time—have promised each other marriage in writing, there is now no longer any doubt. They are certainly, and lawfully, Man and Wife." He turned from his niece, and appealed to Mr. Moy. "Am I right?"

"Quite right, Sir Patrick, as to the facts. I own, however, that your commentary on them surprises me. I have the highest opinion of our Scottish marriage law. A man who has betrayed a woman under a promise of marriage is forced by that law (in the interests of public morality) to acknowledge her as his wife."

"The persons here present, Mr. Moy, are now

about to see the moral merit of the Scotch law of marriage (as approved by England) practically in operation before their own eyes. They will judge for themselves of the morality (Scotch or English) which first forces a deserted woman back on the villain who has betrayed her, and then virtuously leaves her to bear the consequences."

With that answer, he turned to Anne, and showed her the letter, open in his hand.

"For the last time," he said, "do you insist on my appealing to this?"

She rose, and bowed her head gravely.

"It is my distressing duty," said Sir Patrick, "to declare, in this lady's name, and on the faith of written promises of marriage exchanged between the parties, then residing in Scotland, that she claims to be now—and to have been on the afternoon of the fourteenth of August last—Mr. Geoffrey Delamayn's wedded wife."

A cry of horror from Blanche, a low murmur of dismay from the rest, followed the utterance of those words.

There was a pause of an instant.

Then Geoffrey rose slowly to his feet, and fixed his eyes on the wife who had claimed him.

The spectators of the terrible scene turned with one accord toward the sacrificed woman. The look which Geoffrey had cast on her—the words which Geoffrey had spoken to her—were present to all their minds. She stood, waiting by Sir Patrick's side—her soft gray eyes resting sadly and tenderly on Blanche's face. To see that matchless courage and resignation was to doubt the reality of what had happened. They were forced to look back at the man to possess their minds with the truth.

The triumph of law and morality over him was complete. He never uttered a word. His furious temper was perfectly and fearfully calm. With the promise of merciless vengeance written in the Devil's writing on his Devil-possessed face, he kept his eyes fixed on the hated woman whom he had ruined—on the hated woman who was fastened to him as his wife.

His lawyer went over to the table at which Sir Patrick sat. Sir Patrick handed him the sheet of note-paper.

He read the two letters contained in it with absorbed and deliberate attention. The moments that passed before he lifted his head from his reading seemed like hours. "Can you prove the handwritings?" he asked. "And prove the residence?"

Sir Patrick took up a second morsel of paper lying ready under his hand.

"There are the names of persons who can prove the writing, and prove the residence," he replied. "One of your two witnesses below stairs (otherwise useless) can speak to the hour at which Mr. Brinkworth arrived at the inn, and so can prove that the lady for whom he asked was, at that moment, Mrs. Geoffrey Delamayn. The indorsement on the back of the note-paper, also referring to the question of time, is in the handwriting of the same witness—to whom I refer you, when it suits your convenience to question him."

"I will verify the references, Sir Patrick, as a matter of form. In the mean time, not to interpose needless and vexatious delay, I am bound to say that I can not resist the evidence of the marriage."

Having replied in those terms, he addressed himself, with marked respect and sympathy, to Anne.

"On the faith of the written promise of marriage exchanged between you in Scotland," he said, "you claim Mr. Geoffrey Delamayn as your husband?"

She steadily repeated the words after him.

"I claim Mr. Geoffrey Delamayn as my husband."

Mr. Moy appealed to his client. Geoffrey broke silence at last.

"Is it settled?" he asked.

"To all practical purposes, it is settled."

He went on, still looking at nobody but Anne.

"Has the law of Scotland made her my wife?"

"The law of Scotland has made her your wife."

He asked a third and last question.

"Does the law tell her to go where her husband goes?"

"Yes."

He laughed softly to himself, and beckoned to her to cross the room to the place at which he was standing.

She obeyed. At the moment when she took the first step to approach him, Sir Patrick caught her hand, and whispered to her, "Rely on me!" She gently pressed his hand in token that she understood him, and advanced to Geoffrey. At the same moment, Blanche rushed between them, and flung her arms around Anne's neck.

"Oh, Anne! Anne!"

An hysterical passion of tears choked her utterance. Anne gently unwound the arms that clung round her—gently lifted the head that lay helpless on her bosom.

"Happier days are coming, my love," she said. "Don't think of *me*."

She kissed her—looked at her—kissed her again—and placed her in her husband's arms. Arnold remembered her parting words at Craig Fernie, when they had wished each other good-night. "You have not befriended an ungrateful woman. The day may yet come when I shall prove it." Gratitude and admiration struggled in him which should utter itself first, and held him speechless.

She bent her head gently in token that she understood him. Then she went on, and stood before Geoffrey.

"I am here," she said to him. "What do you wish me to do?"

A hideous smile parted his heavy lips. He offered her his arm.

"Mrs. Geoffrey Delamayn," he said. "Come home."

The picture of the lonely house, isolated amidst its high walls; the ill-omened figure of the dumb woman with the stony eyes and the savage ways—the whole scene, as Anne had pictured it to him but two days since, rose vivid as reality before Sir Patrick's mind. "No!" he cried out, carried away by the generous impulse of the moment. "It shall *not* be!"

Geoffrey stood impenetrable—waiting with his offered arm. Pale and resolute, she lifted her noble head—called back the courage which had faltered for a moment—and took his arm.

He led her to the door. "Don't let Blanche

fret about me," she said, simply, to Arnold as they went by. They passed Sir Patrick next. Once more his sympathy for her set every other consideration at defiance. He started up to bar the way to Geoffrey. Geoffrey paused, and looked at Sir Patrick for the first time.

"The law tells her to go with her husband," he said. "The law forbids you to part Man and Wife."

True. Absolutely, undeniably true. The law sanctioned the sacrifice of her as unanswerably as it had sanctioned the sacrifice of her mother before her. In the name of Morality, let him take her! In the interests of Virtue, let her get out of it if she can!

Her husband opened the door. Mr. Moy laid his hand on Sir Patrick's arm. Lady Lundie, Captain Newenden, the London lawyer, all left their places; influenced, for once, by the same interest; feeling, for once, the same suspense. Arnold followed them, supporting his wife. For one memorable instant Anne looked back at them all. Then she and her husband crossed the threshold. They descended the stairs together. The opening and closing of the house door was heard. They were gone.

Done, in the name of Morality. Done, in the interests of Virtue. Done, in an age of progress, and under the most perfect government on the face of the earth.

---

FIFTEENTH SCENE.—HOLCHESTER HOUSE.

## CHAPTER THE FORTY-SEVENTH.

### THE LAST CHANCE.

"His lordship is dangerously ill, Sir. Her ladyship can receive no visitors."

"Be so good as to take that card to Lady Holchester. It is absolutely necessary that your mistress should be made acquainted—in the interests of her younger son — with something which I can only mention to her ladyship herself."

The two persons speaking were Lord Holchester's head servant and Sir Patrick Lundie. At that time barely half an hour had passed since the close of the proceedings at Portland Place.

The servant still hesitated with the card in his hand. "I shall forfeit my situation," he said, "if I do it."

"You will most assuredly forfeit your situation if you *don't* do it," returned Sir Patrick. "I warn you plainly, this is too serious a matter to be trifled with."

The tone in which those words were spoken had its effect. The man went up stairs with his message.

Sir Patrick waited in the hall. Even the momentary delay of entering one of the reception-rooms was more than he could endure at that moment. Anne's happiness was hopelessly sacrificed already. The preservation of her personal safety—which Sir Patrick firmly believed to be in danger—was the one service which it was possible to render to her now. The perilous position in which she stood toward her husband—as an immovable obstacle, while she lived, between Geoffrey and Mrs. Glenarm—was beyond the reach of remedy. But it was still possible

to prevent her from becoming the innocent cause of Geoffrey's pecuniary ruin, by standing in the way of a reconciliation between father and son. Resolute to leave no means untried of serving Anne's interests, Sir Patrick had allowed Arnold and Blanche to go to his own residence in London, alone, and had not even waited to say a farewell word to any of the persons who had taken part in the inquiry. "Her life may depend on what I can do for her at Holchester House!" With that conviction in him, he had left Portland Place. With that conviction in him, he had sent his message to Lady Holchester, and was now waiting for the reply.

The servant appeared again on the stairs. Sir Patrick went up to meet him.

"Her ladyship will see you, Sir, for a few minutes."

The door of an upper room was opened; and Sir Patrick found himself in the presence of Geoffrey's mother. There was only time to observe that she possessed the remains of rare personal beauty, and that she received her visitor with a grace and courtesy which implied (under the circumstances) a considerate regard for *his* position at the expense of her own.

"You have something to say to me, Sir Patrick, on the subject of my second son. I am in great affliction. If you bring me bad news, I will do my best to bear it. May I trust to your kindness not to keep me in suspense?"

"It will help me to make my intrusion as little painful as possible to your ladyship," replied Sir Patrick, "if I am permitted to ask a question. Have you heard of any obstacle to the contemplated marriage of Mr. Geoffrey Delamayn and Mrs. Glenarm?"

Even that distant reference to Anne produced an ominous change for the worse in Lady Holchester's manner.

"I have heard of the obstacle to which you allude," she said. "Mrs. Glenarm is an intimate friend of mine. She has informed me that a person named Silvester, an impudent adventuress—"

"I beg your ladyship's pardon. You are doing a cruel wrong to the noblest woman I have ever met with."

"I can not undertake, Sir Patrick, to enter into your reasons for admiring her. Her conduct toward my son has, I repeat, been the conduct of an impudent adventuress."

Those words showed Sir Patrick the utter hopelessness of shaking her prejudice against Anne. He decided on proceeding at once to the disclosure of the truth.

"I entreat you to say no more," he answered. "Your ladyship is speaking of your son's wife."

"My son has married Miss Silvester?"

"Yes."

She turned deadly pale. It appeared, for an instant, as if the shock had completely overwhelmed her. But the mother's weakness was only momentary. The virtuous indignation of the great lady had taken its place before Sir Patrick could speak again. She rose to terminate the interview.

"I presume," she said, "that your errand here is at an end."

Sir Patrick rose, on his side, resolute to do the duty which had brought him to the house.

"I am compelled to trespass on your lady-ship's attention for a few minutes more," he answered. "The circumstances attending the marriage of Mr. Geoffrey Delamayn are of no common importance. I beg permission (in the interests of his family) to state, very briefly, what they are."

In a few clear sentences he narrated what had happened, that afternoon, in Portland Place. Lady Holchester listened with the steadiest and coldest attention. So far as outward appearances were concerned, no impression was produced upon her.

"Do you expect me," she asked, "to espouse the interests of a person who has prevented my son from marrying the lady of his choice, and of mine?"

"Mr. Geoffrey Delamayn, unhappily, has that reason for resenting his wife's innocent interference with interests of considerable importance to him," returned Sir Patrick. "I request your ladyship to consider whether it is desirable—in view of your son's conduct in the future—to allow his wife to stand in the doubly perilous relation toward him of being also a cause of estrangement between his father and himself."

He had put it with scrupulous caution. But Lady Holchester understood what he had refrained from saying as well as what he had actually said. She had hitherto remained standing—she now sat down again. There was a visible impression produced on her at last.

"In Lord Holchester's critical state of health," she answered, "I decline to take the responsibility of telling him what you have just told me. My own influence has been uniformly exerted in my son's favor—as long as my interference could be productive of any good result. The time for my interference has passed. Lord Holchester has altered his will this morning. I was not present; and I have not yet been informed of what has been done. Even if I knew—"

"Your ladyship would naturally decline," said Sir Patrick, "to communicate the information to a stranger."

"Certainly. At the same time, after what you have said, I do not feel justified in deciding on this matter entirely by myself. One of Lord Holchester's executors is now in the house. There can be no impropriety in your seeing him—if you wish it. You are at liberty to say, from me, that I leave it entirely to his discretion to decide what ought to be done."

"I gladly accept your ladyship's proposal."

Lady Holchester rang the bell at her side.

"Take Sir Patrick Lundie to Mr. March-wood," she said to the servant.

Sir Patrick started. The name was familiar to him, as the name of a friend.

"Mr. Marchwood of Hurlbeck?" he asked.

"The same."

With that brief answer, Lady Holchester dismissed her visitor. Following the servant to the other end of the corridor, Sir Patrick was conducted into a small room—the ante-chamber to the bedroom in which Lord Holchester lay. The door of communication was closed. A gentleman sat writing at a table near the window. He rose, and held out his hand, with a look of surprise, when the servant announced Sir Patrick's name. This was Mr. Marchwood.

After the first explanations had been given,

Sir Patrick patiently reverted to the object of his visit to Holchester House. On the first occasion when he mentioned Anne's name he observed that Mr. Marchwood became, from that moment, specially interested in what he was saying.

"Do you happen to be acquainted with the lady?" he asked.

"I only know her as the cause of a very strange proceeding, this morning, in that room." He pointed to Lord Holchester's bedroom as he spoke.

"Are you at liberty to mention what the proceeding was?"

"Hardly—even to an old friend like you—unless I felt it a matter of duty, on my part, to state the circumstances. Pray go on with what you were saying to me. You were on the point of telling me what brought you to this house."

Without a word more of preface, Sir Patrick told him the news of Geoffrey's marriage to Anne.

"Married!" cried Mr. Marchwood. "Are you sure of what you say?"

"I am one of the witnesses of the marriage."

"Good Heavens! And Lord Holchester's lawyer has left the house!"

"Can I replace him? Have I, by any chance, justified you in telling me what happened this morning in the next room?"

"Justified me? You have left me no other alternative. The doctors are all agreed in dreading apoplexy—his lordship may die at any moment. In the lawyer's absence, I must take it on myself. Here are the facts. There is a codicil to Lord Holchester's Will which is still unsigned."

"Relating to his second son?"

"Relating to Geoffrey Delamayn, and giving him (when it is once executed) a liberal provision for life."

"What is the object in the way of his executing it?"

"The lady whom you have just mentioned to me."

"Anne Silvester!"

"Anne Silvester—now (as you tell me) Mrs. Geoffrey Delamayn. I can only explain the thing very imperfectly. There are certain painful circumstances associated in his lordship's memory with this lady, or with some member of her family. We can only gather that he did something—in the early part of his professional career—which was strictly within the limits of his duty, but which apparently led to very sad results. Some days since he unfortunately heard (either through Mrs. Glenarm or through Mrs. Julius Delamayn) of Miss Silvester's appearance at Swanhaven Lodge. No remark on the subject escaped him at the time. It was only this morning, when the codicil giving the legacy to Geoffrey was waiting to be executed, that his real feeling in the matter came out. To our astonishment, he refused to sign it. 'Find Anne Silvester' (was the only answer we could get from him); 'and bring her to my bedside. You all say my son is guiltless of injuring her. I am lying on my death-bed. I have serious reasons of my own —I owe it to the memory of the dead—to assure myself of the truth. If Anne Silvester herself acquits him of having wronged her, I will provide for Geoffrey. Not otherwise.' We went the length of reminding him that he might die before Miss Silvester could be found. Our interference had but one result. He desired the lawyer to add a second codicil to the Will—which he executed on the spot. It directs his executors to inquire into the relations that have actually existed between Anne Silvester and his younger son. If we find reason to conclude that Geoffrey has gravely wronged her, we are directed to pay her a legacy—provided that she is a single woman at the time."

"And her marriage violates the provision!" exclaimed Sir Patrick.

"Yes. The codicil actually executed is now worthless. And the other codicil remains unsigned until the lawyer can produce Miss Silvester. He has left the house to apply to Geoffrey at Fulham, as the only means at our disposal of finding the lady. Some hours have passed—and he has not yet returned."

"It is useless to wait for him," said Sir Patrick. "While the lawyer was on his way to Fulham, Lord Holchester's son was on his way to Portland Place. This is even more serious than you suppose. Tell me, what under less pressing circumstances I should have no right to ask. Apart from the unexecuted codicil, what is Geoffrey Delamayn's position in the will?"

"He is not even mentioned in it."

"Have you got the will?"

Mr. Marchwood unlocked a drawer, and took it out.

Sir Patrick instantly rose from his chair. "No waiting for the lawyer!" he repeated, vehemently. "This is a matter of life and death. Lady Holchester bitterly resents her son's marriage. She speaks and feels as a frie d of Mrs. Glenarm. Do you think Lord Holchester would take the same view, if he knew of it?"

"It depends entirely on the circumstances."

"Suppose I informed him—as I inform you in confidence—that his son has gravely wronged Miss Silvester? And suppose I followed that up by telling him that his son has made atonement by marrying her?"

"After the feeling that he has shown in the matter, I believe he would sign the codicil."

"Then, for God's sake, let me see him!"

"I must speak to the doctor."

"Do it instantly!"

With the will in his hand, Mr. Marchwood advanced to the bedroom door. It was opened from within before he could get to it. The doctor appeared on the threshold. He held up his hand warningly when Mr. Marchwood attempted to speak to him.

"Go to Lady Holchester," he said. "It's all over."

"Dead?"

"Dead."

---

SIXTEENTH SCENE.—SALT PATCH.

# CHAPTER THE FORTY-EIGHTH.

## THE PLACE.

EARLY in the present century it was generally reported among the neighbors of one Reuben Limbrick that he was in a fair way to make a comfortable little fortune by dealing in Salt.

His place of abode was in Staffordshire, on a morsel of freehold land of his own—appropriately called Salt Patch. Without being absolutely a miser, he lived in the humblest manner, saw very little company; skillfully invested his money; and persisted in remaining a single man.

Toward eighteen hundred and forty he first felt the approach of the chronic malady which ultimately terminated his life. After trying what the medical men of his own locality could do for him, with very poor success, he met by accident with a doctor living in the western suburbs of London, who thoroughly understood his complaint. After some journeying backward and forward to consult this gentleman, he decided on retiring from business, and on taking up his abode within an easy distance of his medical man.

Finding a piece of freehold land to be sold in the neighborhood of Fulham, he bought it, and had a cottage residence built on it, under his own directions. He surrounded the whole—being a man singularly jealous of any intrusion on his retirement, or of any chance observation of his ways and habits—with a high wall, which cost a large sum of money, and which was rightly considered a dismal and hideous object by the neighbors. When the new residence was completed, he called it after the name of the place in Staffordshire where he had made his money, and where he had lived during the happiest period of his life. His relatives, failing to understand that a question of sentiment was involved in this proceeding, appealed to hard facts, and reminded him that there were no salt mines in the neighborhood. Reuben Limbrick answered, "So much the worse for the neighborhood"—and persisted in calling his property, "Salt Patch."

The cottage was so small that it looked quite lost in the large garden all round it. There was a ground-floor and a floor above it—and that was all.

On either side of the passage, on the lower floor, were two rooms. At the right-hand side, on entering by the front-door, there was a kitchen, with its outhouses attached. The room next to the kitchen looked into the garden. In Reuben Limbrick's time it was called the study, and contained a small collection of books and a large store of fishing-tackle. On the left-hand side of the passage there was a drawing-room situated at the back of the house, and communicating with a dining-room in the front. On the upper floor there were five bedrooms—two on one side of the passage, corresponding in size with the dining-room and the drawing-room below, but not opening into each other; three on the other side of the passage, consisting of one larger room in front, and of two small rooms at the back. All these were solidly and completely furnished. Money had not been spared, and workmanship had not been stinted. It was all substantial—and, up stairs and down stairs, it was all ugly.

The situation of Salt Patch was lonely. The lands of the market-gardeners separated it from other houses. Jealously surrounded by its own high walls, the cottage suggested, even to the most unimaginative persons, the idea of an asylum or a prison. Reuben Limbrick's relatives, occasionally coming to stay with him, found the place prey on their spirits, and rejoiced when the time came for going home again. They were never pressed to stay against their will. Reuben Limbrick was not a hospitable or a sociable man. He set very little value on human sympathy, in his attacks of illness; and he bore congratulations impatiently, in his intervals of health. "I care about nothing but fishing," he used to say. "I find my dog very good company. And I am quite happy as long as I am free from pain."

On his death-bed, he divided his money justly enough among his relations. The only part of his Will which exposed itself to unfavorable criticism, was a clause conferring a legacy on one of his sisters (then a widow) who had estranged herself from her family by marrying beneath her. The family agreed in considering this unhappy person as undeserving of notice or benefit. Her name was Hester Dethridge. It proved to be a great aggravation of Hester's offenses, in the eyes of Hester's relatives, when it was discovered that she possessed a life-interest in Salt Patch, and an income of two hundred a year.

Not visited by the surviving members of her family, living, literally, by herself in the world, Hester decided, in spite of her comfortable little income, on letting lodgings. The explanation of this strange conduct which she had written on her slate, in reply to an inquiry from Anne, was the true one. "I have not got a friend in the world: I dare not live alone." In that desolate situation, and with that melancholy motive, she put the house into an agent's hands. The first person in want of lodgings whom the agent sent to see the place was Perry the trainer; and Hester's first tenant was Geoffrey Delamayn.

The rooms which the landlady reserved for herself were the kitchen, the room next to it, which had once been her brother's "study," and the two small back bedrooms up stairs—one for herself, the other for the servant-girl whom she employed to help her. The whole of the rest of the cottage was to let. It was more than the trainer wanted; but Hester Dethridge refused to dispose of her lodgings—either as to the rooms occupied, or as to the period for which they were to be taken—on other than her own terms. Perry had no alternative but to lose the advantage of the garden as a private training-ground, or to submit.

Being only two in number, the lodgers had three bedrooms to choose from. Geoffrey established himself in the back-room, over the drawing-room. Perry chose the front-room, placed on the other side of the cottage, next to the two smaller apartments occupied by Hester and her maid. Under this arrangement, the front bedroom, on the opposite side of the passage—next to the room in which Geoffrey slept—was left empty, and was called, for the time being, the spare room. As for the lower floor, the athlete and his trainer ate their meals in the dining-room; and left the drawing-room, as a needless luxury, to take care of itself.

The Foot-Race once over, Perry's business at the cottage was at an end. His empty bedroom became a second spare room. The term for which the lodgings had been taken was then still unexpired. On the day after the race Geoffrey had to choose between sacrificing the money, or remaining in the lodgings by himself, with two spare bedrooms on his hands, and with a drawing-room for the reception of his visitors—who called with pipes in their mouths, and whose idea of hospitality was a pot of beer in the garden.

To use his own phrase, he was "out of sorts." A sluggish reluctance to face change of any kind possessed him. He decided on staying at Salt Patch until his marriage to Mrs. Glenarm (which he then looked upon as a certainty) obliged him to alter his habits completely, once for all. From Fulham he had gone, the next day, to attend the inquiry in Portland Place. And to Fulham he returned, when he brought the wife who had been forced upon him to her "home."

Such was the position of the tenant, and such were the arrangements of the interior of the cottage, on the memorable evening when Anne Silvester entered it as Geoffrey's wife.

---

## CHAPTER THE FORTY-NINTH.

### THE NIGHT.

On leaving Lady Lundie's house, Geoffrey called the first empty cab that passed him. He opened the door, and signed to Anne to enter the vehicle. She obeyed him mechanically. He placed himself on the seat opposite to her, and told the man to drive to Fulham.

The cab started on its journey; husband and wife preserving absolute silence. Anne laid her head back wearily, and closed her eyes. Her strength had broken down under the effort which had sustained her from the beginning to the end of the inquiry. Her power of thinking was gone. She felt nothing, knew nothing, feared nothing. Half in faintness, half in slumber, she had lost all sense of her own terrible position before the first five minutes of the journey to Fulham had come to an end.

Sitting opposite to her, savagely self-concentrated in his own thoughts, Geoffrey roused himself on a sudden. An idea had sprung to life in his sluggish brain. He put his head out of the window of the cab, and directed the driver to turn back, and go to an hotel near the Great Northern Railway.

Resuming his seat, he looked furtively at Anne. She neither moved nor opened her eyes—she was, to all appearance, unconscious of what had happened. He observed her attentively. Was she really ill? Was the time coming when he would be freed from her? He pondered over that question—watching her closely. Little by little the vile hope in him slowly died away, and a vile suspicion took its place. What, if this appearance of illness was a pretense? What, if she was waiting to throw him off his guard, and escape from him at the first opportunity? He put his head out of the window again, and gave another order to the driver. The cab diverged from the direct route, and stopped at a public house in Holborn, kept (under an assumed name) by Perry the trainer.

Geoffrey wrote a line in pencil on his card, and sent it into the house by the driver. After waiting some minutes, a lad appeared and touched his hat. Geoffrey spoke to him, out of the window, in an under-tone. The lad took his place on the box by the driver. The cab turned back, and took the road to the hotel near the Great Northern Railway.

Arrived at the place, Geoffrey posted the lad close at the door of the cab, and pointed to Anne, still reclining with closed eyes; still, as it seemed, too weary to lift her head, too faint to notice any thing that happened. "If she attempts to get out, stop her, and send for me." With those parting directions he entered the hotel, and asked for Mr. Moy.

Mr. Moy was in the house; he had just returned from Portland Place. He rose, and bowed coldly, when Geoffrey was shown into his sitting-room.

"What is your business with me?" he asked.

"I've had a notion come into my head," said Geoffrey. "And I want to speak to you about it directly."

"I must request you to consult some one else. Consider me, if you please, as having withdrawn from all further connection with your affairs."

Geoffrey looked at him in stolid surprise.

"Do you mean to say you're going to leave me in the lurch?" he asked.

"I mean to say that I will take no fresh step in any business of yours," answered Mr. Moy, firmly. "As to the future, I have ceased to be your legal adviser. As to the past, I shall carefully complete the formal duties toward you which remain to be done. Mrs. Inchbare and Bishopriggs are coming here by appointment, at six this evening, to receive the money due to them before they go back. I shall return to Scotland myself by the night mail. The persons referred to, in the matter of the promise of marriage, by Sir Patrick, are all in Scotland. I will take their evidence as to the handwriting, and as to the question of residence in the North —and I will send it to you in written form. That done, I shall have done all. I decline to advise you in any future step which you propose to take."

After reflecting for a moment, Geoffrey put a last question.

"You said Bishopriggs and the woman would be here at six this evening."

"Yes."

"Where are they to be found before that?"

Mr. Moy wrote a few words on a slip of paper, and handed it to Geoffrey. "At their lodgings," he said. "There is the address."

Geoffrey took the address, and left the room. Lawyer and client parted without a word on either side.

Returning to the cab, Geoffrey found the lad steadily waiting at his post.

"Has any thing happened?"

"The lady hasn't moved, Sir, since you left her."

"Is Perry at the public house?"

"Not at this time, Sir."

"I want a lawyer. Do you know who Perry's lawyer is?"

"Yes, Sir."

"And where he is to be found?"

"Yes, Sir."

"Get up on the box, and tell the man where to drive to."

The cab went on again along the Euston Road, and stopped at a house in a side-street, with a professional brass plate on the door. The lad got down, and came to the window.

"Here it is, Sir."

"Knock at the door, and see if he is at home."

He proved to be at home. Geoffrey entered the house, leaving his emissary once more on the watch. The lad noticed that the lady moved this time. She shivered as if she felt cold— opened her eyes for a moment wearily, and looked out through the window—sighed, and sank back again in the corner of the cab.

After an absence of more than half an hour Geoffrey came out again. His interview with Perry's lawyer appeared to have relieved his mind of something that had oppressed it. He once more ordered the driver to go to Fulham—opened the door to get into the cab—then, as it seemed, suddenly recollected himself—and, calling the lad down from the box, ordered him to get inside, and took his place by the driver.

As the cab started he looked over his shoulder at Anne through the front window. "Well worth trying," he said to himself. "It's the way to be even with her. And it's the way to be free."

They arrived at the cottage. Possibly, repose had restored Anne's strength. Possibly, the sight of the place had roused the instinct of self-preservation in her at last. To Geoffrey's surprise, she left the cab without assistance. When he opened the wooden gate, with his own key, she recoiled from it, and looked at him for the first time.

He pointed to the entrance.

"Go in," he said.

"On what terms?" she asked, without stirring a step.

Geoffrey dismissed the cab; and sent the lad in, to wait for further orders. These things done, he answered her loudly and brutally the moment they were alone:

"On any terms I please."

"Nothing will induce me," she said, firmly, "to live with you as your wife. You may kill me—but you will never bend me to that."

He advanced a step—opened his lips—and suddenly checked himself. He waited a while, turning something over in his mind. When he spoke again, it was with marked deliberation and constraint—with the air of a man who was repeating words put into his lips, or words prepared beforehand.

"I have something to tell you in the presence of witnesses," he said. "I don't ask you, or wish you, to see me in the cottage alone."

She started at the change in him. His sudden composure, and his sudden nicety in the choice of words, tried her courage far more severely than it had been tried by his violence of the moment before.

He waited her decision, still pointing through the gate. She trembled a little—steadied herself again—and went in. The lad, waiting in the front garden, followed her.

He threw open the drawing-room door, on the left-hand side of the passage. She entered the room. The servant-girl appeared. He said to her, "Fetch Mrs. Dethridge; and come back with her yourself." Then he went into the room; the lad, by his own directions, following him in; and the door being left wide open.

Hester Dethridge came out from the kitchen with the girl behind her. At the sight of Anne, a faint and momentary change passed over the stony stillness of her face. A dull light glimmered in her eyes. She slowly nodded her head. A dumb sound, vaguely expressive of something like exultation or relief, escaped her lips.

Geoffrey spoke—once more, with marked deliberation and constraint; once more, with the air of repeating something which had been prepared beforehand. He pointed to Anne.

"This woman is my wife," he said. "In the presence of you three, as witnesses, I tell her that I don't forgive her. I have brought her here—having no other place in which I can trust her to be—to wait the issue of proceedings, undertaken in defense of my own honor and good name. While she stays here, she will live separate from me, in a room of her own. If it is necessary for me to communicate with her, I shall only see her in the presence of a third person. Do you all understand me?"

Hester Dethridge bowed her head. The other two answered, "Yes"—and turned to go out. Anne rose. At a sign from Geoffrey, the servant and the lad waited in the room to hear what she had to say.

"I know nothing in my conduct," she said, addressing herself to Geoffrey, "which justifies you in telling these people that you don't forgive me. Those words applied by you to me are an insult. I am equally ignorant of what you mean when you speak of defending your good name. All I understand is, that we are separate persons in this house, and that I am to have a room of my own. I am grateful, whatever your motives may be, for the arrangement that you have proposed. Direct one of these two women to show me my room."

Geoffrey turned to Hester Dethridge.

"Take her up stairs," he said; "and let her pick which room she pleases. Give her what she wants to eat or drink. Bring down the address of the place where her luggage is. The lad here will go back by railway, and fetch it. That's all. Be off."

Hester went out. Anne followed her up the stairs. In the passage on the upper floor she stopped. The dull light flickered again for a moment in her eyes. She wrote on her slate, and held it up to Anne, with these words on it: "I knew you would come back. It's not over yet between you and him." Anne made no reply. She went on writing, with something faintly like a smile on her thin, colorless lips. "I know something of bad husbands. Yours is as bad a one as ever stood in shoes. He'll try you." Anne made an effort to stop her. "Don't you see how tired I am?" she said, gently. Hester Dethridge dropped the slate—looked with a steady and uncompassionate attention in Anne's face—nodded her head, as much as to say, "I see it now"—and led the way into one of the empty rooms.

It was the front bedroom, over the drawing-room. The first glance round showed it to be scrupulously clean, and solidly and tastelessly furnished. The hideous paper on the walls, the hideous carpet on the floor, were both of the best quality. The great heavy mahogany bedstead, with its curtains hanging from a hook in the ceiling, and with its clumsily carved head and foot on the same level, offered to the view the anomalous spectacle of French design overwhelmed by English execution. The most noticeable thing in the room was the extraordinary attention which had been given to the defense of the door. Besides the usual lock and key, it possessed two solid bolts, fastening inside at the top

and the bottom. It had been one among the many eccentric sides of Reuben Limbrick's character to live in perpetual dread of thieves breaking into his cottage at night. All the outer doors and all the window shutters were solidly sheathed with iron, and had alarm-bells attached to them on a new principle. Every one of the bedrooms possessed its two bolts on the inner side of the door. And, to crown all, on the roof of the cottage was a little belfry, containing a bell large enough to make itself heard at the Fulham police station. In Reuben Limbrick's time the rope had communicated with his bedroom. It hung now against the wall, in the passage outside.

Looking from one to the other of the objects around her, Anne's eyes rested on the partition wall which divided the room from the room next to it. The wall was not broken by a door of communication; it had nothing placed against it but a wash-hand-stand and two chairs.

"Who sleeps in the next room?" said Anne.

Hester Dethridge pointed down to the drawing-room in which they had left Geoffrey. Geoffrey slept in the room.

Anne led the way out again into the passage. "Show me the second room," she said.

The second room was also in front of the house. More ugliness (of first-rate quality) in the paper and the carpet. Another heavy mahogany bedstead; but, this time, a bedstead with a canopy attached to the head of it—supporting its own curtains. Anticipating Anne's inquiry, on this occasion, Hester looked toward the next room, at the back of the cottage, and pointed to herself. Anne at once decided on choosing the second room; it was the farthest from Geoffrey. Hester waited while she wrote the address at which her luggage would be found (at the house of the musical agent), and then, having applied for and received her directions as to the evening meal which she should send up stairs, quitted the room.

Left alone, Anne secured the door, and threw herself on the bed. Still too weary to exert her mind, still physically incapable of realizing the helplessness and the peril of her position, she opened a locket that hung from her neck, kissed the portrait of her mother and the portrait of Blanche placed opposite to each other inside it, and sank into a deep and dreamless sleep.

Meanwhile Geoffrey repeated his final orders to the lad, at the cottage gate.

"When you have got the luggage, you are to go to the lawyer. If he can come here to-night, you will show him the way. If he can't come, you will bring me a letter from him. Make any mistake in this, and it will be the worst day's work you ever did in your life. Away with you, and don't lose the train."

The lad ran off. Geoffrey waited, looking after him, and turning over in his mind what had been done up to that time.

"All right, so far," he said to himself. "I didn't ride in the cab with her. I told her before witnesses I didn't forgive her, and why I had her in the house. I've put her in a room by herself. And if I *must* see her, I see her with Hester Dethridge for a witness. My part's done—let the lawyer do his."

He strolled round into the back garden, and lit his pipe. After a while, as the twilight faded, he saw a light in Hester's sitting-room on the ground-floor. He went to the window. Hester and the servant-girl were both there at work. "Well?" he asked. "How about the woman up stairs?" Hester's slate, aided by the girl's tongue, told him all about "the woman" that was to be told. They had taken up to her room tea and an omelet; and they had been obliged to wake her from a sleep. She had eaten a little of the omelet, and had drunk eagerly of the tea. They had gone up again to take the tray down. She had returned to the bed. She was not asleep—only dull and heavy. Made no remark. Looked clean worn out. We left her a light; and we let her be. Such was the report. After listening to it, without making any remark, Geoffrey filled a second pipe, and resumed his walk. The time wore on. It began to feel chilly in the garden. The rising wind swept audibly over the open lands round the cottage; the stars twinkled their last; nothing was to be seen overhead but the black void of night. More rain coming. Geoffrey went indoors.

An evening newspaper was on the dining-room table. The candles were lit. He sat down, and tried to read. No! There was nothing in the newspaper that he cared about. The time for hearing from the lawyer was drawing nearer and nearer. Reading was of no use. Sitting still was of no use. He got up, and went out in the front of the cottage—strolled to the gate—opened it—and looked idly up and down the road.

But one living creature was visible by the light of the gas-lamp over the gate. The creature came nearer, and proved to be the postman going his last round, with the last delivery for the night. He came up to the gate with a letter in his hand.

"The Honorable Geoffrey Delamayn?"

"All right."

He took the letter from the postman, and went back into the dining-room. Looking at the address by the light of the candles, he recognized the handwriting of Mrs. Glenarm. "To congratulate me on my marriage!" he said to himself, bitterly, and opened the letter.

Mrs. Glenarm's congratulations were expressed in these terms:

"MY ADORED GEOFFREY,—I have heard all. My beloved one! my own! you are sacrificed to the vilest wretch that walks the earth, and I have lost you! How is it that I live after hearing it? How is it that I can think, and write, with my brain on fire, and my heart broken! Oh, my angel, there is a purpose that supports me—pure, beautiful, worthy of us both. I live, Geoffrey—I live to dedicate myself to the adored idea of You. My hero! my first, last, love! I will marry no other man. I will live and die—I vow it solemnly on my bended knees—I will live and die true to You. I am your Spiritual Wife. My beloved Geoffrey! she can't come between us, there—she can never rob you of my heart's unalterable fidelity, of my soul's unearthly devotion. I am your Spiritual Wife! Oh, the blameless luxury of writing those words! Write back to me, beloved one, and say you feel it too. Vow it, idol of my heart, as I have vowed it. Unalterable fidelity! unearthly devotion! Never, never will I be the wife of any other man! Never, never will I forgive the woman who has come between us! Yours ever and only; yours with the stainless passion that burns on the altar of the heart; yours, yours, yours—E. G."

This outbreak of hysterical nonsense—in itself simply ridiculous—assumed a serious importance in its effect on Geoffrey. It associated the direct attainment of his own interests with the gratification of his vengeance on Anne. Ten thousand a year self-dedicated to him—and nothing to prevent his putting out his hand and taking it but the woman who had caught him in her trap, the woman up stairs who had fastened herself on him for life!

He put the letter into his pocket. "Wait till I hear from the lawyer," he said to himself. "The easiest way out of it is that way. And it's the law."

He looked impatiently at his watch. As he put it back again in his pocket there was a ring at the bell. Was it the lad bringing the luggage? Yes. And, with it, the lawyer's report? No. Better than that—the lawyer himself.

"Come in!" cried Geoffrey, meeting his visitor at the door.

The lawyer entered the dining-room. The candle-light revealed to view a corpulent, full-lipped, bright-eyed man—with a strain of negro blood in his yellow face, and with unmistakable traces in his look and manner of walking habitually in the dirtiest professional by-ways of the law.

"I've got a little place of my own in your neighborhood," he said. "And I thought I would look in myself, Mr. Delamayn, on my way home."

"Have you seen the witnesses?"

"I have examined them both, Sir. First, Mrs. Inchbare and Mr. Bishopriggs together. Next, Mrs. Inchbare and Mr. Bishopriggs separately."

"Well?"

"Well, Sir, the result is unfavorable, I am sorry to say."

"What do you mean?"

"Neither the one nor the other of them, Mr. Delamayn, can give the evidence we want. I have made sure of that."

"Made sure of that? You have made an infernal mess of it! You don't understand the case!"

The mulatto lawyer smiled. The rudeness of his client appeared only to amuse him.

"Don't I?" he said. "Suppose you tell me where I am wrong about it? Here it is in outline only. On the fourteenth of August last your wife was at an inn in Scotland. A gentleman named Arnold Brinkworth joined her there. He represented himself to be her husband, and he staid with her till the next morning. Starting from those facts, the object you have in view is to sue for a Divorce from your wife. You make Mr. Arnold Brinkworth the co-respondent. And you produce in evidence the waiter and the landlady of the inn. Any thing wrong, Sir, so far?"

Nothing wrong. At one cowardly stroke to cast Anne disgraced on the world, and to set himself free—there, plainly and truly stated, was the scheme which he had devised, when he had turned back on the way to Fulham to consult Mr. Moy.

"So much for the case," resumed the lawyer. "Now for what I have done on receiving your instructions. I have examined the witnesses;

and I have had an interview (not a very pleasant one) with Mr. Moy. The result of those two proceedings is briefly this. First discovery: In assuming the character of the lady's husband, Mr. Brinkworth was acting under your directions—which tells dead against *you*. Second discovery: Not the slightest impropriety of conduct, not an approach even to harmless familiarity, was detected by either of the witnesses, while the lady and gentleman were together at the inn. There is literally no evidence to produce against them, except that they *were* together—in two rooms. How are you to assume a guilty purpose, when you can't prove an approach to a guilty act? You can no more take such a case as that into Court than you can jump over the roof of this cottage."

He looked hard at his client, expecting to receive a violent reply. His client agreeably disappointed him. A very strange impression appeared to have been produced on this reckless and headstrong man. He got up quietly; he spoke with perfect outward composure of face and manner when he said his next words.

"Have you given up the case?"

"As things are at present, Mr. Delamayn, there is no case."

"And no hope of my getting divorced from her?"

"Wait a moment. Have your wife and Mr. Brinkworth met nowhere since they were together at the Scotch inn?"

"Nowhere."

"As to the future, of course I can't say. As to the past, there is no hope of your getting divorced from her."

"Thank you. Good-night."

"Good-night, Mr. Delamayn."

Fastened to her for life—and the law powerless to cut the knot.

He pondered over that result until he had thoroughly realized it and fixed it in his mind. Then he took out Mrs. Glenarm's letter, and read it through again, attentively, from beginning to end.

Nothing could shake her devotion to him. Nothing would induce her to marry another man. There she was—in her own words—dedicated to him: waiting, with her fortune at her own disposal, to be his wife. There also was his father, waiting (so far as *he* knew, in the absence of any tidings from Holchester House) to welcome Mrs. Glenarm as a daughter-in-law, and to give Mrs. Glenarm's husband an income of his own. As fair a prospect, on all sides, as man could desire. And nothing in the way of it but the woman who had caught him in her trap—the woman up stairs who had fastened herself on him for life.

He went out in the garden in the darkness of the night.

There was open communication, on all sides, between the back garden and the front. He walked round and round the cottage—now appearing in a stream of light from a window; now disappearing again in the darkness. The wind blew refreshingly over his bare head. For some minutes he went round and round, faster and faster, without a pause. When he stopped at last, it was in front of the cottage. He lifted his head slowly, and looked up at the dim light in the window of Anne's room.

"How?" he said to himself. "That's the question. How?"

He went indoors again, and rang the bell. The servant-girl who answered it started back at the sight of him. His florid color was all gone. His eyes looked at her without appearing to see her. The perspiration was standing on his forehead in great heavy drops.

"Are you ill, Sir?" said the girl.

He told her, with an oath, to hold her tongue and bring the brandy. When she entered the room for the second time, he was standing with his back to her, looking out at the night. He never moved when she put the bottle on the table. She heard him muttering as if he was talking to himself.

The same difficulty which had been present to his mind in secret under Anne's window was present to his mind still.

How? That was the problem to solve. How?

He turned to the brandy, and took counsel of that.

---

## CHAPTER THE FIFTIETH.

### THE MORNING.

WHEN does the vain regret find its keenest sting? When is the doubtful future blackened by its darkest cloud? When is life least worth having, and death oftenest at the bedside? In the terrible morning hours, when the sun is rising in its glory, and the birds are singing in the stillness of the new-born day.

Anne woke in the strange bed, and looked round her, by the light of the new morning, at the strange room.

The rain had all fallen in the night. The sun was master in the clear autumn sky. She rose, and opened the window. The fresh morning air, keen and fragrant, filled the room. Far and near, the same bright stillness possessed the view. She stood at the window looking out. Her mind was clear again—she could think, she could feel; she could face the one last question which the merciless morning now forced on her—How will it end?

Was there any hope?—hope, for instance, in what she might do for herself. What can a married woman do for herself? She can make her misery public—provided it be misery of a certain kind—and can reckon single-handed with Society when she has done it. Nothing more.

Was there hope in what others might do for her? Blanche might write to her—might even come and see her—if her husband allowed it; and that was all. Sir Patrick had pressed her hand at parting, and had told her to rely on him. He was the firmest, the truest of friends. But what could he do? There were outrages which her husband was privileged to commit, under the sanction of marriage, at the bare thought of which her blood ran cold. Could Sir Patrick protect her? Absurd! Law and Society armed her husband with his conjugal rights. Law and Society had but one answer to give, if she appealed to them—You are his wife.

No hope in herself; no hope in her friends; no hope any where on earth. Nothing to be done but to wait for the end—with faith in the Divine Mercy; with faith in the better world.

She took out of her trunk a little book of

Prayers and Meditations—worn with much use —which had once belonged to her mother. She sat by the window reading it. Now and then she looked up from it—thinking. The parallel between her mother's position and her own position was now complete. Both married to husbands who hated them; to husbands whose interests pointed to mercenary alliances with other women; to husbands whose one want and one purpose was to be free from their wives. Strange, what different ways had led mother and daughter both to the same fate! Would the parallel hold to the end? "Shall I die," she wondered, thinking of her mother's last moments, "in Blanche's arms?"

The time had passed unheeded. The morning movement in the house had failed to catch her ear. She was first called out of herself to the sense of the present and passing events by the voice of the servant-girl outside the door.

"The master wants you, ma'am, down stairs."

She rose instantly, and put away the little book.

"Is that all the message?" she asked, opening the door.

"Yes, ma'am."

She followed the girl down stairs; recalling to her memory the strange words addressed to her by Geoffrey, in the presence of the servants, on the evening before. Was she now to know what those words really meant? The doubt would soon be set at rest. "Be the trial what it may," she thought to herself, "let me bear it as my mother would have borne it."

The servant opened the door of the dining-room. Breakfast was on the table. Geoffrey was standing at the window. Hester Dethridge was waiting, posted near the door. He came forward—with the nearest approach to gentleness in his manner which she had ever yet seen in it—he came forward, with a set smile on his lips, and offered her his hand!

She had entered the room, prepared (as she believed) for any thing that could happen. She was not prepared for this. She stood speechless, looking at him.

After one glance at her, when she came in, Hester Dethridge looked at him, too—and from that moment never looked away again, as long as Anne remained in the room.

He broke the silence—in a voice that was not like his own; with a furtive restraint in his manner which she had never noticed in it before.

"Won't you shake hands with your husband," he asked, "when your husband asks you?"

She mechanically put her hand in his. He dropped it instantly, with a start. "God! how cold!" he exclaimed. His own hand was burning hot, and shook incessantly.

He pointed to a chair at the head of the table. "Will you make the tea?" he asked.

She had given him her hand mechanically; she advanced a step mechanically — and then stopped.

"Would you prefer breakfasting by yourself?" he said.

"If you please," she answered, faintly.

"Wait a minute. I have something to say before you go."

She waited. He considered with himself; consulting his memory—visibly, unmistakably, consulting it before he spoke again.

"I have had the night to think in," he said. "The night has made a new man of me. I beg your pardon for what I said yesterday. I was not myself yesterday. I talked nonsense yesterday. Please to forget it, and forgive it. I wish to turn over a new leaf, and make amends—make amends for my past conduct. It shall be my endeavor to be a good husband. In the presence of Mrs. Dethridge, I request you to give me a chance. I won't force your inclinations. We are married—what's the use of regretting it? Stay here, as you said yesterday, on your own terms. I wish to make it up. In the presence of Mrs. Dethridge, I say I wish to make it up. I won't detain you. I request you to think of it. Good-morning."

He said those extraordinary words like a slow boy saying a hard lesson—his eyes on the ground, his fingers restlessly fastening and unfastening a button on his waistcoat.

Anne left the room. In the passage she was obliged to wait, and support herself against the wall. His unnatural politeness was horrible; his carefully asserted repentance chilled her to the soul with dread. She had never felt—in the time of his fiercest anger and his foulest language —the unutterable horror of him that she felt now.

Hester Dethridge came out, closing the door behind her. She looked attentively at Anne—then wrote on her slate, and held it out, with these words on it:

"Do you believe him?"

Anne pushed the slate away, and ran up stairs. She fastened the door—and sank into a chair.

"He is plotting something against me," she said to herself. "What?"

A sickening, physical sense of dread—entirely new in her experience of herself—made her shrink from pursuing the question. The sinking at her heart turned her faint. She went to get the air at the open window.

At the same moment there was a ring at the gate bell. Suspicious of any thing and every thing, she felt a sudden distrust of letting herself be seen. She drew back behind the curtain and looked out.

A man-servant, in livery, was let in. He had a letter in his hand. He said to the girl as he passed Anne's window, "I come from Lady Holchester; I must see Mr. Delamayn instantly."

They went in. There was an interval. The footman reappeared, leaving the place. There was another interval. Then there came a knock at the door. Anne hesitated. The knock was repeated, and the dumb murmuring of Hester Dethridge was heard outside. Anne opened the door.

Hester came in with the breakfast. She pointed to a letter among other things on the tray. It was addressed to Anne, in Geoffrey's handwriting, and it contained these words:

"My father died yesterday. Write your orders for your mourning. The boy will take them. You are not to trouble yourself to go to London. Somebody is to come here to you from the shop."

Anne dropped the paper on her lap without looking up. At the same moment Hester Dethridge's slate was passed stealthily between her eyes and the note—with these words traced on it:

"His mother is coming to-day. His brother

has been telegraphed from Scotland. He was drunk last night. He's drinking again. I know what that means. Look out, missus—look out."

Anne signed to her to leave the room. She went out, pulling the door to, but not closing it behind her.

There was another ring at the gate bell. Once more Anne went to the window. Only the lad, this time; arriving to take his orders for the day. He had barely entered the garden when he was followed by the postman with letters. In a minute more Geoffrey's voice was heard in the passage, and Geoffrey's heavy step ascended the wooden stairs. Anne hurried across the room to draw the bolts. Geoffrey met her before she could close the door.

"A letter for you," he said, keeping scrupulously out of the room. "I don't wish to force your inclinations—I only request you to tell me who it's from."

His manner was as carefully subdued as ever. But the unacknowledged distrust in him (when he looked at her) betrayed itself in his eye.

She glanced at the handwriting on the address. "From Blanche," she answered.

He softly put his foot between the door and the post—and waited until she had opened and read Blanche's letter.

"May I see it?" he asked—and put in his hand for it through the door.

The spirit in Anne which would once have resisted him was dead in her now. She handed him the open letter.

It was very short. Excepting some brief expressions of fondness, it was studiously confined to stating the purpose for which it had been written. Blanche proposed to visit Anne that afternoon, accompanied by her uncle; she sent word beforehand, to make sure of finding Anne at home. That was all. The letter had evidently been written under Sir Patrick's advice.

Geoffrey handed it back, after first waiting a moment to think.

"My father died yesterday," he said. "My wife can't receive visitors before he is buried. I don't wish to force your inclinations. I only say I can't let visitors in here before the funeral—except my own family. Send a note down stairs. The lad will take it to your friend when he goes to London." With those words, he left her.

An appeal to the proprieties of life, in the mouth of Geoffrey Delamayn, could only mean one of two things. Either he had spoken in brutal mockery—or he had spoken with some ulterior object in view. Had he seized on the event of his father's death as a pretext for isolating his wife from all communication with the outer world? Were there reasons, which had not yet asserted themselves, for his dreading the result, if he allowed Anne to communicate with her friends?

The hour wore on, and Hester Dethridge appeared again. The lad was waiting for Anne's orders for her mourning, and for her note to Mrs. Arnold Brinkworth.

Anne wrote the orders and the note. Once more the horrible slate appeared when she had done, between the writing paper and her eyes, with the hard lines of warning pitilessly traced on it. "He has locked the gate. When there's a ring we are to come to him for the key. He

has written to a woman. Name outside the letter, Mrs. Glenarm. He has had more brandy. Like my husband. Mind yourself."

The one way out of the high walls all round the cottage locked. Friends forbidden to see her. Solitary imprisonment, with her husband for a jailer. Before she had been four-and-twenty hours in the cottage it had come to that. And what was to follow?

She went back mechanically to the window. The sight of the outer world, the occasional view of a passing vehicle, helped to sustain her.

The lad appeared in the front garden departing to perform his errand to London. Geoffrey went with him to open the gate, and called after him, as he passed through it, "Don't forget the books!"

The "books?" What "books?" Who wanted them? The slightest thing now roused Anne's suspicion. For hours afterward the books haunted her mind.

He secured the gate and came back again. He stopped under Anne's window and called to her. She showed herself. "When you want air and exercise," he said, "the back garden is at your own disposal." He put the key of the gate in his pocket and returned to the house.

After some hesitation Anne decided on taking him at his word. In her state of suspense, to remain within the four walls of the bedroom was unendurable. If some lurking snare lay hid under the fair-sounding proposal which Geoffrey had made, it was less repellent to her boldly to prove what it might be than to wait pondering over it with her mind in the dark. She put on her hat and went down into the garden.

Nothing happened out of the common. Wherever he was he never showed himself. She wandered up and down, keeping on the side of the garden which was farthest from the dining-room window. To a woman, escape from the place was simply impossible. Setting out of the question the height of the walls, they were armed at the top with a thick setting of jagged broken glass. A small back-door in the end wall (intended probably for the gardener's use) was bolted and locked—the key having been taken out. There was not a house near. The lands of the local growers of vegetables surrounded the garden on all sides. In the nineteenth century, and in the immediate neighborhood of a great metropolis, Anne was as absolutely isolated from all contact with the humanity around her as if she lay in her grave.

After the lapse of half an hour the silence was broken by a noise of carriage wheels on the public road in front, and a ring at the bell. Anne kept close to the cottage, at the back; determined, if a chance offered, on speaking to the visitor, whoever the visitor might be.

She heard voices in the dining-room through the open window—Geoffrey's voice and the voice of a woman. Who was the woman? Not Mrs. Glenarm, surely? After a while the visitor's voice was suddenly raised. "Where is she?" it said. "I wish to see her." Anne instantly advanced to the back-door of the house—and found herself face to face with a lady who was a total stranger to her.

"Are you my son's wife?" asked the lady.

"I am your son's prisoner," Anne answered.

Lady Holchester's pale face turned paler still.

It was plain that Anne's reply had confirmed some doubt in the mother's mind which had been already suggested to it by the son.

"What do you mean?" she asked, in a whisper.

Geoffrey's heavy footsteps crossed the dining-room. There was no time to explain. Anne whispered back,

"Tell my friends what I have told you."

Geoffrey appeared at the dining-room door.

"Name one of your friends," said Lady Holchester.

"Sir Patrick Lundie."

Geoffrey heard the answer. "What about Sir Patrick Lundie?" he asked.

"I wish to see Sir Patrick Lundie," said his mother. "And your wife can tell me where to find him."

Anne instantly understood that Lady Holchester would communicate with Sir Patrick. She mentioned his London address. Lady Holchester turned to leave the cottage. Her son stopped her.

"Let's set things straight," he said, "before you go. My mother," he went on, addressing himself to Anne, "don't think there's much chance for us two of living comfortably together. Bear witness to the truth—will you? What did I tell you at breakfast-time? Didn't I say it should be my endeavor to make you a good husband? Didn't I say—in Mrs. Dethridge's presence—I wanted to make it up?" He waited until Anne had answered in the affirmative, and then appealed to his mother. "Well? what do you think now?"

Lady Holchester declined to reveal what she thought. "You shall see me, or hear from me, this evening," she said to Anne. Geoffrey attempted to repeat his unanswered question. His mother looked at him. His eyes instantly dropped before hers. She gravely bent her head to Anne, and drew her veil. Her son followed her out in silence to the gate.

Anne returned to her room, sustained by the first sense of relief which she had felt since the morning. "His mother is alarmed," she said to herself. "A change will come."

A change *was* to come — with the coming night.

---

## CHAPTER THE FIFTY-FIRST.

### THE PROPOSAL.

TOWARD sunset, Lady Holchester's carriage drew up before the gate of the cottage.

Three persons occupied the carriage: Lady Holchester, her eldest son (now Lord Holchester), and Sir Patrick Lundie.

"Will you wait in the carriage, Sir Patrick?" said Julius. "Or will you come in?"

"I will wait. If I can be of the least use to *her*, send for me instantly. In the mean time, don't forget to make the stipulation which I have suggested. It is the one certain way of putting your brother's real feeling in this matter to the test."

The servant had rung the bell without producing any result. He rang again. Lady Holchester put a question to Sir Patrick.

"If I have an opportunity of speaking to my son's wife alone," she said, "have you any message to give?"

Sir Patrick produced a little note.

"May I appeal to your ladyship's kindness to give her this?" The gate was opened by the servant-girl, as Lady Holchester took the note. "Remember," reiterated Sir Patrick, earnestly, "if I can be of the smallest service to her—don't think of my position with Mr. Delamayn. Send for me at once."

Julius and his mother were conducted into the drawing-room. The girl informed them that her master had gone up stairs to lie down, and that he would be with them immediately.

Both mother and son were too anxious to speak. Julius wandered uneasily about the room. Some books attracted his notice on a table in the corner—four dirty, greasy volumes, with a slip of paper projecting from the leaves of one of them, and containing this inscription, "With Mr. Perry's respects." Julius opened the volume. It was the ghastly popular record of Criminal Trials in England, called the Newgate Calendar. Julius showed it to his mother.

"Geoffrey's taste in literature!" he said, with a faint smile.

Lady Holchester signed to him to put the book back.

"You have seen Geoffrey's wife already—have you not?" she asked.

There was no contempt now in her tone when she referred to Anne. The impression produced on her by her visit to the cottage, earlier in the day, associated Geoffrey's wife with family anxieties of no trivial kind. She might still (for Mrs. Glenarm's sake) be a woman to be disliked—but she was no longer a woman to be despised.

"I saw her when she came to Swanhaven," said Julius. "I agree with Sir Patrick in thinking her a very interesting person."

"What did Sir Patrick say to you about Geoffrey this afternoon—while I was out of the room?"

"Only what he said to *you*. He thought their position toward each other here a very deplorable one. He considered that the reasons were serious for our interfering immediately."

"Sir Patrick's own opinion, Julius, goes farther than that."

"He has not acknowledged it, that I know of."

"How *can* he acknowledge it—to us?"

The door opened, and Geoffrey entered the room.

Julius eyed him closely as they shook hands. His eyes were bloodshot; his face was flushed; his utterance was thick—the look of him was the look of a man who had been drinking hard.

"Well?" he said to his mother. "What brings you back?"

"Julius has a proposal to make to you," Lady Holchester answered. "I approve of it; and I have come with him."

Geoffrey turned to his brother.

"What can a rich man like you want with a poor devil like me?" he asked.

"I want to do you justice, Geoffrey—if you will help me, by meeting me half-way. Our mother has told you about the will?"

"I'm not down for a half-penny in the will. I expected as much. Go on."

"You are wrong—you *are* down in it. There is liberal provision made for you in a codicil. Unhappily, my father died without signing it. It is needless to say that I consider it binding on me for all that. I am ready to do for you what your father would have done for you. And I only ask for one concession in return."

"What may that be?"

"You are living here very unhappily, Geoffrey, with your wife."

"Who says so? I don't, for one."

Julius laid his hand kindly on his brother's arm.

"Don't trifle with such a serious matter as this," he said. "Your marriage is, in every sense of the word, a misfortune—not only to you but to your wife. It is impossible that you can live together. I have come here to ask you to consent to a separation. Do that—and the provision made for you in the unsigned codicil is yours. What do you say?"

Geoffrey shook his brother's hand off his arm.

"I say—No!" he answered.

Lady Holchester interfered for the first time.

"Your brother's generous offer deserves a better answer than that," she said.

"My answer," reiterated Geoffrey, "is—No!"

He sat between them with his clenched fists resting on his knees—absolutely impenetrable to any thing that either of them could say.

"In your situation," said Julius, "a refusal is sheer madness. I won't accept it."

"Do as you like about that. My mind's made up. I won't let my wife be taken away from me. Here she stays."

The brutal tone in which he had made that reply roused Lady Holchester's indignation.

"Take care!" she said. "You are not only behaving with the grossest ingratitude toward your brother—you are forcing a suspicion into your mother's mind. You have some motive that you are hiding from us."

He turned on his mother with a sudden ferocity which made Julius spring to his feet. The next instant his eyes were on the ground, and the devil that possessed him was quiet again.

"Some motive I'm hiding from you?" he repeated, with his head down, and his utterance thicker than ever. "I'm ready to have my motive posted all over London, if you like. I'm fond of her."

He looked up as he said the last words. Lady Holchester turned away her head—recoiling from her own son. So overwhelming was the shock inflicted on her that even the strongly rooted prejudice which Mrs. Glenarm had implanted in her mind yielded to it. At that moment she absolutely pitied Anne!

"Poor creature!" said Lady Holchester.

He took instant offense at those two words. "I won't have my wife pitied by any body." With that reply, he dashed into the passage; and called out, "Anne! come down!"

Her soft voice answered; her light footfall was heard on the stairs. She came into the room. Julius advanced, took her hand, and held it kindly in his. "We are having a little family discussion," he said, trying to give her confidence. "And Geoffrey is getting hot over it, as usual."

Geoffrey appealed sternly to his mother.

"Look at her!" he said. "Is she starved? Is she in rags? Is she covered with bruises?" He turned to Anne. "They have come here to propose a separation. They both believe I

hate you. I don't hate you. I'm a good Christian. I owe it to you that I'm cut out of my father's will. I forgive you that. I owe it to you that I've lost the chance of marrying a woman with ten thousand a year. I forgive you that. I'm not a man who does things by halves. I said it should be my endeavor to make you a good husband. I said it was my wish to make it up. Well! I am as good as my word. And what's the consequence? I am insulted. My mother comes here, and my brother comes here—and they offer me money to part from you. Money be hanged! I'll be beholden to nobody. I'll get my own living. Shame on the people who interfere between man and wife! Shame!—that's what I say—shame!"

Anne looked, for an explanation, from her husband to her husband's mother.

"Have you proposed a separation between us?" she asked.

"Yes—on terms of the utmost advantage to my son; arranged with every possible consideration toward you. Is there any objection on your side?"

"Oh, Lady Holchester! is it necessary to ask me? What does he say?"

"He has refused."

"Refused!"

"Yes," said Geoffrey. "I don't go back from my word; I stick to what I said this morning. It's my endeavor to make you a good husband. It's my wish to make it up." He paused, and then added his last reason: "I'm fond of you."

Their eyes met as he said it to her. Julius felt Anne's hand suddenly tighten round his. The desperate grasp of the frail cold fingers, the imploring terror in the gentle sensitive face as it slowly turned his way, said to him as if in words, "Don't leave me friendless to-night!"

"If you both stop here till domesday," said Geoffrey, "you'll get nothing more out of me. You have had my reply."

With that, he seated himself doggedly in a corner of the room; waiting—ostentatiously waiting—for his mother and his brother to take their leave. The position was serious. To argue the matter with him that night was hopeless. To invite Sir Patrick's interference could only be to provoke his savage temper to a new outbreak. On the other hand, to leave the helpless woman, after what had passed, without another effort to befriend her, was, in her situation, an act of downright inhumanity, and nothing less. Julius took the one way out of the difficulty that was left—the one way worthy of him as a compassionate and an honorable man.

"We will drop it for to-night, Geoffrey," he said. "But I am not the less resolved, in spite of all that you have said, to return to the subject to-morrow. It would save me some inconvenience—a second journey here from town, and then going back again to my engagements—if I staid with you to-night. Can you give me a bed?"

A look flashed on him from Anne, which thanked him as no words could have thanked him.

"Give you a bed?" repeated Geoffrey. He checked himself, on the point of refusing. His mother was watching him; his wife was watching him—and his wife knew that the room above them was a room to spare. "All right!" he resumed, in another tone, with his eye on his mother. "There's an empty room up stairs. Have it, if you like. You won't find I've changed my mind to-morrow—but that's your look-out. Stop here, if the fancy takes you. I've no objection. It don't matter to Me.—Will you trust his lordship under my roof?" he added, addressing his mother. "I might have some motive that I'm hiding from you, you know!" Without waiting for an answer, he turned to Anne. "Go and tell old Dummy to put the sheets on the bed. Say there's a live lord in the house—she's to send in something devilish good for supper!"

He burst fiercely into a forced laugh. Lady Holchester rose at the moment when Anne was leaving the room.

"I shall not be here when you return," she said. "Let me bid you good-night."

She shook hands with Anne—giving her Sir Patrick's note, unseen, at the same moment. Anne left the room. Without addressing another word to her second son, Lady Holchester beckoned to Julius to give her his arm. "You have acted nobly toward your brother," she said to him. "My one comfort and my one hope, Julius, are in you." They went out together to the gate, Geoffrey following them with the key in his hand. "Don't be too anxious," Julius whispered to his mother. "I will keep the drink out of his way to-night—and I will bring you a better account of him to-morrow. Explain every thing to Sir Patrick as you go home." He handed Lady Holchester into the carriage; and re-entered, leaving Geoffrey to lock the gate.

The brothers returned in silence to the cottage. Julius had concealed it from his mother —but he was seriously uneasy in secret. Naturally prone to look at all things on their brighter side, he could place no hopeful interpretation on what Geoffrey had said and done that night. The conviction that he was deliberately acting a part, in his present relations with his wife, for some abominable purpose of his own, had rooted itself firmly in Julius. For the first time in his experience of his brother, the pecuniary consideration was not the uppermost consideration in Geoffrey's mind.

They went back into the drawing-room.

"What will you have to drink?" said Geoffrey.

"Nothing."

"You won't keep me company over a drop of brandy-and-water?"

"No. You have had enough brandy-and-water."

After a moment of frowning self-consideration in the glass, Geoffrey abruptly agreed with Julius. "I look like it," he said. "I'll soon put that right." He disappeared, and returned with a wet towel tied round his head. "What will you do while the women are getting your bed ready? Liberty Hall here. I've taken to cultivating my mind—I'm a reformed character, you know, now I'm a married man. You do what you like. I shall read."

He turned to the side-table; and, producing the volumes of the Newgate Calendar, gave one to his brother. Julius handed it back again.

"You won't cultivate your mind," he said, "with such a book as that. Vile actions, recorded in vile English, make vile reading, Geoffrey, in every sense of the word."

"It will do for me. I don't know good English when I see it."

With that frank acknowledgment—to which the great majority of his companions at school and college might have subscribed without doing the slightest injustice to the present state of English education—Geoffrey drew his chair to the table, and opened one of the volumes of his record of crime.

The evening newspaper was lying on the sofa. Julius took it up, and seated himself opposite to his brother. He noticed, with some surprise, that Geoffrey appeared to have a special object in consulting his book. Instead of beginning at the first page, he ran the leaves through his fingers, and turned them down at certain places, before he entered on his reading. If Julius had looked over his brother's shoulder, instead of only looking at him across the table, he would have seen that Geoffrey passed by all the lighter crimes reported in the Calendar, and marked for his own private reading the cases of murder only.

---

## CHAPTER THE FIFTY-SECOND.

### THE APPARITION.

THE night had advanced. It was close on twelve o'clock, when Anne heard the servant's voice, outside her bedroom door, asking leave to speak with her for a moment.

"What is it?"

"The gentleman down stairs wishes to see you, ma'am."

"Do you mean Mr. Delamayn's brother?"

"Yes."

"Where is Mr. Delamayn?"

"Out in the garden, ma'am."

Anne went down stairs, and found Julius alone in the drawing-room.

"I am sorry to disturb you," he said. "I am afraid Geoffrey is ill. The landlady has gone to bed, I am told—and I don't know where to apply for medical assistance. Do you know of any doctor in the neighborhood?"

Anne, like Julius, was a perfect stranger to the neighborhood. She suggested making inquiry of the servant. On speaking to the girl, it turned out that she knew of a medical man, living within ten minutes' walk of the cottage. She could give plain directions enabling any person to find the place—but she was afraid, at that hour of the night and in that lonely neighborhood, to go out by herself.

"Is he seriously ill?" Anne asked.

"He is in such a state of nervous irritability," said Julius, "that he can't remain still for two moments together in the same place. It began with incessant restlessness while he was reading here. I persuaded him to go to bed. He couldn't lie still for an instant—he came down again, burning with fever, and more restless than ever. He is out in the garden in spite of every thing I could do to prevent him; trying, as he says, to 'run it off.' It appears to be serious to me. Come and judge for yourself."

He led Anne into the next room; and, opening the shutter, pointed to the garden.

The clouds had cleared off; the night was fine. The clear starlight showed Geoffrey, stripped to his shirt and drawers, running round and round the garden. He apparently believed himself to be contending at the Fulham foot-race. At times, as the white figure circled round and round in the star-light, they heard him cheering for "the South." The slackening thump of his feet on the ground, the heavier and heavier gasps in which he drew his breath, as he passed the window, gave warning that his strength was failing him. Exhaustion, if it led to no worse consequences, would force him to return to the house. In the state of his brain at that moment, who could say what the result might be, if medical help was not called in?

"I will go for the doctor," said Julius, "if you don't mind my leaving you."

It was impossible for Anne to set any apprehensions of her own against the plain necessity for summoning assistance. They found the key of the gate in the pocket of Geoffrey's coat up stairs. Anne went with Julius to let him out. "How can I thank you!" she said, gratefully. "What should I have done without *you!*"

"I won't be a moment longer than I can help," he answered, and left her.

She secured the gate again, and went back to the cottage. The servant met her at the door, and proposed calling up Hester Dethridge.

"We don't know what the master may do while his brother's away," said the girl. "And one more of us isn't one too many, when we are only women in the house."

"You are quite right," said Anne. "Wake your mistress."

After ascending the stairs, they looked out into the garden, through the window at the end of the passage on the upper floor. He was still going round and round, but very slowly: his pace was fast slackening to a walk.

Anne went back to her room, and waited near the open door—ready to close and fasten it instantly if any thing occurred to alarm her. "How changed I am!" she thought to herself. "Every thing frightens me, now."

The inference was the natural one—but not the true one. The change was not in herself, but in the situation in which she was placed. Her position during the investigation at Lady Lundie's house had tried her moral courage only. It had exacted from her one of those noble efforts of self-sacrifice which the hidden forces in a woman's nature are essentially capable of making. Her position at the cottage tried her physical courage: it called on her to rise superior to the sense of actual bodily danger—while that danger was lurking in the dark. There, the woman's nature sank under the stress laid on it—there, her courage could strike no root in the strength of her love—there, the animal instincts were the instincts appealed to; and the firmness wanted was the firmness of a man.

Hester Dethridge's door opened. She walked straight into Anne's room.

The yellow clay-cold color of her face showed a faint flush of warmth; its deathlike stillness was stirred by a touch of life. The stony eyes, fixed as ever in their gaze, shone strangely with a dim inner lustre. Her gray hair, so neatly arranged at other times, was in disorder under her cap. All her movements were quicker than usual. Something had roused the stagnant vitality in the woman—it was working in her mind; it was forcing itself outward into her face. The servants at Windygates, in past times, had seen these signs, and had known them for a warning to leave Hester Dethridge to herself.

Anne asked her if she had heard what had happened.

She bowed her head.

"I hope you don't mind being disturbed?"

She wrote on her slate: "I'm glad to be disturbed. I have been dreaming bad dreams. It's good for me to be wakened, when sleep takes me backward in my life. What's wrong with you? Frightened?"

"Yes."

She wrote again, and pointed toward the garden with one hand, while she held the slate up with the other: "Frightened of *him?*"

"Terribly frightened."

She wrote for the third time, and offered the slate to Anne with a ghastly smile: "I have been through it all. I know. You're only at the beginning now. He'll put the wrinkles in your face, and the gray in your hair. There will come a time when you'll wish yourself dead and buried. You will live through it, for all that. Look at Me."

As she read the last three words, Anne heard the garden door below opened and banged to again. She caught Hester Dethridge by the arm, and listened. The tramp of Geoffrey's feet, staggering heavily in the passage, gave token of his approach to the stairs. He was talking to himself, still possessed by the delusion that he was at the foot-race. "Five to four on Delamayn. Delamayn's won. Three cheers for the South, and one cheer more. Devilish long race. Night already! Perry! where's Perry?"

He advanced, staggering from side to side of the passage. The stairs below creaked as he set his foot on them. Hester Dethridge dragged herself free from Anne, advanced, with her candle in her hand, and threw open Geoffrey's bedroom door; returned to the head of the stairs; and stood there, firm as a rock, waiting for him. He looked up, as he set his foot on the next stair, and met the view of Hester's face, brightly illuminated by the candle, looking down at him. On the instant he stopped, rooted to the place on which he stood. "Ghost! witch! devil!" he cried out, "take your eyes off me!" He shook his fist at her furiously, with an oath—sprang back into the hall—and shut himself into the dining-room from the sight of her. The panic which had seized him once already in the kitchen-garden at Windygates, under the eyes of the dumb cook, had fastened its hold on him once more. Frightened—absolutely frightened —of Hester Dethridge!

The gate bell rang. Julius had returned with the doctor.

Anne gave the key to the girl to let them in. Hester wrote on her slate, as composedly as if nothing had happened: "They'll find me in the kitchen, if they want me. I sha'n't go back to my bedroom. My bedroom's full of bad dreams." She descended the stairs. Anne waited in the upper passage, looking over into the hall below. "Your brother is in the drawing-room," she called down to Julius. "The landlady is in the kitchen, if you want her." She returned to her room, and waited for what might happen next.

After a brief interval she heard the drawing-room door open, and the voices of the men outside. There seemed to be some difficulty in persuading Geoffrey to ascend the stairs; he persisted in declaring that Hester Dethridge was waiting for him at the top of them. After a little they persuaded him that the way was free. Anne heard them ascend the stairs and close his bedroom door.

Another and a longer interval passed before the door opened again. The doctor was going away. He said his parting words to Julius in the passage. "Look in at him from time to time through the night, and give him another dose of the sedative mixture if he wakes. There is nothing to be alarmed about in the restlessness and the fever. They are only the outward manifestations of some serious mischief hidden under them. Send for the medical man who has last attended him. Knowledge of the patient's constitution is very important knowledge in this case."

As Julius returned from letting the doctor out, Anne met him in the hall. She was at once struck by the worn look in his face, and by the fatigue which expressed itself in all his movements.

"You want rest," she said. "Pray go to your room. I have heard what the doctor said to you. Leave it to the landlady and to me to sit up."

Julius owned that he had been traveling from Scotland during the previous night. But he was unwilling to abandon the responsibility of watching his brother. "You are not strong enough, I am sure, to take my place," he said, kindly. "And Geoffrey has some unreasoning horror of the landlady, which makes it very undesirable that he should see her again, in his present state. I will go up to my room, and rest on the bed. If you hear any thing you have only to come and call me."

An hour more passed.

Anne went to Geoffrey's door and listened. He was stirring in his bed, and muttering to himself. She went on to the door of the next room, which Julius had left partly open. Fatigue had overpowered him; she heard, within, the quiet breathing of a man in a sound sleep. Anne turned back again resolved not to disturb him.

At the head of the stairs she hesitated—not knowing what to do. Her horror of entering Geoffrey's room, by herself, was insurmountable. But who else was to do it? The girl had gone to bed. The reason which Julius had given for not employing the assistance of Hester Dethridge was unanswerable. She listened again at Geoffrey's door. No sound was now audible in the room to a person in the passage outside. Would it be well to look in, and make sure that he had only fallen asleep again? She hesitated once more—she was still hesitating, when Hester Dethridge appeared from the kitchen.

She joined Anne at the top of the stairs—looked at her—and wrote a line on her slate: "Frightened to go in? Leave it to Me."

The silence in the room justified the inference that he was asleep. If Hester looked in, Hester could do no harm now. Anne accepted the proposal.

"If you find any thing wrong," she said, "don't disturb his brother. Come to me first."

With that caution she withdrew. It was then nearly two in the morning. She, like Julius,

was sinking from fatigue. After waiting a little, and hearing nothing, she threw herself on the sofa in her room. If any thing happened, a knock at the door would rouse her instantly.

In the mean while Hester Dethridge opened Geoffrey's bedroom door and went in.

The movements and the mutterings which Anne had heard, had been movements and mutterings in his sleep. The doctor's composing draught, partially disturbed in its operation for the moment only, had recovered its sedative influence on his brain. Geoffrey was in a deep and quiet sleep.

Hester stood near the door, looking at him. She moved to go out again—stopped—and fixed her eyes suddenly on one of the inner corners of the room.

The same sinister change which had passed over her once already in Geoffrey's presence, when they met in the kitchen-garden at Windygates, now passed over her again. Her closed lips dropped apart. Her eyes slowly dilated—moved, inch by inch from the corner, following something along the empty wall, in the direction of the bed—stopped at the head of the bed, exactly above Geoffrey's sleeping face—stared, rigid and glittering, as if they saw a sight of horror close over it. He sighed faintly in his sleep. The sound, slight as it was, broke the spell that held her. She slowly lifted her withered hands, and wrung them above her head; fled back across the passage; and, rushing into her room, sank on her knees at the bedside.

Now, in the dead of night, a strange thing happened. Now, in the silence and the darkness, a hideous secret was revealed.

In the sanctuary of her own room—with all the other inmates of the house sleeping round her —the dumb woman threw off the mysterious and terrible disguise under which she deliberately isolated herself among her fellow-creatures in the hours of the day. Hester Dethridge spoke. In low, thick, smothered accents—in a wild litany of her own—she prayed. She called upon the mercy of God for deliverance from herself; for deliverance from the possession of the Devil; for blindness to fall on her, for death to strike her, so that she might never see that unnamed Horror more! Sobs shook the whole frame of the stony woman whom nothing human moved at other times. Tears poured over those clay-cold cheeks. One by one, the frantic words of her prayer died away on her lips. Fierce shuddering fits shook her from head to foot. She started up from her knees in the darkness. Light! light! light! The unnamed Horror was behind her in his room. The unnamed Horror was looking at her through his open door. She found the match-box, and lit the candle on her table—lit the two other candles set for ornament only on the mantle-piece—and looked all round the brightly lighted little room. "Aha!" she said to herself, wiping the cold sweat of her agony from her face. "Candles to other people. God's light to *me*. Nothing to be seen! nothing to be seen!" Taking one of the candles in her hand, she crossed the passage, with her head down, turned her back on Geoffrey's open door, closed it quickly and softly, stretching out her hand behind her, and retreated again to her own room. She fastened the door, and took an ink-bottle and a pen from the mantle-piece. After considering for a moment, she hung a handkerchief over the keyhole, and laid an old shawl longwise at the bottom of the door, so as to hide the light in her room from the observation of any one in the house who might wake and come that way. This done, she opened the upper part of her dress, and, slipping her fingers into a secret pocket hidden in the inner side of her stays, produced from it some neatly folded leaves of thin paper. Spread out on the table, the leaves revealed themselves—all but the last—as closely covered with writing, in her own hand.

The first leaf was headed by this inscription: "My Confession. To be put into my coffin, and to be buried with me when I die."

She turned the manuscript over, so as to get at the last page. The greater part of it was left blank. A few lines of writing, at the top, bore the date of the day of the week and month on which Lady Lundie had dismissed her from her situation at Windygates. The entry was expressed in these terms:

"I have seen IT again to-day. The first time for two months past. In the kitchen-garden. Standing behind the young gentleman whose name is Delamayn. Resist the Devil, and he will flee from you. I have resisted. By prayer. By meditation in solitude. By reading good books. I have left my place. I have lost sight of the young gentleman for good. Who will IT stand behind? and point to next? Lord have mercy upon me! Christ have mercy upon me!"

Under this she now added the following lines, first carefully prefixing the date:

"I have seen IT again to-night. I notice one awful change. IT has appeared twice behind the same person. This has never happened before. This makes the temptation more terrible than ever. To-night, in his bedroom, between the bed-head and the wall, I have seen IT behind young Mr. Delamayn again. The head just above his face, and the finger pointing downward at his throat. Twice behind this one man. And never twice behind any other living creature till now. If I see IT a third time behind him—Lord deliver me! Christ deliver me! I daren't think of it. He shall leave my cottage to-morrow. I would fain have drawn back from the bargain, when the stranger took the lodgings for his friend, and the friend proved to be Mr. Delamayn. I didn't like it, even then. After the warning to-night, my mind is made up. He shall go. He may have his money back, if he likes. He shall go. (Memorandum: Felt the temptation whispering this time, and the terror tearing at me all the while, as I have never felt them yet. Resisted, as before, by prayer. Am now going down stairs to meditate against it in solitude—to fortify myself against it by good books. Lord be merciful to me a sinner!)"

In those words she closed the entry, and put the manuscript back in the secret pocket in her stays.

She went down to the little room looking on the garden, which had once been her brother's study. There she lit a lamp, and took some books from a shelf that hung against the wall. The books were the Bible, a volume of Methodist sermons, and a set of collected Memoirs of Methodist saints. Ranging these last carefully round her, in an order of her own, Hester Dethridge sat down with the Bible on her lap to watch out the night.

--------

## CHAPTER THE FIFTY-THIRD.

WHAT had happened in the hours of darkness?

This was Anne's first thought, when the sunlight poured in at her window, and woke her the next morning.

She made immediate inquiry of the servant. The girl could only speak for herself. Nothing had occurred to disturb her after she had gone to bed. Her master was still, she believed, in his room. Mrs. Dethridge was at her work in the kitchen.

Anne went to the kitchen. Hester Dethridge was at her usual occupation at that time—preparing the breakfast. The slight signs of animation which Anne had noticed in her when they last met appeared no more. The dull look was back again in her stony eyes; the lifeless torpor possessed all her movements. Asked if any thing had happened in the night, she slowly shook her stolid head, slowly made the sign with her hand which signified, "Nothing."

Leaving the kitchen, Anne saw Julius in the front garden. She went out and joined him.

"I believe I have to thank your consideration for me for some hours of rest," he said. "It was five in the morning when I woke. I hope you had no reason to regret having left me to sleep? I went into Geoffrey's room, and found him stirring. A second dose of the mixture composed him again. The fever has gone. He looks weaker and paler, but in other respects like himself. We will return directly to the question of his health. I have something to say to you, first, about a change which may be coming in your life here."

"Has he consented to the separation?"

"No. He is as obstinate about it as ever. I have placed the matter before him in every possible light. He still refuses, positively refuses, a provision which would make him an independent man for life."

"Is it the provision he might have had, Lord Holchester, if—?"

"If he had married Mrs. Glenarm? No. It is impossible, consistently with my duty to my mother, and with what I owe to the position in which my father's death has placed me, that I can offer him such a fortune as Mrs. Glenarm's. Still, it is a handsome income which he is mad enough to refuse. I shall persist in pressing it on him. He must and shall take it."

Anne felt no reviving hope roused in her by his last words. She turned to another subject.

"You had something to tell me," she said. "You spoke of a change."

"True. The landlady here is a very strange person; and she has done a very strange thing. She has given Geoffrey notice to quit these lodgings."

"Notice to quit?" Anne repeated, in amazement.

"Yes. In a formal letter. She handed it to me open, as soon as I was up this morning. It was impossible to get any explanation from her. The poor dumb creature simply wrote on her slate : ' He may have his money back, if he likes : he shall go !' Greatly to my surprise (for the woman inspires him with the strongest aversion) Geoffrey refuses to go until his term is up. I have made the peace between them for to-day. Mrs. Dethridge, very reluctantly, consents to give him four-and-twenty hours. And there the matter rests at present."

"What can her motive be ?" said Anne.

"It's useless to inquire. Her mind is evidently off its balance. One thing is clear, Geoffrey can not keep you here much longer. The coming change will remove you from this dismal place—which is one thing gained. And it is quite possible that new scenes and new surroundings may have their influence on Geoffrey for good. His conduct—otherwise quite incomprehensible—may be the result of some latent nervous irritation which medical help might reach. I don't attempt to disguise from myself or from you, that your position here is a most deplorable one. But before we despair of the future, let us at least inquire whether there is any explanation of my brother's present behavior to be found in the present state of my brother's health. I have been considering what the doctor said to me last night. The first thing to do is to get the best medical advice on Geoffrey's case which is to be had. What do you think ?"

"I daren't tell you what I think, Lord Holchester. I will try—it is a very small return to make for your kindness—I will try to see my position with your eyes, not with mine. The best medical advice that you can obtain is the advice of Mr. Speedwell. It was he who first made the discovery that your brother was in broken health."

"The very man for our purpose ! I will send him here to-day or to-morrow. Is there any thing else I can do for you ? I shall see Sir Patrick as soon as I get to town. Have you any message for him ?"

Anne hesitated. Looking attentively at her, Julius noticed that she changed color when he mentioned Sir Patrick's name.

"Will you say that I gratefully thank him for the letter which Lady Holchester was so good as to give me last night," she replied. "And will you entreat him, from me, not to expose himself, on my account, to—" she hesitated, and finished the sentence with her eyes on the ground —"to what might happen, if he came here and insisted on seeing me."

"Does he propose to do that ?"

She hesitated again. The little nervous contraction of her lips at one side of the mouth became more marked than usual. "He writes that his anxiety is unendurable, and that he is resolved to see me," she answered, softly.

"He is likely to hold to his resolution, I think," said Julius. "When I saw him yesterday, Sir Patrick spoke of you in terms of admiration—"

He stopped. The bright tears were glittering on Anne's eyelashes ; one of her hands was toying nervously with something hidden (possibly Sir Patrick's letter) in the bosom of her dress. "I thank him with my whole heart," she said, in low, faltering tones. "But it is best that he should not come here."

"Would you like to write to him ?"

"I think I should prefer your giving him my message."

Julius understood that the subject was to proceed no further. Sir Patrick's letter had produced some impression on her, which the sensitive nature of the woman seemed to shrink from acknowledging, even to herself. They turned back to enter the cottage. At the door they were met by a surprise. Hester Dethridge, with her bonnet on—dressed, at that hour of the morning, to go out !

"Are you going to market already ?" Anne asked.

Hester shook her head.

"When are you coming back ?"

Hester wrote on her slate : "Not till the night-time."

Without another word of explanation she pulled her veil down over her face, and made for the gate. The key had been left in the dining-room by Julius, after he had let the doctor out. Hester had it in her hand. She opened the gate, and closed the door after her, leaving the key in the lock. At the moment when the door banged to Geoffrey appeared in the passage.

"Where's the key ?" he asked. "Who's gone out ?"

His brother answered the question. He looked backward and forward suspiciously between Julius and Anne. "What does she go out for at this time ?" he said. "Has she left the house to avoid Me ?"

Julius thought this the likely explanation. Geoffrey went down sulkily to the gate to lock it, and returned to them, with the key in his pocket.

"I'm obliged to be careful of the gate," he said. "The neighborhood swarms with beggars and tramps. If you want to go out," he added, turning pointedly to Anne, "I'm at your service, as a good husband ought to be."

After a hurried breakfast Julius took his departure. "I don't accept your refusal," he said to his brother, before Anne. "You will see me here again." Geoffrey obstinately repeated refusal. "If you come here every day of your life," he said, "it will be just the same."

The gate closed on Julius. Anne returned again to the solitude of her own chamber. Geoffrey entered the drawing-room, placed the volumes of the Newgate Calendar on the table before him, and resumed the reading which he had been unable to continue on the evening before.

Hour after hour he doggedly plodded through one case of murder after another. He had read one good half of the horrid chronicle of crime before his power of fixing his attention began to fail him. Then he lit his pipe, and went out to think over it in the garden. However the atrocities of which he had been reading might differ in other respects, there was one terrible point of resemblance, which he had not anticipated, and in which every one of the cases agreed. Sooner or later, there was the dead body always certain to be found ; always bearing its dumb witness, in the traces of poison or in the marks of violence, to the crime committed on it.

He walked to and fro slowly, still pondering over the problem which had first found its way into his mind when he had stopped in the front garden, and had looked up at Anne's window in the dark. "How ?" That had been the one question before him, from the time when the lawyer had annihilated his hopes of a divorce. It remained the one question still. There was no answer to it in his own brain; there was no answer to it in the book which he had been consulting. Every thing was in his favor if he could only find out "how." He had got his hated wife up stairs at his mercy—thanks to his refusal of the money which Julius had offered to him. He was living in a place absolutely secluded from public observation on all sides of it—thanks to his resolution to remain at the cottage, even after his landlady had insulted him by sending him a notice to quit. Every thing had been prepared, every thing had been sacrificed, to the fulfillment of one purpose—and how to attain that purpose was still the same impenetrable mystery to him which it had been from the first!

What was the other alternative? To accept the proposal which Julius had made. In other words, to give up his vengeance on Anne, and to turn his back on the splendid future which Mrs. Glenarm's devotion still offered to him.

Never! He would go back to the books. He was not at the end of them. The slightest hint in the pages which were still to be read might set his sluggish brain working in the right direction. The way to be rid of her, without exciting the suspicion of any living creature, in the house or out of it, was a way that might be found yet.

Could a man, in his position of life, reason in this brutal manner? could he act in this merciless way? Surely the thought of what he was about to do must have troubled him this time!

Pause for a moment—and look back at him in the past.

Did he feel any remorse when he was plotting the betrayal of Arnold in the garden at Windygates? The sense which feels remorse had not been put into him. What he is now is the legitimate consequence of what he was then. A far more serious temptation is now urging him to commit a far more serious crime. How is he to resist? Will his skill in rowing (as Sir Patrick once put it), his swiftness in running, his admirable capacity and endurance in other physical exercises, help him to win a purely moral victory over his own selfishness and his own cruelty? No! The moral and mental neglect of himself, which the material tone of public feeling about him has tacitly encouraged, has left him at the mercy of the worst instincts in his nature—of all that is most vile and of all that is most dangerous in the composition of the natural man. With the mass of his fellows, no harm out of the common has come of this, because no temptation out of the common has passed their way. But with him, the case is reversed. A temptation out of the common has passed his way. How does it find him prepared to meet it? It finds him, literally and exactly, what his training has left him, in the presence of any temptation small or great—a defenseless man.

Geoffrey returned to the cottage. The servant stopped him in the passage, to ask at what time he wished to dine. Instead of answering, he inquired angrily for Mrs. Dethridge. Mrs. Dethridge had not come back.

It was now late in the afternoon, and she had been out since the early morning. This had

never happened before. Vague suspicions of her, one more monstrous than another, began to rise in Geoffrey's mind. Between the drink and the fever, he had been (as Julius had told him) wandering in his mind during a part of the night. Had he let any thing out in that condition? Had Hester heard it? And was it, by any chance, at the bottom of her long absence and her notice to quit? He determined—without letting her see that he suspected her—to clear up that doubt as soon as his landlady returned to the house.

The evening came. It was past nine o'clock before there was a ring at the bell. The servant came to ask for the key. Geoffrey rose to go to the gate himself—and changed his mind before he left the room. Her suspicions might be roused (supposing it to be Hester who was waiting for admission) if he opened the gate to her when the servant was there to do it. He gave the girl the key, and kept out of sight.

* * * * * * *

"Dead tired!"—the servant said to herself, seeing her mistress by the light of the lamp over the gate.

"Dead tired!"—Geoffrey said to himself, observing Hester suspiciously as she passed him in the passage on her way up stairs to take off her bonnet in her own room.

"Dead tired!"—Anne said to herself, meeting Hester on the upper floor, and receiving from her a letter in Blanche's handwriting, delivered to the mistress of the cottage by the postman, who had met her at her own gate.

* * * * * * *

Having given the letter to Anne, Hester Dethridge withdrew to her bedroom.

Geoffrey closed the door of the drawing-room, in which the candles were burning, and went into the dining-room, in which there was no light. Leaving the door ajar, he waited to intercept his landlady on her way back to her supper in the kitchen.

Hester wearily secured her door, wearily lit the candles, wearily put the pen and ink on the table. For some minutes after this she was compelled to sit down, and rally her strength and fetch her breath. After a little she was able to remove her upper clothing. This done, she took the manuscript inscribed, "My Confession," out of the secret pocket of her stays—turned to the last leaf as before—and wrote another entry, under the entry made on the previous night.

"This morning I gave him notice to quit, and offered him his money back if he wanted it. He refuses to go. He shall go to-morrow, or I will burn the place over his head. All through to-day I have avoided him by keeping out of the house. No rest to ease my mind, and no sleep to close my eyes. I humbly bear my cross as long as my strength will let me."

At those words the pen dropped from her fingers. Her head nodded on her breast. She roused herself with a start. Sleep was the enemy she dreaded: sleep brought dreams.

She unfastened the window-shutters and looked out at the night. The peaceful moonlight was shining over the garden. The clear depths of the night sky were soothing and beautiful to look at. What! Fading already? clouds?

darkness? No! Nearly asleep once more. She roused herself again, with a start. There was the moonlight, and there was the garden as bright under it as ever.

Dreams or no dreams, it was useless to fight longer against the weariness that overpowered her. She closed the shutters, and went back to the bed; and put her Confession in its customary place at night, under her pillow.

She looked round the room—and shuddered. Every corner of it was filled with the terrible memories of the past night. She might wake from the torture of the dreams to find the terror of the Apparition watching at her bedside. Was there no remedy? no blessed safeguard under which she might tranquilly resign herself to sleep? A thought crossed her mind. The good book—the Bible. If she slept with the Bible under her pillow, there was hope in the good book—the hope of sleeping in peace.

It was not worth while to put on the gown and the stays which she had taken off. Her shawl would cover her. It was equally needless to take the candle. The lower shutters would not be closed at that hour; and if they were, she could lay her hand on the Bible, in its place on the parlor book-shelf, in the dark.

She removed the Confession from under the pillow. Not even for a minute could she prevail on herself to leave it in one room while she was away from it in another. With the manuscript folded up, and hidden in her hand, she slowly descended the stairs again. Her knees trembled under her. She was obliged to hold by the banisters with the hand that was free.

Geoffrey observed her from the dining-room, on her way down the stairs. He waited to see what she did, before he showed himself, and spoke to her. Instead of going on into the kitchen, she stopped short, and entered the parlor. Another suspicious circumstance! What did she want in the parlor, without a candle, at that time of night?

She went to the book-case—her dark figure plainly visible in the moonlight that flooded the little room. She staggered and put her hand to her head; giddy, to all appearance, from extreme fatigue. She recovered herself, and took a book from the shelf. She leaned against the wall after she had possessed herself of the book. Too weary, as it seemed, to get up stairs again without a little rest. Her arm-chair was near her. Better rest, for a moment or two, to be had in that than could be got by leaning against the wall. She sat down heavily in the chair, with the book on her lap. One of her arms hung over the arm of the chair, with the hand closed, apparently holding something.

Her head nodded on her breast—recovered itself—and sank gently on the cushion at the back of the chair. Asleep? Fast asleep.

In less than a minute the muscles of the closed hand that hung over the arm of the chair slowly relaxed. Something white slipped out of her hand, and lay in the moonlight on the floor.

Geoffrey took off his heavy shoes, and entered the room noiselessly in his stockings. He picked up the white thing on the floor. It proved to be a collection of several sheets of thin paper, neatly folded together, and closely covered with writing.

Writing? As long as she was awake she had kept it hidden in her hand. Why hide it?

Had he let out any thing to compromise himself when he was light-headed with the fever the night before? and had she taken it down in writing to produce against him? Possessed by guilty distrust, even that monstrous doubt assumed a look of probability to Geoffrey's mind. He left the parlor as noiselessly as he had entered it, and made for the candle-light in the drawing-room, determined to examine the manuscript in his hand.

After carefully smoothing out the folded leaves on the table, he turned to the first page, and read these lines.

---

## CHAPTER THE FIFTY-FOURTH.

### THE MANUSCRIPT.

#### 1.

"MY Confession: To be put into my coffin; and to be buried with me when I die.

"This is the history of what I did in the time of my married life. Here—known to no other mortal creature, confessed to my Creator alone—is the truth.

"At the great day of the Resurrection, we shall all rise again in our bodies as we have lived. When I am called before the Judgment Seat I shall have this in my hand.

"Oh, just and merciful Judge, Thou knowest what I have suffered. My trust is in Thee.

#### 2.

"I am the eldest of a large family, born of pious parents. We belonged to the congregation of the Primitive Methodists.

"My sisters were all married before me. I remained for some years the only one at home. At the latter part of the time my mother's health failed; and I managed the house in her place. Our spiritual pastor, good Mr. Bapchild, used often to dine with us, on Sundays, between the services. He approved of my management of the house, and, in particular, of my cooking. This was not pleasant to my mother, who felt a jealousy of my being, as it were, set over her in her place. My unhappiness at home began in this way. My mother's temper got worse as her health got worse. My father was much away from us, traveling for his business. I had to bear it all. About this time I began to think it would be well for me if I could marry as my sisters had done; and have good Mr. Bapchild to dinner, between the services, in a house of my own.

"In this frame of mind I made acquaintance with a young man who attended service at our chapel.

"His name was Joel Dethridge. He had a beautiful voice. When we sang hymns, he sang off the same book with me. By trade he was a paper-hanger. We had much serious talk together. I walked with him on Sundays. He was a good ten years younger than I was; and, being only a journeyman, his worldly station was below mine. My mother found out the liking that had grown up between us. She told my father the next time he was at home. Also my married sisters and my brothers. They all joined together to stop things from going further between me and Joel Dethridge. I had a hard time of it. Mr. Bapchild expressed himself as feeling much grieved at the turn things were taking. He introduced me into a sermon—not by name, but I knew who it was meant for. Perhaps I might have given way if they had not done one thing. They made inquiries of my young man's enemies, and brought wicked stories of him to me behind his back. This, after we had sung off the same hymn-book, and walked together, and agreed one with the other on religious subjects, was too much to bear. I was of age to judge for myself. And I married Joel Dethridge.

### 3.

"My relations all turned their backs on me. Not one of them was present at my marriage; my brother Reuben, in particular, who led the rest, saying that they had done with me from that time forth. Mr. Bapchild was much moved; he shed tears, and said he would pray for me.

"I was married in London by a pastor who was a stranger; and we settled in London with fair prospects. I had a little fortune of my own —my share of some money left to us girls by our aunt Hester, whom I was named after. It was three hundred pounds. Nearly one hundred of this I spent in buying furniture to fit up the little house we took to live in. The rest I gave to my husband to put into the bank against the time when he wanted it to set up in business for himself.

"For three months, more or less, we got on nicely—except in one particular. My husband never stirred in the matter of starting in business for himself.

"He was once or twice cross with me when I said it seemed a pity to be spending the money in the bank (which might be afterward wanted) instead of earning more in business. Good Mr. Bapchild, happening about this time to be in London, staid over Sunday, and came to dine with us between the services. He had tried to make my peace with my relations—but he had not succeeded. At my request he spoke to my husband about the necessity of exerting himself. My husband took it ill. I then saw him seriously out of temper for the first time. Good Mr. Bapchild said no more. He appeared to be alarmed at what had happened, and he took his leave early.

"Shortly afterward my husband went out. I got tea ready for him—but he never came back. I got supper ready for him—but he never came back. It was past twelve at night before I saw him again. was very much startled by the state he came home in. He didn't speak like himself, or look like himself: he didn't seem to know me—wandered in his mind, and fell all in a lump like on our bed. I ran out and fetched the doctor to him.

"The doctor pulled him up to the light, and looked at him; smelled his breath, and dropped him down again on the bed; turned about, and stared at me. 'What's the matter, Sir?' I says. 'Do you mean to tell me you don't know?' says the doctor. 'No, Sir,' says I. 'Why what sort of a woman are you,' says he, 'not to know a drunken man when you see him!' With that he went away, and left me standing by the bedside, all in a tremble from head to foot.

"This was how I first found out that I was the wife of a drunken man.

### 4.

"I have omitted to say any thing about my husband's family.

"While we were keeping company together he told me he was an orphan—with an uncle and aunt in Canada, and an only brother settled in Scotland. Before we were married he gave me a letter from this brother. It was to say that he was sorry he was not able to come to England, and be present at my marriage, and to wish me joy and the rest of it. Good Mr. Bapchild (to whom, in my distress, I wrote word privately of what had happened) wrote back in return, telling me to wait a little, and see whether my husband did it again.

"I had not long to wait. He was in liquor again the next day, and the next. Hearing this, Mr. Bapchild instructed me to send him the letter from my husband's brother. He reminded me of some of the stories about my husband, which I had refused to believe in the time before I was married; and he said it might be well to make inquiries.

"The end of the inquiries was this. The brother, at that very time, was placed privately (by his own request) under a doctor's care to get broken of habits of drinking. The craving for strong liquor (the doctor wrote) was in the family. They would be sober sometimes for months together, drinking nothing stronger than tea. Then the fit would seize them; and they would drink, drink, drink, for days together, like the mad and miserable wretches that they were.

"This was the husband I was married to. And I had offended all my relations, and estranged them from me, for his sake. Here was surely a sad prospect for a woman after only a few months of wedded life!

"In a year's time the money in the bank was gone; and my husband was out of employment. He always got work—being a first-rate hand when he was sober—and always lost it again when the drinking-fit seized him. I was loth to leave our nice little house, and part with my pretty furniture; and I proposed to him to let me try for employment, by the day, as cook, and so keep things going while he was looking out again for work. He was sober and penitent at the time; and he agreed to what I proposed. And, more than that, he took the Total Abstinence Pledge, and promised to turn over a new leaf. Matters, as I thought, began to look fairly again. We had nobody but our two selves to think of. I had borne no child, and had no prospect of bearing one. Unlike most women, I thought this a mercy instead of a misfortune. In my situation (as I soon grew to know) my becoming a mother would only have proved to be an aggravation of my hard lot.

"The sort of employment I wanted was not to be got in a day. Good Mr. Bapchild gave me a character; and our landlord, a worthy man (belonging, I am sorry to say, to the Popish Church), spoke for me to the steward of a club. Still, it took time to persuade people that I was the thorough good cook I claimed to be. Nigh on a fortnight had passed before I got the chance I had been looking out for. I went home in good spirits (for me) to report what had happened, and found the brokers in the house carrying off the furniture which I had bought with my own money for sale by auction. I asked them how they dared touch it without my leave. They answered, civilly enough I must own, that they were acting under my husband's orders; and they went on removing it, before my own eyes, to the cart outside. I ran up stairs, and found my husband on the landing. He was in liquor again. It is useless to say what passed between us. I shall only mention that this was the first occasion on which he lifted his fist, and struck me.

### 5.

"Having a spirit of my own, I was resolved not to endure it. I ran out to the Police Court, hard by.

"My money had not only bought the furniture —it had kept the house going as well; paying the taxes which the Queen and the Parliament asked for among other things. I now went to the magistrate to see what the Queen and the Parliament, in return for the taxes, would do for *me*.

"'Is your furniture settled on yourself?' he says, when I told him what had happened.

"I didn't understand what he meant. He turned to some person who was sitting on the bench with him. 'This is a hard case,' he says. 'Poor people in this condition of life don't even know what a marriage settlement means. And, if they did, how many of them could afford to pay the lawyer's charges?' Upon that he turned to me. 'Yours is a common case,' he said. 'In the present state of the law I can do nothing for you.'

"It was impossible to believe that. Common or not, I put my case to him over again.

"'I have bought the furniture with my own money, Sir,' I says. 'It's mine, honestly come by, with bill and receipt to prove it. They are taking it away from me by force, to sell it against my will. Don't tell me that's the law. This is a Christian country. It can't be.'

"'My good creature,' says he, 'you are a married woman. The law doesn't allow a married woman to call any thing her own—unless she has previously (with a lawyer's help) made a bargain to that effect with her husband before marrying him. You have made no bargain. Your husband has a right to sell your furniture if he likes. I am sorry for you; I can't hinder him.'

"I was obstinate about it. 'Please to answer me this, Sir,' I says. 'I've been told by wiser heads than mine that we all pay our taxes to keep the Queen and the Parliament going; and that the Queen and the Parliament make laws to protect us in return. I have paid my taxes. Why, if you please, is there no law to protect me in return?'

"'I can't enter into that,' says he. 'I must take the law as I find it; and so must you. I see a mark there on the side of your face. Has your husband been beating you? If he has, summon him here. I can punish him for *that*.'

"'How can you punish him, Sir?' says I.

"'I can fine him,' says he. 'Or I can send him to prison.'

"'As to the fine,' says I, 'he can pay that out of the money he gets by selling my furniture. As to the prison, while he's in it, what's to become of me, with my money spent by him, and my possessions gone; and when he's *out* of it, what's to become of me again, with a husband whom I have been the means of punishing, and who comes home to his wife knowing it? It's bad enough as it is, Sir,' says I. 'There's more that's bruised in me than what shows in my face. I wish you good-morning.'

### 6.

"When I got back the furniture was gone, and my husband was gone. There was nobody but the landlord in the empty house. He said all that could be said—kindly enough toward me, so far as I was concerned. When he was gone I locked my trunk, and got away in a cab after dark, and found a lodging to lay my head in. If ever there was a lonely, broken-hearted creature in the world, I was that creature that night.

"There was but one chance of earning my bread—to go to the employment offered me (under a man cook, at a club). And there was but one hope—the hope that I had lost sight of my husband forever.

"I went to my work—and prospered in it—and earned my first quarter's wages. But it's not good for a woman to be situated as I was; friendless and alone, with her things that she took a pride in sold away from her, and with nothing to look forward to in her life to come. I was regular in my attendance at chapel; but I think my heart began to get hardened, and my mind to be overcast in secret with its own thoughts about this time. There was a change coming. Two or three days after I had earned the wages just mentioned my husband found me out. The furniture-money was all spent. He made a disturbance at the club. I was only able to quiet him by giving him all the money I could spare from my own necessities. The scandal was brought before the committee. They said, if the circumstance occurred again, they should be obliged to part with me. In a fortnight the circumstance occurred again. It's useless to dwell on it. They all said they were sorry for me. I lost the place. My husband went back with me to my lodgings. The next morning I caught him taking my purse, with the few shillings I had in it, out of my trunk, which he had broken open. We quarreled. And he struck me again—this time knocking me down.

"I went once more to the police court, and told my story—to another magistrate this time. My only petition was to have my husband kept away from me. 'I don't want to be a burden on others' (I says); 'I don't want to do any thing but what's right. I don't even complain of having been very cruelly used. All I ask is to be let to earn an honest living. Will the law protect me in the effort to do that?'

"The answer, in substance, was that the law might protect me, provided I had money to spend in asking some higher court to grant me a separation. After allowing my husband to rob me openly of the only property I possessed— namely, my furniture—the law turned round on me when I called upon it in my distress, and held out its hand to be paid. I had just three and sixpence left in the world—and the prospect, if I earned more, of my husband coming (with permission of the law) and taking it away from me. There was only one chance—namely, to get time to turn round in, and to escape him again. I got a month's freedom from him, by charging him with knocking me down. The magistrate (happening to be young, and new to his business) sent him to prison, instead of fining him. This gave me time to get a character from the club, as well as a special testimonial from good Mr. Bapchild. With the help of these, I obtained a place in a private family—a place in the country, this time.

"I found myself now in a haven of peace. I was among worthy kind-hearted people, who felt for my distresses, and treated me most indulgently. Indeed, through all my troubles, I must say I have found one thing hold good. In my experience, I have observed that people are oftener quick than not to feel a human compassion for others in distress. Also, that they mostly see plain enough what's hard and cruel and unfair on them in the governing of the country which they help to keep going. But once ask them to get on from sitting down and grumbling about it, to rising up and setting it right, and what do you find them? As helpless as a flock of sheep—that's what you find them.

"More than six months passed, and I saved a little money again.

"One night, just as we were going to bed, there was a loud ring at the bell. The footman answered the door—and I heard my husband's voice in the hall. He had traced me, with the help of a man he knew in the police; and he had come to claim his rights. I offered him all the little money I had, to let me be. My good master spoke to him. It was all useless. He was obstinate and savage. If—instead of my running off from him—it had been all the other way, and he had run off from me, something might have been done (as I understood) to protect me. But he stuck to his wife. As long as I could make a farthing, he stuck to his wife. Being married to him, I had no right to have left him; I was bound to go with my husband; there was no escape for me. I bade them good-by. And I have never forgotten their kindness to me from that day to this.

"My husband took me back to London.

"As long as the money lasted, the drinking went on. When it was gone, I was beaten again. Where was the remedy? There was no remedy, but to try and escape him once more. Why didn't I have him locked up? What was the the good of having him locked up? In a few weeks he would be out of prison; sober and penitent, and promising amendment—and then when the fit took him, there he would be, the same furious savage that he had been often and often before. My heart got hard under the hopelessness of it; and dark thoughts beset me, mostly at night. About this time I began to say to myself, 'There's no deliverance from this, but in death—his death or mine.'

"Once or twice I went down to the bridges after dark, and looked over at the river. No. I wasn't the sort of woman who ends her own wretchedness in that way. Your blood must be in a fever, and your head in a flame—at least I fancy so—you must be hurried into it, like, to go and make away with yourself. My troubles never took that effect on me. I always turned cold under them—instead of hot. Bad for me, I dare say; but what you are—you are. Can the Ethiopian change his skin, or the leopard his spots?

"I got away from him once more, and found good employment once more. It don't matter how; and it don't matter where. My story is always the same thing, over and over again. Best get to the end.

"There was one change, however, this time. My employment was not in a private family. I was also allowed to teach cookery to young women, in my leisure hours. What with this, and what with a longer time passing on the present occasion before my husband found me out, I was as comfortably off as in my position I could hope to be. When my work was done, I went away at night to sleep in a lodging of my own. It was only a bedroom; and I furnished it myself—partly for the sake of economy (the rent being not half as much as for a furnished room); and partly for the sake of cleanliness. Through all my troubles I always liked things neat about me—neat and shapely and good.

"Well, it's needless to say how it ended. He found me out again—this time by a chance-meeting with me in the street.

"He was in rags, and half starved. But that didn't matter now. All he had to do was to put his hand into my pocket and take what he wanted. There is no limit, in England, to what a bad husband may do—as long as he sticks to his wife. On the present occasion, he was cunning enough to see that he would be the loser if he disturbed me in my employment. For a while things went on as smoothly as they could. I made a pretense that the work was harder than usual; and I got leave (loathing the sight of him, I honestly own) to sleep at the place where I was employed. This was not for long. The fit took him again, in due course; and he came and made a disturbance. As before, this was not to be borne by decent people. As before, they were sorry to part with me. As before, I lost my place.

"Another woman would have gone mad under it. I fancy it just missed, by a hair's breadth, maddening Me.

"When I looked at him that night, deep in his drunken sleep, I thought of Jael and Sisera (see the book of Judges; chapter 4th; verses 17 to 21). It says, she 'took a nail of the tent, and took a hammer in her hand, and went softly unto him, and smote the nail into his temples, and fastened it into the ground: for he was fast asleep and weary. So he died.' She did this deed to deliver her nation from Sisera. If there had been a hammer and a nail in the room that night, I think I should have been Jael—with this difference, that I should have done it to deliver myself.

"With the morning this passed off, for the time. I went and spoke to a lawyer.

"Most people, in my place, would have had enough of the law already. But I was one of the sort who drain the cup to the dregs. What I said to him was, in substance, this. 'I come to ask your advice about a madman. Mad people, as I understand it, are people who have lost control over their own minds. Sometimes this leads them to entertaining delusions; and sometimes it leads them to committing actions hurtful to others or to themselves. My husband has lost all control over his own craving for strong drink. He requires to be kept from liquor, as other madmen require to be kept from attempting their own lives, or the lives of those about them. It's a frenzy beyond his own control, with *him*—just as it's a frenzy beyond their own control, with *them*. There are Asylums for mad people, all over the country, at the public disposal, on certain conditions. If I fulfill those conditions, will the law deliver me from the misery of being married to a madman, whose madness is drink?'—'No,' says the lawyer. 'The law of England declines to consider an incurable drunkard as a fit object for restraint; the law of England leaves the husbands and wives of such people in a perfectly helpless situation, to deal with their own misery as they best can.'

"I made my acknowledgments to the gentleman and left him. The last chance was this chance—and this had failed me.

8.

"The thought that had once found its way into my mind already, now found its way back again; and never altogether left me from that time forth. No deliverance for me but in death —his death, or mine.

"I had it before me night and day; in chapel and out of chapel just the same. I read the story of Jael and Sisera so often that the Bible got to open of itself at that place.

"The laws of my country, which ought to have protected me as an honest woman, left me helpless. In place of the laws I had no friend near to open my heart to. I was shut up in myself. And I was married to that man. Consider me as a human creature, and say, Was this not trying my humanity very hardly?

"I wrote to good Mr. Bapchild. Not going into particulars; only telling him I was beset by temptation, and begging him to come and help me. He was confined to his bed by illness; he could only write me a letter of good advice. To profit by good advice people must have a glimpse of happiness to look forward to as a reward for exerting themselves. Religion itself is obliged to hold out a reward, and to say to us poor mortals, Be good, and you shall go to Heaven. I had no glimpse of happiness. I was thankful (in a dull sort of way) to good Mr. Bapchild—and there it ended.

"The time had been when a word from my old pastor would have put me in the right way again. I began to feel scared by myself. If the next ill usage I received from Joel Dethridge found me an unchanged woman, it was borne in strongly on my mind that I should be as likely as not to get my deliverance from him by my own hand.

"Goaded to it, by the fear of this, I humbled myself before my relations for the first time. I wrote to beg their pardon; to own that they had proved to be right in their opinion of my husband; and to entreat them to be friends with me again, so far as to let me visit them from time to time. My notion was, that it might soften my heart if I could see the old place, and talk the old talk, and look again at the well-remembered faces. I am almost ashamed to own it—but, if I had had any thing to give, I would have parted with it all, to be allowed to go back into mother's kitchen and cook the Sunday dinner for them once more.

"But this was not to be. Not long before my letter was received mother had died. They laid it all at my door. She had been ailing for years past, and the doctors had said it was hopeless from the first—but they laid it all at my door. One of my sisters wrote to say that much, in as few words as could possibly suffice for saying it. My father never answered my letter at all.

9.

"Magistrates and lawyers; relations and friends; endurance of injuries, patience, hope, and honest work—I had tried all these, and tried them vainly. Look round me where I might, the prospect was closed on all sides.

"At this time my husband had got a little work to do. He came home out of temper one night, and I gave him a warning. 'Don't try me too far, Joel, for your own sake,' was all I said. It was one of his sober days; and, for the first time, a word from me seemed to have an effect on him. He looked hard at me for a minute or so. And then he went and sat down in a corner, and held his peace.

"This was on a Tuesday in the week. On the Saturday he got paid, and the drinking fit took him again.

"On Friday in the next week I happened to come back late—having had a good stroke of work to do that day, in the way of cooking a public dinner for a tavern-keeper who knew me. I found my husband gone, and the bedroom stripped of the furniture which I had put into it. For the second time he had robbed me of my own property, and had turned it into money to be spent in drink.

"I didn't say a word. I stood and looked round the empty room. What was going on in me I hardly knew myself at the time, and can't describe now. All I remember is, that, after a little, I turned about to leave the house. I knew the places where my husband was likely to be found; and the devil possessed me to go and find him. The landlady came out into the passage and tried to stop me. She was a bigger and a stronger woman than I was. But I shook her off like a child. Thinking over it now, I believe she was in no condition to put out her strength. The sight of me frightened her.

"I found him. I said—well, I said what a woman beside herself with fury would be likely to say. It's needless to tell how it ended. He knocked me down.

"After that, there is a spot of darkness like in my memory. The next thing I can call to mind, is coming back to my senses after some days. Three of my teeth were knocked out— but that was not the worst of it. My head had struck against something in falling, and some part of me (a nerve, I think they said) was injured in such a way as to affect my speech. I don't mean that I was downright dumb—I only mean that, all of a sudden, it had become a labor to me to speak. A long word was as serious an obstacle as if I was a child again. They took me to the hospital. When the medical gentlemen heard what it was, the medical gentlemen came crowding round me. I appeared to lay hold of their interest, just as a story-book lays hold of the interest of other people. The upshot of it was, that I might end in being dumb, or I might get my speech again—the chances were about equal. Only two things were needful. One of them was that I should live on good nourishing diet. The other was, that I should keep my mind easy.

"About the diet it was not possible to decide

My getting good nourishing food and drink depended on my getting money to buy the same. As to my mind, there was no difficulty about *that*. If my husband came back to me, my mind was made up to kill him.

"Horrid—I am well aware this is horrid. Nobody else, in my place, would have ended as wickedly as that. All the other women in the world, tried as I was, would have risen superior to the trial.

### 10.

"I have said that people (excepting my husband and my relations) were almost always good to me.

"The landlord of the house which we had taken when we were married heard of my sad case. He gave me one of his empty houses to look after, and a little weekly allowance for doing it. Some of the furniture in the upper rooms, not being wanted by the last tenant, was left to be taken at a valuation if the next tenant needed it. Two of the servants' bedrooms (in the attics), one next to the other, had all that was wanted in them. So I had a roof to cover me, and a choice of beds to lie on, and money to get me food. All well again—but all too late. If that house could speak, what tales that house would have to tell of me!

"I had been told by the doctors to exercise my speech. Being all alone, with nobody to speak to, except when the landlord dropped in, or when the servant next door said, 'Nice day, ain't it?' or, 'Don't you feel lonely?' or such like, I bought the newspaper, and read it out loud to myself to exercise my speech in that way. One day I came upon a bit about the wives of drunken husbands. It was a report of something said on that subject by a London coroner, who had held inquests on dead husbands (in the lower ranks of life), and who had his reasons for suspecting the wives. Examination of the body (he said) didn't prove it; and witnesses didn't prove it; but he thought it, nevertheless, quite possible, in some cases, that, when the woman could bear it no longer, she sometimes took a damp towel, and waited till the husband (drugged with his own liquor) was sunk in his sleep, and then put the towel over his nose and mouth, and ended it that way without anybody being the wiser. I laid down the newspaper, and fell into thinking. My mind was, by this time, in a prophetic way. I said to myself, 'I haven't happened on this for nothing: this means that I shall see my husband again.'

"It was then just after my dinner-time—two o'clock. That same night, at the moment when I had put out my candle, and laid me down in bed, I heard a knock at the street door. Before I had lit my candle I says to myself, 'Here he is.'

"I huddled on a few things, and struck a light, and went down stairs. I called out through the door, 'Who's there?' And his voice answered, 'Let me in.'

"I sat down on a chair in the passage, and shook all over like a person struck with palsy. Not from the fear of him—but from my mind being in the prophetic way. I knew I was going to be driven to it at last. Try as I might to keep from doing it, my mind told me I was to do it now. I sat shaking on the chair in the passage; I on one side of the door, and he on the other.

"He knocked again, and again, and again. I knew it was useless to try—and yet I resolved to try. I determined not to let him in till I was forced to it. I determined to let him alarm the neighborhood, and to see if the neighborhood would step between us. I went up stairs and waited at the open staircase window over the door.

"The policeman came up, and the neighbors came out. They were all for giving him into custody. The policeman laid hands on him. He had but one word to say; he had only to point up to me at the window, and to tell them I was his wife. The neighbors went indoors again. The policeman dropped hold of his arm. It was I who was in the wrong, and not he. I was bound to let my husband in. I went down stairs again, and let him in.

"Nothing passed between us that night. I threw open the door of the bedroom next to mine, and went and locked myself into my own room. He was dead beat with roaming the streets, without a penny in his pocket, all day long. The bed to lie on was all he wanted for that night.

"The next morning I tried again—tried to turn back on the way that I was doomed to go; knowing beforehand that it would be of no use., I offered him three parts of my poor weekly earnings, to be paid to him regularly at the landlord's office, if he would only keep away from me, and from the house. He laughed in my face. As my husband, he could take all my earnings if he chose. And as for leaving the house, the house offered him free quarters to live in as long as I was employed to look after it. The landlord couldn't part man and wife.

"I said no more. Later in the day the landlord came. He said if we could make it out to live together peaceably he had neither the right nor the wish to interfere. If we made any disturbances, then he should be obliged to provide himself with some other woman to look after the house. I had nowhere else to go, and no other employment to undertake. If, in spite of that, I had put on my bonnet and walked out, my husband would have walked out after me. And all decent people would have patted him on the back, and said, 'Quite right, good man—quite right.'

"So there he was by his own act, and with the approval of others, in the same house with me.

"I made no remark to him or to the landlord. Nothing roused me now. I knew what was coming; I waited for the end. There was some change visible in me to others, as I suppose, though not noticeable by myself, which first surprised my husband and then daunted him. When the next night came I heard him lock the door softly in his own room. It didn't matter to me. When the time was ripe ten thousand locks wouldn't lock out what was to come.

"The next day, bringing my weekly payment, brought me a step nearer on the way to the end. Getting the money, he could get the drink. This time he began cunningly—in other words, he began his drinking by slow degrees. The landlord (bent, honest man, on trying to keep the peace between us) had given him some odd jobs to do, in the way of small repairs, here and there about the house. 'You owe this,' he says, 'to my desire to do a good turn to your poor wife. I am helping you for her sake. Show yourself worthy to be helped, if you can.'

"He said, as usual, that he was going to turn over a new leaf. Too late! The time had gone by. He was doomed, and I was doomed. It didn't matter what he said now. It didn't matter when he locked his door again the last thing at night.

"The next day was Sunday. Nothing happened. I went to chapel. Mere habit. It did me no good. He got on a little with the drinking — but still cunningly, by slow degrees. I knew by experience that this meant a long fit, and a bad one, to come.

"Monday, there were the odd jobs about the house to be begun. He was by this time just sober enough to do his work, and just tipsy enough to take a spiteful pleasure in persecuting his wife. He went out and got the things he wanted, and came back and called for me. A skilled workman like he was (he said) wanted a journeyman under him. There were things which it was beneath a skilled workman to do for himself. He was not going to call in a man or a boy, and then have to pay them. He was going to get it done for nothing, and he meant to make a journeyman of *me*. Half tipsy and half sober, he went on talking like that, and laying out his things, all quite right, as he wanted them. When they were ready he straightened himself up, and he gave me his orders what I was to do.

"I obeyed him to the best of my ability. Whatever he said, and whatever he did, I knew he was going as straight as man could go to his own death by my hands.

"The rats and mice were all over the house, and the place generally was out of repair. He ought to have begun on the kitchen-floor; but (having sentence pronounced against him) he began in the empty parlors on the ground-floor.

"These parlors were separated by what is called a 'lath-and-plaster wall.' The rats had damaged it. At one part they had gnawed through and spoiled the paper; at another part they had not got so far. The landlord's orders were to spare the paper, because he had some by him to match it. My husband began at a place where the paper was whole. Under his directions I mixed up—I won't say what. With the help of it he got the paper loose from the wall, without injuring it in any way, in a long, hanging strip. Under it was the plaster and the laths, gnawed away in places by the rats. Though strictly a paper-hanger by trade, he could be plasterer too when he liked. I saw how he cut away the rotten laths and ripped off the plaster; and (under his directions again) I mixed up the new plaster he wanted, and handed him the new laths, and saw how he set them. I won't say a word about how this was done either.

"I have a reason for keeping silence here, which is, to my mind, a very dreadful one. In every thing that my husband made me do that day he was showing me (blindfold) the way to kill him, so that no living soul, in the police or out of it, could suspect me of the deed.

"We finished the job on the wall just before dark. I went to my cup of tea, and he went to his bottle of gin.

"I left him, drinking hard, to put our two bedrooms tidy for the night. The place that his bed happened to be set in (which I had never remarked particularly before) seemed, in a manner of speaking, to force itself on my notice now.

"The head of the bedstead was set against the wall which divided his room from mine. From looking at the bedstead I got to looking at the wall next. Then to wondering what it was made of. Then to rapping against it with my knuckles. The sound told me there was nothing but lath and plaster under the paper. It was the same as the wall we had been at work on down stairs. We had cleared our way so far through this last—in certain places where the repairs were most needed—that we had to be careful not to burst through the paper in the room on the other side. I found myself calling to mind the caution my husband had given me while we were at this part of the work, word for word as he had spoken it. '*Take care you don't find your hands in the next room.*' That was what he had said down in the parlor. Up in his bedroom I kept on repeating it in my own mind—with my eyes all the while on the key, which he had moved to the inner side of the door to lock himself in— till the knowledge of what it meant burst on me like a flash of light. I looked at the wall, at the bedhead, at my own two hands—and I shivered as if it was winter time.

"Hours must have passed like minutes while I was up stairs that night. I lost all count of time. When my husband came up from his drinking, he found me in his room.

## 12.

"I leave the rest untold, and pass on purposely to the next morning.

"No mortal eyes but mine will ever see these lines. Still, there are things a woman can't write of even to herself. I shall only say this. I suffered the last and worst of many indignities at my husband's hands—at the very time when I first saw, set plainly before me, the way to take his life. He went out toward noon next day, to go his rounds among the public houses; my mind being then strung up to deliver myself from him, for good and all, when he came back at night.

"The things we had used on the previous day were left in the parlor. I was all by myself in the house, free to put in practice the lesson he had taught me. I proved myself an apt scholar. Before the lamps were lit in the street I had my own way prepared (in my bedroom and in his) for laying my own hands on him—after he had locked himself up for the night.

"I don't remember feeling either fear or doubt through all those hours. I sat down to my bit of supper with no better and no worse an appetite than usual. The only change in me that I can call to mind was that I felt a singular longing to have somebody with me to keep me company. Having no friend to ask in, I went to the street door and stood looking at the people passing this way and that.

"A stray dog, sniffing about, came up to me. Generally I dislike dogs and beasts of all kinds. I called this one in and gave him his supper. He had been taught (I suppose) to sit up on his hind-legs and beg for food; at any rate, that was his way of asking me for more. I laughed—it seems impossible when I look back at it now, but for all that it's true—I laughed till the tears ran down my cheeks, at the little beast on his haunches, with his ears pricked up and his head on one side and his mouth watering for the victuals. I wonder whether I was in my right senses? I don't know.

"When the dog had got all he could get he whined to be let out to roam the streets again.

"As I opened the door to let the creature go his ways, I saw my husband crossing the road to come in. 'Keep out' (I says to him); 'to-night, of all nights, keep out.' He was too drunk to heed me; he passed by, and blundered his way up stairs. I followed and listened. I heard him open his door, and bang it to, and lock it. I waited a bit, and went up another stair or two. I heard him drop down on to his bed. In a minute more he was fast asleep and snoring.

"It had all happened as it was wanted to happen. In two minutes—without doing one single thing to bring suspicion on myself—I could have smothered him. I went into my own room. I took up the towel that I had laid ready. I was within an inch of it—when there came a rush of something up into my head. I can't say what it was. I can only say the horrors laid hold of me and hunted me then and there out of the house.

"I put on my bonnet, and slipped the key of the street door into my pocket. It was only half past nine—or maybe a quarter to ten. If I had any one clear notion in my head, it was the notion of running away, and never allowing myself to set eyes on the house or the husband more.

"I went up the street—and came back. I went down the street—and came back. I tried it a third time, and went round and round and round—and came back. It was not to be done. The house held me chained to it like a dog to his kennel. I couldn't keep away from it. For the life of me, I couldn't keep away from it.

"A company of gay young men and women passed me, just as I was going to let myself in again. They were in a great hurry. 'Step out,' says one of the men; 'the theatre's close by, and we shall be just in time for the farce.' I turned about and followed them. Having been piously brought up, I had never been inside a theatre in my life. It struck me that I might get taken, as it were, out of myself, if I saw something that was quite strange to me, and heard something which would put new thoughts into my mind.

"They went in to the pit; and I went in after them.

"The thing they called the farce had begun. Men and women came on to the stage, turn and turn about, and talked, and went off again. Before long all the people about me in the pit were laughing and clapping their hands. The noise they made angered me. I don't know how to describe the state I was in. My eyes wouldn't serve me, and my ears wouldn't serve me, to see and to hear what the rest of them were seeing and hearing. There must have been something, I fancy, in my mind that got itself between me and what was going on upon the stage. The play looked fair enough on the surface; but there was danger and death at the bottom of it. The players were talking and laughing to deceive the people—with murder in their minds all the time. And nobody knew it but me—and my tongue was tied when I tried to tell the others. I got up, and ran out. The moment I was in the street my steps turned back of themselves on the way to the house. I called a cab, and told the man to drive (as far as a shilling would take me) the opposite way. He put me down—I don't know where. Across the street I saw an inscription in letters of flame over an open door. The man said it was a dancing-place. Dancing was as new to me as play-going. I had one more shilling left; and I paid to go in, and see what a sight of the dancing would do for me. The light from the ceiling poured down in this place as if it was all on fire. The crashing of the music was dreadful. The whirling round and round of men and women in each other's arms was quite maddening to see. I don't know what happened to me here. The great blaze of light from the ceiling turned blood-red on a sudden. The man standing in front of the musicians waving a stick took the likeness of Satan, as seen in the picture in our family Bible at home. The whirling men and women went round and round, with white faces like the faces of the dead, and bodies robed in winding-sheets. I screamed out with the terror of it; and some person took me by the arm and put me outside the door. The darkness did me good: it was comforting and delicious—like a cool hand laid on a hot head. I went walking on through it, without knowing where; composing my mind with the belief that I had lost my way, and that I should find myself miles distant from home when morning dawned. After some time I got too weary to go on; and I sat me down to rest on a door-step. I dozed a bit, and woke up. When I got on my feet to go on again, I happened to turn my head toward the door of the house. The number on it was the same number as ours. I looked again. And behold, it was our steps I had been resting on. The door was our door.

"All my doubts and all my struggles dropped out of my mind when I made that discovery. There was no mistaking what this perpetual coming back to the house meant. Resist it as I might, it was to be.

"I opened the street door and went up stairs, and heard him sleeping his heavy sleep, exactly as I had heard him when I went out. I sat down on my bed and took off my bonnet, quite quiet in myself, because I knew it was to be. I damped the towel, and put it ready, and took a turn in the room.

"It was just the dawn of day. The sparrows were chirping among the trees in the square hard by.

"I drew up my blind; the faint light spoke to me as if in words, 'Do it now, before I get brighter, and show too much.'

"I listened. The friendly silence had a word for me too: 'Do it now, and trust the secret to Me.'

"I waited till the church clock chimed before striking the hour. At the first stroke—without touching the lock of his door, without setting foot in his room—I had the towel over his face. Before the last stroke he had ceased struggling. When the hum of the bell through the morning silence was still and dead, *he* was still and dead with it.

13.

"The rest of this history is counted in my mind by four days—Wednesday, Thursday, Friday, Saturday. After that it all fades off like,

226

and the new years come with a strange look, being the years of a new life.

"What about the old life first? What did I feel, in the horrid quiet of the morning, when I had done it?

"I don't know what I felt. I can't remember it, or I can't tell it, I don't know which. I can write the history of the four days, and that's all.

"Wednesday. — I gave the alarm toward noon. Hours before, I had put things straight and fit to be seen. I had only to call for help, and to leave the people to do as they pleased. The neighbors came in, and then the police. They knocked, uselessly, at his door. Then they broke it open, and found him dead in his bed.

"Not the ghost of a suspicion of me entered the mind of any one. There was no fear of human justice finding me out: my one unutterable dread was dread of an Avenging Providence. I had a short sleep that night, and a dream, in which I did the deed over again. For a time my mind was busy with thoughts of confessing to the police, and of giving myself up. If I had not belonged to a respectable family, I should have done it. From generation to generation there had been no stain on our good name. It would be death to my father, and disgrace to all my family, if I owned what I had done, and suffered for it on the public scaffold. I prayed to be guided; and I had a revelation, toward morning, of what to do.

"I was commanded, in a vision, to open the Bible, and vow on it to set my guilty self apart among my innocent fellow-creatures from that day forth; to live among them a separate and silent life; to dedicate the use of my speech to the language of prayer only, offered up in the solitude of my own chamber, when no human ear could hear me. Alone, in the morning, I saw the vision, and vowed the vow. No human ear *has* heard me from that time. No human ear *will* hear me, to the day of my death.

"Thursday. — The people came to speak to me, as usual. They found me dumb.

"What had happened to me in the past, when my head had been hurt, and my speech affected by it, gave a likelier look to my dumbness than it might have borne in the case of another person. They took me back again to the hospital. The doctors were divided in opinion. Some said the shock of what had taken place in the house, coming on the back of the other shock, might, for all they knew, have done the mischief. And others said, 'She got her speech again after the accident; there has been no new injury since that time; the woman is shamming dumb, for some purpose of her own.' I let them dispute it as they liked. All human talk was nothing now to me. I had set myself apart among my fellow-creatures; I had begun my separate and silent life.

"Through all this time the sense of a coming punishment hanging over me never left my mind. I had nothing to dread from human justice. The judgment of an Avenging Providence—there was what I was waiting for.

"Friday.—They held the inquest. He had been known for years past as an inveterate drunkard; he had been seen overnight going home in liquor; he had been found locked up in his room, with the key inside the door, and the latch of the window bolted also. No fire-place was in this garret; nothing was disturbed or altered; nobody by human possibility could have got in. The doctor reported that he had died of congestion of the lungs; and the jury gave their verdict accordingly.

14.

"Saturday.—Marked forever in my calendar as the memorable day on which the judgment descended on me. Toward three o'clock in the afternoon—in the broad sunlight, under the cloudless sky, with hundreds of innocent human creatures all around me—I, Hester Dethridge, saw, for the first time, the Appearance which is appointed to haunt me for the rest of my life.

"I had had a terrible night. My mind felt much as it had felt on the evening when I had gone to the play. I went out to see what the air and the sunshine and the cool green of trees and grass would do for me. The nearest place in which I could find what I wanted was the Regent's Park. I went into one of the quiet walks in the middle of the park, where the horses and carriages are not allowed to go, and where old people can sun themselves, and children play, without danger.

"I sat me down to rest on a bench. Among the children near me was a beautiful little boy, playing with a brand-new toy—a horse and wagon. While I was watching him busily plucking up the blades of grass and loading his wagon with them, I felt for the first time—what I have often and often felt since—a creeping chill come slowly over my flesh, and then a suspicion of something hidden near me, which would steal out and show itself if I looked that way.

"There was a big tree hard by. I looked toward the tree, and waited to see the something hidden appear from behind it.

"The Thing stole out, dark and shadowy in the pleasant sunlight. At first I saw only the dim figure of a woman. After a little it began to get plainer, brightening from within outward —brightening, brightening, brightening, till it set before me the vision of MY OWN SELF, repeated as if I was standing before a glass—the double of myself, looking at me with my own eyes. I saw it move over the grass. I saw it stop behind the beautiful little boy. I saw it stand and listen, as I had stood and listened at the dawn of morning, for the chiming of the bell before the clock struck the hour. When it heard the stroke it pointed down to the boy with my own hand; and it said to me, with my own voice, 'Kill him.'

"A time passed. I don't know whether it was a minute or an hour. The heavens and the earth disappeared from before me. I saw nothing but the double of myself, with the pointing hand. I felt nothing but the longing to kill the boy.

"Then, as it seemed, the heavens and the earth rushed back upon me. I saw the people near staring in surprise at me, and wondering if I was in my right mind.

"I got, by main force, to my feet; I looked, by main force, away from the beautiful boy; I escaped, by main force, from the sight of the Thing, back into the streets. I can only describe the overpowering strength of the temptation that tried me in one way. It was like tearing the life out of me to tear myself from killing the boy.

And what it was on this occasion it has been ever since. No remedy against it but in that torturing effort, and no quenching the after-agony but by solitude and prayer.

"The sense of a coming punishment had hung over me. And the punishment had come. I had waited for the judgment of an Avenging Providence. And the judgment was pronounced. With pious David I could now say, Thy fierce wrath goeth over me; thy terrors have cut me off."

Arrived at that point in the narrative, Geoffrey looked up from the manuscript for the first time. Some sound outside the room had disturbed him. Was it a sound in the passage?

He listened. There was an interval of silence. He looked back again at the Confession, turning over the last leaves to count how much was left of it before it came to an end.

After relating the circumstances under which the writer had returned to domestic service, the narrative was resumed no more. Its few remaining pages were occupied by a fragmentary journal. The brief entries all referred to the various occasions on which Hester Dethridge had again and again seen the terrible apparition of herself, and had again and again resisted the homicidal frenzy roused in her by the hideous creation of her own distempered brain. In the effort which that resistance cost her lay the secret of her obstinate determination to insist on being freed from her work at certain times, and to make it a condition with any mistress who employed her that she should be privileged to sleep in a room of her own at night. Having counted the pages thus filled, Geoffrey turned back to the place at which he had left off, to read the manuscript through to the end.

As his eyes rested on the first line the noise in the passage—intermitted for a moment only—disturbed him again.

This time there was no doubt of what the sound implied. He heard her hurried footsteps; he heard her dreadful cry. Hester Dethridge had woke in her chair in the parlor, and had discovered that the Confession was no longer in her own hands.

He put the manuscript into the breast-pocket of his coat. On *this* occasion his reading had been of some use to him. Needless to go on further with it. Needless to return to the Newgate Calendar. The problem was solved.

As he rose to his feet his heavy face brightened slowly with a terrible smile. While the woman's Confession was in his pocket the woman herself was in his power. "If she wants it back," he said, "she must get it on my terms." With that resolution, he opened the door, and met Hester Dethridge, face to face, in the passage.

## CHAPTER THE FIFTY-FIFTH.

### THE SIGNS OF THE END.

THE servant, appearing the next morning in Anne's room with the breakfast tray, closed the door with an air of mystery, and announced that strange things were going on in the house.

"Did you hear nothing last night, ma'am," she asked, "down stairs in the passage?"

"I thought I heard some voices whispering outside my room," Anne replied. "Has any thing happened?"

Extricated from the confusion in which she involved it, the girl's narrative amounted in substance to this. She had been startled by the sudden appearance of her mistress in the passage, staring about her wildly, like a woman who had gone out of her senses. Almost at the same moment "the master" had flung open the drawing-room door. He had caught Mrs. Dethridge by the arm, had dragged her into the room, and had closed the door again. After the two had remained shut up together for more than half an hour, Mrs. Dethridge had come out, as pale as ashes, and had gone up stairs trembling like a person in great terror. Some time later, when the servant was in bed, but not asleep, she had seen a light under her door, in the narrow wooden passage which separated Anne's bedroom from Hester's bedroom, and by which she obtained access to her own little sleeping-chamber beyond. She had got out of bed; had looked through the keyhole; and had seen "the master" and Mrs. Dethridge standing together examining the walls of the passage. "The master" had laid his hand upon the wall, on the side of his wife's room, and had looked at Mrs. Dethridge. And Mrs. Dethridge had looked back at him, and had shaken her head. Upon that he had said in a whisper (still with his hand on the wooden wall), "Not to be done here?" And Mrs. Dethridge had shaken her head. He had considered a moment, and had whispered again, "The other room will do, won't it?" And Mrs. Dethridge had nodded her head—and so they had parted. That was the story of the night. Early in the morning, more strange things had happened. The master had gone out, with a large sealed packet in his hand, covered with many stamps; taking his own letter to the post, instead of sending the servant with it as usual. On his return, Mrs. Dethridge had gone out next, and had come back with something in a jar which she had locked up in her own sitting-room. Shortly afterward, a working-man had brought a bundle of laths, and some mortar and plaster of Paris, which had been carefully placed together in a corner of the scullery. Last, and most remarkable in the series of domestic events, the girl had received permission to go home and see her friends in the country, on that very day; having been previously informed, when she entered Mrs. Dethridge's service, that she was not to expect to have a holiday granted to her until after Christmas. Such were the strange things which had happened in the house since the previous night. What was the interpretation to be placed on them?

The right interpretation was not easy to discover.

Some of the events pointed apparently toward coming repairs or alterations in the cottage. But what Geoffrey could have to do with them (being at the time served with a notice to quit), and why Hester Dethridge should have shown the violent agitation which had been described, were mysteries which it was impossible to penetrate.

Anne dismissed the girl with a little present and a few kind words. Under other circumstances, the incomprehensible proceedings in the house might have made her seriously uneasy. But her mind was now occupied by more pressing anxieties. Blanche's second letter (received from Hester Dethridge on the previous evening) informed her that Sir Patrick persisted in his resolution, and that he and his niece might be expected, come what might of it, to present themselves at the cottage on that day.

Anne opened the letter, and looked at it for the second time. The passages relating to Sir Patrick were expressed in these terms:

"I don't think, darling, you have any idea of the interest that you have roused in my uncle. Although he has not to reproach himself, as I have, with being the miserable cause of the sacrifice that you have made, he is quite as wretched and quite as anxious about you as I am. We talk of nobody else. He said last night that he did not believe there was your equal in the world. Think of that from a man who has such terribly sharp eyes for the faults of women in general, and such a terribly sharp tongue in talking of them! I am pledged to secrecy; but I must tell you one other thing, between ourselves. Lord Holchester's announcement that his brother refuses to consent to a separation put my uncle almost beside himself. If there is not some change for the better in your life in a few days' time, Sir Patrick will find out a way of his own—lawful or not, he doesn't care—for rescuing you from the dreadful position in which you are placed, and Arnold (with my full approval) will help him. As we understand it, you are, under one pretense or another, kept a close prisoner. Sir Patrick has already secured a post of observation near you. He and Arnold went all round the cottage last night, and examined a door in your back garden wall, with a locksmith to help them. You will no doubt hear further about this from Sir Patrick himself. Pray don't appear to know any thing of it when you see him! I am not in his confidence—but Arnold is, which comes to the same thing exactly. You will see us (I mean you will see my uncle and me) to-morrow, in spite of the brute who keeps you under lock and key. Arnold will not accompany us; he is not to be trusted (he owns it himself) to control his indignation. Courage, dearest! There are two people in the world to whom you are inestimably precious, and who are determined not to let your happiness be sacrificed. I am one of them, and (for Heaven's sake keep this a secret also!) Sir Patrick is the other."

Absorbed in the letter, and in the conflict of opposite feelings which it roused—her color rising when it turned her thoughts inward on herself, and fading again when she was reminded by it of the coming visit—Anne was called back to a sense of present events by the reappearance of the servant, charged with a message. Mr. Speedwell had been for some time in the cottage, and he was now waiting to see her down stairs.

Anne found the surgeon alone in the drawing-room. He apologized for disturbing her at that early hour.

"It was impossible for me to get to Fulham yesterday," he said, "and I could only make sure of complying with Lord Holchester's request by coming here before the time at which I receive patients at home. I have seen Mr. Delamayn, and I have requested permission to say a word to you on the subject of his health."

Anne looked through the window, and saw Geoffrey smoking his pipe—not in the back garden, as usual, but in front of the cottage, where he could keep his eye on the gate.

"Is he ill?" she asked.

"He is seriously ill," answered Mr. Speedwell. "I should not otherwise have troubled you with this interview. It is a matter of professional duty to warn you, as his wife, that he is in danger. He may be seized at any moment by a paralytic stroke. The only chance for him—a very poor one, I am bound to say—is to make him alter his present mode of life without loss of time."

"In one way he will be obliged to alter it," said Anne. "He has received notice from the landlady to quit this cottage."

Mr. Speedwell looked surprised.

"I think you will find that the notice has been withdrawn," he said. "I can only assure you that Mr. Delamayn distinctly informed me, when I advised change of air, that he had decided, for reasons of his own, on remaining here."

(Another in the series of incomprehensible domestic events! Hester Dethridge—on all other occasions the most immovable of women—had changed her mind!)

"Setting that aside," proceeded the surgeon, "there are two preventive measures which I feel bound to suggest. Mr. Delamayn is evidently suffering (though he declines to admit it himself) from mental anxiety. If he is to have a chance for his life, that anxiety must be set at rest. Is it in your power to relieve it?"

"It is not even in my power, Mr. Speedwell, to tell you what it is."

The surgeon bowed, and went on:

"The second caution that I have to give you," he said, "is to keep him from drinking spirits. He admits having committed an excess in that way the night before last. In his state of health, drinking means literally death. If he goes back to the brandy-bottle—forgive me for saying it plainly; the matter is too serious to be trifled with—if he goes back to the brandy-bottle, his life, in my opinion, is not worth five minutes' purchase. Can you keep him from drinking?"

Anne answered sadly and plainly:

"I have no influence over him. The terms we are living on here—"

Mr. Speedwell considerately stopped her.

"I understand," he said. "I will see his brother on my way home." He looked for a moment at Anne. "You are far from well yourself," he resumed. "Can I do any thing for you?"

"While I am living my present life, Mr. Speedwell, not even your skill can help me."

The surgeon took his leave. Anne hurried back up stairs, before Geoffrey could re-enter the cottage. To see the man who had laid her life waste—to meet the vindictive hatred that looked furtively at her out of his eyes—at the moment when sentence of death had been pronounced on him, was an ordeal from which every finer instinct in her nature shrank in horror.

Hour by hour, the morning wore on, and he made no attempt to communicate with her. Stranger still, Hester Dethridge never appeared. The servant came up stairs to say good-by; and went away for her holiday. Shortly afterward, certain sounds reached Anne's ears from the opposite side of the passage. She heard the strokes of a hammer, and then a noise as of some heavy piece of furniture being moved. The mysterious repairs were apparently being begun in the spare room.

She went to the window. The hour was approaching at which Sir Patrick and Blanche might be expected to make the attempt to see her.

For the third time, she looked at the letter.

It suggested, on this occasion, a new consideration to her. Did the strong measures which Sir Patrick had taken in secret indicate alarm as well as sympathy? Did he believe she was in a position in which the protection of the law was powerless to reach her? It seemed just possible. Suppose she were free to consult a magistrate, and to own to him (if words could express it) the vague presentiment of danger which was then present in her mind—what proof could she produce to satisfy the mind of a stranger? The proofs were all in her husband's favor. Witnesses could testify to the conciliatory words which he had spoken to her in their presence. The evidence of his mother and brother would show that he had preferred to sacrifice his own pecuniary interests rather than consent to part with her. She could furnish nobody with the smallest excuse, in her case, for interfering between man and wife. Did Sir Patrick see this? And did Blanche's description of what he and Arnold Brinkworth were doing point to the conclusion that they were taking the law into their own hands in despair? The more she thought of it, the more likely it seemed.

She was still pursuing the train of thought thus suggested, when the gate-bell rang.

The noises in the spare room suddenly stopped.

Anne looked out. The roof of a carriage was visible on the other side of the wall. Sir Patrick and Blanche had arrived. After an interval Hester Dethridge appeared in the garden, and went to the grating in the gate. Anne heard Sir Patrick's voice, clear and resolute. Every word he said reached her ears through the open window.

"Be so good as to give my card to Mr. Delamayn. Say that I bring him a message from Holchester House, and that I can only deliver it at a personal interview."

Hester Dethridge returned to the cottage. Another, and a longer interval elapsed. At the end of the time, Geoffrey himself appeared in the front garden, with the key in his hand. Anne's heart throbbed fast as she saw him unlock the gate, and asked herself what was to follow.

To her unutterable astonishment, Geoffrey admitted Sir Patrick without the slightest hesitation—and, more still, he invited Blanche to leave the carriage and come in!

"Let by-gones be by-gones," Anne heard him say to Sir Patrick. "I only want to do the right thing. If it's the right thing for visitors to come here, so soon after my father's death, come, and welcome. My own notion was, when you proposed it before, that it was wrong. I am not much versed in these things. I leave it to you."

"A visitor who brings you messages from your mother and your brother," Sir Patrick answered gravely, "is a person whom it is your duty to admit, Mr. Delamayn, under any circumstances."

"And he ought to be none the less welcome," added Blanche, "when he is accompanied by your wife's oldest and dearest friend."

Geoffrey looked, in stolid submission, from one to the other.

"I am not much versed in these things," he repeated. "I have said already, I leave it to you."

They were by this time close under Anne's window. She showed herself. Sir Patrick took off his hat. Blanche kissed her hand with a cry of joy, and attempted to enter the cottage. Geoffrey stopped her—and called to his wife to come down.

"No! no!" said Blanche. "Let me go up to her in her room."

She attempted for the second time to gain the stairs. For the second time, Geoffrey stopped her. "Don't trouble yourself," he said; "she is coming down."

Anne joined them in the front garden. Blanche flew into her arms and devoured her with kisses. Sir Patrick took her hand in silence. For the first time in Anne's experience of him, the bright, resolute, self-reliant old man was, for the moment, at a loss what to say, at a loss what to do. His eyes, resting on her in mute sympathy and interest, said plainly, "In your husband's presence I must not trust myself to speak."

Geoffrey broke the silence.

"Will you go into the drawing-room?" he asked, looking with steady attention at his wife and Blanche.

Geoffrey's voice appeared to rouse Sir Patrick. He raised his head—he looked like himself again.

"Why go indoors this lovely weather?" he said. "Suppose we take a turn in the garden?"

Blanche pressed Anne's hand significantly. The proposal was evidently made for a purpose. They turned the corner of the cottage and gained the large garden at the back—the two ladies walking together, arm in arm; Sir Patrick and Geoffrey following them. Little by little, Blanche quickened her pace. "I have got my instructions," she whispered to Anne. "Let's get out of his hearing."

It was more easily said than done. Geoffrey kept close behind them.

"Consider my lameness, Mr. Delamayn," said Sir Patrick. "Not quite so fast."

It was well intended. But Geoffrey's cunning had taken the alarm. Instead of dropping behind with Sir Patrick, he called to his wife.

"Consider Sir Patrick's lameness," he repeated. "Not quite so fast."

Sir Patrick met that check with characteristic readiness. When Anne slackened her pace, he addressed himself to Geoffrey, stopping deliberately in the middle of the path. "Let me give you my message from Holchester House," he said. The two ladies were still slowly walking on. Geoffrey was placed between the alternatives of staying with Sir Patrick and leaving them by themselves—or of following them and leaving Sir Patrick. Deliberately, on his side, he followed the ladies.

Sir Patrick called him back. "I told you I wished to speak to you," he said, sharply.

Driven to bay, Geoffrey openly revealed his resolution to give Blanche no opportunity of speaking in private to Anne. He called to Anne to stop.

"I have no secrets from my wife," he said.

" And I expect my wife to have no secrets from me. Give me the message in her hearing."

Sir Patrick's eyes brightened with indignation. He controlled himself, and looked for an instant significantly at his niece before he spoke to Geoffrey.

"As you please," he said. "Your brother requests me to tell you that the duties of the new position in which he is placed occupy the whole of his time, and will prevent him from returning to Fulham, as he had proposed, for some days to come. Lady Holchester, hearing that I was likely to see you, has charged me with another message, from herself. She is not well enough to leave home; and she wishes to see you at Holchester House to-morrow—accompanied (as she specially desires) by Mrs. Delamayn."

In giving the two messages, he gradually raised his voice to a louder tone than usual. While he was speaking, Blanche (warned to follow her instructions by the glance her uncle cast at her) lowered her voice, and said to Anne :

"He won't consent to the separation as long as he has got you here. He is trying for higher terms. Leave him, and he must submit. Put a candle in your window, if you can get into the garden to-night. If not, any other night. Make for the back gate in the wall. Sir Patrick and Arnold will manage the rest."

She slipped those words into Anne's ears—swinging her parasol to and fro, and looking as if the merest gossip was dropping from her lips—with the dexterity which rarely fails a woman when she is called on to assist a deception in which her own interests are concerned. Cleverly as it had been done, however, Geoffrey's inveterate distrust was stirred into action by it. Blanche had got to her last sentence before he was able to turn his attention from, what Sir Patrick was saying to what his niece was saying. A quicker man would have heard more. Geoffrey had only distinctly heard the first half of the last sentence.

" What's that," he asked, " about Sir Patrick and Arnold ?"

"Nothing very interesting to you," Blanche answered, readily. " I will repeat it if you like. I was telling Anne about my step-mother, Lady Lundie. After what happened that day in Portland Place, she has requested Sir Patrick and Arnold to consider themselves, for the future, as total strangers to her. That's all."

"Oh !" said Geoffrey, eying her narrowly. " That's all ?"

"Ask my uncle," returned Blanche, " if you don't believe that I have reported her correctly. She gave us all our dismissal, in her most magnificent manner, and in those very words. Didn't she, Sir Patrick ?"

It was perfectly true. Blanche's readiness of resource had met the emergency of the moment by describing something, in connection with Sir Patrick and Arnold, which had really happened. Silenced on one side, in spite of himself, Geoffrey was at the same moment pressed on the other, for an answer to his mother's message.

" I must take your reply to Lady Holchester," said Sir Patrick. " What is it to be ?"

Geoffrey looked hard at him, without making any reply.

Sir Patrick repeated the message—with a special emphasis on that part of it which related to Anne. The emphasis roused Geoffrey's temper.

"You and my mother have made that message up between you, to try me !" he burst out. " Damn all underhand work is what *I* say !"

" I am waiting for your answer," persisted Sir Patrick, steadily ignoring the words which had just been addressed to him.

Geoffrey glanced at Anne, and suddenly recovered himself.

" My love to my mother," he said. " I'll go to her to-morrow—and take my wife with me, with the greatest pleasure. Do you hear that ? With the greatest pleasure." He stopped to observe the effect of his reply. Sir Patrick waited impenetrably to hear more—if he had more to say. " I'm sorry I lost my temper just now," he resumed. " I am badly treated—I'm distrusted without a cause. I ask you to bear witness," he added, his voice getting louder again, while his eyes moved uneasily backward and forward between Sir Patrick and Anne, "that I treat my wife as becomes a lady. Her friend calls on her—and she's free to receive her friend. My mother wants to see her—and I promise to take her to my mother's. At two o'clock to-morrow. Where am I to blame ? You stand there looking at me, and saying nothing. Where am I to blame ?"

" If a man's own conscience justifies him, Mr. Delamayn," said Sir Patrick, " the opinions of others are of very little importance. My errand here is performed."

As he turned to bid Anne farewell, the uneasiness that he felt at leaving her forced its way to view. The color faded out of his face. His hand trembled as it closed tenderly and firmly on hers. " I shall see you to-morrow, at Holchester House," he said ; giving his arm while he spoke to Blanche. He took leave of Geoffrey, without looking at him again, and without seeing his offered hand. In another minute they were gone.

Anne waited on the lower floor of the cottage, while Geoffrey closed and locked the gate. She had no wish to appear to avoid him, after the answer that he had sent to his mother's message. He returned slowly half-way across the front garden, looked toward the passage in which she was standing, passed before the door, and disappeared round the corner of the cottage on his way to the back garden. The inference was not to be mistaken. It was Geoffrey who was avoiding *her*. Had he lied to Sir Patrick ? When the next day came would he find reasons of his own for refusing to take her to Holchester House ?

She went up stairs. At the same moment Hester Dethridge opened her bedroom door to come out. Observing Anne, she closed it again ; and remained invisible in her room. Once more the inference was not to be mistaken. Hester Dethridge, also, had her reasons for avoiding Anne.

What did it mean ? What object could there be in common between Hester and Geoffrey ?

There was no fathoming the meaning of it. Anne's thoughts reverted to the communication which had been secretly made to her by Blanche. It was not in womanhood to be insensible to such devotion as Sir Patrick's conduct implied. Terrible as her position had become in its ever-growing uncertainty, in its never-ending suspense, the oppression of it yielded for the moment to the glow of pride and gratitude which warmed her heart, as she thought of the sacrifices that had been made, of the perils that were still to be encountered, solely for her sake. To shorten the period of suspense seemed to be a duty which she owed to Sir Patrick, as well as to herself. Why, in her situation, wait for what the next day might bring forth? If the opportunity offered, she determined to put the signal in the window that night.

Toward evening she heard once more the noises which appeared to indicate that repairs of some sort were going on in the house. This time the sounds were fainter; and they came, as she fancied, not from the spare room, as before, but from Geoffrey's room, next to it.

The dinner was later than usual that day. Hester Dethridge did not appear with the tray till dusk. Anne spoke to her, and received a mute sign in answer. Determined to see the woman's face plainly, she put a question which required a written answer on the slate; and, telling Hester to wait, went to the mantle-piece to light her candle. When she turned round with the lighted candle in her hand, Hester was gone.

Night came. She rang her bell to have the tray taken away. The fall of a strange footstep startled her outside her door. She called out, "Who's there?" The voice of the lad whom Geoffrey employed to go on errands for him answered her.

"What do you want here?" she asked, through the door.

"Mr. Delamayn sent me up, ma'am. He wishes to speak to you directly."

Anne found Geoffrey in the dining-room. His object in wishing to speak to her was, on the surface of it, trivial enough. He wanted to know how she would prefer going to Holchester House on the next day—by the railway, or in a carriage. "If you prefer driving," he said, "the boy has come here for orders; and he can tell them to send a carriage from the livery-stables, as he goes home."

"The railway will do perfectly well for me," Anne replied.

Instead of accepting the answer, and dropping the subject, he asked her to reconsider her decision. There was an absent, uneasy expression in his eye as he begged her not to consult economy at the expense of her own comfort. He appeared to have some reason of his own for preventing her from leaving the room. "Sit down a minute, and think before you decide," he said. Having forced her to take a chair, he put his head outside the door, and directed the lad to go up stairs, and see if he had left his pipe in his bedroom. "I want you to go in comfort, as a lady should," he repeated, with the uneasy look more marked than ever. Before Anne could reply, the lad's voice reached them from the bedroom floor, raised in shrill alarm, and screaming "Fire!"

Geoffrey ran up stairs. Anne followed him. The lad met them at the top of the stairs. He pointed to the open door of Anne's room. She was absolutely certain of having left her lighted candle, when she went down to Geoffrey, at a safe distance from the bed-curtains. The bed-curtains, nevertheless, were in a blaze of fire.

There was a supply of water to the cottage, on the upper floor. The bedroom jugs and cans, usually in their places at an earlier hour, were standing that night at the cistern. An empty pail was left near them. Directing the lad to bring him water from these resources, Geoffrey tore down the curtains in a flaming heap, partly on the bed and partly on the sofa near it. Using the can and the pail alternately, as the boy brought them, he drenched the bed and the sofa. It was all over in little more than a minute. The cottage was saved. But the bed-furniture was destroyed; and the room, as a matter of course, was rendered uninhabitable, for that night at least, and probably for more nights to come.

Geoffrey set down the empty pail; and, turning to Anne, pointed across the passage.

"You won't be much inconvenienced by this," he said. "You have only to shift your quarters to the spare room."

With the assistance of the lad, he moved Anne's boxes, and the chest of drawers, which had escaped damage, into the opposite room. This done, he cautioned her to be careful with her candles for the future—and went down stairs, without waiting to hear what she said in reply. The lad followed him, and was dismissed for the night.

Even in the confusion which attended the extinguishing of the fire, the conduct of Hester Dethridge had been remarkable enough to force itself on the attention of Anne.

She had come out from her bedroom, when the alarm was given; had looked at the flaming curtains; and had drawn back, stolidly submissive, into a corner to wait the event. There she had stood—to all appearance, utterly indifferent to the possible destruction of her own cottage. The fire extinguished, she still waited impenetrably in her corner, while the chest of drawers and the boxes were being moved—then locked the door, without even a passing glance at the scorched ceiling and the burned bed-furniture—put the key into her pocket—and went back to her room.

Anne had hitherto not shared the conviction felt by most other persons who were brought into contact with Hester Dethridge, that the woman's mind was deranged. After what she had just seen, however, the general impression became her impression too. She had thought of putting certain questions to Hester, when they were left together, as to the origin of the fire. Reflection decided her on saying nothing, for that night at least. She crossed the passage, and entered the spare room—the room which she had declined to occupy on her arrival at the cottage, and which she was obliged to sleep in now.

She was instantly struck by a change in the disposition of the furniture of the room.

The bed had been moved. The head—set, when she had last seen it, against the side wall of the cottage—was placed now against the partition wall which separated the room from Geoffrey's room. This new arrangement had evidently been effected with a settled purpose of some sort. The hook in the ceiling which supported the curtains (the bed, unlike the bed in the other room, having no canopy attached to it) had been moved so as to adapt itself to the change that had been made. The chairs and the wash-hand-stand, formerly placed against the partition wall, were now, as a matter of necessity, shifted over to the vacant space against the side wall of the cottage. For the rest, no other alteration was visible in any part of the room.

In Anne's situation, any event not immediately intelligible on the face of it, was an event to be distrusted. Was there a motive for the change in the position of the bed? And was it, by any chance, a motive in which she was concerned?

The doubt had barely occurred to her, before a startling suspicion succeeded it. Was there some secret purpose to be answered by making her sleep in the spare room? Did the question which the servant had heard Geoffrey put to Hester, on the previous night, refer to this? Had the fire which had so unaccountably caught the curtains in her own room, been, by any possibility, a fire purposely kindled, to force her out?

She dropped into the nearest chair, faint with horror, as those three questions forced themselves in rapid succession on her mind.

After waiting a little, she recovered self-possession enough to recognize the first plain necessity of putting her suspicions to the test. It was possible that her excited fancy had filled her with a purely visionary alarm. For all she knew to the contrary, there might be some undeniably sufficient reason for changing the position of the bed. She went out, and knocked at the door of Hester Dethridge's room.

"I want to speak to you," she said.

Hester came out. Anne pointed to the spare room, and led the way to it. Hester followed her.

"Why have you changed the place of the bed," she asked, "from the wall there, to the wall here?"

Stolidly submissive to the question, as she had been stolidly submissive to the fire, Hester Dethridge wrote her reply. On all other occasions she was accustomed to look the persons to whom she offered her slate steadily in the face. Now, for the first time, she handed it to Anne with her eyes on the floor. The one line written contained no direct answer: the words were these:

"I have meant to move it, for some time past."

"I ask you why you have moved it."

She wrote these four words on the slate: "The wall is damp."

Anne looked at the wall. There was no sign of damp on the paper. She passed her hand over it. Feel where she might, the wall was dry.

"That is not your reason," she said.

Hester stood immovable.

"There is no dampness in the wall."

Hester pointed persistently with her pencil to the four words, still without looking up—waited a moment for Anne to read them again—and left the room.

It was plainly useless to call her back. Anne's first impulse when she was alone again was to secure the door. She not only locked it, but bolted it at top and bottom. The mortise of the lock and the staples of the bolts, when she tried them, were firm. The lurking treachery—wherever else it might be—was not in the fastenings of the door.

She looked all round the room; examining the fire-place, the window and its shutters, the interior of the wardrobe, the hidden space under the bed. Nothing was any where to be discovered which could justify the most timid person living in feeling suspicion or alarm.

Appearances, fair as they were, failed to convince her. The presentiment of some hidden treachery, steadily getting nearer and nearer to her in the dark, had rooted itself firmly in her mind. She sat down, and tried to trace her way back to the clew, through the earlier events of the day.

The effort was fruitless: nothing definite, nothing tangible, rewarded it. Worse still, a new doubt grew out of it—a doubt whether the motive which Sir Patrick had avowed (through Blanche) was the motive for helping her which was really in his mind.

Did he sincerely believe Geoffrey's conduct to be animated by no worse object than a mercenary object? and was his only purpose in planning to remove her out of her husband's reach, to force Geoffrey's consent to their separation on the terms which Julius had proposed? Was this really the sole end that he had in view? or was he secretly convinced (knowing Anne's position as he knew it) that she was in personal danger at the cottage? and had he considerately kept that conviction concealed, in the fear that he might otherwise encourage her to feel alarmed about herself? She looked round the strange room, in the silence of the night, and she felt that the latter interpretation was the likeliest interpretation of the two.

The sounds caused by the closing of the doors and windows reached her from the ground-floor. What was to be done?

It was impossible to show the signal which had been agreed on to Sir Patrick and Arnold. The window in which they expected to see it was the window of the room in which the fire had broken out—the room which Hester Dethridge had locked up for the night.

It was equally hopeless to wait until the policeman passed on his beat, and to call for help. Even if she could prevail upon herself to make that open acknowledgment of distrust under her husband's roof, and even if help was near, what valid reason could she give for raising an alarm? There was not the shadow of a reason to justify any one in placing her under the protection of the law.

As a last resource, impelled by her blind distrust of the change in the position of the bed, she attempted to move it. The utmost exertion of her strength did not suffice to stir the heavy piece of furniture out of its place, by so much as a hair's breadth.

There was no alternative but to trust to the security of the locked and bolted door, and to keep watch through the night—certain that Sir Patrick and Arnold were, on their part, also keeping watch in the near neighborhood of the cottage. She took out her work and her books; and returned to her chair, placing it near the table, in the middle of the room.

The last noises which told of life and movement about her died away. The breathless stillness of the night closed round her.

———◆———

## CHAPTER THE FIFTY-SIXTH.

### THE MEANS.

THE new day dawned; the sun rose; the household was astir again. Inside the spare room, and outside the spare room, nothing had happened.

At the hour appointed for leaving the cottage to pay the promised visit to Holchester House, Hester Dethridge and Geoffrey were alone together in the bedroom in which Anne had passed the night.

"She's dressed, and waiting for me in the front garden," said Geoffrey. "You wanted to see me here alone. What is it?"

Hester pointed to the bed.

"You want it moved from the wall?"

Hester nodded her head.

They moved the bed some feet away from the partition wall. After a momentary pause, Geoffrey spoke again.

"It must be done to-night," he said. "Her friends may interfere; the girl may come back. It must be done to-night."

Hester bowed her head slowly.

"How long do you want to be left by yourself in the house?"

She held up three of her fingers.

"Does that mean three hours?"

She nodded her head.

"Will it be done in that time?"

She made the affirmative sign once more.

Thus far, she had never lifted her eyes to his. In her manner of listening to him when he spoke, in the slightest movement that she made when necessity required it, the same lifeless submission to him, the same mute horror of him, was expressed. He had, thus far, silently resented this, on his side. On the point of leaving the room the restraint which he had laid on himself gave way. For the first time, he resented it in words.

"Why the devil can't you look at me?" he asked.

She let the question pass, without a sign to show that she had heard him. He angrily repeated it. She wrote on her slate, and held it out to him—still without raising her eyes to his face.

"You know you can speak," he said. "You know I have found you out. What's the use of playing the fool with *me?*"

She persisted in holding the slate before him. He read these words:

"I am dumb to you, and blind to you. Let me be."

"Let you be!" he repeated. "It's a little late in the day to be scrupulous, after what you have done. Do you want your Confession back, or not?"

As the reference to the Confession passed his lips, she raised her head. A faint tinge of color showed itself on her livid cheeks; a momentary spasm of pain stirred her deathlike face. The one last interest left in the woman's life was the interest of recovering the manuscript which had been taken from her. To *that* appeal the stunned intelligence still faintly answered — and to no other.

"Remember the bargain on your side," Geoffrey went on, "and I'll remember the bargain on mine. This is how it stands, you know. I have read your Confession; and I find one thing want-

ing. You don't tell how it was done. I know you smothered him—but I don't know how. I want to know. You're dumb; and you can't tell me. You must do to the wall here what you did in the other house. You run no risks. There isn't a soul to see you. You have got the place to yourself. When I come back let me find this wall like the other wall—at that small hour of the morning you know, when you were waiting, with the towel in your hand, for the first stroke of the clock. Let me find that; and to-morrow you shall have your Confession back again."

As the reference to the Confession passed his lips for the second time, the sinking energy in the woman leaped up in her once more. She snatched her slate from her side; and, writing on it rapidly, held it, with both hands, close under his eyes. He read these words:

"I won't wait. I must have it to-night."

"Do you think I keep your Confession about me?" said Geoffrey. "I haven't even got it in the house."

She staggered back; and looked up for the first time.

"Don't alarm yourself," he went on. "It's sealed up with my seal; and it's safe in my bankers' keeping. I posted it to them myself. You don't stick at a trifle, Mrs. Dethridge. If I had kept it locked up in the house, you might have forced the lock when my back was turned. If I had kept it about me—I might have had that towel over my face, in the small hours of the morning! The bankers will give you back your Confession—just as they have received it from me—on receipt of an order in my handwriting. Do what I have told you; and you shall have the order to-night."

She passed her apron over her face, and drew a long breath of relief. Geoffrey turned to the door.

"I will be back at six this evening," he said. "Shall I find it done?"

She bowed her head.

His first condition accepted, he proceeded to the second.

"When the opportunity offers," he resumed, "I shall go up to my room. I shall ring the dining-room bell first. You will go up before me when you hear that—and you will show me how you did it in the empty house?"

She made the affirmative sign once more.

At the same moment the door in the passage below was opened and closed again. Geoffrey instantly went down stairs. It was possible that Anne might have forgotten something; and it was necessary to prevent her from returning to her own room.

They met in the passage.

"Tired of waiting in the garden?" he asked, abruptly.

She pointed to the dining-room.

"The postman has just given me a letter for you, through the grating in the gate," she answered. "I have put it on the table in there."

He went in. The handwriting on the address of the letter was the handwriting of Mrs. Glenarm. He put it unread into his pocket, and went back to Anne.

"Step out!" he said. "We shall lose the train."

They started for their visit to Holchester House.

## CHAPTER THE FIFTY-SEVENTH.

### THE END.

AT a few minutes before six o'clock that evening, Lord Holchester's carriage brought Geoffrey and Anne back to the cottage.

Geoffrey prevented the servant from ringing at the gate. He had taken the key with him, when he left home earlier in the day. Having admitted Anne, and having closed the gate again, he went on before her to the kitchen window, and called to Hester Dethridge.

"Take some cold water into the drawing-room, and fill the vase on the chimney-piece," he said. "The sooner you put those flowers into water," he added, turning to his wife, "the longer they will last."

He pointed, as he spoke, to a nosegay in Anne's hand, which Julius had gathered for her from the conservatory at Holchester House. Leaving her to arrange the flowers in the vase, he went up stairs. After waiting for a moment, he was joined by Hester Dethridge.

"Done?" he asked, in a whisper.

Hester made the affirmative sign. Geoffrey took off his boots, and led the way into the spare room. They noiselessly moved the bed back to its place against the partition wall—and left the room again. When Anne entered it, some minutes afterward, not the slightest change of any kind was visible since she had last seen it in the middle of the day.

She removed her bonnet and mantle, and sat down to rest.

The whole course of events, since the previous night, had tended one way, and had exerted the same delusive influence over her mind. It was impossible for her any longer to resist the conviction that she had distrusted appearances without the slightest reason, and that she had permitted purely visionary suspicions to fill her with purely causeless alarm. In the firm, belief that she was in danger, she had watched through the night—and nothing had happened. In the confident anticipation that Geoffrey had promised what he was resolved not to perform, she had waited to see what excuse he would find for keeping her at the cottage. And, when the time came for the visit, she found him ready to fulfill the engagement which he had made. At Holchester House, not the slightest interference had been attempted with her perfect liberty of action and speech. Resolved to inform Sir Patrick that she had changed her room, she had described the alarm of fire and the events which had succeeded it, in the fullest detail—and had not been once checked by Geoffrey from beginning to end. She had spoken in confidence to Blanche, and had never been interrupted. Walking round the conservatory, she had dropped behind the others with perfect impunity, to say a grateful word to Sir Patrick, and to ask if the interpretation that he placed on Geoffrey's conduct was really the interpretation which had been hinted at by Blanche. They had talked together for ten minutes or more. Sir Patrick had assured her that Blanche had correctly represented his opinion. He had declared his conviction that the rash way was, in her case, the right way; and that she would do well (with his assistance) to take the initiative, in the matter of the separation, on herself. "As long as he can keep you under the same roof with him"—Sir Patrick had said—"so long he will speculate on our anxiety to release you from the oppression of living with him; and so long he will hold out with his brother (in the character of a penitent husband) for higher terms. Put the signal in the window, and try the experiment to-night. Once find your way to the garden door, and I answer for keeping you safely out of his reach until he has submitted to the separation, and has signed the deed." In those words, he had urged Anne to prompt action. He had received, in return, her promise to be guided by his advice. She had gone back to the drawing-room; and Geoffrey had made no remark on her absence. She had returned to Fulham, alone with him in his brother's carriage; and he had asked no questions. What was it natural, with her means of judging, to infer from all this? Could she see into Sir Patrick's mind, and detect that he was deliberately concealing his own conviction, in the fear that he might paralyze her energies if he acknowledged the alarm for her that he really felt? No. She could only accept the false appearances that surrounded her in the disguise of truth. She could only adopt, in good faith, Sir Patrick's assumed point of view, and believe, on the evidence of her own observation, that Sir Patrick was right.

Toward dusk, Anne began to feel the exhaustion which was the necessary result of a night passed without sleep. She rang her bell, and asked for some tea.

Hester Dethridge answered the bell. Instead of making the usual sign, she stood considering—and then wrote on her slate. These were the words: "I have all the work to do, now the girl has gone. If you would have your tea in the drawing-room, you would save me another journey up stairs."

Anne at once engaged to comply with the request.

"Are you ill?" she asked; noticing, faint as the light now was, something strangely altered in Hester's manner.

Without looking up, Hester shook her head.

"Has any thing happened to vex you?"

The negative sign was repeated.

"Have I offended you?"

She suddenly advanced a step; suddenly looked at Anne; checked herself with a dull moan, like a moan of pain; and hurried out of the room.

Concluding that she had inadvertently said, or done, something to offend Hester Dethridge, Anne determined to return to the subject at the first favorable opportunity. In the mean time, she descended to the ground-floor. The dining-room door, standing wide open, showed her Geoffrey sitting at the table, writing a letter—with the fatal brandy-bottle at his side.

After what Mr. Speedwell had told her, it was her duty to interfere. She performed her duty, without an instant's hesitation.

"Pardon me for interrupting you," she said. "I think you have forgotten what Mr. Speedwell told you about that."

She pointed to the bottle. Geoffrey looked at it; looked down again at his letter; and impatiently shook his head. She made a second attempt at remonstrance — again without effect. He only said, "All right!" in lower tones than were customary with him, and continued his occupation. It was useless to court a third repulse. Anne went into the drawing-room.

The letter on which he was engaged was an answer to Mrs. Glenarm, who had written to tell him that she was leaving town. He had reached his two concluding sentences when Anne spoke to him. They ran as follows: "I may have news to bring you, before long, which you don't look for. Stay where you are through to-morrow, and wait to hear from me."

After sealing the envelope, he emptied his glass of brandy and water; and waited, looking through the open door. When Hester Dethridge crossed the passage with the tea-tray, and entered the drawing-room, he gave the sign which had been agreed on. He rang his bell. Hester came out again, closing the drawing-room door behind her.

"Is she safe at her tea?" he asked, removing his heavy boots, and putting on the slippers which were placed ready for him.

Hester bowed her head.

He pointed up the stairs. "You go first," he whispered. "No nonsense! and no noise!"

She ascended the stairs. He followed slowly. Although he had only drank one glass of brandy and water, his step was uncertain already. With one hand on the wall, and one hand on the banister, he made his way to the top; stopped, and listened for a moment; then joined Hester in his own room, and softly locked the door.

"Well?" he said.

She was standing motionless in the middle of the room—not like a living woman—like a machine waiting to be set in movement. Finding it useless to speak to her, he touched her (with a strange sensation of shrinking in him as he did it), and pointed to the partition wall.

The touch roused her. With slow step and vacant face—moving as if she was walking in her sleep—she led the way to the papered wall; knelt down at the skirting-board; and, taking out two small sharp nails, lifted up a long strip of the paper which had been detached from the plaster beneath. Mounting on a chair, she turned back the strip and pinned it up, out of the way, using the two nails, which she had kept ready in her hand.

By the last dim rays of twilight, Geoffrey looked at the wall.

A hollow space met his view. At a distance of some three feet from the floor, the laths had been sawn away, and the plaster had been ripped out, piecemeal, so as to leave a cavity, sufficient in height and width to allow free power of working in any direction, to a man's arms. The cavity completely pierced the substance of the wall. Nothing but the paper on the other side prevented eye or hand from penetrating into the next room.

Hester Dethridge got down from the chair, and made signs for a light.

Geoffrey took a match from the box. The same strange uncertainty which had already possessed his feet, appeared now to possess his hands. He struck the match too heavily against the sand-paper, and broke it. He tried another, and struck it too lightly to kindle the flame. Hester took the box out of his hands. Having lit the candle, she held it low, and pointed to the skirting-board.

Two little hooks were fixed into the floor, near the part of the wall from which the paper had been removed. Two lengths of fine and strong string were twisted once or twice round the hooks. The loose ends of the string, extending to some length beyond the twisted parts, were neatly coiled away against the skirting-board. The other ends, drawn tight, disappeared in two small holes drilled through the wall, at a height of a foot from the floor.

After first untwisting the strings from the hooks, Hester rose, and held the candle so as to light the cavity in the wall. Two more pieces of the fine string were seen here, resting loose upon the uneven surface which marked the lower boundary of the hollowed space. Lifting these higher strings, Hester lifted the loosened paper in the next room—the lower strings, which had previously held the strip firm and flat against the sound portion of the wall, working in their holes, and allowing the paper to move up freely. As it rose higher and higher, Geoffrey saw thin strips of cotton wool lightly attached, at intervals, to the back of the paper, so as effectually to prevent it from making a grating sound against the wall. Up and up it came slowly, till it could be pulled through the hollow space, and pinned up out of the way, as the strip previously lifted had been pinned before it. Hester drew back, and made way for Geoffrey to look through. There was Anne's room, visible through the wall! He softly parted the light curtains that hung over the bed. There was the pillow, on which her head would rest at night, within reach of his hands!

The deadly dexterity of it struck him cold. His nerves gave way. He drew back with a start of guilty fear, and looked round the room. A pocket flask of brandy lay on the table at his bedside. He snatched it up, and emptied it at a draught—and felt like himself again.

He beckoned, to Hester to approach him.

"Before we go any further," he said, "there's one thing I want to know. How is it all to be put right again? Suppose this room is examined? Those strings will show."

Hester opened a cupboard and produced a jar. She took out the cork. There was a mixture inside which looked like glue. Partly by signs, and partly by help of the slate, she showed how the mixture could be applied to the back of the loosened strip of paper in the next room—how the paper could be glued to the sound lower part of the wall by tightening the strings—how the strings, having served that purpose, could be safely removed—how the same process could be followed in Geoffrey's room, after the hollowed place had been filled up again with the materials waiting in the scullery, or even without filling up the hollowed place if the time failed for doing it. In either case, the refastened paper would hide every thing, and the wall would tell no tales.

Geoffrey was satisfied. He pointed next to the towels in his room.

"Take one of them," he said, "and show me how you did it, with your own hands."

As he said the words, Anne's voice reached his ear from below, calling for "Mrs. Dethridge."

It was impossible to say what might happen next. In another minute, she might go up to her room, and discover every thing. Geoffrey pointed to the wall.

"Put it right again," he said. "Instantly!"

It was soon done. All that was necessary was to let the two strips of paper drop back into their places—to fasten the strip to the wall in Anne's room, by tightening the two lower strings—and then to replace the nails which held the loose strip on Geoffrey's side. In a minute, the wall had reassumed its customary aspect.

They stole out, and looked over the stairs into the passage below. After calling uselessly for the second time, Anne appeared; crossed over to the kitchen; and, returning again with the kettle in her hand, closed the drawing-room door.

Hester Dethridge waited impenetrably to receive her next directions. There were no further directions to give. The hideous dramatic representation of the woman's crime for which Geoffrey had asked was in no respect necessary: the means were all prepared, and the manner of using them was self-evident. Nothing but the opportunity, and the resolution to profit by it, were wanting to lead the way to the end. Geoffrey signed to Hester to go down stairs.

"Get back into the kitchen," he said, "before she comes out again. I shall keep in the garden. When she goes up into her room for the night, show yourself at the back-door—and I shall know."

Hester set her foot on the first stair—stopped—turned round—and looked slowly along the two walls of the passage, from end to end—shuddered—shook her head—and went slowly on down the stairs.

"What were you looking for?" he whispered after her.

She neither answered, nor looked back—she went her way into the kitchen.

He waited a minute, and then followed her.

On his way out to the garden, he went into the dining-room. The moon had risen; and the window-shutters were not closed. It was easy to find the brandy and the jug of water on the table. He mixed the two, and emptied the tumbler at a draught. "My head's queer," he whispered to himself. He passed his handkerchief over his face. "How infernally hot it is to-night!" He made for the door. It was open, and plainly visible—and yet, he failed to find his way to it. Twice, he found himself trying to walk through the wall, on either side. The third time, he got out, and reached the garden. A strange sensation possessed him, as he walked round and round. He had not drunk enough, or nearly enough, to intoxicate him. His mind, in a dull way, felt the same as usual; but his body was like the body of a drunken man.

The night advanced; the clock of Putney Church struck ten.

Anne appeared again from the drawing-room, with her bedroom candle in her hand.

"Put out the lights," she said to Hester, at the kitchen door; "I am going up stairs."

She entered her room. The insupportable sense of weariness, after the sleepless night that she had passed, weighed more heavily on her than ever. She locked her door, but forbore, on this occasion, to fasten the bolts. The dread of danger was no longer present to her mind; and there was this positive objection to using the bolts, that the unfastening of them would increase the difficulty of leaving the room noiselessly later in the night. She loosened her dress, and lifted her hair from her temples—and paced to and fro in the room wearily, thinking. Geoffrey's habits were irregular; Hester seldom went to bed early.

Two hours at least—more probably three—must pass, before it would be safe to communicate with Sir Patrick by means of the signal in the window. Her strength was fast failing her. If she persisted, for the next three hours, in denying herself the repose which she sorely needed, the chances were that her nerves might fail her, through sheer exhaustion, when the time came for facing the risk and making the effort to escape. Sleep was falling on her even now—and sleep she must have. She had no fear of failing to wake at the needful time. Falling asleep, with a special necessity for rising at a given hour present to her mind, Anne (like most other sensitively organized people) could trust herself to wake at that given hour, instinctively. She put her lighted candle in a safe position, and laid down on the bed. In less than five minutes, she was in a deep sleep.

*      *      *      *      *      *      *

The church clock struck the quarter to eleven.

Hester Dethridge showed herself at the back garden door. Geoffrey crossed the lawn, and joined her. The light of the lamp in the passage fell on his face. She started back from the sight of it.

"What's wrong?" he asked.

She shook her head; and pointed through the dining-room door to the brandy-bottle on the table.

"I'm as sober as you are, you fool!" he said. "Whatever else it is, it's not that."

Hester looked at him again. He was right. However unsteady his gait might be, his speech was not the speech, his eyes were not the eyes, of a drunken man.

"Is she in her room for the night?"

Hester made the affirmative sign.

Geoffrey ascended the stairs, swaying from side to side. He stopped at the top, and beckoned to Hester to join him. He went on into his room; and, signing to her to follow him, closed the door.

He looked at the partition wall—without approaching it. Hester waited, behind him.

"Is she asleep?" he asked.

Hester went to the wall; listened at it; and made the affirmative reply.

He sat down. "My head's queer," he said. "Give me a drink of water." He drank part of the water, and poured the rest over his head. Hester turned toward the door to leave him. He instantly stopped her. "I can't unwind the strings. I can't lift up the paper. Do it."

She sternly made the sign of refusal: she resolutely opened the door to leave him. "Do you want your Confession back?" he asked. She closed the door, stolidly submissive in an instant; and crossed to the partition wall.

She lifted the loose strips of paper on either side of the wall—pointed through the hollowed place—and drew back again to the other end of the room.

He rose and walked unsteadily from the chair to the foot of his bed. Holding by the wood-work of the bed; he waited a little. While he waited, he became conscious of a change in the strange sensations that possessed him. A feeling as of a breath of cold air passed over the right side of his head. He became steady again: he could calculate his distances: he could put his hands through the hollowed place, and draw aside the light curtains, hanging from the hook in the ceiling over the head of her bed. He could look at his sleeping wife.

She was dimly visible, by the light of the candle placed at the other end of her room. The worn and weary look had disappeared from her face. All that had been purest and sweetest in it, in the by-gone time, seemed to be renewed by the deep sleep that held her gently. She was young again in the dim light: she was beautiful in her calm repose. Her head lay back on the pillow. Her upturned face was in a position which placed her completely at the mercy of the man under whose eyes she was sleeping—the man who was looking at her, with the merciless resolution in him to take her life.

After waiting a while, he drew back. "She's more like a child than a woman to-night," he muttered to himself under his breath. He glanced across the room at Hester Dethridge. The lighted candle which she had brought up stairs with her was burning near the place where she stood. "Blow it out," he whispered. She never moved. He repeated the direction. There she stood, deaf to him.

What was she doing? She was looking fixedly into one of the corners of the room.

He turned his head again toward the hollowed place in the wall. He looked at the peaceful face on the pillow once more. He deliberately revived his own vindictive sense of the debt that he owed her. "But for you," he whispered to himself, "I should have won the race: but for you, I should have been friends with my father: but for you, I might marry Mrs. Glenarm." He turned back again into the room while the sense of it was at its fiercest in him. He looked round and round him. He took up a towel; considered for a moment; and threw it down again.

A new idea struck him. In two steps he was at the side of his bed. He seized on one of the pillows, and looked suddenly at Hester. "It's not a drunken brute, this time," he said to her. "It's a woman who will fight for her life. The pillow's the safest of the two." She never answered him, and never looked toward him. He made once more for the place in the wall; and stopped midway between it and his bed—stopped, and cast a backward glance over his shoulder.

Hester Dethridge was stirring at last.

With no third person in the room, she was looking, and moving, nevertheless, as if she was following a third person along the wall, from the corner. Her lips were parted in horror; her eyes, opening wider and wider, stared rigid and glittering at the empty wall. Step by step, she stole nearer and nearer to Geoffrey, still following some visionary Thing, which was stealing nearer and nearer, too. He asked himself what it meant. Was the terror of the deed that he was about to do more than the woman's brain could bear? Would she burst out screaming, and wake his wife?

He hurried to the place in the wall—to seize the chance, while the chance was his.

He steadied his strong hold on the pillow.

He stooped to pass it through the opening.

He poised it over Anne's sleeping face.

At the same moment he felt Hester Dethridge's hand laid on him from behind. The touch ran through him, from head to foot, like a touch of ice. He drew back with a start, and faced her. Her eyes were staring straight over his shoulder at something behind him—looking as they had looked in the garden at Windygates.

Before he could speak he felt the flash of her eyes in *his* eyes. For the third time, she had seen the Apparition behind him. The homicidal frenzy possessed her. She flew at his throat like a wild beast. The feeble old woman attacked the athlete!

He dropped the pillow, and lifted his terrible right arm to brush her from him, as he might have brushed an insect from him.

Even as he raised the arm a frightful distortion seized on his face. As if with an invisible hand, it dragged down the brow and the eyelid on the right; it dragged down the mouth on the same side. His arm fell helpless; his whole body, on the side under the arm, gave way. He dropped on the floor, like a man shot dead.

Hester Dethridge pounced on his prostrate body—knelt on his broad breast—and fastened her ten fingers on his throat.

\*　　\*　　\*　　\*　　\*　　\*　　\*

The shock of the fall woke Anne on the instant. She started up—looked round—and saw a gap in the wall at the head of her bed, and the candle-light glimmering in the next room. Panic-stricken; doubting, for the moment, if she were in her right mind, she drew back, waiting—listening—looking. She saw nothing but the glimmering light in the room; she heard nothing but a hoarse gasping, as of some person laboring for breath. The sound ceased. There was an interval of silence. Then the head of Hester Dethridge rose slowly into sight through the gap in the wall—rose with the glittering light of madness in the eyes; and looked at her.

She flew to the open window, and screamed for help.

Sir Patrick's voice answered her, from the road in front of the cottage.

"Wait for me, for God's sake!" she cried.

She fled from the room, and rushed down the stairs. In another moment, she had opened the door, and was out in the front garden.

As she ran to the gate, she heard the voice of a strange man on the other side of it. Sir Patrick called to her encouragingly. "The policeman is with us," he said. "He patrols the garden at night—he has a key." As he spoke the gate was opened from the outside. She saw Sir Patrick, Arnold, and the policeman. She staggered toward them as they came in—she was just able to say, "Up stairs!" before her senses failed her. Sir Patrick saved her from falling. He placed her on the bench in the garden, and waited by her, while Arnold and the policeman hurried into the cottage.

"Where first?" asked Arnold.

"The room the lady called from," said the policeman.

They mounted the stairs, and entered Anne's room. The gap in the wall was instantly observed by both of them. They looked through it.

Geoffrey Delamayn's dead body lay on the floor. Hester Dethridge was kneeling at his head, praying.

———◆———

# Epilogue.

## A MORNING CALL.

### I.

THE newspapers have announced the return of Lord and Lady Holchester to their residence in London, after an absence on the continent of more than six months.

It is the height of the season. All day long, within the canonical hours, the door of Holchester House is perpetually opening to receive visitors. The vast majority leave their cards, and go away again. Certain privileged individuals only, get out of their carriages, and enter the house.

Among these last, arriving at an earlier hour than is customary, is a person of distinction who is positively bent on seeing either the master or the mistress of the house, and who will take no denial. While this person is parleying with the chief of 'he servants, Lord Holchester, passing from one room to another, happens to cross the inner end of the hall. The person instantly darts at him with a cry of "Dear Lord Holchester!" Julius turns, and sees—Lady Lundie!

He is fairly caught, and he gives way with his best grace. As he opens the door of the nearest room for her ladyship, he furtively consults his watch, and says in his inmost soul, "How am I to get rid of her before the others come?"

Lady Lundie settles down on a sofa in a whirlwind of silk and lace, and becomes, in her own majestic way, "perfectly charming." She makes the most affectionate inquiries about Lady Holchester, about the Dowager Lady Holchester, about Julius himself. Where have they been? what have they seen? have time and change helped them to recover the shock of that dreadful event, to which Lady Lundie dare not more particularly allude? Julius answers resignedly, and a little absently. He makes polite inquiries, on his side, as to her ladyship's plans and proceedings—with a mind uneasily conscious of the inexorable lapse of time, and of certain probabilities which that lapse may bring with it. Lady Lundie has very little to say about herself. She is only in town for a few weeks. Her life is a life of retirement. "My modest round of duties at Windygates, Lord Holchester; occasionally relieved, when my mind is overworked, by the society of a few earnest friends whose views harmonize with my own—my existence passes (not quite uselessly, I hope) in that way. I have no news; I see nothing—except, indeed, yesterday, a sight of the saddest kind." She pauses there. Julius observes that he is expected to make inquiries, and makes them accordingly.

Lady Lundie hesitates; announces that her news refers to that painful past event which she has already touched on; acknowledges that she could not find herself in London without feeling an act of duty involved in making inquiries at the asylum in which Hester Dethridge is confined for life; announces that she has not only made the inquiries, but has seen the unhappy woman herself, has spoken to her, has found her unconscious of her dreadful position, incapable of the smallest exertion of memory, resigned to the existence that she leads, and likely (in the opinion of the medical superintendent) to live for some years to come. Having stated these facts, her ladyship is about to make a few of those "remarks appro-

priate to the occasion," in which she excels, when the door opens; and Lady Holchester, in search of her missing husband, enters the room.

### II.

There is a new outburst of affectionate interest on Lady Lundie's part—met civilly, but not cordially, by Lady Holchester. Julius's wife seems, like Julius, to be uneasily conscious of the lapse of time. Like Julius again, she privately wonders how long Lady Lundie is going to stay.

Lady Lundie shows no signs of leaving the sofa. She has evidently come to Holchester House to say something—and she has not said it yet. Is she going to say it? Yes. She is going to get, by a roundabout way, to the object in view. She has another inquiry of the affectionate sort to make. May she be permitted to resume the subject of Lord and Lady Holchester's travels? They have been at Rome. Can they confirm the shocking intelligence which has reached her of the "apostasy" of Mrs. Glenarm?

Lady Holchester can confirm it, by personal experience. Mrs. Glenarm has renounced the world, and has taken refuge in the bosom of the Holy Catholic Church. Lady Holchester has seen her in a convent at Rome. She is passing through the period of her probation; and she is resolved to take the veil. Lady Lundie, as a good Protestant, lifts her hands in horror—declares the topic to be too painful to dwell on—and, by way of varying it, goes straight to the point at last. Has Lady Holchester, in the course of her continental experience, happened to meet with, or to hear of—Mrs. Arnold Brinkworth?

"I have ceased, as you know, to hold any communication with my relatives," Lady Lundie explains. "The course they took at the time of our family trial—the sympathy they felt with a Person whom I can not even now trust myself to name more particularly—alienated us from each other. I may be grieved, dear Lady Holchester; but I bear no malice. And I shall always feel a motherly interest in hearing of Blanche's welfare. I have been told that she and her husband were traveling, at the time when you and Lord Holchester were traveling. Did you meet with them?"

Julius and his wife looked at each other. Lord Holchester is dumb. Lady Holchester replies:

"We saw Mr. and Mrs. Arnold Brinkworth at Florence, and afterward at Naples, Lady Lundie. They returned to England a week since, in anticipation of a certain happy event, which will possibly increase the members of your family circle. They are now in London. Indeed, I may tell you that we expect them here to lunch to-day."

Having made this plain statement, Lady Holchester looks at Lady Lundie. (If *that* doesn't hasten her departure, nothing will!)

Quite useless! Lady Lundie holds her ground. Having heard absolutely nothing of her relatives for the last six months, she is burning with curiosity to hear more. There is a name she has not mentioned yet. She places a certain constraint upon herself, and mentions it now.

"And Sir Patrick?" says her ladyship, subsiding into a gentle melancholy, suggestive of past injuries condoned by Christian forgiveness. "I only know what report tells me. Did you meet with Sir Patrick at Florence and Naples, also?"

Julius and his wife look at each other again. The clock in the hall strikes. Julius shudders. Lady Holchester's patience begins to give way. There is an awkward pause. Somebody must say something. As before, Lady Holchester replies:

"Sir Patrick went abroad, Lady Lundie, with his niece and her husband; and Sir Patrick has come back with them."

"In good health?" her ladyship inquires.

"Younger than ever," Lady Holchester rejoins.

Lady Lundie smiles satirically. Lady Holchester notices the smile; decides that mercy shown to *this* woman is mercy misplaced; and announces (to her husband's horror) that she has news to tell of Sir Patrick, which will probably take his sister-in-law by surprise.

Lady Lundie waits eagerly to hear what the news is.

"It is no secret," Lady Holchester proceeds —"though it is only known, as yet, to a few intimate friends. Sir Patrick has made an important change in his life."

Lady Lundie's charming smile suddenly dies out.

"Sir Patrick is not only a very clever and a very agreeable man," Lady Holchester resumes, a little maliciously; "he is also, in all his habits and ways (as you well know), a man younger than his years—who still possesses many of the qualities which seldom fail to attract women."

Lady Lundie starts to her feet.

"You don't mean to tell me, Lady Holchester, that Sir Patrick is married?"

"I do."

Her ladyship drops back on the sofa; helpless, really and truly helpless, under the double blow that has fallen on her. She is not only struck out of her place as the chief woman of the family, but (still on the right side of forty) she is socially superannuated, as The Dowager Lady Lundie, for the rest of her life!

"At his age!" she exclaims, as soon as she can speak.

"Pardon me for reminding you," Lady Holchester answers, "that plenty of men marry at Sir Patrick's age. In his case, it is only due to him to say that his motive raises him beyond the reach of ridicule or reproach. His marriage is a good action, in the highest sense of the word. It does honor to *him*, as well as to the lady who shares his position and his name."

"A young girl, of course!" is Lady Lundie's next remark.

"No. A woman who has been tried by no common suffering, and who has borne her hard lot nobly. A woman who deserves the calmer and the happier life on which she is entering now."

"May I ask who she is?"

Before the question can be answered, a knock at the house door announces the arrival of visitors. For the third time, Julius and his wife look at each other. On this occasion, Julius interferes.

"My wife has already told you, Lady Lundie, that we expect Mr. and Mrs. Brinkworth to lunch. Sir Patrick, and the new Lady Lundie, accompany them. If I am mistaken in supposing that it might not be quite agreeable to you to meet them, I can only ask your pardon. If I am right, I will leave Lady Holchester to receive our friends, and will do myself the honor of taking you into another room."

He advances to the door of an inner room. He offers his arm to Lady Lundie. Her ladyship stands immovable; determined to see the woman who has supplanted her. In a moment more, the door of entrance from the hall is thrown open; and the servant announces, "Sir Patrick and Lady Lundie. Mr. and Mrs. Arnold Brinkworth."

Lady Lundie looks at the woman who has taken her place at the head of the family; and sees —Anne Silvester!

THE END.

# APPENDIX.

I HAVE no desire to encumber the concluding pages of this book with needless references to newspaper reports which are accessible to everybody. But the riot at the Oxford Commemoration of 1869, and the sacking of the Christ Church Library, at the same University, in May 1870, present themselves so remarkably in the relations of cause and effect, that an abridged report of the proceedings on these two occasions may be admitted here, as forming an episode in the social history of England in our time. For the benefit of my foreign readers, it may be necessary to explain that the "Commemoration" at Oxford is an annual assemblage of the Heads of the University, of the Students, and of Visitors; the object of the meeting being to confer honorary degrees, and to hear the recitation of prize compositions in poetry and prose. Let it be further remembered in this connexion—by English as well as by foreign readers—that the riotous proceedings in the students' gallery have been customary and licensed proceedings for many years past. The destruction of the works of art in the Christ Church Library some months later will then appear in its true aspect, as the necessary result of a system of University misgovernment, which is happily without a parallel in the civilized world.

## MANNERS AND CUSTOMS OF YOUNG ENGLISH GENTLEMEN.

### [First Specimen.]

*Abridged Report of Proceedings at the Oxford Commemoration of 1869. "The Times," Thursday, June 10, 1869.*

". . .The storm opened with a few preliminary growls at 'hats' retained on the heads by strangers who had recently entered the area; but these murmurs were soon superseded by a furious onslaught on an unfortunate bachelor who had happened unthinkingly to adorn his neck with a somewhat conspicuous kerchief. Shouts of 'green tie' arose, and were repeated for the space of fully three quarters of an hour. The person was asked to retire; those in his neighbourhood were invited to 'turn him out;' he was entreated to change his tie or to take it off. All seemed for nearly an hour to be in vain; but importunity at length prevailed; the offender, amid volleys of applause, quitted the house, and the academic youth were able to turn their attention to other matters.

". . .The Vice-Chancellor opened the proceedings in tolerable quiet, but the delivery of the Crewian Oration by the Public Orator was the signal for the renewal of disturbance; the speaker was interrupted by a running fire of questions and remarks, which were more witty than complimentary, and very little of his speech reached any other ears than his own. When he

finally sat down, the Vice-Chancellor rose, and, having with great difficulty obtained silence, announced that if the proceedings were interrupted any more the Encænia would be abruptly closed. The recitation of the prizes (there being no honorary Degrees) then commenced; but very little could be heard of any, except the Newdigate, which was listened to with tolerable attention, and interrupted less than usual. The series of recitations approached completion, when attention was unfortunately attracted to a 'white hat,' held, though not worn, by a gentleman in the area. The Undergraduate (that is to say, the Oxford Student) is afflicted by a disease, which, for want of a better name, we may term *'Pileo-albo-phobia.'* At the sight of a hat of the obnoxious hue, he foams, he shrieks; he is no longer master of his actions. The solemn warning had been given by the Vice-Chancellor; the warning was understood to imply a probability, at least, of the abolition of Commemoration in time to come—a terrible consequence this, which those present would, one might have thought, fully appreciate. But all was in vain. With the hated 'white hat' before their eyes, the infuriated mob of Undergraduates could do nothing but rave and hoot; and the Vice-Chancellor, unable to obtain attention, rose from his seat, and, accompanied by the Doctors, left the building."

### [Second Specimen.]

*Amusements of the Students in their leisure hours. Materials for a University bonfire, taken from a University Library. Remarks on proceedings at Christ Church, Oxford. "The Times," May 18, 1870.*

". . .The most brutal and senseless act of Vandalism that has disgraced our time has been committed by members of the great foundation of Christ Church, young men belonging to the higher classes of England, brought up in the midst of the most refined civilization, and receiving the most costly education that the country can provide. The account of the matter is that on the night of Tuesday in last week, the Library of Christ Church was entered, and several busts, together with a marble statue of Venus of great value, were carried out by certain Undergraduates. In the course of the night a pile was made of fagots and mats, the sculptures were put upon it, the whole set on fire, and the works of art totally destroyed. There has been as yet no official statement concerning the outrage and its perpetrators, but of course the facts are tolerably well known in Undergraduate circles. The report is that two distinct sets of men were engaged in the business. The one took the statues out of the Library and stuck them up about Peckwater (one of the principal Quadrangles) as a joke. The other set found them in Peckwater, took them down, made the bonfire, and destroyed them.

". . .The thought necessarily suggests itself, that there must be faults of discipline where the freaks of Undergraduates thus culminate in an indictable offence. If no one becomes all at once very bad, so no society can produce such a set of rioters unless a great deal in the same style, though less serious, has been tolerated in former years. If this be so, we cannot but think that it is the duty of the authorities to intimate to the Undergraduates that excesses of the kind will be more seriously dealt with in future. These things are simply a stupid tradition which each year hands on to the next. The men cannot, and we are certain do not, feel any strong desire to engage in these so-called 'larks,' but there is a fashion, and it is followed. It used to be worse in the Army not many years ago; an unpopular newcomer, for instance, was subjected, in property and person, to persecutions that were almost incredible. Public indignation at a particular case, forced the Horse Guards to act, and the smashing of furniture and so forth was put an end to at once. The same firmness would produce the same effect at the University."

It is necessary to add, that the persons actually concerned in this outrage have since received such punishment as it is in the power of the University authorities to inflict. What those authorities, after this warning, will do towards improving the discipline of the University generally, and spreading "the blessings of civilization" among their own Undergraduates, remains to be seen.

# A CATALOGUE OF
# SELECTED DOVER BOOKS
# IN ALL FIELDS OF INTEREST

# A CATALOGUE OF SELECTED DOVER
# BOOKS IN ALL FIELDS OF INTEREST

RACKHAM'S COLOR ILLUSTRATIONS FOR WAGNER'S RING. Rackham's finest mature work—all 64 full-color watercolors in a faithful and lush interpretation of the *Ring*. Full-sized plates on coated stock of the paintings used by opera companies for authentic staging of Wagner. Captions aid in following complete Ring cycle. Introduction. 64 illustrations plus vignettes. 72pp. 8⅝ x 11¼. 23779-6 Pa. $6.00

CONTEMPORARY POLISH POSTERS IN FULL COLOR, edited by Joseph Czestochowski. 46 full-color examples of brilliant school of Polish graphic design, selected from world's first museum (near Warsaw) dedicated to poster art. Posters on circuses, films, plays, concerts all show cosmopolitan influences, free imagination. Introduction. 48pp. 9⅜ x 12¼.
23780-X Pa. $6.00

GRAPHIC WORKS OF EDVARD MUNCH, Edvard Munch. 90 haunting, evocative prints by first major Expressionist artist and one of the greatest graphic artists of his time: *The Scream, Anxiety, Death Chamber, The Kiss, Madonna*, etc. Introduction by Alfred Werner. 90pp. 9 x 12.
23765-6 Pa. $5.00

THE GOLDEN AGE OF THE POSTER, Hayward and Blanche Cirker. 70 extraordinary posters in full colors, from Maitres de l'Affiche, Mucha, Lautrec, Bradley, Cheret, Beardsley, many others. Total of 78pp. 9⅜ x 12¼. 22753-7 Pa. $5.95

THE NOTEBOOKS OF LEONARDO DA VINCI, edited by J. P. Richter. Extracts from manuscripts reveal great genius; on painting, sculpture, anatomy, sciences, geography, etc. Both Italian and English. 186 ms. pages reproduced, plus 500 additional drawings, including studies for *Last Supper*, Sforza monument, etc. 860pp. 7⅞ x 10¾. (Available in U.S. only)
22572-0, 22573-9 Pa., Two-vol. set $15.90

THE CODEX NUTTALL, as first edited by Zelia Nuttall. Only inexpensive edition, in full color, of a pre-Columbian Mexican (Mixtec) book. 88 color plates show kings, gods, heroes, temples, sacrifices. New explanatory, historical introduction by Arthur G. Miller. 96pp. 11⅜ x 8½. (Available in U.S. only) 23168-2 Pa. $7.95

UNE SEMAINE DE BONTÉ, A SURREALISTIC NOVEL IN COLLAGE, Max Ernst. Masterpiece created out of 19th-century periodical illustrations, explores worlds of terror and surprise. Some consider this Ernst's greatest work. 208pp. 8⅛ x 11. 23252-2 Pa. $6.00

UNCLE SILAS, J. Sheridan LeFanu. Victorian Gothic mystery novel, considered by many best of period, even better than Collins or Dickens. Wonderful psychological terror. Introduction by Frederick Shroyer. 436pp. 5⅜ x 8½. 21715-9 Pa. $6.00

JURGEN, James Branch Cabell. The great erotic fantasy of the 1920's that delighted thousands, shocked thousands more. Full final text, Lane edition with 13 plates by Frank Pape. 346pp. 5⅜ x 8½. 23507-6 Pa. $4.50

THE CLAVERINGS, Anthony Trollope. Major novel, chronicling aspects of British Victorian society, personalities. Reprint of Cornhill serialization, 16 plates by M. Edwards; first reprint of full text. Introduction by Norman Donaldson. 412pp. 5⅜ x 8½. 23464-9 Pa. $5.00

KEPT IN THE DARK, Anthony Trollope. Unusual short novel about Victorian morality and abnormal psychology by the great English author. Probably the first American publication. Frontispiece by Sir John Millais. 92pp. 6½ x 9¼. 23609-9 Pa. $2.50

RALPH THE HEIR, Anthony Trollope. Forgotten tale of illegitimacy, inheritance. Master novel of Trollope's later years. Victorian country estates, clubs, Parliament, fox hunting, world of fully realized characters. Reprint of 1871 edition. 12 illustrations by F. A. Faser. 434pp. of text. 5⅜ x 8½. 23642-0 Pa. $5.00

YEKL and THE IMPORTED BRIDEGROOM AND OTHER STORIES OF THE NEW YORK GHETTO, Abraham Cahan. Film *Hester Street* based on *Yekl* (1896). Novel, other stories among first about Jewish immigrants of N.Y.'s East Side. Highly praised by W. D. Howells—Cahan "a new star of realism." New introduction by Bernard G. Richards. 240pp. 5⅜ x 8½. 22427-9 Pa. $3.50

THE HIGH PLACE, James Branch Cabell. Great fantasy writer's enchanting comedy of disenchantment set in 18th-century France. Considered by some critics to be even better than his famous *Jurgen*. 10 illustrations and numerous vignettes by noted fantasy artist Frank C. Pape. 320pp. 5⅜ x 8½. 23670-6 Pa. $4.00

ALICE'S ADVENTURES UNDER GROUND, Lewis Carroll. Facsimile of ms. Carroll gave Alice Liddell in 1864. Different in many ways from final Alice. Handlettered, illustrated by Carroll. Introduction by Martin Gardner. 128pp. 5⅜ x 8½. 21482-6 Pa. $2.50

FAVORITE ANDREW LANG FAIRY TALE BOOKS IN MANY COLORS, Andrew Lang. The four Lang favorites in a boxed set—the complete *Red, Green, Yellow* and *Blue* Fairy Books. 164 stories; 439 illustrations by Lancelot Speed, Henry Ford and G. P. Jacomb Hood. Total of about 1500pp. 5⅜ x 8½. 23407-X Boxed set, Pa. $15.95

THE AMERICAN SENATOR, Anthony Trollope. Little known, long unavailable Trollope novel on a grand scale. Here are humorous comment on American vs. English culture, and stunning portrayal of a heroine/villainess. Superb evocation of Victorian village life. 561pp. 5⅜ x 8½. 23801-6 Pa. $6.00

WAS IT MURDER? James Hilton. The author of *Lost Horizon* and *Goodbye, Mr. Chips* wrote one detective novel (under a pen-name) which was quickly forgotten and virtually lost, even at the height of Hilton's fame. This edition brings it back—a finely crafted public school puzzle resplendent with Hilton's stylish atmosphere. A thoroughly English thriller by the creator of Shangri-la. 252pp. 5⅜ x 8. (Available in U.S. only) 23774-5 Pa. $3.00

CENTRAL PARK: A PHOTOGRAPHIC GUIDE, Victor Laredo and Henry Hope Reed. 121 superb photographs show dramatic views of Central Park: Bethesda Fountain, Cleopatra's Needle, Sheep Meadow, the Blockhouse, plus people engaged in many park activities: ice skating, bike riding, etc. Captions by former Curator of Central Park, Henry Hope Reed, provide historical view, changes, etc. Also photos of N.Y. landmarks on park's periphery. 96pp. 8½ x 11. 23750-8 Pa. $4.50

NANTUCKET IN THE NINETEENTH CENTURY, Clay Lancaster. 180 rare photographs, stereographs, maps, drawings and floor plans recreate unique American island society. Authentic scenes of shipwreck, lighthouses, streets, homes are arranged in geographic sequence to provide walking-tour guide to old Nantucket existing today. Introduction, captions. 160pp. 8⅞ x 11¾. 23747-8 Pa. $6.95

STONE AND MAN: A PHOTOGRAPHIC EXPLORATION, Andreas Feininger. 106 photographs by *Life* photographer Feininger portray man's deep passion for stone through the ages. Stonehenge-like megaliths, fortified towns, sculpted marble and crumbling tenements show textures, beauties, fascination. 128pp. 9¼ x 10¾. 23756-7 Pa. $5.95

CIRCLES, A MATHEMATICAL VIEW, D. Pedoe. Fundamental aspects of college geometry, non-Euclidean geometry, and other branches of mathematics: representing circle by point. Poincare model, isoperimetric property, etc. Stimulating recreational reading. 66 figures. 96pp. 5⅝ x 8¼. 63698-4 Pa. $2.75

THE DISCOVERY OF NEPTUNE, Morton Grosser. Dramatic scientific history of the investigations leading up to the actual discovery of the eighth planet of our solar system. Lucid, well-researched book by well-known historian of science. 172pp. 5⅜ x 8½. 23726-5 Pa. $3.50

THE DEVIL'S DICTIONARY. Ambrose Bierce. Barbed, bitter, brilliant witticisms in the form of a dictionary. Best, most ferocious satire America has produced. 145pp. 5⅜ x 8½. 20487-1 Pa. $2.25

THE CURVES OF LIFE, Theodore A. Cook. Examination of shells, leaves, horns, human body, art, etc., in *"the* classic reference on how the golden ratio applies to spirals and helices in nature . . . . "—Martin Gardner. 426 illustrations. Total of 512pp. 5⅜ x 8½.　23701-X Pa. $5.95

AN ILLUSTRATED FLORA OF THE NORTHERN UNITED STATES AND CANADA, Nathaniel L. Britton, Addison Brown. Encyclopedic work covers 4666 species, ferns on up. Everything. Full botanical information, illustration for each. This earlier edition is preferred by many to more recent revisions. 1913 edition. Over 4000 illustrations, total of 2087pp. 6⅛ x 9¼.　22642-5, 22643-3, 22644-1 Pa., Three-vol. set $25.50

MANUAL OF THE GRASSES OF THE UNITED STATES, A. S. Hitchcock, U.S. Dept. of Agriculture. The basic study of American grasses, both indigenous and escapes, cultivated and wild. Over 1400 species. Full descriptions, information. Over 1100 maps, illustrations. Total of 1051pp. 5⅜ x 8½.　22717-0, 22718-9 Pa., Two-vol. set $15.00

THE CACTACEAE,, Nathaniel L. Britton, John N. Rose. Exhaustive, definitive. Every cactus in the world. Full botanical descriptions. Thorough statement of nomenclatures, habitat, detailed finding keys. The one book needed by every cactus enthusiast. Over 1275 illustrations. Total of 1080pp. 8 x 10¼.　21191-6, 21192-4 Clothbd., Two-vol. set $35.00

AMERICAN MEDICINAL PLANTS, Charles F. Millspaugh. Full descriptions, 180 plants covered: history; physical description; methods of preparation with all chemical constituents extracted; all claimed curative or adverse effects. 180 full-page plates. Classification table. 804pp. 6½ x 9¼.
23034-1 Pa. $12.95

A MODERN HERBAL, Margaret Grieve. Much the fullest, most exact, most useful compilation of herbal material. Gigantic alphabetical encyclopedia, from aconite to zedoary, gives botanical information, medical properties, folklore, economic uses, and much else. Indispensable to serious reader. 161 illustrations. 888pp. 6½ x 9¼. (Available in U.S. only)
22798-7, 22799-5 Pa., Two-vol. set $13.00

THE HERBAL or GENERAL HISTORY OF PLANTS, John Gerard. The 1633 edition revised and enlarged by Thomas Johnson. Containing almost 2850 plant descriptions and 2705 superb illustrations, Gerard's *Herbal* is a monumental work, the book all modern English herbals are derived from, the one herbal every serious enthusiast should have in its entirety. Original editions are worth perhaps $750. 1678pp. 8½ x 12¼.
23147-X Clothbd. $50.00

MANUAL OF THE TREES OF NORTH AMERICA, Charles S. Sargent. The basic survey of every native tree and tree-like shrub, 717 species in all. Extremely full descriptions, information on habitat, growth, locales, economics, etc. Necessary to every serious tree lover. Over 100 finding keys. 783 illustrations. Total of 986pp. 5⅜ x 8½.
20277-1, 20278-X Pa., Two-vol. set $11.00

SECOND PIATIGORSKY CUP, edited by Isaac Kashdan. One of the greatest tournament books ever produced in the English language. All 90 games of the 1966 tournament, annotated by players, most annotated by both players. Features Petrosian, Spassky, Fischer, Larsen, six others. 228pp. 5⅜ x 8½. 23572-6 Pa. $3.50

ENCYCLOPEDIA OF CARD TRICKS, revised and edited by Jean Hugard. How to perform over 600 card tricks, devised by the world's greatest magicians: impromptus, spelling tricks, key cards, using special packs, much, much more. Additional chapter on card technique. 66 illustrations. 402pp. 5⅜ x 8½. (Available in U.S. only) 21252-1 Pa. $4.95

MAGIC: STAGE ILLUSIONS, SPECIAL EFFECTS AND TRICK PHO-TOGRAPHY, Albert A. Hopkins, Henry R. Evans. One of the great classics; fullest, most authorative explanation of vanishing lady, levitations, scores of other great stage effects. Also small magic, automata, stunts. 446 illus-trations. 556pp. 5⅜ x 8½. 23344-8 Pa. $6.95

THE SECRETS OF HOUDINI, J. C. Cannell. Classic study of Houdini's incredible magic, exposing closely-kept professional secrets and revealing, in general terms, the whole art of stage magic. 67 illustrations. 279pp. 5⅜ x 8½. 22913-0 Pa. $4.00

HOFFMANN'S MODERN MAGIC, Professor Hoffmann. One of the best, and best-known, magicians' manuals of the past century. Hundreds of tricks from card tricks and simple sleight of hand to elaborate illusions involving construction of complicated machinery. 332 illustrations. 563pp. 5⅜ x 8½. 23623-4 Pa. $6.00

MADAME PRUNIER'S FISH COOKERY BOOK, Mme. S. B. Prunier. More than 1000 recipes from world famous Prunier's of Paris and London, specially adapted here for American kitchen. Grilled tournedos with anchovy butter, Lobster a la Bordelaise, Prunier's prized desserts, more. Glossary. 340pp. 5⅜ x 8½. (Available in U.S. only) 22679-4 Pa. $3.00

FRENCH COUNTRY COOKING FOR AMERICANS, Louis Diat. 500 easy-to-make, authentic provincial recipes compiled by former head chef at New York's Fitz-Carlton Hotel: onion soup, lamb stew, potato pie, more. 309pp. 5⅜ x 8½. 23665-X Pa. $3.95

SAUCES, FRENCH AND FAMOUS, Louis Diat. Complete book gives over 200 specific recipes: bechamel, Bordelaise, hollandaise, Cumberland, apri-cot, etc. Author was one of this century's finest chefs, originator of vichyssoise and many other dishes. Index. 156pp. 5⅜ x 8.
23663-3 Pa. $2.75

TOLL HOUSE TRIED AND TRUE RECIPES, Ruth Graves Wakefield. Authentic recipes from the famous Mass. restaurant: popovers, veal and ham loaf, Toll House baked beans, chocolate cake crumb pudding, much more. Many helpful hints. Nearly 700 recipes. Index. 376pp. 5⅜ x 8½.
23560-2 Pa. $4.50

AN AUTOBIOGRAPHY, Margaret Sanger. Exciting personal account of hard-fought battle for woman's right to birth control, against prejudice, church, law. Foremost feminist document. 504pp. 5⅜ x 8½.
20470-7 Pa. $5.50

MY BONDAGE AND MY FREEDOM, Frederick Douglass. Born as a slave, Douglass became outspoken force in antislavery movement. The best of Douglass's autobiographies. Graphic description of slave life. Introduction by P. Foner. 464pp. 5⅜ x 8½. 22457-0 Pa. $5.50

LIVING MY LIFE, Emma Goldman. Candid, no holds barred account by foremost American anarchist: her own life, anarchist movement, famous contemporaries, ideas and their impact. Struggles and confrontations in America, plus deportation to U.S.S.R. Shocking inside account of persecution of anarchists under Lenin. 13 plates. Total of 944pp. 5⅜ x 8½.
22543-7, 22544-5 Pa., Two-vol. set $12.00

LETTERS AND NOTES ON THE MANNERS, CUSTOMS AND CONDITIONS OF THE NORTH AMERICAN INDIANS, George Catlin. Classic account of life among Plains Indians: ceremonies, hunt, warfare, etc. Dover edition reproduces for first time all original paintings. 312 plates. 572pp. of text. 6⅛ x 9¼. 22118-0, 22119-9 Pa.. Two-vol. set $12.00

THE MAYA AND THEIR NEIGHBORS, edited by Clarence L. Hay, others. Synoptic view of Maya civilization in broadest sense, together with Northern, Southern neighbors. Integrates much background, valuable detail not elsewhere. Prepared by greatest scholars: Kroeber, Morley, Thompson, Spinden, Vaillant, many others. Sometimes called Tozzer Memorial Volume. 60 illustrations, linguistic map. 634pp. 5⅜ x 8½.
23510-6 Pa. $10.00

HANDBOOK OF THE INDIANS OF CALIFORNIA, A. L. Kroeber. Foremost American anthropologist offers complete ethnographic study of each group. Monumental classic. 459 illustrations, maps. 995pp. 5⅜ x 8½.
23368-5 Pa. $13.00

SHAKTI AND SHAKTA, Arthur Avalon. First book to give clear, cohesive analysis of Shakta doctrine, Shakta ritual and Kundalini Shakti (yoga). Important work by one of world's foremost students of Shaktic and Tantric thought. 732pp. 5⅜ x 8½. (Available in U.S. only)
23645-5 Pa. $7.95

AN INTRODUCTION TO THE STUDY OF THE MAYA HIEROGLYPHS, Syvanus Griswold Morley. Classic study by one of the truly great figures in hieroglyph research. Still the best introduction for the student for reading Maya hieroglyphs. New introduction by J. Eric S. Thompson. 117 illustrations. 284pp. 5⅜ x 8½. 23108-9 Pa. $4.00

A STUDY OF MAYA ART, Herbert J. Spinden. Landmark classic interprets Maya symbolism, estimates styles, covers ceramics, architecture, murals, stone carvings as artforms. Still a basic book in area. New introduction by J. Eric Thompson. Over 750 illustrations. 341pp. 8⅜ x 11¼.
21235-1 Pa. $6.95

YUCATAN BEFORE AND AFTER THE CONQUEST, Diego de Landa. First English translation of basic book in Maya studies, the only significant account of Yucatan written in the early post-Conquest era. Translated by distinguished Maya scholar William Gates. Appendices, introduction, 4 maps and over 120 illustrations added by translator. 162pp. 5⅜ x 8½.
23622-6 Pa. $3.00

THE MALAY ARCHIPELAGO, Alfred R. Wallace. Spirited travel account by one of founders of modern biology. Touches on zoology, botany, ethnography, geography, and geology. 62 illustrations, maps. 515pp. 5⅜ x 8½.
20187-2 Pa. $6.95

THE DISCOVERY OF THE TOMB OF TUTANKHAMEN, Howard Carter, A. C. Mace. Accompany Carter in the thrill of discovery, as ruined passage suddenly reveals unique, untouched, fabulously rich tomb. Fascinating account, with 106 illustrations. New introduction by J. M. White. Total of 382pp. 5⅜ x 8½. (Available in U.S. only)     23500-9 Pa. $4.00

THE WORLD'S GREATEST SPEECHES, edited by Lewis Copeland and Lawrence W. Lamm. Vast collection of 278 speeches from Greeks up to present. Powerful and effective models; unique look at history. Revised to 1970. Indices. 842pp. 5⅜ x 8½.     20468-5 Pa. $8.95

THE 100 GREATEST ADVERTISEMENTS, Julian Watkins. The priceless ingredient; His master's voice; 99 44/100% pure; over 100 others. How they were written, their impact, etc. Remarkable record. 130 illustrations. 233pp. 7⅞ x 10 3/5.     20540-1 Pa. $5.95

CRUICKSHANK PRINTS FOR HAND COLORING, George Cruickshank. 18 illustrations, one side of a page, on fine-quality paper suitable for water-colors. Caricatures of people in society (c. 1820) full of trenchant wit. Very large format. 32pp. 11 x 16.     23684-6 Pa. $5.00

THIRTY-TWO COLOR POSTCARDS OF TWENTIETH-CENTURY AMERICAN ART, Whitney Museum of American Art. Reproduced in full color in postcard form are 31 art works and one shot of the museum. Calder, Hopper, Rauschenberg, others. Detachable. 16pp. 8¼ x 11.
23629-3 Pa. $3.00

MUSIC OF THE SPHERES: THE MATERIAL UNIVERSE FROM ATOM TO QUASAR SIMPLY EXPLAINED, Guy Murchie. Planets, stars, geology, atoms, radiation, relativity, quantum theory, light, antimatter, similar topics. 319 figures. 664pp. 5⅜ x 8½.
21809-0, 21810-4 Pa., Two-vol. set $11.00

EINSTEIN'S THEORY OF RELATIVITY, Max Born. Finest semi-technical account; covers Einstein, Lorentz, Minkowski, and others, with much detail, much explanation of ideas and math not readily available elsewhere on this level. For student, non-specialist. 376pp. 5⅜ x 8½.
60769-0 Pa. $4.50

AMERICAN ANTIQUE FURNITURE, Edgar G. Miller, Jr. The basic coverage of all American furniture before 1840: chapters per item chronologically cover all types of furniture, with more than 2100 photos. Total of 1106pp. 7⅞ x 10¾.     21599-7, 21600-4 Pa., Two-vol. set $17.90

ILLUSTRATED GUIDE TO SHAKER FURNITURE, Robert Meader. Director, Shaker Museum, Old Chatham, presents up-to-date coverage of all furniture and appurtenances, with much on local styles not available elsewhere. 235 photos. 146pp. 9 x 12.     22819-3 Pa. $6.00

ORIENTAL RUGS, ANTIQUE AND MODERN, Walter A. Hawley. Persia, Turkey, Caucasus, Central Asia, China, other traditions. Best general survey of all aspects: styles and periods, manufacture, uses, symbols and their interpretation, and identification. 96 illustrations, 11 in color. 320pp. 6⅛ x 9¼.     22366-3 Pa. $6.95

CHINESE POTTERY AND PORCELAIN, R. L. Hobson. Detailed descriptions and analyses by former Keeper of the Department of Oriental Antiquities and Ethnography at the British Museum. Covers hundreds of pieces from primitive times to 1915. Still the standard text for most periods. 136 plates, 40 in full color. Total of 750pp. 5⅜ x 8½.
23253-0 Pa. $10.00

THE WARES OF THE MING DYNASTY, R. L. Hobson. Foremost scholar examines and illustrates many varieties of Ming (1368-1644). Famous blue and white, polychrome, lesser-known styles and shapes. 117 illustrations, 9 full color, of outstanding pieces. Total of 263pp. 6⅛ x 9¼. (Available in U.S. only)     23652-8 Pa. $6.00

*Prices subject to change without notice.*

Available at your book dealer or write for free catalogue to Dept. GI, Dover Publications, Inc., 180 Varick St., N.Y., N.Y. 10014. Dover publishes more than 175 books each year on science, elementary and advanced mathematics, biology, music, art, literary history, social sciences and other areas.